Claire was born and raised in London. She graduated with a BSc (Hons) in Social Sciences from the OU, and a Creative Writing MA from Royal Holloway. She now lives in Surrey with her family where she is fulfilling her lifelong dream of writing, full-time. *Vanilla Kisses* is her debut novel.

Vanilla Kisses.
C. C. Burns

Copyright

www. ccburns.co.uk

Acknowledgments.

With loving thanks to Jon, for holding the fort whilst I finally got this finished. Gratitude for all your unwavering practical support, and belief in me.

Thanks to my brother, Mathew, and my dad, James, for your time spent beta reading, and for your generous praise and encouragement. - Much love.

Thank you to my fellow MA students, for being my first audience, and for all your helpful feedback and encouragement in our workshop sessions.

Thanks to all collaborators involved in making this publication possible:

Editor: Kemone Brown at THPeditingServc

Cover artist: @premiumsolns

Dedicated to Mathew.

Prologue.

March 1821. - Surrey, England.

The gallery swarmed increasingly. One title announced after another, another low bow or graceful curtsy before disappearing into the crowd of satins and silks. I watched on above the rim of my glass, disappointed. They seemed a bore on the whole, high society or not.

I was not the first to notice her. It was in following the distracted gaze of all the gentlemen about me that caused me to break my conversation to discover the spectacle that caused the room to lull and skip a beat.

'Who is she?' I turned away a moment to ask Felix, whose expression made no secret of having registered the exquisite beauty.

'I am not certain,' he said without looking away. 'But I shall be sure to find it out—that blasted master of ceremonies speaks in such monosyllabic accents. Damned if I know what he's saying.'

I turned back to the sight of her, somewhat obscured now by the throng gathered about her: A crowd of eager greeters, her dance card already being drawn from her reticule. It was impossible to conceive from such a distance what colour her eyes were, but I felt drawn to the sparkle of them the instant they stole about the room surveying it. I narrowed my focus, making a study of her face, a glow of radiance in her complexion but no crimson blush upon her fine set cheek; she was neither shy nor overwhelmed by these attentions; an amiable and patient smile upon her lovely mouth, but failing to disclose any clue as to her thoughts or feelings. Perfect measure. Perfect control. Too polite and well bred, I think, to publicly snub a gentleman cruelly, yet no doubt of adequate consequence and favour to be permitted to do so.

I turned to Fawkham instead now, he would surely know. 'Who is that?' I asked, as I put my glass down upon the mantle and stood a little straighter.

'Who, her? The Baron's daughter, I believe.'

'The Baron's daughter,' I nodded nonchalantly as she passed in a rustle of taffeta, without lifting her eyes to notice my waiting smile. She was uncommonly beautiful, I confirmed, catching a closer glimpse, not like those stiff faced wallflowers she took a seat with presently.

At first it seemed too ambitious, even for me. I sank my glass and watched her dancing the opening quadrille. The chances of succeeding to her notice, let alone beyond it, seemed little more than fantastic. But with a little help, it might be managed. It *must* be managed. Though it would need to be handled carefully. I was certain she would be naturally disposed to disliking those below her stamp. I would need to figure out just the right way in. I must watch and wait yet a while should I wish to succeed in this. Then as my cousin drew up beside me, the scheme become instantly clear to me.

An inclement night.

August 1821.

The rain came fierce, pounding against the water logged grassland, pooling in sunken hollows of mud; a merciless lashing. Eleanor felt her way up to the trunk of a tree, tracing it blindly from its twisting roots, snaking up from the ground until she found the rough bark beneath her palms and steadied herself against it. *Where exactly am I?* she considered with a searching glance about her, the scent of rain disturbed earth in her nostrils, the acrid tang of the amber draught upon her tongue.

It was a moonless night. The dense black clouds had swallowed it up entirely, and even the intermittent cracks of lightening splitting through it, failed to orientate her. She would have to guess her way, let her instincts guide her. She knew these woods well. If her head was not so fuzzy and the light not so poor, she might have remembered the route.

She wiped the rain streams from her eyes, hitched her dress up above her knees and waded her way barefoot through the mud, taking care to lift her feet properly as she trod, to avoid tripping on a creeping vine or tree stump. *Giles, you monster,* she thought, as the pain coursing through her brought with it the memory of his violence. *I wish you dead.* She had never wished anyone dead before, not in seriousness. But these words came to her in earnest. She felt the rough bulge of a fallen branch beneath the sole of her foot and bent to pick it up. She could not be sure if he had learned of her escape. *He might come after me.* She tested its weight and circumference in her hand to make sure it was up to the task should she need it. Yes, it would do. *If you happen upon me, I shall spear it through your liver without a moment's hesitation.*

For now, she used it as a prop to support her body weight and push aside vines and nettles. *Oh god, let this be the right way.* She sighed inwardly, the prospect occurring to her now as she walked farther, that she could find herself back on the lawns of Beaulieu as easy as Cuddington. It was impossible to tell with only the out sprawled hands of trees craning above and around her to navigate. Had it been winter, she might have stood a chance at recognising one bare and bony skeleton of bark from the next. But despite the inclemency of this night, it was summer and the trees blossomed thick with leaves, altering their shape and filling out gaps of demarcation only revealed in colder seasons.

She paused to check the viability of the way ahead, poking at the ground and bracken when she started; heard a rustling from a bush. She lifted the stick now, into the air. Poised. Ready. Wishing the volume of her thumping pulse quiet so she might hear another clue as she strained her ears to the direction it had come. Silence. *A bird or rodent perhaps?* Nothing more gave it away and as she searched the blinding darkness, she looked up ahead and noticed as her eyes readjusted, a path that led to a clearing in the trees where the density dispersed a little in the cleft between them. *Could it be?* Could this be the clearing onto Cuddington, the one so familiar to her in daylight hours? She changed course, surged on in its direction, the promise of relief tangible, hurrying her steps towards it until she lost her footing in the rush.

She knew she was foredoomed to slip before she hit the ground, thudding down an unseen embankment in a mud slide, her skirts catching on something as she landed, the drag of snagging muslin pulling her back as her bodyweight propelled her forwards. 'Ouch,' she groaned, untangling her twisted limbs from beneath her with careful manoeuvre. She had landed badly, and instantly feared a dreadful injury at her ankle. But as she wrested it from beneath her, rubbing and prodding at it, she realised it was more a matter of shock than injury. A tentative circling of the joint reassured her it was weight bearing, and carefully, very carefully now, she folded onto hands and knees before lifting to stand again.

She strained her eyes against the ground to check for any further trappings before continuing. The wind whipped in and out from time to time, threatening her balance, plucking the woodland into a strange symphony with the creak and crack of branches bending and snapping. She was calf deep in a slippery ditch, she had to navigate carefully to avoid another mishap. She flexed her toes and focused on balancing her steps to avoid sliding into the nettle bushes on either side of the narrow channel. She wished she had not lost her stick in the fall. She wished so many things in this moment, remembering in piecemeal fragments, the overheard conversations, the revelations that sprung from them, and the horrors that followed them. She shook the memory and refocused on the path. She would just have to go slowly. Inch her way along it. *Steady.* She would soon land either on home ground or on that of her enemy. Either way, she would know the case in just a few moments more.

Keep going, she willed herself on with the last of her resolve. The wind determined to pull her back with each heavy step; her body threatening to give in to the exhaustion, her breaths so sharp they were burning in her chest like a quaff of straight liquor.

She had no idea how long she had been out in this, how long she had lay in the woods until her consciousness had returned to her. It could have been merely minutes or hours since she slipped out through the jib door. The night sky gave no clue. But she could not allow herself to dwell on it, or the gravel indents on the soles of her feet, or the icy stabs of air that prickled her skin to numbness. Home: that was all that she could think of, like a distant mirage. *Sanctuary. Safety. Respite.*

Clearing the woodland at last, her heart rejoiced as she felt the grass between her toes and saw the familiar shape of Cuddington carved against the night sky. Her instincts had not failed her, not in this at least. She was arrived onto the front lawns; flashes of lightening were illuminating the vast and towering walls before eerily casting them back into shadow. A candle still burned beyond a window of the left wing; with desperation, she clung to its every flicker and looked to the moment she could be safely inside the walls too. *He* could not reach her there, not under her parents' protection. She clung to her sopping skirts that had begun to slip from her grasp, the muslin feeling more like slime in its mud slickened coating, rather than Mrs Oliver's finest muslin weave. It had been such a pretty dress; one that was certain to become a favourite, when she had been fitted for it just weeks ago. Now its hem hung in tatters and she ran with it flapping against the prickled skin around her knees. The rhythm of the thunder quickening her pace, even though her legs were trembling so exceedingly they threatened to give way with every step. The night storm seemed to chase her, rumbling and cracking behind her like a horse whip, echoing louder the closer she drew to the house.

Home. She had never expected to feel such relief from beholding Cuddington again. But then there was a great deal that had come to pass of late, she had never expected. She tried the door, carefully, but as she feared, she had found it locked. She could not disturb the house at this hour: If it was locked, it must be somewhere between the hours of midnight and six, although whereabouts she could not say. Even if she could bear the raucous and subsequent assumptions of waking the servants in the dead of night, she had had no time to contemplate what she would say to them or what she would tell her parents. No, it would not answer. A window perhaps might have been forgotten?

She made her way back down the steps and surveyed the building, one window at a time. She had never really paid attention to just how many there were. But despite their number, it seemed hopeless. The basement windows were barred and barely peeped above ground level. The windows above were too high to consider. For a moment, she felt hopeless, as the rain continued to pelt at her, her clothes sagging, the floor slippery and difficult to navigate in bare feet. But after a moment of helpless sobbing, she remembered why she was fleeing—the feeling of being pressed faced down against the mattress, the constriction of her breath against the sheets, the muffle of her screams—and prompted herself on, until she found the stairway down to the servants' entrance.

It too was locked, but beside it, a small box like window that seemed implausible at first, had been forgotten, and its sash remained an inch or so lifted from its frame. She seized the opportunity and forced it all the way up and pushed herself headfirst through the narrow gap provided. She was either going to get stuck midway and have to cry out for help, or gravity would deliver her to the ground with a thud.

It was the latter which prevailed. She managed to break her fall somewhat by hooking her feet either side of the windowsill as she tumbled down. She was in. *She was home.* A little more ruffled and bruised, but nothing to answer in the scheme of things. The promise of dry clothes and a soft bed to sink into awaited her now, and she was safe; safe from him.

She caught her breath and composed herself briefly, before pulling up from her semi-clumsy landing and tried to work out where to go from here. She crept through another door and into the sanctuary of the basement corridors and bustled along the hall past the servants' quarters.

The darkness was even denser inside with each blind turn of what seemed an endless maze of unfamiliar corridors. She had never had cause to visit the service levels of the house before, but now, in the dimness of its walls, she wished she had. It was all the more eerie for its unfamiliarity. The stifled smell of tobacco burning and facetious laughter strayed from beyond the closed doors as she passed silently through the darkness, hoping that the pounding of her heart and slippery footsteps would not disturb them. If she could just make it to her room, nobody would suspect a thing and she had 'till morning to work out what to do from there.

ANNALISE WAS ON HER way back from her rounds, extinguishing the last of the fires and candlelight. She rubbed a tired eye with the back of her hand; careful not to contaminate it with one of her sooty fingertips that were ashen grey from putting out the candles and fires. Her shoes were tight around her feet and had been rubbing against her heals all day. She had been putting off buying a new pair for months, but wondered if now might be classed as a time of necessity after all, feeling another stroke of the leather upper sear across her heel as she took to the servants' staircase to make her way back down to the basement. She paused and sat upon the top stair to give herself a moment's respite from the pain. She did not know what time it was but the silence about the place suggested it a late finish. She had been on the go since six a.m., and bodily weariness was slowly overtaking her conscious efforts to allay it. She unlaced her left shoe with one hand, the other preoccupied with holding the candlelight over it, hot wax slipping and dropping its glossy petals over her apron. As expected, her healing blisters had been torn open again and were bleeding through her stocking. She sighed and slipped her foot back in, deciding that she must give in to visiting Mr Phelps' shoe stall on her next morning off.

With her laces roughly re-tied, she pulled herself back up off the cracked stone stair which had been growing cold against her bottom, and lifted her light to guide her down the remainder of the winding stairway. She had savings enough to spare a few shillings, she reminded herself as she winced again with each tentative step. But the longer she squirreled away her wages, the harder it seemed to disrupt the now-weighty-feel of her purse. She would soon have enough to pay the deposit on a headstone for her mother's grave. Perhaps not a very grand one, but at least something to mark the spot, to ensure she was never forgotten to the world. If it was not for Mr Harrison's benevolence, her mother would have been buried in a common grave and she wouldn't have a hope of identifying her resting place. Such a privilege was not to be wasted. She would soon have a headstone too. The stonemason had told her it would take a year for the grave to settle and she had resolved that in her new job, with the better pay and careful economy, she could save enough towards the deposit to have it commissioned by the end of summer. The rest he would accept in instalments.

As she rounded the corner of the last flight, she froze suddenly, noticing a shadow against the wall further down the staircase. She must be mistaken. Everyone else would long be retired now. She rubbed her eyes with the heel of her hand, careful not to smudge them with her ashen fingertips. She must be overtired from all these extra tasks, her eyes playing tricks on her. She called out instinctively, 'Hello...is someone there?' She blew gently at the candle flame which had been flickering to a low burn and jumped as the rising flame illuminated the shape of someone at the foot of the stairway. Good grief! She felt suddenly aware of her heartbeat and stepped on, close enough to further examine the silent figure but at length enough to flee, should she need.

'Hello?' she said again, but noticed how much weaker her voice had become. Her mouth suddenly seemed dry and she felt her pulse quickening. 'Are you well?' She took another cautious step down and lent in closer. She could see better now and recognised the outline of a gloved hand, part shielding a mass of drenched and tousled hair.

'Miss?' This was not another servant; the clothes were too fine to permit that possibility.

Silence.

'I can see you,' she said, and this time the figure removed her hand from her face and squinted at the imposing light.

Annalise gasped. 'My Lady! It is you.' She felt relieved to see a vaguely familiar face and not some housebreaker or ghost her imagination had first begun to conjure. Although what she saw before her was equally disconcerting, and before she could quell the over excitement in her voice, she blurted out in the same flustered tone; 'Goodness me, what is the matter, why are you hiding? You are very... Wet!' It seemed a preferable recovery to saying: in an utter state.

Annalise could not claim to have been overly familiar with the Ashlyn daughter—what was her name? Eleanor? She wasn't certain, she had never seen her closely before or even spoken to her. In any case, she certainly could not fathom what might account for such a circumstance as finding her here, like this at such an hour.

'Hush, will you keep your voice down!' came the reply. 'I just got caught in that terrible downpour is all,' Eleanor stuttered, almost tripping on the bottom stair. 'And I was not hiding!' she hissed. But even as she spoke, it was apparent how ridiculous she sounded, looking about herself in the light, realising that her attempt to hide herself in a stairwell wide enough for one, was at best; curious.

'Yes of course, sorry miss.' Annalise looked her over in more detail now she was level with her. She was in a shocking state. Her thick curls tangled around her neck and her shoulders with the weight of the water pulling the ends almost straight. Smudged kohl marks around her eyes, an earring missing from her left ear, the fine damask fabric of her evening gown sodden, torn and frayed at the hems and her bare feet caked in mud. She couldn't tell if her face was wet from the rain or what she thought might be tears streaming down her cheeks. She opened her mouth to speak, then thought better of it, noting Eleanor's changed expression. Even a face so comely did not hide its scorn well.

'Well, don't just stand there gawking, girl. Do something!'

'Yes, yes of course miss.' She wasn't sure what a lady's maid would do in such a situation but knew better than to hesitate further. 'I will bring some towels up to you right away. Anything else I can—?'

'The candle,' Eleanor interrupted her, snatching for it.

She released her grip upon it and headed off to the linen store in the pitch-black darkness. She was fast becoming aware that never having had any direct interaction with the family might be something to be grateful of. Of course, usually, she would not need to. She was only above stairs to pick up the surplus duties since Molly's dismissal. But she had not, from anything she had heard from others who had closer contact, considered them to be of a cruel disposition: Stiff-rumped perhaps, but not cruel.

Was she not supposed to be gone from the house and married off now anyway? She could not rightly say. The constant gossip below stairs was something she had found tedious and often closed her ears to, although it could never be altogether avoided in such a busy kitchen.

When her arms were heavy with the weight of a pile of towels still holding the faint scent of lavender water, she trudged her way back, desperately trying to ignore how much more her feet were hurting. She should be in her bed now. Her sore feet bathed and dressed, the weight off her tired limbs and the blissful hum of sleep beckoning her to its restoration. Her timing was ill. If she had worked just a few minutes faster, or slower, she would have avoided this calamity. Avoided having to wait on a bad-tempered miss...

She was surprised to find Eleanor had not gone on up to her quarters and was now sat on the stairs where she had left her, candle holder clasped between both hands, staring blankly ahead; so preoccupied that Annalise had slipped right beside her when she turned and jumped at the notice of her. Annalise took a towel from the top of her pile, putting the rest of them down on the step beside her.

'You are shivering,' she said and draped it around Eleanor's shoulders.

She stood up quickly. 'Do hurry,' she snapped, pulling it around her neck and waving Annalise to go first up the stairs.

'Yes miss,' she said, hoping she remembered the way through the main house. It would probably be against protocol to take her up the servants' stairs.

They did not speak again on what felt to Annalise like a very long and uncomfortable journey as they traipsed the dark corridors. The creaking of the old grand oak staircase was all that disturbed the deafening silence as they light footed their way up to the first floor. Annalise was still no clearer as to what on earth she was doing out on her own at such an hour, or why she looked only mildly distinguishable from a vagrant. But she got a strong sense that the last thing she wanted was to disturb her parents from their beds and bring such questions to *their* minds.

When they finally reached the bed chamber, she heard Eleanor's stomach growl and stood aside as she pushed hurriedly through the door with her hand cupped over her mouth.

She had not signed up for *this*. Dusting, rug beating and the putting out of fires and lights she had agreed to undertake alongside her ordinary kitchen duties. But dealing with impromptu episodes of inebriation, rude missish behaviour and vomit, had not been part of her agreement with Mrs Crawford. She rolled her eyes and huffed out her breath; she was not going to see her bed a while yet. She closed the door softly behind her, put her towel bale on the nearest surface and watched Eleanor run to the basin and lower her face to it, just in time for the first wave of retching.

If this is what a lady's maid was to endure, she felt relieved, for once, to be a kitchen maid. She took a facecloth from the pile and willed herself to follow Eleanor over to the washstand, despite the pungent stink that was already catching at the back of her throat. When she got there, she kept a tentative distance: she was throwing up into the basin so violently it made Annalise flinch.

When the episode finally lulled, Annalise took a breath and moved in to hand her the cloth and noticing her hair was in danger of bathing in the contents, she gathered it up into a bunch, pretending not to notice the stench of strong liquor on Eleanor's breath as she drew her head up from the basin and swept a sticky curl from her cheek.

'I can manage!' she spat and snatched her hair from Annalise's grasp before being seized by another guttural groan.

'Of course, miss, I was only trying to...' She didn't bother finishing her sentence. *She's impossible!* Had she ever met anyone so discourteous before? She did not think so. If it wasn't for the fact that she knew what her job was worth, she would have marched herself down to her bed and left her to deal in her own mess. But she did know; she knew exactly what it was to work in miserable circumstances every day and this was the first she had encountered in six months of working here. So, instead, she went off to light some of the candles and oil lamps about the room and start up a fire in the grate.

It is a beautiful room, more so by daylight, Annalise thought, with its large windows filling it with light that brought out the earthy tones of the wooden furniture and showed off the polish of the mirrors, ceramic vases and artefacts that were organised skilfully about the room. She fiddled with the wick on an oil lamp and nearly knocked its glass top off and burnt her hand. She shook the pain out silently, hoping Eleanor hadn't noticed. If she could be so belligerent over her gestures of help, she daren't think how it would be if she gave her a reason for such scolding.

She could see her through the dressing table mirror and watched her struggle over to the bed and slump upon it in a shivering heap. She felt a hint of sympathy rising in her but warned herself not to get carried away with such feelings for one with such a lack of gratitude, not to mention such a spiteful tongue. But when she walked around to the other side of the bed and watched as she buried her face into the pillow and began to cry, her conscience got the better of her. No matter how unpleasant her manner, it simply did not feel right to see anyone in such a sorry state. She might be quite out of character for all she could tell; she could be suffering a shock or the coming of a fever? Perhaps she should suggest that the doctor be called? Something warned her though, that this suggestion would not be a welcome one.

She bought herself some time to contemplate her actions by cleaning up the vomit spattered washstand and litter picking the rug of muddy fragments that had dried and flaked off of Eleanor's muddy feet. Whatever could have happened to her shoes? This seemed, above everything else, such a difficult thing to make sense of. Even if they had grown too wet or uncomfortable to go on wearing, surely, she would have been carrying them with her? It did not signify. She would not get answers to her questions, however pertinent, and however embroiled she found herself in dealing with the situation. She was of no consequence and in no position to even ask such questions, let alone expect to have them answered. She must try harder to remember this: she was not in the kitchen now. Although she had to mind her tongue to an extent below stairs, above them, she must behave like she didn't have a tongue in her head.

She was out of her depth and she knew it. She wanted so much to defer this to someone better equipped to deal with it. To lend comfort to her own people in despair was one thing, but to console someone so above her touch, not to mention so volatile, was unknown territory. These people rarely exposed themselves in this way to anyone. How could she possibly know what to say or do? She had only been at Cuddington for six months, and even at twenty years of age, the closest she had come to undertaking her 'ladyships' duties was to prepare their meals. She thought about calling upon Watts, Lady Ashlyn's maid. She would surely know how to handle such a predicament. Not that she much envied the task of disturbing her from her bed either, for she was a miserable and disobliging sort of person too; although she would only be the messenger, she reminded herself.

'Madam, please; permit me to call upon your lady's maid. I fear I am of little help to you,' she said after awaiting a long enough gap in her sobs.

'No... no you must not call on anyone!'

'Very well, I shan't,' she agreed, sighing inwardly. 'But you will permit me to get you some water to wash in and see you ready for bed then?' She could hardly leave her unattended and if there was no getting out of the task being foisted upon her, then she would prefer to get it over and done with as swiftly as it could be managed.

A slightly less hostile nod came as her answer.

Annalise offered out her arm. 'Come and warm by the fire. I'll go down and heat the water, and we'll get you set to rights so you can go to bed.' She waited silently for her reply for a few moments before Eleanor dropped her suspicious glance, rose and took her lead to the armchair by the low burning fire she had managed to stir back to life from the waning embers. Once she had dispatched her there, Annalise set upon the unenviable task of fetching the sick bowl to dispose of the contents downstairs. Covering it as best she could with the discarded hand towel, she held her breath and took care to hold it steady so its contents did not spill out.

As she made the arduous journey back down to the basement for the water, her heels chaffing, hot wax dripping, burning her hands as she struggled to balance the basin and her candlestick, her eyes stinging with the need for sleep; she mulled over the strangeness of it all. She might not be at liberty to ask questions, but she could not help theorising as to what might have caused her mistress to be found in such peculiar circumstances. She had clearly been in her cups tonight, but that did not answer to this alone. Indeed, she had rarely seen women of her own class in such a condition after a night spent at the Three Tuns, but never a lady. It would not be borne.

She went straight to the scullery and washed out the basin, glad to finally be rid of the stench as she swilled the water about it and watched it spiral down the plughole, congealed lumps catching in its grate. She would deal with those after. Right now, she needed water on to boil so she could begin looking to the prospect of her bed again.

Her back ached as she held the heavy kettle beneath the tap to fill it. She slipped her heel out of her shoe momentarily and moaned as a slow trickle of water began to fill it. It was going to be a long night yet. She sighed, having no patience at such an hour for the hopeless new taps that had been recently installed in the scullery. This new apparatus may sound impressive over tea, and certainly the idea of them was sound, but when it came to functionality, they put out barely above a meagre drizzling of water, no matter how many times they'd had the installation man back out to them. But as usual, the Ashlyns' would be the first to jump at such nouveau ideas, and since they never faced the unfortunate task of operating them, why should it matter to them if they weren't fit for purpose? They probably had no realistic idea of what kind of continuous use they were in during the day, catering to their never-ending needs.

She was too tired to go out to the old pump in the yard, which might have been more labour intensive, but would fill the bucket in half the time. She considered the less of evils and decided against it; the night looked unfriendly, angry perhaps, and she didn't want to get soaked. She already had enough to contend with, without getting herself into a state too.

Her efforts were not completely to her disadvantage though. As the water was put to boil, she afforded herself a few moments to make a tincture for her blisters and pick at her untouched meal which Cook had left upon the stove for her. So busy her chores had kept her, she had missed supper and quite forgotten how hungry she was until the smell of cold cuts and bread caught her notice. As the sound of the water bubbled in the copper kettle, she looked about her, realising now how alone she was.

She had never been in the kitchen so late and unoccupied; it seemed changed, sinister in such darkness with sears of lightening illuminating random corners of the room and the rain rapping against the windowpanes with such violence. Even the back door shuddered in its frame every now and then from the might of the wind. She turned up her oil lamp and told herself to stop being silly. Besides, it was rare to enjoy such peace; there was never peace below stairs during the day. The chopping, scrubbing, clanging of pots, chatter and general mayhem of the kitchen could be felt along the corridors of the basement, so that even on mornings off, it was impossible to sleep in. Not that she would want to in any case; her two mornings off a month were sacred. Every minute was pre-planned with errands and she would now have to squeeze in the market stall, she reminded herself, pouring some warm water from the—not yet boiled—kettle, over the salt and marjoram leaf mixture she had just prepared. She took the liberty of taking a clean folded cloth from the fresh pile she had just assembled to take up to Eleanor's room and dabbed it in the fizzing tincture. She flinched as she pressed it to her bloody heel, the sting and relief so soothing and long awaited she ignored the over-bubbling of the rest of the water upon the stove when it at last came to the boil.

When she was done nursing her wounds and binding them in muslin rags and the kettle threatening to spill out, she reluctantly put her shoes back on, added the kettle to the cold water she had waiting in the pail and plodded her way back up to what was fast becoming a familiar route, even in the darkness.

When she returned, Eleanor barely looked up at her beyond casting a quick glance to confirm her identity, her gaze slipping back to the fire on ascertaining this. She was sat precisely as she had left her and despite seeming somewhat calmer, there remained something odd in her manner. She couldn't put her finger on precisely what seemed so disconcerting but it seemed an uneasy type of calm, not of a restful or relaxed kind, but vacant, paralysing.

Setting out the things she needed, Annalise realised now, that despite her accepting this undertaking, she wasn't sure where to start, or how to interrupt this peculiar reverie. She walked right past her quite unnoticed and stood at her side a moment, watching her stare into the flames unblinking.

'Miss?'

No reply came.

She placed a hand on her shoulder to prompt her attention. 'Your toilette is ready miss. Shall we get you out of those muddy clothes?'

She looked up then, shuddered and pulled away from Annalise's hand, throwing her an icy glare. But she didn't say anything.

Poppy was right; there was much improved upon in this family's employ, they had a comparatively good "lot", but they were certainly not so easy to please,' Annalise thought, stepping back from the armchair where Eleanor was still sat stiffly in it.

Was this why there was always such relish in gossiping over the family's affairs? She had never understood it before; had even thought them an ungrateful bunch, not realising they could do a lot worse. It had seemed to her, ill-mannered to speak so of your employers when your portion was fair. If they had worked for a monster like Mr Gint, like she and Poppy had in the past, they would know what it really was to have complaint. But nonetheless, this encounter was causing her to question if perhaps it was an inevitability of the profession to be so treated in one way or another and perhaps the kitchens really were the best place after all.

She had begun to hope, since coming here, that one day she might earn promotion to housemaid, the chance to be above stairs and admire all the finery around her, see the sunlight through the windows, and if she was lucky, have the chance to get outdoors a bit more, even if it was just to beat the rugs. She had thought doubling up on Molly's chores and proving herself worthy might have paved the way to such a promotion after a time, especially as she had such a range of experience under Mr Gint's employ. But maybe it was not the kind of promotion she wanted after all. The kitchens may have been dank and chaotic, but at least the vegetables couldn't talk down to you, continually reminding you of the lowly order in which you were assigned at birth.

She went back over to the washstand and poured the water into a china basin adding some soft soap and rose water. She wondered if she should leave her to wash herself since she seemed so averse to her help and would not allow her to call on Watts. But even a kitchen maid knew what her job was worth and she was not to be responsible for leaving her mistress in a poor state. She went back to her and asked again.

'What is your price?' Eleanor snapped, rising from the seat quicker than her body seemed to anticipate and stumbling a few paces. She reached quickly for the fire mantle and straightened herself up, shooing away Annalise's arms that were outstretched to catch her.

Annalise frowned and took a step back. 'Pardon me madam?'

Eleanor rolled her eyes, 'I am in no fit mood for negotiations, so name your price and we'll be done.'

What could she mean? 'Madam, I do not mean to irritate you, but I have no 'price' as you describe it.'

Eleanor stared at her a moment; 'All of you have a price,' she snarled, then staggered over to the washstand without her assistance.

Annalise wasn't sure if it was simply her temperament or the amount of liquor in her blood but decided she must try to ignore her unkindness rather than let it upset her. She did not like confrontation; it was not in her nature and situations like this made her feel uneasy. So she decided she would not speak beyond what she must and began to help her out of what remained of her evening gown, the fabric drying stiff and chalky, mud flakes cracking and spilling to the ground with it. It seemed such a tragedy to Annalise, to see the ruby damask in tatters, such a waste. If she was ever fortunate enough to own such a marvellously embellished dress, she would certainly have a care to keep it in better order than this. She examined the ragged hems and wondered what on earth she must have done to get it in such a state. She could see from the stitching and still-neat shape of the body that it was a new dress, which until tonight had seen little wear, if any at all. She had grown so used to fashioning and refashioning fabric over and over until the amount of darning repairs rendered it no longer possible, she could hardly believe her eyes. To have such new and beautiful fabric, such fine weave and weight, and treat it with such indifference, seemed to her an act of utter negligence. But looking up at her now, considering the disorder she was in; a patch of blood upon the back of her shift, it seemed as though she had neglected more than just her dress tonight.

She would have to burn the shift; she could hardly send it to the laundry like that without raising suspicion. Of course, the laundry maids were used to washing all kinds of muck, including the monthly kind. But it would likely seem strange to them to have no matching bloody rags or bed sheets to accompany it. And from what Annalise could gather, this seemed the result of more of a one-off kind of incident rather than the routine kind.

'Throw it away... The dress.' Eleanor told her when Annalise began folding it.

Annalise nodded . Their eyes met uncomfortably for a moment as she removed some stray hair pins that were dangling from Eleanor's tangled curls. She could not help wondering what misery lurked behind those dark eyes that seemed at first so endearing and yet clouded over with such ferocity in a flash. She pushed away the thought and lifted her chemise over her head, surprised to find it laid over her stays, but saying nothing of this peculiar arrangement of her clothes. She began to un-strap the soggy stays as Eleanor offered her her back. She was about halfway down when she stopped and frowned, noticing bruises on her arm in the shape of what must be fingerprints; she quickly silenced her open mouth. It was none of her business in any case and she was surely making her curiosity transparent judging by Eleanor's suspiciousness of her. She should have long been curled up in bed now, she remembered as the joints in her fingers began to ache. She tugged at the last row of lacing and at last they slackened and slid undone, but as the corset fell loose, Eleanor raised her hands to her breasts to conceal them.

'Miss, might you prefer Watts to attend you? I confess I am not familiar with a lady's toilette; my work is in the kitchens. If I am doing this all wrong, I am sorry for it. Let me go to her now and she can set things right.'

'No. That won't be necessary,' she said, removing her hands. 'Let us just get this over with. I'm very tired,' she added.

You and me both, Annalise thought. She wondered if she was like this with Watts or if it was just her own ineptitude to blame. She had only ever seen her from afar, but had always thought she had noted a kind of charm about her, beneath all the customary propriety. They seemed to be of similar years. She had always imagined that if ever they were to cross paths and speak, that it would be a cordial exchange. *Looks really can be deceiving,* she thought, as she turned her around until they were face to face. It was an uncomfortable proximity. More so since Eleanor had not noticed the blood stain upon her chemise and Annalise had to make a discreet effort to roll it quickly into a bundle so she did not notice. If she knew her secret was out, she might feel exceedingly embarrassed or, turn very ill tempered. Either way, Annalise had no wish to find out. She tossed it beneath the dress under the guise of going to the dressing table for the hairbrush.

Eleanor's hair had dried well in the fire's warmth, save a damp patch at the nape of her neck. Annalise began at the ends and watched how her tawny curls tumbled as she lifted them, then settled about her shoulders. She had thought her curls must be the result of the efforts of the curling irons, but she realised now it was not. No matter how often she smoothed them out, they bounced immediately back into shape. She brushed them back gently into a bandeau, rung out a facecloth and handed it to Eleanor; she held it to her forehead and let out a little sigh. It was only when she patted her face dry that Annalise noticed the large bump and sticky line of blood just above her temple.

'Miss, you are hurt,' Annalise said, pointing. 'I think you have hit your head?'

She palmed her forehead tentatively. 'Oh yes, I'd forgotten that. Is it still bleeding?'

Annalise drew in closer to examine it. 'No, the blood has clotted, but the swelling is bad.'

'That's good.'

Annalise stepped back and considered that topic closed. She looked her over and considered where to start upon the task of cleaning her up, but when she noticed Eleanor raise her eyebrows into perfect arches, she realised she'd been staring and quickly dipped her cloth into the water and began. She hadn't meant to stare of course, but this was all quite new to her. It was hardly like scrubbing the kitchen table down. Her softness and crevices would require a delicacy of touch she was not sure she knew how to apply. If her touch was too soft, it would irritate her, too hard and it would chafe. Moderate; that must be her attempt. Gentle enough to glide over the cuts and bruises she was littered with, but firm enough to wipe away the stubborn grime and mud that clung to her.

She sponged down the length of each arm, in between her fingers and down the length of each, continuously rinsing out clouds of filth into the water until it turned a murky shade of grey. She could have done with some help, someone to keep a fresh supply of warm water on the go, if nothing else.

As the muddy residue slipped away beneath the cloth and tiny droplets of water bubbled on Eleanor's skin, there seemed now to be a glow to it. She wondered if it was really as flawless as it looked or if it was perhaps some trickery of the candlelight. If it was, it certainly failed to have the same effect on her own pale skin which seemed even more lacklustre than usual.

She had never washed anyone except herself before, and was sure she was doing it all wrong. She studied Eleanor's expression for a signal of disapproval, but her face remained vacant as if she was somewhere else entirely: Responding only in perfunctory ways, lifting an arm or turning one way or the other, wincing occasionally when the cloth smoothed over a cut or bruise.

It was better this way, Annalise decided. It was nerve wracking enough to be tasked with such a duty without an assiduous eye upon her.

As she worked away at the grime, she realised how her hand begun to tremble now with each stroke, trying not to snag her rough and calloused fingers against her softness and the more fragile cuts and scrapes that punctuated it. She concentrated harder to steady it but it seemed only to make it worse. *Calm down, you're being silly,* she repeated until the trembling at last subsided.

She rinsed again then brought the washcloth up to the narrow channel between her breasts and took extra care to be cautious where she touched her. So when Eleanor's eyes shot open and with an alarming glare of indignation in her expression, she shrank back immediately. *What is it?* Had she made some mistake she could not fathom?

'I will manage that,' she scowled and snatched the cloth from her hand.

Annalise glared at her and stepped back. 'Sorry miss, I thought...'

She made no reply but tears rolled down her cheeks as she washed herself down clumsily, lacking all the carefulness Annalise had so deftly trifled over. Her tears fell thickly now. She seemed embarrassed by them, but unable to stop them falling.

Her natural instinct was to reach out to her, comfort her, offer some words of consolation perhaps. But there was a stealthy divide between them that could only be felt, one that somehow managed to wield itself powerfully enough to prevent the care of one human reaching out to the other.

Annalise turned away and busied herself with setting out a clean chemise upon the bed having found them neatly folded in one of the drawers. When the sounds of her sobs subdued, she turned back around and offered her a towel to step into.

Eleanor wiped her face with her hands, stood up and wrapped the towel around her and sat down in the chair. An awkward silence lingered while Annalise moved the basin to the floor, knelt down at her feet and rinsed the cloth out in the murky water, flakes of mud rising to the surface. She held the back of Eleanor's calf in the palm of her hand and felt her flinch again but pretended she hadn't noticed. She was sure she had done nothing wrong *this* time.

The mud was thick and up to her knees; it had dried to a crust and clung stubbornly to her before melting beneath the cloth to reveal more cuts and grazes all over her ankles and feet. She dried them carefully with a pat and tried to pay no attention to the sound of Eleanor's sobs which had recommenced. *Ignore her: she does not like my presence as it is.* But when she looked up and saw her face buried in her hands and tear streams rolling down to her elbows it became too much to bear.

'Miss, are you quite well?' she decided on, after minutes of mulling it over.

Wiping her eyes, Eleanor looked up mistrusting, 'What business is it of yours?'

'None. I just thought I may be able to—'

'Earn a better bribe?' Her eyes were wide with rage.

What? 'No!'

'Take it; take it all, anything you want,' she snatched up a handful of her discarded jewellery that was sat upon the dressing table and threw it to the floor. 'You think I care about this? Take your payment; keep your silence and go. Don't just stare at it, girl, take it!' She laughed like a madwoman and threw another handful down.

Annalise leant over and picked it up. She could hardly believe the turn. What had she done to give her the impression she expected any type of special payment? Did she really believe she would not keep her silence and her secrets without trinkets? Did she think her integrity was for sale?

Their eyes met. A menacing silence brewing in the pause.

'You have judged me badly miss,' she said, knowing she should hold her tongue but feeling so misread she was unable to. She walked over to the dressing table and placed them back upon it.

'Get out... GET OUT!' Eleanor screamed, kicking the basin over in her rage.

The water spilled and splashed the bottom of Annalise's skirts before she had the chance to move out of its path. She peered momentarily at the mess and then back at Eleanor. *She was actually insane.* Her charming looks and genteel façade was but a camouflage for a lunatic. A lunatic that no less, had a dagger for a tongue. She felt her own eyes fill with tears now and her lip quiver. Without further hesitation, she fled from the room, catching her tears upon her lips as she ran.

THE ROOM WAS DARK AND Poppy was in bed when Annalise burst in snivelling.

'Annalise?' She reached out blindly to turn up the oil lamp.

Dash! 'Yes...it's me,' she managed, sniffing back her tears, sinking onto her bed.

Poppy sat up and squinted in the now, dimly lit room. 'Are you crying?'

'No,' she snivelled, trying harder to sniff them back.

'Oh Annalise, what is it?' Poppy rushed over and draped a comforting arm across her shoulders.

She struggled over a few more sobs. 'It's silly really.'

'Silly enough to get yer into this state? Tell me what's 'appened.'

Annalise caught her breath and began to relay the strange events that had lead to her being so late to bed. She left out what she thought she should not convey; the blood stains, the cuts and bruises, the lack of shoes, and kept to the broader details.

'That wretched girl!' Poppy gritted her teeth when she had took it all in. 'You shouldn't o' wasted your good nature on the likes o' them; they'll never afford you the same courtesy.'

'I didn't know what else to do.'

'Shouldn't you have been finished anyhow? I've been in bed for near to two hours.'

'I've been on Molly's chores.'

'On top of your own?' Poppy shook her head.

Annalise nodded and slipped her shoes off at last, flexed her toes and felt the relief.

'You shouldn't 'ave been expected to take them on for this long, you can't manage both.'

'Yes, Cook has promised me to Mrs Crawford for the week. The new girl should be here by then.'

'Tut, we'll see about that,' Poppy said defiantly. 'You must be exhausted, and still you offered to help that snooty Miss.' She shook her head again and wiped a tear stream from Annalise's cheek. 'They're not like us sweetheart; your kindness is wasted on them. Take my advice, and save your energy, do only what you must. We are not at Mr Gint's anymore. There's an army of us here and no need for anyone to manage so much alone.'

Annalise nodded her agreement. At Mr Gint's, there was no end to what was expected and she must learn to drop this mindset now. Poppy was quite right.

'And don't take it to heart and upset yourself, luv; they are as cold as stone, even to their own, never mind us. I know you are new to all this, but don't be fooled by all the finery. Fine houses, fine looks and fine manners but they are no better than Mr Gint really, it's just that he made no bones about what he was. They like to hide it beneath airs and graces, but they don't care for us anymore than he did.'

She supposed not. The better conditions and wages were probably just to sweeten the pretence and, if tonight was anything to go by, keep their not so sweet secrets from getting out. 'No indeed. I should not be so green.'

'You are anything but that. You have the wisdom of at least twice your years; I've seen it with my own eyes. You're just used to plain behaviour, and so was I before I came here. But you adjust; you learn their ways and can start reading between the lines.'

Poppy sat with her a while before Annalise snuggled up beneath her blankets and the lamp died out once more. Poppy always made her feel better, she had become like a sister to her over the years. They had lived and worked together in a much smaller house for a miser of a man where her mother had been head housekeeper for years. How glad she was not to be there anymore, and that was thanks to Poppy.

It had seemed fine in the old days of course, when her mother was alive; she had such fond memories of those days. But after her death, soon followed Poppy's departure from the house and life at Hurley Street changed and fast became unbearable. Annalise was doing the work of three with little help from the few staff that remained. Ironically, she had become so multi-talented in switching between every kind of servant role, except that of lady's maid, for there were no ladies to wait upon in the house. Being the late housekeeper's daughter had left her with a promotion she neither earned, wanted or could cope with for a difficult man like Mr Gint. Nor had it been taken kindly by the older staff who resented her for it. Pushing her to making threats against their employment before lifting a finger under her command, and then taking twice as long as needed for the task, leaving her to pick up the slack. It had been a hellish few months and not just for the grief of her mother.

Cuddington had fast become a happy home. It wasn't perfect, of course, but the house was so huge that the staff numbers formed an entire community of its own, so you were not forced to be amongst those you did not favour since there were many others company you could keep, and most were friendly and welcoming. The wages were a little better; even the work wouldn't have normally been that bad, only Molly had been unexpectedly dismissed and she supposed that still being considered the 'new girl' it was no surprise the extra burden was passed to her. She hadn't minded, she was to have an extra shilling a week for it, and it was a privilege to have the chance to explore above stairs: it was so beautiful, like a palace, she thought. But after tonight, she wasn't so sure.

How had she managed to provoke this on her first proper encounter with the family? Perhaps it was her lack of experience with these people as Poppy had said. Mr Gint might have been considered a gentleman, but it was an entirely different league working under a wealthy Barons household. And with these thoughts, Annalise's tiredness overcame her.

Coming Out.

March 1821.- Eleanor.

'This is it Eleanor, your official becoming of a lady and look at you: I could not be prouder.' Mama fussed about with the position of my veil. We were sat in our carriage outside Buckingham House in the longest queue I had ever seen. Our overly prompt arrival for my court presentation had seemed quite unnecessary now with the procession of coaches pouring in through the palace gates ahead like a creep of tortoises

'Thank you, Mama.' Sentimentality suited neither of us well. 'How much closer are we now?' I asked, and she wound down the small window of the coach to see better in the dimness. The morning light had barely broken on our departure and was only just beginning to brighten. I had questioned the necessity of such an early departure for an appointment hours ahead, but it was only now I was beginning to realise why.

'We are approaching the gates,' she told me and I sighed a long drawn-out protest against the delay.

'Is it always this busy?'

'It is always busy, but after a lull in drawing rooms being held, it always creates a back log and it has been a while since the King's death now. At least we are not at the back end of the queuing, for it now extends twice farther than the point from which we began waiting.'

Small mercies, I thought. Her enthusiasm for the event seemed suddenly quite remarkable to me, given she had had to sit through this ritual three times before for both my sisters, and her own presentation. I would have to hope for sons and not daughters if I was to escape the responsibility of attending this rigmarole again. It had all seemed quite the disappointment so far. All the months of looking to it. All the preparations and expenditures. Hours of dress fittings and practice runs, all to sit in such a queue; and after such a long wait to be officially out, I found it all the more disappointing. Of course, with so long to look to the day whilst I waited for my sisters to progress through their own, I had perhaps had a little longer than most to build such expectation and fantasy of this occasion into something quite unrecognisable from the reality of it. But no less, I had found it to be a great deal of fuss over what had so far proved to be little deserving of the effort.

Despite the numerous fittings for my court dress and careful arrangement of it in the coach, already my skirts had become creased and crumpled from sitting so long in the carriage. Almost as many hours devoted to sitting for a portrait in it, weeks in rehearsal of walking backwards with my train, days of writing out invitations to this evening's celebratory coming out ball and now it would seem I must add to it, a lengthy hour queuing to execute it.

'Do not look so downcast Eleanor; this is your special day. You might try for a better mood.'

'I am sure I will once I am journeying my way back through these gates and I am finally free to enjoy the consequences of it.'

'And in those you will find no end of contentment. The metropolis is yours for exploring now, chaperoned of course. Here, I was going to save it until after, but since you are in greater need of the cheer now, you may have it early,' she said and pulled out a small sealed letter with a length of carmine ribbon tied around it.

I did not recognise the seal as I turned it in my hand. 'Thank you, Mama,' I said, and carefully unwrapped it. Inside, I found my first ever voucher to Almack's bearing my own name and the official stamp upon it.

'Thank you, Mama! This is definitely a worthy cause for a better mood.'

She smiled her satisfaction at my response which took no effort to orchestrate. This was precisely the kind of thing I had looked to in great anticipation, and I knew whatever else, my subscription to Almack's would not fail to enamour me. I had long heard the tales of my siblings and friends, of many nights spent happily in its entertainment and that was quite in spite of the dreadful offerings of the supper rooms. I had longed to dance a German waltz upon its ballroom floor and join Betsy and the rest of our set, who had preceded my coming out by a year or two already. I could now look to Wednesday evenings with the same anticipation I had seen in their faces, but until now, had only been able to look upon with great envy and admiration. Of course, I had an advantage over most, in knowing with certainty I would obtain my voucher eventually, for Mother's position as a Patroness had afforded me that assurance and spared me the turmoil of awaiting the trial of an application that many suffered. But no less, to hold it in my hand and see my name upon it, felt just as satisfying as if I had toiled over the worry of applying for it myself.

And the day continued hereon in the same good spirit once we had left behind the monstrous queues along the mall and the equally trying wait in the crowded, airless antechamber and finally made it into the Throne Room.

'Lady Ashlyn and the Honourable Miss Eleanor Ashlyn,' called the chamberlain in turn, and I had managed to walk and bow as gracefully as in my most well practised rehearsal; I had not tripped on my train, or as I had often managed in practice; my own slippers, as I stepped back.

I had not failed to impress the Princesses in my deportment, nor did it appear, the gentleman onlookers with my looks, as I glided my way in and out in a bob of neat and timely curtsies.

When I later stood at the doors of our London home greeting the unrelenting flow of guests that had paid me the compliment of attending my coming out celebration, I felt equally as admired, and it was liberating to at last be able to receive these attentions officially. For some of them had been paid to me unofficially before now (a detail I had not disclosed to mama or Delores) and it was only now I was free to acknowledge them and give thanks, or as was in the case of Mr Hinkley (who seemed to have an indomitable fondness for us Ashlyn Ladies) make my indifference perfectly plain. I ushered him quickly on to mama as I held out my hand to the next guest in line. His was a new face to me and not one to be overlooked, I noted as the Marquis made us the introduction.

'Miss Ashlyn, I give you Mr Aldingham.'

'Pleased to make your acquaintance, Sir,' I said to him as he took my gloved hand and held on to it and my gaze, a moment longer than he ought. This was a liberty he would have earned my mama's contempt for, but she was still much detained by Mr Hinckley and it had slipped quite past her notice.

'Miss Ashlyn, congratulations. You look exquisite. I am very honoured to at last make your acquaintance,' he said to me, as smooth as newly spun ribbon, a dangerous slant to his smile.

He was all dark featured, heathen looking handsomeness and I could see from the sparkle in his eye, he was quite the rake and not to be trusted for a second. No less I would dance with him later if he asked me and enjoy toying with the notion, now I was at liberty to do so. 'Mr Aldingham, you are too kind,' I said slipping my hand from his grasp and returning his smile: Relieved that we had not been seen and stifling the temptation to laugh out loud at his brazen audacity.

'I will seek you out later,' he said low enough that only I could hear him now Mr Hinckley had moved on and the Marquis was distracted in small pleasantries with Mama.

'I shall save a space on my card.' I dropped an easy curtsey, but inside I was fit to burst with the excitement this new power already promised to me. Of course, I knew his type spelled danger. I was not so green. But I intended only to dance in the smoke a while, not to be burned by the flame. I meant to dance all night, with as many as I could fit onto my card this evening, if their looks and manner pleased me well enough. Which would be good for my constitution, for I would need to do something vigorous enough to expel the overflow of energy inside me from both the excitement of today and too many idle weeks spent in vapid preparation. It was time to forget those irksome weeks of court deportment tutoring, and embrace the coming months, which promised much greater diversion now all the formalities were taken care of.

The night was half spent by the time I was released from my hosting duties and the doors were finally closed. I looked around at the room full of colourful bouquets and a crush of bodies that would have been better suited to the more generous space our country home offered. I fought my way through a secondary flow of well-wishers as I made my way to the punch trolley to take a glass before the next set. I waited only the time it took to empty my cup, to accept new dance partners for the next three, and as I cavorted about the ballroom floor to the first Quadrille, I was in no doubt from the glimpses I caught of other onlookers, that I would indeed have my wish and be dancing all the night.

'Well, it was a good job we did not rely on your company tonight,' Betsy said when I went to them during the interval.

'Forgive me, ladies, I have been so detained this evening I have quite neglected you, and I have not had the opportunity to thank you for the kind gift you left me this morning.' They had left me a parcel with the footman this morning containing *The Mirror of Graces by a Lady of Distinction*. It was not really to my taste of reading. I had a greater preference for novels or books on foreign cultures. Anything there was to learn in terms of conduct for the haut ton had been impressed upon me in multiple manifestations in the course of my mother's position at Almack's and the recent seasons of my two older sisters, notwithstanding my own fatiguing instruction in it.

'It is the new edition,' Clara assured me, but I knew it would have been Betsy's choice. Betsy and I were the closest of our set and, for the most part, we went along very well together. However, there was something of a steely sense of propriety I did not much like in her character and something of a wildness beneath mine, she was not too keen on either. I understood the meaning of the book and her narrowed glance. 'I look forward to reading it,' I said to them as I took my seat amongst them.

It felt good to take my rightful place amongst them at last. We had not really been apart at any length, but as the rest of the group had come out before me, we had grown used to more disparate opportunities to congregate as we once did in the years before it: Me often left to fester indoors whilst they attended London and the season events. It was pleasing to settle into our old ways but with an equal balance in circumstances now we were all out together. There could be no more envy or frustration to divide us as it had often seemed to more recently. We would at last receive all the same invitations and attend all the same soirees. The only thing left now to cause such calamities would be any differences that might arise in the balance of our dance invitations, and that was perhaps more inevitable now than before, given that some of our party were looking to this season with the view to making it their last, whilst others (like me) were ready to indulge in all the frivolities afforded by the luxury of being in the first. The next of which, I was about to set out on, as Mr Aldingham came to collect me for my next dance.

WHEN WE RETURNED TO the country that weekend; my come-out celebrated and flaunted to its fullest extent, I was quite exhausted by so much dancing, dressing, talking and flirting. Although my exertions in London had been very happily spent, I was now looking forward to the respite of Cuddington again. I was not used to keeping London hours, but Mama assured me I would adapt to it quite comfortably once the preliminaries were over and it was in full swing. As for this taster, I would consider it a rehearsal for the real season and use this time in the country to replenish myself in preparation for it. It would be quiet and slow here, as it always was, except this time, with an understanding of its counterpart, I might for once appreciate the calm waters of Cuddington, for just a short while.

Aside from Sheldon's home-coming surprise dinner, I had little else to look to this weekend and was actually pleased for it. Far from complaining for more society, I planned to do nothing more than spend long mornings riding out upon the Downs on Samson's back and lounging about at Anna or Betsy's in idle gossip.

Faithful to my word, the first thing I did on waking Saturday morning was have Samson saddled up. The freedom and seclusion of trotting the Cuddington deer park or the wilder terrain of the Epsom Downs was one I missed greatly when away. Although I would settle for rides along the Serpentine in Hyde Park, I could not tolerate the crush along rotten row for long, before I longed for these undisturbed meadows where we could spirit off on a gallop unhindered. It looked prettier under a blue sky, and I rejoiced at the generous warmth of the long-awaited spring sunshine as I felt the first hint of it on my back.

When we were back on Cuddington ground, I slipped down from Samson's back and led him the short cut through the denser woodland by his reins. I enjoyed the peace it brought to me when I walked in clement weather through the trees with the birdsong about me. There was something soothing in it that I missed sorely during the darkness of winter. As I stepped amongst the tousled layers of crêpey brown leaves that had been long left over by autumn, I noticed the little sprouting blades of green clover, daffodils shooting up in great swathes of yellow, dog roses pledging to bloom from tight buds and cow parsley pushing through the ground, stretching up to bask in the sun's generosity. Spring was late in coming this year, yet it seemed I had been too preoccupied with my presentation arrangements to notice how suddenly it had blossomed. Still, I rejoiced at it, for it was my favourite season: natures promise that the cold, dark bareness of winter was behind us, and as I saw the brightness crack through the woodland in dappled sunbeams, I felt the new hope it brought with it.

When we reached the flat terrain of the formal front lawns, I climbed back up on him and gave him one last trot to reinvigorate us both before I stabled him. As I rode into the courtyard and slowed, I was surprised to see what I thought—at first glance—was Delilah, harnessed to the stable gate. I summoned the groom to help me and to find out what on earth the Elmbridge's horse was doing in our stable, for I was certain now, noticing the white patch at her chest and running down the length of her nose, that it was definitely her. 'Thomas,' I called out again, a little louder and less patiently.

'He is busy, I'm afraid and I take the blame for it,' came a voice from inside which I recognised, but could not at first place, so long since I had heard it. Then as I turned to seek it out, Sheldon came through the stable door smiling widely at me.

'Sheld— Mr Elmbridge!' I corrected myself; we were certainly not children anymore. 'You are returned early?' I gasped and as I began to clamber down in the excitement of seeing him, he came over to assist me.

'Yes, a day early,' he said and as he put me down on the floor and let go of me, I forgot myself amidst the excitement of seeing him and squeezed him back into my embrace. He looked different, felt different: sturdier and less boyish than I remembered him. It had been almost three years, I reminded myself. I pulled back a little to see his face better. His skin was brown with tan, his hair a few inches longer than I'd ever seen him wear it, and the rounder features of his face had grown more angular. 'It is good to see you after such an age,' I said, studying him still, convincing myself this man was my lifetime friend and playmate and not some imposter. He had matured in his absence, but I found him in a bloom of health that was either new or had previously gone unnoticed. It seemed we were both so much changed and yet somehow, for the briefest moment, still the same.

'You look well Eleanor, very well indeed,' he said, peeling my arms from around his neck and stepping back to inspect me. There was a radiance in his eyes as he spoke, and although he was better composed than I in all my overexcitement, I could see his own, shining back at me.

'I saw your new portrait hanging; I wish I could have been there to see you on your coming out.'

I could feel the blush in my cheeks although I didn't understand why. I supposed we must remember each other again—properly—before our familiar ease would return to us. 'You have been greatly missed. But have not missed much here. Up until my drawing room, it has been a dead bore. I could have done with your company before now when Bets and Anna begun abandoning me for their season two years ago. It seemed to me a conspiracy you should all desert me at once for such adventures.' We both laughed and whilst it was meant in humour, there was a dash of truth in it. He was perhaps the only friend who could have been relied upon in my former loneliness, and whilst my lady friends could not help the necessity, he had abandoned me for the adventures of the continent.

'I had hoped to arrive yesterday, but the sea was rough and the packet took above nine hours from Calais.'

'Dreadful inconvenient,' I said with an air of sympathy, although I had no experience to consider what time it might normally take or if it was dreadful at all. 'But I'm sure the toils of travel are lightened by the opportunity afforded to see so much of the world. You will have to tell me the whole when you have time to.'

'I will.' He brushed his hair off his forehead. 'So, it seems I have finally achieved—in disappearing for a while—what I never could when I was here.'

'Oh, and what's that?'

'For you to miss my company.'

I laughed.

'That is what you just confessed?' he said with an affected accusatory tone.

'I own I did.'

'You pretend you did not mean it?'

'No,' I said more seriously, 'But I did not state the degree.'

'Then indeed you must.'

'Well...' I paused for effect. 'You were mostly missed in the battledore pairings, and also a little, at the card table,' I said teasingly. 'But you do not say that I have been much missed, sir?'

'A little; at the pianoforte,' he retorted and we both laughed again.

'Well, I cannot imagine you have ridden the journey over from Nork Park on the day of your return to partake in a sing song?'

'Of course not. I...felt it was time Samson and Delilah were reunited.' Our laughter settled into something more puzzling, and for a moment we stood staring at each other pondering it. I could still remember us as children, when we were taken to Mr Scriminger's stables to choose them when they were only foals. We had all grown up since then, but I could still see the cheeky face of the little boy he once was; same blue eyes and hair a few shades fairer than it was now.

'Are you coming in for tea? My parents will be pleased to know you are arrived home safe and well.'

'Actually, you find me leaving their company.'

'Of course, you said so.' I suddenly felt a little embarrassed by the notion that he had come only for my sake. I supposed we were not the childhood playmates we once were. He was certainly every part the gentleman now. I could note the change in him, an air of a wise and learned mind from his years at Cambridge, and the cultivated experience of life gained on his travels. Both suited him well, and I was as jealous of him now as I was the day we fought in Mr Scriminger's stable because he chose the only female foal that was ready. I wanted her so much I teased him for having a girl's horsey. When that failed to deter him, I changed tactics and impressed him almost enough to retract his claim on her when I told him that my horse would be the strongest, fastest horse ever known and I would call him Samson. I had as good as convinced him into swapping when his papa returned and announced her as his.

I cried all the way home in the carriage and he was so sorry for it, he spent the whole journey trying to give her back to me. By the time I saw him again, I was so in love with Samson I had quite forgotten about it altogether, but he had not. He told me he had named her Delilah in my honour, and when I said I did not like the name because Delilah betrayed Samson, he helped me see it differently.

'Yes, but Samson loved her so much, he told her his most precious secret even though he knew it would give her the power to betray him,' he explained, and I was sure that if Samson really did love her as much as that; he deserved to see more of her, and so I gave the name my blessing. Of course, we had, during our playtimes changed the story to suit us, with them having a horsey wedding and living happily ever after, and suddenly we were stood here as adults, wondering what was to become of our own fairytales...

'El,' he said, and I realised then I had been daydreaming. It had been a long time since I had answered to that, he was the only one who called me by it. Had he not been holding a wrapped package out in front of me, it would have sent me on another tangent of reminiscence.

'I brought this back for you. I hope you like it.'

I took it from him. 'Thank you, Sheldon.'

'Every place I went to, I collected a little keepsake, for I know how well you enjoy foreign things. Each has a little tag tied to it where I have written the place from where it came.'

I peeled back the layers of elegantly wrapped paper and found a small trove of little treasures neatly sectioned into a felt lined box. 'I cannot believe you remembered me so often to gather so many things. So many interesting things,' I said, fingering the contents, finding myself embarrassed at him offering me such a thoughtful gift and then remembering, we were after all, old friends: it could not be considered altogether inappropriate.

'Two and a half years is a long time, but I remembered you often.'

'Thank you, Sheldon, I have never been given such a considerate gift. I will treasure it.'

He beamed at me and I returned it.

'I trust you are not aware that your family have planned a surprise dinner to welcome you home tomorrow?' I remembered he was not minded to appreciate such surprises thrust upon him, and I was happy to find a change of subject.

'Ah, well I had suspected such a trick, which is why I am come early, to see the most important persons today, since I will be forced to slight better conversation tomorrow in favour of the many that will be thrust upon my society.'

I was an important person. I wasn't precisely sure how to understand the meaning of that. 'Well, since you are not staying, I hope you will find some time to tell me all about your travels tomorrow and educate me in the ways of our continental cousins.'

'Of course; I always have time for you El.'

And he was as true to his word. As guest after guest competed for his attentions at Nork Park the next evening, it was I who was afforded the lion share and made to feel quite the guest of honour. We spent much of the evening sat with Mama and a few of the dames around the game table over a freshly dealt pack of cards we had long abandoned in favour of hearing his many tales and descriptions of all the places we never had, and likely never would, get to see. He promised us a private exhibition of his artefact collection when it was arrived back from the continent, so we might better understand his descriptions and references, and I looked forward to the prospect of getting to know him again. Our separation had been a long one; between his years at Cambridge and his tour, it suddenly seemed we missed the part where we both became adults, and here we were now; familiar strangers.

'Forgive me for breaking up the party,' the Viscountess came over to us and put her hand on his shoulder, 'but I must insist we make some more introductions Sheldon, since this evening is in your honour.'

'Yes Mother, of course,' he said obediently, and made his apologies to us.

I watched the expectant wallflowers brighten as his mama paraded him about the saloon. The turnout had been significant and I doubted Lady Elmbridge had suffered any letters of apology to her invitations. The amount of females, particularly of the unmarried kind, reminded me a lot of the King's drawing room.

It didn't take long for his empty seat to render me incomprehensibly bored. I could have listened to his descriptions of the Palace of Versailles or the ancient remains of Rome and Pompeii for as long as they were offered. These were places I had studied in books and seen in portraits, spoke the languages of with reasonable skill, and yet was never likely to require the use of them on any practical level. My brothers had taken their tours years before and returned home with trunks full of relics and portraits with great stories to accompany them too; it was the only time I had ever been interested in anything they had to say, for there was nothing more than the connection of our parents between us. Their growing up was well on course by the time I was arrived in the world, the youngest of five. I was too young to remember the brief years they were at home, it seemed always in my memory, they were away to boarding school. Now they kept their own rooms in London and were rarely seen beyond the obligatory family gatherings. From what I had gathered in recent years from these brief reunions, (and father's complaints), they were spending too much of his money and doing too little to settle down in the city.

Edmund had at least begun to find his way in the world as a man of Law, whilst Henry, the older of the two, had previously spent a great deal of time in the company of Prinny as part of his set (before he turned king) and was the poorer for it, father always complained. Mother wouldn't hear of it of course, and on the increasingly rare occasions either of them returned to Cuddington, she would afford them all the fuss and praise of the devoted sons they had so far failed to deserve.

I did not miss them at all. My childhood days had been full of the warmth of my sisters' company and of course dear childhood friends like Sheldon, who made up for both of my brothers' absences in droves. I looked at him now, his mama on his arm, puffed up with all the pride she could enjoy from a deserving son, and realised how the divisions of our sex would alter things betwixt us now we were so far beyond our years of juvenescent play. Where once we might be looked upon with innocent eyes, now we must be suspected for sitting too close or dancing too much. It saddened me to think it.

'Ladies,' I said putting down my glass beside theirs on the table. I had sought out Betsy and Clara to escape the dull conversation of Mama's set, now Sheldon had abandoned us. I had spent enough years limited to the older company at the occasional country events I had been permitted to attend. I was free now to join the other Debutantes and eligibles at last, and I had no intention of wasting it.

'Well, well, well, the fledgling finally joins us!' Betsy said as I took an empty seat beside them in the row formed around the dance floor.

The orchestra were busy setting up their instruments and I presumed this marked the coming of the long-awaited dances. They were practiced enough to know it was a good time to make themselves available to being asked, whereas I was still learning. I smiled at the welcome and said, 'She has finally left the nest and is ready to make up for the delay!'

The smiles made in reply were of a mixed tone. Martha and Beth seemed quite genuine for they were too mild natured to be wilfully scornful. In Clara's and Anna's, I sensed thinly veiled resentment, for I supposed, to have further competition in their second season was an inconvenience that could not be overlooked, even as my friends. Betsy, who was planning to make this her final year, was pleased enough to have her best friend back to overlook the inconvenience of additional competition. Besides, we all knew that however long she meant to keep him dangling, she would eventually give in to the Colonel and accept his offer.

We were all that remained 'out' in our small town, so it was strange to be amongst so many visiting debutantes tonight, given this was but a country affair. The rest of our childhood set had already been dealt their fate in making matches and moving away to the marriage home like my own dear sisters, or the few that received the unfortunate hand of being passed over for three seasons or more and relegated to the sidelines to sit in the company of the old maids or take up as companions or governesses to the married women. This was the fate of mother's companion, and my recently inherited chaperone, Delores. She certainly had a comfortable lot, and yet it was clear she desired so much more than her position offered her.

'So, who do you have your sights on for the first dance?' Betsy asked from behind her fan and I noticed by the widening eyes of the others that they had also heard her question.

'I cannot presume to know, let's see who applies to my card.' In terms of male company, the offering was relatively small and I could not pretend to be overly thrilled with the bachelors in attendance. The disproportionate number of debutantes would easily outweigh them in any case and I sensed an unhappy number would not dance at all tonight. Clara, who had complained at the offering, took it upon herself no less, to give me a rundown of each and every one of them, with all the necessary details of their birth, connections, annuity, and character where she had the knowing. The looks at least, she left to my own judgement.

'Clara, Eleanor might have been kept behind, but she has lived here as long as the rest of us!' Betsy said exasperated, and we were all glad when the music began to play, putting an end to this irksome prattling.

I danced the first set with Mr Woods (a dull streak of a man who was destined for the clergy). I agreed for the sake of getting it out of the way, for I knew his application was coming and I had no wish to put him off and scupper my chances of dancing the rest of the evening. In London company, his asking might have felt quite the insult, being so much below my touch, but in the more limited society of the country, I could not easily dismiss his invitation however much I desired to. He was followed by an applicant I did not recognise and surprisingly, one Clara had missed from her extensive list. He was introduced to me as Mr Harper-Craythorne of Beddington Park, and only a moderate improvement on Mr Woods.

'Now, he is one worth the gossiping,' Betsy told me once he escorted me back to my chair. Mother had been watching us quite distractedly, but I could not understand what I had done wrong; I remembered all my steps and remained impeccable in my manners. We had danced a short quadrille and I was glad for its duration because although amiable enough in manner, there was something in his gaze that I found disconcerting in its over familiarity. So I was all ears for this run down in order it might explain my natural dislike of him.

'New money: a Nabob, father says,' she began, and I was relieved to find the justification of it immediately. The rest I entertained for the sake of politeness, half listening and half considering who the better-looking fellow in the coquelicot tailcoat and oriental cravat was, and thinking I would be happy for a petition in his direction.

'Once an officer in the Navy,' she rattled on about this Craythorne fellow, '...made a handsome fortune through his commission and time in the Indian subcontinent. He has just come into Sir Radcliff's estate at Beddington and is said to have twenty thousand a year. His only redeeming feature it appears. His stepfather has just bought a Rotten Borough to which he has invested, so it seems he means to make a political career, but continues some merchant shipping trade abroad I believe.'

With this enlightenment, I understood mothers piqued interest in my dancing with him and regretted my naivety. I still had more to learn despite my commitment to the cause. I looked at her now and she was beaming from above her wine glass and it confused me until I followed the direction of her stare.

'Miss Ashlyn.' Sheldon had slipped beside me quite without my notice. 'Will you do me the honour of this dance?'

I smiled in earnest. 'Yes, of course, Mr Elmbridge.' It seemed strange; us both putting on such airs when we had never required such formalities before. We would grow used to it eventually I supposed. But would we also grow used to this altered expectation of us now we were grown? I felt eyes upon us from every direction and feigned ignorance to them all. I would have sooner gone back to the days we could play Battledore on the lawn. It was so much easier to be in his company then, without society's glances. Back then, I might have stolen his company for the entire evening to hear more of all his tales from abroad, without anything beyond a friend's interest being drawn from it. Now, I was in constant danger of evaluation whenever in the company of his sex. Whether I was in it for the sake of friendly regard, an inescapable duty or a playful flirtation; all would be construed as a potential romantic interest and judged accordingly. I must try harder to get used to it.

'It seems you will dance all night Miss Ashlyn, despite our humble gathering,' he said taking my hands in his for the dance and it felt odd to feel him through the satin of my gloves when I could still remember the sight of our grubby smaller fingers, deep in some muddy patch, hunting for worms to make a makeshift home for.

'Yes, I think the novelty of a new Debutante on the scene is owing to it.'

He laughed a little. 'Yes, I think I have not been the only one waiting for your come out.'

Waiting?

We broke and changed partners momentarily and when we returned together, I saw something in his eyes that told me he had meant what he had just said. I felt quickly unsettled by it and almost forgot my steps as I was swept away by another dance partner before being twirled back toward him.

'Well, Mr Elmbridge,' I said thinking on my feet, '...You yourself have been given quite the welcome back with so many debutantes having turned out for the occasion of your homecoming. I think you too must expect to be dancing merry!'

'No. I shan't be. I mean only to dance a couple of sets tonight to appease my mama's coaxing and to not seem wholly uncivil to our guests.'

'Come, you say it as though I do not know how much you was used to like dancing.'

'You speak of when I was little above my tender youth.'

'So you say you have since altered and here you are looking quite like someone having a jolly enough time, if I might take the liberty of saying so.'

'Well of course I am,' he said and I frowned. 'I am dancing with you.'

A new position.

February 1821. - Annalise.

'Oh Poppy, I am so happy to see you!' Annalise flung her arms around her with such enthusiasm she almost knocked them both off the doorstep.

'There now, no tears,' Poppy said, slipping an arm into hers. 'Where's the ol' git? Shall we go in or can you nip out?'

'Let's nip out; he's in his study, but I wouldn't put it past him to overhear us.' Mr Gint had a remarkable talent for hearing through walls and floorboards. The staff had learned over the years not to speak on anything of consequence unless he was out or to bed. Annalise closed the door soundlessly, holding back the latch until it met the jamb before releasing it and stepping quietly into the basement yard, gently up the steps, and taking care not to let the gate snap back and clang against the iron railings as they spilled onto Hurley Street. They did not speak again until they had walked to the end, crossed onto Bourne Street and into Cadogan Gardens where there stood a wooden bench in a prettyish spot between the ornamental shrubbery and a bed of violets. Strictly speaking, it was intended for the inhabitants of Cadogan Square, but was always used by its neighbours, since it was the only one in the vicinity.

'Now,' Poppy said at last, taking a seat on the bench and Annalise settling beside her. 'I have some good news. It is not perfect mind, I know you're not so keen on kitchen work, but the position is open for kitchen maid and Cook is desperate to fill it now all the pre-season events are firing off.'

'Really? That is wonderful news, Poppy. Thank you!'

'As bad as that then, is it?' They both knew it would have to be for Annalise to be so enthused at settling for the prospect of a kitchen maid's work in order to escape from beneath Mr Gint's roof, but then they both, having worked in this household, knew what a trial it was to remain under such a roof where the staff were few, the work demanding and moreover, the master never content with his maids fulfilling the usual duties, but always ready to seize the petticoat of any he could get away with so doing.

Poppy had drawn the line at *that* 'duty' six months ago when he had, upon ringing the bell for the warming pan before bed, chanced upon her. She had worked for him for fifteen years or thereabouts and although she had seen things she mightn't wished, and had heard whisperings she preferred not to attend to, she had, until that night, never had direct cause for complaint: Could not attest to him having ever made such demands upon her person, and as such, thought nothing untoward in having to attend him at his chamber, given he kept no proper valet and they were short on staff that night. So, having heated the pan and placed it beneath the blankets to warm up the bed, she did not expect to find his long-fingered hand creep about her waist like a snaking vine of nettles as she tucked in the disturbed sheets. She stood up with a start and watched the bony, warped joints retract back into a fist. It had taken all her constraint not to ball up her own fists and attack him with them, so furious she was at him daring to touch her. It wouldn't take much, him so twisted up with rheumatism and yelping with gout, she was surprised he even looked to such activities, had the capability; the thought turned her stomach. But she was not a murderess, even if he deserved to be murdered: and so, she settled for giving him a sharp setting down and threatening him with a word to her brothers on this head.

She had left the next morning, up bright and early to the registry and never looked back. Her appointment at Cuddington had been a doubly happy occasion, for not only had she escaped Mr Gint's, she had bagged herself a promotion to Under Cook and a pay increase to go with it. Technically, it would be considered a like for like position, but coming from a household of eight staff to one of over forty, it was certainly a promotion in duty, if not in title. Her only sorrow through it all had been in leaving Annalise behind. They were like sisters, better in fact. Mrs Tullier had always told them that real sisters often squabbled and nipped, but Poppy and Annalise never had. Those had been the good days, not that they realised at the time just how precious those days were, until they were no more. Until Mrs Tullier was no more; and the house fell into disorder of every kind.

She had been the binding that had held it all together, even in her frailty and to her deathbed she had managed, commanding from it, to keep things running smoothly. Poppy had grieved for her own sake and for Annalise's, for even though Mrs Tullier was the housekeeper, she had been like a mother to her too in the many years of her employ there, kept so far abroad from her own. She at least still had her real mother, but Mrs Tullier was all Annalise had in the world when she left it, and to abandon her to that hellish house knowing her to be so alone and what kind of house it was, had blackened Poppy's days in her new job. Days that should have been happy ones—that were certainly kinder ones than she had been used to—felt curiously tainted with the loss and fear for her surrogate sister.

She understood of course, why Annalise was reluctant to leave it. It was not just the worry of finding another post or grieving her mother's loss; she had grown up in this house. All her memories of her mama were sketched within these walls, even if all her nightmares were now also contained within them. "To leave behind one was to leave behind the other," she had told Poppy on their many discussions, or persuasions as they had more accurately become. But this time, it was Annalise who had sought out her help, asked her to keep a look out for a place. Poppy had done so eagerly, enquiring of the housekeeper and the cook in not just Cuddington, but all the other households she had connections with. Weeks had passed with no news, no hope and no half days off left for Poppy to visit her on, until today.

'So, the position is open for interviews now and even though it's not what you might wish, and by gad I know it's far below your talents, but it's a way out eh? And you'll be with me. I even 'ave a spare bed in my room now the other maid's left.'

'Poppy, it sounds perfect, and I am so much grateful for all your efforts.'

Poppy smiled but had failed to hide the concern behind it.

'What?' Annalise asked, noting it. 'Is something the matter?'

'No love. I just 'ate to see you so reduced to this.'

'I am not reduced, Poppy. We both know I was never really meant for housekeeper and I would certainly be thought too young and too inexperienced to offer myself out to such a position in any other household. Besides, I prefer to see it as a means to sparing the reduction of my character, not as a podium to reach from.'

'You don't know what a weight off my mind it'll be t' know that you're safely away from this place. It'll be the first good night's sleep I'll have in months.'

'Well, let's not forget I must first manage to be offered the position.'

'Of course you'll get it. You'll out trump the rest naturally, and you have the advantage of my putting in a very good word for yer.'

'I know. Thank you, Poppy. I wonder what I might have done if it were not for your help. I have had not a moment to spare to make replies to the adverts in the paper and they are so few now the country folk are preparing to abandon to London.'

'Don't be daft, you don't need t' thank me. You know what music it is t' me ears at last.'

'Then why do you look so heavy hearted when at last we may rejoice?'

She shuffled in her seat a little, looking down at her boots that she was scuffing back and forth against the gravel pathway, scattering stones. 'I just can't help but think 'bout what a brute 'e must 'ave been to change your mind, that's all.'

'He has not been, that's the thing.'

She looked up now, brow knitted, eyes narrowed.

'I mean, he has been his ordinary cantankerous self, I own. But, well, not in the way you mean Poppy, he has not proposed to me the things he attempted upon you.'

'He 'asn't?'

'No. Quite the contrary in fact. It's quite a puzzle. I seem to be the only one safe from such attempts.'

'Truly?'

Annalise nodded. She was equally mystified, but it had given her little comfort having to beat back his continuous attempts at the other staff, who she had now, with the exception of the older staff, managed to reduce to the employ of two village women coming in for day work and a girl for the scullery at half days. It had been arduous to effect such changes, knowing she herself must stay behind a while to see off the younger or more vulnerable maids into other households, bringing such positions to their notice and encouraging them on to them. She knew she must stay a while so that she could vouch for them and secure them places by her references when Gint took offence at their rebuffs and put them out. It was in this she had seen the opportunity her new position presented to her, to reconfigure the staffing in such a way as to protect them from his advances. There had been few advantages to this unsolicited promotion to housekeeper, slipping into her mother's old shoes without wanting to or even being asked. The tasks unrelenting, the older staff put out by her new standing. But there was this one justice afforded her. Of course, her mother had done just the same, in her own way, although she had done her best to hide it from Annalise. Her method of protecting the younger staff was to self-sacrifice.

Annalise had no intention of resorting to that. She had seen what that did to a person. It was only when she had worked this out that she truly understood why her mother could never let go of the spirits, even when they were killing her. Because without them to medicate her senses, she could not bear what she had to do, what she had to become. "Never, never ever be free with yourself Li-Li—promise me," she would beseech her often as she grew older. "There are men that will tell you anything, promise you anything to make a bed fellow of you. Trust none of them until there is a ring upon your finger. They will as soon as leave you with a babe in you and turn their backs if you do not have a care." And that, Annalise understood, although it remained unuttered, was how she had come to be: the product of some rake's broken promises and her mother's broken heart. That also unspoken, was the reason she knew her mother stayed at Hurley Street and tolerated the things she had learnt to in the course of her duties; because of *her*, because she had to think of how she would put a roof over her head and food in her belly if she left this house. Mr Gint was a "tolerant" master she had said when Annalise had first found out the true way of things. Most respectable households would not take in an unmarried maid with a child to support. Most would not cover the expense of an extra mouth to feed, an unproductive one at that, which had accounted for most her younger years. But she was no longer a child, and now she was set to work anyway, it needn't be here.

How she begged her mama that they leave, find positions elsewhere. They could save up, rent a room somewhere and take up day work or take in sewing and laundry. Annalise did not mind what, she would adapt, it would be worth it to see the pain fade from behind her mother's eyes, to see her off of the drink when it begun to ravage her health.

But she was already too weak by then; too broken and too much used to her lot to even dream of any possibility beyond it. All her dreams had been invested in her daughter's future, her own was of little consequence to her now. Annalise had accepted that eventually, stopped nagging and instead turned her head to saving up her own wages and keeping a look out for other places that might have two positions to fill. But by the time she found such a prospect, her mama was too sick to leave her bed.

'Are you alright luv?' Came Poppy's voice, reaching her from her unanticipated reverie.

'Yes. Yes, sorry Poppy, I was just...thinking. What did you say?'

'I says its time you put yourself first and make a clean break, luv. I dunno why he's kept 'is 'ands off you, but I'd expect it's only a matter o' time.'

'Yes, to be sure. I am ready to go now, Poppy, to look ahead at last. Now you must brief me on how to please the cook. You know I haven't a great deal of experience in the kitchen, and in a grand house like that I'm sure they ask for much fancier things than Gint does.'

She laughed at this. 'Indeed, they do! I've never seen the like of what is set upon those tables. Even on an ordinary day, never mind when theys 'ave guests to dine.'

On their walk back to Hurley Street, Poppy briefed her on so many things she must now attempt to commit to memory, her head was in quite a spin for want of remembering it all. She was determined she must not fail. She must do her utmost to impress the cook and win herself her ticket out of here, whatever it took. Poppy was right, now that she had ushered away his other prey, it was surely only a matter of time before he turned upon her.

Whatever it took came easier than she had supposed it might. There was one matter that neither she nor Poppy could quite see how to overcome and one that would not be dismissed in a household like Cuddington. Who was to provide her a reference? Her dear mama was no more. Mr Gint would sooner blacken her name than let her leave, and she was the only other one of authority in the house to write such a thing. It was then the idea came to her. She would have Pike write it.

Pike was of late, her arch enemy. She had been in service to Gint for more than twenty years and despite her long standing, he had put Annalise ahead of her natural promotion to the position, to everyone's bewilderment. Of course, Annalise had been doing the work, in her mother's place when she had been at her worst, but Pike was just as capable of so doing. She and Mr Clifford; the butler -come -footman, -come -valet, and the only male staff member excepting the hall boy, had set their faces violently against her since she stepped into the role. She had not meant to put their noses out, she had even tried to refuse the job altogether, but it was not to be. Gint said she would take it or be put out. Why she could not fathom. Perhaps out of some peculiar regard for her mama's service to him, guilt perhaps? She did not know. But now she had an idea that would set things to rights. Pike could be her reference, because she was soon to become the new housekeeper.

'OW'S I EXPECTED TO write a reference when I can't even write's my name?' she said, peering ugly faced back at Annalise when she met her with the proposition.

'I will write it Pike, you need only vouch for it should anyone enquire.'

She looked at her mistrusting. 'And you say I'll be housekeeper here, just like that?'

Annalise nodded.

'And that's all you want. Me to swear to your character?'

'Yes, that is all.'

'And to your word, I'll be 'ousekeeper?'

'Yes.'

There was a moment's pause where Pike shuffled around various expressions upon her face, calculating the plausibility perhaps, before eventually saying, 'Fine, you 'ave a bargain.'

And so it was. Annalise traded her housekeeper's chatelaine for a kitchen apron. Annalise got her reference and her new position at Cuddington and Pike, got what she no doubt considered, to be her rightful place. It suited everyone well. Everyone except Mr Gint perhaps, but he was left with no other choice and she would lose no sleep on his account. Annalise could only hope the little good she had done would be upheld. That Pike would take heed of what she had said and keep the young maids to day work below stairs and out of the master's reach.

In any case, she could not dwell upon it. It was now beyond her contrivance and therefore, as Poppy told her often, was little to be gained in feelings of guilt or melancholy. It was for Gint to indulge in such feelings, Pike too if she did not keep her word, but not she. She had done all she could. More than most, and was not to live out her life as a shield of armour as her mother did for her. Her mother did it so she would never have to; she raised her not as the illegitimate child of a servant girl, but in the way that she was raised: to become a young woman endowed with skills and understanding above and beyond the ordinary. Out of the common way. Few of her class could read, write, play at the piano and speak another language. Few could make their own clothes with such flair. But she could. She could because of what her mama had always intended for her; to reclaim her rightful place in society, to restore to their lineage, that which was lost to her in the war; a respectable existence. A life that was not in constant want and shackles, servitude and limitation. A life that could be enjoyed, cultivated, rejoiced in for its own sake. That was the life Mrs Tullier had once known; had been born to, and the life she wanted to give her daughter; not the one she had been forced to suffer into since that mighty fall from grace. Of course, all was relative; a daughter of a book binder was hardly of the demi-monde. But it had been a happy existence. Her mother had always told her this with such fond reminiscence in her eyes, as if she were gazing into an altogether different dimension.

It was hard for Annalise to understand it, it was the only life she knew and it had not seemed a hard one to her, for the most part. Not until the blissful ignorance of youth was lost to her alas, those days of never considering what it took to keep a roof and full belly, what labours were exchanged for this small mercy. How much sweeter it tasted back then, when it appeared it just 'was' in the same way the sun rose every morning and the darkness fell at dusk; it just 'was', always had been, always would be she supposed. Bacon and eggs at the breakfast table and good meat and vegetables from the garden each night, perhaps even a trifle or bread pudding now and then. Fresh linen, the softness of a cosy bed and her mama's cuddles and bedtime stories. It had all seemed so natural. So necessary that she could hardly imagine these comforts as something denied to others. The idea that she was luckier than many scratched and scathed at her when she learned of it. The realisation that the invisible price tag attached to these things was so alarmingly high: Too much to bear the paying of and yet no recourse to do otherwise. It was only then, Annalise began to resent these happy comforts. The bacon seemed too salty and the bed too full of lumps and dips. It was then she vowed she would carve them both a way out of this existence.

She must keep that promise now and break free, Poppy told her. She must not waste all her mother's painstaking years of devotion to her cause. All the endless hours spent teaching her her letters between ironing linen and beating Chinese carpets. The diligence spent in encouraging Annalise to know and speak her native tongue in French and not slip only into the default of the English words spoken all about her. The nights she would sit up in the dimness, squinting over a needle and thread, her joints aching from her toil, directing Annalise's hand, showing her how to make up patterns and then dresses. "Promise me Li-Li, promise me you will leave this place when I am gone. Promise me you will go out into the world and make your mark. You are worthy, you know. And the war will one day fade from people's minds, the French will once more be known, not as only enemies, but the fine chefs and Modistes they are celebrated to be. Then you will understand the world as it once was, no better: a better world is coming, I think. And you will live it Li-Li, you will seize it and live a good life, a happy life. I know it. I feel it."

Annalise did not know how she was to achieve such a feat, especially now with her dear mama gone from the world. She did not know what kind of world was to rise from the ashes of the war that had marred her mother's life so cruelly, or how it may come to alter, or how it once was before Napoleon. Only that Poppy was right, her mother had a dream for her and it was in a brighter future. She had fought to give it to her, her whole life and it would not be wasted. She would not let her down.

New neighbours.

March 1821. - Eleanor.

It never took much to induce Cuddington into a furore, but news of the Craythorne's' arrival had sparked intrigue and speculation amongst the town and surrounding parishes. We were a familiar set of well-established old families that occupied these sleepy Surrey villages. There were few comings and goings here, so to have new neighbours was expected to spark some interest I supposed.

My father put down the invitation he had finished reading out, to the Craythornes' introductory ball, and swiftly reached for his newspaper.

I wasn't particularly interested in the hearing of it over breakfast, as I sipped on strong black tea and buttered still-warm rolls. As far as Mama was concerned, the nouveau riche were beneath our acquaintance, even if they had taken residence at Beaulieu Manor and were to become our nearest neighbours.

They were rumoured to have an even more obscene fortune than their relative Mr Craythorne of Beddington, but even that did nothing to improve Mama's opinion.

'Whatever is it coming to with all these nabobs and cits! First this Mr Harper-Craythorne inheriting Beddington and now these other Craythornes at Beaulieu! I think we will have to move to Stapleford Hall at this rate, if this is the way things are to go here,' Mama complained into her plate of devilled eggs as my father took refuge behind his copy of *The Times*.

'Mama, what fancy!' I said, repressing a smile behind my teacup. 'I have not known you even visit Cambridgeshire in what must be five years since father purchased Stapleford for you.'

'Well, that's may be, but it is not through want of going!' she said rather pointedly to the back sheets of my father's newspaper.

'You could take Delores and make a holiday of it,' father said from behind them.

He had only brought it to keep peace with her. I think the intention to make an additional summer home of it was hers alone.

'Holiday indeed! Mr Ashlyn, if it has not escaped your notice, I have Eleanor to bring out this season and have been engaged in the very same these past years with Harriet and Caitlin. When you expect me to take up such holidays I don't know.'

I bit into one of my rolls; I knew precisely how this was set to go.

'Anyway, I shan't be put off the subject. You must make answer to this invitation and you know full well that I shall not go!'

'The Elmbridges will attend Beaulieu, so it's hardly our place to create a fuss,' my father said flatly, abandoning his paper now and casting a determined glare across the table.

'So you knew of this already then?' Mama accused him. 'Already given our answer I suppose! I see how it goes.'

'It was a passing comment in Brooks, nothing more.'

I saw Mother's scorn building in her face, a branch of capillaries colouring beneath the corner of her right eye, the only blemish upon her otherwise flawless complexion. But the Elmbridges were our friends as well as our superiors, and father knew as well as I, that their going would seal her acceptance, whatever the rant we might suffer for it.

'You cannot simply buy your way into society, Mr Ashlyn. Twenty thousand a year or no, he is a nabob and I shan't be persuaded to sit at his table!'

'Helena, they are to be our closest neighbours now, whether it is liked or no. We would do well to get along with them since our land shares the boundary with theirs.'

'The taking up of a respectable residence does not entitle one to the respect of your neighbours when you are without good connections, Mr Ashlyn!'

'They are not without connections, they have simply been abroad a long while.'

'Puh! Yes, abroad in the pursuit of trade. A nabob like I said. Connections indeed. And if you speak in the name of neighbourly goodwill, then perhaps we should start taking up invitations from the tenant farmers!' She abandoned her plate and flicked her fan out and vigorously fanned herself. 'I am still the daughter of an Earl you know!'

It was Mother's favourite phrase in the face of impropriety.

'Lest us ever forget,' he said exasperated.

Father, a mere Baron, was not quite of Mama's pedigree, a detail she rarely permitted him to forget. His fortune, which was vast enough, and increasingly growing, was in part the bargain of a good match but in equal part, the fruit of a wise head for good investments and a modern approach to managing his estates. Not that Mama ever considered such investments with the taint of 'business' about them, for Father had a steward to take care of such details.

I looked across to her, she had set her face at an angle against him; red blotches had risen about her jaw line. This, I knew, was far from over.

I sat silently and pensively feigning disinterest, flicking through *La Belle Assemblee* and nibbling at plum cakes throughout the rest of their exchange; which consisted, as per usual, of Mother's best amateur dramatics and Father's sparse grunts, sighs and eventual disappearance behind his paper. Yet no less we would go, and all of us knew it.

We made the usual round of morning calls, the Fitzroys, Lady Claremont, left a card for the Marchioness who was out, and paid our duty to the dowager. In each case staying no more than fifteen minutes, which suited me well since there was less time to dwell on the Craythorne gossip, which seemed the only conversation on everyone's lips. It was as if this small quarter had quite forgotten that the season was just about to fire off and we would soon be abandoning the country for London. Although it seemed our departure would now be delayed if we were to accept this invitation, and this had not gone down well with anyone, myself included.

We were scheduled to have only another week here before we were back in Berkeley Square ready for Mama to take up her Almack's interviews and me, my first assembly. Now it seemed we must either delay it by another, or rattle up to London and back down again in a flash. Everybody was displeased and yet it seemed that everyone was minded to accept the unfortunate circumstance. I was puzzled as to why they should. It was not as though it was an invitation from Carlton House.

I was looking forward to escaping all the vexation on our journey home, and decided I would take a walk on the park before breakfast. I was just about to summons Molly to have my walking dress laid out when the Viscountess, Lady Elmbridge, was announced and mother beckoned me to the drawing room to take tea with them.

When I entered the drawing room, Mama was flapping around the Craythorne invitation in her hand and protesting (much more politely than I had heard her do in private) at the audacity of these, "strangers" turning up out of the blue and expecting society to jump at their invitation.

Lady Elmbridge sipped quietly on her tea and listened patiently to the revised edition of Mama's complaint. I envied her countenance, for even though I shared Mama's disappointment, I had little patience with her when she was in one of these passions.

'We thought...' Lady Elmbridge said gently, 'perhaps it was a neighbourly gesture. And felt it our duty to set a good example. We wouldn't want them to feel that this was not a...forward thinking place,' she said evenly, settling her cup soundlessly back into its saucer.

I glanced at Mama; she looked like she had been stung by a wasp. I had certainly seen little of country society that would induce me to call it forward thinking, I considered.

'Well, yes of course,' Mother said quickly to this, 'and were it not in the chaos of the start of the Season, I would have taken the trouble myself to have paid them a call by now, but we have so many invitations in London, I am quite inconvenienced to have to delay our going to Berkeley Square to attend theirs,' she said more reasonably and busied herself at the tea tray.

I could see the word nabob in her thoughts, even though she had left it out for Lady Elmbridges hearing.

'Yes,' the Viscountess cut in, 'I do indeed sympathise. I myself had planned to leave for London on Wednesday, as Lady Jersey said in her letter; we are much needed in the interviews, but they shall have to manage without us for a few more days. It seems with the rise of trade we must try to embrace the future and rise to the challenges as they present themselves.'

It sounded precisely like something my father would say, and I had no doubt she spoke Lord Elmbridge's words and not her own. For the most part, men seemed to me disinclined to employ such cunning methods, preferring a more straightforward way of going about matters. But Mother was quite skilled in exercising her disapproval, and I would not have put it passed Papa and Lord Elmbridge to have jointly instigated this visit to help bring mama around, although I couldn't fathom why they should want to take such pains for the sake of these mushrooms.

Despite Lady Elmbridge's honeying efforts, after she left, Mother was in quite the rage, in spite of smiling through it at tea. For the next half hour, I was subject to her pent-up complaints; that my father's parliamentary interests should not come before his sense of propriety. For it quickly became clear that the tolerance of these climbers was due to the financial and political support Mr. Craythorne's trade connections would bring to the Whigs campaign, and they were still sore over Liverpool's re-election. It was not the first time Father had been known to associate with men of the rising classes in his political quests, but it was the first time he had ever brought such affairs into our private company. The former could be overlooked, the latter most unforgivable in Mama's view.

It was a welcome relief to eventually escape out onto the park when I finally prised myself from the stale confines of the house. It was not the same as being able to ride out to Epsom as I had been permitted to enjoy pre come-out, but I was to take the rough with the smooth now and accept that along with the novelty of joining the marriage mart, I must too accept being closely guarded in preservation of my reputation. So I accepted it, however disagreeable I found such restrictions. I looked forward to when Delores would return home and I would be free to enjoy much of my regular pastimes once I could be properly chaperoned again. She had been given leave to tend her sick aunt just before my presentation in London, leaving me with Mama to fill the void. I had never thought I would see the day when I wished for such surveillance. But if it was left much longer to Mama and her dislike of little beyond tea sipping calls, I should quickly lose my head.

Moving on.

March 1821. - Annalise.

As the last of her trunks were loaded onto the carriage, she stepped into the hack and closed the door behind her, a conflicting sense of relief and sadness at leaving what had, for all its shortcomings, been her lifelong home. She peered through the small carriage window, taking one last glimpse at the house: a mist of condensation blooming on the glass from her frosty breath. The sun was up but it remained a crisp early March morning, and she considered for a moment, that this view she knew so well, would soon diminish in familiarity. An unexpected tear rolled down her cheek as the horses started off and the house faded from her view; first the black front door, then the row of terraced houses, then Hurley Street itself, as they pulled onto the stirring High Street.

It had been an unceremonious parting. No farewells or well wishes. Pike would be glad to see the back of her and step into her new role with the eagerness of one who had lay a long time in wait for such an opportunity. She had spotted her at the window as the hackney carriage pulled up outside. Checking, Annalise supposed, that she was actually leaving, at last. And it was at last. What she had longed for. So why, she wondered, choking back another wave of tears, did it feel so sad, so terrifying?

She consoled herself with a few of her fonder memories of the place, memories of her childhood, her mama, reminding herself that those resided not within those walls, but within her own heart and mind and that nothing could ever separate her from them. Yet somehow, despite her holding onto this fact, she couldn't help feel that she had left something there, something inexplicable, indefinable, but certainly something.

She had put her melancholy mood down to the fact that having spent the past few days packing up and sorting through her mother's things—a job she had until now refused to do—it had at last taken its toll on her. Her own things had taken very little time to assemble, a couple of dresses beyond the one she was in; one tired but still pretty, one she had never gotten around to re-trimming, and her best, usually reserved for church on Sundays, she had decided to wear today. She would be furnished with new work clothes on arrival, Poppy had told her, so she could leave

Gint's old clobber behind. She would have new dresses and aprons aplenty and never have to toil over the laundering of them since they had a whole army of maids whose sole job it was to see to all the household laundry. This would be a welcome benefit, Annalise considered. She had grown used to doing her own since Gint was too tight fisted to pay the washer woman for any longer than it took to see to his own wardrobe.

She wondered, as she left the familiar roads behind her and found herself meandering down country lanes unknown, how long it would take her to shake the memory of that awful man, of the last few years of horror from her memory. She prayed it would be quick. She looked to the day when they seemed so distant and removed from her daily life that she could hardly summons them. She only hoped that as she let go of those, she would hold firmer to her mama's.

When they pulled through the gates of Cuddington and began rattling up the long driveway, it at last all seemed real to her. She watched through the carriage windows as the sun cast its rays across the meadows and woodlands, feeling the promise of spring in the air. This, she thought as the house came into view, was her new home and how marvellous it was; from its well-manicured gardens, to its magnificent façade. It seemed already such a world away from Hurley Street, she was certain that it was here, she could begin to put her life back together again.

As they pulled around to the side of the house, parallel with the servants' entrance, she saw, as the coachman lowered the footplate and helped her out, a fine lady, dressed in her habit, patting down the mane of a handsome looking bay across the stable yard. She had first assumed her to be the Lady of the house, but soon realised, as she caught a better look at her face, that she was likely far too young, seeming not much beyond her own years. The family didn't involve themselves in the business of interviews or meeting of staff, Poppy told her. Not in grand houses. It was only their personal staff they took the trouble over; the rest were left to the judgement of the cook, the housekeeper or the butler. Poppy had met Lady Ashlyn once though, when Cook was ill and she had been tasked to step in and meet with her for the week's menus. 'Other than that,' she said, 'you never saw them below stairs.'

'Good morning,' said a footman slipping in beside her, quite without her notice.

'Good morning, Sir,' she said surprised at the prompt reception.

'You can call me Will,' he said brightly. 'Miss?'

'You can call me Anna,' she said, returning his smile as he began unloading her things from the hack. Cook had decided that Annalise Tullier was too fussy for a maid and she would be called Anna below stairs and Tulley above them. Annalise had of course, made no protest to this, but couldn't help but wonder if, like her mama had often told her, folk were still weary of French sounding names, even though the war was over.

She was quickly shown into the basement and then to her room by one of the housemaids, since the kitchen staff were already busy to work on the day's tasks and couldn't step out to receive her. She had hoped to see Poppy on her arrival, but looking across to her bed on the opposite side of the room to her own, she felt at least some comfort in knowing they would soon be reunited. She was to have an hour to settle in and unpack, then get changed into her new kitchen clothes and join the kitchen staff for their one-o-clock sustenance break. After which, she would then be set to learning the work for the rest of the day.

She would have sooner set to work right away. It seemed strange when the housemaid closed the door behind her, to find herself in the unfamiliar room all alone. She sat down upon the bed and sat thoughtfully a moment, getting used to the shape of the small room, its plain plaster walls and flagstone floor with a well-worn rug stretched across the middle between the beds. It was not lacking in practicality as such, she considered, examining the small hanging rack which she assumed they were to share, a washstand with a cracked mirror above it, a stack of fresh towels folded upon the shelf below. A stocking laden wooden drying rack beneath the tiny window that shafts of sunlight broke in through, illuminating what would have otherwise been a very dully lit room. A mismatched chair and a side table was tucked into a corner too small to accommodate it comfortably. It had everything they needed she supposed, but it seemed to lack the homeliness she was used to; papered walls and pictures upon them, a vase of flowers or stack of books upon a shelf. She reminded herself, as she sunk back onto the bed, that she had been used to the best room in Gint's—the housekeeper's room, with its double bed that she had shared with her mother until it became only hers.

She was sure she would grow used to it, however strange it felt to her now. They were lucky, Poppy said. There were only three rooms in the basement for female staff; one belonged to the cook, the other to the housekeeper, and this one. The rest of the female staff resided in the attic and were always squabbling and complaining of each other since they shared one large room, dormitory style. Being the first up in the morning to light the kitchen stoves, get the water on to boil and prepare the breakfast, was what afforded them this privilege of enjoying their own private space down here. And for the privacy at least, she felt grateful.

JUST BEFORE ONE-O-CLOCK, she was dressed in her new clothes and set out for the kitchen. The skirts were much heavier than she was used to and a little too big for her in places, but she had tied her apron strings tighter to improve it and planned to alter them in the evenings to procure a better fit. She was not sure how long the brilliant white of her apron would hold up against kitchen work, and was glad it would not be her task to launder it at least.

It was only when she closed her door behind her and was faced with the dilemma of which way to head, she realised she had forgotten to ask the way to the kitchen. She had only been once on her interview and it had all seemed such a labyrinth, it had never occurred to her to attempt to record its direction to her memory.

Finding the corridor vacant and realising there was no one to ask for directions, she tried to retrace her steps. She was sure they had come in from the left and so headed back in that direction, only to find herself stuck at a new junction she did not recognise. She scanned the rows of doors for a clue, some were unmarked, some carried a brass plate upon them: "STORE", "DEED ROOM", "STILL ROOM", she read as she passed them. When she got towards the end of the corridor and the plaques read " BUTLER'S PANTRY", "HOUSEKEEPER", she realised she was off course and turned to try the other way. This end, consisting of only unmarked doors, was even less helpful and she began to despair at the prospect of arriving late. No sooner had she considered this, she heard the din of the stable yard clock sounding the hour. She looked around her and took a breath, *'Calm. Think.'*

As the chiming waned, she paused and listened for the direction of the stifled echoes of noise rippling along the corridors and decided she must follow its direction; it would surely lead to the right place. She recalculated her steps, her ears strained to every reverberation as she walked quicker now, the sounds growing closer, a shifting of feet against flagstone and...wheels turning over, she thought, creaking and rattling. After a few more turns, she found them tangible and as she turned to follow them, found herself amongst a throng of servants navigating a very busy passage in both directions. Maids carrying buckets one way, boys rolling small carts carrying milk churns the other. She sighed her relief. 'Excuse me,' she said to one of them when she gained on him, 'where is the kitchen, please?'

'Back the way you came,' he said without stopping and continued rattling the milk churns along until he was lost in the throng.

''scuse me miss,' came a voice from behind her then and another lad, a little older than the other, overtook her with his trolley and she pressed back against the wall to give way to him.

'Are you headed for the kitchens?' she called out after him, but her voice seemed lost amongst the drum and he did not look back to make an answer. She was beginning to despair and felt the heat of frustration and panic flushing to her cheeks when she heard someone say from behind:

'We're headed for the kitchens. Are you lost?'

Annalise turned to see a trio of maids coming up in her direction. 'Yes!' she said relieved, to the blonde one who spoke to her. 'Could I come with you?'

She smiled. 'O'course. Like a maze when you're new in't it.'

Annalise returned her smile and felt the relief of having been rescued. 'I'm sure I don't know how I'll ever come to know it,' she said, keeping pace with them, heading back in the direction she had just come.

'You'll know it like the back 'o your hand before the weeks out. I take it you're the new kitchen girl?'

'Yes, Annal—Anna,' she corrected herself.

'Lizzy and this is Bea and Tabby,' she pointed to the other two girls who smiled back in her direction.

'Pleased to meet you.'

'We work in the dairy, that's where you were headed.'

'Oh?'

'Yeah. It's a long way off, good job you bumped into us when you did, this corridor runs all the way beneath the stable courtyard and out to the farm and dairy buildings. We're on our way to the servants' hall for our break, its right beside the kitchen. I suppose cook will be expecting you?'

'Yes, although I dread to think how late I must be. Do you know what time it is? I was supposed to be there at one.'

She looked at Annalise with a hint of pity in her eyes. 'We left at one. We're ne 'er on time by the times we get over to the house anyway, but I'd guess we are usually there about ten minutes after.'

'Ten minutes!' This was not the first impression she intended to make and when she was at last delivered to the kitchen where Cook was waiting, hands upon hips, cheeks flushed crimson, she realised quickly that her anxiety had been quite justified.

'Forgive me ma'am,' Annalise said sheepishly. 'I left in good time, but got lost on my way.'

'Lost? We are but a minute from your room!'

'I realise that now, ma'am, I set out in the wrong direction. I am ever so sorry.'

She considered her carefully. 'I do not know what kind of house you are used to, but here, we keep to the clock precisely. Do you think the bread cares for excuses if you over bake the loaf for ten minutes? No, it burns! If you cannot keep to the clock, you won't be long for my kitchen. '

Annalise swallowed. 'Of course, ma'am, it won't happen again.'

You shall take the fifteen minutes remaining of your break and present yourself to Maggie for your work. Now, get out of my sight.'

'Thank you, ma'am.' She dropped a curtsey and left swiftly in the direction of the servants' hall, fighting back the urge to let her tears fall. It was the sight of Poppy, when she saw her through the glass paned door and stepped inside, that helped dispel them. So happy to see a familiar face at last, they faded almost instantly.

'There you are!' she said, standing up from the table and putting down her cup.

'Poppy,' she said, exhaling her relief as she met her around the table in a quick embrace. 'I am so glad to see you.'

'Me too, luv, me too. Now, sit yourself down and get this down your neck,' she gestured, pushing her towards the untouched place setting.

'Did she give yer a setting down?' asked Lizzy, who along with the other two dairymaids was sat amongst a row of less familiar faces.

Annalise nodded.

'Don't worry about it, luv, the upper servants are all uppity here. But you'll get used to it,' Poppy said.

The others nodded their agreement.

'But you're in good company,' said Lizzy. 'We all stick t'gether down 'ere at the lower rungs.'

Annalise smiled and exchanged introductions with the other staff at the table before filling her plate. She hadn't much of an appetite despite her lack of breakfast, but it was a long time off 'till dinner yet, Poppy told her, so she made an effort all the same. It was the nerves, the anxiety she thought, that had stirred up nothing but nausea in her stomach as she took a bite of bread.

It did not take long though, for her reservations to fade. She sat over a plate of cold cuts, immersed in chatter and instantly felt the warmth of kind and friendly company.

Maggie was tasked with showing her the ropes that afternoon and they got along merrily enough; peeling and chopping vegetables and plucking guinea fowl, whilst Cook and Poppy set about cooking for the evening meal. The work was relentless, but the company merry. Even Cook, who Annalise had made her best attempts at keeping her distance from, seemed too absorbed in her tasks to take much notice of anything else.

The kitchen was a vast one, nothing like the one at Hurley Street. It had rooms coming off of rooms, and large tables more than double the length of the ones she was used to. Being one end of the table allowed enough distance from the other end for your conversation to be lost among the din and clatter of pots and pans. It was that which permitted her and Maggie to chat upon all sorts of subjects whilst appearing to be conversing on the work she was being instructed in. The peeling and chopping had been self-explanatory, but it had never been her task to pluck and butcher fowl before and it was trickier than it looked. She hoped, in time she might prove herself worthy of more interesting work, like that which Poppy and Cook were engaged in on the far table where they were decorating sweetmeats, constructing structures out of sugar paste and tipping out moulds of trifles and jellies. It was exquisite work. *Too good to eat,* Annalise thought when her and Maggie were tasked with taking the trays of the completed works of art into the cold larder to keep away from the heat of the huge ranges that stretched half the length of the room. These minute long journeys between the table and the larder seemed instantly calamitous to Annalise as she struggled to steady her trembling hands as they balanced trays of delicacies she was petrified of dropping. She didn't though. However much she feared she would, especially when the other staff seemed to have little regard for what you were carrying as they dashed past with pots and pans and baskets of produce.

'Here,' said Maggie once they returned to the cold larder with the last round. 'Try some.'

Annalise stared at her outstretched hand as she broke one of the delicate looking lemon shaped sweetmeats between her palm and offered her a handful.

'Maggie, I'm sure we must not,' Annalise said, astonished at this act of vandalism. The other staff had obviously not had the necessary fear instilled into them by Cook's gruff set downs, she thought, watching Maggie shrug and tip the contents of her palm into her mouth.

'They never miss the odd one here and there,' she said, speaking with her mouth full.

'I suppose not,' Annalise said, looking at the vast number set upon the many trays as they slid them onto the shelf. She, however, was not willing to put herself in the way of anymore trouble on her first day and as Maggie chewed down the last mouthful, licking the powdery sugar residue from her palm, Annalise pointed out the dusty traces upon the corners of her mouth and littered down the collar of her dress before they returned to the main kitchen.

The next task was to gather up all the discarded feathers into one bucket and all the innards into another and take them down to the farm buildings, Maggie said. This task, Annalise realised, was every bit as unpleasant as it sounded, but, as Maggie also explained on their journey over to the farm, it afforded them a sniff of fresh air for a bit if they went across the courtyard rather than through the basement underpass. They weren't really supposed to, she advised her when they were more than halfway there. The family preferred them to be out of the way during calling hours so they were supposed to go through the underpass. But the kitchen staff usually got away with it, as it was not very often they were sent about such journeys and they had no choice but to visit the kitchen gardens in plain sight anyway.

When they had dumped their buckets with the farm hand, Annalise asked; 'What will be made use of those scraps?'

'I thinks the innards go to the dogs and the feathers are ground down for fertiliser or somein.'

'Oh.'

'Over there,' Maggie pointed to a high walled enclosure, 'is the kitchen garden. The tatties, roots and stuff are sent over from the farm but's the herbs and salad greens are all planted in there and it's our job to get them when they're wanted.'

Annalise made a mental note of its location as they walked their way back.

'In the summer, when it's busy and all the berries and fruits start ripening, we sometimes get asked to 'elp with the picking too, especially if it gets really warm and everything starts bolting.'

Annalise liked the sound of this and for the remainder of the journey, envisaged balmy summer days with a basket on her arm, plucking strawberries and blackberries from their stems.

This daydream was quickly usurped however, by the next task set upon them, which Maggie told her was to scrub the kitchen table down with salt before they would be needed to help with the batter mixes and broths for the gravies.

The day went on in this way, one task leading to the next and when at last all the kitchen staff, under Cook's assiduous direction, delivered the many dishes, steaming tureens and piping hot cloche's to the small serving hatch where they turned the responsibility of their labours over to the finely dressed servants on the other side, was the end in sight.

Poppy, now free at last to speak to her, whisked her back to the room once the serving hatch was at last shut.

'We've got about a twenty-minute break to get washed up and get out of these aprons before we sit down to dinner,' she told her, untying her apron strings and discarding it into the linen basket before slumping onto her bed and letting out a sigh. 'I could go to sleep right now.'

'It's certainly a lot faster paced than Gint's. Is it always this busy?' Annalise said, sitting down on her own bed and examining her pruney looking fingers.

'This my luv is an ordinary day, it's when they start up with the parties and visitors we really know what work is. We were lucky, the last one they had was in London for the daughter, so we were spared that, but it shan't be long before it's our turn.'

Annalise dreaded to think how the kitchen could possibly cope with more demand, when it already appeared to her, after just one day, how many things there were to manage. They were well managed at least, and she supposed that was the key. Rather than the pitch in approach at Hurley Street she was used to, here everything had been neatly divided into delegated duties. It seemed to her there was a taskforce for every duty and everyone (except her) knew what their role was and what was to come next.

'Don't we need to help with the servant's dinner?' Annalise said, it suddenly occurring to her that they were the kitchen maids.

'No luv, Maggie and Susan are tasked with that. You and me have the pleasure of serving the upper servants at seven, in their private dining room.'

'So we eat separately?'

'Yes, from them. But the rest of us—the good folk—all sit down together. You'll get to meet them all soon. The footmen are often a little late if the family dinner drags on, but Grantley usually dismisses them once the last plates are sent back to the scullery and it is only their glasses that need tending to.'

It seemed to her, like a beast that never rested, the cogs always turning and needing someone or the other to peddle them. 'So once we have served the upper servants, are we done for the day?'

'Almost. We just need to have a few cold cuts and the like on hand for supper if it's called for. But it's rarely more than a few trays to prepare if it's only the family. There's only three of the family in the house nowadays, although it was once a family of seven. Last daughters about to fly the nest this year, then, Cook always says, our load will get very easy. Without all the marriage mart entertaining and society affairs to cater for, it will likely be dinner for two with the occasional party to manage.'

It seemed absurd to Annalise suddenly, what a workforce it took, just to keep the three of them catered for. What an expense it must have been too, so much money on the food and wages. Even Gint's accounts used to shock her but she dreaded to think of the numbers that must be recorded in these estate ledgers.

It was later that night, once they'd stripped off their aprons for the final time and sat about the servant's hall with mugs of beer in hand, that Annalise at last began to understand the cause of Poppy's satisfaction here. All the servants (except of course the upper echelons who relaxed in their own parlour) were crammed around the table together. Chatter and laughter filled the room, the fire burning bright in the hearth. Some (most of the manservants) played cards and puffed on cigarettes, others took up sewing and others sat sipping and talking above their mugs. *Community*. That's what it was. That which was missing from Gint's where there seemed only division and thinly veiled scorn. Here there was friendship, laughter, a little complaining here and there too, but unlike at Gint's where the staff pitched themselves against each other, here their seemed to be solidarity. Their grumbles were directed at the upper servants or family rather than amongst each other. It was in that moment, she realised that she would indeed come to like it here after all. Where she had of late known great loneliness and isolation, here, she would remember the warmth of good company and friendship.

Mushrooms.

March 1821.- Eleanor.

When the Craythorne ball finally arrived and my ears were fatigued at the mention of the thing, I was braced for it to prove quite the ghastly affair. I think everyone was, and no doubt hoped (and of course everyone was there, the attendance of the Elmbridges ensured that). But when we arrived on the lantern lit portico of Beaulieu, we were much surprised to see the hubbub of so many persons pouring into the place. It was indeed as good a crush as any we might expect to attend in London, if I allowed myself to admit it.

Mama said nothing as we climbed the stairs; windows aglow above us with silhouettes moving beyond them. The exterior stonework had been cleaned and seemed dazzling white against the night sky, the marble colonnades polished to a fine shine so as to catch the colours of passing gowns and coats and trick the eye into thinking its shade momentarily altered.

'Good to see the old place back up to the knocker again,' said my father as we crossed the vestibule.

'Yes,' I said to break the discomfit of my mother's enduring silence. It seemed quite resurrected to its former glory, having sat vacant and neglected these past years. I remembered then, a flash of my coming here to play with the Braithwaite's daughters in childhood; Mama and Lady Carlton sipping tea on the lawns. It seemed sad to remember it now they were gone. I wondered if that was part of Mama's protest, beyond the mushroom line; that her friend's home was to be taken over at all, (lest still by such persons) having still not come to terms with their loss. It was once thought Caitlyn might be matched with their eldest, before the ravages of war claimed his life. I shrugged off the memory and my pelisse, handing it to the outstretched arms of a footman as we awaited our turn to be announced.

I could hear the music now, a string ensemble plucking up a dulcet symphony I did not recognise. I followed the sound over to the gallery doors and beheld a glimpse of the swarming of the large saloon ahead.

'What a ridiculous painting.'

I turned to see what my mother referred to. The wall behind us, comprised of white wood panelling with heavily decorated gilt pattern work, set in an even more elaborate gilt frame as the centre piece, hung a family portrait of the new occupants. Quite possibly the most over-sized and overstated picture I had ever seen. It took the place of Lord Carlton's portrayal of his fine set stallion who I remembered now, was poised on two back feet about to leap somewhere off yonder.

'Keep your voice down, Helena,' my father cut in, turning her away from it.

I, however, paid it some curious notice. I had not before had the opportunity to put faces to these phantom upstarts responsible for this unwelcome delay to my first season. I should like to know them in advance to better avoid their company. I studied the scene: the father proudly poised in red coat and sash, hand upon his hip, stick propped in the other. The mother dressed in a gown of sea green silk with crimson and gold thread embellishments and a bandeau of pearls across the forehead. She seemed small, shrunken against the figure of her husband, pale face framed with mousy curls tumbling from a height. Two sons, not dissimilar of looks, not quite twins; both baby-faced, sporting fine navy coats and crisp white neck cloths: One a fraction taller than the other, the other stouter. Not un-handsome, not anything to account, however. Then on a sofa, one arm crossed to meet the other as it rested upon the plump upholstery: the daughter; auburn curls, small hazel eyes, a faint spattering of freckles about the nose; fine bone structure but not an exquisite beauty. In the background some exotic view outside a window. Peacock feathers in a gold trimmed vase in front of it.

'Eleanor!' my father scolded, and I stepped away to go in with them seeing the queue had now dissipated.

'Lord Henry, Lady Helena, The Honourable Miss Eleanor Ashlyn.'

We made our way into the saloon, nods and hellos in multiple directions as we crossed the floor. It was finely decorated, that which I could note from what was not already so much obscured by the throng of persons crammed about it. Exotic looking drapery, chandeliers I had stopped counting at six and the leafy heads of towering plants fanning out above the crowds. I looked at my parents; smiles fixed, outwardly sanguine. How our announcement had shrunk, I considered then; my sisters and brothers all out in the world, and me, only a step behind them. Then it would be just the pair of them left with no one else to despair of except each other.

'Miss Ashlyn.'

I turned to see Sheldon at my shoulder, eyes bright, smiling.

'Mr Elmbridge, good evening.' We had gotten quickly used to this formal address now, however unnatural it had at first seemed. I watched my parents proceed on without me. *Yes, quite happy to abandon me now.*

'Good evening, I did not mean to separate you from your company.'

'No matter.'

'I just thought you might like to know, my collection from the continent has arrived.'

'How exciting.'

'When you are able, you must come to Nork Park and let me show it to you.'

'Yes, to be sure. I will look to it.'

His smile was beaming wide. 'And I.'

There was a lingering about his gaze that caused me to suddenly feel most aware of its singularity and I searched for something to say to dispel it. 'So, are you finding yourself well settled into country life again after being so long in far more exciting places?'

'I am acclimatising.'

'You do not long to go back and abandon this dreary parish now the reality of its docility has taken its effect on you?' I said in earnest, for if I had a choice between the attractions of the continent and the stagnant goings on of Cuddington...

'No,' he said quickly. 'At least, for now, I am quite content to be reacquainted with those much missed ...and a climate far more genial.'

'Of course. Well, if you will be so good, I must find my party and a glass of something.'

'Yes, forgive me for detaining you. I will escort you, if you will allow me?'

I took his arm and wondered how such a simple gesture felt so peculiar. There was nothing to answer in the propriety of it, but the hairsbreadth between our shoulders seemed charged with some invisible current I could neither fathom nor ignore. When he deposited me back with my mama and her set, having taken pains to secure my dance card before taking his leave, I noted how the ladies paid particular attention to his presence and offered approving smiles in our direction.

Not you as well?

'Pray, what was that about?' Mama said to me as soon as he was gone. She had brightened suddenly too.

'Mama, keep down your voice,' I said, with a reprimand in my own.

'Well?' she said a little quieter.

'Well, what?'

'Well, what did Mr Elmbridge want?'

'I own I'm not entirely sure.' This was true, what he did was to invite me to view his collection, and make claim to my dance card, but somehow, that seemed not equal to the measure of what he *wanted*. That, I was still trying to determine. 'Something about his collection arriving.'

'Well then, perhaps we can call tomorrow to see it.'

'But we have plans tomorrow?'

'Nothing pressing my dear.'

I let out the beginning of a sardonic laugh. Now I should be worried. My mother did not alter plans for anything that could not be avoided. 'You will excuse me, Mama, I must find a drink, and my friends.'

I quickly found a passing tray to snatch a glass from and sunk it quicker than I knew was polite to. I was sure I had never seen so many man-servants in attendance except for at court. The sour tang of orange wine on my tongue steadied me as I paused to consider where they would likely congregate. *Well, where are you ladies? I must have some diversion from this madness.* I stood, surveying the saloon, so much in a swell of bodies I could not think what direction to begin in. I drained another glass and allowed myself a moment to consider. The gossiping whispers of mamas set still about my ears:

'I am told Craythorne is already promised a seat in the Commons, how can it be?' said Mrs Turner behind her fan.

'He has his stepfather to thank for that I believe. They have jointly purchased that rotten borough out Reigate way, Gatton. Its suspected they mean to take a seat each.'

'So they do have family connections here then?'

'Well, the stepson is as much in trade as them, although he at least has some credible connections; I believe he's inherited Beddington Park. Twenty thousand a year I heard.'

'Twenty thousand! Well!'

'I heard thirty thousand was the number.'

'Yes. I think you are right Mrs Turner, I too heard something of that order. On the prowl for a wife no doubt, now he has Beddington.'

'You should make an introduction to Bethany, Mrs Jameson.'

'I do not think so!'

'Twenty thousand is twenty thousand.'

'Eliza, you cannot mean it?' I heard my mother put in a plea for sanity.

'Precisely, Helena!' Mrs Jameson concurred. 'Well, I find this lavish extravaganza quite vulgar from persons of their class—money or no—exhibiting themselves as some kind of royalty,' she snapped, with such wickedness in her tone it silenced them quite abruptly and put an end to that line.

I pushed along the meandering rows of bodies stood back-against-me in conversation, looking for my set. I had not noticed even one of them yet. In fact, I did not recognise half the faces I passed in the search as I crossed from one end of the saloon to the other. It was quite unnerving to have to exchange so many polite acknowledgments with strangers when I could not place them, nor could I risk offending someone of significance. This was the rub. Everything else would have tricked the eye into thinking this some regular kind of tonish affair. It could have fooled anyone, on the surface. The problem was precisely that; you did not know who you were amongst; what sort of persons. Who you could accept on your dance card; who you must decline. Whose smiles you must return, who should get the cut. What a labyrinth it suddenly seemed to me, a very dangerous one at that. Why, the stakes must have been so much higher than we could fathom for our parents to subject us to such danger. Of course, danger was inevitable at such large affairs, but at least when attending on respectable hosts, you could feel some assurance as to the vetting of their guest lists.

'Forgive me!' I exclaimed. I had stumbled into a gentleman as I turned back on myself, finding my friends not to be in this quarter either.

'Quite forgiven,' he smiled, far too familiarly for such an occasion and I stepped back and patted my skirts. 'Can I escort you somewhere?'

'No Sir, I thank you but I do not think we have been introduced. You must excuse me.'

'Shame indeed,' he said smirking, stepping aside.

Rake.

I was growing impatient with this search now. *You better have not wriggled out of this!* I could see Betsy contriving the means to manage such a thing. But the others would surely not dare; besides, I had already seen several of their Mama's with my own.

I found them eventually, sat upon a long sofa, tucked away in a recess so concealed by the squeeze, I was lucky to have discovered them at all.

'Hiding, are we?' I said when I was close enough not to be overheard.

'What else are we to do if we must endure it?' said Betsy, shifting to make room for me beside her.

'Well, you certainly picked a safe spot; I have been searching for you at least ten minutes now!'

'Good,' said Anna flatly. 'If you could not easily spot us, let's hope no one else will.'

'You will not dance tonight?' I said to her, knowing how much she liked to dance at every opportunity.

'I may, so long as it is the right kind of invitation.'

'Indeed, who are all these persons? I do not recognise many at all,' I said, lowering my voice.

'Well how could you?' said Betsy incredulously, 'these are hardly of the polite world.'

'No, but they do seem to be all-the-crack,' said Clara, more impressed than was wise to let on. 'I have seen no less than three of those new Parisian ball gowns that have only just been published in *La belle*. They must have come direct from Paris.'

'Clara, surely I do not need to spell out the difference between being plump in the pocket and of good society?' Betsy scowled. 'Besides, I find them all so vulgarly bedizened I fear a headache will ensue from just the looking at them. That's of course if the Lombard Fever does not take me first.' She sighed into the rim of her glass before consoling herself with a long sip from it.

'I do not think it so very shabby,' said Beth in that defiant tone she often tried to press against Betsy's. 'There are many officials here of the East India Company and the Viceroys office, diplomatic sorts, my father told me.'

I noted that my parents were not the only pair to be in discord over this issue, remembering Mrs Jameson's rebuff, just a moment ago.

'Did he indeed?' said Betsy rolling her eyes. 'I wonder, does he expect you to make up to them in the hope of finding you a match?'

I could have warned her not to push her luck with Bets in such a mood; indeed, she should not have required such a warning. I watched Beth flick out her fan and turn to Martha.

'Well, you can all dance your slippers to threads and play up to these mushrooms if you wish, but I intend to give the cut sublime for the entirety of the evening if I must. That was the condition of my coming I set out to my parents, who seemed to prefer it over my refusing altogether.'

'You will dance if the Colonel is here though?' I said to rouse her from her mood.

'I shall credit him with enough sense not to come here at all. But then this is the Elmbridges doing, so anything is possible I suppose. No offense Eleanor,' she added quickly.

'Why would you offend me?' I asked, puzzled.

Anna let out a snort but before I could give her a setting down, I was interrupted.

'Miss Ashlyn.'

I saw Betsy about to spring to my defence, so I quickly made answer, although I would have preferred not to. 'Mr—' I searched my memory for the name. 'Craythorne,' I added with a smile, more for the apology of forgetting him than any earnest regard for seeing him again. Our brief set at the Elmbridges was the slightest of recollections and I had not known at the time, the significance of his namesake and his relationship with our new neighbours. I saw nothing to denote a family resemblance.

'You are well I hope, Miss Ashlyn, and your family?'

'Yes, I thank you, sir, quite well. And yourself?' I tried to ignore the heat of Betsy's gaze. The others were upon me too but their disapproval did not signify.

'Yes, well thank you. I wonder Miss Ashlyn, could I trouble you for a space on your dance card this evening, if you are inclined to dance this night?'

I looked at my card, Sheldon's name already marked upon it. 'Yes sir, I shall be free after the first set,' I told him and bid him away. 'Well, what else could I do? Sheldon has already engaged me in the first set so I could hardly put him off!' I said in answer to Betsy's bewilderment. But before we could continue, another gentleman I had danced with at my coming out was before me. He had seemed to open up the flood gates, and for the next fifteen minutes we found ourselves detained by some fellow or another putting down his name on our cards. For the most part; not strangers, even if hardly friends. But a few had dared to make bold introductions to us, until all but Betsy's card was nearly fully claimed.

'These gentleman are far too coming!' Betsy complained when we seemed at last to be left alone a while.

'To be sure,' I agreed, wondering how I would keep up with the pretence of civility for such a time.

Then, came old Mr Wilmott to seek out Martha, and we all fell silent when she accepted him. I was surprised to think him capable of a jig in his years. 'Whatever was that?' I asked bewildered, turning to the others for an explanation. Wilmott would often attempt to secure Martha's interest, but never before had she entertained such endeavours.

'Oh, you have not heard then?' said Anna behind her fan.

'Heard what?'

'Mr Nash, finds himself in dun territory; squandered the Baronets fortune and more besides. If they can't put up for the debts, he will be headed to the Fleet, and Martha and her mama quite ruined,' said Anna with a disturbing note of delight in her tone as she recounted it.

'It cannot be!' I said astonished. 'Sir Thomas provided well for his wife, surely—'

'He did, but that blaggard Nash is never away from the hells,' Clara added.

'If you ask me, that paper scull of a mother of hers should have never remarried,' Betsy said, jabbing a finger at no one in particular. 'I mean, what need had she beyond her own vanity? The Baronet had come up to scratch in settling upon them in his death. Besides, she was far too old for such dalliances.'

'She was only eight and thirty,' said Beth.

'And having a settled estate and daughter to bring out, need not have concerned herself beyond that endeavour. She must have known a man of his years could only be on a fortune hunt and yet she let his flummery win out, and now look at poor Martha, no dowry and soon to be in the suds,' Betsy concluded, quite exasperated to have to explain what was so obviously wrong about the whole affair.

I looked across to Martha, entertaining Mr Wilmott's conversation with all the good grace of one so well bred and felt a pang of regret on her behalf. 'You don't truly think it as bad as to cause her to wed him, do you?'

'Well, I am of a hope some other solution might be found before the scandal breaks. But it shan't be long I fear.' Betsy reclined back in her seat and tucked a chestnut ringlet behind her ear. 'I only knew of it because my father has had the lenders petitioning him order a writ, he holds them back by a thread now. But if some solution is not fast found, and he is forced to issue it, then there will be no hiding the news.'

'Poor Martha, she was not the greatest catch with her fortune, whatever will she do without it?' I put down my empty glass.

'What is the sum?' asked Clara.

'I do not know and Papa will not tell me. But it must be vast for I think a trifling amount he might have been willing to settle for the honour of an old family.'

If the sum was too vast for her father to reason, then it must be dire, I considered.

'Oh, we cannot let it break!' Clara said astonished. 'There must be something your father can do?'

'Clara, my father is a magistrate, not a magician. He will do all in his power to be sure, but he cannot neglect his duty. He has given the Nashs' fair warning to set their affairs in order.'

'Will Wilmott settle the debts, do you think—if she will have him?' Beth cut in, genuine concern in her face.

'I doubt he has enough even in his coffers. But we might hope he will settle on Martha and she at least be spared the infliction of their misery.'

'Spared? There is surely nothing to be spared of misery if the offset is her having to marry him,' I said with more volume than I intended and lowered my voice now: 'he is so near to the grave she may as soon as order a fitting for her mourning clothes at the same time as her wedding gown. Nay, it cannot be all,' I complained, quite put out by this notion that she would have to settle for such an unhappy bargain.

'She is in her third year and I don't see a queue forming, do you? Besides, he will have ample put aside to keep a good widow, and I doubt she will have to tend him for long,' Betsy said flatly as if able to premeditate the direction of my thoughts. *We were in a room full of money, new money, but money no less.*

'Is there no dowry at all?' There was a note of desperation in Beth's tone I recognised in my own.

Betsy crossed her legs and settled back more comfortably against the sofa. 'Martha tells me not.'

'Well, Wilmott certainly isn't going to need her dowry, but I am surprised his family would permit the arrangement of her coming empty handed when we all know he would be lucky to last another five years.'

'Well, Anna, they cannot know, and they must not. Nobody must hear a word of this, or it will be her last shot at a match over with,' Beth warned us, now re-joining the conversation having tended her dance card and apparently decided on forgiving Betsy.

'Indeed. Although I'm not sure the old pervert would care much for her situation, I think he would be happy to pay the price for a few kicks before he keels over,' Anna put in.

'Anna!' Beth exclaimed.

'Well, she is a walking disaster, who else would have her now?'

Betsy shrugged and I saw she was of Anna's mind, even if not sharing in her delight in the drama of it.

'Perhaps not, she is of good birth, her family is old, despite her mother's frivolity she would still be a happy prospect for someone in need of connection,' Beth said thoughtfully and the same thought must have struck us both at the same moment as we looked over to the Craythorne men.

'Don't even entertain the idea,' Betsy warned us, following the direction of our stare.

'Who is in greater need of good connections than they?' petitioned Beth. 'And they would not care a whit for the dowry; it is purely the connection they have come here for. Besides, they will be less fussy than most regarding the Nashs' circumstances.'

'Outrageous!' Betsy sat up stiff and slammed her glass upon the side table. 'You will have her cut from society over suffering out a few years as Mrs Wilmott and ending a settled widow? Do not encourage the notion, not if you want to be able to call her your friend again!'

Nobody responded. Not even I, who could push the boundaries with greater ease. Closest friends or not, I knew when she had her face set against something and she was resolute in this. I could understand her concern. I shared it, but as much as Martha was a hen-witted kind of girl, I had no wish to see her suffer cruelly or to have to cut her. But the idea of—I looked up astonished to find the Craythorne 'twins' in front of us, as if conjured by our very words.

'Ladies,' they chorused and bowed. I was quite shocked to see them so bold as to make their own introduction even if it was their own house.

'Would you care to dance this evening Lady Elizabeth?' said the taller of the two, to Betsy.

'Sir, save your flummery. I have no wish to dance this night,' said Betsy with not the slightest hint of regret in her tone.

I did not know whether to laugh or apologise for her display. Poor fool. He went into the lion's den without realising that Betsy was not one to set aside such protocols, nor concern herself with polite refusals when they were transgressed.

'Our cards are quite claimed sir, sorry,' I offered to the stouter one, who was eyes fixed upon me.

'Then I am sorry indeed for coming too late,' he said to me with a bow.

'Mine is not quite full,' Anna said looking like she might swallow the words back up as Betsy's chilly glare slid towards her.

We watched him lead her off onto the dance floor as the music started up in a change of rhythm, signalling the start of our first dance set. Our own petitioners, coming close behind to claim us, leaving Betsy sat alone with a poorly repressed scowl upon her face.

Despite the odd mood, the dances proved a gay distraction. The music well played, the dance floor well claimed and suitably chalked for good merriment. I was no aficionado, stepping only furtively into my first season, but I could not feel the Craythornes had failed to put on a good drum, even if, like Betsy, I had wished it the case.

There were of course the odd faux pas that a meticulous eye could spot and of course the forwardness of introductions had been quite astonishing, but it was the exception rather than the rule. Even their deportment had proved disappointingly reasonable.

I learnt through my prattling with my dance partners that the Craythornes were English born (somewhere up north I gathered, contrary to mothers claims that they were 'foreigners') even though they had spent most their lives abroad in India and later in France. And yes, it was clear that Mr Craythorne Senior had serious plans to make his mark in his newly promised seat in The Commons, but his connections among the diplomatic sorts were quite renowned.

Of course, their coming at the beginning of the season was indeed a timely entrance having two unmarried sons and a daughter, but they seemed not to suffer any shame on that account by the looks of things. Not that they could 'come out' in society in the traditional way of course. But it was not unheard of that even classless people such as they, might drag up well enough with the giant settlements they were rumoured to have (and I had heard varying accounts of sums, none of which might be called modest).

Certainly, no one without troubles would give any of them a second glance with the stench of trade all over them. But Martha, Martha might just be the one amongst us who could look to them for some relief, if we could work upon Betsy. –This of course, I had no wish to press tonight.

When we returned from our first session of dancing, she was no better improved and the conversation went on in much the same fashion, Anna finally receiving her cut for accepting the Craythorne fellow's dances, not one, but two! Even I received a smacked wrist for not keeping with her example and issuing a proper set down. But we were distracted from all the drama of it when the Craythorne daughter took to the side of the pianoforte and began a vocal recital that no one seemed to recognise, yet apparently, could not fail to be enchanted by. She sang in French and scaled three octaves with relative ease, and although I had heard better, it could not be called unpleasant. In fact, as she entered the second verse, all the indifferent chattering had fallen away and the room was silent save the melody. And when the applause broke out, even Mama and co could not refuse to make some involuntary effort towards it.

She accepted it graciously before stepping away to her brothers' company and I wondered who she had her eye on impressing, or if indeed they were attuned to their parents (presumed) marital intentions for them at all. She certainly did not appear to be on the prowl. I had seen her decline many a petitioner to her card and yet here she was claiming the notice of the party, dressed in her finely trimmed satin gown with gossamer overlay and curling feather plumage.

Whatever could be found wanting in them, it was not their style. They were a well-dressed set and had outdone us all with their extravagant Parisian fashions. This ruffled more than a few feathers, for we were not average country folk. Most of our families spent as much time at London addresses, as here in the country and were hardly ignorant of the latest modes. Yet somehow, we seemed sadly outdated against the freshness of their wardrobes.

I had managed to avoid an introduction to the daughter through half the evening when an ill-timed visit to the buffet table put an end to my avoidance.

'Miss Ashlyn,' squeaked the unmistakable voice of Miss Ponwiker. She was a well-meaning type of prattle-box, but I was not in the mood to be detained by her now. I half turned to see her smiling widely at me, blinking through her spectacles with more enthusiasm than was necessary.

'Miss Ponwiker,' I dipped a polite nod. 'Are you enjoying the evening?'

'Oh yes, Miss Ashlyn, marvellous! Are you?'

'Well enough,' I said carefully, noticing the Craythorne girl at her side as I turned around fully to face her.

'Miss Craythorne, have you met Miss Ashlyn yet?' she turned to her right and disturbed her from her conversation.

'I don't believe so,' I said quickly, trying to quell my displeasure at the prospect as she spun around to notice me. I don't know why she prickled at me so, when I had not found much complaint in her relatives' behaviour. But she seemed a stiff-rumped creature. A chin far too upturned for her standing, and letting off an heir of repulsion to any who dare approach her. With such un-extraordinary features, small hazel eyes and a small pout mouth, I wondered why she felt the need to try so hard at repelling the company when most of us would have rather been anywhere than here. Unless she was not in accord with her parent's intentions and this accounted for her frosty countenance.

Her hair redeemed her somewhat, I considered, its auburn curls pinned up in an elaborate style with colourful feather plumes, and her bone structure was as fine as in the portrait, but there was a chilliness in her features I did not like at all. 'Miss Craythorne,' I coaxed a smile from my own reluctant mouth and she looked up blankly before meeting it.

'Miss Ashlyn. Pleased to meet you,' she said with an accent more noticeable now than in her vocal performance. A peculiar, perhaps eclectic blend that I was not quite able to identify. 'We are neighbours, I am told.'

'Yes,' I agreed. *But that is the only commonality we share.* 'You sing well,' I added quickly to change the direction, before our neighbouring proximity assumed some future pledge of calls or further association beyond what must be endured for civilities sake.

'Thank you. Do you sing, Miss Ashlyn?'

'Only when I must.'

'Then I trust you play?'

I nodded.

'Well, perhaps I might get to hear you some time.'

'Perhaps,' I agreed thinking it most unlikely we should cross paths again anytime soon. She was cordial enough in speech but her expression remained unmoved, and if I was not mistaken, seemed most uninterested in my conversation, which I thought quite the cut since she was clearly too ignorant to understand the courtesy I paid her. This seemed a good moment to make my excuses before my façade faltered. I had not been brought up to speak with Betsy's acidity, but schooled to make snubs and protests with dignified subtlety. But I was not beyond doing so when provoked. I picked up my half-filled plate from the table to leave, but before I could speak the words to excuse myself, Miss Ponwiker began rattling on in her usual style, detaining me further.

'Miss Ashlyn is our newest debutante to come out this season,' she said with the over inflated pride of a close relative, despite her being the merest of connections.

'Oh?' Miss Craythorne feigned interest, but Miss Ponwiker, I could tell, did not detect this. Her own meek nature would probably render such suspicions impossible. She was one of Cuddington's old maids, holding a record for seeing through an entire decade of seasons without a successful conclusion, in the days of Mama's youth. After her brother's death, who had sheltered her from the harshness of her station, she was forced to live in much reduced circumstances in her nephew's humble estate cottage. Had it not been for her handsome pedigree, coming from a family as old as the village itself, it may have proved a miserable existence. But what her lack of means rendered impossible, her birth forgave her and she would be found on every respectable guest list. Was this the fate Martha would endure if she did not find a solution? I hoped not.

'She is expected to make a very good match!' Miss Ponwiker tugged gently at my arm.

I smiled but was sure it had not reached my eyes.

'Such a handsome girl, so well accomplished. Oh I have embarrassed you, forgive me Miss Ashlyn.'

Miss Craythorne smirked; it was the first time I had seen her face move more than a twitch and I was fast forming a strong dislike of her which was becoming increasingly difficult to contain.

'Not at all Miss Ponwiker.' I patted her hand gently and released myself from her grip. Her I could forgive with ease, however excessive this regard, it was at least well intended. But this Craythorne mushroom I could not excuse and I was grateful when I found Mr Elmbridge at my side. *A well-timed rescue.*

He greeted us with an apology for interrupting the company then turned to me to remind me of the next set which I was promised to him.

'Mr Elmbridge?'

I turned back to Miss Craythorne. Her voice came as a surprise after so much silence. Her eyes were alight with intrigue and her attention remarkably perked up. I watched her bob a polite curtsy in Sheldon's direction and saw the curve of a genuine looking smile upon her face as he returned the greeting with a bow. *So, she was capable of a polite disposition even if vulgar enough to introduce herself to a gentleman.*

'Have you met Miss Craythorne?' Miss Ponwiker quickly cut in, realising Miss Craythornes faux pas and carrying it off as her own idea in acquainting the pair, 'He is to be the next Viscount Cobham.'

'I have had the pleasure of meeting your parents, but not you sir,' she said in her strange accent that I still could not fathom. 'This is my stepbrother, Mr Harper-Craythorne,' she added, pulling him from his conversation behind her.

'Mr Elmbridge,' he said and offered his hand for a gentleman's handshake.

'Mr Harper-Craythorne, of Beddington Park, is it not?' Sheldon reached out and Craythorne nodded. 'I think you have already been introduced to my...friend; Miss Ashlyn.'

'Miss Ashlyn,' he bowed briefly and I acknowledged it. We had danced, yet I decided we would not again, noting the flash in his eyes as he caught sight of me. I wasn't sure how to interpret it, but I disliked it and regretted accepting his dance invitations now. Perhaps Mama had not been so much out of her wits when suggesting the place gone mad and we might retreat abroad to Cambridgeshire.

'I thank you again for the honour of your dance,' he said with an exaggerated bow.

'Mr Craythorne.' I bobbed a curtsey and ignored Sheldon's stiffening arm, set now beneath my own. 'You are welcome, sir.' I watched his gaze settle deeper upon us. *At least he understood the generosity of our attentions; he would do well to teach Miss Craythorne.*

'I look forward to the next,' he offered.

I gave answer only with a brief smile. I was not minded to set up expectations I had no intention of keeping.

'Well you must excuse us. I hope you will forgive me for stealing your company,' Sheldon said to the rest of the party when the orchestra struck the first strings of the second half, 'but the next set is about to begin.'

'Thank goodness you came when you did, what a dreadful bore that Craythorne girl is,' I whispered once we were out of earshot.

'I did not like that Craythorne fellow. I wish you would not favour him with your dances,' he said distracted.

We took our place on the dance floor. 'Oh? Well, I preferred him over his sister; I found her manners in want of some redress!'

'Yes, well she was not set upon impressing your liking of her. I noticed her stepbrother was though.'

'Mr Elmbridge, if we were not such good friends you would indeed offend me. You cannot have the notion I should entertain him beyond my duty, besides I have in mind the perfect introduction to make him.'

He seemed satisfied by this but I could not help feeling annoyed that he felt it his place to dictate my dance partners. In our younger years I would have simply told him so, but it seemed an uncomfortable prospect now. I would let it slip this time, principally because I was minded to agree with him and had no wish to advance my acquaintance with any of these upstarts beyond making Martha's introduction. But should he do so again, I could not promise to be so forgiving.

We danced well together; our bodies at least seemed at ease where our speech was not. I had sensed such a change in his manner towards me since his return, I found it quite hard to know how to speak to him of late. Something in the way his gaze would linger a little longer over me, or how I would sometimes catch him staring from over the shoulders of his company when not in mine. It was flattering, but a rather peculiar shift that I had not quite adjusted to. He had long been a dearly missed friend, but the chemistry between us seemed changed somehow and I wasn't sure how much of our former friendship could be salvaged in light of this alteration.

WHEN I TOOK A BREAK during the dances and sat alone on a chair to throw off any suspicion that may be forming after our rather long preoccupation in each other's company, the others were still detained by their dance partners. Even Betsy had been induced by the late coming of the Colonel. I searched the room for a sign of Martha—she, I was certain, would not have been dancing since Wilmott had spent the entirety of his efforts in the first half. But before I could locate her through the crush, I was surprised to see Miss Craythorne take up one of their empty seats beside me. *You, again.* I took care not to roll my eyes. 'Miss Craythorne.' I could hardly protest at her lack of invitation, in her own house.

'You left your fan at the buffet table; I kept it for you while you danced,' she offered it out to me and I thanked her.

'How careless of me,' I said, examining the mother of pearl.

'It is a Brise fan, from Paris?' she said wisely and her recognition of the fact impressed me. There was something altered in her manner towards me now. Perhaps her notice of my acquaintance with the Elmbridges was to account for the improvement, after all, they must know who they should look to thank for this sponsorship.

'Yes, it is. It was a gift,' I replied, running my fingers over its perforated design. Even though the impropriety of it would have likely evaded her, I knew better than to confess it was from Sheldon. That it was one of the many trinkets he had brought back for me in that gift box I had told no one about.

'They are very popular out there at the moment. I have a similar one, but I think this is a rarer kind. It is a generous gift,' she said more wisely than I liked. 'Have you ever been to Paris Miss Ashlyn?'

'Sadly not. Mama said we will consider the journey once the memory of Waterloo is further faded from her mind, but I'm not sure how long that will take, it has been six years already I think.'

'I think you would like it well.'

'I daresay I would. Sheld—Mr Elmbridge,' I swiftly corrected myself, 'has promised me an exhibition of the art he has collected on his tour, so I hope to see more images of it.'

'You must also see ours; my father brought a great collection home from our Chateau in France.'

I un-creased my furrowed brow. 'You are very generous Miss Craythorne, perhaps another time.' *Or not.* I was hoping she might leave me alone now. If this was her apology, I was willing to accept a truce. I was mildly interested in the exotic artefacts I had noticed around the house; Sheldon's tales from afar had certainly reawakened my interest in such things, but the others would soon return and I did not want them to find her here when they did. When I withdrew my conversation beyond monosyllabic answers, she seemed to take the hint and made her excuses. I sat thoughtfully a while, wondering if she had a fancy for Sheldon, if that was her reason for trying at making up to me.

'Ugh, that was quite exhausting,' Betsy said dropping into the chair next to me. 'I have danced one Reel too many tonight and I shan't fatigue myself with another,' she complained and charged the Colonel to bring her a drink.

'You cannot allow your enthusiasm to fade so early when you started so far behind us!' I teased her. Pleased to see how well his coming had improved her mood.

'That is easy for you to say, you have not spent the last two years dancing so much your feet remember the steps to every version of the Scotch Reel!"

'True, but I look forward to the thrill of the number of names I will get through on my dance card by then,' I laughed and she raised her eyebrows to reproach me.

'You will not get that far: I give you to the end of the month at most, before the Banns are read.' She cast a glance over her shoulder. 'What did she want with you?'

'Oh her,' I said, watching Miss Craythorne repair to her brothers' side. 'She returned my fan to me,' I said holding it out. 'And you are mistaken; I intend to fully enjoy the entertainments of at least one season before I am open to anything.'

'I'd say he has other plans,' she said in her simple, to the point manner, tilting her own fan in Sheldon's direction. He was standing with the older gentleman now, in conversation amongst them, but his eyes were upon me.

'Betsy,' I protested. I did not want to broach this topic, not with her, or within the realms of private thought. There was something uncomfortable, almost incestuous in thinking of him as such a prospect and I could not permit it.

'You know it is true and so does everyone else, he is come home for your benefit. Well...and his of course,' she smirked.

'Nonsense,' I said flatly, hoping to dismiss this line. 'He would not make a journey from half the way into the continent to petition my dances. He could hardly venture on to Greece in the midst of the Ottoman rebellion, so of course he must come home. The timing is but a mere coincidence.'

'Maybe, but it's clear he intends to petition your hand, and he won't waste any time in it, I assure you. Your sisters have kept him waiting long enough for your debut, and we both know he could have been snapped up long ago if he had a mind to it. Yet he has danced with only you since his return.'

'We are old friends.'

'We are *all* old friends, but I do not see him favouring us with such attentions. Eleanor, you know I speak as I find, and what I see is that he has been in love with you since he was a boy.'

I took a long sip from my glass and watched him from over the top of it. 'The fondness of a dear friend is what you see Betsy; that is all.'

'No, it is what you see. I see the look of a man who has come home to claim the woman he has been waiting for, and you would be a fool not to wake up to the matter before the end of this season or you might find his head turned in another direction.'

I scanned the ballroom and understood her meaning. Every debutante's eyes were upon him as intensely as his were on me and the realisation was sobering and uncomfortable. If Betsy was right (and admittedly she was not often wrong) I appeared, by all accounts, to be in an envious position. Yet, somehow, I hoped we might just go on as we were. For whatever was regulating his pace, to continue to do so, because I did not feel ready to receive his affections and I wasn't sure it was even possible I could be. He was like a brother to me, in my mind, and I had long awaited the chance to be seduced by all the attractions of my first season. I peered down at my dance card, the petitions had been forthcoming and we were not yet in London. I would take care to put some distance between us from now on. I did not want to give him any encouragement and nor did I wish to lend any substance to such notions in the minds of others.

When Beth, Clara, and Anna regrouped with us, I was relieved for the natural change of subject.

'Eleanor?'

I looked at Clara to find a clue to the question she must have asked me whilst I was caught in my own musings.

'You waste your time on her conversation; she has other matters on her mind,' Betsy told her and they pulled teasing, smirking faces at me.

'Balderdash! What did you say?' I said quickly, shaking myself back into the present.

'The Craythornes, what do you make of them?'

'Oh. Well, I can't say they have made much of an impression on me either way, but I suppose it will be called a success, for neither have they made as much a hash of it as we were all expecting.' I looked across to Betsy who was now detained by the Colonel who had arrived with their cups. I leaned into the others to draw them in to a tête-à-tête. 'But, I have made one acquaintance tonight that may prove promising...where is Martha?'

'Detained in conversation with Mrs Ponwiker.'

'Poor creature,' Clara cut in. 'I see her ending up just like her at this rate.'

'Well, that's just it.' I gathered them closer still. 'I think I may have found someone to whom we can introduce her.'

They all glared back with intrigue.

'But you know Betsy will never support the Crayth—'

'Not they, the stepbrother.'

'Oh, you mean the mystery Beddington heir?' said Clara.

I nodded.

'But surely he will not be so much in need of her connections if he has inherited the old squire's place,' Anna considered.

'Well, I hear it is a precarious inheritance indeed and he is of no proper birth, so I think you may be on to something Eleanor,' Clara added.

'In which case, he will not approve of the Nash's scandal when it breaks?' Anna pointed out.

'Well, this man does not seem much of society from what I gather, always abroad on some business duty or another, he tells me,' I said, thinking back to our broken conversations over the ballroom floor. 'I can't imagine so much of a sniff of her family's troubles will land on his ears before our work is done at introducing them.'

'I don't think she would like a foreigner,' said Anna flatly.

'He's not a foreigner,' Beth corrected her. 'He's a merchant of sorts I suppose?'

'Yes, and I know you will disapprove of him, Anna, but what do you say to his twenty thousand a year. Even you can overcome your prejudice for Martha to make such an unlikely recovery. And before you make your complaint, he is obviously not wholly without family either, whatever the inheritance situation may be.'

'His family connections are weak at best. He comes from generations of trade, the only reputable connections he can claim are through marriage, and those distant.'

'But how can they be if he was made heir to Beddington?' I asked, surprised.

'Well, there are two versions I have on-dit. The first would make him a barely passable prospect, but the second would render it impossible. It is said he was the squire's bastard through some petticoat fling in his youth.'

'And the other?' It was just like Anna to prefer the most scandalous of the two.

'Well, I don't remember all the details but like I said, there is some rather drawn out distant connection though the marital line of course.'

'Anna, it seems that in either case, he would be suitable for Martha. I mean, if he was the squire's bastard, it is still a traceable, if unorthodox claim to a good bloodline,' Beth pointed out.

That was doing it a bit brown even by my standards but I was pleased to have her in my corner. I felt certain this could work.

'I'd say I would sooner meet my fate like Miss Ponwiker than be tainted with the stench of trade, twenty thousand or no,' Anna piped up.

'Here, here, sense at last. I have begun to think everyone gone mad tonight,' Betsy cut in, surprising us with her return and everyone laughed except Beth. She was perhaps the only one who truly understood the prospect of the ruin young Martha faced. Beth's prospects were only marginally better with the meagre dowry her family had lay upon her having had to stretch their fortune thinly in pursuit of seeing their other seven daughters off their hands. And unlike Betsy, who was on her third season out of choice rather than lack of interest or dowry, Beth was not so fortunate to snub 'reasonable' offers. She would at least make a match. Likely she would end up destined for a clergyman or the like, but Martha, truly might become the Miss Ponwiker of our generation if something was not done soon.

And right on cue, Martha made her way back to her seat. 'I have been missing out?' she said patting her skirts and taking up her chair, bringing our laughter to a swift close.

'Eleanor has been matchmaking on your behalf,' Anna said unashamedly and everyone glared at her.

'Oh, I see: The Craythorne sons. Well, I am to be a laughing stock soon enough, so I suppose I must get used to it!' she said, cutting a glare at Anna.

'Martha, Anna is just jealous, she has been quite taken with the taller of two all night but is too ashamed to confess it,' Beth said with a hint of vengeance in her face I could not help but find amusing.

The colour rose in Anna's cheeks. 'What a notion!' she retorted.

We all fell silent at that and shared a look of uncertainty.

'I was simply considering his suitability for Martha, by god, I have no interest in any of them!'

'Well lucky you, Anna. Not all of us can be so choosy,' said Beth.

'Martha, pay no head to this lot, you must not even think of accepting his dances,' Betsy told her flatly as though the decision was her own to make.

'How charitable of you all to take such pains on my behalf! Now, tell me, are your matchmaking efforts to rescue me from my unhappy fate, or simply an attempt at rescuing the disgrace of our attachment before the news breaks? In fact, let me spare you the trouble of having to break our acquaintance yourself,' she stood up, almost knocking her chair over with the force with which she rose. 'Goodnight!'

'Well, I suppose it makes things easier in the long run.'

'Anna, really!' Beth stood up as Martha broke into a fit of tears and departed our company behind the cover of her fan. 'That was very bad form, even for you!' she cut her a look of such outrage I thought she might attack her before she finally departed to go after Martha.

'What?' Anna lifted a glass from a passing tray. 'I only said what you all were thinking.'

'That was not the way Anna.' Betsy spat the words as if the taste of them was bitter on her tongue. 'Well, I think we shall leave our matchmaking attempts there for this evening. Who's for the card table?'

We all nodded in eagerness of the diversion.

AS WE SAT IN A DRAWN-out game of whist for small money, the atmosphere around the table was little improved. It would be of no use tonight of course, but I was sure the answer to this problem lay in the introduction of Martha to this Beddington heir. This I felt Betsy could eventually be brought to, a preferable alternative to the Craythorne twins alas, for there was no mystery about their birth, they were simply of trade lines. I would have to contrive a way to make it possible, once the dust had settled on this evening's events, but I would look for a way.

I was quite fagged and looking to our departure when the 'way' presented itself to me quite unexpected. The men had long since retired to the billiards room to sip on brandy and blow a cloud, the ladies either engaged in gossip or gaming. It was all such a bore since the dances had ended and I had meant to petition my mother for our leaving on my return from the water closet. But as I made my way back towards the saloon, I found the Craythorne girl lurking in the hallway.

'You managed to escape your party then?' she said.

I was surprised at her address after our brief introduction. 'Whyever should I wish to?'

She rolled her eyes, 'Because you have seemed positively bored by your company for hours.'

I did not like the presumption of her speech or her tone. Who did she think she was? 'I do not know what you mean to refer to?'

'Shame. My mistake perhaps. I thought a tour of the long gallery now would be well timed to divert you.'

I paused. It was true; it seemed a more favourable prospect to my return to the card table and there was no one around to notice me in her company out here. I supposed I must try to craft some amicability between us if I was to gain her allegiance in setting up the match between Martha and her relative. 'Very well,' I agreed. 'I would like to see the paintings.' I did not like the triumphant smile that formed at her puckered mouth upon my answer, but I followed her on all the same.

We climbed two flights of stairs in deathly silence, before arriving at the picture gallery. It was quiet and derelict, a small fire burning in the grate and dim lights in just the measure to make the paintings out.

'You will forgive us; we have not finished all the work yet,' she said, removing some dust sheets from a few that had not yet been hung, but were propped against the walls and the furniture.

'This is Paris, down by the Seine. You see the Eiffel tower there,' she pointed and I followed her guidance. Thinking that perhaps her own portrait had not quite done her justice, now I could inspect her more closely.

'Is that a true likeness of its height, to scale I mean?'

'No. It is far greater. I suppose the artist found it impossible to capture fully from this aspect.

'And where is this?' I said, moving on to the next. It was a pretty scene of cobbled streets, brightly coloured flower boxes set below shuttered windows, doors to what seemed to be shops and cafes lining the main road.

'I don't recall. It could be a great many places, this is typical of the style.'

We moved on in this fashion, sparse commentary and questions as we went from one scene to the next. The truth was, I didn't know what to say to her.

'It seems a beautiful city, you must be sorry to have left it,' I managed eventually.

'Indeed. I intend to return one day.'

I wondered if this pining for such a city could be the cause of her Friday-faced demeanour. Was she longing for the home she had left? I wanted to ask why they left at all if it was as much loved as her distant gaze gave away, but I knew our acquaintance far too shallow to permit such questions. 'Where is this place?' I asked instead, pointing to a painting so vastly different in landscape that it caught my notice.

'This is Madras, India, where I grew up.'

'Fascinating, and what is the name of these flowers?' I asked noting the scene of a lush looking forest set behind a white building, red and white flags set upon its roof and red carpet under its pavilion styled reception area with turbaned men in gowns all about it.

'They are flame lilies. They are everywhere there: enticingly beautiful but deadly poisonous.'

'They are very fine colours,' I replied, to counter the strange expression that accompanied her words.

'I think travel will suit you well Miss Ashlyn, your interest is keen.'

'I intend to make some such journeys, to the continent at least, once I am married.'

'Then you must hope your husband will prove fond of travelling.'

'Well, that will be one of the necessary requisites.'

'You are not yet promised then?'

It seemed she did not grasp a proper understanding of what lines of questioning were appropriate to our acquaintance. 'Miss Craythorne, the season has only just commenced, I am barely a moment out.'

'You seemed to have a great many dance invitations tonight.'

It seemed wise to me that they would take as great pains in learning the proper conventions as they had in refurbishing Beaulieu and putting on lavish parties, I considered. 'Well, one must dance when asked to. I assume you are not fond of dancing?' I was in danger of falling into bad territory here, allowing the conversation to progress in this style.

'I am very fond of it. I danced a great deal in Paris, and in the Bengal, we dance such merry dances, not at all like these English country dances.'

'You do not approve of English dances?'

'I did not approve of my invitations tonight,' she said flatly.

'Is that why you only permitted your stepbrother a set?'

She nodded.

'Well, I don't know why you should complain at the petitions of your own guest list?'

'Not mine, Miss Ashlyn. These are my father's associates, not my friends, my friends I left behind. You see, he would have me marry an Englishman from a "good family" and takes great trouble to encourage it.'

'You do not wish it?'

'No. Why should I?'

'Well, if not for your own sake, then for your family's I suppose.'

'Is that what you intend, to appease your family's wishes?'

'No. I mean to make a love match on my own terms. But that it will permit me to do my duty to my family is a happy consequence, is it not?'

'It might be, if you can manage to find both love and their approval in the same man.'

'Whyever wouldn't I? I am of no mind to pursue acquaintances outside of their approval.' *Present company excluded*, I considered. If she was sizing up my intentions for one of her brothers, I should like to tell her she was wasting her time, though I could not. 'And the rest of your family, the unmarried amongst them, do they intend to make matches this season?'

'Well of course, they are men, what objection can they have?'

A great many apparently, if my brothers' disinclination was anything to go by.

'It is but a trifling thing for a man to take a wife and have to give up nothing in the bargain. Not quite the same arrangement for our sex.'

It seemed a true enough case in my mind; it was the women who had the harder part of the bargain should the match turn out ill. 'And your relative, Mr Craythorne, is he looking for a wife?'

Her eyes flashed at the mention of him and I wondered if I should have taken more care than to single him out. 'He is indifferent to the idea, but the family encourage him he must leave some heirs, and so he will no doubt seek to do as much.'

'Good,' I said without meaning to. I did not want her to mistake my interest for my own sake. 'What I mean is; it is only natural he should hope to leave his line well established. A good match too, someone of good pedigree perhaps?'

'He is not much thoughtful of such things. In truth, I do not see him as the marrying type; too much used to his own company, always about on his travels. He's a merchant you know, a great shipping company that keeps him so much occupied.'

I wished she would not speak of trade with such a misplaced regard for it. Did she not realise that these were the very things that would turn society off of them, not promote them as they might in their more middling circles? 'Well, even a travelling man must set up home somewhere.'

'Yes, and I believe he means to, although he is terrible lax in taking any pains towards the task.'

'Then Miss Craythorne, you must help, I think. Press him to the task of it. I mean, if you do not intend to employ your time in your own endeavours, then you may as well do service to your family in this way, don't you agree?'

'Oh, I mean to. I have already made my feelings plain to him on the matter.'

'And you hold influence with him?'

'A great deal.'

This was heartening and confirmed to me I was on the right track. 'Well then, perhaps Miss Craythorne, I may offer my own assistance, in making some introductions to you both: good ladies, of course, excellent families.'

'You are too kind.'

Short-staffed.

March 1821. - Annalise.

The first two weeks flew by and Annalise had fallen into step with the routine of the kitchen at last. There were still things to learn, but they had become fewer and farther between as the days turned over into the next.

'What's wrong with Poppy?' Maggie asked her, setting down her freshly filled bucket and starting on the floor.

'She's been frightfully ill all night; a fever and her jaw is swollen,' Annalise replied, putting down her scrubbing brush and rolling her sleeves up a fraction higher. 'She's been in agony, hardly slept an hour. Crawford thinks she needs to have her tooth pulled.'

'Poor Poppy. What's she gonna do?'

'The surgeons been called. I suppose he will end up extracting it.'

Maggie let out a deathly squeal of sympathy, which echoed Annalise's thoughts precisely. She dreaded to think of the suffering. She could only hope that having a surgeon do the task as opposed to the local Farrier that had always been relied on at Gint's, would be some improvement on the process. She was sorry not to be there to comfort her through the trauma of it. But with Poppy down, there was no possibility of being spared today.

'I 'opes she's alright,' Maggie said looking a fraction paler. 'Whatsa matter with you?'

'Nothing. Just my hands again,' Annalise said, flexing her fingers a moment and examining them. She was scrubbing the table down after breakfast, her fingers chaffed and chalky from the salt and the cracks stinging every time she had to dip her hand back into the bucket, seeping into them. She would get used to it eventually, this rougher type of work she was not so well adjusted to. It had been the same for all the kitchen staff and laundry maids in the beginning, and now, Maggie told her as they took a momentary pause; Maggie had skin like well-worn leather. They never cracked anymore. She could put them in scalding water and put out a candle flame with her bare fingertips, they were so much improved.

It was not a prospect Annalise found particularly comforting, but to be able to get through the day without this torment would be some consolation. For now, she would just have to keep covering them in Bear's grease at any interval they were permitted out of water for a long enough spell.

Beyond that one complaint, she had no others. The work was hard on the body but her mind had not known such ease in recent years. The days were long but she slept soundly. The basement was noisy and chaotic but she had company, friends. She had settled well into Cuddington and liked most of the staff. Most of all, she was back with Poppy, which felt like home again. Being with her seemed to somehow strengthen her feeling of connection to her mother's memory, as though in having someone who shared in her memory and regard helped her to hold onto it better. So, when she felt herself slipping into the doldrums, it would only take for Poppy to whisper some happy reminiscence or quote her mother's sayings or sentiments to bring her back about again.

This new equilibrium was precious to her, something she had thought impossible to regain after so many months of sorrow and isolation. But she was lighter again at Cuddington. By degrees she felt the shift. The crack of hope to light her way through her grief and loss. She had much progress to make yet, but the difference was, that this time, she trusted that she would.

When the servants' hall was set to rights again and they came back from emptying their buckets into the cess pit, Cook was flapping around, hurling orders about the kitchen as she speed rolled pastry across the flour dusted tabletop. 'You two,' she said, looking up briefly as they tramped the mud off their boots upon the doormat and shook the rain streams off their sleeves. 'Over here.'

'Yes ma'am?' Maggie said.

'You know how to do the pie crusts don't you?'

Maggie nodded.

'Right then, you take over from me,' she said, handing her the rolling pin and throwing a dusting of flour over Maggie's shoulder in the process.

'You,' she turned to Annalise now, 'I need these diced up small, as soon as you like.'

She lifted a basket brimming of potatoes, onions and carrots onto the next table and when Annalise looked up and said, 'Yes ma'am,' she had to stifle a grin as she noticed Maggie making impressions of Cook from behind her.

'Polly, Polly—' Cook called out, moving around the table now and marching over to the scullery. 'Rights, you twos will have to leave that for now. Polly, you're to go find the hallboy and have him fetch up some more tatties from the farm and then you can peel them once he's gotten them. Chop chop!' She clapped her palms together—a cloud of flour puffed into the air and Polly quickstepped into the corridor to find him. 'Myrtle. Leave them pots in soak and come and help me get these birds up on the spit jacks,' she said stooping and clutching the severed necks of three birds up from the bucket and lugging them over to the fireplace.

Annalise knew from then on, it was not going to be an ordinary kind of day. Chaos seemed to be in the air and no one was to escape it. They would all have to work harder, over and above the ordinary to make up for Poppy's absence. What she hadn't expected was for Cook herself to join the absentee list the very same morning.

She had been helping Maggie fill the pies and trim the pastry tops when they heard an almighty thud and yelp. It seemed, from Cook's accusatory cursing as she lay flat between the table leg and brick stove, that Polly, the scullery girl who had just this morning been recruited to kitchen peeler, had left a trail of slippery vegetable skins about the floor and Cook had slipped upon them carrying a pan of white sauce from the hotplate. It all happened so quickly that by the time anyone had realised something was amiss, Cook was upturned on the flagstones, copper pot bouncing along the floor and white sauce spattering into the air and raining down like snow.

She had at least evaded anything of serious burns with the ranges taking the greater measure of the contents. But her back was out, an arm likely broken and an ankle sprained from the cursory evaluation. The surgeon's visit would be worth his coin today it seemed.

Once the initial calamity was dealt with and Cook heaved up onto a hessian sheet and carried off by the footmen to her bed, she later, with a hearty draft of brandy and opium in her blood, directed the kitchen staff from her bed as she fidgeted and squealed every now and then.

'Maggie, I am relying on you to take the helm now,' she said to her and Maggie nodded sheepish and wide eyed. It was no trifling responsibility and Annalise was certain that however well adept Maggie was, this was more than a touch above her skill set. She listened as Cook run off a list of things to which must be attended and when Cook asked her if she would remember it all, Maggie looked as though she might burst into a fit of tears. It was this, that moved Annalise to saying, quite without any forethought: 'Perhaps ma'am, I might write it down so we don't forget or get muddled.'

As all eyes turned upon her and Cook's gaze dilated as she cast a most perplexed frown upon her, she then realised how foolish she had been in offering up such a suggestion and in so doing—offering up a confession of something Poppy had long since warned her to keep to herself here.

'Back to work Cook said without answering her. Not you,' she pointed to Annalise, lifting her good hand from the mattress, 'the rest of you are dismissed.'

Annalise swallowed and fidgeted as she watched the other staff filter out of the room. It was a very pleasant room Annalise observed. Twice the size and thrice as homely and comfortable as her and Poppy's.

'Write?' Cook said once the door was closed shut and only the two of them remained.

Annalise nodded. She had expected some severe admonishment to be delivered: was sure that if it were not for the desperate calamity of the kitchen and perhaps the more sedate condition of Cook's usual temperament owing to her draft, then indeed there would have been.

Instead, though, she found herself covertly hovering about the kitchen table as Maggie sat with Lady Ashlyn, taking instructions on the menu for Friday's dinner party. Annalise was forbidden—Cook had said—to write anything down in her presence, but she must overhear the conversation, commit it to memory and write it all down as soon as Miss Ashlyn was gone. This way, there were two pairs of ears to rely on and the instructions cast on paper.

Annalise listened carefully as Lady Ashlyn swanned into the basement in a rustle of skirts and took a seat opposite Maggie. 'Who are you?' she said when Maggie dropped her curtsey and was given leave to sit.

'I am Hobbs, miss, kitchen maid.'

'You are not the undercook?'

'No ma'am, she is not well today, she's with the surgeon. Cook asked me to step in.'

'I see,' she said, uncertain. 'I do hope these unfortunate circumstances will not compromise Friday's dinner party. It is very important you know.'

'You may rest assured ma'am, everything will be taken care of.'

Annalise could tell by the briefest flash of relief on Mrs Ashlyn's expression that these were indeed the words she wanted to hear, even if, Annalise thought as she heard them—she was not at all convinced how they might manage it.

She was impressed with Maggie though, who had remembered the correct words to say, with a calmness of tone Annalise knew she had to feign. She had been a nervous wreck at the prospect of dealing with Lady Ashlyn and having got a sense of her presence now, Annalise quite understood why. She was a pleasant looking woman with manners to match, but there was an exactness and precision about her that made Annalise uncomfortable. Maggie had kept her composure though, had even took care to pronounce her words fully and carefully and her speech was almost unrecognisable. This, Annalise had helped school Maggie in once she had left Cook's chamber and Annalise found her in a veritable panic over having to undertake the meeting. 'Can't you tell Cook you'll do it? You'll be much better; you already speak fancy enough and understand all them long words. I's probably won't even know what she means,' she pleaded, red faced and clutching the ends of her apron ties.

'Maggie, you will do just fine and I will be right there with you,' Annalise told her, proceeding to offer her some tips and guidance on speaking more clearly and calmly. They hadn't had long to practice before Mrs Ashlyn came into the room and Annalise took up her cloth and feigned some light cleaning of the dresser shelves. But as she peered over to her, sat upright with her hands in her lap and nodding to Lady Ashlyn's speech, she felt proud of her.

'Well then,' Mrs Ashlyn said more breezily, 'let us move on to the arrangements,' and set her notebook and pencil upon the table and flipped the cover. 'The guest's will arrive at seven, we shall dine at eight, our party shall comprise of eleven in total. We will have five of them to stay and so the same number will be expected for breakfast the next morning in addition to us three.'

Annalise concentrated hard on committing the details to memory and Maggie said nothing above the necessary in order she may keep this meeting as brief as could be made so she did not forget or muddle some detail of importance. She was aware too, that as Miss Ashlyn umm'd and ahh'd over which soup precisely would best suit, and which fish should be served for the fish course and other such fripperies, that every moment she spent with her, was another moment the kitchen was left without their help.

When at last, after something like a quarter of an hour had passed, Mrs Ashlyn rose majestically from her chair and told Maggie she was satisfied with the arrangements and was to go to Mr Grantley now to consult upon the wines. Maggie stood, bobbed a parting curtsey and exhaled.

All in all, it went smoothly enough, Annalise thought. Cook having briefed Maggie on a few fail-safe suggestions for the main courses should Mrs Ashlyn be in one of her less decisive moods, which was useful since she had relied upon them once or twice in the course of the discussion. Annalise wondered, as she joined Maggie at the table now, scribbling down—in some parts verbatim—the details, whether this revealing of her literacy would come back to bite her. She was not sure if in a more sober head, Cook would admonish her for the very same when it was not so useful. It was this thought that led her, with such relief once she had discovered the close mistake, to rewrite the instructions in a different hand. It occurred to her suddenly that the very reference her place was granted upon was written in her own hand, even if Pike did make her mark upon it. She shook her head at the dangerously close mistake she had just foiled as she tossed the original page into the fire and watched it smoulder into cinders.

'What was wrong with that?' Maggie asked her, gazing into the fire as the paper edges turned to cinders.

'A mistake,' Annalise said quickly and continued writing.

'Oh,' Maggie replied, peering over to her now. 'Looks complicated. How did you learn to do it?'

'My mother taught me,' Annalise said and carried on writing before she forgot the thread of it all.

Her mother had taught her so many things over and above the average skills for a girl of her class, she had realised all the more since coming here. She had never had occasion to think on it before, but how clever and well accomplished her mama was, how unjust that she should live out the latter part of her life as a housekeeper. She wondered how her life might have been if her grandfather's bookbinding business had not gone to ruin. Would she have turned out to be the kind of lady that sat at the kitchen table discussing menus for her guests. Perhaps not in a house as grand as this one, but certainly something comfortable and well situated would have been expected for her back then. But that was before the war. French émigrés were not well liked in England when Napoleon set upon his rampage and business did not last long after that, and with it, died all her mama's promise of a kinder life. And so began a life much unlike the one she had been born to.

Annalise was not brought up in such luxury of course; she had lived at Mr Gint's in Hurley Street for as long as she could remember. But that had not always been a bad thing. She had fond memories along with those she tried harder to repress. And however busy her mama was in her duties, she had always found time to care for Annalise with tireless devotion. She had been given years of tuition in Needlecraft, French, Music and Literacy, through her childhood. Mr Gint had even permitted her use of his pianoforte for her lessons. Odd, since he had never seemed a very generous man to Annalise's memory and yet this was one time she could vouch for. Her mother was of a mind that if she taught her well and brought her up with gentility, as she herself had been; Annalise would be able to raise herself back up to her rightful station one day, when the war was over and the French forgiven. Of course, she could not have known then, just how long the war would endure, nor that she would leave this world so prematurely.

FRIDAY HAD COME ABOUT in a blink and it had been a stressful few days managing without Poppy and Cook in the kitchen. But managed they had, and Poppy, having rested her swollen jaw after the surgeons aggressive yanking out of her back tooth, insisted she was to come back to the kitchen today and not leave them with the dinner party to deal in on their own. This was welcome news. The family had accepted with equanimity the plainer dishes Maggie and Annalise had served up in their stead, but it would not do for their guests.

Cook had already given them a breakdown of how to execute the many elements of each recipe for every course. Annalise had scribbled down every instruction for fear of forgetting them, but there was knowing and doing. What had emerged from their experiences of the past few days was that the two did not always readily equate. Even when they had followed the directions to the letter, things had gone wrong; sauces had curdled, fowl had not been cooked through and had to be returned to the spits whilst the other courses cooled and congealed awaiting them. Sponges had sunk in the middle or failed to rise altogether and there had been more than one or two moulds that had tipped out a semi-set mush rather than the glossy blancmange towers anticipated. It had certainly proved a learning curve. But nobody had been poisoned or starved and they had got better with each meal, learning from the errors of the last.

So, when Poppy put her apron on and took command of the kitchen, she had a much wiser and more capable team at the helm than when she had last left it. This, Poppy said, had been a blessing in disguise, for today they would all have to work in perfect tandem and share the tasks, both simple and complex, if they were to have any hope of seeing this menu through the hatch by eight.

Under Poppy's superior management however, the task did not seem half as daunting and doomed to failure as the previous days. The scullery maids had been set to pluck, peel and chop and Poppy expertly tutored her, Maggie and Susan in the making of sweetmeats, the cutting of sugar-craft, the stacking of *Apples a la Parisienne* amongst many other things that were new to them. *Patience is her superpower,* Annalise thought as she followed Poppy's instruction on how to mix the batter for rout cakes. That is what Cook lacked, the patience to teach them how to do things properly and permit a little breathing room for early errors or taking extra time with unfamiliar tasks.

No one could deny Cook's mastery in her domain, it was all there in her head, automated, hundreds of recipes recorded to memory, years of experience and intuitive knowing of when something looked 'done' or 'right'. It was her failure to transmit this knowing to the rest of them that made what could often be shared, a task of chaos and reprimand. But Poppy had a gift for it, the showing and nurturing of effort until you caught on. *It transforms chaos into occupied calm, fear of failure into pride,* she thought, watching Maggie burst into a wide smile as Poppy applauded her flavouring of the flummery as she poured it into moulds.

'Delicious,' she told her, wiping her finger on her apron. 'Spot on,' and went over to the scullery girls who were chopping samphire and scorzonera root at their table. 'Lovely job girls,' she hummed over one of their shoulders. 'Don't bother trying to peel that yet—we'll do it once it's boiled,' she added and shuffled back over to her own workstation where she was starting on the apple soufflés.

Not only did Poppy's easy manner keep morale high, despite the relentless tasks afore them, they had taken to singing as they worked. With Cook not there to hear or forbid it, what had started out as a stifled humming had soon turned into a task of its own with them taking turns of starting up a new song or ditty and in chorus too when they all knew the words of it.

WHEN THE TROLLEYS WERE at last rolled out and the mountains of sculptures and stacked cloches started leaving the crowded tables through the hatch, it seemed a shame they would not come to see the lavish spread set out upon the fine table upstairs, after all their hard work. But it was done, on time and in perfect order, and so long as it tasted as well as it looked, they could be proud of such a feat.

'Well done girls,' Poppy said, flinging a teacloth over her shoulder and shutting up the hatch door.

'Well done to you Poppy,' Annalise replied, 'how well you kept us going and everything in such order.'

The others chimed in with their own words of praise and agreement.

'Well, I might not be Mr Caréme, but aye, we pulled it off alright,' Poppy said and the relieved smile was one they all shared in as they shuffled towards the scullery to start on the mammoth task of cleaning up. This was the arrangement they had come to so the scullery maids had a hope of getting to bed before the early hours, having been prevented from their own jobs most of the day. They were all to form a team, working in a line, one scraping off pots and plates, two washing, one drying and one putting away. This way, what would otherwise take several hours might be done in just a couple.

Still, they retired much later than usual, even with the extraordinary efforts and lack of reprieve all day. As fast as they had set the kitchen back to a semblance of order, the trolleys from the dining room began to roll back in, and when they were attended to, the staff dinner plates weren't far behind them. But they had done it. Not only pulled off the impossible without Cook in sight, but kept calm heads and even received the Ashlyns' compliments on their repast. The plain meals they had supped on the previous days, was no doubt, a point of relative contrast for them.

'I don't care how tired we are, we deserve to sit up for at least a mug of beer to salute ourselves,' Poppy said as they hung the teacloths over the stand by the fire, and they all agreed that whilst they were fit for bed, they could stretch to a very well earned cup, especially since they were in the company of the guests travelling staff today. It was always exciting to have other servants to stay, with their own tales of other places and houses to exchange.

An exotic new friend.

March 1821. - Eleanor.

'Good morning, Delores, you are back at last.'

'Good morning, Eleanor, indeed at last!'

A *real* chaperone would not have gotten away with missing her debutantes coming out presentation. But Delores was not a *real* chaperone; she was Mama's companion and quite possibly the most well indulged part-time chaperone in the county.

'Oh Delores! How cheerful it is to have you home again,' Mama said, pushing her letters aside. 'I wished I might see you last night on your return, but we got home so horrid late I did not want to risk disturbing you after your journey.'

This was lucky for Delores, although she did not realise it, for she would have only suffered Mama's complaints. Her mood had not improved all night, bar the odd smile in her eyes as she watched Sheldon and I dance at Beaulieu.

'And so it is to be home Helena. That journey is not one for the faint of heart. I do not have the constitution anymore to endure such rattling about at my age,' she took her seat at the table and poured a cup.

They began on an exchange of woes then: Delores despair of her aunt's condition, the perils of the New Direct Road and bothersome relatives, Mother's recounting of the immense sacrifice in having attended the Craythornes' "odious" affair.

I flicked through my copy of *La Belle* and read a letter from my sister through the greater length of this reunion.

'And Eleanor, I hope I have not missed too much in your quarter?'

'Nothing at all,' I told her, earmarking my page. 'How could it be when we have been detained here instead of going to London?'

'Dreadful inconvenience,' my mother put in. 'But Mr Ashlyn would not hear of our going sooner with this ball to attend. But now it is over with, we shall set out on Tuesday next. I mean, nothing much has fired off yet at least, and everyone here has suffered the same inconvenience, so we will hardly be alone in our coming a little late. Besides, we have friends amongst us: I did not tell you, Sheldon Elmbridge is returned from his tour.' She raised her brows a flicker. 'Home less than a week, but quite keen to reintegrate into society,' she looked pointedly at me as she said this, with some emphasis about her glare and I caught a sense about her glance, that she would elaborate further on this point, when I was not around for the hearing.

'Oh,' Delores cooed.

'You will excuse me. I must change into my habit and take Samson out on the park,' I said, standing up and pushing in my chair.

Yes, yes my dear, don't stay out too long mind.'

I RODE OUT FOR OVER two hours, although it had not seemed so long at the time. I always lost track of time when I was riding. I think that's what I loved most about it. Besides, it often proved a good remedy in working out my thoughts when they felt to be in a muddle. Despite my preoccupation with other things last night, I had tried to put out of mind all the strangeness with Sheldon to little success. But my head seeming clearer for some fresh air and exercise, I was minded now to ignore all the presumptuous talk, and put off his invitation to Nork Park. It was with a pang of regret, for I wanted to see his collection, had until now, been excited by the prospect. But I needed time to accept this possibility of his marked attention and would not play into it prematurely; whatever ideas my mama had allowed herself to run away with.

A card I did not recognise the style of was left on the salver in the drawing room when I returned from my exercise. I was surprised to find it had been left by Miss Craythorne. I looked at the neatly curving hand in which a message was written on the other side of it:

I am at home today between the hours of 12-2pm if you should like to continue our previous conversation?

I knew I should dismiss such an invitation, but I was compelled by the possibility of distraction and the opportunity to form a greater understanding of her stepbrother's circumstances. I was sure that between both of our efforts, we could hatch a means to make Martha and Mr Craythorne's introduction. She was no doubt of a similar mind, having considered the benefit of my assistance, since I put it to her.

'What is that?' mother said as I slipped it quickly beneath the pile. 'Nothing of interest, just the usual callers.'

'Nothing from Mr Elmbridge?'

'No, why should there be?' I demanded as Betsy's words came back to me at the implication of hers.

'I just wondered,' she said more carefully.

'I was planning on paying some calls to Beth and Martha later on.' More honestly, I was planning to pay a call, not to, but in service of Martha, but I could not be plain, for Mama would never permit me paying calls at Beaulieu voluntarily; she coped ill enough with the obligatory visit. I should likely send her quite over the edge to even pose the suggestion. So, I would not. I would spare us both the inconvenience of such a conversation.

'But you never go to them my dear.'

This was true: it was not the most likely cover. I should have perhaps said Betsy's or Anna's for better conviction, but it would be easily foiled since our mama's kept such frequent company. 'I know. But I fear it is my duty. Some great unpleasantness occurred between our set last night, and now Martha fears we will cut her once the scandal about Mr Nash breaks.'

'Terrible business. But I cannot see what's to be done. Poor girl. I suppose you could take her on once the dust settles and you are married. You will be in need of a companion then,' Mama said as if Martha's fate was already sealed.

She probably meant it as a kindness, just as she had rescued Delores from her fate. Sometimes I wondered if it was the other way around, if Delores was the crutch that held my mother up enough to endure her married life; whether she would have withered long ago through loneliness and despair without her support. But my concern for Martha, however much at mind, did not extend to my having to take her into my employ. We were not *such* close friends. We had never quite bonded like Bets and I. I felt sorry for her though. There was a naivety and pathos to her character that made it difficult not to hold her in some gentle regard, like a chick fallen from its mother's nest. 'I will go to her this afternoon, Beth can wait until tomorrow.'

'*This* afternoon dear?'

'Yes, whyever not?'

'Nothing in particular, only Delores will be attending me at tea with Lady Elmbridge at two and I had hoped you would go with us, perhaps to see Sheldon's collection?'

I could understand her motives plainer than I would have liked to. Prior to Sheldon's arrival home, she would often go to Nork Park without requiring me to accompany her. Betsy was right, everyone else seemed to have the notion firmly set in their mind, even if it had arrived a little late to my notice. I had not thought myself such a greenhorn, but I was fast beginning to wonder. 'Well, I will come next time. But it is more pressing that I see how Martha does.'

'Can you not postpone the visit, or perhaps go now and be back in time for our leaving?'

'No Mama, I will be much too rushed. This matter requires great delicacy, not a fifteen minute call.'

'Very well,' she acquiesced and returned to her needlework.

'I shall take Watts and then it will not interfere with Delores going with you,' I offered as a compromise. Now that I was 'out', any hope of escaping beyond the park alone seemed quite impossible. But the advantage to having poached my mother's companion for a chaperone was that she had to balance her own comfort of having Delores wait on her, against her obligation to safeguard me. I supposed it was favourable to having some harridan at my side like a shadow, but the prospect of such molly coddling seemed already stifling. I had always been used to enjoying walks in the country with my sisters or friends, the occasional ride out on the downs with only the groom in tow. Now all these activities had been restricted. How I would suffer the duration of the season in such captivity, I didn't know. But taking Watts (Mama's Abigail, who was not indifferent to a bribe) was of great convenience, for Delores would not hold a secret back from Mama for any trinket or sum. And that was the disadvantage of inheriting your mother's companion for a chaperone, even if her role had so far proved more a matter of theory than practice.

'As you wish. But you will come in the coach with us and we will drop you off on our way and send Coombs back for you to deliver you home.'

'Mama, I am quite capable of walking back, it is but half a league and Watts will be with me.'

'Perhaps you may walk home with Watts, so long as the weather is fair and the hour not late.'

This was as much of a compromise as I could hope for, so I didn't protest, but made a note to put on my walking boots. If I was to be dropped half a league away from my true destination, I must at least be equipped for the journey. I peered through the nearest window to check the sky for an indication of the weather. Soft hues of pale grey threatened the otherwise clement looking sky.

I let the coach deposit me and Watts to the gates of Glyn, which was Martha's ancestral home, although for how much longer who knew. I waved as Mama and Delores watched us walk through them, and as soon as they drove on, took Watts by the elbow, turned around and walked the entire journey back in the direction of Beaulieu, with instructions to Watts not to return home for a couple of hours. She was less impressed with our seemingly pointless walk back, but her newly acquired ribbon had seemed to placate her for her troubles and I'd no doubt a spell at the inn on my purse would not be passed in ill temper.

BEAULIEU SEEMED DIFFERENT in the daylight, without the clatter of people all about it and vague memories of my coming here as a child resurfaced as I waited to be received.

'Miss Ashlyn. I am glad you came,' Miss Craythorne said when she found me waiting in her drawing room. I smiled mildly and wondered if she could fathom the trouble it had taken me to get here, despite our neighbouring proximity.

'Miss Craythorne, you will forgive my returning your call so late; I was out riding when you called.'

'I confess I hardly expected it returned. You must be much engaged. But I am glad you did. Come along. I will show you straight through to the library and send for our tea to be taken there. I found some books you might like, on Paris.'

This genial reception much surprised me, but I returned it all the same. A certain allowance of intimacy must be permitted if we were to align in the cause, and if she preferred to go about it under the guise of her Paris books, then it suited me well enough too.

The house, set back in perfect order from last night's soiree, grew increasingly familiar as we walked its halls, without all the bells and whistles of decoration and masses of guests swarming about it. Much had remained unchanged since the Braithwaite's days, even if it had been a little further embellished and certainly spruced up since their coming. I followed her on obediently, eyeing the strange ornaments and artefacts they had contributed to it as we walked. There were all manner of exotic looking things I wanted to stop and linger over on the journey: wood carvings and painted porcelain in styles I had never seen before, bronze statues, elegant marbles and brilliant sprays of colourful fabrics and carpet. But I must not lose my focus. The purpose of today's visit was to contrive a way to place Martha and her stepbrother in each other's paths, nothing more.

'You will forgive me for being so disorganised, I should have set them out before, but in truth, I did not really expect you to come,' she said to me when we sat at the oversized writing desk and she rummaged through the book piles searching for those intended for my perusal.

'Why do you say that Miss Craythorne; we are neighbours are we not? It is no trouble,' I lied. I could already hear Mama and Betsy's scolding words if either had discovered how I had really spent my afternoon.

She smiled at my answer but I could tell she did not believe a word of it.

'So, you are quite recovered from the party?'

'Yes, we were a full house only a few hours ago, but our overnight guests left after breakfast.'

'Oh, was there many to stay?' I wondered if their number included Mr Harper-Craythorne.

'Yes quite a few, but only relatives, we have been a long time abroad so it was an overdue reunion for my parents. I cannot pretend I know many of them at all for I cannot remember my life in England, I was so young when we awayed.'

'Indeed. It must seem as much a foreign land to you as Paris is to me!'

'Quite possibly.'

'So have you any connections here you are well acquainted with?'

'A few of my father's diplomatic connections. Families who have, like us, since returned from their service there. Daughters who attended the same convent school as me in Madras, but they are scattered all over the country. Realistically, I'm not sure how much I will see of them now. So now I have only my stepbrother within reach. So, you see, you find me quite alone and friendless here.'

I was so relieved at her bringing his name into the conversation and sparing me the need to prove fast in getting to the matter. 'You kept in touch then, during your years abroad?' I assumed his naval career had meant he had not been much about.

'No, not in India. We did not grow up together. He is my senior by one and twenty years you know. I became acquainted with him in France. His business takes him regularly abroad and he would sometimes break his journey with us, on his way onto Venice.'

'Venice?' the frequenting of the city of sin, hardly added to his potential as a candidate for Martha. She was poor now, but well-bred and quite above any such habits in a husband.

'Yes, it is the base of his shipping business.'

'I see,' I was relieved to hear this explanation for his visits, even if there was more talk of business than I was comfortable with. 'So, you must be pleased to have him so close now you're here. Does he have any other family nearby?' I tried not to sound overly interested.

'No. Not anymore. But we hope he will settle to a wife now and stay less abroad.'

'Now he has Beddington you mean?'

'No, now we are returned home. He is no stranger to Beddington, he spent a great deal of his childhood there in fact.'

Now we were getting somewhere, but recalling Clara's intelligence last night, I feared this news was the worst of the possibilities. I had pinned my hopes on him proving a distant marital connection. Could he really be the squire's bastard? 'Oh, what is his relationship to the squire, may I ask?'

She flashed me a searching glance that unnerved me: had my prying become too plain to her? She was more astute than I had given her credit for. I shifted in my seat and turned the pages in one of the books she had slid across to me.

'He was the squire's only living heir, of course.'

'Well, of course.' I wanted to press her further on these details for they were vital in the potential match, but I feared I had already said too much. So, when a manservant came in to deliver her a note, I took this as my cue to relent in my inquiries and finish my barely disturbed cup of tea.

When I had agreed upon the loan of a couple of her books, she offered me a tour of the house and this, I thought, would prove the perfect opportunity to take a more casual approach and inquire after what invitations she had received and where, potentially, we might place Mr Craythorne and Martha in the same soiree. If she was as dependent upon his company as she seemed, I was sure that one might follow the other. Besides, I had told Watts two hours at the inn and I had barely took up half an hour. It was a good job the family's additions to the place had piqued my interest, for I probably knew the layout of the house even better than she, so many years spent here in the Braithwaite's days. 'I really should be on my way,' I told her just to feign propriety. I did not want to seem over keen and give her the idea I had nothing better to be getting on with.

'Everyone will be out for at least another hour; your company would be a great favour to me.'

'You are here alone?' I had assumed her mama at least in her quarters or her younger brothers undertaking some sport on the park. I mean, it was not as though they could have much to entertain them, so new to local society they were, even if they were moving remarkably fast to alter the circumstance.

'Of course, it is my home now.'

I should have been appalled but I was impressed. What I would have given for such freedom now I was of age and struggling to escape the house for even the slightest of excuses. But it was necessary, I had a reputation to protect and it was temporary, until such a time as... 'Miss Craythorne, I hope you don't mind my saying so, but it would be very good form for your parents to employ a chaperone to protect your reputation here. Cuddington is perhaps a less forgiving society than Paris, and it will not be liked if you stand out quite so much from the rest of us.'

'Thank you, Miss Ashlyn, your words are wise. But we have been well accustomed to standing out our entire lives. There were not as many white faces in Madras when I was growing up as there are now. Besides, I have no care for protecting my reputation. I told you, the marriage mart could not be further from my mind.'

'Even if you are not disposed to—'

'People will take me or leave me as they see fit, and I will make no effort to alter their opinion. Particularly if that means having some old dame hovering at my shoulder. I think not.'

'I see.' There was something in her countenance that seemed far more inflated with pride than it deserved to, and yet I could not help but find it compelling, impressive even. She was certainly not the desperate damsel on the hunt for a husband, we had all put her down as. Unless...I considered her words again; unless she was already engaged to someone, some clandestine affair or betrothal perhaps? No one knew enough about this family to understand their past, and I certainly knew the limits of our acquaintance did not stretch to any further prying in that quarter.

'But still, I think that since you have been good enough to educate me in the ways that are familiar to you, you might allow me to repay the courtesy. Come, let me show you how we dress in Madras,' she held out her arm and hesitantly I took it. I still had a while yet before I risked either Watts or mama returning ahead of me. So I did not refuse her and I did not regret it when she opened up her dressing room and showed me colours and cuts of fabrics I had never seen the like of before.

'These are Sari's,' she said and draped some intricately embroidered fabric over my shoulder.

'The patterns are exquisite,' I told her examining the brilliance of the colours and their unusual combinations, the intricacy of the embroidery and richness of the embellishments which were unlike anything I had ever seen before. Suddenly, my own dress seemed incredibly plain against the contrast of the fabrics as I caught a glimpse of them in the full-length looking glass.

'Would you like to try it?'

'I don't know, I really should get home soon.'

'You said yourself, we are neighbours; the journey is short and if you like, I will have the groom drive you back?'

I ran a finger across the sparkling gold sequins and rich red and gold brocade. 'Very well; a few more moments then. But it is a trifling distance, no cause to trouble your groom with; I will make the journey on foot.'

'As you prefer,' she pulled out the red sequined one I had been fingering. 'Well, turn around then. I think we can manage this without a maid since we are in a rush.'

I hesitated a moment then turned around to offer her my back and wondered how she managed to reduce me to a state where I felt the more unreasonable of the two of us. I felt her fingers work open the buttons of my dress and it was only when I watched our reflection in the glass, I felt suddenly aware of how much I had succumb to her peculiar instruction and wondered what on earth had got into me. I watched my dress fall to a heap at my feet. I felt the laces of my half stays release me. But when she put her hands on my shoulders to push down the sleeves of my shift, I pulled away instinctively. 'Surely this can stay on?'

'Not if you want to wear it correctly,' she said and when I did not reply, she put her palms over the frilly cotton straps again and slid them along the length of my arms until I was standing there with not a thread upon me except my stockings. It was no different than what I endured several times a day in my own dressing room in front of Molly, but she was a servant and used to the task. But when I felt her eyes on me, it seemed somehow different. I felt a strange sense of awareness I had not before now, as if I was being sized up, measured against some invisible standard for which I did not know the bar.

'Raise your arms up,' she said, stepping round to the front of me and I could no longer see us in the mirrors reflection because she was a fraction taller than I. She seemed quite unconcerned by this duty, but I could not be comfortable with it. I lifted them anyway and she slid a small garment over them that looked like the top of a gown with all the skirts missing. When she stepped away, I looked in the mirror at the bottom hem which hung a little higher than my navel. It was a strange look and I was relieved when she returned with her arms full of a fabric that looked as it does when cut from the roll in Mrs Oliver's boutique. But as she began some clever weaving of it around the rest of my lower body, I was impressed when I looked back in the mirror and saw the shape of an unusual skirt take form from her working of it. What a novel idea, to wrap the skirt into style rather than sew it that way. She wrapped the last length of it across my left shoulder and let it hang loosely like the end of a scarf.

'Well, how do you like it?' she said, stepping back to better see her handiwork.

'You cannot be finished dressing me?' I looked at the bare flesh of my midriff that was visible at the sides and small of my back where the fabric of the scarf failed to fully conceal me.

'We are quite done.'

'But—'

'It reaches over forty degrees in the Bengal at its peak; I assure you that if you understood the discomfort of such a climate, you would wish to wear less still.'

It was difficult to imagine such a temperature. As extreme as it sounded, I could not be convinced it would justify this kind of exposure. 'And this is a morning dress?' It surely must be undress, although its quality seemed extremely extravagant for romping around the house in, yet, it also seemed impossible such a revealing costume could otherwise be worn beyond the house.

'No.'

I was perfectly baffled, not that such a garment existed, but that somewhere in the world it was possible and acceptable to wear it. I turned in circles to examine it further and as peculiar as I found its design, I loved the lightness of it upon me. It was so becoming. I felt more beautiful in this than I had when stepping into my court dress only a week ago. I envied the ladies of Bengal for having the opportunity to feel this beautiful every day, even if I would never dream of stepping outdoors in such a scant garment. 'So, what would you wear this type of costume for?'

'There is little distinction in the fashions of day or night there or indeed between the men and women: look. This is a churridar suit, it is for a lady but not dissimilar to the kurta my brothers have which is the gentleman's version.'

I was entirely astonished when she held up what appeared to be a pair of gentleman's pantaloons but in a mode of silk brocade I could not imagine well suited to a man's deportment.

'I think you mean to gull me, Miss Craythorne.'

'In earnest I do not.'

'You mean it is acceptable for ladies to wear men's clothes there?' I said with a repulsion I could not filter in time not to offend her.

'They are not men's pantaloons, although admittedly they resemble them. They are quite the thing at celebratory affairs. Wait here.'

I watched her disappear out of the room. Once the tap of her footsteps vanished beyond my hearing, I walked over to the glass and tried to pull the scarf a little wider around my midriff, but however I fashioned it, it would not stretch enough to cover me up.

When she returned with a more demure fabric that appeared to be of the same cut of template pattern, I wondered if she really was playing a trick upon my ignorance, but when she ushered me over to help her out of her dress, I complied anyway out of the curiosity for seeing how it was worn. I hadn't realised my curiosity at seeing her bare before me until I saw the bounce of her modest bosom as she lifted her arms for the sleeves. I had never before looked upon anyone else's nakedness and it was strange to note both the similarities and differences between our bodies. I tried only to look when she would not notice, but curiosity got the better of me and when she caught me in the mirror, I felt the colour rise in my cheeks.

'It's quite alright,' she said with a smirk and I wished she had spared me the humiliation of her comment for I would have preferred to allow for the possibility she had missed it, however unlikely.

I pulled the sleeves of the dress over her outstretched arms and helped her wriggle into the shape of the fabric. I was more eager than she was to have her flesh covered up safely out of sight now. I stepped back to watch as she pulled the oversized silk pantaloons over her legs and flattened the high hemmed skirt over her knees. I could not decide what was more peculiar; seeing her dressed in this bizarre hybrid of male and female garment, or the idea that either sex could wear such a like thing.

'Well? Don't look so puzzled, it is quite the ordinary attire out there, I assure you. As normal as the day dress you arrived in,' she was stepping into some gold slippers that were too big for her and curled into a peak at the toe.

'I am not sure what to make of it.'

'You do not think it handsome?'

'Yes, I like the colour a great deal. But how are the men to be distinguished from the women if they wear the same attire?'

'There are differences, for a start, gentlemen would wear a pagri turban on their head whereas you would wrap your head in a scarf called a dupatta, and of course there is the embellishment of the fabrics which sets them quite apart.' I compared the lighter coloured, plainer style of the one she was wearing to the bright peacock like patterns on the lady's version weaved with beautiful gold thread and sequins.

'Wait here, I will show you,' she wondered out of the dressing room to some other part of her chamber and I heard her fumbling about and the opening and closing of drawers. I used the privacy of her absence to step up to the mirror and make a closer examination of the exposed parts of flesh around my midriff which I just could not grow used to seeing. There was something dangerously daring in the style of such a look and however much I should have found it outrageously outré, I could not help being fascinated: Thrilled by it.

'You look well in it.'

I jumped and tipped the looking glass a fraction. I did not realise she was back in the dressing room with me and felt that familiar wince of mortification that I had been caught out again.

'Very beautiful,' she stepped up close behind me and examined me in the mirror from behind my shoulder. 'You have the taut navel and strong hips to wear it without your dupatta, as the dancers of the Middle East dare,' she unwrapped the draped end of it from my left shoulder exposing my midriff completely.

'In only this?' I said with the appropriate level of outrage.

'Oh, the dancing ladies would wear the cut of their choli much higher,' she tucked the hem of the top up under itself a few times so that it hung but an inch lower than my breasts and clung tightly to them. 'But it is certainly not suitable dress for a lady of your position,' her hands were rested at my hips and it was strange to see them there, feel them there. 'My my, what would your gentleman friend Mr Elmbridge say if he could see you like this?'

I stepped away from her. 'I don't know what you mean to refer to.' I was far too defensive to convince her I did not understand her reference, but she did not linger. She sensed the change in my mood and was quick to abandon the subject.

'And then there is the alternative option; to be rid of the choli altogether like the ladies of Kerala,' she unravelled the folded hems now and pulled it up over my breasts to expose them once again. I lifted my arms quickly in the air to assist her in removing it and once she had, held my arms across them instinctively.

'I did not think you were the shy type, Miss Ashlyn, you should have said and I would have taken far greater care with you.'

I let my arms fall back to my sides. 'Of course I'm not shy, but the air is chill in here.' I did not know what it was I heard in her words or sensed in her demeanour that unsettled me. There was something in her every movement and every syllable that told me her meaning was something far more precarious than the simple implication of it, and it made me uncharacteristically nervous. I moved my arms aside as she knelt at my waist to find the end of the fabric she had moments ago let go of. Before she stood back up, she glared up at me and I tried to understand the meaning in her eyes as I studied them between the peripheral view of my breasts. She looked away again and busied herself in the task of unwrapping and re-wrapping my body in the layers of fine muslin cloth until she was level with me again. This time, when she met my eyes and told me to lift my arms out of the way, I was better composed, until I felt the brush of her own body against mine as she passed a length of muslin around my back. I was frightened by the feeling of it, by how much it alarmed me; by how much it *excited me*.

She passed another layer around that covered my breasts entirely and then she tucked the end of it inside with them and I felt her hand moving against my skin as she folded it down to secure it.

'There,' she said and stepped aside for me to see. 'You wear the Mundum Neriyathum just as well.'

Mundum what? I would never remember the names of all these things. I looked over my body wrapped in layers of swirling, twisting muslin as before, but now it gathered at the décolleté leaving my arms and shoulders entirely bare. I looked like something from an old Grecian sculpture I had seen in one of my brother's paintings brought back from the continent. 'I cannot believe anyone walks publicly in such dress in this day and age. Miss Craythorne, I think you are teasing me.'

'Come,' she said and took a seat on the chaise. I watched her take up a book and untie the ribbon from it.

I sat down beside her. 'Watercolours?'

'Mostly sketches. You will forgive my hand but it is a record of my observations growing up in Bengal. You will see I do not tease you after all.'

I took the open book from her without invitation and began turning the pages in my lap. Her hand was reasonable, certainly in comparison to my own, but the images depicted were incredible. The colours and scenes were beautiful, rich in colour and detail and beyond my expectations of the exotic. I continued through the pages, momentarily stopping to peruse in greater detail some of the interesting scenes: a woman carrying a jug upon her head in some lush looking forestry with plant life I did not recognise. A busy dust covered street full of stalls of foods and unusual offerings. A crowd of people stood about a strange blue elephant-like statue.

'What is this?' I asked stopping to consider several portraits of patterned hands.

'Mehndi patterns: A decoration of the skin using henna dye.'

I frowned at the intricate swirls and floral details. 'What is it for?'

'It is traditional decoration for the brides and grooms. I was at a wedding and this was part of a long series of celebrations leading up to the actual marrying of the pair. You see here, the artist is painting the bride's feet. It went on for hours, but see the finished result.'

She flicked forward a few sheets and I was impressed with what looked like beautifully patterned black lace gloves upon the bride's hands, creeping halfway up the length of her forearm like twisted vines. a matching design upon her feet. 'How is it done?'

'I will show you another time if you would like it?'

'You can do this?'

'Not as well as the artist who did these, but well enough to impress you further, I'm sure.'

You do care to impress me? 'Very well, I will come tomorrow,' I told her and continued thumbing the pages and listening to her commentary of them for another hour.

When I realised the time and that both Watts and mama would be back by now, I decided the best way home would be to cross Beaulieu's grounds on foot through the woodland until they led to the borders of my own. I refused her offer again, to send for a coach and had her take me through to edge of the woodland until I found my way through the trees into Cuddington.

It took a while to find the route for it had been an age since I had crossed between the boundaries in my childhood. But I was pleased to see that no fence or demarcation had been since erected and that it was much as I remembered, even if a little more overgrown and unkempt.

I made a conscientious effort to remember the features of the journey as I walked it; an ancient oak strewn on its side where it had fell, a muddy ditch that had to be carefully crossed to avoid slipping in and a narrow one that was small enough to be leapt. As the rooftops of Cuddington's East wing appeared in the distance through the bare branches of trees that had still not blossomed, I noted the alignment of it all so I could use the same path to go to her tomorrow. That way, I would not need to pretend at going somewhere that required a chaperone or use the company of my friends as an alibi. A morning walk on the park would be sufficient cover. *Was she a friend of mine now? Had my tactical acquaintance now transcended the decent realms of polite tolerance and fallen into the margins of friendship?* I was not certain how it had happened, but I knew I looked forward to going to her again tomorrow, and not only to contrive the meeting between her brother and Martha, which I had seemed to have failed to carry off today, despite my hours spent there.

The truth was I had become distracted...engrossed even. Although I was careful not to add any hint of that opinion to the post party gossip that evening as I sat with Betsy and the others around the Dowager's drawing room. I had duly noted Martha's absence and when I had the chance to steal a private word with Beth, I convinced her to encourage Martha back out again. I had not made quite the progress I had meant to today, but I had certainly advanced the cause in befriending Miss Craythorne; I was certain we could carry this off soon.

But for the rest of the evening, I had to keep my silence. I listened nonchalantly to their opinions of the Craythornes without contribution, as they reflected on their feats and blunders in pulling off, what none of us could rightly deny, quite the successful crush, whatever else. Betsy had afforded them all the contempt I had expected her to, Anna only slightly less, and the others nodded along as I did with relative disinterest. I knew I would have to end my acquaintance with the Craythorne girl as soon as I had achieved Martha's introduction, it simply could not be justified. But for now, we had a common purpose, and I was content to indulge in the diversion of her company, along the way. She was different. Odd yes, but interesting in ways I was not used to.

Whilst the households away...

March 1821. - Annalise.

'Sorry!' Annalise said, stumbling back in surprise, finding Molly and the footman tucked into the recess beneath the stairs as she ran out to the bell board to respond to the kitchen summons. It was her night to be on call, and even though she had spent many a night on call, the shift rotating every four nights between herself, Poppy, Maggie and Susan, this was the first time it had ever rung on her turn. She had barely drifted into sleep when it woke her with a start and she came hurtling out into the corridor, housecoat pulled tight about her, a candle wax trail burning lines down her forearm as she strained her eyes against the gloom. The last thing she expected was to bump into any of the other staff on her way, especially, she considered now, Molly, who was a long way from the attic dormitory.

'Was just fetching my lady a hot brick, probably be hot enough by now,' Molly said, stepping guilty faced into the glow of Annalise's candlelight and disappearing into the kitchen. The footman, who Annalise thought was Jack, but couldn't be sure, had turned just as quickly in the direction of the manservant's corridor and vanished into the shadows.

If she hadn't been so tired, she might have thought more of it. But she was tired. Exhausted in fact, and knew, having read the bell board, that the summons had come from Lady Ashlyn's chamber, and the request, might well be a fussy one. She at least, didn't have to seek it out. The custom, Maggie had explained to her, was for the valet or lady's maid to be summoned first, and it was they who would pull the bell to alert the kitchen their services were wanted, and they too who would usually come down to give the instructions and deliver the trays to them. This, she said, was to limit the below stairs staff from invading the privacy of the family by attending them in their private quarters. It was their personal servants that held this privilege and unless in the case of some irregular circumstance, you should never actually go to the room except if the bell continuously rings and no one comes in answer of it.

She hoped someone would come and supposed that she must give it at least five minutes for Watts, Lady Ashlyn's Abigail, to make her way down to the service halls. So, in the wait, she went into the kitchen, lit a few more tallow candles and washed her hands in the scullery whilst contemplating what task she was to perform in her half-conscious state. She hoped for something simple, like a warm milk posset or the like, but she had heard a story of Lady Ashlyn calling for ices in the middle of the night during the summer months. She did not know how true it was, but she was glad it was only March. Not that she knew the direction of the ice-house in any case.

'Goodnight,' came a voice suddenly and she turned to see Molly slip back into the corridor as she dried her hands on a cloth and hung it back on the drying rack. Odd, she thought then, noticing that the fire curfew remained in place and none of the stoves or fire boxes had been lit. It seemed she had somehow managed to heat a brick out of thin air.

By the time she had found the tinderbox and struck the flint to light the stove plate, she heard footsteps padding down the basement stairs and felt relieved that it would not fall to her to go wondering about upstairs in the night when she had never so much as set foot above stairs before, let alone find her way to Lady Ashlyn's chamber.

'Good evening,' Annalise said when Watts stepped into the kitchen, looking equally inconvenienced at having been called from her bed at this hour.

'Her Lady requires a thin plain broth; she is a little out of sorts. Have you any to hand?' she said, her tone as perfunctory as her expression.

'Yes ma'am,' Annalise replied and headed straight to the cooling larder to find the right jar. She scanned shelves with the aid of the lamplight until she found the bone broth they had only finished boiling up yesterday for the gravy base. It slopped into her waiting pan in cold congealed lumps and oily liquid thudding against the copper. It certainly smelled better than it looked, she considered, adding a few plucked sprigs of rosemary and a little seasoning. It took little time to warm upon the stove as Watts pulled a stool up to the table and held her head in her hands.

'Will she have it in a cup or a bowl ma'am?' Annalise said as the pot began to bubble.

'A bowl,' she said with a note of irritation, as if it was patently obvious. Mr Gint, she recalled had always taken his in a mug. She set out the tray with one of the fine china sauce tureens, and poured the steaming liquid into it, careful not to make splash marks around the rim—this, Cook had reprimanded others for upon serving and taken her cloth to wiping away the renegade droplets before it was sent out. It was a shame to have Cook back at the helm, having enjoyed so many days of Poppy's more patient direction. She inspected it before popping the lid on it to keep it warm and propping a napkin and a spoon beside it. 'Will there be anything else ma'am?'

'Yes, better pour a fresh carafe of soda water whilst we are at it and spare us both another summons,' she said dryly.

MORNING CAME ABOUT in a blink. When Poppy nudged her into consciousness, she was certain it must still be halfway through the night. 'Is it the bell again?' she said, half slur, half decipherable.

'No luv, it's the morning.'

'Urgh,' she sighed and rolled over, burying her head back into the pillow, 'it can't be.'

"fraid so.'

The mood about the breakfast table was a marked happy one today, owing to the fact the family were to away to London this afternoon for a week. This, was seen as good as equating to a week's holiday for the staff, who, with the exception of the few that would be travelling with them, meant no bell calls, meal sittings or parties to tend to. Yes, there would of course be some work, Poppy told her. They would still need to prepare the staff meals and Cook, never liking to have her staff too much lapsed in routine, would often set them on some other kind of work, spring cleaning, pan polishing or the pickling of vegetables or boiling up of jams. But the work was easy, unrushed. The bedtimes early and break times unhurried. The best part, Poppy explained, was the merriment about the house and the hum in the servants' hall in the evenings. There had, from time to time, even been secret parties held there late into the twilight hours.

'Really?' Annalise said astonished as she swallowed down a spoonful of porridge. 'And the upper servants permit it?'

'No,' Poppy leaned in, lowering her voice a tad. 'Some says they turn a blind eye to it and some says they are up to not much better themselves and too distracted to notice. Not parties I mean, but Agnes once found 'em in the middle o' a card game for stakes with the upper servants from Beaulieu and Mr Ashlyn's good brandy in their cups.'

Annalise was unconvinced. She had seen nothing but rigidity and propriety from the upper servants. The very notion seemed unlikely. She thought it more likely—coming from Agnes—that the story had been embellished for either entertainment or retribution's sake. Nonetheless, the high spirits of the staff were contagious and Annalise looked forward to the lightening of the workload and the prospect of some extra rest. She had adapted to the routine well enough now, the short staffing of the kitchen had brought her quite up to speed and she had not the slightest doubt in her mind that moving to Cuddington had been the right decision; she hadn't been so happy in years. But the days were long and work relentless, and she did sometimes miss the liberties she had at her disposal at Hurley Street, such as stepping out into the yard to enjoy the sunshine or fresh air, running errands in the town and the peace of mind of knowing bedtime generally meant bed, no bells to await the call of, except on rare occasions.

Since her arrival, there had been days on end where she had not stepped out into the fresh air or beyond the kitchen and her room. That was the gripe that nipped her. It was a happy place to work, of that she was certain. But she wondered if she might be better suited to a different post:

One that would include going outside beyond the occasional stolen visits to the farm or kitchen garden. Even one above stairs where she at least might see something beyond the gloom of the basement plaster walls and stifled daylight.

But these were small gripes she had exchanged for much larger ones and when she felt herself slipping into such a head, she would remind herself of the fact. And today, it seemed, she would at last come to know what all the hysteria of the family awaying might amount to in compensating some of those shortcomings.

The only one displeased—she noticed as she gathered up her tray and stacked it on the trolley—was Molly, who sat amongst the other housemaids in what appeared to be a fit of fury. Her face flushed, her spittle flying into the air as she spoke with speed and severity, tears glistening in her eyes. She thought back briefly to last night and wondered if there had been more to her odd behaviour than she had paid mind to at the time.

It turned out, Maggie told her as they stood chopping gherkins for the pickling jars that afternoon—Molly was in a rage over being tasked to go to London with the family.

'Doesn't she always go to London with them then? I thought she paid attendance on the daughter?'

'She does, well unofficially anyway. She 'as none of the pay or the perquisites of an Abigail, and gets no relief from the 'ousemaids' chores when she's not tending her, you see.'

'That does seem a little unfair. But I would have thought that going off to London would count as a perquisite.'

'Aye, and most of us would jump at the chance but,' she lowered her voice and seemed to weigh Annalise up a moment before continuing. 'You won't utter a word of it will yer?'

Annalise blinked her confusion and put down her knife a moment. 'No. What is it?'

'Well, Bea reckons that Molly's always slipping out of the dorm at night, all kinds of strange hours and not only when the bells been rung.'

'To tend her mistress?'

'Well, that's what she says 'o course. But Bea has had it from the others that her and that footman Jack has been seen about together, ya know.'

'I see,' Annalise said reflecting back upon last night. She was almost certain it was him she saw in the hall with Molly. It explained the mismatched alibi of the hot brick and cold firebox, she supposed.

'You mustn't breathe a word of it mind, promise. Mrs Crawford would have her out on her ear if she got wind of it.'

'Of course not Maggie, you have my word,' she reassured her.

'Anyways, she was looking forward—like the rest of us—to the family setting out to London, thinking her and Jack would enjoy a little freedom probably. But instead she gets told last night that she's to go with them, as Mrs Ashlyn's Abigail is not up to the task of seeing to the pair of them now Miss Ashlyn is to be presented and 'ave all them fancy things to attend. She's to go to court yer know, the daughter, see the princesses and all that.'

'How exciting. Surely Molly will be excited to hear all about it and the experience will be good for her. She must want to work her way up to the position?'

'Nah. 'ousemaids never get made up to Abigail's. It's 'appened too many times before when the other daughters were at home. Theys start off with the 'ousemaids tending the daughters and when's they gets married, they advertise for their own Abigail and take them to their new houses with them.'

'How strange.'

'Saves money Prue reckons. Abigail's cost a lot more than 'ousemaids and the Ashlyns have three daughters.'

It made financial sense, Annalise supposed, waiting for the new husband to take on the additional expense and making do until then. It seemed quite the paradox to her though, having seen the extravagance of the food menus. 'So that's what Molly was upset about this morning then?'

Maggie nodded and scooped a handful of chopped gherkins into the jar.

LATER THAT AFTERNOON, when the footmen and upper servants made their way out to the front of the house to see the family off, Poppy called them out to the basement yard to get a view of the spectacle. Two coaches, each with four horses to pull them were stationed along the driveway, footplates lowered ready to receive the family. The servants, stood in a line like statues as first Lady Ashlyn, stepped into one of them, followed by her husband. The daughter came next, followed by her Chaperone and the door was closed behind them. Into the next coach, The Valet, Watts, and a sour faced Molly, followed suit.

The mood of the house had shifted the moment the coaches disappeared down the drive and the staff filtered back into the basement. There was a hum of chatter and merriment that only usually surfaced after hours in the servants' hall. A sense of unimportance when the courtyard clock sounded the hour, as if the keeping of time had somehow been rendered irrelevant. Even the dinner table seemed more generously catered with foods that would usually be reserved for the family finding their way onto the servant's plates. This, Cook had assured them as they prepared it, was simple economy, ensuring that anything that was unlikely to last out the week and could not be preserved, must be eaten or end up wasted.

In the case of the uncured meats and already baked foods, Annalise saw the sense in the idea. But it was the good ham and fancy cheeses they served in the upper parlour that evening, she was less convinced by.

Whether it was the digestion of their extra courses to blame or the rumoured brandy sipping card games that kept them to their quarters, the upper staff did not surface again for the remainder of the evening. This was as everyone else expected. The butler's usual duties had been delegated to the under butler, the housekeeper's to the head housemaid and the cook's, to Poppy. Not that there was much to be done beyond cleaning up after themselves anyway. Even the scullery maids enjoyed an early finish without the family dining to wash up after, and by eight-o-clock, everyone was around the table with their beer mugs in hand.

It all made sense to her then, sat hands clasped about her mug with the fire crackling and warming her toes. The excitement had been justified, underestimated in fact. *Is this*, she wondered for a moment, *what it was like to be at liberty? To just be.*

The conversation flowed easily about the table, smiles upon faces, candlelit eyes aglow, not only with the sparkle of flame dancing in them, but something else: something like contentment. Even people's features seemed to change; soften, brighten a little. Even old Agnes, who rarely stopped to breathe when she had an audience for a story, was relaxed and well humoured tonight.

'The best jobs,' she explained, 'were the 'ouses on board wages where the family were 'ardly in residence for more than a few weeks of the year.' She had a friend, (Agnes always had a friend or relative to substantiate her tales) whose master would come back for just three weeks of the year with a shooting party and for the rest of the year they were at their leisure.

This story, unlike her usual more outlandish style, was welcomed by the audience and gave birth to excited conversations about finding such posts and whimsical questions such as, 'Did they used to sleep in the masters chamber and take the drawing room for their parlour?'

SHE SLEPT SOUNDLY THAT night despite going to bed late. And there was a different quality about the sleep; it was restful, rejuvenating. And when she rose, at the usual hour, she did not find herself stumbling about, bleary eyed at the washstand as she usually did. Today she felt fresher; effervescent with possibility.

The morning was spent polishing the copperware and scrubbing down the larders. But in the afternoon, once the stew was set to boil for dinner, they sloped off to the kitchen garden, collecting herbs to be hung and dried, taking at least thrice as long as they needed to. Then Maggie found excuse in delivering the peelings over to the farm for the pigs and they spent a while meandering about the woods before coming back. This part of the journey had been of Maggie's contrivance, but Annalise did not put up much of a protest once they got there. She had often looked over to the woodland in want of exploration. She had noticed the bluebells rising at their periphery and although not quite in bloom, looked ready at any moment to erupt from their clenched buds into vibrant sprays of colour.

When they got back, they spent a little while baking fruit crumbles and boiling up custard, which Cook said was for their betterment and learning, but she was certain she would be serving them up in the upper parlour this evening for evaluation.

After dinner the retirement to leisure began more promptly tonight. Fanny, one of the housemaids, had offered to the below stairs maids, an unofficial tour of the house. This seemed to Annalise an opportunity too good to pass up, until she realised it was little more than a guise for mischief; prancing about the rooms, trying out the beds and chairs, flapping about in Lady Ashlyn's wardrobe and impersonating her. This was not to Annalise's taste and when she realised how it would be, she decided to slip back down to the Servants' Hall.

She wasn't against a little funning, but it seemed to her a step too far of an invasion of their privacy. She had hoped to tour the library and see what portraits hung in the gallery. Catch a glimpse of the saloon and a view from the large windows she had often peered up at and wondered at the aspect. But this did not seem to be part of Fanny's plan.

She enjoyed the walk back down though, tempted enough by the vacancy to find her way back via the grand oak staircase rather than the servants' stairs. She padded gently along the soft carpets, inhaling the scent of oak wood and polish, pausing to stare up at the marvellous fresco ceiling a moment and taking her steps slowly down the stairs to admire the portraits that hung all about her. She stopped to consider a few and lingered over what she was sure were the current family's portraits. It was difficult to tell for certain, having only seen them in brief or from afar. She spent a while considering the likelihood against her memory. They all looked very fine, some were very handsome too. She wondered what it must be like to live as they did.

When she found herself in the entrance hall, she caught her breath. It was beautiful. The marble floor polished to a glimmer, the colonnades and statues casting up towards the ornate ceiling, the whitewashed shutters at the windows and cushioned seats below them. She had never seen such a beautiful room in all her life. She stood mesmerised by it, suspended in a fantasy of curling up in one of the window seats overlooking the gardens, book spread out across her knees. She daren't sit down, but she could imagine it, that she could do without restraint at least.

'Anna?' came a voice echoing to the heights of the ceiling and she gasped at the fright and pressed her hand to her throat.

'Will!' she said, a little embarrassed at being caught, but relieved that it was not someone else. 'You frightened the daylights out of me!'

'Sorry,' he said sheepishly before brightening into a smile. 'What brings you up here?'

'I—I just wanted to have a look, see what it was like up here,' she replied, remembering to stay quiet on the subject of having abandoned half a dozen over excited maids romping about in Lady Ashlyn's chamber.

He held his hands up in surrender. 'I wasn't quizzing you. Honest.'

This reassured her a little. She was sure not all the servants were as wild as Fanny or would share her disregard of the family, even if they permitted themselves to enjoy the extra leisure it afforded. She didn't want him to think her taking wild liberties or mention her being above stairs to anyone else.

'It's fine alright, i'nt it,' he said to the ceiling.

'It's beautiful. And you get to see it every day.'

'Yes, that's true.'

'You must know your way around it all?'

'Yep, carried enough trunks up and down them stairs to draw a map o' the place.'

'You're so lucky.'

'They're heavy trunks you know,' he said in jest and then more seriously; 'Are you unhappy in the kitchens?'

'Not always, I don't mind the work really; I just don't like being cooped up in the same place all day, that's all.'

'You won't leave, will ya?'

'No. Why?'

'Cause I like seeing you about the place. You brighten it up.'

She wasn't sure how to respond to this. It was not the most articulate of compliments, but what his words lacked, his eyes compensated for. 'I suppose I should get back downstairs before someone else discovers me. Can you tell me how to get to our staircase from here?'

'I can. It's just through that jib door,' he gestured. 'But, if you'd like it, I could show you about some of the other rooms first?'

There was a moment of temptation, the possibility of the tour she had hoped to go on. She was certain Will would not be minded to mock the family and rummage through their things. But: he could have other intentions that were no less precarious. 'You're kind, Will, but it is late enough for me. I think I shall take advantage of retiring early.' She saw the disappointment in his expression, but pretended not to understand it. If he thought her of Molly's stamp, then he would be sadly disappointed.

'Aye, make the most of it while we can. I'll walk back with you,' he said. 'Perhaps tomorrow, eh? It's better to see it in the daylight anyway.'

'Perhaps,' she said noncommittally. 'I'll have to see what extra work Cook can find for us tomorrow.'

'Like that is it? Grantley's not been too bad. A bit of moving around furniture for Mrs Crawford so the housemaids can clean behind things and beat the rugs, but there ain't been much to do since this afternoon.'

'Then I think, yet again, you have the better bargain,' she teased.

When they returned downstairs to the gloom of the basement, which seemed even more wanting, having the upper bounds to compare it to, she decided to make her excuses and go straight to bed. Partly, because the idea of an early night, wrapped up cosy in her bed and chatting away to Poppy, seemed too good an opportunity to pass up; partly because she was struggling to understand Will's intentions towards her. She had initially thought him too forward in his approach to her and suspected him of some unsavoury intent, but had since considered him perhaps a little overfriendly and fond of her perhaps, but without such objectives. She wasn't decided and wasn't sure it was of any consequence either way. Provided she did not leave herself in risky situations, it mattered not. She was of no mind to be walking out with anyone, even if she did like them. Her position in the world now, was her sole responsibility. She no longer had her mother's protection or provision, and any risks she took to dice with her character or employment could land her destitute if she was not careful. And so careful she would be; in all things that posed a threat to that security.

Mehndi Art.

March 1821. - Eleanor.

The journey took only fifteen minutes to make this time, thanks to my careful navigation of it on my way home yesterday. I met her in the same place she had left me, in the clearing by the fallen oak trunk. I knew she was not such a goose as to fail to understand the true reason I could not come through the front door instead. No more than I was dim-witted enough not to realise that she hoped to win her way into my circle of friends through her pandering to my intrigue. However much she might have set her face against the marriage mart, I was under no illusion she was intent on elbowing her way in to society. Friendless as she was, and if in earnest about not meaning to try for a match, what else could she look to, to sustain her here? It was not Paris, but the sleepy English countryside. If you were without society here, it would prove painfully dull. Torturous. I should know, I had two insufferable years of reduced society behind me.

I did not see the likelihood of her admittance, and was not sure I wanted to campaign the interests of someone so peculiar, even if I could manage the task. But I could not deny that she fascinated me and I could not resist it.

We sat in her chamber dressed as the bride and groom in one of her pictures, mixing what looked to me like a mud paste to make the Mehndi patterns. It was agreed that she would go first and in my observation of her method, I would practice my own attempt on her afterwards.

'It is ready,' she said stirring at the dark brown paste she had constructed from a mixture of things from her mother's spice cabinet, which I had to confess held the most elaborate variety I had ever seen. I shuffled in closer and offered her my hand. We had been sat upon cushions on the floor, which was unusual to me, but she assured me quite the norm in the Bengal. But now she pulled me up and directed me to the armchair, plumping cushions that we had flattened on the floor.

I sat obediently.

'I cannot do it on your hand,' she said laughing as I offered it again. 'It can last for weeks.'

'Oh, you mean it will leave a stain even after I wash it?'

'Of course, that is the purpose of so many hours spent in the detail of it. It will not fade for at least a fortnight. Now, sit up in the chair and give me your foot instead so it won't be noticed beneath your stockings.'

I hesitated. I wasn't sure I wanted the evidence of this lasting upon me for any extended period, but I supposed the only one who would see me without my stockings would be Molly and she was always willing to keep secrets for trifles.

'How long did you say it will it remain?'

'A couple of weeks or thereabouts.'

I considered this.

'Do you want to learn or not?' She was knelt at my feet now, looking up at me with such a determined gaze I could not meet her eyes for long. *What was she about?* I looked her over with a mistrust she probably did not deserve, before I gave in to her and withdrew my hands from my knees, which I only noticed now, how I had grasped at them in some strange defence. She smiled at this and pulled a footstool over, first one to rest my foot on, and then another she took for own seat.

I watched her gather the tray, check the arrangements of her implements, and then, without further warning, she lifted the hem of my skirts high into my lap, instructing me to keep them there or risk them being stained beyond laundering. They were her fine Indian skirts I was adorned in, and so I could not be complacent in their preservation. I saw the pale flesh of my thighs below the gold trimmed coquelicot silk as she looked up at me, her head now in perfect alignment with my perched knee.

'What pretty shoes,' she said, as naturally as if she were paying a casual compliment to my shoemaker and yet there was something so very unnatural I sensed in every glance, every touch.

'*Wood* at Cornhill,' I told her. 'Probably not as smart as your Parisian boutiques, but its good silk and leather...'

'Oh, I don't know,' she slipped the shoe off and held it up to examine it a moment before setting it down on the floor, 'I think it very pretty.' Then she parted my knees wider and placed her fingers around the ribbons of my stocking. 'I have to say I have been so far impressed with the handsome things I have discovered here.'

I felt the heat of her palms against the flesh of my thigh as she slowly rolled my stocking down the length of it, before discarding it to the floor.

'Your colour is up Miss Ashlyn, are you too warm? I can call for some refreshment?'

'No, thank you.'

'Or some air perhaps? I'll call Francine to open up the windows?'

'I am quite well!' I pulled my skirt down an inch to cover my thighs better. 'Please do not trouble your maid.' I considered the scene her maidservant would behold on being summoned:

me sat with my skirts gathered up, her crawled up in the space between my knees. *I have truly lost my senses.* It was a strange proximity to be in with anyone beyond a servant, but it disturbed me how comfortable she seemed, despite the intimacy of it.

'Relax, Miss Ashlyn, it is not painful,' she told me, as she positioned her tray a fraction closer and held fast about my ankle.

I was not concerned that it might be painful; I was concerned that...I was not quite sure *what* unsettled me. Only that *something* did.

The paste was cold against my skin as she began piping it on from a small cone in dainty sweeps and curls that had yet to take shape into something recognisable or impressive. It tickled my toes but I made an effort not to flinch at it. I observed her movements carefully and patiently to begin, following her commentary with them, but I soon grew bored of watching what consisted mostly of the sight of the back of her head in the way of her handiwork, once she became engrossed in it.

I picked up her sketchbook to amuse myself and flicked through more of her pictures as I felt the paste making its way further up my toes, then across my foot and up to my ankle. This seemed an arduously slow craft, but I was content to thumb my way through the depictions as she continued. It was a cultural feast for me to see so much of the intricate ways of life she had captured in them. They were more than the admirable likenesses depicted in many of the portraits and prints that hung in private galleries. What they captured was the daily life and workings of a world so foreign to my senses I found exhilaration in the most humble of scenes. I could see the story of the subjects' lives documented in the pages before me and I wanted to step into them and understand the feeling of a heat so scorching that such beads of sweat would gather above their brows despite their scant dress. I wanted to understand the vast perspective of beholding the sight of an elephant in my midst, or the fear of observing a tiger sleeping on a distant rock from a tree-house view, or understand the deportment required to balance a jug of water on my head without using my hands to hold it: books had proved tricky enough in my school room days.

I could have studied them for hours without tiring. They may have called her father a nabob but I would have traded the grounds of Cuddington to understand the things she did, and recall the memories she had, of such exotic places. I understood now, why the gentleman had bemoaned so appallingly over the war hindering their tours. I had always understood the want for adventure and folly, the opportunity for sightseeing and learning beyond our culture. There was much to be learned in the way others lived—beyond the landscape and the language—that could not come from book learning or masters. There was something to be absorbed perhaps, from the immersion of living amongst a foreign culture, not only a foreign landscape. And now I had glimpsed these finer details, witnessed how well they had informed Miss Craythorne's learning, I was jealous of it and hankered to set out upon a packet and know it for myself. Of course, it would be impossible, until after my marriage...

'Keep still.'

'I cannot,' I complained, shuffling in my seat. 'I must get out of this chair for a turn if you are not soon to be finished.'

'Very well,' she acquiesced and shuffled to let me up.

The chair had turned to stone beneath me and as I walked past the fire mantle and checked the clock, I was not surprised at it, realising I had already been sat for more than an hour. I took care as I padded along the floorboards bare foot, having been warned not to crack the art that was still drying; congealed half-finished swirls that were forming into something quite impressive.

Miss Craythorne stood up too, stretched and flexed her fingers before crossing the room and peering out of the window. I wondered what she was looking for, she seemed much mindful of something unspoken.

'You are expecting a call?' I asked her, feeling recovered now the blood seemed better distributed through my limbs once again.

She peered back at me vacantly a moment before answering. 'No I—I'm still not used to the view of this place.'

'You will grow used to it, in time.'

'Perhaps.'

'What do you have planned for the—' I almost said season, 'coming weeks?'

'I'm not sure. My father seeks a house in London presently, so I suppose we are to be whisked off there once he arranges everything. But for now, I must make do with what you call: country life.'

I pitied her the wait. I knew all too well what it was to be kept back in the country when society had abandoned it. I had spent enough years in the circumstance whilst first Caitlyn, then Harriet awayed to Berkeley Square for their come outs. At least when it was Caitlyn's turn, me and Harriet had each other for company, but when it moved to hers, how painfully I had spent those springs, since most my set had come out with her by then.

'Well, I daresay it will not take too long for your father to make such arrangements and I suppose you have your brothers for company, in the meantime. Does your stepbrother keep much in society?' I tried for nonchalance, sinking back into the chair now I had a sense of circulation again.

She laughed dryly. 'Not unless you mean in sporting circles.'

'Oh.' This was unfortunate. I did not know how she would manage this, or how I would engage he and Martha in the same place if this was true, and time was of the essence with London ever closer on the horizon.

She sat back down upon the stool and returned to her work. This time, I did not flinch when she lifted my skirts to above my knees.

'Does your stepbrother not keep a London residence?'

'No, he finds a hotel when the need arises. He is rarely in one place for long enough to warrant it. Beddington shall be his first stable home, although I doubt he'll be kept to it.'

The notion of this nomadic style of living did nothing to improve his prospects at all. 'If he is looking to make a match, you might encourage him to consider it. I know it is an expense to keep an empty place, but it would greatly improve his circumstances, for I cannot think of any wife who would not wish to look to spending at least half of the year in the city. Once you have grown accustomed to country life, you will understand the significance.'

'I fear I already do. It is good of you to think of him.'

'I think of you both. It is your hope he will marry soon, is it not?' I was sure she had hopes that her stepbrothers match might do more than bring him up in the world, but allow her a way into it too, to be related to persons who could not refuse to send her invitations.

'Yes, it will be the best thing for it, for him, I mean.'

Her answer seemed to me a strange one, but I could not see her face to read the accompanying expression. 'You do want him to settle to it, do you not?'

'Yes, the sooner the better I suppose.'

'If you encourage his attendance to London for the season, he shall likely not be long in the wait, there is every opportunity to make such acquaintances.'

'You have some candidates in mind for him?'

'Well, I had not given the matter a great deal of thought,' I said nonchalantly. 'But now you press me, there is one that comes to mind.'

'Oh? Then we must contrive a way that they might chance upon each other soon.'

I had expected her to answer with the question of, 'Who?' but her ambivalence gave me hope that either she did not expect him to be particularly picky, or trusted in any recommendation I would make to her. 'Yes, to be sure!' I said. At last, we could expedite the arrangements now we had taken the pains of clearly understanding each other.

'Now, Miss Ashlyn, I must insist you let me keep to my work, or we shall be here all day.'

Perhaps not *so* swiftly then. I decided not to press too far ahead; I did not want her to think Martha's need quite as desperate as it was. So, I sat quietly then, went back to the sketch book, although this time my thoughts turned from one matchmaking scheme to another.

I had no wish to spend the entirety of the day here, nor any fitting alibi to account for such an absence, so I was relieved when she switched to my other foot, working quicker now, and then eventually, finally declared her work complete. My back was aching, despite the many cushions I had stuffed into various crevices of the chair. But my complaints were soon forgotten when I examined the intricate work she had completed. I lifted my feet to look closer at the patterns. A complex design of so many meandering swirls amongst a river of dots in jewel like formation that covered my toes and crept at varying degrees to my ankles. It gave the look of a delicate slipper made of black lace, with a strap around my ankle that reminded me of the shape in which a chandelier hung. I had never conceived such a beautiful adornment possible upon one's skin; it seemed a shame to think it would fade away and that I would be forced to hide it until such a time. I meant to enjoy the spectacle of it, privately at least, for as long as it remained.

'It pleases you?'

I had quite forgotten her.

'Yes! You are very talented Miss Craythorne, it is a marvel.'

'Oh Miss Ashlyn, you have no notion of the talents I have yet to share with you.' She smiled that slightest of a curve through almost pursed lips, that I had come to learn had some measure of warning to it, although I was yet to understand for what purpose. I quickly picked up the sketch book at the page I had left it open on. 'Miss Craythorne, I did not want to interrupt your work, but I must know: what food is it they eat here? I cannot make it out,' I said holding up the page so she could see it.

'Jalebi. They are sweets given at special occasions,' she said with disinterest.

'And what is the occasion for it here?' I pointed.

She took up the book to refresh her memory of it. 'This was the last Diwali celebration I attended, before we left Madras.'

I noted the hint of reminiscence in her gaze.

'Di-wali?'

'It is the festival of light. See the little candles she lights, they are called divas,' she traced them on the page with a Mehndi-stained fingertip. 'It is something like a version of Christmas, although celebrated in far greater spirit, not to mention extravagance.'

'I see. Do you miss it terribly?'

'Sometimes. In the deep of European winter, I long to feel the warmth of the hot sun, hear the strings plucked on a sitar, the beat of the tabla drum, the smell of a fiery dhal coming from the cook's pot.'

'What does a sitar sound like?'

'It is plucked like the strings of a harp, but the sound is quite different, vibrating in a tone most singular and the drums have such a rhythm you cannot resist moving to their beat whatever it is you are doing when you hear the call of them.'

'And what dances are made to their playing?' I asked, thumbing through pictures of what I guessed were the rest of the Diwali celebrations where women and men were captured mid pose in dances I did not know the steps to.

She did not answer but got to her feet and pulled me up to mine.

'I do not know the steps?' I protested, as she began bouncing and turning in energetic bursts to a tune I could not hear, but I somehow felt the rhythm of in the beat of hers.

'Follow what I do,' she said, and took one of my hands to encourage me.

'Miss Craythorne, I cannot risk the Mehndi work, not after how long you—'

'So long it must be nearly dry. Come now, it is you that posed the question. Come see how it may answer!'

I followed suit and lifted my skirts above my ankles to take care with them and pranced around in the same peculiar manner she did, and however badly I replicated it (and I was quite sure it was certainly bad) and however funny I found the look of her movements: it was strangely liberating to move with such gaiety, making strange shapes with our hands and then our steps at such a speed. I soon found her joy in it quite contagious. Or perhaps it was how sparingly I noted joy in her at all before now. It was like glimpsing through a crack in her otherwise steely façade. There was something compelling in her softening a fraction, something difficult to resist in its relent.

When our energy was spent, we collapsed upon the rug and lay on our backs staring at the fresco ceiling and catching our breath.

'Well, you will not see that on any London ballroom floor!' I said between gasps and we both laughed a little. It was the first time I had seen her laugh in earnest and it improved upon her features vastly.

'I think Miss Ashlyn, we must host a party, like the ones I remember in Bengal and you can invite your lady friends and together we can show them how to dress and dance. I will even ask the chef to make some simple Indian foods for us to try.'

'And exhibit your drawings,' I added to the fantasy that was growing rapidly in my mind at her suggestion, however much I doubted the possibility of it.

'They are not worthy of an exhibition.'

'They are. If you will forgive my saying so, your hand is not so extraordinary, but the detail and the subjects you capture, most certainly are.'

'Thank you, Miss Ashlyn, I see the credit in your honesty. Now, will you do me the same courtesy in telling me if your friends will come?'

I could not deny that the diversion of it would be far more greatly received than one of Dowager Beauvoir's card parties, or some other dry amusement we could expect to keep us entertained until we were in London. But nor could I deny the implausibility of bringing them around to accepting her into our set. 'I do not know—I doubt it.'

'I understand.'

'It is the complicated matter of turning Betsy, Lady Elizabeth to the notion. If she could be persuaded to attend it, no one else would refuse, but if she says it cannot be then...'

'No one else is to be persuaded.'

'I do not think so.'

'I see.'

'But I will try.' I was as surprised at this pledge as she was; even I felt such a task was beyond me. But for Martha, I wondered if they could be convinced to make a singular exception. I knew I could count upon Beth and Clara in the pursuit. Anna would align with Bets, always looking for an opportunity to out trump me and claim my spot as Betsy's nearest friend, but if she could be persuaded, Betsy might come around. Not in earnest of course, but in tolerance of it being a one-off attempt to introduce Martha to Mr Craythornes notice. It was still a long shot, but there was no better cause I could find in inducing them to relent. 'I think there is a way, Miss Craythorne; if you could contrive a means for some male company to be present, it could make the prospect much more appealing.'

'Of course, I forget how impossibly you are separated from the men here. But the difficulty is, who would I invite?'

'Well, there are your brothers.' This I knew would pique Anna's interest, however much she denied the implication. 'They surely must have some gentleman acquaintances, and your stepbrother of course, now he cannot be without friends here, for you said it yourself, he has lived here longer than us both! And I am sure that if there were to be other gentlemen present, I could persuade Mr Elmbridge to attend, which would make it all the crack.'

'Consider it settled. I will ensure their coming worthwhile if you will work on your acquaintances. And I think we must work quickly to plan it before you are all gone away.'

'Yes, impossibly quick at that. Mind, it needn't be above a small affair. Of course, we cannot suggest it as such a cultural festivity either.' I could not imagine anyone's mama's agreeing to them indulging in some foreign bazaar of an entertainment under their roof...unless. 'I have another idea. You must hold a small dinner party, nothing out of the ordinary, that would be the way of it.'

She frowned, drawing her thinly arched brows into flat lines. 'A dinner party?'

'Yes, something modest—no one can take offense to such a simple gathering. And when we withdraw whilst the gentleman puff a cloud, that is when *we* will withdraw to the *real* event: your Indian party. It is perfect. It will also keep the chaperones out of the way, you don't want them fussing over the scant costumery and wild dancing, or we shall not have a moments fun. Once they have relaxed about their armchairs and perhaps settled on the game table or some prattling, we can slip away.'

'To the Orangery perhaps? They shall not see nor hear us from the house.'

'Perfect! And so long as the gentleman remain at their Brandy, who will care. You will give the excuse of taking us to see your gallery or some such harmless diversion.'

She rolled over onto her side and craned her neck to look at me. 'You surprise me with your cunning Miss Ashlyn.' I felt her finger trace my chin to bring me to look her in the face. 'And yet you seem so much the proper lady I can hardly think you capable of such scheming.'

There goes that smile again. I sat up quickly and looked for my shoes. 'It is late, I think I must go.'

'But you haven't tried at the Mehndi yet?' She sighed and got up from the floor. 'And we have so much to plan.'

'You deal with the arrangements your end, we don't have long: Cuddington will be abandoned by Tuesday. You tend to fixing a date and planning the entertainments and I will get to work on the guests. We can discuss the details tomorrow. I will come to you at three and I will try the Mehndi then.'

'Excellent,' she said as I found my shoes and stockings strewn beside the armchair. 'Miss Ashlyn—'

'Yes?'

'You might want to change back into your own clothes before you go home?'

I looked down at my brilliant red skirt. 'Yes, yes of course, Miss Craythorne, I own I quite forgot.'

Matchmakers.

April 1821. - Eleanor.

Despite looking to it, I was not able to make it to Beaulieu the following day and I was annoyed at feeling so disappointed by the fact, as I examined the drying Mehndi pattern on my feet which had now begun to crust and flake about the ankle. So when Anna paid me a call that morning, I decided to use the opportunity to my advantage and bring up the plans for Miss Craythorne's little soiree.

'Have you lost your mind?' she said, when I put the scheme of Martha and Mr Craythorne to her. We were sat in the small sitting room that overlooked the knot garden. 'Why ever did you go there? You will have enough difficulty explaining that to Bets, let alone bring her around to the idea of going there again.'

'I know that will be her initial reaction, Anna, but if we all nudge her in the same direction, she might surprise us both.'

'Nudge her in to attending on them again? Why would I wish too?'

'Because we owe it to Martha to make a try for her. And I hear the young Mr Craythorne may be about the house...'

'Well, that is quite beside the point. In any case, you hold far more sway with Bets than I do, Eleanor.'

'Perhaps, but it is a great deal to ask and it will take more than the power of my influence alone. Anna, please. I know you are not keen, but don't you think that with all Martha is likely to face, we can bear this little inconvenience if there is even the slightest possibility it may prevent her ruin?'

She paused and considered me. 'Why do you concern yourself so much with that pudding headed girl anyway? I do not think you the nearest acquaintances.'

'Anna that is not fair. She is, I own, a little cakey. But she does not deserve to be so vilely punished for it. Besides, we have all grown up together as friends and if anyone owes her the inconvenience, it is you and Bets after the other night,' I reminded her.

She sat considering me a moment. 'Oh, very well. On one condition.'

'Name it.'

'You will not again make any reference to my tendré for the young Mr Craythorne in company. In fact, you will refute the notion entirely, ridicule it and swear against if you have the cause.'

I raised a brow. 'So, you do intend to pursue him then?'

'We both know I cannot be seen to: he would make a poor choice for a husband. Besides, Mr Barrington has already spoken to my father, so I expect my offer to soon be on its way: any hint of suspicion would be very ill timed. But what Mr Craythorne lacks as a marital candidate, does not prevent him proving a satisfactory choice for a lover,' she smiled and I laughed with surprise at this admission.

'You may rest assured. We have an agreement.'

'And should I need your assistance in bringing it off: my acquaintance with Mr Craythorne—you will owe it to me by then,' she added, finishing the last of her cup.

WITH ANNA ON SIDE, I put my efforts towards encouraging a slightly higher opinion of the Craythornes' when the opportunities to do it were presented, and where they were not, I sought a way to look for one. It was only with Betsy I struggled to make any progress. The others were reasonably satisfied to be open to the possibility of her invitation for Martha's sake, but Betsy seemed unable to hear a reasonable word said in their favour and was so unbending I thought one of us was soon to snap.

'I do not care if the Elmbridge's are supporting them or why, for that matter. I will not be encouraged to depart from decency to please them or anyone else,' she said pointedly, when I suggested that I may have been fast in deciding against them.

'But why did you attend their ball if you felt so, Betsy?'

'I went for the same reason we all did: to see the spectacle of their vulgar attempt at breaking into society. Besides, the Elmbridge's left us little choice.'

'I did not think it so displeasing I confess, it was quite a crush, with the best entertainments we have seen in Cuddington for some time,' Anna added to lend support to me and I was grateful to her for remembering her promise.

'Anna, please, not you as well. What is this madness I say? It was a crush in the same way those travelling circus acts are, with every man and his dog queuing up to know the spectacle of it!'

It was enough to silence us all for a while.

'Mr Barrington is returned home at last, Anna, did you know?' I said eventually to break the silence. Betsy did not approve of him either, him being a second son, and although with lands in trust and a respectable income, she insisted Anna could do better.

'Yes, he left his card,' Anna replied, a blush blooming at her cheek.

We looked on as Betsy got up from her seat, let out an exasperated sigh and excused herself from our company beneath a flutter of her fan. Anna and I exchanged a look of consolation that told us we got only what we expected. But at least with her departure we were free to bring around the others to the scheme without her influence to prevent it.

Beth was a breeze, as expected: her concern for Martha easily outweighed the obstacle of the Craythornes' station and she was happy to bring Martha around to attending. Clara was a trifle reluctant, but willing to follow the consensus. Betsy, I was not willing to give up on just yet. I would go to her tomorrow and try again, when we were not in company.

But through all my business in bringing off the scheme, I had failed to notice the plans my mama had been accomplishing in my distraction.

When our tea sipping calls were over with and I was about to change into my riding habit and deliver a progress report to Miss Craythorne, she threw upon me at the last, the news that we were promised to Nork Park for luncheon and reminded me of Sheldon's collection. I had quite forgotten about it entirely.

'Come Eleanor, not more excuses, you already had your way on Tuesday with your outing to Glyn, if I turn up at the Elmbridges' without you again, they will start to think you uncivil,' she complained as Molly set to laying out my riding habit upon the bed.

'But mama, I have so much to do today. I'm sure I will not be much missed at a luncheon.' I offered my back to Molly to dress me.

'I cannot imagine what you have to do that must keep you so much from your engagements Eleanor. Molly, go and fetch the Rose Pompadour silk. I think it will become you well in the outdoor light,' she said, looking me over.

'Molly, carry on as you are. Mama, I am not coming with you. I have my ride now, correspondence to catch up on, and I really must pay a visit to Betsy today, we have important matters to discuss.'

'Oh?'

'Anna's pending engagement. You must not whisper a word of it, nothing is formal yet.'

'Well, at least someone's daughter shall make a match this season, even if it will not be my own at this rate.'

I pretended not to understand her implication. 'My habit, Molly.'

'It shan't be needed, the pink silk. You will be pleased to know that the Mowbrays' are also invited, so your meeting with Lady Elizabeth need not be delayed by your coming, and I'm sure your correspondence can wait until we return.'

My protest now was futile and into the bargain, I would now have to play a normality game with Bets in order to keep up appearances with the company. It was a conversation much better suited to a private meeting. I only hoped she would be as keen to feign normality as I.

After a drawn-out toilette, I soon found myself sat on the Elmbridge's lawn taking compliments on my rose-coloured silk.

'Oh Eleanor, I am so glad you could come,' said the Viscountess. 'I hope you are feeling much improved?'

'Yes, thank you, Lady Elmbridge.' This feigned illness, Mama had failed to brief me on, so I looked quickly to change the subject in order to staunch any further inquiries on that head. 'You have changed the arrangement of the gardens, Lady Elmbridge: how beautifully set the alliums look.' I turned my head a fraction admiring the view of them a moment: Their gigantic purple globular heads standing up in towering rows above the shrubbery. They were quite fantastic it was true, and yet when I studied them, it was the image of the fire lilies I imagined there.

'Yes, Paxton started them early in the glass house, they have taken quite brilliantly I think.'

I smiled and nodded my agreement. 'It has perhaps been a little warmer than usual too this spring.'

'Yes, and you must be in need of refreshment. Won't you join Lady Elizabeth and take some? Sheldon will soon be joining us, once he has finished dressing.'

When I had well enough appeased the Viscountess, I went over to the small wrought iron table where Betsy was sat picking at a Queen cake. I waited for the footman to pull a chair up for me to join her.

'You are surprised to see me?' Betsy said.

'No, I knew you would be here, but I did not expect the whole family. What is the occasion?'

'Can't you tell?'

I frowned. 'No'

'Well, we are here for the same purpose as you, of course.'

'Oh?'

'Must you look so bamboozled? Honestly Eleanor, you are no paper skull, but I do not know you of late, must everything be spelled out to you?'

This insulted me a little and if we had not been so recently at odds, I would have made it plain, but I thought better of it under the circumstances.

'Lady Louisa is almost of age. My brother is ready to marry, or so my father insists.'

'Oh, I see. I did not realise they were...intended.'

'Yes, not as intended as you and Sheldon perhaps, but our parents have a fancy for the idea.'

I shot her a narrowed glance. 'Pardon me?'

'Well, it is hardly a secret Eleanor. Don't you see? This is a marriage market of a luncheon gathering. You are here to be encouraged in your match, or to support the efforts in my case.'

I looked about the table uncomfortably. 'Sheldon and I are barely reacquainted. Why must everyone assume...'

'Well, no doubt the assumption is that you must be given ample opportunity to become so.'

When we were called to the dining room, I took my place at the table and peered over to Lady Louisa who had been conveniently contrived to sit beside the next Lord Mowbray. I too had been conveniently placed at Sheldon's side. It seemed to me a waste to invest so much effort in schooling me in protocol and etiquette, only to throw it all asunder when it suited.

I unfolded my napkin and wondered as I watched Louisa chatting, if she had a clue as to what was happening here. She did not appear outwardly aware, innocent smiles and easy conversation flowing from her to her neighbours. But then, why should she feel concerned, she was not yet out, and would not suspect this priming so prematurely. I supposed that had Sheldon not been so long absent, that a similar course would have been contrived between us: which may have been gentler than this hard rushed attempt they used to compensate it. I considered her age by working back from her brother's. I had her as four years my junior: at about fifteen. She was, no doubt, much greener than even I and had not set her mind to such matters yet.

'Eleanor?' A voice slipped into my awareness and I looked up. Sheldon nodded me in the direction of the footman at my shoulder, poised with tray and spatula in hand to serve me.

'Thank you,' I said, offering my plate. 'Sheldon, is it true that Louisa is intended for Mowbray?' I asked quietly when the footman was gone.

He cast a fleeting glance in their direction. 'I believe so.'

'Don't you think someone ought to tell her? I'm sure she does not understand the fact.'

He frowned a little thoughtfully as he unfolded his napkin. 'Unlikely, but there is no need to fill her head with such notions. Surely, she will not have her drawing room until next year.'

'I know, but if she is to be pushed into his company like this, surely she will grow suspicious.'

He spread paté onto dainty toasted breads. 'Well, it shall take its course I suppose and she will discover it after a time.'

'To be sure, but I cannot help but feel she has a right to know.'

'There will be time for that later.'

I didn't respond beyond a nod and took up one of the toasted breads and reached for my knife. It irked me that he didn't see the significance of my point: she had a right to know what everyone else was taking for granted all about her.

'What's wrong?' he said when I went back to my plate to layer my toasts.

'Nothing.'

'There is something on your mind, I can see.'

I didn't have a chance to reply. As I was contemplating how to form my answer, my mama knocked my toast from my hand as I lifted it towards my mouth. 'Mama!' I exclaimed as it scuttled across the table and landed upon my father's napkin.

'Crab!' she shrieked, and although I understood her meaning, our company paused and frowned, confused at this spectacle. If it was not so awkward, it might have proved comical. 'In the paté, there is crab meat.'

I pushed my plate aside. 'Crab does not agree with me,' I said to enlighten the audience.

'Forgive me,' Mama said, returning to her seat now, slightly red faced. 'Footman, take her plate away please. I did not mean to alarm anyone, only she is so sensitive to shellfish that the last time she ate it, it nearly took her to her death bed!' Mama explained and I saw the faces about the table relax into understanding and relief now the context was made plain to them.

'I'm dreadfully sorry Eleanor,' said the Viscountess looking concerned, 'had I known, I would have altered the menu.'

'Thank you, but the fault is mine, I should have checked. I was not paying attention,' I said apologetic and instantly wished I could retract those words, for I could tell that I had been misunderstood and my distraction imputed to be on Sheldon's account when it was actually on Louisa's.

I edged away enough for the footman to clear my plate and cutlery and by the time he returned to replace them, Mama was so busy telling the whole epic tale of that fateful day I grew ill from the shellfish, that I decided not to try to rebuff it. It was all so embarrassing, not just the descriptions of my swollen lips and windpipe that nearly choked me to an early death, but the atmosphere of heavy presumption that I felt in every knowing or approving glance or smile. I momentarily wondered if I might have preferred to have taken a bite of the crab pate and be given excuse to escape this affair entirely. I kept as quietly to my plate as I could for the rest of the ordeal.

'Who's for Cricket?' called Lady Charlotte when scarcely given leave from the table.

'Charlotte, perhaps in a little while,' her sister reminded her and Charlotte went off in a little sulk, stomping away in disappointment as children of her years often did on not getting their way.

'I would very much like to play,' I called out to her and as she turned back, she dropped her poised hand from her hip and a smile crept across her sulky face. 'Will you, Miss Ashlyn? Will you?'

'Yes. Let us see if we can summon up a team,' I said to her with a wink.

'You are very kind,' said Lady Louisa. 'But you must not feel obliged. She will have us playing games 'till dusk if she has her way.'

'I was much the same. It's perhaps a malady of being the youngest in a family where everyone else is grown up.' *Anything to break up the awkwardness of this façade was most welcome to me this day.*

'Well, I shan't leave it all to you. I will join the team and see who else I can muster up.'

'I'll see you over there,' I said and ran ahead to catch up with Charlotte.

IT TOOK SOME TIME TO broach the intended subject with Betsy once we were sat alone again at last. It seemed half the afternoon was spent before I found the opportunity for us to speak comfortably in private, and then to contrive the nerve to drop the subject into our conversation.

'It will be a simple affair, with just our set and a few gentlemen,' I explained carefully, trivialising it in the extreme.

'Are you ill, Eleanor?' she said in that caustic tone she rarely used on me, but often used on others in my presence.

'Before you think me gone mad, just hear me out.' I offered her my best speech on Martha's need for our support, but I could tell that despite my (perhaps slightly overzealous) efforts, they produced no happy effect on her and she seemed more concerned with my condition at being induced to such bidding.

'It is but a small dinner party, Bets, no great deal. I cannot see what harm it can do, and besides, we are in the country for less than a week now.'

'Forgive the interruption, ladies.' Sheldon came upon us from the pitch. 'It's your turn Eleanor.'

I had quite forgotten the game altogether until he handed me the cricket bat.

'What party is this?'

'A small dinner party at Beaulieu this week,' I said taking the bat and watching Betsy roll her eyes to the sky.

'At Beaulieu...and you will go?' he asked a little surprised.

'Yes, a small affair, but an opportunity for us all to get together intimately before the season gets into swing. You are invited of course.'

'Then I look forward to it.'

I took up my space at the wicket to spare Betsy the humiliation of her (now necessary) acquiescence in the light of Sheldon's agreement to the event. If the heir of Elmbridge saw no obstacle in going, she could hardly persist in her complaint. I lifted the bat to strike the ball as it was served and hit it clean beyond the pitch. I was on a winning streak now, I smiled to myself, as I lifted my skirt a fraction to make my run.

When the game was finished, the Mowbrays made their excuses and bid us farewell. Betsy had remained distant, but I knew her pride had been scratched by having to accept the Craythornes' invitation or ostracise herself in the face of everyone else's going. We were better used to serving each other as allies rather than coming up against each other and it was an uncomfortable circumstance for us both. I was happy in my triumph and she would get over it—it was but a flea bite really—but a short reprieve from each other's company was for the best, to let things settle. And now, I felt relieved for the prospect of getting home and delivering the happy news to Miss Craythorne at long last.

But after the Mowbray's departed, much to my irritation, Mama and Delores continued to sip tea and busy themselves in conversation with the Viscountess whilst Papa disappeared into Lord Elmbridge's study with him. I sighed inwardly and agreed to Lady Charlotte's request for me to join her and her sisters in a game of Battledore. I was not much in the mood for it now. I longed to go home, but with Betsy now departed, leaving me and Sheldon quite alone, her words came back to haunt me and I wanted to keep our seclusion minimal.

I played absentmindedly, hitting the shuttlecock in turn, leaping now and then to catch it. No matter how much I tried to divert it, I felt my mind turned only towards the hour growing near until I went to Miss Craythorne's again.

'Eleanor?'

I turned around just in time to bat the shuttlecock that was hurtling towards me.

'Not you as well now?' said Lady Charlotte, who, despite her years, had quite adeptly gauged the direction of my stare and distraction: Sheldon had been lingering about the side-lines, watching us.

'I don't know what you mean Lady Charlotte! Now, whose turn is it to serve?'

'Well, it is not my brother's since he is not playing!' She laughed and her older sister scorned her for her cheek and suggested we break for some refreshment.

As we journeyed to the marquee, Lady Louisa came up beside me and took my arm in hers. 'You must forgive her Miss Ashlyn, she has a habit of speaking the things no one else would care to mention, no matter how much we attempt to free her of the habit.'

'It's quite alright, Lady Louisa, there is no harm in it at such an age, I am sure.'

'You are very kind not to take offense, Miss Ashlyn.'

'Why ever should I?' I said accepting the glass of offered lemonade and taking a sip from it.

'Well, it is no secret between us of course that we might one day become sisters, but Sheldon has had us all on a strict warning not to question you over the matter. Unfortunately, Charlotte is the only one who would consider the temptation too much.'

I nearly spat my drink out, and in my attempt to prevent the urge, ended up choking on it instead.

'Oh Miss Ashlyn, are you alright?' She put down her own glass and begun fanning me until I recovered.

'Thank you, I do not think I am thirsty after all,' I said and handed it back to the footman and dabbed the spillage from my dress with his offered handkerchief. 'Lady Louisa, what did you mean by that, about us being like sisters?'

'Well, what do you think I meant, Miss Ashlyn? There is no need to be coy about it for my sake, it will be my own coming out next year, so you will not find me ignorant of such affairs.'

'I see.'

'Of course, I would not let Mama or Papa realise it yet, but even they cannot expect us not to notice such details when it is all that is ever talked about since Sheldon's return.'

I inwardly sighed at the irony. She would not wish her parents to know she was of an age to work out such things, and they did not yet wish her to realise they intended her to marry the next Lord Mowbray. 'Talked about by whom?' I asked her casually.

'My parents, your parents too when they are here, and I must confess: Julia and I, have on occasion, discussed how well we would like to have you for a sister over anyone else, which I fear may be responsible for Charlotte knowing a little too much.'

I smiled. 'You are very generous, Lady Louisa.' I looked at her face: it was a handsome resemblance to her brother's and the rest of her sisters', with their pale blue eyes and fair golden hair. I saw not the slightest comprehension in her face that she had any understanding of what she had just plainly confirmed to me, what her words had just done. Speculation and presumption was one thing, this quite another. I looked over at Sheldon who had gone back to the table but was still watching us: watching *me,* as he had been all day. But it was only now I could no longer placate my denial of it with excuses. 'Lady Louisa, would you be so kind to permit me sit the next half out, I think I am over fatigued.'

'Not at all, Miss Ashlyn. Let me take you to the table.'

As she led me over towards the small table where a light tea was sat half eaten on its surface, flies buzzing around it and Sheldon, his mama, mine and Delores sat around its edge beneath a small marquee, I hadn't the slightest notion of what I would say to him, but I wanted no less, to test the truth in the idea everyone around me seemed to take for granted. It was one thing to tolerate the teasing and presumptions of Betsy and the others, but another to be spoken to so frankly by his own sister.

'Miss Ashlyn, have they quite worn you out?' Lady Elmbridge said with her usual smile, although I sensed something more in it now, more meaning than I had noticed before. Was it the smile of a soon to be mother-in-law she offered me now?

'I am afraid so,' I admitted. But I did not confess that I was worn out of all this matchmaking, meddling and gossip. The lawn games I could have played on at, but this scheming was becoming a harder game to navigate.

'Then you must sit with us and recover. Sheldon, will you have some refreshment brought for Miss Ashlyn?' said the Viscountess, sliding her glance to him.

He summoned a footman to take my order, but I wanted nothing and excused him.

'Now, you two must excuse us. I have promised your mama and Delores a tour of our refurbishments to the east wing and have become quite distracted from the matter. I would invite you to go, but I think Sheldon means to show you his collection. Shall we?' she said getting up, and I knew by Mama's delayed expression that this was no pre-existing plan at all, but yet another plot to force us into solitude.

As Mama and Delores rose with her, and Lady Elmbridge ushered Louisa on to return to her sisters, I knew I truly was the last to understand what mischief had been going on right before me for the past week. It was not just a hopeful whim of my mama's, a suspicious inference from my friends: but an orchestrated plan by all involved parties, except, it seemed: me.

'I hope they have not overexerted you, El, not now you are well again,' Sheldon said when everyone had left us quite alone and there seemed suddenly nothing left to talk about.

'No, no. It has been most enjoyable, and I expect the fine air has done me a great deal of good Mr Elmbridge, but I thank you for your concern.'

'You were greatly missed yesterday, but it is good to see you today.'

'Of course, I was sorry not to come, but these things have a way of taking you by surprise,' I answered and flinched at the suggestion I had unintentionally made. As if I would discuss such a subject as the monthly curse in a gentleman's company. The usual ease was already under strain, now I had somehow managed to degrade it further.

I looked over to the game his sisters continued in and considered Louisa's words again. Did they really all believe that we knew anything enough of each other's character now we were grown? That either of us would wish to court such an idea? A childhood friendship was no foundation on which we might choose to marry, even if I could still see the same tenderness in his eyes when I dared to look at them. And I, well it seemed I was fast outgrowing any straightforward notion he might still hold of knowing much of my character. The years of absence may have been few, but they were not any old years, but formative years. Years of our becoming, years of our own transformation where much of what once was, had long since altered.

'Well, if you are minded to, you might consider permitting me to accompany you on your morning ride tomorrow, if you are still as much in the habit of it as I remember?'

'I am.' *That is one of the few things that remain unchanged in me.*

'I am glad to hear it. It's been an age since we last rode out on the Downs together. If it will please you?'

'Well, of course, Mr Elmbridge, we are old friends are we not? I see no reason why we shan't continue to be so acquainted now you have returned. Although I must tell you: I am no longer permitted beyond the park un-chaperoned.'

'Then I will come to you and we can ride on the Park at Cuddington if it will satisfy you better?'

'Not I, I should much prefer the Downs. I certainly miss that route.'

'Then permit me to speak to your mama and see if she cannot be brought to reason.'

'Very well,' I smiled. She was clearly willing to permit many a protocol to slip in aiding this attempt at matchmaking, but that would be doing it too brown even for her. 'So, tell me, will you be staying with us for some time or do you plan to resume your travels?'

'I have not ruled out the possibility of returning to the continent again once this Ottoman affair is settled and I can travel to Greece, although who can tell when that will be?' Then more soberly, he added, 'But I would prefer to find a reason to stay behind.'

I turned towards the battledore pitch and offered some applause to Charlotte's victory in the match.

He took me into the house next, eager to show me his collection, or eager to be so much alone with me? I was not sure. But I felt nervous of it as I sat in the drawing room pottering with his foreign ephemera. The paintings, we had already toured at length, and although admirable, in their own way, and surely of great rarity and value, they did not compare to the scenes I had observed in Miss Craythorne's sketch book. The artist's handiwork of course was greatly superior, but the scenes themselves, the capturing of the minutiae of detail was not to be seen in these works, and I found it hard to sustain my interest much beyond the primary glance.

When Mama and Delores finally summoned me from the drawing room, it was a quarter past six and I realised we had been left quite alone for more than an hour without so much as a servant to check up on us. There was no further confirmation required of how this was all meant to go. But he had not spoken at least. I had hung on every fresh sentence fearing some spontaneous declaration, but I was relieved now I was to go home, that it had not come to pass.

It was a shame, for if I had not been so preoccupied with the impending threat of the possibility, I might have actually enjoyed our conversation better. He was civil and easy in his manner, offering up accounts of the stories of his acquisitions and the highs and lows of his time abroad. Explaining the arduous journeys, the poor inns and the sometimes poor repast on the journey. But he had also described to me the brilliance of the scenery, the magnificence (and perils) of the Alps and so much more that I paid only half my attention to, mainly for fear that any engrossment may be misconstrued, but also being so distracted for the ever growing want of going to Beaulieu.

Oryantal Dansi.

April 1821. - Eleanor.

We were home by seven-o-clock and I debated the possibility of getting to Beaulieu and back before dark. The evenings were getting lighter now, but I reckoned I had an hour at most. Arriving five hours later than promised was hardly fashionably late, but I knew she would overlook it for the happy news I came to bring her.

When I made my way through the adjoining woodland, she was not there and I wondered how I expected she would be at such an hour. Perhaps Betsy was right; I had become feather-headed of late. I found my way around to the front of the house but hung back, seeing a coach poised on the driveway. I did not want to go in if they were in company and risk being seen paying a call, so I turned upon my heels when I heard the butler's voice. But then I heard the mumblings of farewell and turned back and saw her stepbrother, Mr Craythorne, step up on to the footplate and vanish into the waiting coach.

Once the horses carried him off through the gates, I rounded the corner and rang the bell. I supposed she had long given up on me now and however impertinent my visit, I did not think it would be much minded under this roof.

I was shown into the reception room and when I had spent nearly ten minutes pacing its length and considering the newly hung paintings in it, the footman returned with a maidservant to tell me Miss Craythorne was in the Orangery and had given leave to bring me to her. I was in half a mind to depart at once with the audacity of her failing to receive me properly, but then I remembered who was at fault in such a late visit and followed the maid the short journey through the house, across the courtyard and beyond the furthest extent of the ornamental pond.

As we approached, I could see movement beyond the glass and hear strange sounds coming from it. I considered asking the maidservant what was going on, but then I remembered she did not speak much English. Their staffing arrangements were as odd as them I supposed. From what I could gather, they seemed to have made a collection of them along their travels with Indians and French amongst the few English ones they had taken on with the house. I wondered how they could need so many and what an interesting ensemble it made below stairs, especially when it came to communicating with each other.

When the maid opened the door to show me in, my ears were flooded with strange music quite unlike any I had ever heard. I turned back to the maidservant to ask her to announce me, but she was already gone. This lack of address would certainly need to be remedied before any invites were sent out.

Miss Craythorne was prancing about in steps not dissimilar to the ones she had shown me yesterday, except these were far more flamboyant and, if I cared to admit it, provocative in nature. It was not helped by the matter of her having only the bottom half of a sari skirt on and what looked like a scarf tied around her back, covering only her bosom—that daring Mundum thingy she had fashioned on me only days ago. And whilst I was relieved to see she was not in company, I was so aghast at the sight of this display, I thought I might go out again and await its conclusion. I began to back out of the doorway. *Who knew my court practice would come in useful beyond my presentation?* But before I could remove entirely, she caught sight of me and came prancing towards me in the steps of the dance.

I paused. 'Miss Craythorne,' I said to greet her in the reasonable expectation she might stop and return the courtesy. She only smiled and continued right before my gaze in an even more illicit style; gyrating her hips and stretching her arms up above her head in swaying movements, leaving her torso wriggling and jerking in front of me. I had never seen such a thing before, and I knew I hid my astonishment badly, even though she seemed indifferent to it. She took a scarf from around her neck and hooked me about the waist with it in a swift move that gave me no time at all to evade it as it looped over me. Then she pulled me farther into the room by it and pushed me gently into a seat, although I only realised there was one when I landed in it.

I should have set a better example and punished her for this appalling disregard. I would be perfectly justified in my leaving, yet I did not want to go without giving her the news. *Have you no regard for the pains I have taken to come here, or the time constraints set upon me by the fading light?* I remained seated as she danced her way back into the centre of the room and watched her continue this impromptu demonstration.

I looked across to the place the sounds were coming from and saw, sitting on the floor, an Indian boy tapping away on some drums with the palms of his hands with extraordinary speed. Another plucking away at the string instrument that was strumming out these exotic noises that made me instantly hunger for the faraway scenes I remembered from her sketches. I may not have approved of her dancing, but I did like the music. When I looked up from my examination of these musicians, I saw her leaping her way back in my direction and braced myself. I did not know where to look or how to behave when she stared at me so boldly, shaking parts of her body so close to my face, I had to lean back in my chair to avoid being whipped by the fabric of her skirts.

It was now I noticed where the jingling sound of bells was coming from: a string of them tied about her waist and around each of her ankles.

I was relieved when she turned her back to me, but I had not expected her to stay in such proximity as she shook her posterior several times and rolled her hips around in ways I knew were obscene but found no less fascinating for its vulgarity. *Why was she taught such lessons?* I could not imagine there were hop merchants in Madras or even Paris who would be called upon for such learning. Indeed, what kind of father would be willing to pay tuition for his daughter to be taught such strange accomplishments?

I watched on a little more freely now, knowing she could not see me staring, and regarded the perfect curve of her back, the small of her waist, and the taut flanks either side, as they moved with the beat of the drum. She seemed suddenly beautiful to me in a light that I had not seen her in before, for I had never thought her comely. But there was some other trick that made her charming now, and this performance (which I should have disowned her for), exacerbated my notice of the fact, and I was completely enchanted by it.

I had never considered how wildly a woman might shake and move her body beyond the country dances I was used to, nor how compelling such a look of unashamed brazenness could seem upon her face. If there had been gentlemen present to witness such a thing, I was sure they would all be in love with her, for no other reason than this disgracefully captivating dance.

She eventually wiggled her way back over to the other side of the room, and at last I could breathe again. She took up a scarf and started waving and weaving it about in her routine, a swathe of shimmering colour sweeping through the air. The drumbeat shifting into a new pattern and the strings' vibration fully diminished before another was plucked.

When she came close again, she wrapped the scarf around my neck this time, and I did not understand the invitation, nor how to escape her eyes when she held me there right in front of her.

She let me go in the end and what she did next, I was wholly unprepared for. I watched her take the scarf between her legs and pull it from front to back as she shook her head in every direction, letting the lengths of her hair whip up around her face and sweep the ground. Her sari skirt lifted higher than her knees, revealing the clench and release of her thighs as she thrust the scarf between them. I had never seen anything like it. I knew I should have left long before this, but I could not take my eyes off her or settle the nerves in my stomach. After a vigorous repetition of this odd routine, she slowed into swaying pulls from side to side, before dwindling to her knees and collapsing into a huddled ball over them.

I had never been so astonished. Never had I had witnessed anything so absurd. I waited for the music to completely decrescendo before I found the courage to applaud her dancing. It seemed a peculiar thing to do for such an outrageous demonstration, and yet I did not know what other response might answer.

'Thank you, Miss Ashlyn,' she said, panting. 'You are very kind and remarkably tolerant. I am pleased I judged your character well.'

I could feel nothing but offence to that notion.

'I was not expecting an audience, I confess.'

I certainly hoped not, but it was really the least important detail after so much else. I watched her unfurl herself from the ball she had become and rise to take a bow.

'Miss Craythorne, those were indeed interesting steps. May I ask you where you learned them?' The question seemed ridiculous to me, but I was still trying to compose myself as I watched her tame her bedraggled locks back into a bandeau, the sweat glowing upon her skin, her chest rising with her recovering breaths.

'In India.'

'Of course.'

'Although the dance is not an Indian one. It was an Ottoman girl who taught me the Oryantal Dans. There was not much diversion at my convent school, so we often had to make do with making our own entertainment. But as you might imagine, that particular style of dancing is only intended for very specific audiences.'

This much, at least, relieved me, for it suddenly occurred to me that my friends were in agreement to attend a party of her organising. Although I could not see the point in learning such a complicated dance that was too indecent to be shown to others, nor understand why I was considered a suitable audience to such a thing. 'I see,' was all I could say. Words were not forthcoming.

'Did you enjoy it, Miss Ashlyn?'

There was a suggestion in her question I did not like. 'It was most *unexpected* Miss Craythorne.'

'I thought you would appreciate it.' She smiled, and again I saw the suggestion beyond her words. It frustrated me that I could not rebuff them without making my interpretation of them plain. 'Perhaps you will let me teach you another time.'

I could not begin to imagine that! 'I am better suited to ordinary dancing: country dances suit my taste very well. Now, I know I am late coming, but I must tell you my delay was a profitable one.'

'Oh?' She picked up a long cloak and wrapped it around herself. I was pleased to be able to look her in the eye at last. 'Then we must go back to the house, so you can tell me all about it.'

'I cannot. I must be back before sunset.'

She drew in close to me and lifted the cap of my bonnet a fraction to better see my eyes. 'Now, that is a disappointment.'

'Yes, but the news I bring is not at all disappointing, Miss Craythorne. It is what I am come to tell you. You shall have your party!'

A wide smile broke across her glowing cheeks. 'Then we have a lot of planning to do. But first, we must celebrate!'

'Celebrate?'

'Yes! We must dance!' she said with renewed enthusiasm, throwing the cloak back off.

'You have danced enough,' I complained.

'That? A mere warm up! I crave some real celebratory dancing. Rakesh—' she said something to him in his native tongue and he began strumming out a new tune before the other boy came in on the drums.

She stood up in front of me and pulled me from my seat. 'Come, let us see how well I have taught you?'

I kicked off my shoes and let her lead me to the middle of the room, half reluctant, half intrigued.

'Follow my lead if you wish,' she said, and I began imitating the beat at which she crossed one leg over the other alternatively as she twisted her hands in small circles and turned her elbows inwards and outwards to coordinate with her feet.

This kind of dancing I was agreeable to, even if the steps were a little fast. It was of an altogether different tone to the one I had just witnessed. It had been designed for innocent merriment. The last, I did not know for what purpose it was designed but knew it to be nothing of decent purposes...

'Relax, let the music guide your body!'

I thought I was, but it was so quick it took me 'till the proceeding steps to get the hang of the last. After a few rounds, I caught up a little better for the practice.

When we had worked up a sweat from moving so fast in leaps and bounces, she gave Rakesh another instruction and the rhythm fell off to a slower more sedate pace and the movements turned in to elongated sways and pulls. At first, I was relieved for a reprieve to catch my breath and keep in time, but the mood was turning, both in the music and her movements. Her sways slower, more deliberate, more gyrating and provocative and I knew I would soon have to find a reason to be excused before she attempted to teach me the steps of the Oryantal Dans.

She unpinned the top of her sari from her shoulder and tucked it into her skirt so her midriff was showing again as she began lowering herself down to the ground and working her way up again in a sequence I had no wish to replicate. It was my cue to make an exit, but as I tried to make my way, she came up close in front of me and presented herself as a barrier between me and my exit. I made a few failed attempts to dodge her, but she was persistent, as was her gaze that distracted me to the point I could not make the protest I had planned. I had stopped moving altogether but she continued swaying her body indecently in front of me without a hint of shame. My breaths and temperature were rising again even though I had almost recovered from my exertion now. She inched so close to me I could feel her body brushing against mine and every time I stepped back to create some distance between us, she stepped into it again and closed it.

'Miss Cray—' I shouted to try to speak above the volume of the music.

'Don't go,' she said, and took up the ends of my shawl to pull me closer to her until I felt her hips circling against mine. 'Unless you really want to?'

When I made no reply, she put her hands on my hips and moved mine in sync with hers. 'Don't be afraid, you move well. Close your eyes and feel the music, answer its call, do what your body wants it to do,' she said and closed her own eyes. She leaned back so far, her hair swept the ground before she came back up again, coaxing my hips a little closer, a little more vigorously.

My mouth had become suddenly dry. 'I do not have your talent for it, I really must—'

She silenced me with a fingertip pressed against my lips and part of me rose up in outrage at her audacity, but the greater part placated it, and would not let me move from her grasp, from this feeling rising in me at the proximity in which we swayed and moved together.

'You have so many talents, but you are yet to realise them all, Eleanor.'

The audacity. Eleanor? It seemed impossible to protest at the use of my Christian name in the light of such interactions.

'Let me help you. Let me show you how to let go, how to be free of all these fears that hold you back.'

'Nothing holds me back.'

'Oh? Well then you will not object to proving it.'

'Very well.' It was not only the challenge in her tone that made me pledge it, it was the danger promised in it that I seemed to have an unnatural appetite for.

She smiled that cunning wide smile and tightened the shawl in her hands so I was pulled by it so close against her I could not exhale without feeling the bulge of her bosom against mine, or the pain of her bruising me with the grinding of her hip bones into my own.

'The pleasure will be mine,' she whispered in my ear, and a shiver ran through the length of me at the sensation of it, 'maybe yours too, if you permit it.'

I was fighting a losing battle to prevent it now. Our bodies had become so entwined they moved as one in small circles, swaying and writhing slowly with the music. When she let go of my shawl and it fell away, I did not step back to pick it up or try to escape her. I was too enchanted, too much under this spell and too much beyond the possibility of forgiveness to not permit myself the full extent of this degradation.

Her now empty hands moved quickly to my rear and when she pulled it towards her, I tried not to show my surprise. Her hands moved quickly to my hips, then my back, in light stroking movements that felt so soothing I could not stop my breaths from escaping into long held sighs and gasps. I was embarrassed by it until I realised how it encouraged her and the exploration of her hands which were moving over my back, circling my shoulders and playing with the hair at the nape of my neck.

'Touch me if you want to Eleanor, do not be afraid.'

I was afraid. I was petrified, even though a part of me felt curious at the invitation. I tried to lift my hands from their position hanging at my side but they were reluctant and rigid and I could not persuade them to shift.

'Hold my body against yours and see if you like the way it feels.'

Despite my curiosity, I could not find the nerve to satisfy it. It seemed somehow greater the crime that I would instigate such a thing, despite my permitting her to set her hands upon me in such a way. I could not do it and I could not tell her, so I pretended not to hear her words at all above the drumming and the plucking of strings. But she soon took the initiative, in this too: found my hands at my side and lifted them to her hips and rested them upon them. The bulge of her flesh beneath my palms felt strange, foreign.

'You are scared, but there is nothing to fear,' she said again, and when I failed to reply or move my hands from the place she had put them, she began moving them beneath her own.

I should have stopped her, but I did not. I felt the full curve of her back, the soft round flesh of her bottom as she circled it and then the smooth taut skin of her flanks. She had rested her head on my shoulder and I could hear the deepening of her breaths as I began to move with her, feeling the planes of her waist, the bumps of her ribcage, the trim depression of her navel. I was just beginning to relax, just coming around to enjoying the feeling of her when she moved her own hands across my clavicle and swept them lightly down the swell of my breasts. I withdrew instantly, stepped back and looked at her with utter alarm.

'There is nothing to fear, Eleanor. Come here,' she reached for me again and I resisted. I could not convince myself to accept her request, to accept that I was as corrupt as she was... I drew in a deep breath to steady myself. *What was the meaning of this? What was I permitting?'*

'No, I must go now. It is dark outside,' I told her flatly.

'Shame,' she said sobering. 'I have pushed you too hard, you must forgive me, Eleanor.' She leant over and kissed me quickly on the cheek. 'Go home now,' she said, and led me to the door by my arm with instructions to one of the musicians to escort me back to the house. I had entirely forgotten their presence and wondered what they made of our behaviour. It was only now the thought occurred to me that we were watched, and it disturbed me greatly.

'Do not worry, Miss Ashlyn,' she pushed me on towards the door. 'They cannot speak a word of English.'

This knowledge did not comfort me however when I walked the short journey back to the house alone with him, nor did it comfort me to see how well *she* could presume to know my thoughts, even if she had guessed them correctly on this occasion. It made me feel vulnerable somehow, as did having to walk in the presence of someone who had just witnessed me succumb to something so peculiar, I would rather die than have the details repeated, even if they were in some other language I could not fathom. 'Go. Leave me,' I had tried to tell him several times as we walked, but he stared blankly at me and continued at my side.

When I returned home, having managed to navigate the woodland in the merest hue of dissipating light, I went straight to my chamber and gave Molly the instruction to inform Mama that I was indisposed and too unwell to go down for supper tonight. She was not the only one who could feign illness for me to make excuse. The thought of having to face anyone now seemed too much to bear as I sobered to the realisation of my actions. I was certain that anyone who looked upon me would see the shame in my face and question me on it. I wasn't sure precisely what had passed between us. There was nothing in dancing between friends and yet this was different somehow. I did not know how, what it meant, what was so shameful specifically, only that I was uncomfortable with having permitted it. *Enjoyed it...*

The dread of this transparency increased when both Mama and Delores took their turns in tending me. 'I wonder if you have a fever coming on, or perhaps you have eaten something ill? Perhaps it was the crab! Or maybe you have overexerted yourself? You would insist on playing lawn games all day in such heat!' Mama said searchingly, sat at my bedside.

'No Mama, it is simply the monthly ills, there is nothing to concern yourself with.'

'If you are sure. But I can have Delores sit up with you tonight, just to be certain you are not...'

'Mama! I just want to go to sleep! Please, stop fussing,' I hissed through my blankets. I was determined to keep my face from her, so she could not see the shame in it.

Stifled Sigh.

April 1821. - Eleanor.

I had quite forgotten my agreement to go riding with Sheldon the next morning until he was announced. I was at least already in my habit, although my intention had been to go to Beaulieu. Part of me felt disappointed at his arrival and another part of me, grateful for distracting me from the odd night of thinking and dreams I had suffered since Miss Craythorne's peculiar behaviour yesterday. I still did not know how to understand it, or how I would face her now. It had thrown me quite out of countenance. But there were plans to be made that could not wait and I would have to face her again eventually, even if I had been offered a momentary reprieve. I sent Molly to take her a note, explaining that I could not come to her as planned this afternoon and that I would send another to tell her when I could.

I went downstairs and bid Mama farewell, crop in hand. I had suspected she would at least have our ride chaperoned and I would have no chance of getting out on the Downs, but when she as good as pushed me out of the door with Sheldon quite alone, with a casual request that we stick to the park, I felt a new anxiety altogether. *He is going to propose to me!*

The astonishment of this made me quite dizzy and as I saddled Samson, I tightened my grip on the reins to keep steady. We took a gentle trot out towards the deer park, at a comfortable enough speed to converse, although I was finding it difficult to hold much conversation with my head swimming with so many thoughts.

'There is something I would like to ask you,' he said, once we reached the bracken boundary by the lake and slowed to turn the horses back.

My throat instantly felt dry and constricted like one of the twigs Samson crushed beneath his hooves had clipped off and lodged itself in my windpipe. 'Oh,' I said as nonchalantly as I could, fiddling with Samson's mane to avert my gaze. *Beg him not to ask it, beg him wait a while.*

'I know you have always wanted to go to the Derby,' he said.

'Yes,' I said, mildly puzzled and letting my breath out now.

'Well, I have had the fortune to reserve some seats in the King's Stand for the occasion. I thought you might like to go with me?'

'Really?' I felt a child like excitement rise in me at the prospect, but then remembered back to the time I snuck off the park and rode out to catch a glimpse of the races on Samson's back, only for my brother Henry to discover me there and report me to my parents. 'I would love to, Sheldon. And it is very generous of you to ask me, but by no means would mama permit me go to such an event. She has no sympathy for sporting affairs—'

'Well, I have taken the liberty of seeking her permission before asking you, and she is agreeable to the scheme, if Delores attends you of course.'

Part of me wished to cheer at such a triumph in bending my Mama to the impossible, but the greater part of me was unsettled by her making such allowances. Mama hated sporting events with such a passion and thought them no place for a lady amongst the gamblers, drinking, and trouble such events brought with them. But she had bid me go to appease Sheldon's wish, which confirmed to me over again that it would only be possible on the understanding of far greater intentions. 'I see,' I said when I realised he was anxious of my silence.

'You do not want to go?'

'Yes, I do—' I corrected him. *I do. But as friends, not potential suitors.* It seemed impossible to add this caveat to my acceptance though, without offense.

'Then it is settled.'

'It is,' I said with the best smile I could summon. But I could not feel the natural delight such an occasion warranted. I hoped he did not think me uncivil in my gratitude for I was grateful...for the opportunity to see the races.

'HOW WAS YOUR RIDE?' Mama came to me as Molly changed me out of my habit. She never asked after my rides. She had little sympathy for my love of riding, having given up the habit in her youth.

'Fine,' I said evenly and turned to offer Molly by back.

'It was nice of Mr Elmbridge to call on you.'

'Yes, I suppose it was.'

'Well, you were not gone very long dear, are you well recovered this morning?'

'Perfectly well, Mama; I feel better today. I did not think it appropriate I stay out long given how un-chaperoned we were. Besides, the park is not so large when on horseback.'

'Very proper. But, well...you and Mr Elmbridge are more like family; so closely brought up you have been.'

'Yes, but I know how you hate me to forget my manners, Mama, so I thought I did right to make it a brief affair.'

'Yes, and would you have been in any other company—'

'Mama, I don't know what the meaning of this is; but I don't like it a bit!'

'Whatever can you mean?'

'You have always refused me going to the Derby, no matter how many petitions, even when my own brother and uncle would vouch for taking me, you have never permitted it.'

'Well, yes, but my dear, you will not be amongst the rough common sorts, you will be in the King's Stand. Even I cannot protest to that.'

'And yet you did when Henry made the same case to you.'

'That was different, my dear, your brother could not be trusted to the task. Always fooling around in the princes set, as he was then. I had your reputation to consider.'

'And now you do not?'

'Eleanor, Mr Elmbridge is a sensible man. I know you will be in very good care, and Delores will go with you. There can be no argument against it.'

'No. I suppose not.'

'Well, you might be pleased? You have wanted so much to go over the years, I thought it would produce a better effect on you than this. I own I do not see the attraction in it, but I know you have always had a greater appreciation for these things.'

'I am.' It was half true. Of course, I was happy to go, but this pushing and coaxing of the pair of us was having quite the opposite effect of the one intended. I liked Sheldon, and he was not himself at fault here, yet it was he I shrunk from for feeling so much pushed towards him. If our parents did not take care, I feared they may do some serious injury to our acquaintance, for romantic feelings had never surfaced for me, even if I could understand why he was held in such esteem. Green or not, I was certain such things could not be evoked or conjured at will, but must occur naturally of their own accord. I was willing to consider whether such a thing had the possibility of flourishing between Sheldon and I, but not at such a pace and not like this: So coaxed and meddled in.

DELORES WAS NOT SO impressed with the news that she would be lumbered with attending the race track. I could see it in her tight-lipped smile when mama apprised her of the details. But she was in high spirits today, for the Squire of Dorking had invited us to dine and whenever his name was in the mention, Delores was in good spirits.

Mama did not tell me this invitation had been extended to the Elmbridges and Mowbrays. This I only learnt on my arrival.

Betsy was still in a sulk with me, I noted from her unwillingness to be detained in my conversation beyond brief pleasantries, and so it seemed I would be left to Sheldon's for the night. I took his offered arm into the dining room with a feeling of such foreboding it took all my measure to counter it. The general mood about the table was genial and relaxed, but I felt anything but, as I tried to keep within the spirit of it. It seemed the harder I tried, the more difficult it became to smile easily or find the natural flow of conversation on my lips. The laughter and conversation all about me, fading into a distant muffle of indecipherable sounds as I lifted my spoon to my mouth and tasted the salty liquid of the soup upon my tongue. Salt, it had a way of overpowering every other flavour when a little too much was used. I wondered if the same could be said of other feelings; could they be washed in salt until their effect was neutralised to something far less potent? I knew it could not, and yet I sipped from my spoon until all the salty liquid was gone, as if it could somehow be transported through my digestive tract into other parts of me; the parts of me responsible for all the strange and uncomfortable thoughts and feelings that were making it hard for me to compose myself...contain myself.

'Ma'am, can I offer you the salmon?'

I looked up at the footman, only just seeing him, wondering how he had managed to clear my soup bowl without me noticing. 'Forgive me. Yes, I will have a small helping,' I told him and edged out of his way as he filled my plate with a slab of salmon. Steam rose up from it, misting the stem of my wine glass, lemon and dill wafting with it.

'You seem far removed,' Sheldon said to me when the footman moved along.

'Do I?' I said with a vagueness that probably confirmed, rather than dispelled the notion.

'Have you something weighing on your mind?'

'Yes,' I said sitting up straighter, making a more conscious effort to respond. 'Nothing to account; only I am anxious to away to London now.'

'You are finding the country a little dry now you have had a taste of the Season.'

'To put it mildly.' I picked up my glass. 'I would say less a taste and more of a sniff.'

He offered me a small laugh and his eyes brightened with it. It was not just the candlelight I saw reflected in them. They were familiar eyes, but I had grown used to not seeing them. 'Well, Wednesday is not so far away, and hopefully not *all* the company is so irksome that we might not keep you entertained until then?'

I knew I should offer some gentle rebuff or compliment on the merit of his, but I felt unable to on his account. 'Not all of the company,' I told him, but I did not think of him when I said it. It was her; that peculiar, uncouth Miss Craythorne that sprung to mind, swaying and writhing in the orangery. *Curse her for her strange ways! Disturbing me so ill.*

His smile ate it up all the same.

'Eleanor, I have to say; you look most becoming this evening.'

I swallowed the mouthful of wine I had just taken in a gulp. It burned like acid down my gullet. 'Thank you, Mr Elmbridge, you are too kind.' I did not say that I wished he would keep the use of my Christian name for when we were not in company. His voice was low but I did not want to risk being overheard and giving off any such impressions.

'And you, too modest.'

'Well, I am not sure about that Mr Elmbridge. I am, after all, at last at liberty to flaunt my wardrobe and so I mean to, for it has been a long time coming.'

He laughed again. 'And how well you manage it.'

'Well, whilst your sex gets to enjoy other kinds of sport, mine take pains over such trifles.'

'To be sure. But it is not your wardrobe I meant to pay compliment to, fine though it is.'

I searched for my voice and for my glass of water to cool the flush of heat that flamed in my cheeks. 'You are full of flattery today, Mr Elmbridge; I'm sure I do not know you.'

'Well, I think we have both changed a great deal since we were last so much in each other's company.'

I wished it otherwise now. I was much more comfortable with him poking his tongue out at me or making cross eyed faces. 'Perhaps you have, Mr Elmbridge, on such travels and finding your way in the world, but I am still not fully out of leading strings!' I wondered if he took my hint, his expression, so puppy-eyed, I could not tell.

'You are about to be, no less, and must have turned your mind to the fact.'

'I have had time to do little else: I have every intention of seeing all of London's pleasures and dancing my slippers off, just as soon as Wednesday comes.' Yes: this seemed to throw him off.

'Is that all you have thought of?'

'Quite,' I said quickly, 'along with dresses and ribbons and shoe roses. I am in no rush to think beyond such follies, there will be time enough for such musings later on. But for now, I mean to enjoy the small things.'

'Well. Then you must brace yourself for an open reception El, for your dance card is much exhausted in our society, I can only imagine how it will be in London.'

'Merry, I hope. And you too, Mr Elmbridge, you must mean to make a merry time of it after such an absence and so long estranged from society?'

'I cannot say I am much minded too. Although I will attend.'

'Perhaps the spirit of it will tempt you once you have arrived!'

'No, that shan't tempt me,' he said thoughtfully and went back to his plate.

I cut into my salmon, it was cold now.

WHEN WE SAT AT THE card table later, it was her I thought of still. Part anxiety in not attending her today, and trusting her to set upon the arrangements without me, part replay of the strange dancing...

'A penny for your thoughts?'

'Forgive me, Sheldon. It has seemed a long day indeed and I do not think I have the concentration left to focus on our game.'

He put his hand down on the table and I noticed from his cards that he would have claimed the game. 'Well, what say we quit this and I take you for a turn about the balcony? A little air may reinvigorate you?'

'Yes. A good idea, an airing will surely cure it.'

Of course, it did not, and I hadn't the slightest notion what the cure was for such a malady of one's thoughts. But it seemed that turning in small laps across the balcony was only good for disappointing Delores in tearing her away from receiving the squire's attentions, which I was not much sorry for, since his late wife was not long buried. I was surprised that a woman of Delores years did not have a greater sense of decency. I was sure it should be noticed and remarked on, but there was little hint of any attention being paid to this flirtation, all eyes being focused on detecting a hint of ours.

I remembered in my youth, overhearing rumours that Delores had been the squire's paramour, something that had seemed so absurd and ridiculous to me at the time, I had paid it no mind. Yet it was only now, that I saw them in each other's company, I pondered the matter more seriously.

'Do you think the squire means to remarry?' I asked Sheldon, quietly.

He frowned. 'I could hardly say. Why?'

'I don't know precisely, it just seems to me that Delores acts strangely since he became a widow: Girlish at his mention, or company.'

'It's possible, they were once promised.'

'They were?'

'Yes. If my memory serves me right, I recall my mama mentioning as much. Some matter of her losing out to the late Lady Forester on account of her dowry being more favourable.'

I looked between he, and then Delores, quite stunned. She was standing at the balcony's edge, staring out into the night; although not to simply feign disinterest in our movements, but seeming much adrift in thought. *So that's why she never married: she was heartbroken.* I had always thought some scandal to be to blame, for I knew her birth was no mystery. Perhaps by the time she got over it—if indeed she ever did—her time was up. 'How horrid.'

'Yes. I believe there was some devastation on both sides.'

'They must have been much in love.'

'It is a cruel thing.'

'Yes,' I agreed, still taking in the shock of it.

'We must be grateful, I think, that things are much different now. That love can prevail in these modern times.'

Could it? I wonder if Louisa or I would concede once our banns were read. I wondered just how much flexibility there was in our families' minds, even if in ours we hoped for romance and affection. 'I do hope you are right, Sheldon. There are too many ill matches I could name to increase the number.'

'Indeed. I think it important to consider feeling as well as duty in these matters.'

I wondered what category he had me in, or whether in his mind I was equal to both. 'So do I. I do not mean to be made to choose between the two.'

'I hope you shall not have the need to court such anxieties,' his head was cocked at an angle that made it difficult to subvert his meaning.

'I don't, that is; I do not have the cause to presently. I am neither in love, nor in the suds.'

'Well, let us hope the former will soon be altered and the latter never come to pass.'

I WAS NOT ABLE TO VISIT Miss Craythorne that day, or the next. With the run up to our London departure and being pushed beneath Sheldon's nose at every opportunity, I could not find a moment to visit her again for two days. I was growing increasingly concerned at what wild notions she might have planned without me to tame them, and begun to question my sanity in involving myself in such a scheme that now seemed incredibly mad-brained to me. At the time, it had seemed something of an adventurous attempt at bringing something lively and exciting to Cuddington whilst throwing a lifeline out to Martha. Now it felt like an insufferable risk I had bound myself to and would have to be content to limit the damage now.

We exchanged covert notes using our servants who rebounded back and forth each time either of us made a new discovery of attendance or had some query or suggestion to pass between. But where I took pains with mine to be clear and comprehensive, hers were brief and perfunctory, and images of her wild dancing came back to me with the dread of what she might plan in my absence. When I opened an invitation for the event, set for Saturday evening, I knew I must act quickly: So, I rose early the next morning to gain an advantage on the day. Whatever itinerary Mama had cooked up for me today would not be scheduled until after breakfast at least.

Miss Craythorne had barely risen when I arrived.

'Well, I don't know, Miss Ashlyn: I do not see you in days, and then you stir me from my bed!' she said, when I was announced in the middle of her toilette. She was stood in her chemise over the washstand as her maid poured the jug.

'Forgive the intrusion; I have been so much detained. I came as soon as I could. Is there somewhere else I might wait while you dress?'

'Not if you want to keep out of sight?' she looked up and took the offered cloth to pat her face dry.

'Very well,' I agreed, taking the offered seat she gestured to. When she stepped away from the stand and offered her back to the maid, I did not know where to look when she stripped her of her shimmy and took the cloth to her. *The Mehndi.* I examined the embellishment of her bare flesh from the back of her thighs up to her waist, her pale buttocks seeming to hang from the mock chandelier of its design. I was sure I had never been more astonished.

'You like it?' she asked, and I looked up to see her reflection in the mirror, watching me.

'But how did you—?'

'I had Geeta do it,' she said simply.

I looked at the Indian maidservant who was mixing her lotions and did not know whether to feel disgust or admiration at this strange talent she seemed outwardly incapable of. But when Miss Craythorne turned around to face me, I gasped, realising that this was not the full extent of her maidservant's talents.

'Oh. You have not seen this look before?' she asked, and however much I did not want to confess to understanding her reference, I knew it would be even more humiliating to cause her to spell it out.

'I have not,' I said, turning away from the sight of the smooth, hairless mound between her legs as she was helped into a satin peignoir. She waved the maids away and came closer to me. 'It is normal practice in Asia you know.'

'I do not think it is here.'

'No, that was the very thought that crossed my mind when we were costume trying, the other day.'

I felt the embarrassment of her words instantly as I thought of her noticing the thick curling mound of hair I was used to—and had been perfectly happy with, until now. It had never occurred to me before that one would take pains to consider its style, and from such consideration, make efforts to remove it. 'You trust your maid to take a razor blade to your—?'

She laughed. 'No, silly. It is done with a paste made from sugar that sticks to the hair and is pulled away to remove it. There is no risk of being nipped! Perish the thought. I can have Geeta school your maid if you wish to try it.'

'Thank you: no,' I said flatly. I could not begin to imagine the look on Molly's face at such a request and I did not wish to find it out. I had heard of maidservants tutoring each other in some new hairstyle at the bequest of their lady, but this...

'As you prefer. It is not without its benefits you know.'

'Benefits? I am not a scarlet woman, Miss Craythorne, what possible benefit could such a practice possibly—?'

She put down the towel she had been patting her face dry with and crossed the room to where I was sitting until she was stood right before me. 'I simply meant it is far cleaner and smoother, see for yourself,' she moved aside the satin of her robe. A faint scent of lavender soap drifting.

'Forgive me, I did not mean to suggest—'

'No offense taken. Give me your hand,' she said holding hers out in front of me.

They were glued to my reticule, wrapped neatly around it in my lap. My instinct warned me I should refuse, but it was caught up in a debate with my curiosity that failed as soon as she peered at me so darkly. I lifted one—now slightly trembling—hand and gave it to her.

'See,' she said triumphantly as she brushed my fingertips over that pale patch of skin at the corner of her thigh.

I jumped at the sensation and withdrew my hand so fast I could barely test the smoothness.

'It is just skin, there is nothing to fear,' she said and pulled it back.

How did she always manage to make me feel the fool? I circled an inch of the area cautiously—smooth velvet beneath my touch—and I was surprised at how different it seemed from the wiry tangle of my own.

'Do you approve now?' she asked, and I did not appreciate her choice of words.

I withdrew my hand and buried it beneath my thigh. 'It is very neat. But Miss Craythorne, you will grow cold, you really must get dressed. We have so much to arrange and I do not have much time.'

She withdrew from me, walked away and sat down on the chaise in front of the window and peered out of it. 'Neither I, so let us go over things now. I can dress after.'

This was a surprise. I wondered what engagements called her away. I surely did not expect her at the Dowager's this afternoon.

'So, let us get to business,' she said, turning back to look at me. Her robe remained un-drawn and I wished she would tie its ribbons. 'I have made all the arrangements, I think; the invitations are sent, the servants have their instructions.'

'I thought we might go over the plans more carefully. What exactly is the schedule?'

She smiled incredulously and bit her bottom lip. 'You are worried aren't you, Miss Ashlyn, that I am not capable of making the proper arrangements?'

'Of course not,' I held up my hand in protest.

'It is quite alright. I understand. You have put your reputation on the line for me, it is only right you wish to be certain of me.'

'I do not doubt your intentions, Miss Craythorne, but you see, things are done differently here, and I would be failing in my duty to you if I did not check that your entertainments will be suitable for society's constitution. I do not say it for my own sake, but the truth is; the rest of Cuddington will not share my sympathy in the more extraordinary things you have shown to me. And I fear that perhaps I have done you a disservice in permitting you to think it acceptable, when I assure you, it would prove quite the shock for them to witness the things I have, and they will not welcome it at all.'

'And yet it does not seem to disconcert you, Miss Ashlyn. I wonder why that is?' she smiled a wide cunning smile at me. 'You know, Miss Ashlyn, we are a very good fit. With all that you know of *good* society and all I can teach you of *other* types of society, we might learn a great deal in the exchange and be much the wiser for it?'

'Perhaps, Miss Craythorne. But for now, I think we might just concentrate on this one.'

'Of course,' she rose and went over to her writing desk and pulled a notebook from it. 'Let me run the format by you, and if there is anything you do not consider appropriate, it must go!'

'Thank you,' I said, pretending not to notice the flashes of her naked flesh as she strode past me with her still undone robe. A small pale breast bobbed from beneath it as she sat back down and opened the book in her lap.

'Seven-o-clock arrival. Drinks and canapés in the drawing room before we take our seats at the table, this is the menu I have planned.'

I took it from her and scanned it quickly, seeing nothing amiss.

'Then after dinner, I will have card tables set up in the drawing room, mainly as a guise and to keep the chaperones entertained whilst the men keep to the dining room. This will be our opportunity for our smaller party to disappear...'

I quickly grew bored and distracted from the list she ran off as she detailed every sequence of events, and it pleased me, for I had heard nothing worthy of concern. Perhaps I had allowed myself to be unduly anxious after all.

As she continued in these details though, I found the words blurring and evading me: my eyes searching over the details of *her* instead. The fine sculpting of her jaw line as it jutted with the words she spoke. The shape of her lips as they mouthed sounds I seemed no longer able to hear or decipher. The line that formed and quivered in her cheek as she spoke. The pale skin that stretched across the length of her neck, the ridges in her gullet and the dip in her clavicle...

I was quite aware that this was entirely the wrong direction for my attention to be fixed, and yet I could not seem to persuade it back to the task. *What was happening?* Perhaps I had risen a little too early and I was a little dozy still? The trim of her robe, Lavender stitching, finely crocheted lace at the sleeves, embellished with little sprigs of Lavender thread over the palest shade of lilac. I followed the line of trim from where it gaped at the neck, rose over the shape of her bosom and fell slack at her navel.

'Eleanor?'

'Yes?' I said almost jumping at the sudden audibility of her voice and lifted my gaze to her face.

One brow was raised and her expression waiting. 'Are you quite well?' she asked.

'Yes.'

'You seem distracted.'

'Do I? I—I was just admiring the style of your dress robe. It is unusual and quite beautiful, what is the shade?'

'Thank you,' she said unconvinced. 'The shade is: Stifled Sigh.'

I nodded and smiled, feeling somehow diminished by the gaze she cast over me.

'There will be maids and changing curtains set up for the costume trying,' she said then, consulting her list, and I realised we were back to the topic of the party and made a marked effort to show my notice now.'

'Very good, with shifts on though, Miss Craythorne; you must instruct your servants that it is to be done this way for the guests.'

'Of course. We will dance a while—'

'Modest dances, very modest, Miss Craythorne. No Oryantal Dans!'

'I assure you,' she said with a grin in her eyes I didn't like.

'Then some simple Indian snacks to try.'

'Not too fiery mind.'

'The cook has already been instructed to keep the flavours mild.'

'Excellent. You have done very well, Miss Craythorne. I congratulate you.'

She looked up from the pages and smiled. 'There is one small matter.'

'Oh?'

'I have not the slightest idea of how to game.'

I frowned. Could it be true? That with all her many (albeit often bizarre) accomplishments, she could not sit out a quick round at the card table?

'Don't look so surprised, Miss Ashlyn. I have never had the time or need for such pursuits.'

I supposed a life as colourful as hers had provided enough distraction not to require the learning.

'But I have the matter in hand; my stepbrother is taking care of those arrangements and will try to give me a lesson beforehand. What game shall I tell him to teach me?'

'So, he is definitely coming?'

'Of course.'

'And your other brothers?'

She nodded.

'A game of whist will suit.'

'Very well.' She scribbled down a note in her book. 'Now, I really must get dressed.' She rung the bell for her maidservant. 'Unless of course you wish to stay?' And she pulled her robe from her shoulders and I watched the satin slip down the length of her back, land upon the chaise then slide off and gather in a pile by my feet.

I swallowed hard. I was not sure how I could answer this without lending insult to her or suspicion of myself. 'Like you said, we are both in a hurry.' I reached down to the floor to pick up her robe which I could not otherwise avoid stepping on in getting out of my seat. She was already walking away from me as I held it out to her. 'Your robe, Miss Craythorne.'

She turned around and we were suddenly colliding rather close to each other.

'Thank you,' she said, taking it from me, her small eyes wide, something bold about them, as if challenging me to something I'd failed to fathom out. 'Where did you get such an unusual peignoir?' I asked then, hoping it would cause her to break her stare and let me pass.

'Why, Paris of course,' her eyes glazed over with what I imagined to be some fond reminiscence from the past, before they cleared and she came back to me.

'Of course.'

'Perhaps you might like it as a gift, Miss Ashlyn, I have a sense that it would suit you better.'

'You are very good, but I could not.'

'Whyever not?'

'Well, for a start, I would have no occasion for it,' I answered without thinking. 'I mean—'

'Suit yourself,' she said, returning to the washstand where her maids had started up mixing her lotions, letting off a scent of rosewater into the room.

'Well, thank you, Miss Craythorne. I shall be on my way.'

'Anytime.'

Almost everything that came past her lips seemed tainted with the dangerous hint of some innuendo. Whereas, at first, I had considered them no more than a cultural misunderstanding, a lack of being socially adroit and just about any other rational excuse I could find to explain it away, now I was beginning to wonder if she enjoyed being so inflammatory. 'Good day,' I said, slipping back through the jib door and letting out a sigh.

Her plans at least; did seem safe—on paper anyway—and she'd made no protest to my restrictions... and yet, despite this, I still felt a great deal of dread at the prospect she might let some erratic behaviour or detail slip that would be enough to plunge us both into disrepute. My character was as much on the line for this as hers; if I was found lacking in my judgment, they would all turn on me.

Probation complete.

March 1821. - Annalise.

'Is that oyster sauce done yet?' Cook said, expectant faced, looking up from the tray of roasted woodcocks, steam rising and gathering about her brow. She wiped her forehead with a cloth and swung it over her shoulder.

'Yes,' said Maggie, shaking out the spoon against the side of the pan.

'Well! Don't just stare at me, you nit wit, bring it over!' she scowled.

Tensions had suddenly seemed to rise again since the family's return from London this afternoon, and it was as if, Annalise considered, they had never been away. The relaxed peaceful pace that had patterned the majority of the week had vanished promptly after breakfast this morning. Not just in the kitchens either, all through the estate. The gardeners had risen early to tend the grounds, the housemaids had been set to blacking the grates and polishing every surface and vase. The footman shined the silverware and polished brass plates and handles upon the doors. Mrs Crawford had set to distributing clean linens for the bed chambers and dining rooms, whilst laundry maids boiled coppers ready for the discarded ones. In the kitchen, the ranges had been burning bright and the spit jacks had been turning since dawn broke. Bread, cakes and pies had been baked, all manner of fowl and joints had been set to roast, soups bubbled over in pots and syllabubs were set in glasses.

The smell of the kitchen had been deliciously rich and fragrant, even if the atmosphere was not so cordial. If this marked the struggle back to regularity after only a week's leisure, Annalise wondered how it would be after the family awayed for the whole season in a couple of weeks' time. This—Maggie explained—was the greatest reprieve, for they would usually stay in London consistently for two to three months. With Mr Ashlyn being wanted often in London to sit in parliament, the house was used to the family rushing off and meandering back with regularity through the winter. But for the Season, they could comfortably rely on no one heading back between mid-March and June. There would, occasionally be a weekend of disruption if they came back for the Derby weekend, and there was the unfortunate year when one of the daughters was matched and wed within a few weeks of the seasons start. 'That,' Maggie told her with severity in her tone, 'was the year nearly all the kitchen staff left.'

'Left?' Annalise frowned as she trimmed silvery fins off the fish.

'Yep. Cook was in a rage and even more impossible than usual. We'd spent the first couple of weeks shutting up the house and setting everything in order, then just as everyone 'ad got used to the peace, suddenly, there was the family back, the bell ringing, engagement parties and wedding breakfasts to prepare, guests to stay,' she pulled a spine of bones out from the fish, held it up to the light a moment and flung it aside. 'Out in one,' she said impressed with herself. 'We'd had not a moment's notice. Half the undercooks left cos they couldn't cope with the impossible work, the other half cos they couldn't cope with Cook's scolding. That's when I got brought up from the scullery into the kitchen.'

'I see,' said Annalise, and she was pleased to note that promotion was possible here, even if it was based less on merit than necessity. 'So they didn't send you back to the scullery once they had found new kitchen maids?'

Maggie shook her head. 'Nah. I 'ad a knack for the kitchen, Cook said. Never complaining, just getting on with whatsever I was asked to. Who wouldn't if they knew what it's like to be in the scullery all day?'

This at least, gave Annalise some perspective. It was easy to consider what jobs might be the better ones, but she had not considered those that would be worse. After spending more time around the table with Will this week, she had decided that he had her ideal job: Going about the house, serving at the table, waiting on the family and guests. Nowhere was out of bounds to him, so long as there was a need of him there. On account of her sex, this was obviously unobtainable. But she could ponder it anyway, as she stood at the table, cracked hands covered in fish scales.

'But don't worry, thats was an unusual fing to 'appen,' Maggie said, gauging a fisheye out and catching it before it rolled off of the table. 'Usually, the season goes along just merrily. Just as this last week's been. So long as *this* daughter can hang on about getting leg shackled for a few months, we'll 'ave nothing to worry about.'

'I suppose we will have to wait and see.'

'Not that it'll be any better if we've all the wedding stuff to do over summer, but at least we'll be better for having had a long rest before it.'

Annalise couldn't help but wonder if that would make it worse, not better. If the contrast, she felt able to draw now, between yesterday and today was anything to go by, she could only consider such extremities even more difficult to adjust to.

'If,' Maggie told her as they flung the last fish upon the tray and gathered up the bones and guts from the table, 'you think it 'ot in here in now, you wait an' see what's it's like in the summer.'

Annalise slid the tray of neatly trimmed and filleted soles across to Poppy who was frying them off on the hot plate.

'You can 'ardly breathe in here!' she said, picking little bones from the cracks in the wood grain and adding them to the bucket too. 'Mostly everyone gets excited for the warm weather, but not us kitchen girls. Winter is our saviour.'

AFTER THIS RATHER GLOOMY start to the day and the less than cheerful conversation Maggie had imparted, she was pleased to get out for a moment to take the scraps over to the farm. She went alone now. Cook was past permitting two for a job where only one was needed. She took it as confirmation that she had come up to scratch now and her training considered complete, her duties competently dealt in. She would never tell Cook of course, that her improvement was owing to Poppy's instruction, and of course neither would anybody else. But they all knew that whilst Cook reigned superior in her cooking skills, Poppy reigned superior in their teaching and supervision and was ever catching up with the cooking skills to match it. There would be a day, Annalise thought, when Poppy would be the cook, and she looked to it as eagerly as she looked to the thought of her own promotion one day, even if it would never be to footman.

She was grateful for the moment's peace from the noise of the house in chaos and walked slowly, inhaling the balmy spring air and admiring the neat beds that had been weeded and turned only this morning.

The farm was as it usually was; they seemed to her, the only ones who gained no benefit from the family's comings or goings. It was a cog that must always turn with routine regularity and it had remained unaltered throughout. As she set down her scraps and headed back, she saw, marching up from the basement steps, Molly, looking no better pleased today, than she had on the day of her leaving.

Annalise watched her empty a bucket down the cess pit.

'Morning,' Annalise said as she passed her.

'You got a minute?' she said, not returning the greeting.

'I suppose so.'

'Good,' she said holding out the bucket. 'Take this to the laundry room, will you.'

Annalise peered into the bucket, noting the content and the smell. Soiled rags sloped about in the bottom, brown with blood.

'Stink, don't they? I think I'm going to throw up if I am near them a moment more,' she said, turning her head away from them.

Annalise took the bucket. 'Alright. Give them here,' she said, realising as she looked her over that it seemed not a guise for getting out of an unpleasant job, but the pallor and clammy look of her complexion suggesting it a genuine emergency.

When she came back from the laundry, she found Molly crouched over at the wall, dribble dangling from her chin and a trail of vomit upon the gravel. 'Are you alright?' she asked, crouching down at her side.

She shook her head and Annalise noticed now, she was crying.

'Let me help you back into the house.'

'No,' she said, wiping her sleeve across her chin. 'I'll be alright in a minute, I just need some fresh air.'

Annalise nodded. This she could quite understand, although she would have thought her opportunity for it better, having spent a week paying attendance on the family. 'Was it the rags?'

She nodded. 'I'm sick o' it. The rags, the chamber pots, the six changes of clothes a day for that fussy Miss, the bell ringing, the packing, the rattling around in the coach for hours. And now I'm back at last, Crawford expects to put me straight to work when all the other housemaids have been at leisure all week.'

It did seem a little unfair to Annalise. She would have thought the remainder of the day to recover from the journey would not be so unreasonable. When she was housekeeper at Gint's, she would have given leave of such a respite. That was why Poppy said she was ill-suited to the position. Because she would always take up work that wasn't hers and work her own fingers to the bone, whilst the others grew slack. Perhaps it was true. But it seemed to her there must be a balance between your duty to your employer and your duty to being human. 'Do you want me to help you to your room and tell Mrs Crawford you are ill?'

'Would you?' she said, looking up surprised.

Annalise nodded and held out her arm.

India comes to Cuddington.

April 1821. - Eleanor.

When I arrived to inspect the preparations on Saturday morning, I was pleased with what I saw, and it put to rest my qualms that had been resurfacing since our meeting and taunting me when I let myself get carried off in such thoughts. She was busied with the Indian servants making colourful garlands, laying out diva lights along the paths edge and making rangoli patterns out of chalk upon the floors to embellish the room in the Indian style I remembered from her pictures. It was quite fantastic, even incomplete. She had even managed to get some peacock feathers from the farmers to make an exotic centre piece on the table that was most artfully displayed. A good selection of costume for our guests to try had been hung on a rail behind a screen of luxurious drapes which formed quite a beautiful feature for its own sake. I reminded her again to counsel her maidservants in how to politely dress my friends in ways sympathetic to our modesty, and she assured me that they could be trusted to the task.

I don't know why I placed so much faith in her: a foreigner, an eccentric and someone so below our notice I would have been as obstinate as Betsy in rebuffing her only a week ago. Besides that, there was a great deal of danger in her influence that I had sensed almost immediately, but seemed curiously attracted to, however hazardous the scent of it. Her company was refreshing and unique, and it was for those reasons I craved it even though they were equally good reasoning to justify why I should avoid it altogether. But it was set now, there was nothing to be done but commit to the task. So I put on a borrowed apron and sat upon the flags and helped with completing the chalking of the orangery floor.

WE WERE SOON BUZZING about the drawing room making small talk before dinner, and I knew I had little time to waste in the introduction, so in spite of Betsy's assiduous gaze upon me, I hooked my arm into the crook of Martha's elbow and with my best nonchalance, marched her over to where Mr Harper-Craythorne was standing and made the introduction. It was not my usual style, bold and unreserved. But time was in short supply and it had taken a great deal of effort on my part, to get us finally here.

'Mr Craythorne, you have met Miss Brownlow?'

'Miss Ashlyn, very good to see you again. No. I do not believe I have had the pleasure. Miss Brownlow, very pleased to make your acquaintance.'

'And you, sir,' she dipped a curtsey, and returned her gaze to the ground.

'I trust you are both in good health?' he said to the awkward silence.

'Yes, sir. I am quite well, I thank you,' I said when Martha did little more than offer a nod in answer. If she was going to continue in this fashion, I felt already the frustration of my efforts. I jabbed her a little more than gently in the ribs and was relieved when she took up the hint and inquired at last after Mr Craythorne's health. It was no wonder to me that her past two seasons had been fruitless if this was how she conducted herself in gentleman's company. That, or perhaps, she did not like him and did not mean to make a civil impression on him. I supposed that could be the case, although it was hard to fathom that she should prefer to be left to a fate with old Wilmott than make a try to any better possibility, however fractional.

When the gong was struck and the butler announced dinner, I conveniently drifted beyond their company so he was left to escort her in. I had, after some deliberation advised Miss Craythorne against a formal seating plan, for the simple fact that it would have been quite impossible to sit them directly together if we had followed protocol. Conversely, having neglected to provide one, also left open the possibility that it would be taken as a lack of propriety or oversight on the Craythornes' part, however, I hoped that for such a small and informal affair it would not be much thought of at all, and even if it was, that by the time they had enjoyed what had been so painstakingly put together for their entertainment, they would quite forget it altogether. Besides, there could be nothing argued on that head after the same had been the case at recent dinners where seating plans could be happily overthrown in our own society, for matchmaking purposes.

As I watched Mr Craythorne pull out Martha's chair and settle into his own beside her, I caught his searching gaze about the room. Sheldon, having seized me the instant I removed myself from their company, had directed us to the furthest extent of the table. Before I could protest, or try to move us down to the opposite end, Anna and one of the Craythorne twins had settled in precisely the spot I had my eye on. Surveillance or contrivance would be impossible from here. I sighed and sat down in the chair Sheldon directed me to, spreading my napkin across my lap and trying to see beyond the obstruction of the candelabra, whether Martha was making an effort towards conversation.

'You wish yourself in other company?' came Sheldon's voice at my ear.

'What?'

'You seem more preoccupied with that quarter of the table than this.'

I turned to him now, noting the acerbity in his tone. He was eyes narrowed across the table in Mr Craythorne's direction.

'If you must know,' I said, trying to curb the irritation in my own, 'I have taken great pains to put those two in the way of each other and now I cannot see or hear what is happening!'

'Miss Brownlow and that Craythorne fellow?'

'Yes, now, stop looking, you are not being discreet.'

'So that is your plan, is it? To match the pair.'

'Yes. What is so absurd about that?' I said, forgetting that he was perhaps not privy to Martha's calamity, having only just returned home.

'He seems to me to have his sights set somewhat higher, I think.'

'Oh? You know this?'

'I suspect it.'

'Well? On whom?' I demanded, feeling at once concerned of any threat to the already shaky looking prospect of their hitting it off. But before he could furnish me with an answer, Betsy sank down in the chair the other side of me and cut in.

'I see it's a free for all,' she said, sulky faced and disapproving.

'Hardly worth the trouble at such a trifling affair don't you think?' I said to appease her.

'It was your bright idea to drag us here,' she replied, brows arched, accusing.

'Well, I thought it preferable to another irksome evening in the country, I confess. Still, we are soon to be in London and such trifling entertainments quite beyond us.'

'I will drink to that!' she agreed, offering up her empty glass to a footman.

DESPITE THE DOUBTFUL start, dinner went smoothly and civilly enough, with a full attendance around the table. But with Sheldon so much in my ear, and being so far separated from the pair, I could not further attempt to bring Martha and Mr Craythorne beyond a polite introduction even though I had planned to. I had hoped that they would soon grow comfortable and talkative of their own accord, but in the sparse glimpses I caught of them, Martha said little, staring sheepishly into her soup and Craythorne seemed disinterested in anything beyond civility. When I did see them talking at all, it was not to each other but their other neighbours, Martha to one of the Craythorne twins who she seemed to have no difficulty finding conversation with, and Mr Craythorne turning to Beth. If Sheldon could have only let me be a while, I knew I could have coaxed some further discourse between the pair, but he was relentless: guarding me and nipping at me every time I turned from him, like an over indulged lap dog. I was quite beside myself with stifled rage by the time the first courses were removed.

Beth had made a small attempt to connect them, but was sat the other side of Mr Craythorne, pulling him away, and not towards Martha's notice. Was this what Sheldon meant to imply before—that it was Beth Mr Craythorne had his sights set upon? I could see his point: he certainly seemed to have more time for her. But Beth was Martha's closest friend and I was certain that any efforts on her part would be solely dedicated to Martha's interests and not swayed towards her own.

Anna, who was the other side of Beth, had totally abandoned her in preference of the other Craythorne twin's company, which had been much more forthcoming, and Betsy sat in a sulk, scratching the plates with her cutlery and sipping silently on her wine beside me.

It was a relief to leave the men to the dining table when the time finally came and we distributed our chaperones about the gaming tables in the Parisian style drawing room. They were reliably at ease and consumed with their stakes or gossip, now the gentlemen were out of sight and they could withdraw their beady watch from us.

When we finally snuck away from the gaming tables and lead my friends carefully down to the orangery, we arrived to the beat of the tabla and immediately I could see the intrigue in their searching glances and furrowed brows. The beat echoed to the heights of the orangery which was dressed in such opulence it was hardly recognisable. Grand and beautiful as it was with its glass dome ceiling and generous windows, something came to life in it now, beyond the plants and otherwise usually vacant space of it.

We could see the decoration through the tall glass windows as we approached beneath the rose tunnel which had been embellished with a canopy of bright garlands draping from it. We stepped in onto a length of mazarine blue carpet at the door, acting as a pathway through the patterned floor with colour bursting from it like a reflection of fireworks. Flickering divas marked the carpet's boundary as it led us to the centre of the room where the low table was set beneath tumbling canopies of red and gold cloth that gave the illusion of a suspended ceiling below the glass dome overhead. A small ensemble of their Indian maidservants formed a line, dressed in traditional Indian clothes, echoing the colours of the peacock feathers upon the table, and they furnished each of us with our own flower garland to wear around our necks, and at the end of the line, we received our Tilaka mark upon our foreheads. It was precisely the kind of entrance they would all approve of and their curious smiles confirmed this.

'Welcome ladies, or should I say: namaste, as we say in the Bengal.' Miss Craythorne was palms pressed together and head bowed.

'Namaste,' they returned with varying degrees of accuracy and headed for their offered seats on the floor which had been furnished with co-ordinating silk cushions around the table.

'Well, this is quite something,' Anna said, taking it all in.

Clara was eyeing the plates on the table with distrust, Beth still admiring the maidservant's dress, and Martha was trying not to knock anything over.

'It is beautiful!' Beth agreed.

'Most irregular, but not unpleasant I suppose.' That was as good as a compliment from Betsy who had only just seemed to notice Miss Craythorne's costume. I saw a frown distort her face. 'Miss Craythorne, are you wearing pantaloons?' The astonishment on her face reminded me of my own, the day she had stripped me to my skin and dressed me in her clothes.

'Yes, Lady Elizabeth, but these are not considered only for men in the Bengal.'

She was wearing baggy satin trousers beneath her matching dress that was cut above her knee. I had felt it the more modest of her selections in terms of limiting the exposure of her flesh, but no less, I knew it would cause a stir. I had hoped it would be better accepted once we afforded them a perusal of the other costumes behind the curtains and they had a means of comparison. And I had not failed in my presumption that they would be as easily seduced by them as I was, and took no persuading to try them for themselves. All but Betsy at least, who sat pensively on the chaise outside our mock dressing room considering it all, as the rest of us were wrapped and unwrapped in various swathes of opulent fabric.

We took turns in parading them up and down the narrow path of carpet, applauding each other and listening to Miss Craythorne's running commentary of what was exhibited. I was grateful to note I was not the only one who struggled with the names of them. Even Betsy could not disguise her interest from the safety of her chair, and appeared to be drinking it all in, however much she maintained her silence.

I had every confidence that if Miss Craythorne could stick within the limits of the itinerary tonight, this could indeed be the making of her, for I saw the hunger in their eyes for the welcome diversion of it all. It was not only I that craved to break away to London, so tired of the country Lombard fever and the monotony of country dinners. Cuddington had never seen entertainment like this before.

After the costumery, a perusal of some Indian jewels; rich gold and bright gems in abundance, and a demonstration of the Mehndi art, Miss Craythorne and her maidservants entertained us with some Indian dances that were much more modest than the styles she had exhibited to me. Bouncy flouncy merriment abounded, and no obscene jiggling of indecent body parts. It was very well received, and I realised when all but Betsy joined in, we were on a winning streak.

The evening rounded off with the exotic refreshments and Miss Craythorne's retelling of many tales from her life abroad which she had a knack for narrating in such a way that transported you to the moment. I was sure they would have happily sat around the diva lit table for the whole evening if we were not on borrowed time.

WHEN WE RETURNED TO the card party and one by one, the guests made their departure, we were left sipping Ratafia, congratulating ourselves on the day and nibbling on some savoury dried snacks leftover on the buffet table that I could not remember the name of. I saw for the first time, a hint of gratitude in her eyes. I returned it. I was as grateful for the lack of faux pas as she was for the opportunity to shine.

'If it was not for Lady Elizabeth's disapproval, I would have been sure we had won them all over today,' she said to me.

'Oh, that's just Betsy, even she was not nearly as indifferent to the affair as she would like us to think; her silence speaks volumes. She even danced the final set. I think it went well, but I will know for certain tomorrow when they pay their calls,' I told her.

'I owe you a great deal of thanks, Miss Ashlyn, for making this possible.'

I smiled. 'You are welcome, Miss Craythorne. I cannot say I have not enjoyed assisting you in it. It has been quite the adventure.'

Then she leaned over, wrapped me up in her arms and squeezed me. I felt a little triumphant for managing to break her usually cool composure, but when she kissed both my cheeks and did not let go of me for such a long time, I felt other things I did not like and bid her to release me.

'I think I must go too.'

'Must you?' she said with a gravity about her expression that felt intense in some inexplicable way. Like her gaze was boring into me to see past my eyes and into my head.

'Yes. It is late.'

'Shame,' she lifted a hand and held my cheek against her palm.

I wondered what it meant.

'You know you could stay a little while longer.' I felt her fingers slide to my chin, holding it fixed in position whilst the others traced my jaw line, turning in small circles. 'You look tired. You could come and lie down upon my bed a while.' Her hand smoothed its flat palm down the length of my neck, resting in the crook of it before massaging it in deft strokes, pressing into the bones and muscles enough to cause my head to sway with the giddiness of the motion. 'A little rest before you journey back?'

I could lay down now; I could certainly rest my eyes a moment. 'But Delores—'

'Shhh,' she said, her strokes growing wider, the pressure working deeper until I felt the heaviness of a muscle in my shoulder smoothing out beneath the warmth of her palm. How good it felt. How easy I could fall into some beautiful reprieve right now. I sighed deeply.

'That's it, relax,' she said, and although I had my eyes closed, I felt the shift in her movements until I felt her come behind me, coaxing me to lean against her as she spread her fingers wide across each shoulder's breadth and began to work them simultaneously.

I felt my breathing shallow into an effortless hum. I was relaxed. So relaxed I felt like I was melting into the shape of her as my back slouched and my head sunk a little further.

'In Ayurveda, we are encouraged to make a regular habit of receiving massage. It is good for the constitution,' she said, and I felt her breath against my ear as she spoke.

'Oh,' I murmured. It seemed too laborious to make answer when I was so much immersed in the sensation of it, her hands sliding the planes of my back and the lengths of my upper arms, heat blazing beneath her palms and soothing my body into compliance. I did not know what kind of place Ayurveda was, but it seemed a very sensible notion to make a regular habit of such a practice. I could see that feeling so much at ease would be conducive to good health. I let out another deep exhale and my head lulled and rolled to one side, resting against her.

'You know,' she said, almost a whisper, leaning in at my ear and causing me to twitch at the surprise. 'It is much easier to massage without your clothes on.'

I did not reply to this, but it shocked me enough to cause me to open my eyes and call my senses back to order. If she thought I was willing to be undressed, she was quite mistaken.

'We could go up to my room, in private.' I felt her hands slipping beneath the sleeves of my dress now. 'I could massage you properly then, all over.' Then I felt the brush of her fingertips sweep the line of my décolleté and sat up with a start.

'No,' I said quickly, recovering my composure. 'I really must not be any later.' I pulled myself to my feet feeling a little lightheaded and unprepared for such an abrupt rising. I steadied myself and brushed creases from my skirts. 'Delores will be wondering at our going. Goodnight, Miss Craythorne.'

An odd invitation.

April 1821. - Eleanor.

When Grantley came for me at the breakfast table, I was relieved to be interrupted by a succession of calls from my friends who came bearing their compliments to the success of yesterday's entertainments at Beaulieu, which of course they could not pay directly to the host (for fear of sending Betsy quite over the edge) but no less wished for me to pass on in their stead.

Of course, I was happy to take the news to her, and as soon as they left, I had Molly dress me in my sprigged coral day dress, so I could deliver the news before we received the Elmbridges this afternoon. I spent the journey through the woodland fantasising over her reaction to it. Even she could not feign such a cool façade to such exceptional news, I was certain. The success of the party was more than a simple triumph of a good evening's entertainment; it was a breakthrough in her eventual acceptance among us. It was that simple: favour could be denied or granted as easily as that, with the right patronage. Of course, we were all about to desert the country and finally get to London, but at least when we returned, she would not be entirely friendless.

I was so excited at our triumph, I could hardly bear the pain of the disappointment at the butler telling me she was not home when I arrived. I asked him to permit me to make a note upon the back of my calling card before I left it, and I wrote 'Success!' before handing it to him.

I thumbed through the cards left for me when I returned home and was not surprised to find nothing left from Betsy, who was usually punctual to the hour of two if she was calling. I would let her sulk at me a little longer before I attempted to placate her and bring her around. It was not the first time we had disagreed and would surely not be the last, but we rarely allowed it to endure beyond a few days. It had seemed a worthwhile sacrifice to permit Miss Craythorne to draw closer into our acquaintance. Although, it seemed it had done little to further Martha's cause which I had found sadly lamentable. I was certain it required only a little more opportunity where I could encourage it further, although it seemed unlikely we would find it now until we returned from London, and by then, it would most likely be too late.

THE SUSPENSE OF HER whereabouts did not leave me all day, as I sat over two games of whist with the Elmbridges and played several games of Battledore with Sheldon's sisters. Mama's dislike of my participating in such things had, along with much else, vanished under such circumstances.

It was our turn to play host today, so I knew my excuses for disappearing would fail and tried to bear up to it as best I could. It seemed we might as well inhabit the same house and spare the horses, so much our households had been forced to merge of late. I could not wait for London. *This* could not continue there with so much else to amuse us. I was determined to be as flighty and fleeting as I could be to dispel this oppressive pairing which had took such a regular pattern now as to seem quite ordinary yet felt anything but. It seemed however I was engaged, or whoever I was with, it was always *her* that took up my thoughts.

I was cross and curious at her not being at home to receive me on a day as important as this. I considered her lack of telling me of any plans and the possibilities of whom she might pay a call on with so little acquaintance here. I presumed, perhaps some charitable invitation from the Rector and his wife, or maybe some duty to her family. Whatever it was, I knew it would have to be of some significance for her to slight me when I had spent the greatest part of a week giving her the compliment of my company and bringing my friends about to her cause. She must surely be as keen to hear the verdict as I was to deliver it? Then I thought of the disappointment in her face last night when I refused her request to stay longer and go to her room and considered the possibility that this was some kind of deliberate punishment for it.

When the Elmbridges were at last gone, I sought out the salvers and still found no card left by Miss Craythorne returning my call. I checked with Grantley and Mary too, to make sure. *Nothing.* I felt quite aggrieved, but considered the likelihood that she was not familiar with the correct protocol and there was nothing more in it than her ignorance. If it were not for the fact that I had barely enough time to get changed before leaving for the Glenthornes' musical concert, I would have paid her another brief visit to help her understand the correct courtesy. But Mama would not permit my going out in the dark, and Delores was in my chamber finding me things to wear, so I knew it would have to wait until the morning.

I had long accepted the fact of this delay and set my mind towards making the best of the soiree ahead. There would at least be musical entertainments tonight to dilute the need for so much prattling. So I accepted the wardrobe Delores had picked out and tolerated Molly plucking and pinning at my head for what felt like an age, in resigned acquiescence. I had barely finished dressing when I was called down from my chamber to receive her. I was surprised she had taken the liberty of calling here at such an hour when I was sure it must be plain to her that neither Mama nor Delores approved of her. But I was so glad at the sight of her, after waiting all day for a response, that I ignored Delores' arched eyebrows as I passed her in the hall.

'Forgive me Miss Ashlyn, I know you must think me quite uncivil for taking so long to return your call. I have been in but a half hour today. I hope it is not too late?'

It was outrageously late and we were soon to leave the house; but I had been guilty of as much, so there was little to be said. 'It could not be helped then, Miss Craythorne. Where have you been?'

'Beddington. My brother has begun on the works there. A great many renovations and he needed a female eye to pick the drapes and wallpapers. Just as well too; dreadful, dreary taste he has.'

'Should that not be left to his wife if he is soon to marry?' or at least someone more suitably qualified to such domesticities. I could not imagine Miss Craythorne paying notice to such trifles as house décor.

'Perhaps. But the problem is there is no time to waste; the house is so much in need of renovation before it will even resemble a home, that he shall have no fit place to promise to a new bride if he does not set upon it soon. It is likely to take months in the least, but he means to make the east wing habitable to begin with so he can at least set up there. No doubt the west wing will leave his future wife with such choices of papering and fabrics.'

I did not think Martha would much mind either way, under the circumstances. 'I see. Well, you are come now and you must know how well we brought it off. They all loved it!'

A wide grin stretched from ear to ear.

'Except Betsy of course, but then her silence speaks to the credit of it, even if her words cannot.'

'Oh Miss Ashlyn!' she said leaping towards me and embracing me like a child when given a new plaything. 'Thank you.'

I pulled back from the intensity of her excited grip, remembering how this had gone yesterday. 'You are quite welcome, Miss Craythorne, please do sit down,' I said, pushing her towards a chair and stroking wrinkles out of my sleeves that she had managed to dishevel. 'But you, too, are to be congratulated for,' *Moderating* is what I wanted to say, 'keeping to such a happy program and carrying it off in good style.'

'Well, how could I fail with you as my guide?'

This was true; it had never been my counsel that concerned me. 'Well, it was a happy collaboration then.'

'I wonder what other types of happy collaboration we might find ourselves capable of, Miss Ashlyn? It seems such a shame we will be so soon parted from each other when we are just beginning to understand each other better.'

It was indeed a shame, but I could not agree that I had come to understand her well at all. Her character and her intentions were still curiously obscure to me, and it was speeches just like this, that threw me into a puzzle between what her words said and what I thought she meant to indicate. However much I had become accustomed to excusing this to some ill-use or misunderstanding of the English language, I grew ever more doubtful of this being the case.

'You must tell me how I might ever repay you?' she said, a sparkle in her eyes.

This at least I could make out and I thought instantly of Martha then, but I could not directly put her in the mention. Miss Craythorne would surely be suspect as to why I would continue to particularly single her out with neither of the pair having shown the slightest of interest in the other in the brief exchanges they had shared at the table the other night. No, it must be a more subtle occasioning that hinted at the possibility; no suspicions must be raised regarding Martha's desperation for a husband. However inept Miss Craythorne's social understanding often seemed, even she would plainly comprehend the strangeness of a Baronets daughter wishing to court suitors so beneath her touch.

I was searching for a delicate way to pitch the idea when Mama came bustling into the room in a rustle of silk taffeta. Her hair had been made up in a new style and I could smell the wafting of her scent as she came in closer, flashing me a glare that only I would understand as to signal her displeasure.

'We must leave presently,' she said, looking at me and avoiding the notice of Miss Craythorne sat upon the sofa. 'Or we shall be late.'

'Very well, Mama.'

'Lady Ashlyn, how well you look,' Miss Craythorne offered, and I saw the pinch in my mother's cheeks as she was forced to turn to her and say: 'Miss Craythorne, how do you do?' Before disappearing from the room as quickly as she had come into it.

'Well, it seems I must be on my way,' she said, standing up and clutching her reticule.

'Sorry about that,' I felt obliged to say, although I did not know why. 'You find us on our way out.'

'It is quite alright, Miss Ashlyn. I realise not everyone is as forgiving towards me as you are,' she said, before pressing a lingering kiss against my cheek that I had not expected. I had been told it was a continental custom, this kissing of cheeks and I was not wholly unfamiliar with the idea when some distant relative came to break a journey or attend an occasion. But there was something about the lack of depth to our acquaintance and the intention with which she did it that unnerved me slightly.

I drew back before she immediately went to the other cheek and when both had been graced with the gesture, she leant forward and kissed me on the lips. The former I was happy to excuse to foreign custom, the latter I did not know how to interpret or excuse. 'Miss Craythorne,' I said, jumping back in such alarm I almost tripped upon the tassels of the Chinese rug. I looked around to check nobody, not even a servant, was in the vicinity to witness it.

'No need for such ceremony, Miss Ashlyn, it was just a little kiss, I thought you might appreciate it. After all, I do not know when we will meet again, with you away to London in a couple of days.'

I rang the bell and was glad that Mary arrived almost instantly to show her out.

COME MORNING, WHEN I awoke early and found myself at a gallop over the still-dewy meadows, the morning sunlight breaking through a mist of hazy cloud, I had come to two realisations: the first was that it was true; it would be some time before we were reacquainted once I departed to London, and the second was that in the light of this, I perhaps could forgive her for last night and make a detour on my way back.

'She is not at home,' said the butler, which, although I thought very odd at this early hour, took with equanimity. However, when I returned later that afternoon and again in the evening, leaving a card for her each time, I had started to wonder if this was some deliberate slight and she was watching me from a window above with a smirk upon her pout face. 'Has she returned home today at all, sir?' I asked on my final attempt, to be told that yes, briefly she had. This had the effect of infuriating me that she had not at least bothered to send her maid with a note to acknowledge my calling. But perhaps she had been busy and it was my own anxieties I grew impatient with.

But when I was turned away again the following day, I was unwilling to consider anymore excuses. 'Perhaps you will tell me when she is due to return, sir?' I said to the butler as he took another card for me.

'I do not know my lady.'

'Of course, you don't! Very well. 'You may tell her that this is the last time I will trouble myself to pay her a call when you pass my card on to her!'

'Very good, madam.'

'Good day!'

It was another day later when I had quite given up on her, that I found her card left for me after breakfast. I turned it over in my hands as I wondered what to do about it. My instant reaction was to tear it up, toss it into the fire and forget her name altogether, but as I lifted it toward the amber flames, I prevented myself from letting go of it.

It was followed by another, later that day and I ignored that one too; *Now, at least we were even.* On the next day, she left me a sealed letter and when I opened it, I found the strangest invitation I had ever received.

"Miss Craythorne invites you to come to her chamber at the hour of nine to have your hair removed with a paste of sugar."

I did not know whether to laugh or pronounce her a lunatic, for I had never seen such a peculiar request in my life. No less, after mulling over the attendance (not the hair removal, this I was decided firmly against) I made excuse with Delores to pick some wildflowers to take to Nork later, and instead went straight through the woods.

'What on earth were you thinking writing down such a thing and leaving it with the butler?' I declared when she met me in the reception room and led me up to her chamber.

'I was thinking; what might catch your interest enough to make you come? And it seems it served its purpose. Now, I have the paste cooling, it is not quite ready because you are a half hour earlier than the invitation required you be and if I am not mistaken *that* is not 'correct protocol' either? So, we are even, and quite without occupation, so I suggest you come here and let me kiss you again to show you I am sorry.'

'We are not even, and I am not come for that pasting thing, so you do what you will with the paste and put the notion out of your head.'

'And yet you are here in answer to my invitation?' she walked over to me and ran her fingers across my collar bone and I quite forgot my words. 'You are even more beautiful when you are cross, Eleanor.'

She had never sought or been given the permission to call me by my name, and yet she said it so casually it was difficult to correct her. 'If you are to persist in calling me by my Christian name, then I suggest you at least have the good enough manner to tell me yours!'

'Very well. I will give you three opportunities to guess it. If you guess it correctly, you will get to know my name and also to escape the sugar paste. However, if you cannot guess within three attempts, I win and I shall take you into the dressing room and remove all this hair,' she brushed her hand briefly against my crotch as she said this and it made me flinch with a great deal more than just surprise.

'Arabella?'

'No.'

'Jane?'

'No'

'Isabel?'

'Mariella. Now, *Eleanor*, you are coming with me.' She took me by the hand and led me to the dressing room where her Indian maidservant was busied with the preparation of various pomades. She said something to her in Hindi and she poured some water from the jug and added something from a small glass bottle into it.

'You will lay here, Eleanor; on your back with your legs raised at the knee.'

I swallowed my protest and my nerves, even though the horror of what I had just agreed to seemed to manifest now I was able to see all the preparations around me. The chaise was covered in sheets, a bowl of water at the foot of it with clean towels folded and the tray of things upon it I did not recognise. It was clear there was no doubt in her mind I would come, and I hated the idea that I was so predictable and easy to lull. This was no usual trait of my character and reflection upon the fact only further irritated me.

'Now, will you prefer just to lift your skirts or go down to your chemise? You might find the latter more comfortable for the task, for you must realise the positions you will have to take will not always be comfortable.'

'I will stay as I am I think.'

'Very well. Now, for the teaching of it, I will have Geeta demonstrate it on my thigh so you can see it clearly should you like to practice it yourself another time or school your own maid.'

Ridiculous notion that I should desire to repeat something I never desired to do in the first place! How had I given in to this, to her? I shuffled against the pillows and fidgeted with them until I felt as comfortable as I could contrive. I was grateful for the excuse to prolong the moment, for I needed more time to brace myself and master the nerves of so many things, of which letting her see me *there* was currently the most disconcerting.

'Now, you begin by a cleanse of the skin, making sure your water is not too warm and you are properly dried from it.'

I nodded as she settled beside me on the chaise and Geeta lifted Miss Craythorne's skirt mid-thigh and began according to the commentary she was giving: washing, drying then applying an amber paste to the skin just above her knee, before pulling it away and lifting it to show me the hairs that had come out with it. I felt instantly nauseous at the idea that I was about to have them ripped out like that from such a place, but I was determined that I could withstand whatever she could, and was not minded to look a fool.

When I learnt that it would be Mariella and not her maid that would carry out this forfeit and she was ready to begin on me, I requested Geeta leave us in private, for I was even less comfortable to show another stranger the view of me with my skirts raised and my legs opened out so wide.

She helped me into the position and told me to relax as she brought a washcloth to me and started cleaning me. I was as good as buried in my skirts, having rolled them so far up to avoid their ruin. Perhaps it would have been better to strip down after all. It was not very comfortable to be so buried, but at least I could not see her face now, without lifting my head to look over the heap of white cambric balanced upon my navel.

It seemed such an odd thing, to have her doing the task of a maidservant as I felt the thoroughness at which she undertook the task. Droplets of tepid water dripping down onto my buttocks as she dabbed. When she patted my skin dry, I felt the brush of her hand a few times and leapt at the fleeting sensation of it. I had felt the brush of Molly's hands *there* before and it had never induced such a fever in me, but hers, somehow, I longed for her to repeat the mistake and I despised myself for it.

'You must brace yourself my sweet, this part is not kind, but I promise you, I would not subject you to such discomfort without every intention of soothing it again.'

I did not know if it was the fear of the impending pain or the perverse excitement at her insinuation that made me tremble and hold my breath in a little too long. I lifted my head, watched her reach down to the tray and come up again with her fingers covered in a gooey ball of paste. Then I felt her smoothing it on to the corner of my groin which was warm but pulled and snagged a little, before I felt her tear it away from me again.

'There, there,' she said.

I felt my bottom lift in the air with the shock of the pain: it was actually worse than I had imagined and as I felt her applying more of it to me, I was petrified with how I would actually get through it now I had the measure. I sunk my fingers into the upholstery of the chaise and held the sheets so taut I could hear my nails dragging against the cotton weave as she ripped another patch away, and then another.

'You are doing very well, Ma Cherie, it will never hurt so much again: I promise you,' she said and leant over to kiss my cheek before she continued. Another time and I may have reproached her for that impromptu kiss, but right now, I was stiffened with the anticipation of more of the tearing pain against my skin and already I could feel the injured areas sting and inflame in response to this attack. I squeezed my eyes shut and clenched my body as she continued, working faster and more aggressively. Pulling and pushing my legs up and out in all directions, delving in to and pulling apart the delicate parts of me and ripping hair from them with great concentration as she lowered her face to stare into my deepest places. I was quite past the embarrassment of it now, it was only the trauma that remained constant, and the longing that she would finish it before I lost to my failing nerves and beseeched her to give up on it altogether for fear of throwing up with the pain. But I could not have her think me so feeble. So, beyond the beads of sweat at my brow, I kept my protest to an internal dialogue. Silent expletives and reproaches bubbling in and out of my consciousness as I stared into the ceiling.

In the pauses, I tried to divert myself with other thoughts, happier ones, and drifted from time to time from the contemplation of the promise she had made to soothe me afterwards. *What did it mean?* But every time I was induced into some distracting, tantalising thought, I would be seized by the surprise of another attack of the paste and lose my train of thought entirely. It was fast exhausting my body and my mind and when she finally announced we would soon be finished, I thought I might cry with the relief at hearing it.

'But I will need your help for this last part,' she told me as she parted my bottom with her palm and replaced it with my own hand. 'You must keep the position so I can work the opposite side of it.'

'But why ever do you apply it here?'

'Ma Cherie, the hairs grow from places you would not believe unless you could see them for yourself. Give me your other hand,' she pushed my fingertips into a small fuzz of hair that I could not deny was in the place I thought it could not be. I endured a further few assaults to that area before she said the words I feared would never come, and I finally felt my body collapse in exhaustion at the news of it.

'You are sore now, but in a day or two you will be healed and ready to learn the benefits of what you have endured. You will not be disappointed. But for now, you must recover.'

I lent up upon my elbows. 'What is that?'

'A balm to soothe the soreness. You must apply it morning and night for the next couple of days and you will soon be restored.'

She rubbed it across her palm and fingertips before gently smoothing it over my stinging skin in gentle strokes, and despite the soreness, I could feel at last the pleasure in her touch which she made no brief matter of as she circled and stroked, smoothing the lotion into folds and crevices. If this was the soothing she referred to, I was quite willing to endure the unpleasantness of it again. She poured some more balm into her hands and spread me apart with the other as she slickened the deeper folds of me with the same gentle strokes she had the rest. A sigh escaped me and the sound of it came as a surprise for it had been entirely involuntary.

'Oh my. If this provokes you, just wait until you have healed and I can place my kisses there, now you are prepared to receive them,' she pressed a fingertip against the middle of me and it coursed through me with a charge I could hardly contain.

Kisses? There? Prepared? I was trying to take in these words that seemed so ill-suited to the topic, but she had begun stroking me in some more determined fashion that made my legs start to tremble and my breaths faster. She had caused me to endure this...*Oh*...in preparation...*Oh my God*...to kiss me...*ahh*...there? Something strange had seized my body, like I was no longer in possession of it and moved and jerked to its own command.

'Uh, uh,' she said, moving more gently now. 'Not now.'

I thought I might not let her stop if she continued any further. But she did not. She wiped her hands on a cloth and pulled my skirts back down and helped me to sit up.

'Now, shall I send for tea?'

Good Sport.

April 1821. - Eleanor.

My head had been a spin since my odd forfeit, and every time I felt the chaffing of my sore inflamed skin, or was forced to hide that part of myself from Molly in my toilette, I was reminded, not just of my uncomfortable ordeal, but the part I had found more agreeable too. I did all I could to quell the thought as I prodded at the sore rashy patches of skin as I set about my own bathing. The lotion Miss Craythorne had given me was nearly half used up with how often I was called to reapply it and I dreaded to think how I would manage without its soothing reprieve.

Molly had seemed disinterested in my insistence that I would see to my own washing in the morning and only require her help once I was fresh and carefully covered with a neat, clean shift. After I had managed this, I rang the bell for her to help with the lacing of my stays and the rest of my dress. I had expected to get a sense of her suspicion at this new routine, especially after how curious she had been with her questions about the Mehndi pattern about my feet that was starting to fade now to an orange-coloured stain. But she had seemed distracted these past days, in her own thoughts, and engaged in little conversation with me at all beyond what was cordial or necessary. It suited me, although I could not help but wonder at her ever-declining mood.

When she had finished pinning my hair into a simple bun, she tended to the knock at the door and as I leaned up to the mirror to push a plain pearl stud into an earlobe, she returned, telling me Miss Craythorne was in the drawing room, waiting for me.

My heart sunk. I had promised myself I would take pains not to see her again until after London now. The time and distance between us, seemed to me, a welcome and well-timed interruption in this peculiar friendship that grew ever more dangerously intimate with each passing day. But I knew a part of me longed to see her before I left on Tuesday, and so I rose from the dressing table and set out to find her.

I was pleasantly surprised to find her address formal and plain when I found her sat upon the sofa, looking out towards the grounds. Her manner was so at ease that I could have questioned whether the whole affair had happened at all, if it were not for the stinging reminder I felt as the fabric of my shift caught against my skin as I took my own seat opposite her. Still, I was happy to feign normality along with her, it was easier than acknowledging anything more sinister and when she handed me an envelope, I was quite surprised to receive an invitation to Mr Craythorne's sporting event the next morning, being the merest of acquaintance. 'For me?' I said, staring at it, bewildered.

'I confess it was offered on account of my asking. I shall be quite alone hosting for a party of gentleman at Beddington and I own I find myself rather out of my depth. I thought I might rely on your help?'

'My help?' I said astonished. 'I have never hosted a single party in my life, Miss Craythorne, less still a party of sporting gentleman, and I would advise you not to put yourself in such a precarious position either. Just think of your reputation, you are not a married woman. Can't he hire a hostess; it is certainly what he should have done.'

'Too short notice it seems. I shall bring my servants, of course. It was a little moral support I was hoping for, in your quarter. I thought perhaps Martha or Beth might be persuaded to join you if you asked them.'

I was close to citing a host of reasons why it would be impossible, our preparations to leave, my parents' refusal of my attendance at such an affair, and so on, but I could not resist the opportunity to secure Martha's invitation and try at one final shot at throwing the pair together before we departed. So, when Miss Craythorne agreed she would not tell anyone I was to go, and that I would bring Martha as my own companion, I found myself determined to find a way of going. 'If my parents will permit me, I will certainly come,' I told her. What I didn't expect was to actually gain their agreement, or to the well-attended gathering that turned out for the event, set out upon the vast lawns of Beddington Park when we arrived there the next day.

It was all the part the grand country seat in size and stature, but faded glory hung in the décor and furnishings I glimpsed as we were taken through the house and delivered to the bustle of the sporting pitches by a footman. I now understood the need for Mr Craythorne's swift action and Miss Craythorne's assistance, in bringing the place about. This was no suitable home to offer to a new bride in its present condition. It was clear Mr Craythorne's 'relation' had not made any investment in the place for many years. I was pleased to note the neglect of the interior did not extend to the grounds at least; they were, pleasant and well kept.

When we arrived at the cricket pitch, a game was already in play, so we took a seat at the sideline and joined the audience. Martha had been easily persuaded to come. I wasn't sure if it was for the sake of escaping what must be a despairing atmosphere at home with all the bad business, or the novelty of my paying her such singular attention which was normally reserved for Betsy. I did not invite any of the others, on account that I did not want Betsy to chip away at the newly won progress the Craythorne's had recently earned with her more acetic observations of such a host, nor did I wish her to poison Martha's view of him if I was to have a hope of bringing about the scheme of their match when she had, insofar, shown so little interest in him.

So, when I spotted Mr Craythorne on the pitch, I pointed him out to Martha with some kind comment or observation on his behalf to direct her interest. 'What an excellent score!' I declared, clapping my hands together and standing up to join the applause when he made a winning run. As I had hoped to encourage, Martha stood up beside me and joined me in the applause and Delores shot me a sharp look that told me to moderate my manners.

'I understand him to be quite the sportsman, I can see it now,' I said to Martha behind my fan when the applause de-crescendoed and we settled back into our seat. 'I mean I am sure I have not seen a greater pair of calves before.'

'No indeed,' Martha agreed a little perplexed. I supposed she must have taken my interest to be for my own sake and wondered why I would say so, having Sheldon's affections so firmly in my favour. 'I think you are quite well acquainted with Mr Craythorne now? I noticed how much he kept to your company at the dinner party.'

'Did he? I own, we did talk on some small matters, but...'

Her surprise was well founded. I had noticed only the briefest exchanges. 'Ah, so that explains it.'

'Explains what, Miss Ashlyn?'

'Well, I hope you will take no offense at my saying so, but I own, I was a little surprised that when Miss Craythorne conveyed the invitation, that of our set, only you and I were included on it!'

She looked even more perplexed now. 'You mean the others did not decline to come?'

'No, they were never invited in the first place. I mean, I knew, for my part, the invitation came on Miss Craythorne's account, you understand she has few friends here, but I must own, it was not until now it becomes clear why you were invited.'

'Oh...I see, well—'

'Indeed!' I said excitedly before she could raise some objection to my implication.

Delores' suspicion at our excited whisperings drew her between us at just the right moment to silence Martha and afford her some introspection on the matter just proposed.

'Miss Ashlyn, I do not think we know anyone here,' Delores said to me with a questioning scan of the party. 'Is Mr Elmbridge coming?'

'Oh no, sadly not. I learned only this morning that he cannot come, he must make a journey to Oxford today before joining us all in London, a last-minute obligation, I gather.'

'How sadly disappointing,' she said with a wise air of mistrust and I understood exactly why she should suspect me. It was not that I was lying per se, Sheldon had indeed been invited at my bequest, but only once I knew him to already be engaged in some business in Oxford. I saw no need to inform my parents of his apologies when Grantley brought me his note at breakfast. I had simply mentioned in my petition to my parents that he was invited, not that he would be able or inclined to accept the invitation. I could not feel sorry for the deception, it seemed just to see their over presumption turn against them for a change. Usually, I was the subject to be forced into something I had no wish to be. I held in a sigh. I detested the way their meddling had caused me to wish to detach myself from Sheldon so much. I had been happy at his return and was sure I would have much enjoyed having him about again after such a time, if only it could be as it was before I was 'out' and before everyone seemed so determined to push us together. 'It is disappointing,' I agreed. 'But I understand it to be a short trip at least. 'Oh look, they have won!' I joined in the applause and noticed Miss Craythorne, for the first time, step out from the crowd and congratulate her stepbrother with a rather hearty hug that surprised me, for I had not noticed them to be an intimate family. 'We must go and congratulate them!' I said, taking up Martha's arm and directing her on to where a small party of well-wishers surrounded them. Delores followed behind with the look of a sulk on her expression. She had grown so very weary of having me in her charge and yet we had barely begun.

I understood why she tried so much to convince my mama's coming with us, when I overheard them discussing the invitation yesterday. Quite by accident, I came upon them in the small parlour to ask if we could make a stop at Glyn to convey Martha along with us, when I heard the low conversation coming from the room as I approached it.

'If Mr Elmbridge is there, there will be no need to be distressed. He will do most of the work for you in keeping her closely guarded. You need only concern yourself with supervising them,' Mama had said to her complaint, which I had not heard.

'Very well Helena, I hope you are right, for you know how difficult it is to keep her in tow and I have no notion of what kind of affair this will be at this man's house who we know so little of.'

'I sympathise, Delores, but Mr Ashlyn takes no offense to them, and so it seems we must suffer them as best we can. Besides, we cannot be in wait much longer now. I understand Mr Elmbridge's affections are resolute, his only wish, Lady Elmbridge tells me, is that he awaits Eleanor's showing him a similar regard before he petitions an interview with her.'

I had been astounded to hear this, and Delores relieved, if her sudden pacification was anything to go by.

'So now it remains for you to do a good job of making sure they are kept as much in each other's company tomorrow as you can manage.'

I had long lost such innocent ignorance of our matchmaking, but I could not help feeling shocked to know the question was so close to coming. However, if he was truly waiting for such a sign, I would take great care now, to make no such indication to him to encourage it.

'Miss Ashlyn!' Miss Craythorne exclaimed when she noticed me amongst the crowd. 'I am so pleased you are come. You must excuse the excitement, my brother has just won the game!'

'Yes, I saw, very well played Mr Craythorne, I congratulate you,' I said as he turned to notice us.

'Miss Ashlyn, you are very kind,' he bowed. 'I hope you are enjoying the sport? It is very good of you to come, you honour us greatly.'

'Thank you, Sir, yes, very much so. Mr Craythorne, you remember my friend, Miss Brownlow,' I pulled her out from behind me.

'Yes, of course, Miss Brownlow, thank you for coming, a great honour.'

'Mr Craythorne, I am much obliged for your invitation,' she said sheepishly and I was glad to notice a blush of colour at her cheeks as she spoke to him. Her introspective pause had served her well.

'My pleasure indeed. Now, shall we take some refreshment before the archery begins?' He directed us out of the crowd, nodding to well-wishers along the way until we left them behind and journeyed to a marquee where lemonade and ale was being served.

'I am so glad you are come,' Miss Craythorne said, taking up my arm as we walked. 'When I received Mr Elmbridge's apology, I thought perhaps yours would follow.'

Not you as well. 'Don't be daft, Miss Craythorne, you already had my answer, why should Mr Elmbridge's coming alter the fact?'

'Well, then, I must be quite mistaken and you must forgive me it. I thought that was why you agreed.'

'Is it impossible that I come with no ulterior motive?'

'I don't know, Miss Ashlyn, you tell me,' she smiled a cunning smile laden with an innuendo she usually did not display in company and kept for our private meetings.

I freed myself of her arm. 'Miss Craythorne, I own there might have been some small agenda on my part today.'

Before she could make some discomforting comment or glance, I pressed on, checking we were out of earshot. 'In fact, I had hoped to petition your assistance in the matter.'

'Oh?' she was not easily read but I noted a hint of intrigue about her gaze.

'I presume your stepbrother is still seeking a match?'

She nodded.

'I wonder, is it still the case that there is no particular person in mind for this match?'

She stopped and turned fully to me. 'No, I do not believe there is. Miss Ashlyn, am I to understand, you have such a person in mind?'

'Yes,' I said relieved not to have to spell it out with Delores hanging so much on my heels to glean the subject of our conversation.

'My, my, what interesting news!' she said, encouraging. I was impressed at her seeing the sense in my design, for I had thought her ignorant enough of societal affairs to not properly understand the prudence such a match could make, even though I had been so far reluctant to put Martha directly in the mention. It seemed now I had little choice but to at least make the hint, since we would all be gone to London by morning. If she was to have her chance at all: it must be now. I looked about the place. I could easily place her here as mistress of it, she could not have looked for a more comfortable situation now, and Mr Craythorne might have been a touch on the coarse side in the company he kept, but he could not be called uncivil and had at least a thirty-year advantage on old Wilmott.

'So, you understand me?' I said, sliding a sideways glance towards Martha when I noticed Delores was fussing over Martha's muddy skirt hems.

'I think I do, and I most certainly will do everything I can to assist.'

'Thank you, Miss Craythorne, I knew I could rely on you. But we must save the planning of the scheme until later when I can find a moment to shake off my Chaperone; she is so very ill at ease today, she suspects me of some plot at every moment.'

Miss Craythorne turned to notice Delores' attempts at evading her stepbrother's conversation, and her efforts to gain on us closely enough to listen in on ours. 'You need not fret, I know just the thing to keep her busy for an hour.'

Sadly, her attempt to intervene, however well intended, did not go to plan. When she intercepted Delores and Mr Craythorne's conversation, which I gathered was focused on the subject of the house renovations; I could see what she intended and knew it would fail. For although she had correctly read Delores for being a nosy sort of busy body and much more at ease touring the house than on a muddy field, Delores was on to me, and we both knew it.

'Brother,' Miss Craythorne said to him loud enough for us all to hear, 'you must have Barton take Ms Parkes on a tour of the house. The plans are quite extraordinary if I might say so,' she appealed. 'My brother has just lately instructed Crace and Sons.'

Whatever else had not impressed Delores insofar, the mention of the Crace company's involvement had managed to pique her interest and for a fleeting moment, she had me fooled the scheme had succeeded.

'How famous!' she said. 'I think I should like to take a tour after all Mr Craythorne, if you would be so good to instruct your servants. Come now you two—' she fingered at Martha and I. 'You have much need for the learning of house renovations now you are of age. Let us hope you will have your own households to instruct soon enough!'

This latter part of her speech was directed unashamedly at me, and I did not know if the purpose was to toy with me at having foiled us, or to warn Mr Craythorne of the fact of my intended betrothal. How incredulous that she could think he would need it in my regard, when

Martha was the object of our design. Either way, as she marched us off to the house, refusing my complaint and protest to sign up for the Archery instead, the decoy had failed.

It was war!

If she thought I would not find a way to avenge her for it, she would be in for a surprise when I found the means.

Realising her plan had failed miserably and having dispatched us to the care of the servants, Miss Craythorne made excuses on her and her brother's behalf, on account of already being signed up to shoot the first round of arrows. I was disheartened at her leaving me to endure her failed scheme, for I had no interest in the admiring of houses or in the Crace's designs and was much better suited for the sports field. But I had noted a twinkle in her eye as she stole her brother away, that told me she was to set to work on our plans, despite my absence. This, if nothing else, was of some consolation.

Once we had endured a rather dry and unenthusiastic tour from Mrs Pemble, the housekeeper—a dull woman, who I supposed had spent so long on board wages, she had lost the art of indulging visitors—I felt at last the promise of our return, until Delores turned to her and said, 'Thank you, Mrs Pemble, you have been very attentive. But I wonder, is the clerk of the works about the place? I should very much like to see the new designs?'

You witch!

'I think he is, Ms Parkes. If you will permit me to make inquiries with him, I shall return to you directly.'

AN HOUR LATER AND HAVING been so long bored sitting over sketches, samples and descriptions of the plans, even Martha looked like she was hungering for the merriment of the sports fields as we finally re-joined the gathering.

I said barely a word to either of them, as I struggled to contain my fury with Delores as she sauntered about triumphant in punishing me so cruelly. It was well timed then, when the opportunity to avenge it came upon me quite by chance. We were back amongst the crowd and seeking out Miss Craythorne when a gentleman approached me.

'Miss, miss—'

I turned to look at him and realised his question directed at me.

'How dare you address her, Sir!' Delores cut in before he reached me. 'Be gone with you. Outrageous!' she declared.

'Delores, please! You must forgive my chaperone Mr—'

'Huxley.'

'Of course, I remember now. Mr Huxley, I am afraid my chaperone did not realise we have already been introduced, she was away when we were.'

Delores looked at me with a mix of surprise and contempt.

'Now, pray tell me, how are your family?'

'Very well, miss, I thank you.'

'Good, now, what have you come to tell me?'

'Our team is short on the Pall Mall game, I thought you might like to make up the number?' he said brightly.

I looked at Delores who was so offended by this idea that I turned to him and told him, 'I would very much like to Mr Huxley. Thank you indeed!'

'Miss Ashlyn, do you know this man?' Martha whispered when I relieved my reticule and fan to her care.

I drew in close to her. 'I have never seen him before in my life, but you mustn't tell Delores!' I smiled as I marched off to the pitch with a rather confused Mr Huxley at my side.

I was pleased, when shown to my post that we were to play a joint game of Pall Mall against Miss Craythorne and her stepbrother, although being on opposing teams would unlikely permit me opportunity to exchange whispers with Miss Craythorne on how she had got on. But it had not proved much an inconvenience, for I was certain by my observations of Mr Craythorne's marked good humour, leniency when we come head-to-head in the game, and seemingly grateful glances; that he was quite certain of the service I had rendered to him and most obliged. It was such a happy relief: Both Martha and he had seemed to come round so effortlessly today to the possibility, with the least of exertion, that I could not quite believe how successful we had been. I knew I was right to make one last attempt before giving up on them.

'So, Miss Ashlyn, can I bring you a glass of something?' said Mr Huxley more keenly than I thought polite when the match was over, our rivals defeated by only a point.

'Thank you, no,' I smiled evenly.

'Then perhaps you will permit me a turn?'

'No, sir. Forgive me, I am quite fatigued and must return to my party.'

'Then I hope I will see you later, madam.'

I smiled. *You will certainly not, I think.*

I joined Miss Craythorne and her brother walking from the pitch and sought out Delores and Martha amongst the crowd. I was surprised to spot her laughing and engrossed in conversation with one of the Craythorne twins, who she had shown a fondness for at the table, the other night. I should have to send him on his way, the progress insofar had been hard won, without his interference. 'You are not a sore loser are you, Miss Craythorne?' I said teasing, as I listened to them both attributing each other blame for their defeat in the match.

'No,' she glared at her brother accusingly, for we all knew it was his letting me off, by not hitting my ball when so many opportunities were afforded him to do so, that accounted for it. 'But I could have hoped for better teammates,' she said pointedly.

'Still, it is all in good sport,' he replied, and I drew him instantly towards Martha as we approached and teased the younger brother away in some contrived conversation to separate them as soon as I could.

Far from this being an onerous duty, he proved surprisingly genial company and I quickly found myself forgetting I was acting as decoy. I had never spoken beyond a few words to him, in passing. But now I found myself comfortably prattling with him, without realising how I had got here. I could see why Martha appeared so agreeable to his company. He was an amusing sort, full of innocent candid speech and blundering foolishness, but in the most endearing fashion possible, and without a hint of self-importance about him. I could not fail to find him enchanting, and felt relieved to understand that it must be this innocent regard for him to blame and nothing more ominous, as I had feared. I could have stood a while longer with him, even with Delores buzzing about impatiently at my shoulder, had he not excused himself on account of setting off for a change of his mud-clad clothes.

We all agreed to sit out the next round of gaming and Mr Craythorne had a picnic blanket set out for us, and a chair brought over for Delores who complained that the ground was damp and would get into her joints. It was a warm afternoon, so I ignored her whinging, for I knew she would complain on any little account she could find, for she wanted so much to abandon the place. How I wished she would abandon me.

'So, did you enjoy the tour?' Mr Craythorne inquired, and I told him that we had, and how much impressed Delores was by the plans and she sat, still sulking, contributing a rare and contrived nod or smile of agreement now and then. Martha seemed to have lost her voice altogether in his presence and Miss Craythorne was still annoyed at losing the game, and so it left me and her brother to contrive all the civil conversation we could manage. If their other brother had not abandoned us, it might have proved a pleasure, but he was not blessed with his younger brother's easiness, and I felt quickly exerted by the effort and wished it over with.

When a footman came about, calling for subscriptions to the bowling game, Mr Craythorne agreed it and offered me to join him and I could not think of anything more insufferable.

'Martha, you have not tried out a sport yet today, will you not be encouraged to join Mr Craythorne and make up the number? I own I am quite in need of a rest,' I said instead. I was glad to see his gratitude for my service paid so well in his kind attention to me, but he had made his point and I had no wish to be slow about bringing them together.

Martha looked as though she might swoon. 'Well, I am not much for sports Miss Ashlyn, I, I—'

'Nonsense, you were always one of the better players amongst our set. I am sure you have not forgotten the skill,' I said accusingly.

'Oh, very well, if you wish it Mr Craythorne.'

'Why, yes, Miss Brownlow. Miss Ashlyn, I hope you will feel recovered enough to join us soon?'

'Perhaps,' I feigned exertion in my tone. I could of course happily find the will to play another ten games, but I had much sooner speak to Miss Craythorne and leave the pair to get better acquainted.

It was not until they left, that Delores relaxed her hawk-like watch upon us and reclined in the deck chair, leaving us at last to a little peace. We chatted on trivial things and made observations on the games, placed a bet on which side would win for chicken stakes, and eventually noticed Delores grow complacent, then bored, and eventually snoozing.

'Dear god, I thought she would never let us breathe,' I said, in a low voice, just in case.

'Yes, she does not seem at ease here. I own I am surprised you get to dance as much as you do with her to gate keep on your behalf.'

'Indeed,' I did not wish to explain that it was quite another matter entirely when the company was of a standard she approved of. 'Now, I have been dying to pick up our conversation earlier, we must get to work on how we will encourage this match!'

She seemed shocked at my enthusiasm. 'Well, I don't think there is anything more to be done, but watch and wait,' she said simply, and I had to remember to keep my voice down as the excitement threatened to bubble over into it: 'You cannot mean it? You have spoken to him then?'

'Yes.'

'And he feels inclined to the match?'

'Of course, you cannot really be so surprised at the fact.'

'No, not entirely, I mean Martha's family are so very well connected and such a respectable line. I mean, the dowry is not very much I own, but I think your brother a wealthy enough man to overlook the fact?'

She was frowning at me, and I assumed that she was not sure this news would be insignificant. But what she said to me next, I could hardly believe and gasped so loud it roused Delores from her nap.

'Miss Ashlyn?' she said to me with great seriousness, 'whatever does Martha's dowry signify?'

'Well, I am glad you see it as I do, but you fear your brother will not share our view?'

'My brother will not care a fig if Martha is with a dowry of five thousand pounds or five shillings.'

'Really? What a credit he is to your family, Miss Craythorne; generous of spirit indeed.'

'Generous? Miss Ashlyn, you are puzzling me a great deal. It is *your* dowry that is of significance here, not Martha's. But I do not think he will care for the number if that is what you mean?'

There it was, the very moment I realised what had been so very sorely mis-conveyed.

'My goodness, Miss Craythorne, you cannot mean you thought—I mean you did not tell your brother, that it was me, and not Martha, that was inclined towards a match with him?'

Her eyes widened at the realisation. 'Miss Brownlow? Well of course not, he would not look at her for the world with all her difficulties.'

How could they know of her troubles? 'You mean you thought...he thinks I—' I had never felt so insulted in all my life, but I had to relent in my protest that was already made through gritted teeth as Delores took a notice in what was starting to form a commotion betwixt us.

'Is everything quite well, Miss Ashlyn?' she said, lifting up to examine us with one of her beady glances.

I smiled. 'Yes, quite well. We are just having a little debate over our wager; it seems I have lost Delores,' I said with such a hard look at Miss Craythorne, she could not fail to understand my distemper.

When the game was finished, I as good as dragged Martha from the pitch and announced our leaving to her. 'You will forgive me,' I said to Mr Craythorne at his protest, 'My chaperone is so much in complaint I cannot bear another moment of her moaning. She is quite fatigued and not much used to being in the sun, we really must away,' I explained, ignoring the suddenly apparent disappointment I had caused.

'Then you must let me escort you to your coach.'

'No, please do not trouble yourself, Mr Craythorne, you cannot neglect your guests on our account. Miss Craythorne can show us the way.'

She shot him a warning glare that seemed to acquiesce any insistence on this head, and instead he bowed gracefully and bid us farewell.

When the coach pulled up, I took care to let the others step in before me, and in the brief moment it afforded me to: I turned to Miss Craythorne and whispered to her as I feigned a friendly embrace: 'You will come to me tomorrow before our leaving and tell me you have undone this error!'

WHEN AT LAST THE COACH pulled along the gravel driveway, I felt some small relief. But this was to be very short lived, I soon realised as all the words Martha had kept to herself all day, now seemed determined to come out.

'Oh Miss Ashlyn, it is so very kind of you to bring me along today, what a marvellous day I have had!'

Delores rolled her eyes and held an expression that said she could not agree to the sentiment, and certainly I could not either, now I understood just how terribly wrong everything had turned out. 'I am so glad you did.'

'I own,' she said fidgety in her seat, 'I am not much for sports, but what a great affair it was, and you were quite right, I am not a bad player at bowling. Mr Craythorne noticed the fact himself for he told me so.'

'Well, I am glad I could encourage your taking it up again,' was all I could say to her brightly lit eyes, holding behind them by a thread all her excitement and conflated wonderment at this new prospect of a man who had the power to rescue her from so much misery, yet it appeared, he would not be brought to.

I pinched the flesh between my brows. I must still find a way to right this.

'And what a very pretty house it will be when all that clever work is done to bring it about,' she continued.

'Indeed, it will be.'

'Of course, it will take a great deal of time, Mr Craythorne tells me. In fact, he does not even habitate there presently because of it.'

'He doesn't?'

'No, he has a long-standing room at the Greyhound Inn in Carshalton, so he can keep an eye on the project without having to suffer the inconvenience of all the building works.'

'The Greyhound Inn,' Delores said with distaste.

'Oh, I think it must be a respectable place, Ms Parkes, Father always mentioned what a famously good landlord it has. The best for miles I believe.'

'Yes, Miss Brownlow, I see that the Greyhound Inn is a perfectly respectable place to stop on a journey, but for a permanent lodging, well!'

'Well, it is not permanent you see, he is much away anyhow, but he will settle into Beddington as soon as he returns from his business affairs and his apartments are suitable—'

'Miss Brownlow, I have such a terrible headache,' Delores held up her hand and complained to silence her.

I considered the irony that Delores would take so much offense to the discussion of Mr Craythorne's lodgings and 'work' commitments when she herself worked for her living. Or so Mama always insisted to my father when he questioned exactly what indeed Delores actually does. Today, I supposed she had earned her keep and how arduous I had found it. I was glad that she did not usually manage the task so well.

When we finally delivered a very over-excited Martha home, I was pleased Delores seemed too fatigued to make such a fuss as I expected. She said very little on the whole, but the few sentences that passed between us were so poignant I was stunned at her quiet observations.

'Eleanor, I do hope you are not so insensitive to notice the damage you may have done to that girl today.'

I sighed. 'Oh Delores, just because he is a merchant, it does not mean the circumstances will not suit Martha's predicament well.'

'Oh indeed, even I cannot disagree with you under the circumstances.'

'Then how can you object?'

'I do not object at all. In fact, I would congratulate you on the idea myself if I thought it could be managed.'

'Then what other possible disagreement can you have on the subject?'

'A very great one indeed! Oh, I do despair at you, Eleanor. Can you really be so insensible?'

This did provoke my anger. 'How exactly do you mean?'

'You cannot see? You have filled that girls head with the notion that Mr Craythorne has a care for her, when it is clear, he only has such a regard for you.'

I swallowed hard. 'How insufferable you should say such a thing!'

'I own it is outrageous he could dare to look to you, but he does not have the breeding to recognise his folly. Take care Eleanor, the damage you could do to your own reputation may not be so easily undone.'

WHEN ANNA PAID A CALL to me the next morning, I let out the whole. She was the only one I could trust for her secret tendré for the older Craythorne twin was equally abhorred. Betsy, I feared, would never speak to me again if she understood the situation. Miss Craythorne would be insulted at my outrage, and I would break Martha's heart if she got a scent of this calamity. Beth and Clara might be trusted to this confidence, but they had already left for London ahead of us.

She sat puzzled for a moment, taking in all the details I had thrown at her in my hysterical account as she sipped at her teacup. Eventually she said, 'Well, I own this is every part the calamity you say, on Martha's account, but come, she has only herself to blame for believing it possible. But you, what harm can be done if no one of polite society attended the gathering, and you will hardly be forced to see him about if you keep to more respectable gatherings hereafter.'

'But if you had seen how taken Martha was by him, you would understand how terrible it all is.'

'What should you care on Martha's account? She is a liability to herself, I don't mean her situation, she is a walking disaster in every sense of the word. She has been out two seasons already. Don't look at me like that; we all know it to be true. She will get over Craythorne and we must do our best to settle her sights on Wilmott.'

I too had accepted this to be the only course open to us now, even though I could not easily stomach the idea of owning how badly I had hashed the scheme. If only I could have escaped Delores long enough to explain things to Miss Craythorne in greater clarity rather than sparse whispers.

I slowly came round to the realisation that I would have to speak to Martha as soon as possible and make it clear to Miss Craythorne, to call her brother to heal.

So, I rode over to Beaulieu early, having conveyed a note to her the night before. Mama and Delores were in a drawn-out meeting with Lady Elmbridge, over the Almack's applications, and I knew they would not be expected to emerge from the small parlour for at least a few hours as they sat over their scandal broth and applicants.

When I arrived to find Mr Craythorne in her company, I could have swooned at the sight.

'Miss Ashlyn, good day,' he stood up from the sofa as the footman announced me.

'Good day, sir. Miss Craythorne,' I curtsied and took the offered seat.

'I trust you are well?' he said.

'Yes, thank you,' I stared into my lap.

All fell uncomfortably silent.

'Well, you find me about to leave. I bid you both good day.'

'Good grief, Miss Craythorne!' I said when he was gone.' I wish you would have told me to come at a different time if you were receiving your brother here!'

'Forgive me, I thought you were departing for London soon and I did not know to expect him at all. He came to convey Bertram home now the surgeon has set his arm.'

'Set his arm? Whatever happened?'

'Oh yes, you were long departed when they got up the idea to play some goals of football, dreadful fierce it was, Bertram broke his arm and another fellow his nose, can you believe it? And that was without the general bumps and bloodiness of the team.'

'Oh my! I hope he is well soon,' I offered. I felt sorry to think the jolly fellow put out, for I realised Bertram referred to the Craythorne twin of which I had been fond of, but the greater part of me was more relieved that no such games were played with Delores present, or I should never hear the end of it. She had already delivered the unimpressive account of the day to Mama who was unhappy that Sheldon was not present, but at least she was spared an account of bloody sports.

'Thank you. He will recover well I believe.'

'Good. Now, Miss Craythorne, please tell me you have clarified matters with your stepbrother.'

'Yes,' she shifted uncomfortably in her seat. 'I explained my confusion in the affair yesterday.'

'And he understands fully that my intentions for him, were always set in Martha's direction?'

'He does. He was most embarrassed, I don't deny it.'

'Well, I fear that Martha will be in just the same mind when I go to her next to break the news.'

'You mean she does not know?'

'How could she?'

She did not answer this.

'In fact, I must go to her now, I have not long to make the journey before we depart.'

'Must you go so soon? I had thought we might—'

'Miss Craythorne, you will forgive me I hope, but I cannot help but think my going abroad to London will provide the perfect pause to our visits for a time, until the dust has settled on this affair. You understand, as much as I might like to keep your company; with your connection to your brother—a little distance will prove quite the thing until everything is quite forgotten?'

'When will I see you again?'

'I cannot say when. I suppose we must return for a brief spell over the Derby weekend, and then, I can't imagine us back in Cuddington until late June. July even, if my parents plan to stay on for the Kings Coronation.'

'So long?' she did not hide the disappointment in her eyes at all and I could not believe this display of emotion, and so openly, when it was so unlike her.

'Then you will be very much missed, I confess.'

'Come, we are not much for sentiment you and I. We will see each other again when I return.'

As I turned to leave, she grasped at my wrist. 'I will miss you.'

'I really must—'

And before I could speak the words, she was there, close against me, holding my face between her hands and placing the lightest kisses, first upon each cheek and then one lingering kiss upon my mouth.

I did not go to Martha's on my way back, my senses were too scattered to think or do anything much at all, let alone face such unpleasantness. I would pack the last of my things and await my summons to the coach.

London Hours.

April 1821. - Eleanor.

I was excited when our coach pulled up in Berkeley Square after a sluggish journey into London in the early spring rain. It was not cold at least, just miserable looking in the grey gloom of stifled light and rain streams. I lifted my dress to step through puddles and climb the stairs up to the house; the servants ready and waiting with outstretched arms to take our coats and hats, and hand towels distributed to pat ourselves dry. Everyone else went straight into the little parlour to take some refreshment, but I went directly to my chamber.

It was just as I had left it two weeks ago, with the exception of the new bed drapery that had been hung in our absence. I lifted a weight of it in my hand; the heavy brocade in canary yellow was much to my liking. Mama had been opposed to the colour scheme, thinking it too striking a shade, but I wanted something bright to cheer me. London, for all its fantastic offerings, was not always the brightest place with its many grey stone buildings and smog tainted air. I had heard it more brilliant in the summer with the improvement of the weather, but my parents were always back at Cuddington by mid-June, and so I supposed we would hardly note it. Although it had proved an uncommonly warm spring insofar.

I went over to the fire to spread my hands out to the heat and admired the new colours from afar. Then Molly came in, followed by the footman lugging up my trunks and bandboxes, so I moved aside and took a seat out of the way upon the window cushion, and peered out onto the Square through rain misted panes of glass. I hoped it would dry up by this evening; I had the perfect wardrobe picked out in my mind for my first assembly at Almack's and did not want it spoiled by drab-soaked hems and damp spatters about the pretty gauze overlay.

I needn't have troubled over the possibility, by a quarter past five, a warm glow of evening sunshine broke through the clouds and by eight-o-clock, when we left for King Street; the ground was perfectly treadable. The assembly rooms, however, were an altogether different matter with over five hundred persons about them to navigate without tripping on a toe or skirt. When my first dance partner was introduced to me by Patroness Lady Jersey who was hosting tonight, I wondered where at all anyone might dance when it was hazardous enough just to pass between the rooms. The supper room, I knew I should never repeat the going of, I decided instantly as I thumbed a humble plate of bread and butter and had nothing more than tea or lemonade to choose from in quenching my thirst. It was an abysmal offering and I intended to make my complaint known to Mama when we were home. But otherwise, the night was as merry as I had dreamt it. So many new faces, introductions, dance partners and excitement that I wished we might stay in London all the year. I was sure to have made such a happy number of new acquaintances after such a time in this kind of company. And not the kind I would have to worry over, for I was certain of its vetting and I relaxed in the knowing that when a gentleman was introduced to me, he was of god ton, Betsy could not sulk at our invitations and mama and Delores need not make a fuss.

I wondered, as I made curtsey after curtsey, if somewhere amid the crowd, my husband-to-be was amongst the number huddled about the red roped rooms. No one had stood out yet as a particular favourite, but it was only my first attendance. At least with Sheldon absent tonight, I was free of the need to avoid him. His mama had told me there had been a change of plan and he was expected to arrive from Oxford the next day now. I gave her my regret's whilst privately rejoicing at this extended reprieve.

He would be limited to a single dance per soiree from hereon, not only to give way to other invitations, but to dispel the matchmaking attempts we had suffered in Cuddington being permitted to flourish here. I was minded to hold everyone to the letter of propriety now and speak promptly against any oversights or shortcomings in our being chaperoned. I did not want to give him any of the hints he required to induce his asking me to marry him. I had no desire to accept him and yet for the sake of our once fond friendship, no heart to want to refuse him either and injure his feelings. If I could contrive the right balance of distance and platonic amiability, I hoped we might both be spared the uncomfortable circumstance altogether. And where the limitations of country society could keep us closely pressed in each other's company, here, I knew, the same could not be so well contrived.

I WAS DESPERATELY FAGGED when we returned home that night, having danced until past midnight at Almack's and supped until three in the morning at the Jersey's thereafter. It was this I blamed on rising so late and being caught out.

Molly came to me as she usually did, filling the washstand with warm water, fresh cloths and towels. Drawing back the drapes and flooding the room with blinding light my tired eyes were not ready to adjust to after so little sleep.

'Morning miss. Will you take something in your chamber today or wait for breakfast since it shall soon be served?' came Molly's voice in a musical trill that seemed too much for my hearing, my ears still ringing with the music from last night. Keeping London hours again would take a period of readjustment, I realised.

'Hmm, no... breakfast will be fine. What time is it?' I asked, shrinking beneath my blanket to filter out the harshness of the light.

'Why, it's just past ten-o-clock miss,' she said brightly, a swish of skirts rustling by the bed, the clatter and chink of her replacing glassware and then the swill and slosh of her refilling the barley water carafe.

Someone was in better spirits this morning.

'I thought best to let you sleep in miss, you were so late to bed and when I came at seven you didn't so much as blink.'

'Thank you, Molly.' I could have easily drifted back to sleep for hours still. But I could not indulge. I had things to attend to now that already strained the hours in the day, without my setting upon them late. So, reluctantly and with a concerted effort to convince my limbs to move, I lifted myself from the bed, pushed my feet into my slippers and staggered over to the washstand, my legs still remembering how to coordinate themselves.

I was so tired, all I could do was slump in the chair beside it, letting out a series of yawns as Molly set upon my toilette: tugging the brush through the lengths of my hair, patting me down with wet cloths and dabbing me dry. I did not need to pay much mind to it; we had the sequence down to an art, she always following the same routine, me always anticipating the next lift of a limb or turn. So it was easy to permit myself a little further period of resting my eyes and letting my consciousness stir into life.

Except, more lately, I had altered that routine entirely to prevent the exposure of myself. Today I entirely forgot this stipulation altogether, until, having stood up from the chair and felt the draught of my shift rise over my head, I was startled by Molly gasping in astonishment.

'Oh miss,' she said, freezing and staring wide-eyed at the sight of me, the cloth laying limp in her hand and dripping over the floorboards. 'What's happened to you, miss?'

At first, I too was startled, wanting to know what had happened to me to cause her so much alarm. But it was a brief moment indeed, for instantly then, sobering from my sleep now, I noticed the direction of her stare and the horror of the memory came flooding back. I felt instantly my cheeks aflame and searched for an excuse. It had been easy to forget about it now I was recovered. 'I – I had a case of lice and this was given to me as the remedy,' I said, cringing as I spoke, realising this was not much of an improvement on the actual truth. But what could I say? I'd lost at a dare and the bare mound before her was the bargain? That I allowed my new acquaintance who I should not have even been visiting, to do this to me? That it was quite the thing in Paris or Bengal?

'Oh miss, I am sorry, I didn't know. I didn't mean to—'

'It's quite alright Molly. How could you know. I have spared you the task for I did not want to risk contaminating you with the infection until I had taken the cure.'

'To be sure miss. Thank you.'

'You will not tell anyone, will you, Molly? You understand how embarrassed I would be?'

'Oh no miss, not a word.'

'Thank you, Molly,' I said and reached eagerly into my fresh shift and covered myself up again.

Once I was dressed, I said to her before she left: 'Molly, what do you think is the scent of this new toilette water—I do not think it suits me.' I pumped a spray of it from the atomiser across her sleeve and wafted the scent with my hands to help it settle.

'Oh, it's very agreeable miss, I'm not sure what's in it; patchouli perhaps, orange blossom?'

'Ah...patchouli; that is the issue. I'm sure that is the aroma I cannot quite like in it. What a dreadful waste, the bottle is practically full.'

'Oh, but it smells lovely,' she protested, sniffing at her sleeve.

'Would you like it, Molly?'

'Oh, I couldn't miss.'

'What a shame, it shall have to be disposed of then.'

'In the bin miss?'

'Well, if you don't want it...'

'I do want it miss, if you please.'

'Excellent. It shall not go to waste after all,' I said, pressing the bottle into her palm.

THE EMBARRASSMENT OF it all had not left me, even as I sat over a salver of calling cards and invitations at breakfast. Another unwelcome effect of this was to remind me of Miss Craythorne, and of that peculiar morning in particular, and the strange sensations she stirred up in me. I had been happy to forget about it, about *her* now I was in London, but this discovery had set me back on both accounts.

I had Molly's promise that my *lice* problem would not be spoken of, but I could not help fret over the possibility she might mention it to someone. I had at least the comfort of knowing that not only were the staff here, less than half the number of Cuddington, but that she was new to the house too, with this being only her second time of coming and I thought it unlikely she would have drawn anyone into a suitable level of confidence already. I hoped that by the time she might, it would be quite forgotten.

It was decided over breakfast that we would have to put off half the days invitations since we could not be in two places at once and had already R.S.V.P'd to a number adequate to busy us again until the small hours. I left the sorting of the rest of the week's affairs to Mama and Delores, who had the measure of the better offerings that could be relied on, and the hosts we could not afford to slight. But as one costume change and carriage ride turned to the next, I wondered how we might sustain the effort of scuttling back and forth, however pleasing these invitations proved. We no sooner left one soiree before being promised at the opening of another and it was in this mad dash I came to better understand the meaning of being fashionably late: For we were late for almost everything after nine-o-clock when the toll of the day began to show itself.

After more than a week of repeating my sleep deprived routine in keeping up with the itinerary, I begged to be let off of going to church to do nothing more than sleep away the only day not promised to someone else. It was granted as a one-off and appeased by my agreement to entertain the Elmbridges in our drawing room this evening for a few hours after an early dinner. I accepted the compromise of a lazy day for this bargain, although I looked to tonight with a sense of foreboding, having spent very little time in Sheldon's company at all since his delayed arrival. This had only had to be half contrived by my own regulation, the rest originating from the ever-increasing number of new acquaintances I had to divide my attentions between. But I knew him unhappy with me, and as we sat over the chess board before the fire, I felt sorry to see him so Friday faced on my account.

I did not openly acknowledge it or question him however, for I knew he had grown jealous and frustrated at me. But it seemed not to encourage him off in other directions as I had hoped, instead, he seemed to withdraw further from the society of others and brood increasingly over my movements. I had even tried at making introductions of my new lady friends who had expressed their admiration for his looks and manner, and although he would make polite and charming prattle with them about the ballroom floor, he would not invite any of them to dance, even when I encouraged it.

After another week, it had grown out of all proportion and become all too much to bear, for both of us, I think. How could I tell him, I wanted only to be his friend without consigning the very same, to irreparable damage?

It was on account of a Mr Drake that this tension was brought to a head in the end. Mr Drake having only become acquainted with me in the past couple of weeks through an introduction made by Countess Lieven, had got the crack-brained notion into his head to propose to me. I had of course refused him instantly after such a brief acquaintance and having no particular regard for him above the ordinary, but despite my trying to keep the matter private, unbeknownst to me; he had not been so discreet.

I was parading along Rotten Row the next afternoon, arm in arm with my new lady friends and a couple of my Cuddington set, when Sheldon appeared red-faced and marched me off quite unapologetically and made me sit beside him on a bench out of the way of any company.

'Whatever has gotten into you?' I asked, releasing myself from his grip about my arm and sitting down upon the bench.

'Is it true El?'

'What?'

'That Drake has asked for your hand?'

'Yes, and to no avail, I might add.'

The relief that washed over his expression indicated that he had only half the account and did not know I had refused him. *So that was what this was about.*

'Truly?'

'Of course. You cannot think me so frivolous to marry a man I've barely known for a fortnight. Give me some credit, Sheldon.'

'I do. What I cannot understand, however, is why you will not receive the attentions of a man you have known all your life.'

This was where I faltered and wished for an escape. I stared out across the Serpentine a while before deciding I must end this insufferable discord between us. 'You're my friend, Sheldon, it's different. I don't think of you in that light.'

'But could you, be brought to it: to think of me as something else?'

'I honestly don't know. We are much changed and find ourselves as much strangers as friends I feel, since your return.'

'It's true. But I want us to grow to know each other again El, in all ways, not just as we once were.'

'But why me, Sheldon? You could have anyone of your choosing.'

'I choose you.'

I had no answer for this. I could not return the sentiment even though I found this frankness between us moving. 'You hardly know me now. I hardly know myself anymore.'

'And how can I get to know you again when you push me away and prevent it?'

I shrugged, 'I don't know.'

'Look, I know you are not minded to rush up the aisle, and I think it prudent, this early on. But El, one day you shall be ready to make the step, and I want to know if it's possible we might be happy together?'

'You ask me questions to which I have no ready answer, Sheldon. I am fond of you my dear friend, you know it, and I am sensible of the compliment you pay me, I am: But I am fatigued by the matchmaking attempts of our families, and the further they set their minds to pressing the matter, the further I wish to flee.'

'To the devil with them, El, what do *you* want?'

'A chance to understand my own mind. To discover what it is I want; because when I settle to it, I want to mean it with all my heart. I want to feel it with all my being.'

'Then I shall not ask you what I wanted to.'

I was relieved to hear this.

'So, I will ask you something else instead.'

I braced myself and stiffened.

'Forget your family, and mine. Take the time you need to come to know what it is you want; but will you let me back in, El? Take down this divide. Let us be friends once more and keep an open mind to where that might be led to flourish in some future time.'

'I will,' I said and reached out and squeezed his hand a fleeting moment.

This honest speech between us had proved so cathartic, I wished it had come to pass sooner, for I could see in the passing days how much better we went along: How much easier our conversations came to mind, how much kinder our smiles. Only as friends of course, but it was nice to feel that simplicity betwixt us after such a time. And whilst I still found myself no closer to knowing my own heart, I found comfort in the new understanding between us and his handling of the matter.

Molly's Indiscretion.

May 1821. - Eleanor.

As the April showers began to whimper off and the generous blue skies of May cast their brilliance outside my window, I was full of all the buoyancy of the season and fully adjusted to its demands. It had taken some time to fall into to step with it, but here I was, capable of paying attendance on three to five hosts a night, as many costume changes and still finding time to pay morning calls on my ever-increasing circle of friends and promenade along Rotten Row in the afternoon.

It was all a matter of fine management and logistical planning, and of course, learning just the right amount of time to spend in one saloon before slipping off to the next. Something I had become quite artful at, of late. Delores was not so impressed by my new skills, always complaining to Mama that I was becoming something of a *persona grata* about the ton, and whilst that was all very well in the day time, Delores could barely keep up with me of an evening. Thus rendering her job as protectress and spy, more than a trifle tricky. Mama, however, had no concern over it, so long as I was keeping to good company and having a care to not be overly flirtatious. I had taken a great deal of care on this head since my heart to heart with Sheldon. Things had much improved between us, not in any romantic direction, but his loosening his selfish grip on me, had induced me to flirt much less and only dance for the sake of gaiety nowadays. I supposed I had at last found the balance and culled the wilder excitement that had burned bright in me at the start of the season. Between the two, Sheldon and I, had, by degrees, begun to remember our friendship again: Been able to laugh and prattle comfortably as we once did as well as share a few confidences and converse more seriously. It was nice to have his friendship back, and even though I still could not imagine him as anything more, I held this in high regard once more and had a care not to upset him.

I was just returned from my second outing of the evening and had approximately thirty minutes to permit myself a quick change of clothes and make the journey over to Almack's before they closed the doors at eleven-o-clock. I rang for Molly and rustled about in the dressing room trying to find my new blush gown with the peasant bodice, for I wanted something new to show myself in tonight. I was beginning to run out of new things to present myself in, I thought, peering at the three remaining boxes that had not yet been opened since Mrs Oliver had delivered them. It was perhaps true that I should have to try out one of the London Modiste's now, or risk running out of fresh gowns before the season's end. I had always been happy with Mrs Oliver's at Ewell, even if I did sometimes procure the fabrics in London, I was never disappointed with the result when I described or showed her some new pattern or fashion plate. But I could not trundle back and forth to the country now for dress fittings and it was still another three weeks before we made a weekend visit back for the Derby. I decided I must take Lady Belmonte's recommendation of the Modiste in Tyburnia she had spoken well of, if she was to be found at the assembly rooms tonight.

By the time I had found the right box and opened it out on the chaise, Molly was still nowhere to be seen. I checked the clock and realised I had already spent ten minutes of my time. Whatever was she about keeping me waiting for such a time when she knew how hard-pressed we were. I yanked the bell pull again and after a few more moments I heard footsteps upon the stairs.

But it was not Molly who came into the room in a fluster, but one of the housemaids bringing a story of Molly being in an interview with the housekeeper and my mama. It seemed most irregular to my mind, particularly at such an hour, but I did not have time to ponder it. I recruited the housemaid instead to assisting me with my rushed toilette and dress change and had to be satisfied with the hair design I had returned in.

All the same, I had got to King Street just on time and stayed a few merry hours before coming home and finding once again, no answer from Molly when I rang to be put to bed, but the same housemaid arrived to answer it.

'Is she ill?' I asked her as she unbuttoned me.

'I don't think so ma'am.'

'Then whatever is the matter? I have not seen her all evening.'

'I've not been told, miss. All I know is that she was kept to the housekeeper's parlour all the day and I have been asked to come in her place ma'am.'

'Very well. I will find it out in the morning. It is late enough as it is.'

I HAD JUST SETTLED comfortably to my armchair to take a quick browse of my diary and check tomorrow's itinerary before going to bed when I had a tap at the door so quiet I could hardly tell if I had imagined it. I got up and called through the door: 'Hello?'

'It's me miss, Molly,' came the reply and I opened the door to find her standing there in the darkness in her bedclothes.

'Molly, whatever are you come so late for?—I have already been set to bed by one of the housemaids. Where have you been all day?'

'Miss, I'm sorry to come to you like this, but I haven't a choice.'

'Whatever do you mean, Molly? What is wrong, why are your eyes all red?' I stepped back and let her into the room and closed the door behind her.

'I's been given the boot, miss. Mrs Elkins and your mama are awful cross with me and I'm to be sent back to Cuddington in the morning to get my things and be gone by dinner time.'

I was perfectly astounded. I had never heard of anyone being put out under our roof. 'Whatever has happened?'

'I know I shouldn'ta done it miss, I didn't mean no harm. But—'

'Do what?' I said with some insistence in my tone, realising that it must indeed be something quite terrible for this to be the consequence.

'I was walking out with one of the footman at Cuddington miss. I didn't know it wasn't allowed. I mean, I knew it wasn't permitted on Mrs Crawford's time, but I thought, well, on my own time—'

'I see.' Of all the things she might have done, this was perhaps the only one I could not get her out of, that and stealing, perhaps. These were the prime matters of character my parents had neither tolerance nor compassion for. 'But how did my mama and the housekeeper here come to know of it when we left the country weeks ago?'

'One of the stable fellows here had found it out miss, and blackmailed me about it since I got here.'

'Blackmailed you?'

'Yes, miss. Said if I did not show him such favour as he'd heard me famous for, then he'd tell the butler.'

'Famous for—Molly, how many footman?'

'Just one, miss, just Jack until that blaggard stable boy made me pay him attentions. Pardon me my language ma'am.'

Her language was the least of my concerns right now. I was trying to think of a way that I might salvage this and not be left without an Abigail at the greatest hour, and yet the more she spoke, the more impossible I knew it.

'So how was it discovered?'

'Mrs Elkins found us in the stable this afternoon and took us straight to your mama. The butler sent the stable boy packing and now I'm to follow in the morning. If it weren't for an express needing to go ahead of me to Cuddington to warn them of the situation, then I would be gone too by now.'

It was hopeless if she had been found out by the housekeeper herself. A rumour or suchlike, I might have been able to counter or at least cast some doubt upon.

'Please help me, miss. Will you speak to Lady Ashlyn for me, please? I've nowhere to go and she won't give me a reference neither.'

'Molly, I—'

'I'll give it up with Jack, I already have, miss. It will never happen again.'

'What did happen, Molly?'

'You know, the things you do when you're walking out with a gent.'

I wondered what these were in her world. 'You mean romantic meetings?'

'Well, kinda. They weren't really very romantic miss.'

I did not know what to make of this precisely. Only that I had heard enough to convince me my mama would not hear a word of protest in her going. 'Molly, there is nothing I could say to convince my mama to change her mind. Not in a matter of this gravity.'

'Miss, you have to, please.'

'Molly, if I could, I would try for it. Indeed, I am sorry it has come to this. But I know my mama and of all the matters of character and reputation, she thinks this kind of digression the very worst. She simply will not hear it.'

'Then I have no choice.'

'What do you mean?'

'If you will not help me keep my place, then I might as well tell the whole house about you having lice down there!'

'Lice?' I frowned.

She pointed to my groin accusingly and I was quite thrown out of countenance.

'And don't think you can deny it, the proof is beneath your skirts, you've hardly a whisper of hair since.'

I was quite beside myself in understanding her at first. The excuse I had given to her those weeks ago had been quite forgotten to me now. 'How dare you speak to me in threats!'

'Oh, don't think I don't know how you get them either. You only get them from stepping out with gents and them trying to put a babe in you. So perhaps me and you are not as different as you'd like to think, except you won't be thrown out for it.'

I did not know if this was true or not; if lice might only be transmitted through such acts and if it was then I had chosen poorly in my excuse to her, but this was not the time for such considerations; I was in such a rage I might have throttled her.

'So, either I stay, and so does your secret, or I go, letting it out on my way. What would your mama say to that if she gets mad as fire over a maid, what will she have to say of her own daughter?'

'I have had no bedfellows I'll have you know and as for your threats, I've a mind to have you sent out of the house tonight and write to all the registry's I know, warning them of you—'

'Oh, please don't miss,' she began to cry. 'I didn't mean to, it's just Fanny says I could have a baby in me, and if I do, then I'll not get another place again.'

I considered her a moment. My heart still racing with fury, my jaw clenched, and vitriol building upon my tongue, but as I considered her words, the fact that she might be with child, I knew I could not carry out my intended threat. I paused a while, making laps about the perimeter of the rug, trying to calm myself with drawn out breaths and thinking over what must next be done. 'What of the footman?' I said eventually, 'I think you must get him to marry you.' It seemed to me the only viable solution. A married couple might get work on a farm or the like.

'He won't, miss, he said he won't lose his place over a petticoat fling.'

'You mean *he* has not lost his place too?'

'No, miss. He's to have a warning.'

I looked her over, the pitiable sight of her, her face all blotchy and smeared with dirty tears. I could never forgive her for this attempt at blackmail. I certainly could not like her now I knew her so disloyal. I could not approve of what she had done. Nor did I wish to attempt to spare her her position here, now. But, and this was fast proving the greater feeling; there were two things that could not be overlooked and I could not permit her suffer for: The fact that she and she alone, was to take the blame for this, despite it being an act committed by two, and that she now might be landed with a child and no support. Both were insufferable to me. She now seemed insufferable to me, but to a somewhat lesser degree than her punishment would warrant if I did not step in and do something to ease it.

I was not sure what must be done. I knew mama would not be moved to even giving her a character. I knew too that whilst it was right the footman should go too, she would probably not hear of it if I pressed the point and even if she would give in to my protest, what good would it do to send him out too? I should better like to be certain of his wage and see a share of it sent on for the child.

I could not make a recommendation of her to any of my own friends after this. Who would want such a disloyal maid? 'Stop crying will you,' I said, shoving her a handkerchief and going over to my escritoire, plucking from beneath its lid a fresh sheet of paper and decanting some ink into the well. 'Sit down by the fire and pour yourself a cup,' I told her.

I wrote out, through her sobbing and whimpering, a reference. A very good character indeed and one I was certain should get her out of a spot—at least for now. If she was with child, I wasn't sure what she would do once it became apparent, for there was no obvious sign of it yet. But that was beyond my power, and certainly beyond my immediate concern.

'What's this miss?' she said when I handed it to her.

'This is a character. A character you are not worthy of, but if you accept it, you will strive to be in your next place!'

'Oh, I will miss, truly, I will.'

'I hope so, Molly, for if you try any of this business you have tried with me today, you shall deserve to be thrown out by your next mistress without a second glance.'

'Yes, miss. You're very good.'

'Well then, you shall remember that when keeping my secrets.'

'Yes, miss. I shall never utter a word.'

'Now, take this reference, take this money and in the morning once you are back in the country, you can go to the registry and seek a new place. That should be enough to see you through any travel or board expenses until you settle to one. And don't go to the Epsom Registry, take a coach out far enough that my writing of your character shall not prove suspect. Everyone knows it should be my mama performing such duties in Cuddington. Go somewhere we are less likely to be known—even come back to London if you must, once you have gathered your things from Cuddington and visit a registry here.'

She held out her grubby hand and accepted the coins into them, turning them to count their number. 'Thank you, miss. I'm sorry again.'

'Once you are settled, if you do find you are with child, you shall need to write to me and provide me your new address. I shall see that the footman, Jack, forwards to you, your dues each month. It does not seem just that he shall escape that duty, even if he intends to escape the others.'

'I can't write miss. But I shall look for someone who can.'

'Very well. Goodbye, Molly,' I said as evenly as I could manage.

The whole affair threw me off for the entire day when I awoke to the housemaid's attendance and remembered it all. A sense of gloom hanging over me, no matter what I did or where I was to go. As mad as I was with her, and it was very mad indeed, I felt a deeper fury bellowing beneath even that, at the fact that my mama and Mrs Elkins saw fit to make an example of her, but not the footman at Cuddington. Was our sex to bear the brunt of such injustice even by our own sex? It would not surprise me so much if my father or brothers were to make such a decision, but there seemed something of a betrayal to me in my own sex permitting it. I shook off the thought. One thing that was clear to me, was I should not be so careless around servants in the future if this was how easy it was for them to turn and break your trust.

Leaky pipes.

May 1821. - Annalise.

It had been many weeks since the family departed for London, and it had taken a long time for the lull in duties to fall into a routine of complaisance, owing to a concealed burst pipe in the kitchen scullery, which until this morning, had been out of action for weeks. It was not a case of simple inconvenience; of going out to the yard pump to fetch the water, which had proved a revelation on how inconvenient not having the taps functioning in the scullery was: But dealing with the leaking water flooding the basement floors and having to drag every pot, pan and plate to the dairy sinks for washing. It had been chaos for everyone. All the furniture that could be moved, having to be taken upstairs to spare it, constant mopping and staunching to prevent the deterioration of anything that could not be, like the heavy kitchen tables and ranges. Odious amounts of laundering to do to recycle the staunching and drying linens and soaked clothes. Extra cleaning for the housemaids who were called to clean the kind of dust and grime that builds in crevices and corners where furniture had long stood and had now been moved. It had disrupted them all when they had so looked to this as a time of welcome respite.

Even when the source of the problem was finally discovered and corrected—over weeks of having the kitchen pulled apart and overcrowded with tradesmen puzzling over it and clanging away—when the workmen had finally departed the house, it had taken a long time to dry everything out and set it all to rights again.

'Well, it looks like we shall have to have a new rug, but, otherwise, I think everything is well enough to go back in,' Poppy said to Mrs Crawford as they undertook an inspection of their abandoned room that had finally dried out.

'We'll have Grantley send for the furniture to be put back then, and you can both go and fetch your things from the attic later.'

'Thank you, ma'am,' Poppy and Annalise chorused.

'What a relief!' Poppy said when she was gone. Neither of them had liked having to share the attic dorm. They could not sit up chatting as they often did, without risk of keeping the others awake, or enjoy the desertion of the servant's hall if they had a fancy for a cup of chocolate or to warm in front of the fire awhile on a chilly night. There was also the inconvenience of having so far down to go in the morning to start on the breakfast, and not being able to nip back for a ten-minute lie down on a break.

'I will be very glad to have our own space back, to be sure,' Annalise agreed, thinking how much she had hated having to keep all her mother's private things upstairs all this time. Not that she believed anyone would take anything. She had no reason to think herself amongst those kinds of persons, but she had seen the curious glances as all her boxes had been carried up and shoved beneath her bed. She thought they must have considered her plump in the pocket to have so many things when most only had a single bag or box to their name, but they were not her own. They were not even worth a great deal, for the most part, with the exception of a fine turquoise cabochon broach her mother had been given by her grandfather on her sixteenth birthday, and a few well-read books. Most of what her mama had salvaged from her once abundant life, she had sold over the years to pay for Annalise's clothes and shoes and to take her about on the odd trip to somewhere fancy on her birthday. The remainder of the boxes were filled with things of sentimental value, like her letters and watercolours, a few bound files of musical manuscripts which Annalise had learnt to play from, and a great many clothes that had gone quite out of mode by the time Annalise was in leading strings. She had got the idea up of one day turning them into a patchwork quilt, to remember her by, when time permitted the crafting of it.

She felt a happy sense of relief when she returned to the room in the afternoon to find all the furniture set back in place and unpacked her things again, and made up the beds with the fresh linens which had been left upon them. It would have usually fallen to Fanny to do, but with everyone having been recruited to all sorts of tasks beyond their prescribed ones recently; it was no trouble to see to this herself.

It was a pleasant afternoon with the sun casting its warmth over the kitchen yard flagstones, and when she returned from unpacking, she sat outside with Maggie, peeling potatoes into a bucket for this evening's stew. Even Cook had been minded to keep things as simple as could be, after all the recent disturbance.

'I was speaking to the farm 'and earlier when I went to take the pigs scraps, and he said that some of the strawberries have started to ripen. So, I told Cook, and she said we might as well go and pick 'em for jam since they'd not keep 'till the Ashlyns come back.'

'What fun, well done Maggie,' Annalise said, wiping a trail of sweat from her brow as she tossed another potato into the bucket. 'It's a lovely day for it too.'

'Aye, and we can take our time about it, cause their ain't much to do once we've got these into the pot.'

Annalise nodded. 'Looks like we might finally get the break we all looked to at last.'

'Aye, and Fanny has arranged a secret little gathering in the barn after supper, to try out a little dancing. Says Peter can play the 'armonica and he will do it for us to all dance to. Will you come?'

'I'm not sure. I will let you know at supper. I am rather looking forward to an early night now we are back in the basement.' She remembered too, that Will had asked her if she wanted to walk to the Three Tuns with him this evening, now the nights were growing lighter, and she was still undecided on the answer. He had insisted it would be his treat since he had benefitted from some good veils from guests before the Ashlyns departed, and he had promised he had no intentions she need be concerned with; just good conversation over a mug or two of beer and then straight back home. She had thought about seeing if anyone else would want to go along with them, so there were no false impressions given; either to him or anyone that might notice them missing. But she hadn't got around to asking about yet, and if a barn dance was already planned, it was likely anyone minded to stay up a while, would have promised their attendance to Fanny already.

As she sat over the peelings, she contemplated her answer. Will had proved such a gentle natured fellow and easy friend; she could hardly suspect him of any funny business now she had got to know him. But it was no secret he was overly fond of her, something he himself had never denied, but always professed at being a gentleman in such matters and never crossing lines that should not be crossed. So their encounters had been innocent and friendly, consisting of cosy chats in the servant's hall and the occasional sitting out to a cup of beer on the kitchen doorstep before bed. But in every case, nothing out of the ordinary had occurred, and so she reasoned she could probably trust him to keep his word if she did decide to go. And she fancied she would like to. The trouble was; she wanted no whispers to strike up about them if they were thought to be too much in each other's company. And whilst it seemed less likely they would be missed if everyone was to be in the barn, and she could give the excuse of going off to bed now she was back in her own room, she still felt anxious.

'Shall we take these over to the farm then?' said Maggie, picking up the bucket of potato peelings as Annalise set the other bucket of peeled spuds inside the kitchen door. 'We can have a nose at the berries too and see how many baskets to bring with us later.'

'Baskets? How many berries are we to pick?' Annalise asked with a note of a laugh and wiped her hands on her apron.

'As many as make it into them, once we have checked 'em for quality of course.'

They set out through the yard, and up the steps into line after line of drying linens stretched out to navigate through, flaying about in breezy gusts and catching them every now and then as they edged and ducked to avoid them. Hopefully the lines could be pegged down to their usual number soon, once the back log had been caught up with.

As they passed beyond them, they caught sight of others about, finding excuses to dawdle in the clement weather; the housemaids beating rugs and curtains at sloth speed, footmen and hallboys loading barrows for the coal cellar, briquette by briquette, bootboys at a makeshift table blacking and polishing every shoe in the house, faces turned to the sun. It was a mood of gentle occupation; the embodied exhale of finally acclimatising to a relaxing pace of duty after so much calamity and delay.

They passed through the rose garden and admired the varying shades of pink and pale, the smell of the warming earth rising from it, as Maggie gave a demonstration of the dance steps she intended for tonight, Annalise clapping her along and the crunching gravel being kicked and crushed beneath their feet. It would be merry now; the scent of this shift carried in the air and caught everyone's notice as they turned their thoughts to the possibilities of a remaining month of liberty.

They calmed their easy laughter and gay talk as they approached the stable courtyard and heard suddenly the creak and turn of carriage wheels and a rush of hooves behind them. They stepped immediately aside and watched the carriage slow and creep by them, before halting.

'We's not expecting anyone are we?' Maggie said, frowning at the sight.

'Is that not the Ashlyns' own coach? I'm sure that is their coat of arms, I saw it in the stained-glass window of the grand staircase.'

Maggie shrugged. 'Dunno. But I hope you are wrong. Probably means the daughters gone and got leg shackled early and there goes any hope of a break.'

'Surely if the family were back they would have been set down at the vestibule, but that coach did not stop until the courtyard?'

Maggie shrugged and they resumed their steps, but slowly, watching sideways beneath their lashes. A groom jumped down from the driver's box, let down the footplate and opened the door. When Molly stepped out from it, and quite alone, they were both puzzled.

'Molly!' Maggie called out and turned in her direction, 'Is it just you, Molly?'

Molly nodded but did not look up and smile back, and set off across the cobbles with an alacrity about her pace.

'Molly?' Maggie persisted and burst into step to catch her. 'Why you back so early, as she got 'erself an Abigail at last? Are you free to come home now and stay with us?' she asked brightly, but Molly did not stop or answer.

Annalise tugged gently at Molly's sleeve to slow her, but she paid no mind in her excitement.

'We're to 'ave a barn dance tonight. How merry we can celebrate your home-coming—'

Molly stopped and turned, eyes heavy with tears. 'I shan't be staying.'

'Are you alright, Molly?' Annalise asked. She did not know her well at all but it was clear something was starkly amiss.

She shook her head. 'I've been given the boot. I'll be gone by tea-time.' And she broke into a fit of sobs.

'Oh, Molly...' Annalise said, and Maggie flung her arms about her.

'It can't be true,' Maggie said. 'What's 'appened?'

Annalise had a sinking feeling she already knew.

'I'm not supposed to talk of it. The upper servants know and will make an announcement once I'm gone. I'm to go in discreet through the tunnel and directly to Mrs Crawford. I shouldn't even be talkin' to yer.'

'We shan't tell,' Maggie pledged, with tears in her own eyes.

'Is it about Jack?' Annalise said and Molly nodded.

'What about Jack?' Maggie asked looking between the pair.

'He's gone and put a babe in me Maggie, and the Mistress has found it out and I'm to go. There it is, I'm ruined.'

Annalise put a hand to her throat. She hadn't realised it as bad as all that. 'Oh, Molly, where will you go?'

She shrugged. 'Got to set about finding me a new place and 'ope they don't cotton on for a while. After that, who knows...'

'Have you somewhere to go tonight?'

'Miss Ashlyn's given me some money to put up for a bit whilst I find something, and Crawford's to settle my wages before I go. It should last a while, but I dunno what I'm to do if I can't get a place before my belly's noticed.'

Maggie stood in stunned silence, stroking Molly's shoulder and Annalise searched her pockets for a handkerchief to offer, but finding it covered in potato starch she slipped it back into her apron. 'There is a place you could try. Although I don't know what hours they keep anymore. Do you know the bookshop *Harrisons,* in town?'

She shook her head. 'I don't need no books.'

'I know. But at that shop, in the back rooms, there is a lady there, a Miss Lockheart, she teaches girls their letters there, twice a week, Tuesday and Thursday mornings, if it is still the same routine.'

"ow's learning her letters gonna 'elp?' Maggie re-joined now.

'It's not. But that same lady helps girls in all sorts of...difficulties, including the kind you find yourself in. If she can't help you herself, she will no doubt know of someone who can.'

'Do you mean for getting rid of the babe?'

'God no. That's not what I meant at all, Molly. That is not what you intend to try is it?'

She shrugged again. 'I dunno what I'm gonna do.'

'Please don't do that, Molly. You're as likely to end up as dead as the baby.'

She was taken aback by this and Annalise hoped it had startled her enough not to think of it again. She had heard some dreadful stories on that head she didn't want to even think about again. There'd been a lady on Old Mill Street who'd been hung for it just last year; she remembered her friend Rosie telling her. Five women she'd 'helped' all dead in as many weeks.

But Miss Lockheart was a good woman, the rector's daughter and of a nature far more Christian and charitable than her own papa's. Her mother had used to volunteer at Harrisons, once a week on Tuesdays, before she got sick, and made a friend of Miss Lockheart over time. 'She is one of the good one's Li-Li,' her mother had told her one day as she was introduced to her in the backrooms. She usually preferred to sit out and wait for her mother in the bookshop, browsing the new titles and chatting to Mr Harrison as he sat at his counter. But on that particular day, she sat in with the other girls to learn to improve her grammar. 'If only there were more like her,' her mother had said as they walked home: 'the world would be a happier place indeed.'

WHEN THEY RETURNED to the kitchen after, sworn to secrecy on the matter, their mood had altered drastically, all the hope of the day faded in this learning. It had made Annalise's mind up that she would definitely decline Wills invitation tonight, after all, she thought as she watched over the fly solution in the pan: The peculiar waft of milk, sugar and pepper simmering beneath her nose. Maggie assured her it worked a treat at combating them and with the warm weather and need to have the windows and doors open to cope with it, it was inevitable they should suffer such swarming with so much to attract them into the rooms.

'It suffocates them, Cook says,' Maggie informed her as she laid out several saucers ready for the mixture.

Conversely, Cook had been nowhere to be seen half the day. When Maggie had gone to find her in her parlour, she was sat at her table with a ledger spread open and a copy of the newspaper tucked beneath it. 'It's not all boiling and baking you know, I have other work to do. I'm sure you two can manage a simple jam boiling between you,' she had said when Maggie asked if she would show them how to do it, for it was Poppy's half day off.

'Here, take this and give it to Anna, she'll know what to do.' She passed her a piece of paper, which Annalise told her, once she came back with it, was instructions on how to make jam.

By evening, the news of Molly's departure was announced by Mrs Crawford, with a stiff message of warning to the rest of the staff. Of course, she had not disclosed the details of her condition or named the footman involved, but everyone knew it was Jack. He was a regular rakish type of fellow and Annalise had made a point of keeping well out of his way since the night she had found the pair in the corridor on her night duty. It seemed after this, the rest of the maids were minded to do the same as he was refused to dance with everyone he offered to in the barn that evening. Annalise was glad to see it and made a point of setting out to Maggie that she should have a care around him, whilst shying away from Will's conversation most of the evening herself.

EVEN A WEEK LATER, there remained an air of cautiousness and misery on account of the Molly situation, partly because of the effect Molly's dismissal had had on the upper servants whom had been behaving more circumspect and unrelenting than usual. It was as if they were striving to prove themselves worthy masters in compensation for this mishap that occurred under their watch.

No one had heard from her since she had set off last Thursday afternoon with her bags packed and tear streamed cheeks as they waved her off, and many had regularly asked about to check for news. There were of course some that took the view that such a fate served her right, but for the most part, there was more pity for her than anything else. And the secret collection that was gathered for her before her leaving, was testament to what a warm-hearted community they were, on the whole, and Annalise felt glad to be amongst them.

They had spent another happy morning out in the sunshine, picking close-to-bolting rhubarb and asparagus on the farm fields. Maggie had struck up quite an eager friendship with the farm staff and had offered up their services willingly. Annalise left her chatting to the farmer's wife as she headed back to the house to start on washing her basket full. She'd had a little too much sun and felt a touch dehydrated and looked to taking a drink. She walked the long way by shadowing the edge of the woodland perimeter, to benefit from its shade. It was a short stroll, but in the heat, it seemed taxing and she welcomed the cooler air against her skin. She was but half the journey on when she heard the thud of paws against the ground and momentarily, feared some wild beast amongst the deeper woodland, she could not see. When a pair of Labradors came bounding out of a clearing, chasing each other in circles, before being distracted by some scent about the oak tree, she caught her breath.

'Maximus, Bess,' she heard behind her, followed by a whistle, to which the pair looked up, sniffed the air and darted back through the trees at the very moment Will stepped out of the clearing.

'Anna,' he called out, pleased to see her.

'Will, I didn't know dog walking was amongst a footman's duties.'

'Aye, it is when the master's valet is away with him. I don't mind it though, it's quite nice when it's not raining.'

It seemed to her increasingly, that footmen got all the best jobs and some of the best veils too. She'd a mind to dress in men's clothes and try her luck at a trying for a position, although she didn't have the stature or the calves to pass it off, she told herself in this private joke she entertained as the dogs gathered about her ankles to sniff her and she bent to ruffle their backs.

'Handsome fine pair of hounds, aren't they?' he said indulgently.

'They are indeed. I see you have made friends of them.'

'Hard not to, I shall miss our little walks when the family return. You should come wiv us one day, now things are slower. It's beautiful down by the lake. We go three times a day, so you can take your pick to suit you.'

'Thank you, Will, I'll see about it.'

'Ah, I know what to make of that kind of answer. As good as a no, without the sting,' he teased. 'Not all of us are like Jack you know. We're a pretty decent bunch apart from him, and the Steward.'

'The Steward?'

'Don't ask,' he said, and stooped to pick up a stick. 'So, you've been out to the farm again I see.' He stepped away a fraction and threw the stick across the lawns for the dogs.

'Yes.'

'You got some colour on your cheeks.'

'Have I?' she pressed a palm to one of them and felt the heat in it. 'Oh no, I haven't burned have I?'

'Nah, just a little pink about the cheek.'

'I'd better get back and see for myself. It doesn't take much to turn me pink. I should have taken better care.'

'I don't think it's as bad as that. I'll walk back with yer, we were coming to the last of it anyway. They look like they could take a bowl of water.'

She was hoping he would not do that, but did not know how to put him off, so instead she hoped that the others were inside and wouldn't see them approaching.

When she came in through the basement door, however, leaving Will at the hand pump seeing to the dogs, she was glad to find the staff happily distracted in news of Molly, who had sent a message to say she had found a place in Kingston-upon-Thames and was doing alright, and thanking everyone who collected for her. It had been post marked from the Rectory at Ewell and Annalise smiled to see it, for she knew that if Miss Lockheart had assisted her in finding it, it was likely to be on honest terms and the likelihood of her being set off again on account of the baby, was slim.

Derby Day.

June 1821.- Eleanor.

Our weeks in London had flown by, and even though we still had a few remaining, our little trip back to the country for the weekend seemed to highlight how close we were drawing to its end. It felt sad to think my first season to be almost over and in such a flash, and as much as I intended to make the most of the respite and riding whilst we were here, I was equally determined to make the most of the remainder of the season when we returned to the city. *It might, after all, prove to be my last.*

We journeyed a day ahead of the races to prepare for the early start and I was up with the excitement of going, long before I needed to be, and even once I'd taken my morning exercise and been set ready in my fanciest day dress and bonnet, there was still an hour to spare before our going.

When our relatives arrived with their weekend bandboxes in tow, I was happy to be disturbed from my early breakfast, for their company was never irksome or disappointing.

'Well look at you!' said Aunt Orlagh when I passed over her Redingote and gloves to Mary and embraced her. 'Looking every part grown into her status,' she said to my uncle.

'Oh, Aunt, you too look very well,' I told her, leading them into the drawing room and sending Mary for tea. I was very fond of my aunt and uncle. There was something about their easy manner that was always so refreshing. Most of my family were a stiff-rumped bunch, with a rare few exceptions, but none as notable as my aunt and uncle. In their company, you were free to be at ease, speak whatever was in your head, and since they were minded to always do the same, laughter was often in abundance when they were about. It was a sad shame the opportunity to see them was always a rarity, but I intended to set aside time to enjoy their company whilst I could. 'I hope the journey was a smooth one?' I asked.

'Oh hideous busy,' she said in that strong Irish accent that had never much diminished in the many years of their living between London and Cork. 'The local roads are heaving with coaches and riders already, it's a wonder they can all find a place to stay in these small villages!' she complained.

'Well, it shall be the worse still in another hour, I fear,' I told her, remembering the impossible crush along Tattenham Corner the *unmentionable* time I snuck out to watch it. Later, of course, I would be conveyed in the Elmbridges' coach, and not upon Samson's back clambering for a spot in which to see.

I had quite forgotten the prospect of our solitude until now. London had managed to set some well needed distance between us, and I had found myself favourable to small moments in his company; the odd dance or ride in Hyde Park now it was so much dispersed and punctuated by other things... other admirers. But this weekend would be different again, set us back on a path of contrived intimacy I had spent the last six weeks shedding. But whilst I remained unsettled by the forced encouragement between me and Sheldon; after the misunderstanding with Mr Craythorne the last time we were here, I was suddenly quite glad to have occasion for Sheldon publicly parade me, just in case any whispers came to surface over the debacle. I was, for the most part, doubtful they should. As Anna said: it was so many weeks ago, there was no one of good society present, and nothing untoward had occurred to give rise to any gossip. Certainly, nothing had reached our ears in London, which I took to be a good sign, although I knew the country to be much slower in moving from one topic of gossip to another, whilst in London, it seemed to turn by the hour. In any case, today, in keeping exclusively to Sheldon's company, I would wash away any such whispers if there was anyone paying heed to such topics.

He was punctual to the hour of ten and we made our way through the quiet lanes as far as Ewell before we descended on the expected crush of coaches, riders and walking crowds clambering for space along the London road. The roads were a rickety coach ride on an average day, but they seemed far worse today with the tumult of every type of vehicle trying to push its way through them: pedestrians forced up against the bushes and bramble for their safety. Delores was with us, so the conversation on the journey remained formal, but I could see the relaxed indifference in her disposition today, safe in the comfort of relieving the burden of my safekeeping onto Sheldon and having little concern over our own interactions.

My uncle's family had already departed for the Downs half an hour earlier, on account of finding a good aspect in which to park the Barouche and enjoy the view from. They were not, as they pointedly reminded me (in good humour), fortunate enough to have a seat in Prinny's stand. I envied them now though, thinking they must already be happily settled in their spot and looking to the joys of the day ahead, whilst we made our painfully slow and rattling journey towards them. I would have rather gone with them and enjoyed it in authentic style amongst the rambling and roaring crowds rather than watching them from above, quite apart from all the real fun. But to be permitted here at all I knew I must be grateful.

No races had begun when we stepped out of the Elmbridges' coach and made our way to Prinny's stand. But the trackside was teaming with thousands of spectators. Seas of gentleman in top hats, some sat upon the roofs of their coaches to gain a better view, many stood around horses, examining them in consideration of where to stake their money ahead of the races. Ladies sat in the back of Barouche's with the hood pulled back. Families with the youngest and oldest generations afoot, carrying picnicking hampers in search of a free spot of grass to claim for the day. Jockey's parading horses up and down the ring and showing off their colours. Blacklegs stands queuing several yards back and that was without the hubbub of the many other stalls I could not well make out through the crowds.

The weather did not look too promising; the sky was hazy with grey cloud, although it had not begun to rain yet at least. I wondered what the thousands of spectators would do for cover if there was a downpour, since there was little provision in the event of one, unless you had come in your own vehicle or, like us, were fortunate enough to be in the stand.

We were admitted at the door upon Sheldon giving his name and trod what seemed a great many steps until we came into a salon where large gothic windows looked out upon a clear elevated view of the finishing line. The people now seemed vast and swarming like an insect colony from such a perspective and I took in just how huge the whole affair was. There were doors leading off from the main drawing room, to sit trackside under cover. I supposed everyone would migrate towards them once the races begun. But, for now, they seemed content to take refreshments and chat amongst themselves in the comfortable environs of comfy chesterfields and low-burning grates.

The salon was only hall full, with many faces I recognised from society and some I did not. I smiled and waved fleeting greetings to those who knew me, as we found a charming spot to settle with a view out to the track.

The King was not in attendance and it seemed a great deal like what I would have imagined the scene to be at Brooks or White's; men gathered in clusters of conversation over their stakes or some parliamentary affair or the other whilst they sipped on dark spirits or port wines and chugged on a cigar. There was a scattering of ladies about at least, so I did not feel completely out of place, but it was definitely a gentleman's salon for the greater part.

'Ah, the young Lord Elmbridge, how d'you do?' said Lord Grafton as we passed.

'Your Grace, very well I thank you.'

'And who is this young maiden?'

'May I present, Miss Eleanor Ashlyn.'

'Pleased to meet you, Your Grace,' I curtsied.

'Ah, Henry's girl? Yes, I see it now, your mother's fine features,' he said looking me over with an impressed, but twitching eye and offering Sheldon a congratulating look as though he had just made a bid on a good Filly. I supposed to men of the Duke's years, women and fillies were not so different.

'So have you entered your horses?' asked the Duke expectantly, the crêpey skin about his nearside jowl still aquiver.

'Yes,' Sheldon answered and they set upon a rather dull and drawn-out conversation on what horses they were running and what stakes.

'And will you pick a horse, Miss Ashlyn?' he turned and said to me after a time.

'Yes, I have backed Mr Elmbridge's horse.'

'It's like that is it. Well, loyalty is all fair and well in some matters, but mark my words, there's no place for it at the stakes. My Regi's a fine horse, but I've put an insurance stake on the favourite all the same. Here's a tip Miss Ashlyn,' he tapped his nose and winked at me: 'Put a side bet on Gustavus—Hunter's grey, just won at the Newmarket Guineas, smashing good stepper.'

'Thank you, Your Grace,' I smiled appreciatively, trying to convey adequate gratitude for what he obviously considered no trifle of a tip-off. I liked horses as much as any gentleman, but the gambling and competition stakes were of little interest to me. I would perhaps put a guinea or two on Gustavus for the fun of it, but such drawn-out conversations on these matters I found a bore, and since that was all the conversation that filled the room, I longed for some diversion.

I looked over to Delores; without Mama or some other lady friends to converse with, she looked positively bored too. She was not minded for placing bets beyond the occasional rubber of whist and nor was she a fan of horses beyond their usefulness of transport, so I supposed she must be suffering more than I. I should have liked to get down to the trackside where I could see, through the window, such fine breeds being paraded about.

A footman carrying champagne flutes caught my notice as he passed by with a tray, but as I took a glass from him, Delores narrowed her gaze giving me a warning glare, took the glass from my still outstretched hand, and thanked me for it. I wanted to scowl at her as I watched her take a sip from it instead, but offered her a tight-lipped smile, noticing Sheldon watching me. When the Duke drew his attention back, I turned to Delores and said in a whisper; 'I suppose I am expected to go thirsty!'

'Shall I have some orange wine or chocolate brought out for you?'

'Thank you: No!' I said through gritted teeth and turned away from her entirely. We were both fed up, but at least she could enjoy a few cups to divert her ill mood. I was about to excuse myself from the party in search of something more interesting to capture me, when the Duke bade us farewell and Sheldon turned back to me catching me before I could go too far adrift.

'Sorry,' he said sheepishly. 'I tried to keep it brief.'

I smiled at him, at his knowing my mind. I knew my thoughts were not plain upon my face to ordinary onlookers, for I had been too well schooled to betray myself so vilely. And yet he understood what was behind my cool gaze as I dropped a parting curtsy to the Duke. 'It can't be helped,' I told him. 'Although I should really like to see the horses and get out of here before the races begin.'

'Then let us go whilst we have time.'

I shook my head. 'And give Delores a seizure. She might actually have to do something beyond putting up such a sulk.'

But when the squire arrived some moments after, Delores perked up remarkably and left us quite to ourselves, allowing him to steel her away to his table and fetch her another glass. I was grateful for his effect on her, and wandered out of her view, perfectly unnoticed. I took the opportunity to request Sheldon obtain me a glass of Champagne too. She would have kept me to orange wine all season if she had her way, save risking me getting a little squiffy and cause her any exertion in her duties.

Sheldon summoned a footman, procured a glass and handed it to me, our fingers brushed briefly and he paused a moment and looked at me with searching eyes. I took the glass to my lips and almost drained it.

'Thank you. This is just the thing.' I took another sip.

'Slow down, Miss Ashlyn. You will have me in bad credit with Delores if I return you in your cups!'

'Oh, dash it, she is far to engrossed with Sir John's company to pay me a groat of notice now. What say we go down to the fair and see what draws those crowds? I think us a little late for the horses,' I said, peering out to the track where they were taking their positions in preparation for the first race.

'Do you want me out of favour?'

'It is so full in here now,' I said looking around at how the salon had suddenly seemed to shrink in the masses that now filled it; 'she won't even notice our going. She will think us somewhere amongst the throng, finding a view to see from. Where is your sense of adventure, Mr Elmbridge?' I asked, putting down my empty glass and pulling him on towards the door.

A crack of sunlight that was breaking through a heavy expanse of cloud, warmed my face as we exited the grandstand and stood out upon the trackside. *Now, this is where the real merriment is to be found.* We squeezed our way through the crush of bodies to make our way over to the stalls and tents lining the perimeter. There were musicians, fire eaters, acrobats, performing dogs, stalls selling ale, wines and slices of suckling pig. Stands for games of pitch and toss and many blacklegs stands where people queued to place their bets. It reminded me for a moment of an evening at Vauxhall Gardens, a shabbier version indeed, but the spirit of the varied entertainments bore a resemblance, even if the guests were generally more heathen. 'I think I might place a little stake on the Duke's suggestion, if it will not offend you,' I said as we passed a stall with a more agreeable looking queue.

'You offend me deeply, Miss Ashlyn,' he put a hand to his heart and flashed a smile of jest. 'But I am a gentleman, and I shall not deny a lady her whim, even if she is about to lose her guinea!'

'How good you are, Mr Elmbridge.' I gave him a playful shove of rebuke, forgetting myself momentarily. *We are not in the school room anymore,* I reminded myself, and changed the subject, noticing the hope that blossomed in his blue eyes at my brief lapse in conduct.

The stakes were high. I wondered how many fortunes would be made and lost today. My own humble guinea bet was no more than a little jest for the sport of the occasion, but I had overheard sums as high as a thousand guineas spoken of up in the stands.

'Sir, will you buy some flowers for your lady?' I looked around to see a girl with flowers tied into neat bunches in a basket far too large for her small arm.

'I think that a very good idea indeed,' Sheldon said to the girl with a wink and bent down to pass her some coins and pick out a neat bunch of white chrysanthemums.

'For my lady,' he said with mischief in his eyes as he handed me the flowers.

'Thank you, they are very pretty,' I told him, patting them gently with my gloved fingers and smelling their fragrance as it wafted beneath my nose. *His Lady. Is that what he considered me?* 'Come, let us see what stalls there are,' I encouraged him.

'Keep your reticule concealed beneath your shawl.'

'Why?'

'There are pickpockets all about,' he said, and I searched the crowds no wiser for his saying so. I supposed the race winnings were not the only bounty at stake on a day like this.

We were stood on the edge of a gathering crowd, marvelling over an acrobat treading a high rope when I noticed Miss Craythorne, arm in arm with her stepbrother perusing the stall of a cigar seller. *So, she was about after all.* I had left her my card on our arrival yesterday, only to be told she was away and yet here she was. Should I consider it some intended slight, or perhaps that my message had not yet reached her? The sight of her brought me instantly back to our strange parting all those weeks ago; those odd kisses goodbye that had unnerved me somehow. I had revisited the memory several times since my departure, searching for a clue of what it was that shook me so. I had missed her company quite faithfully in the first few weeks, however much I had tried to resist the confession. London was exciting, chaotic and full of new faces and places, but somehow, even that had been no solid diversion from my longing for the wildness and irregularity of her company. The possibility that came with not knowing what must be expected next when I was around her, left me wanton. What had, at the time, seemed to be so shocking and uncomfortable, I now revisited with something of a diminished horror, even longing. I could not answer why her effect had left such a strange impression on me, and yet I felt it keenly as I looked her over from beneath my bonnet. She was dressed in fine fashion as usual; a Nakara day dress trimmed with blush ribbon. She seemed to be at ease and in happy spirits as she considered her brother's cigar choices with him, handling them and sniffing them like he did.

I looked to the blacklegs stall beside them and urged Sheldon on towards it. 'I think I must place my bet before I run out time,' I told him, not indicating that I had noticed Miss Craythorne or her brother in the queue beside us.

'Allow me,' he said, and I put my guinea in his palm and reminded him it was to be placed on Gustavus.

'I know, I know,' he said in mock disapproval and stepped up to the stand and waited for our turn behind a grubby looking man wearing a tattered sheepskin coat, which I could smell from here.

I peered across to Miss Craythorne; I watched the sun catch the gleam of her hazel eyes as she lifted a gloved hand to shield the glare. She looked up and laughed at whatever her brother had spoken next, and I saw the luminosity light up her face, softening her features. I was used to her more poker-faced demeanour, and noticed now, how much better this suited her.

'There you are,' Sheldon said stepping away from the stand and stuffing into my hand a small square of paper. 'A Guinea on Gustavus, to win,' he declared, and as we stepped out of the line, he led us directly in the path of Miss Craythorne.

'Oh, Mr Elmbridge, Miss Ashlyn, good day,' she said surprised, catching sight of us.

'Miss Craythorne, Mr Craythorne,' Sheldon and I chorused.

'You did not say you were back in town.'

'I left you my card only yesterday,' I said in a tone more accusatory than I had intended.

'Oh, well I have not been home. I am at Beddington presently, hosting another sports party.'

Had it endured at such length? At least it was not a slight. 'I see. Who did you bet upon?' I asked.

'My brother's horse: Ginger Neath, but I own,' she stepped away a little and lowered her voice, 'I had my groom go to the legs and put a side bet on Reginald, just in case,' she winked. 'Who is your money on?'

'I am backing Sheldon's *Lady Aruba*, and the grey colt over there with Mr Hunter: *Gustavus*. I am told he is a favourite.' I was aware I was rattling on, talking for the sake of it. I was nervous of seeing her again and I couldn't explain how she managed to reduce me to such a state even after such a time apart. But time had done nothing to neutralise the strange chemistry. I watched her lips moving as she spoke in her calm and cool manner, and remembered her pressing them against my own.

'Are you enjoying the day?' Mr Craythorne said, now stepping away from the stall and tucking his purchases into his coat pocket, directing the question and his gaze more pointedly in my direction than Sheldon's.

I gathered up closer to Sheldon. I had briefly forgotten our little misunderstanding, but now he looked at me—eyes sparkling—the calamity came rushing back. 'Yes, isn't it marvellous fun. Mr Elmbridge has procured us seats in Prinny's stand,' I said with a pride as though the triumph was my own. I caught him eyeing up the flowers I held and was glad he had noticed them. Anything to remind him of his error and my staunch disinterest was agreeable.

'Excellent,' he replied, but I got the impression he meant something altogether different. I hoped Miss Craythorne had done as bid in clarifying matters, but had this uncomfortable feeling from something lingering in his gaze that it had not had its full effect despite the time since elapsed. I still felt offended that he could have ever thought it possible...

'Yes, indeed. Have you entered any horses today, Sir?' I said for the sake of politeness.

'Yes, I have my filly running today. In fact, you must forgive me; I must change, I am set to race in the next heat.'

'You are racing yourself?' I asked surprised.

'Yes, I like to race my own horses.'

How irregular. He surely had the means to employ a Jockey.

'My brother has a love of being in the action, he trains the horses himself and although he is unwilling to admit it, he has a competitive streak, I think,' Miss Craythorne said with a fondness in her tone I was not used to.

Competitive streak. I hoped he did not think he had any hope of competing against Sheldon for my attentions, although I could not help notice something of a steely resolution behind his gaze that told me otherwise.

'I confess I am in the habit of winning when I have a prize in mind, Miss Ashlyn, wish me luck.'

'Good luck,' I said indifferently.

'Good day,' Sheldon wished him with outward equanimity, although I could feel how he had stiffened slightly and raised a protective hand over mine, which was resting upon his forearm.

He tilted his hat and set off into the throng.

'I must re-join my party: It was good to see you again,' Miss Craythorne excused herself, following on after him and taking up his arm.

Was it, good to see me? It was good to see her, but I felt her indifference in our re-acquaintance and it disappointed me. It had been much on my mind since our arrival and yet she seemed to have little care for staying back to converse a little further or suggest paying a call before us awaying again. I couldn't explain why I wanted to steel her away from her company and spend the day with her instead of Sheldon, but I felt it.

'I really don't like that fellow,' Sheldon said reflectively as we turned away and headed in the opposite direction.

'They are not sensible of our ways; that is to be sure.'

'No, it's not that. There's something, I cannot quite put my finger on it...'

'Well, let us be thankful that we are of the merest acquaintance,' I said quickly, in an attempt to put an end to the subject. I had a suspicion that whilst he could not have learnt of the previous misunderstanding betwixt Mr Craythorne and I, he had noted something in his demeanour that gave away a hint to it.

We walked on through the crowds and I paused as we passed a pitched tent draped with purple curtains, embellished with gold stars. I read the sign above its opening: *Madame Zola: Fortune Teller'*. 'We must have our fortune's read!' I said excited by the prospect of a little adventure.- Well timed to divert us, too.

Sheldon raised an incredulous eyebrow. 'What stuff and nonsense. You are funning.'

'I am certainly not funning. What's the harm in it? Come, let us have a turn, it might be amusing.'

'Amusing?' he was unconvinced, but obediently, even if with a hint of reluctance about him, let me lead him in to inquire.

'Hello,' I called out as we stepped beneath the heavy canvas drapes of the tent. The daylight shrank away as they fell closed behind us, only candlelight illuminating the cloaked figure who sat at the small round table with closed eyes, in silence and stillness. The interior was dressed in further layers of drapery, red velvet and the occasional swathe of orange cloth hung like a shrouding partition, setting a backdrop against the candlesticks and table laid with crystals of many varieties and sizes, strewn flower petals and burning sticks letting out an earthy, but not unpleasant scent as it wafted in curling grey swirls about the place.

'Welcome, welcome. Be seated,' came a voice from beneath the cloak suddenly as her eyes peeled open wide and abruptly, causing me to jump back a step after such a delay. We took our offered seats around the table and as Madame Zola dropped the hood from about her and her face flashed into the glow of candlelight, I was surprised not to see some old hag like creature, but a woman of moderate years, bright faced and fine featured, even if a little oddly decorated with over exaggerated ornaments at her neck and ears, her hair tied in an elaborate scarf so I could not tell the colour of the hair beneath it. Her voice carried an accent I guessed originated in some eastern European region, although whether it was authentic or for effect, I could not tell.

'Who would like to go first?' she spread a pack of cards across the tablecloth.

Sheldon offered me up and I nodded my agreement.

'What is your name child?'

'Eleanor,' I told her.

'Choose ten cards, Eleanor,' she directed me, and I did as bid and slid them across the table.

She scooped up the remainder of the pack and swept them away expertly, turned over each of my selected cards in turn, pausing momentarily to consider them, then closed her eyes.

I looked over to Sheldon and frowned my confusion, at which he shrugged his shoulders in response. I turned back to Madame Zola, she remained shut eyed, breathing long drawn-out breaths and saying nothing. I fidgeted a little in my chair and searched the room for some diversion. I noticed there were small pictures containing geometric style symbols, a brass bowl containing what appeared to be a variety of herbs and some kind of handheld drumming instrument and mallet.

'Eleanor.'

I jumped again at the sudden sound of my name and returned to her wide-open eyes again.

'I am connecting to your spirit guides.'

I repressed the urge to let out a laugh at this and bit down on my bottom lip to prevent it.

'You are sceptical. That is alright,' she smiled warmly then picked up one of the cards and considered it. 'I am told you are embarking on a new phase of your life, an exciting new beginning.'

I nodded.

'Your prospects are bright, Eleanor. But you must take care, when the world throws its many choices at your feet, you must be careful to make the correct one. Some will lead you to happy ends and others will just as soon lead you to depart from them.' She moved onto the next card and drew a deep breath before continuing. 'You have a traitor in your midst Eleanor,' she said with a start, as if hearing or seeing some invisible thing I could not and taking in its input before speaking. 'They will make themselves known to you in time, but by then it will be too late. Trust your instinct over those that call you to question it. Do not be careless in this Eleanor; it is vital you keep your wits for it is a wolf dressed in sheep's clothing that threatens you.'

'Come now,' said Sheldon in protest and I had quite forgotten his presence at all.

Madame Zola did not look over to acknowledge his speech but pressed on to the next card. 'I see you at a crossroads Eleanor, you are wise in many ways and yet still you have a great deal to learn about the world, about yourself, your own essence and truth has yet to make itself known to you. It will become plainer to you soon. You will come to question that which you thought would secure your happiness and realise that perhaps all that glitters is not the gold you are seeking after all. There is a happy conclusion to this realisation, however, there is a beautiful soul waiting to awaken you to your own.'

I swallowed hard and remembered Sheldon sitting next to me. Despite my curiosity and desire to question her on this further, she had already said too much for his hearing. I cleared my throat and thanked her for her insights, bringing the reading to a close. She understood my uncomfortable glance, smiled in acknowledgment of it and gathered up the cards.

I had not expected such a serious tone to the affair. I had entered the tent in mind for a diverting jest and found myself somehow taking in her words with a conviction I had not anticipated. A beautiful soul, was Sheldon that person she spoke of?

'Now, Sir, what is your name?' she had turned her attention in his direction.

'Thank you: no,' he said flatly. I could not tell if he was disturbed or disinterested, but I did not feel inclined to press him to it. I slid some coins across the table to Madame Zola, thanked her, and bid her farewell.

'Well, that was a waste of ten minutes and as many shillings,' Sheldon said once we had stepped back into daylight and the hustle and bustle of the trackside which had seemed quite a world away from the still little den of Madame Zola's tent.

'There is no harm in a little diversion.'

'Perhaps, but paying for such empty words. Charlatan!' he declared as if the words left an unpleasant taste in his mouth and he was spitting it out with them.

'Perhaps, but we must all do what we can to get along in the world?' I said reasonably, but I was really thinking that I was not convinced that she was a charlatan at all. I could not place a clear context to her words and they were indeed arbitrary enough to be suited perhaps to any person who sat in the chair in front of her, but there was something about her presence; her eyes, that persuaded me she intended at least, to speak the truth. 'Besides, it cannot be any worse than the man who collects a shilling for watching his dog do a trick or to stare at a freak. It's all folly.'

He could not disagree with this and seemed to shake off his distemper, for I could sense that even though he remained a sceptic, there was something altered in him since our going. He seemed contemplative and thoughtful but did not voice it. I wondered if, like me, he was considering whether it was him she referred to in her reading; "the beautiful soul" that would awaken me to mine, or whether he feared he was the glittering gold that would not turn out to make me happy after all? I pondered both possibilities.

'Shall we have a game of pitch and toss?' I offered to lighten the mood, then I dropped my posy with the surprise of hearing the gun sound to signal the commencement of the races.

I stooped to pick them up.

'I think, El, we should go back to the grandstand before Delores grows concerned for your whereabouts.'

'Very well,' I agreed. I had considered making a protest on account of her being only concerned for the squire's company, but decided against giving him the impression I had grown wholly radical in our few years apart. There was time yet, for him to adjust to that element of me that had perhaps grown a little stealthier in the years of our estrangement.

'We'll get a better perspective on the races up there too, there's no hope of making it out from here,' he said and I nodded my agreement, watching the thickly mounted crowds that clustered towards the tracks. They were cheering and chanting names of their chosen horses, elbowing each other out of the way to advance on a better view. A pistol had fired a second time and the thud of hooves upon the mud sounded through the hubbub. It was at least easier to navigate our way back now, with the majority of the masses migrating over there, leaving the sideshows and stalls abandoned. We made our way back, me clinging to his arm as he led me and trying to protect my bunch of flowers from a rising wind in the other. I caught sight of Miss Craythorne amongst a crowd of gentleman stood at the rail, leaning over and cheering the race as we passed them. I thought back to Madame Zola's words for a fleeting moment before I was whisked into the lobby of Prinny's stand.

'HOW WAS THE DERBY MY dear?' Mama asked when I came into the drawing room that evening.

'Good fun.'

'Oh, I am pleased you enjoyed it. Delores said you and Mr Elmbridge were getting along merry.'

'I am surprised she noticed. Perhaps, Mama, you might think of having someone chaperone Delores when the squire is about.'

'What nonsense, Eleanor, hush with such vulgarities. Delores and the squire have long been friends. You cannot blame her for showing some sympathy now his dear wife is departed.'

It was more than sympathy I had observed. 'Is my aunt and uncle back yet?'

'No, not yet dear. I daresay they have come upon acquaintances. I'm sure they will be home soon. Did you see them there?'

'I did not. There were thousands on the trackside. I daresay it will take them some time to make their way through the traffic.' We had benefited from a head start, owing to the rear exit of the King's Stand, I supposed purposed for the King's own swift departures whilst the masses made their exodus in the other direction. But I doubted they were stuck in a coach crush and considered it more likely they had stayed behind for the cock fighting and prize fights, but since they were now illegal, I didn't share this suspicion with Mama. She had enough qualms with this side of Father's family as it was, and was better left ignorant to such goings on. 'Besides, Uncle must retrieve his horses once they are rested. You know they did not come in for him,' I told her and took up my sewing.

I went back the next two days to the Derby, but insisted we sit out with my uncle's family on the trackside from now on. Had the weather proved ill, I could see the benefit of having access to the stand, but beyond that, I would much rather be out in the open air, enjoying the spirit of the event. It was far more exhilarating from this perspective than stuck up high with a brood of old gentleman getting in their cups and speaking wagers and politics most of the day. Sheldon was not minded to abandon me to such matters, where he could avoid it, but it could not always be avoided and anyway, I did not wish to stay solely in his company either. It was one thing to make a show to dispel any ideas in Mr Craythorne's imaginings, but another to be seen so much with Sheldon exclusively to form other opinions I was not sure I wanted to lend credence to. London had permitted me to distribute my attentions widely, but back here I was at risk of seeming in some way attached to him if I wasn't careful.

'I see you and Mr Elmbridge are becoming more and more the thing,' Miss Craythorne said to me with a teasing grin when I met her at the drinks tent during the finals. She was wearing a Pomona green dress today and pink and lilac feather plumes in an elaborate head dress that was neither quite turban nor bonnet.

'We are old friends; that's all. I see you have a number of gentleman *friends* of your own,' I said, referring to the fact that she was the only female in Mr Craythorne's party of a great many gentleman I recognised from his sporting event that day at Beddington. Mr Huxley, I was pleased to note, had not made the mistake of approaching me again, and I was relieved at not needing to explain myself to Sheldon on that head. Then it occurred to me; was this how it would be to be married to him? A pre-emptive fear of displeasing him arising whenever any gentleman moved into my presence? Something told me it was not just the way of the season, but would be the way of things to come. Would I shed one proctectress only to inherit another?

'Ha...them. No, they are not my friends. But my brother has not the first knowing of how to play host, so I could hardly abandon them all to his arrangements. Besides, Cuddington is a ghost town now you have all deserted it and I have little to occupy my time here. They have been very good company though, it's been a jolly few weeks.'

'Your father has still not procured a London residence?'

'He has been much occupied in The Commons, but assures us he has made viewings. He keeps to his hotel and insists it is no proper place to establish his family and so we must be patient.'

'But at this rate, the season will be spent before you join it?'

'Miss Ashlyn, I have no intention to participate in this marriage mart: I told you, nothing could be further from my mind. Although, to escape this dead bore of a town, I will go, when my father sends word.'

'I wonder why you would not hasten it. It is the best excitement I have enjoyed in all my years. I have never danced so much.'

'Oh, Miss Ashlyn, I have told you before; I have very particular tastes in the kind of entertainments I find amusing,' she swept a curl from my cheek and walked away, leaving me, as she often did, with a confused frown upon my brow and further questions rattling around my head.

My uncle's barouche was parked only a few yards away from Mr Craythorne's party. I had suggested the spot myself, remembering the reliability in which they had remained in theirs the past two days. I could see her from there comfortably, but with enough distance that our parties did not need to interact and I could remain entirely clear of Mr Craythorne. I had noticed how much together they were, but I supposed it was her way of keeping out of the grasp of the rest of the male party. She was certainly not fazed at being amongst so many men, as I observed her causal mannerisms, hearty cheers and laughter. She was so peculiarly odd in every way, although I could not quite decipher why it impressed me so when I knew it should have appalled me.

When the last races were announced and Craythorne departed to ride his horse, she found me in the crowd and took up my arm, casually, as if she had been with us all along. And when Gustavus came in first place after lagging in joint first for most of the race, I leapt up (much to Delores chagrin) and Miss Craythorne hugged me in congratulation. I saw the envy in Sheldon's eyes as she let go of me, I saw clearly how much he wished to have leave to do the same and it sobered me quickly.

'I will remember to give the Duke your thanks when I next see him at Brookes,' Sheldon said, a smile beaming.

'Yes, do. Although I have your Lady A to thank for yesterday's win,' I smiled back at him.

'Yes, you do seem to be on a lucky streak, but Gustavus has proved more lucrative for you,' he said.

'Has he?' I asked, searching for the betting slip inside my reticule.

'Yes, you have tripled your investment, if I remember correctly, the odd's were three to one, here, let me see,' he took the paper and nodded confirmation. 'Yes, three guineas due to you, shall we go and collect it?' he offered and I took his arm, in quiet disbelief at my trifling, but no less exhilarating win.

But on our way, I bumped into Mrs Ponwiker and sent him on ahead of me to make the collection whilst we exchanged polite prittle-prattle, that bored me swiftly and would have no doubt bored him all the more. When I made my excuses and sought out Sheldon's direction, in my peripheral vision, I caught sight of Madame Zola's tent and changed my course.

'I've been waiting for you to return,' she said with her eyes still closed as I stepped into the familiar tent with its opulent drapery and odd accoutrements. This strange greeting startled me though and as she gestured me to take a seat, I felt how stiffly I lowered myself into it.

'I would like another reading Madame, I—'

'Now you are not in company. That is better, yes.'

'Yes,' I agreed tentatively.

'Close your eyes, Eleanor.'

Her remembrance of my name surprised me too, for I was sure she must have seen many other persons since my coming two days ago.

'I feel your anxiety, just try to relax. Trust yourself, if you cannot trust me. Your soul would not have brought you here were it not for to give you this message. That's better, breathe slowly and deeply. There is nothing to fear, you are just tuning into yourself, your own energy, your own nature. Now, I want you to place your feet flat upon the floor, connected to the earth, imagining roots growing out from the soles of your feet, reaching down into the earth, the mud, the insects, the stones, the clay, the rock, deep into the earth's core, anchoring you to it.'

Maybe Sheldon was right, perhaps this was a crackbrained idea.

'There is nothing to fight, nothing to resist.'

I pushed aside the thought and focused on following her instructions, imagining green shoots sprouting from my feet and pushing their way into the soil.

'That's it. Just breathe and feel that connection.'

It seemed a peculiar instruction; I was sure I must have always just breathed since my birth, for I was not dead. Then I smelt the burning smoke of something freshly alight and opened my eyes. She was holding a bunch of tied herbs that were smoking light plumes of fragrant scent and wafting it around me.

'It's white sage,' she said as if communicating directly with my mind, for I had hardly said a word since my coming and, despite this, their definitely seemed to be a dialogue between us.

'It's cleansing.'

Was I in need of "cleansing"? I had always followed in the fashion of the Beau Brummell and took a particular care to maintain a good standard of toilette.

'Close your eyes. Imagine from your heart, a spring of golden light emanating from it, swirling its way around you like this smoke, above you, below you, beside you, until you are entirely shrouded in this beautiful light from every angle.'

I followed her voice, her imagery and created the vision she described whilst the sceptic in me fought to distract me from it. Then I felt her hands at my shoulders, a warm gentle pressure, then she let go, sweeping the air around me in strange movements, blowing then mumbling some strange words I could not fathom. As I considered calling a halt to this strange ritual, I was overcome with a sudden sense of calm and felt how light and easy my breaths were now.

'That's it, that's it,' she said, approving. 'Now—'

I opened my eyes to see what came next and was relieved to find her back in her seat, sat opposite me.

She spread the cards across the table and instinctively I picked out ten and sat patiently whilst she went into her trance like silence. I supposed she was "connecting with my spirit guides" again.

I glared at the selected cards with their exotically decorated backs face up to me, and wondered what strange illustrations and messages lie beneath them. When Madame Zola, several seconds later, opened her large, hooded lids and flipped each card over in turn, the pictures upon them left me none the wiser for the revealing. I frowned at a picture of a skeleton riding a horse with the word 'Death' written upon the bottom. *I should never have come!*

'Do not be alarmed,' she said without looking up. 'Change is in the air for you, Eleanor, do not be afraid. You see, in order to transform, we must first let the old self die.'

I let out an involuntary gasp.

'There is nothing to fear, it is a metaphorical death. For when we die, we are reborn. We must be willing to part with the old, in order to embrace the blessings of the new. The death card symbolises, not your physical death, but the death of an aspect of your life that no longer serves your truth, the person you need to become.'

I had no intention of changing or being "reborn", whatever I was supposed to make of such a statement.

She slid her gaze across to another card, depicting a burning tower and I rolled my eyes. I did not come for ill-news. I came for answers; all I seemed to receive were further questions.

'You will get the answers you seek, Eleanor.'

She *is* reading my thoughts. I was not imagining it.

'Great change is afoot. I know you have not accepted it yet, you may not even realise it yet, but your soul yearns for deep change, for liberation. You will not be the same person you are now, by the time this process has run its course.'

Well, that at least was realistic, I would likely be married soon, much was bound to change and I would be liberated, from my parents, Delores, and their protocols and close guarding, I supposed. 'You said, last time, that there was a traitor in my midst?'

'Yes.'

'Well, who is it?'

'Someone you will not expect, so you must be vigilant. There are people around you who would lead you astray to ill ends. It is inevitable your paths must cross, it cannot be avoided, but their purpose is to light your path for you, not to walk it with you.'

Well, that narrows it down…

'I do not see the faces or the names, but I can feel their presence; their jealousy, their cunning. Your own wisdom will guide you if you allow it. If you pay attention and take care not to get swept up in their plans for you.'

'It is expected I will marry soon, can you tell me anything from these cards about that?'

'I do not see a wedding just yet, but I do see great love in your future, deep devotion, a very beautiful connection,' she paused as though listening and smiled. 'But you have not yet met, it is not yet time. There are things that must alter before you are ready, some challenges ahead before you unite.'

So, it could not be Sheldon, he was not the beautiful soul she described previously. 'So, I am to wait for this knight in shining armour, without knowing who he is, or when we shall meet?'

'I cannot tell you what to do; only what I see. But I can tell you that you will not marry this love.'

'I will not marry them?'

She shook her head.

So, I was either going to end an old maid in the wait, or marry someone I did not love and what, take a lover? I was not Anna and it was certainly not how I envisaged what I or my parents had in mind for me. I did not want a loveless marriage, nor did I want to be unmarried past my prime. 'Whyever, will I not marry them, if our love is to be so deep and devoted, it does not make any sense?'

'There is an obstruction, I believe, a class divide. In fact, they would usually fall beneath your notice.'

Great. So, I was going to fall in love with some middling sort that my family would not approve of when I had the opportunity before me, to perhaps become the next Viscountess. I was certainly regretting my digression to come here now. Sheldon! He must be wondering where I have gotten to.

'I must go, I—'

'Before you do...'

I sat back in the chair. There was something serious in her tone that I did not question.

'I have one last word of counsel.'

'Yes?'

'You must not rush into accepting a proposal, it is imperative, that should you choose to marry at all, you are certain, absolutely certain, that this person has your interests at heart; it must at least be a match of great care and consideration for it cannot be one of love.'

I felt my furrowed brow ache with the riddle of all this. 'But you said there would be no wedding yet?'

'I said I did not see a wedding, not that you will not marry. Eleanor, the reading shows me insights, they are there to guide you, not to walk the path for you. You have free will and you can decide which path to walk at any given crossroads. But be warned, some roads we begin to tread cannot be easily un-trod. If you marry the wrong person, you may, unwittingly tread upon such a path.'

'Are you saying I am in danger of doing so?'

'I am saying that I can see you will have many options, many competitors for your hand, and this variety, could lead to many different outcomes. Some mediocre, some slightly more satisfactory and some, downright dangerous. The former, I am guided to warn you from.'

'But you must tell me how to know such a man, how to see him coming so I can avoid it!'

'I'm afraid that is beyond my knowing.'

'So, you warn me of oncoming danger and then give me no means by which I can recognise it!'

'You already have the means: your insight, your gut feeling; that will be your guide, if you take care not to silence it.'

When I stepped back outside the tent I felt disorientated and regretted going only to receive such a puzzle of unpleasant news.

'Good Grief! Where on earth have you been? I've been searching high and low for you!' came a voice, startling me as my eyes readjusted to the daylight glare.

'Sheldon.' I held a hand to my throat in fright. 'Forgive me, I—I got distracted.'

'I thought something had happened to you, we were about to send out a search party!'

'I'm sorry. I did not realise I had been gone for very long. I needed to use the chamber pot and then there was this dog doing all sorts of clever tricks and I...'

'Well, you gave me a fright. I wish you would have told someone; taken a chaperone. I only turned my back on you for a moment and found Mrs Ponwiker quite abandoned. Why did you wonder? There are all sorts of fellows here.'

'I'm sorry, I didn't think.'

He took my arm up protectively and led me back towards our party. Well, if he was not to be my true love, I could at least discount him from the dangerous' suitors category and relegate him to either the satisfactory or mediocre realms. Did I want a mediocre or satisfactory marriage? Would it be better to remain unmarried so I was at least unclaimed for my true love's arrival? It seemed outrageous that I could even think of falling in love with someone so below my station it would prevent our marrying. I did not even mix in such circles that would permit such opportunities, did I?

The season was not yet done. I supposed not every person with an invite to society events was a good candidate. I supposed there would be second sons without good prospects and a few rakes. It seemed so terribly tragic: I would find the kind of love my heart longed for, but when I found it, it would be beneath my grasp. Of course, she could well be a charlatan as Sheldon had seemed convinced. Nay, I knew she was not. But mistaken, yes, I was sure that was a possibility, that she had got some details muddled or misinterpreted the messages somehow. She said herself, she could not see everything.

Invitation to London.

June 1821. - Eleanor.

A letter was waiting on the salver when my morning chocolate was left at the bedside when I awoke.

Miss Ashlyn, I know you away back to London later, but I really must speak to you before you go. Please meet me in the usual spot at 10, if you can make it. Miss Craythorne.

I told myself I would not go: that I should not go, and I wondered as I stood under the cover of the trees at nine-forty-five, how I had managed to talk myself in and out of the meeting so many times.

'Thank you for coming,' she said with some relief about her expression when I found her pacing the clearing of woodland in a pale blue morning dress.

'I do not have long, pray what is so urgent?'

'Have you spoken to Martha over that misunderstanding with my brother?'

'No,' I frowned, 'I confess I could not find the words. I felt so dreadful after how it ended up, I thought better she forget about it now she was of out of town,' I said with a brief reminiscence of our uncomfortable parting, that day at Beddington. The truth was, I had tried and failed to confess my blunder to Martha more than once since then, as she indulged in animated recollections of our day at Craythorne's estate and complaints at him not seeming to be about London. I hadn't the heart to correct her, to tell her to put him out of her mind, besides, with him not about, there seemed no need to intervene when the attachment would be thought to naturally fall away after such an absence.

'Good,' she said, in that matter-of-fact way I had grown used to accepting. 'Now, I cannot give false assurances, and I cannot pretend he was not disappointed at the confusion, but I do hold some influence with him and, although he has not agreed to the match with Martha, I have tried to bring him around to see the sense in *considering* it.'

'You have?'

'He is a sensible man, Miss Ashlyn. I cannot own that he was at all taken with her, for her circumstances are difficult, but, he does not need to make a money or a love match. Nor does he have time for such wooing or attendance on societal affairs that might assist in him finding a wife. I am convinced a prudent match would suit him well, and now that I am helping him to see the matter more wisely, I think I can bring him about to Martha and the benefits of joining our family to one of such a name. Whatever her troubles are now, I understand her family name to be well known and well regarded.'

For a moment, I wanted to snatch her up and squeeze her, but I composed myself remembering that was not such a sensible thing to do. Things had not improved for Martha, even in London, despite the greater audience. 'This, Miss Craythorne, is very happy news indeed.'

'I will need your help; you understand.'

'But what can I do?'

'Nothing too taxing, just helping me to find the means to bring them together in each other's company a little. Of course, they need only a chance to see if they might go along tolerably.'

'But that will be quite impossible now; we are off again this afternoon. And it is certain we must go today since Mama will be busy hosting at Almack's this week—'

'That is a shame. I own if I am to have his ear, I will need the opportunity to encourage his consideration of her and that is quite impossible if–'

'You must find a means to come to London Miss Craythorne! Has your brother procured a place there yet?'

'Sadly, no. But I have pressed him to look more keenly, and he assures me that now the Derby is over and his guests departed, he will go to London directly to settle things—he means to travel up this week. I have marked out several advertisements in *The Times* for him to make viewings of.'

'That is very good, but you cannot stay in his lodgings until then; most impolite for a lady, you will need a more respectable address. Have you some acquaintance that will be in London? You might stay with them a while.'

'Unfortunately, not. My father, only this morning, conveyed a letter home, informing us that he has now instructed his attorneys in regard to the purchase of a place on Wimple Street, and he will send for us as soon as things are settled, although it could be yet a few weeks.'

'But the season will be done with by then and everyone headed back here anyway.'

'There is that. But it could wait I suppose until you all return. Although it would be tight, I know he is to away abroad on business in July.'

'Then I wonder, Miss Craythorne, if until then, I could petition my parents to agreeing the matter, if you might perhaps come with us, as our guest, just until your father's affairs are settled?'

'I could not impose...'

'Leave it with me; I shall make a try, and if I manage to win them, you will have but three hours to be packed and ready.'

Mama of course did not like it well, but Papa was so much in Mr Craythorne Senior's pocket, I knew he would not refuse me, however much mama sulked, and she did; for the best part of the week. Delores was not best pleased either at the prospect, learning that Miss Craythorne was quite without her own chaperone and not even 'out' in society. But it had been agreed for her to stay a week, so I reminded Delores of the fact that her additional burden would be a short one, and she tolerated it as well as could be expected.

Mama and Delores' sulk had a very happy side effect that suited me so well, I wish I had understood its effect earlier and had invited her back in April: with the exception of guarding us at season events, neither of them wished to be much in our company at all, which left us free to make our own plans during the day, even if we did have to drag the groom and maids along for them. I took her to parade with me on Rotten Row in the barouche and to pay calls to as many acquaintances as I thought would not mind my bringing her, and we even managed a few shopping trips when time allowed for it, leaving us much opportunity for planning and scheming on Martha's behalf.

But the evenings were more difficult to appease, as she had so few invitations to fill them with, whilst I was never about above a costume change, however well I tried to sponsor her. So I sat out a few of the later affairs when I could, and spent them with her instead. But I was not willing to give up my Wednesday at Almack's, or my invitation to Lady Rossiter's on Saturday night. She did not seem to mind this and said she was happy to entertain herself and would take an early night.

It seemed that the bustling society of London, despite being her true homeland, was as foreign and fascinating to her, as her travels across Asia and Europe were to us. And it was indeed the case that wider circles than ours had become interested in her tales and travels from faraway places since my friends' retelling of the success of her small party in Cuddington. There had been some suggestion that the Craythornes should throw a proper affair with the theme, but Miss Craythorne was quite disinterested in the notion and I am not sure, grateful enough of the compliment of such a suggestion.

Martha, being in her precarious circumstance was spending this season in Curzon Street as Bethany's guest. The cost of another season was hardly feasible under the circumstances, and she would have otherwise missed out on her last shot of trying to turn her fortunes. Not that she was having any success so far. She was not the greatest catch without her troubles, and although Mr Nash remained out of the Fleet by a whisker, their house on Mount Street being put up for auction, but a week into the season, had not helped matters.

But Mr Craythorne had come to London at last, and even though we had seen him only twice: I was pleased at the more deliberate attentions he afforded in Martha's direction now. It was clear he meant to make a favourable impression on her and whilst he was clearly no romantic, he paid her the proper attentions and she received them gracefully now. I was only grateful that it was Beth and not I, that had to hear out the greater share of the fuss over it, after being afforded a couple of dances or brought a glass by him, for I knew what it was to endure her excitement after a great deal less.

Miss Craythorne's company had been far less taxing, even if, sometimes unnerving. But she knew to behave much more prettily under mama and Delores care, for their dislike of her presence was so thinly disguised it often made me uncomfortable and I knew she had the measure of it. We had already passed five of our seven promised days here, and I knew better than to attempt petitioning an extension, having pushed my luck already.

But it seemed this was not to be despaired over now, since she now had updated news that the house in Wimple Street was expected to be ready any day now, and she was invited to go and see it today, whilst her father had a rare moment to spare from The Commons.

Her father's valet picked her up in his carriage at eleven and I took the opportunity to slip off to Almack's to petition a stranger's ticket, in the hope of procuring one for her, since it seemed she would now be about for this week's assembly. I had thought better than to try through Mama. I had a hope that Lady Sefton might be at King Street today, in which case my application might be simple enough.

When I stepped from the coach and joined the line around the building, I had not expected to find Anna in the queue. 'What are you doing here?'

'I am charged with getting tickets for Martha since her family can't trump the voucher price and her May voucher has expired.'

'Oh, I see. Is that what the donations were for?' I remembered now the covert collection Beth had orchestrated amongst us the other night at Grosvenor House.

'Why have *you* come?' Anna said puzzled, and I assumed that she thought having mama amongst the patronesses would spare me such inconveniences. I explained to her that I was hoping to obtain a stranger's ticket so that Miss Craythorne could come as my guest and she rolled her eyes.

'Then where is she?'

'Oh, at Wimple Street, her father has just taken a house there.'

'Well then, how do you expect to get her one? She is supposed to come with you.'

'Is she?'

'She is expected to have an interview with the patroness to decide it, so I don't see how she can do it in her absence. But—well, you might get special treatment on your mama's account I suppose. I would have thought you would have asked her to arrange it anyway over standing about in queues.'

'Mama has no wish to grant her an application at all, so I could hardly use her connection.'

'Oh? I had it on-dit that Lady Elmbridge was endeavouring to support their applications—outrageous that she should—but all the same, I would have thought that would have brought your mama around?'

'Not so, and believe me my father has as good as instructed her to do so, but she cannot bear the idea of having them wriggle in. And whilst my mama is quite powerless against my father's head in most matters; she knows that even *he* has no power to sway her vote at Almack's.'

'Well, I cannot fail to understand her concerns, they are justified—I mean, *I* would not object to the odd dance with Felix Craythorne, but let's face it; if they gain entry, they may as well open up the floodgates to anyone with a purse to pay the voucher fee. But, if you do not share them, then you must not petition the Patroness for a ticket at all; unless you wish to cause Miss Craythorne harm?'

'Of course not, but whyever should it?'

'Because if you apply for her guest ticket and she is blackballed, as sounds likely if any of the other patronesses are in accord with your mama's sentiment, and I'm sure your mama may rely on Lieven whatever else, then so will her voucher application be denied and she must suffer the scandal of it.'

'Truly? Just for a guest ticket?'

'Yes. I forget this is your first season. You will not remember Florence Lovell last year, but a similar affair ruined her, and *she* was at least worthy of a voucher, although Lieven voted otherwise—you ask Betsy for the details, she will happy recount the tale for she did not like Florence at all, owing to them both setting their sights at Colonel Delaware.'

I vaguely recalled a memory of Betsy's complaint against some debutante, but I could not recall the details.

'I mean, you might stand a hope since it's Lady Cowper in the Blue Room today, and if anyone shall grant it, she might, given she let Caroline Lamb through the door, but do not be surprised if she is later blackballed by the other patronesses,' she shrugged.

'In that case Anna, I shall not go to her. Thank you for your counsel; I should have made quite the blunder if I had not happened upon you.'

'Indeed—Eleanor, what is it about you and that family?'

'I don't know what you mean?'

'Yes, you do, and don't say it is on Martha's behalf for there is something more to it than that!'

'I happen to like the Craythorne girl, her company is diverting, that is all.'

'I own her conversation is refreshing, and I even understand the novelty of your acquaintance to some degree, but surely, Eleanor, you must see that it is one thing to tolerate her in the country but quite another to try to sponsor her in London... Almack's?'

'What harm can it do to show a little charity?'

'Well, I hope you are right. For if you succeed in this campaign, Eleanor, and she disgraces herself, she will by default, disgrace you too.'

'Thank you for your warning, Anna, but it really is not necessary. You have seen that for yourself.'

'So far perhaps...'

WHEN WEDNESDAY CAME, I struggled to quell my excitement at the prospect of the assembly, as it still remained, above all else, the highlight of the week. But owing to the fact that Miss Craythorne still had no voucher, I took pains to try to moderate it in her company. I was tempted to petition Mama myself to submit to her application, but having already inconvenienced her so much with taking her in as our guest, I thought better of it. Besides, although our agreement had been for her to stay just a week, I had, after much consideration, decided to make a try to extend her stay after all, and would save mama's nerves for that petition instead. It turned out that the house in Wimple Street, although now in her father's possession, needed new furniture for the bedchambers before they could move into it, and so it was likely take a little longer yet. I hoped that if mama could be convinced to agree another week, since this one had gone smoothly, then she would be able to stay in town and maybe put on some little soiree's of her own, so that Martha and her brother could be more in each other's company: For although a few liberal hosts had permitted them entry, there had been no more invitations in their direction yet, and the opportunities for them growing more intimate were fading fast. If we could not rely on the Almack's applications, then the house in Wimple Street, they could play host at, at least, beds or not.

'IT IS GOOD TO HAVE your company to myself this evening,' Sheldon said before the opening Minuet. 'I take it your new protégé will not be joining you tonight?'

'Ha, well she is not my protégé; but I did consider trying for a guest ticket, but I was warned better of the effort. I thought your mama had intentions to support them in it?'

'Yes, I believe she means to bring it off eventually, so I suppose I must make the most of the advantage of her lack of presence whilst it lasts.'

'So you have taken against her too?'

'I was never *for* her in the first place, but if you must know; my protest is solely on account of how much her company keeps you from mine.'

'Fustian! How can it? I am hardly at liberty to roam London at my leisure in your company Mr Elmbridge, and she hardly makes it out of an evening as it is. Last night was quite the rare exception.'

'For now, perhaps.'

'Well, we have only a couple of weeks or so left, so you've had a good run,' I teased, jabbing him playfully with my fan, before I abandoned it to my chair and took his arm.

The next dance he had pledged to Martha, and I was grateful to him and remembered why we were fond friends and felt glad we had repaired the damage to our friendship. I watched him line up with her for the Cotillion as I took my partner's arm to join them; Mr Stanton had offered me this set and he was pleasant enough company, although I was certain he had his gaze fixed upon Clara. Which was a sad shame for him, because she was but a few days from taking her vowels and as I watched Mr Allerton lead her into the dance, their glittering glances all for one another, I could see theirs was a love match and she only had eyes for him.

Exhausted by the dancing and the heat in the assembly rooms tonight, I was very ready for my bed on our return home at three. I had quite forgotten Miss Craythorne altogether, until I noticed the glow of candlelight from the crack beneath her closed door, as I journeyed to my own chamber. My aching feet told me to go straight to my room, but a hint of sympathy for her being up and alone at such an hour, induced me to knock at her door and at least bid her goodnight. I gave the door a gentle tap and when no answer came, opened the door a crack. 'Oh my, Miss Craythorne! I did not know you were engaged in your...your toilette, or I should not have troubled you,' I said, stepping back and trying to pull my senses together at seeing her laid out upon the chaise with her maid knelt at her feet, her shimmy pulled up to her waist and her legs spread asunder.

'Nonsense, come in. It's nothing to answer, it is simply that dreaded time when I must attend to the task,' she said, unruffled as her maid spread another layer of sugar paste upon her. The very smell of the stuff was enough to evoke the pain of the memory and cause a shudder to creep over me. 'Now, sit down beside me and tell me all about Almack's, I should be happy for a diversion.'

I hovered undecided. I supposed I must be glad that it was not someone else that walked in and discovered her in this fashion. Although it would not occur to Mama or Delores to do so at least. 'I will tomorrow, I am so fatigued and you are busy.'

The maid pulled the paste from her groin and I watched her wince a little as she tore it away again.

'Your conversation would be a welcome distraction.'

'It's a mystery to me why you endure it. I own I cannot see the need?'

'I like to keep myself in good order. Besides, it is more uncomfortable the longer it is left, so I prefer to keep on top of the chore.'

I came fully into the room now and perched on the edge of the armchair and watched her wince again as the maid pulled another ball of paste from her. Another shiver crawled up my spine.

'So, I gather you shan't want another try at it?'

'Thank you: No!' I was quite satisfied to stick with my own fashioning, rather than endure such a trial again. I had been grateful at my re-growth now I was lumbered with Watts or the housemaid for my assistance. If Molly had found the shock too much, I could only imagine what Watts would have made of the scene. It was still short and sparse compared to usual, but I was happy to see the evidence of its removal gone.

'It wasn't all bad, was it?' She smiled and narrowed her eyes.

This time, I took satisfaction in the jarring wince she expressed at the next pull. 'I am quite certain it is not to my taste. Anyway, I am to bed now. Goodnight,' I said quickly.

IT WAS TO BE HER FINAL day with us before it was planned she return to the country tomorrow, and I still had not found the nerve to petition an extension. To make matters worse, our invitations today were impossible, and it seemed as though she would spend much of the day, as well as the evening, in our absence. I scanned my journal over breakfast, looking for something that might be possible to put off to spend even an hour or so in her company if it was to be her last, but there was nothing to be done. We were invited to Clara's Wedding Breakfast just after noon, and then, allowing to spend a couple of hours there, I had about an hour's turn around before we were due at Lady Sefton's musicale, and then at best, another hour and a half gap, before the first ball of the evening.

She had said she did not mind the fact when I explained to her the difficulty when she joined me in my chamber whilst my hair was being fashioned. She would take a peruse along the shops at Bond Street, for she had a fancy for some new hats, and to see what inspiration she could find for her new bedroom furnishings, and I made sure to put a housemaid and a footman at her disposal before our going.

It had been a happy morning spent, seeing Clara as a bride in her beautiful gown and glowing smiles, and how well suited the pair seemed about the table. Even Betsy, had relented and had agreed that they seemed well fitting, after all. But the breakfast had finished late, setting the whole day up for calamity and setting us on a pattern of unpunctuality for everything else.

It had been beyond fashionably late to walk into Lady Sefton's drawing room half an hour into the concert and distract everyone from the opera singer, with our shuffling to our seats. And on the way back from it, we were held in a tailback leaving Arlington Street, where a carriage had turned over at the junction of Piccadilly, forcing us to turn about and take a detour up St.

James's Street, to cross it. It seemed everyone else had resorted to the same and we crawled along it painfully as the time ticked on. It would have been quicker to walk the journey back at this rate. Still, this was my most generous break in the day and we had a little time to play with at least. I drew the window down on the coach to let in some air and held in a gasp and double glanced at the sight of a familiar figure, crossing the road a little way up. 'It cannot be!' I said without meaning to.

'Whatever is the matter?' asked Delores, sitting up in her seat and following my gaze with beady eyes.

Thankfully, she was on the wrong side of the carriage to glean my view with any clarity. 'Oh, nothing to concern us,' I said swiftly and shut down the privacy blind. 'Women, walking up the street alone here.'

'Vulgar creatures,' Delores hummed, relaxing back and I was relieved she had not managed to check my observation, for she too would have recognised Miss Craythorne, if she had done so. Mama would put her out this very night if it got back to her that she had taken to walking St James' Street and alone. I wondered what she must be thinking, for I had taken great pains to put the servants at her disposal.

'Probably a street walker,' I said vaguely and settled my gaze on the view out of the opposite window instead.

'And what do you know of street walkers?' Delores bristled, turning to me and staring at me boldly.

'Nothing in the least really,' I lied, 'only that was what Edmund would always tease Henry about.'

'Well, your brothers did like to taunt each other. Pay no mind to it. That is no such language to pass a lady's lips.'

I nodded my agreement. *Whatever was she doing in such a place?*

Any notion that I may have mistaken her for some lookalike was abandoned when we arrived back in Berkeley Square and I marched straight to her room and found it empty. Bentham advised me she had been gone all afternoon and had not said where she was to go— refused the offered chaperone of the maid and the groom he had made her. I bid him to keep the fact to himself and admit her quietly into the house when she returned, which I suspected would be any moment soon, since it had taken us so long to get back.

I sat in the receiving room over a pot of tea so I could hear her come in and counter any catastrophe should Mama or Delores emerge from their chambers and discover the situation. Thankfully, when I heard the ring of the door, they kept to them, and I was out in the hall quicker than Bentham, pulling her into the receiving room before she could say a thing.

'Wherever have you been?' I said to her more scolding than I had realised until I saw the defensiveness rise in her expression.

'Out for a walk, what is the matter?'

'I saw you, Miss Craythorne.'

She held her hands up in front of her. 'So, I didn't take the maid, adzooks!'

'That is bad enough, I own, but to be seen walking in Piccadilly; St James's Street! Have you gone mad?'

'What of it?'

'I told you plainly on our arrival: ladies do not walk about such quarters where all the gentleman's clubs are, you must know it?'

'Your customs here are so very odd,' she said with a frown, peeling off her gloves. 'But if you must know, I went to visit my brother, and since he lodges at the Grenier's, I had little choice in the district.'

'You went to a hotel? Did anyone see you?'

'I have no idea, I did not pay attention.'

I sighed into my palms. 'My God Miss Craythorne: If you cannot have a care for your own reputation, at least have a care for mine. You are our guest and my friend, what you do reflects upon me!'

'I am sorry for it then, I did not mean to do you any harm. I am sure I have not.'

'Whatever was of such urgency you had to go to him at this hour?'

'Nothing urgent.'

I noted a shifty glance about her eyes.

'I simply wanted to see how he was coming along with Martha.'

'Oh.' This appeased me a little. 'And how is he coming about?'

'Not as well as I hoped. He has made no effort to call on her. Indeed, he has not seen her since we last did. I do despair at him, unless I lead him to it directly, he does not act. I think we must initiate some excuse, some outing to put them together.'

'Very well, but you may have to go without me; it is all too busy now and as it stands, you are to be leaving tomorrow, unless you are able to go to Wimple Street?' I had still not found the words to approach Mama, and given today's calamity, I had begun to doubt whether I should.

'Not yet, but not to worry, I will think of something. Now,' she crossed the room and took off her Spencer, 'I hope I am forgiven?' She brushed a hand upon my cheek and stared hard at me until I felt unable to look at her. 'I hate the idea I have upset you. Tell me you forgive me it and I promise not to repeat it.'

'Yes, quite,' I said, pulling back. 'But please have a care, Miss Craythorne, and abstain from meeting him in such places at least.'

'Whatever will please you, ma chéri;' she said in a tone that toyed with me in some compelling yet uncomfortable way. I went directly to my dressing room in a pucker. I could not shake this ambiguity in her intentions whenever she behaved in these flamboyant styles that confused me so...

A goodbye kiss.

June 1821. - Eleanor.

It seemed I was to be spared any inconvenience in making an appeal to my mama (even though I had decided against making one anyway) for Mariella had the bold audacity to go to my mother herself, without even warning me. If I was not so annoyed with her for sneaking about without my knowing, I might have found it comical to think of her putting her case to my mother and compelling her into agreement of extending her visit.

She had brought me this news, and a note from her father over breakfast, which I was taking in my room today on account of an early morning ride with Sheldon. Mr Craythorne Senior had asked her to enquire as to whether Lady Ashlyn would have any objection to keeping her to stay another night, as a delivery of furniture was expected at Wimpole Street tomorrow, and she might be spared the journey of going back to Cuddington for the sake of a night. I understood then how my mama could not have refused such a reasonable request, especially one made so directly on the spot.

I handed her back the note and reminded myself it was just one more night, and I was again, to be out most of the day. There had been a lull in the schedule I had pencilled in, to see her off on her way, after my ride this morning, but it was only an hour, for I had promised myself to accompany one of my newer friends, Miss Pembroke, to see the Elgin Marbles at the British Museum this afternoon. And whilst I supposed I could have included Miss Craythorne in this outing now she was to stay, I did not feel inclined to, given yesterday's howler. Besides, Miss Pembroke was of very good ton and I could not be certain of trusting Miss Craythorne to behave well about her.

So, I went about my day as planned and spent only the hour set aside for her, in her company. She knew I was displeased with her, even though I made no further mention of the affair. She spent the time—which we went walking about in Hyde Park—trying to make it up to me, behaving prettily and amiably throughout. But I could not take the risk with her, even if I had relented a fraction through the morning. She was proving too much of a liability, just as everyone had warned me she would, and now I was so well known in London, I could not afford to be disparaged on her account. It had been a mistake to bring her here, and very little had been achieved by it; her brother and Martha still no further on than genial terms, and my having to abandon her to the house for the greater part.

Perhaps once she was set up in Wimpole Street, it would be easier to find more time to be about her, for any misdemeanours on her part would not reflect directly on me as her host, if I took a step back and let her find her own feet here. But as far as my own sponsorship went, I was minded to take much greater care now.

SHE WAS STILL HALF awake when we arrived back from the Cowper's in the early hours of the morning. I found her slumped over a copy of *The Epicure's Almanack* on the library chaise with the candle burned out. I felt a little sorry for her then; seeing that one of my brother's old books was all she had for company tonight. I was minded that tomorrow I would spend the morning with her until she went off to Wimpole Street, perhaps even go along with her and see her home.

'How was your evening?' she asked, sitting up, rubbing her eyes, when I stirred her to tell her to go to her bed.

'Good.'

She reached into a stretch and afterwards, grinned and said, 'Ah, do I sense that Mr Elmbridge may be responsible for your answer?'

'I do not spend all my time in his company you know.'

'You must tell me everything,' she said standing up and gathering her shawl.

'There is nothing to tell.'

'Nonsense, I saw how happy you were when the pair of you rode back this morning.'

I had not realised she must have been watching us from a window.

'I am coming to your chamber, and you will give me all the evening's news since I could not see it all with my own eyes!'

'It is past two in the morning,' I protested, but I felt a little sorry for her that the most exciting part of the evening would consist of my retelling of it. 'Very well,' I relented, 'but half an hour, and we will have to be quiet or Mama will complain.'

We both went off to our separate chambers to be undressed and made ready for bed, and shortly after the refreshments I had sent for had arrived, she knocked at the door. We sat on the rug by the low fire and arranged the trays about it. It reminded me of happy days, before my sisters left to begin their married lives. It seemed somehow impossible that I would soon be following suit, and yet there was still a great part of me that longed to be back in the time we would all sit around in Harriet's chamber eating cakes and ices when Mama thought us tucked up asleep.

Tonight, we snacked on sugared almonds and jellied fruits. Miss Craythorne was propped against the foot of the armchair upon the cushions pulled down from it. She fingered a sugared lemon slice before dropping it into her mouth and wincing at the bitter-sweet tang.

'So, will you tell me what has put such a smile on that sweet mouth?' she asked when she had finished chewing.

I frowned at her description and swallowed my half-chewed almond in a gulp. I sometimes wondered if her time abroad had deprived her of a proper comprehension of her own language, with some of the odd references she made.

'How many dances did you favour Mr Elmbridge with tonight?'

'Two. Why?'

'Don't think I have not noticed how well you have begun to enjoy each other's company of late, just because I am kept at home in the evenings. You seem remarkably changed from how I remember you at Cuddington.'

'Well, we are becoming somewhat better reacquainted but—'

'Stuff and nonsense! What passed between you this night?'

'Nothing of significance; it was the usual affair. We chatted and danced a little, and then Delores got side-tracked with the squire's invitation to dance the waltz, leaving us quite alone in each other's company, so we went for a turn about the place, that's all.'

'Then why do you look so distracted?'

'I am not distracted. I am only tired.'

'Puh! You kissed him, didn't you?'

'Of course not!' I said far louder than I intended, snatching the carafe from her hand. 'You have some very strange notions, Miss Craythorne.' I poured us both a glass of lime cordial and pushed hers towards her on the tray. 'You must take pains to abandon this habit of saying such extraordinary things.' It was this I feared would hold her back the most in society. I was only grateful she did not make such errors beyond our own company or the others would cast her off in an instant. For, with the obvious exception of Betsy, they at least, had been good enough to accept our calls in London, even though they had made no effort to pay them in return.

'Well, what did he do then? You cannot think to blow me off without answering when your face tells me that something has passed between you this night.'

I let out a sigh. 'It is his birthday tomorrow and he has invited me to dine at Park Lane and afterward to go to the theatre with him.'

'Well.' She shrugged.

'The thing is, he has not invited anyone else to go, and I know for certain his mama is not at home tomorrow as I heard her tell my mama so.'

'And that is all?'

'All?' *How could she fail to understand the meaning of such a request?* 'What else did you expect? Miss Craythone, you are quite impossible sometimes. I wonder why I bother to tell you things at all.' I could hear the ringing of my exasperated tone in my ears. I should have known better than to seek her counsel on matters she was insensible of.

'So, will you go?'

'I do not know. I am in a quandary over it. Even with Delores in tow, it will seem too intimate. I wish he would have thought to get a small party up at least. But it shall be just the three of us if I accept. When I asked what he wished for on his birthday, he said: that I would accept his invitation. I said, I will think about it.'

'Well, then think, and if you decide against it; get him a snuffbox or some such thing.'

I laughed behind my hand. 'My goodness. The things you say. It is no more appropriate for me to buy him such a gift, as it may be thought to sit alone in his box with him at Drury Lane—and anyway, he does not take snuff.'

She shrugged and filled her palm with sugared almonds. 'Perhaps let him kiss you then: I am sure that would make a birthday present he would not object to, and it may be managed in secret without the Drury Lane audience, unlike your singular attendance upon him.'

'I am grateful he would not try such a thing.'

'Would you dislike it if he did?'

'It is not a question of what I would or would not *like* Miss Craythorne, it would be a scandalous thing indeed, regardless.'

'It's a shame; you would have an even greater smile on your face now if he had taken the trouble.'

'I would be perfectly mortified.'

'Perhaps for a second or two, but then you would come to adore the sensation of it and forget your anxiety altogether.'

'How is it you have so much to say on the things that go between a man and a woman when you remind me often, you shall never marry?'

'I understand more than you might expect and more than perhaps, I should, however regrettable.'

I sat up a fraction. 'Miss Craythorne, do you mean to say you have done such things with a gentleman?'

'Yes, I have been kissed before and not politely.'

That explained a lot, and as disgraceful as I found it, I could not feign disinterest or resist the welcome distraction from my own anxieties. 'By gad!' I exclaimed, spilling a trickle of cordial down my arm and onto the rug. I hoped it would not stain but was too enthralled to pause to wipe it up.

'I own, I had thought him in love with me; until my father broke the engagement on the grounds he had debts beyond Paris that would only be settled by a doubling of my dowry.'

'Good grief, what a scoundrel. I am sorry for it, Miss Craythorne.' I supposed that explained her resistance to the idea of marriage now.

'Do not be. He meant little to me indeed. I have been far more aggrieved by lesser acquaintances I assure you.'

'Then why ever would you agree to engage yourself to him if you felt so little regard?'

'I cannot be sure now I think back on it. A moment of folly perhaps; that I shall not be repeating.'

'Well, I see why you would feel so reluctant now after such an unfortunate experience. But you must know that not all gentlemen are so contemptible. You must simply find the better ones.'

'I am in no mind to think of it at all. I have realised since my brief liaison with Monsieur di Patrierre, that it was in fact a narrow escape to be relieved of him, rather than the slight and scandal my parents considered it.'

At last, I understood the reason of their coming to London; in Paris she was tainted with the dishonour of a failed engagement to a rake. 'I feel quite aggrieved for you; I did not know your family had suffered so much.'

'We do not suffer. As I said, I celebrate the turning out of things the way they have, for it would have been a miserable existence to be tied to such a man before I understood enough of myself, of what it was to know true love.'

'You have been in love with another?'

'I have known love.' Her eyes clouded over with a longing I was astonished to witness. 'Anyway,' she said, dissolving it and refocusing her eyes in my direction. 'We have talked quite enough on that head. Now, pray tell me the strength of your regard for Mr Elmbridge?'

'I do not know in truth. I am flattered and fond of him of course, and he is no way disagreeable but, I am confused—'

'You forget to say handsome—I think?'

I felt myself colour a little. 'Yes, I suppose he is.'

'You do not feel a greater affection toward him?'

'Sometimes I wonder if I do, but how would I know it if I did? What does it feel like, to be in love, how can you tell it apart from any other kind of fondness? For there is a great deal of fondness between us, but there always has been.'

'You can tell because you will be full of no other thought or feeling that does not relate to their being, because your heart will beat faster in their presence and when you are separated from them, the grief is more to bear than you thought possible to manage.'

'It seems, I am not in love with Mr Elmbridge then.'

She laughed a little. 'It does not begin that way of course; it starts from something more subtle and grows into the way of it over time. That is the difficulty in the knowing in the beginning.'

'When did you know you were in love?'

'When the only thing that mattered anymore was being attached to them.'

'But you are not attached, are you?'

'It is impossible that I can be in the usual way, but in my heart, there is a great attachment.'

I wondered who she could mean and why this mystery object of her affection could be so disagreeable to even the Craythornes that they would deny their daughter the match of her choosing with a fortune as great as theirs and no name to trifle over. 'I did not mean to bring so much melancholy to mind.'

'You have not. In any case, I am grateful for the diversion of hearing your news. So, are you certain of Mr Elmbridge's affections towards you?'

I nodded.

'He has spoken then?'

'Not exactly, or not directly at least, but he has made the hint.'

'Hmm. So do you know whether there is any real intention behind it?'

'What can you mean? Mr Elmbridge would never be so unfeeling as to pay false attentions to a lady, I assure you.'

'Well of course not, intentionally. But perhaps he is, like you; coaxed into it by his family and has little choice.'

So, it was obvious even to her, kept so much out of it, all the meddling to throw us together. 'I had never thought of that.' I felt suddenly foolish for never having considered the possibility that he was in the same position as me: Pressed and prodded into settling. It would make so much sense; his delay in asking for so many months, seeming always to be on the cusp of so doing but putting it off, his frustration at me, all that nipping and watching over me before. Had he just wanted to get the matter settled and over with? Oh, how dreadful that I had taken for granted that all his attentions must be a matter of genuine regard, when he might only be doing his duty to his family. He was their only son, and they must be keen for him to leave his own heirs early under such a circumstance. Indeed, men of Sheldon's years were not much minded for marriage, yet a while. I thought directly of my brothers who had made no attempt whatsoever to settle down, even though they were almost eight years his senior. But he was not like them. I knew him to be a dutiful son, and how little choice an only son had when they were destined to fill such big boots; when the line might die out without your haste to insure against it. I felt suddenly queasy at the imagining of his parents and mine, beating him into this all. Not realising he might be under the same weight of pressure I had felt myself. *More*. Perhaps that was why he had seemed so improved of late since our clearing the air and growing more comfortable; maybe he was relieved I felt the same way and was grateful of it. He had been so much more relaxed since then.

'Are you alright?' Mariella asked.

I had forgotten her altogether. I nodded.

'It is not to be despaired of, Eleanor. You simply need a little proof, a sign of something to reassure you.'

'Like what?'

'Some *real* affection. A little kiss would not hurt to test his feeling or yours.'

'I told you, things are not done that way here. And if they were, I would not wish it anyway when I myself am not certain of my own affections yet.'

She let out a sardonic laugh. 'Of course they are; they are done here as they are all over the world in matters of the heart, the difference of course, is that here, things are done with far greater discretion.'

'Maybe it is so in the society of Paris, but I think you are much mistaken that it is so here. I have heard of ladies and gentlemen thrown out of Almack's for a great deal less than what you speak.'

'Only because they were careless enough to be caught. I have no doubt that if either you or Mr Elmbridge attempted to undertake the mischief in some private place where you could not be discovered, you could very plainly know what each other's true feelings were.'

'That may be, but I should never think of it. To make such a bold attempt and have him think me fast would be reason enough, besides—'

'Then you must provoke him into the temptation of trying it: then it would be quite impossible you could be blamed? You must simply provide a private enough opportunity and enough enchantment to test whether he can resist you.'

'Even if I knew how to play such tricks, I would not.'

'Then you know not your own power; for you would have to put very little effort into the trying.'

'I think solitude has driven you to insanity. I cannot believe we are speaking on such subjects.'

'I speak from experience, not insanity.'

I was desperate to hear the details; however disinclined I was to attempt to replicate her example. 'Monsieur di Patrierre?'

'Yes, but I was not aware of his intentions when he came upon me. It was only after his attentions that I began to understand my own power and learned to better use it. Once you have mastered this, everything else is simple.'

'What did he do to you?'

'Come here and I will show you.'

I moved in towards her expecting some form of abstract demonstration. Not the light movement of her lips trailing the length of my neck and my shoulders before bringing them to my mouth. I recognised instantly the excitement I had felt on other occasions when she had pushed the boundaries of our intimacy to peculiar heights. But tonight, I was not simply surprised by it; *I willed it.*

'You see,' she moved back enough that her lips were now only brushing mine, 'there is nothing to a simple kiss.'

I was not ready for her to stop for it seemed there was a great deal more to it than nothing. Something inside me had begun kindling at the pit of my belly, and I liked the sensation.

'Now, you imagine I am Mr Elmbridge, and try it on me.'

I did not want to pretend she was him, but I did want to try it again, so I brought my lips to hers so they were touching and tried to mimic the movements she had just demonstrated.

'That will not do,' she said, pulling back. 'You are like a shrinking violet. You must do it with confidence; with meaning. He will see in your eyes something that will take his breath away before you even touch him. Look, stand with me and see how I approach you.'

I rose with her. She was standing proud, her chin dropped slightly at an angle but her gaze raised seductively to mine. In her eyes there was ferocity, a determination in them I had seen briefly before but not at such length and such intensity before. It was affecting and intimidating in just the right measure to startle and compel simultaneously. When she came closer and kissed me again, I felt the improvement in it.

'Better?'

I nodded.

'Now, you try.'

I was nervous, but intent on finding another excuse to enjoy the sensation again, so I ran through what she had done in my mind before imitating it; the courage, the intent, the promise and then the purpose in the movement as I seized her mouth. Even I felt the difference in the passion of it.

'Well. If you do to him as you just have to me, I am sure he would not deny you anything.'

Him. I had quite forgotten the object of this practice. 'I cannot do this to him.'

'You cannot or you do not will it?'

'What difference does it make? Anyway, he would think me so fast that even if he did have serious intentions, it should certainly put him off of them. No one wants a dasher for a wife.'

'Believe me; if he wants you, he shall like nothing more than to taste your mouth and much more besides.'

I raised an eyebrow.

'I guarantee it. And I guarantee you will be a nervous wreck when he pops his tongue into your mouth, if that is how you react to a gentle motion of the lips.'

Tongue in my mouth?

'Shall I show you, Eleanor, and kiss you like a gentleman will wish to, with true passion?'

I swallowed the nerves as the intention in her face resurfaced and I realised that this time was not a rehearsal.

'Yes,' I murmured.

She took me by the chin and pushed her tongue into my mouth in one smooth movement that left me quite astounded. I could taste the faint tang of sugared lemon upon it as I adjusted to the strange sensation of feeling it against my own. She pulled back, paused to look at me again. 'Will you let me touch you like a gentleman would wish to?'

I did not know exactly what I was agreeing to, but I nodded and watched a devious smile spread across her face. But before I could reconsider, she took to my neck and began licking and nibbling at it. I jumped at the surprise and then thought I would fall down with the pleasure of it. But she held me up with her strong slender arms, took my weight against her body as I weakened and fell into tremors of delight and longing, a longing she was working up intentionally, I knew. I also knew that she understood its effect, and how to quell it, and I did not know whether that was to be feared or rejoiced in, for both emotions were competing against each other as I felt her devouring me, touching me, loosening the ribbons at the neck of my chemise. This was not a practice, this was not for Mr Elmbridge's sake, this was a determined attack on my senses for its own sake and I did not know how to contain it as it spun out of control. Her hands were fast, her kisses determined, growing hard and unrelenting. She let go only to take me to the bed and in that brief moment of our separation, I began to panic. She sat me down on its edge but stayed on the ground standing in front of me.

'So many gentlemen would like to do what I am about to do to you. Do you know that, Eleanor? Have you seen the desire in their faces as they behold you?'

'Of course not.' She was undoing her own ribbons as she said it and I watched as the neck fell wide and slack around her shoulders: Her breasts only half covered by the muslin.

'Well, you will see it hereafter,' she said, and she seized my mouth and my breasts in one violent movement that stunned me so much I could not stop her. Even when I felt her pull the neck of my chemise wide open and her hands beneath the muslin, coaxing my nipples out from beneath it. She was twisting them between her finger and her thumb as she pushed her tongue into my mouth and feasted on me with a lack of restraint I had not thought possible. It made me so dizzy I could barely believe it was happening at all, let alone find the strength to make any protest.

'My god, you are a delight, aren't you?' she said between kisses, pushing and grappling at my breasts still, leaving me in no doubt that everything that had come before was intended to permit I let her ravish me in such a way. She pushed me back onto the mattress and clambered over me, and as I attempted to sit back up and refuse her, she pushed me back down and I felt her mouth at my breast, licking and nibbling at it as she had my neck and it froze me: Suspended me in the delight of it.

What was this persuasive corruption she attacked me with? How could I want so much to let her continue when I knew it so contemptible? I felt her kisses disappearing from my breasts, moving down between them, further towards my navel. I wriggled around beneath her wet mouth in shuddering spontaneous jerks of pleasure, but even through it, the fear had grown more palpable and I put my hands on her head to stop her and brought her back to my mouth. Then she stopped altogether, lifted her face to look at me before pulling me back up to sit. It suddenly seemed so much worse now I could see her face. She was still smiling but her eyes were glazed over with a hue of tenacity she had never allowed to show before. But it was quickly replaced with amusement as she observed my reaction to her taking her bare breasts out and bringing both my hands up to touch them. I recoiled from it moments later than I had meant to, but suddenly her power over me was lost, and I felt nothing but panic and disgust as I watched my tentative fingers hold the weight of her breasts.

'I want you to touch me, Eleanor. I want you to do to me what I have done to you. Don't be afraid. It will bring us both such relief.'

'No, Mariella.' I had always refused to use her *Christian name*, but it seemed just to come out now of its own accord, 'I cannot do what you ask.' I was struggling to find the ribbons around my shoulders to retie them as I pulled the sleeves back up and ushered her away so I could stand. The disappointment in her face was poorly concealed as she stepped aside to let me pass.

I went straight to the window and opened it to get the fresh air I suddenly longed for. The curtains flapped around me and I closed my eyes and let the force of the breeze engulf me. *What are you doing? What have you done?*

'Eleanor?'

The sound of her voice made me wince. She was up close behind me, reaching around my waist. 'Do not be afraid, nothing is changed?'

'Everything is changed. I think you should go to your bedchamber now.'

'If it is your wish. I only wanted to please you, Eleanor. But we can soon forget this ever happened if you want it to be that way.'

'Yes, yes that is what I wish.'

She fell silent but I did not query her.

The relief of her going was immediate, but with her departure came waves of shame and disbelief I had not anticipated. I closed the window and slumped into the nearest chair. I already knew I would not sleep for hours even though I needed my rest if I was to stay out late again tomorrow. I thought of Sheldon then, and I could not even consider how to proceed in that direction with my head swimming with so many thoughts. *I will tell Mama I am unwell in the morning.* That would both relieve me of seeing him again until I had time to think things through and spare me going to her new house with her in the morning as promised. I could not even think of how I would manage to bear such proximity to her now. I wanted never to see her face again. The sooner she was packed off to Wimpole Street, the better.

Betsy's ill-timed relent.

June 1821.- Eleanor.

The next day when I awoke, I was pleased to feel some subsidence from the shame of the previous night's antics, but when I rose for breakfast and found her note left for me on the mantle, I realised she had already been in my room before I had risen, and the revulsion returned in floods.

Dear Eleanor, I have just popped out to Bond Street (with the maid) to collect some of the furnishings I ordered the other day. I did not want to wake you, as you seemed so very tired. I shan't be long and hope you will still be about for me to say farewell to. My papa is sending his coach for me at five. M x

I tossed it into the fireplace and picked up the newly arrived edition of *La Belle* to distract myself. But as I turned the pages and sipped on lukewarm chocolate, I could not prevent the replay of it all in my mind or decide upon how to comport myself with her until she was gone. Why five? Why not first thing in the morning? I sighed and scratched around in my head for ideas, immediately discounting the easy way out, which would be to feign illness to avoid her. I had the displeasure of the monthly curse today, but I couldn't afford to play that line since it was Sheldon's birthday today, and whilst I remained undecided on that count, I would want to wish him well today, whatever was decided.

I heard the shuffle of hooves outside and stood up from the table to get a view out the window. It was her stepping out of the coach and directing the groom to load her boxes down for the footman. I sighed and found myself soon ushered into the drawing room to see her wares, or at least that was what I suspected, when I came into the room.

I had not expected to find my Mama and Delores sitting on the sofas and making an audience to her shopping exhibition. I sat down quietly so as not to interrupt her animated speech as she fished around in a band box.

'This,' she said to my mama, 'is for you, Lady Ashlyn, a token of my gratitude for having me to stay,' and placed into her reluctant hands a small box. She followed suit turning to Delores, 'And this is to thank you for keeping watch over me,' and then she turned to me and said; 'and for you Miss Ashlyn, for being so good as to invite me and show me about London.'

I forced a smile and peeled back the paper to find a pretty silk bookmark with a scene of Paris embroidered into the centre with a pretty beaded trim and tassel fringe. 'Thank you, Miss Craythorne,' I said complaisantly, 'it is very good of you, but you really should not have taken the trouble.'

'Indeed, what a pretty pastille burner,' Mama said, turning about a fine celadon porcelain in her hands.

'Thank you, Miss Craythorne,' Delores added, it is most thoughtful of you. She was holding a delicately crafted needle case in ivory.

An announcement came at just the right moment to interrupt this uncomfortable scene of thanks giving, which, once spent, mama and Delores took pains to trouble over questions about Wimpole Street and her other purchases, whilst I sat quietly reflecting on things I would rather forget. But when Mary announced our caller to be Lady Elizabeth, it had not been the welcome diversion of mama's callers I had hoped for, and I wanted to vanish altogether. Could this get any worse? I could not see how. But I could not turn her away with excuses: things were fragile enough between us as it was, and if she was here at all, it was a peace offering, I knew. So I braced myself to receive her.

'Betsy, what a happy surprise,' I said when she came into the room behind Mary. It would have been if it were not for the company she found me in. I wanted to tell her I was sorry, she had been right all along about Miss Craythorne. Instead, I sent Mary for refreshments and offered her to sit.

Mama and Delores took her arrival as an opportune moment to slip away to the small sitting room after some polite exchanges with Betsy, and suddenly, it was just the three of us sat stiffly about the sofa's, sipping on lavender lemonade.

'So, Miss Craythorne, how do you like London?' Betsy said as she put her glass upon the small table and settled back into her chair.

I was positively astounded.

'I have found it most agreeable,' Miss Craythorne said with a smile I did not like the shape of. I knew this smile well, understood the innuendo it conveyed. I could only hope that Betsy would not consider it anything out of the ordinary.

'Well, you have had a good host.'

I shifted in my seat and did not look at Miss Craythorne. I had expected eventual forgiveness from Bets, even an improving tolerance of Miss Craythorne if I persisted in our acquaintance, but I had never imagined Betsy making a contrived effort to show a change of heart. Under better circumstances, I might have privately revelled in this moment of Betsy making up to me, in an attempt to put our friendship back in favour, but today it was all I could do to wish it otherwise.

'Indeed. She has been most attentive,' she smiled in my direction this time and I feigned interest in reaching for my glass. I momentarily had the thought of throwing the contents of it over her for toying with me publicly like this. If things were not bad enough. *Betsy, of all the company to make an audience of.*

I sat passively listening to their awkward exchange. I knew Betsy's tolerance was a long way from her liking of the matter, and she was too used to her own way to hide it well from me. But she was trying. I reached for the carafe and refilled my cup: I must have finished the last without notice, for their cups were barely diminished when I looked to them. A week ago, I might have felt relieved, grateful of Betsy's efforts, but how could I say that I did not want her accepted amongst us now. Now that I had come to realise what a terrible idea it had been to try to help such a person find their way into good society. I could just imagine it: the shock and scandal of her pulling such stunts on one of my friends given the opportunity. I thought back to how quickly she had progressed in her actions upon me: the strange pictures, dances, Mehndi patterns; it had all been leading to her attack on me last night. Now I had refused her, who would she prey on next? Anna, Beth, Martha? And who would they look to, to blame for such a vulgar acquaintance when it all came out? *They* would not afford her the discretion I had. The thought made me nauseous. *What have I done?*

'Well, Miss Craythorne; it seems to me you have been very fortunate to have seen so much of London already. I think Miss Ashlyn has done you a great service. I do hope you are grateful of it.'

My consciousness re-joined the conversation just in time to intercept. 'Not at all,' I said quickly, offering about the plate of plum cakes.

'You are too modest Miss Ashlyn; you have been so generous to me, I half wonder how I might deserve you,' Mariella put in and I managed to contrive a fleeting smile in her direction.

This double entendré was becoming intolerable now, as had become the sight of her face, the sound of her voice or even the rasp of her breath. For a moment I imagined tipping the plate of cakes into her lap. I carefully placed it on the table instead and shot a glance over to Betsy to make sure she could not detect her meaning. It was not easy to get something past her notice, but it seemed she was appeased with Miss Craythorne's apparent show of gratitude. Of course, Betsy would never consider the likes of her to be deserving of as much, but to be sufficiently grateful for it would prove some consolation in her mind.

'Well then, perhaps Miss Ashlyn would be so good as to bring you along to our card game tomorrow evening at my house. It is a small affair, but a popular one no less. Unless of course; Miss Ashlyn has forgotten my address of late?'

I laughed along with her. 'I would of course be happy to bring Miss Craythorne, except she will no longer be my guest.'

'Oh?'

I understood Betsy's relief at this news; it was but the briefest flash in her eyes that gave it away.

'Yes, she shall be busy I think, furnishing and packing into her new chamber at Wimpole Street where her father has just taken a house. Perhaps another time, when you are not so busy?' I said pointedly to Miss Craythorne now.

'Actually,' said Miss Craythorne, finishing her mouthful of cake. 'I would be grateful of something to look to after so much dull organising. Thank you, Lady Elizabeth, you must give me your direction.'

Impossible. I attempted to make reply but must have inhaled a crumb of cake into the wrong part of my throat for I was suddenly seized by a most violent coughing fit.

'Take a drink,' Betsy encouraged me whilst Miss Craythorne tapped at my back until it gradually abated.

'Are you well, Eleanor? You seem out of sorts?' Betsy asked, offering me a handkerchief with which I dried my streaming eyes whilst steadying my breath.

'Yes; just the usual monthly ills.'

'Ah that. Well then, I shall leave you to rest and recover and see you tomorrow. Come for eight-o-clock won't you,' and she passed a calling card to Miss Craythorne to furnish her with her address.

'Indeed, I shall. But Miss Craythorne, you are not much for cards, are you?'

'It is true I am very poor at gaming, but I would greatly appreciate the improvement of watching you all play well at it.'

'Excellent. Until then,' Betsy stood to take her leave of us.

I felt my heart sink, *How had I let this happen?*

When she tied her bonnet and made for the door, I made an excuse to follow out after her and catch her up. 'Betsy, I don't understand?' I said, running up beside her and tugging at her elbow.

She paused at the front door and looked at me. 'Of course, you do. I have not seen you for more than a week and I have heard nothing else but her name and her tales in my ear from the others, so I will tolerate her, for your sake. That is the best I can do. After all, if I cannot have faith in your judgment, then who can I?'

'I cannot ask that of you, Betsy.'

'Well, you seem to be asking it of everyone else, so unless we are no longer friends; I think you shall.'

'Of course, we are friends, Betsy, you are my closest friend and it will take a great deal more than a new face in Cuddington to set that apart.'

'I'm glad to hear it. For a moment you had me wondering. I was beginning to fear I would suffer no greater conversation than the others could offer in your absence.'

I laughed, even though there was nothing at all funny about this situation I had sunk us all into.

'Well, you could at least look pleased at your triumph?'

'Forgive me, I am grateful.' What else could I say? That she was not fit for our company after all? That I had been mistaken? That my judgement was in want and out of sorts just lately? That she was not the straight-forward eccentric I had first considered her, but a debauchee who had induced me into lewd behaviours I had never before contemplated? That I feared she might try to corrupt us all with such tricks?

IT WAS ONLY WHEN WE sat in the barouche in the afternoon (on Mama's insistence that a ride and some fresh air would do me good as I had seemed rather pale today) that it dawned on me that those were not my only complaints at Betsy's invitation. Firstly, there was the fact that although I was minded to avoid Miss Craythorne once she was gone from the house, I would now be forced to endure her company as soon as tomorrow night, which would be as disconcerting as I felt it now; being forced into polite prattling for the sake of convincing Mama and Delores all was well. But more worryingly, was the great benefit it would do her in being received at Grosvenor Square by Betsy. The other invitations it might lend to, if she appeared to have not one, but two prominent sponsors. It would certainly indicate to the others of our set that they could now make visits upon her and include her in invitations. Cumulatively, the effect could be more far reaching then I could permit myself to imagine with all of them extending her these courtesies.

I came up with various ideas on how I might try to backtrack or counteract this outcome. There was the obvious one of asking her directly to decline the invitations, but I knew she would not. There was the option of asking Betsy to retract the invitation, but she would want an explanation that I was not willing to offer. I could make my excuses not to go and hope she might cry off too, but if she did not, there would be no one about to regulate her at all. It seemed an impossible bind, and I had tied the knot myself.

I reluctantly accepted the ice the waiter held out to me, the melting pistachio cream dripping onto his white gloves as he passed it into the carriage. Just when my relief at returning to Berkeley Square was tangible, Mama decided on a whim, that we should first stop at Gunter's and park beneath the trees to indulge in eating ices before returning home. I spooned the melting cream back into shape as it attempted to escape the goblet and ruin my own gloves. I was usually amenable to such folly, but today I had no taste for it; nor for anything beyond my solitude.

'Well, I must say, I quite understand the novelty of this fashion better,' Mama told Delores. She usually complained at having Gunter's as a neighbour and at all the traffic of having parked carriages all about the square in the afternoon from such custom, but now she had quite succumbed to the novelty herself, it seemed to matter not.

'In fact, I think Mr Elmbridge might like to join you next time for such a trip.'

I held in a sigh. I had enough to think of without revisiting that dilemma just now. I looked at Mariella, spooning her ice in small and delicate mouthfuls, outwardly seeming quite the proper lady. Either Mama and Delores were learning to become tolerant of her, even if not favourable, or I was in a horrid nightmare and I would roll over and open my eyes to my canary bed drapes any moment.

It had all seemed such a battle to bring about, making her acceptable, tolerable even, and here I was having suddenly succeeded in it. If only I might undo it all. If only I might go back to the night in the picture gallery and decline to see those paintings. Or tear up the calling card she left me for the next day and refused to go to her. Even after that, there was still time and opportunity to retract, but I had squandered them all, and now I could not see a way out. I contemplated scheme after scheme but could find nothing but blind alleys or dangerous consequences. In the end, I gave up scheming altogether, reminding myself that I may not need to do anything at all; in time, she would show herself up. Hopefully, just enough to provoke distaste for her company with some small solecism that might prove sufficient to avoid any sizeable scandal that would implicate or reflect upon me. But then it occurred to me, as I watched her showing courteous deference to Mama and Delores, just how capable she could be of the correct behaviour in company. If there was something else I had learned of her since coming to London, it was her chameleon-esque talent for adapting her behaviour to her audience.

I looked up again and caught her staring in my direction. Quickly, I looked to Mama and Delores to check their notice and was relieved to find them too engrossed in their own conversation to care for the lack of ours. I leaned back in my seat and closed my eyes against the sun's glare. It was all I could do to stop meeting hers and reading the desire in them. I longed to be home so I could escape to my chamber and have at least the protection of walls set between us for a time. Oh, how I longed for the clock to chime five-o-clock.

When it did, and her father's coach pulled up in Berkeley Square, her things loaded into it, I let out a sigh, moved away from the window and sat back down to my toilette. I had decided, upon consulting my mother, that I would attend Sheldon on his birthday after all, if she would be persuaded to accompany us to pair the party and take some of the heat off the affair. And so, I sent him a note, telling him such and wishing him many happy returns.

This proved a welcome antidote to such a taxing day and as the curtains drew back at Drury Lane to signal the beginning of *Dirce: or The Fatal Urn,* I felt myself starting to forget my troubles in his easy company. We had a good view of the stage from the Elmbridges' box, being mid aspect and in alignment with the dress-circle, but the heat inside the auditorium was somewhat dense and suffocating tonight with the increasing June warmth, that whilst had so far proved hot during the day, still had a chill about the air at night, enough to require the kindling of a very low fire. Tonight, however, with the press of so many bodies into the space and the extravagance of so many candle lights burning bright, it felt how I imagined the Bengal heat to feel in Miss Craythorne's sketches. I pushed the thought away as it began to lead to other thoughts I did not wish to entertain. But the more I tried to quell them, the more they began to taunt me and attempt to rise up and mount an attack on my consciousness.

As I watched the actors upon the stage cross it in shrill and bellowing song, they were interrupted by scenes of my holding her breasts in my hands, then the opera would startle me back to the stage set before it was replaced with another; the view of her face as she kissed me and I opened my eyes to peep at her as she broke away. Then I remembered the taste of sugared lemon and the feeling of her kisses at my neck. The heat seemed almost to smother me now, and when the orchestra de-crescendoed and the curtain fell to signify the interval, I knew I must step out to take a little of the night air if I was to manage to sit through the next act. I accepted Sheldon and Delores' escort as Mama stayed behind, stepping into the Sefton's box beside us and prattling on some Almack's matter that seemed of some importance.

Delores shadowed us as we paced in front of the theatre house whilst crowds spilled out from the theatre entrance and formed about us; groups of gentlemen lighting up cigarillos and a few, like us, remaining beneath the portico and taking a reprieve of evening air.

'Are you enjoying your birthday?' I asked him as we found our eyes settling upon each other's.

'It is the best birthday I have had in an age,' he said, without affectation.

'Well, I am glad to hear it. But I shan't set too much store by it since the last couple you have spent rattling about other the Alps or some such other terrain, supping on Inn fare.'

He laughed a little. 'Very true. But this one will prove memorable for greater reasons than the fare. Although you shall never hear me confess so in front of my mama, who is quite taken with her new French chef and always singing his praises.'

I smiled. 'The dinner was very fine. I shall have a care to make mention of the fact the next time I am in your mama's company.'

'You've no need to flatter my mama; she is already won over in your favour.'

At this, Mariella's words came back to me and I was certain the horror of them must have shown in my face, for he said to me then:

'Don't be so surprised by the fact, why shouldn't she think well of you?'

I shrugged. 'Well, you know I have a patroness for a mama too and they are very particular creatures I find.' We settled into laughter but this haunting thought did not disperse with it. I studied him carefully; the way his eyes glittered and shined in the light of the theatre entrance gas lamps, a smile not just at his mouth but in the contours of his face beyond it. Could he really be pressed into this by his parent's wishes, and if so, was he in accord with them for their sake or in his own right? I hated the ambiguity but knew I would make us both so uncomfortable to enquire so frankly. And if I did, what would I say? I could level with him perhaps and say that if his parents were behind this, then he may be at ease and relieved of any burden in that direction, only...only I was not entirely sure anymore if that's what I wanted to say. I had allowed my preoccupation with her company to divert me from so many things, I now realised. And I found myself wishing to make amends for such neglect. In many ways, he was still Sheldon the boy as I remembered him, but there were other parts of him I did not recognise at all. There was a time when I could guess his response and opinion in most matters, but now I lacked the knowing and was surprised and impressed by how he had altered. I recognised in him the development of his character as Sheldon the man; he had grown wiser and more confident in the understanding of not only the world, but who he was and where his future was heading. I had often wondered how he might grow into his father's footsteps and become the Viscount one day, but I could see it now: the possibility, the capability.

I saw him searching for clues to understand how I had altered over the years, but I knew he had no greater hope of fathoming that quandary than I did. I was neither Eleanor the girl he remembered, nor Eleanor the woman who understood herself or her future well anymore.

Gaming.

June 1821 - Eleanor.

The house on Wimpole Street was incredibly grand with its six storey high and five window wide facade. They didn't seem to do subtle. I got the groom to slow the horses to a canter as we passed it so I could peep behind the window blind and take in the view. She had left me her card this morning whilst I was out walking with Miss Pembroke; an invitation to come to her at my leisure and the address scrawled upon the back of it. I had no desire to return the call having just re-acclimatised to her being gone from our house, but as I returned from conveying Miss Pembroke back to Cavendish Square, the temptation to take a small detour to sneak a look, won out. The roads were not very busy and so we did not linger long, but hastened to a gallop once I'd caught a glance of the number and checked it against the card I had slipped into my reticule this morning. A sinking feeling overcame me as I reflected on the possibility that she had left cards for others of our set too. And even if she hadn't already, I was certain that tonight's invitation to Betsy's meant it was only a matter of time. But I had wrestled with this dilemma so much I was fatigued at the irresolution it always resulted in, and had decided I must put it out of mind and hope for the best.

When I saw Sheldon later that afternoon and he offered to convey me to Grosvenor Square and spare our horses, I found myself minded to accept his generous offer and felt some relief to arrive in his company when we entered the saloon, seeing Miss Craythorne's expectant gaze raised at our entry. We found most of the party already there, seated about the tables that had been set out and labelled with their game offerings: Piquet, Quadrille, Loo, Pharon, Whist, Backgammon, Draughts, it was all catered for in pristine style. Delores went off immediately to sit with Anna's chaperone and I realised as he led me the length of the room, that we must seem quite the couple, from the smiles and glances we received.

'Ah, there you are,' said Betsy, an approving glance cast between us. 'It is nice to see you both and looking so very well,' she said with a hint of overemphasis on "both".

'Thank you, Lady Elizabeth,' Sheldon replied. 'A nice little drum you've gathered up. I hope we have not missed the pairing and you are ready to be challenged to a rematch this night—I own I have improved my game significantly since you beat me last,' he teased.

'Well, that was about three years ago if I recall, and I've no doubt you've improved, visiting all those continental hells on your tour, but, your challenge is accepted, Mr Elmbridge, so long as I can name the game.'

He laughed. 'I don't deny the charge. Name it.'

She paused and scanned the tables in contemplation. 'Backgammon, I think, best of three?'

'Come, Lady Elizabeth, Backgammon? And where will all the maids and chaperones sit if we usurp their tables?'

'Nice try,' I added, 'but on your honour, you agreed she might name the game.'

'It's very true, and on my honour, you shall have your game of Backgammon, Lady Elizabeth, but I own, I had credited you with better taste.'

'Not a consideration of taste in the least, Mr Elmbridge, purely strategic,' she smiled and we all laughed along as she found seats for us and summoned a footman to wait on us.

'Well, that served you right,' I said to Sheldon with a gentle prod. 'Nobody likes a sore loser you know.'

'Not sore...only keen to reclaim my title,' he teased and our smiles settled easily on each other.

His high spirits were contagious and I had noticed the marked good humour he had been in of late and realised how it had helped me to remember him again, with the fondness that had never really gone, but had seemed lately overshadowed. I was grateful of it, for he helped me remember my own better humour and in doing so, forget some of my troubles, even as they stared at me from across the room. But I knew it would prove merry tonight, this little rendezvous Betsy put on was always so much fun and so I was determined not to let Miss Craythorne's presence spoil it. Even when she approached us to say hello, I took a breath and put on my most serene smile. 'Miss Craythorne, you came after all,' I said to her in the most cordial accents I could contrive. I noted she had the sense to bring her maid to attend on her now we were at Betsy's. The French one she called Francine, I had noticed she sometimes used to double up as a companion, on the rare occasions she bothered to keep herself chaperoned. It was always her she would take on shopping trips, and I wondered if she might have the sense to keep to the habit more widely after her stunt along St. James'.

'Eleanor, such formality. You know you have leave to address me as a close friend now,' she said sounding innocent enough, but privately, I knew she meant to toy with me. I watched Sheldon raise his brows at this and thought better than to tell her she did not have leave to address me so.

'Miss Craythorne,' he said with a bow, but I could tell he had no wish to linger in her conversation.

'Mr Elmbridge, good to see you,' she said more stiffly and, in that moment, I saw the briefest flash of jealousy sparkle in her eyes before she settled them back on mine. It surprised me. And whilst in usual circumstances such a clue I would attribute to her being jealous on account of Sheldon, I knew it was on account of me, and it gave me an idea. 'How are you settling into Wimpole Street Miss Craythorne? There must be so much to do, I'm surprised you could be spared.'

'Very well actually, there is not much to see to at all beyond sending for and unpacking things as they arrive. It turns out most of the house was only refurbished two years ago and in fine enough style, that beyond some lacking furniture here and there, all is quite ready.'

'How convenient for you. Pray tell me, have the rest of your family joined you yet?'

'My mama has arrived this afternoon and my brothers are to follow tomorrow.'

'I see,' I replied, but was grateful to be spared the need to contrive any further conversation as Betsy tapped a glass and called us all to order. I turned away from Miss Craythorne, inching in a little closer to Sheldon. I hoped that if I stayed close to him, she would eventually take the hint that I had no interest in her.

'Thank you all for coming,' Betsy began. 'Now, I know most of you are familiar with our little gaming format for tonight, but for those who have joined us for the first time; welcome, and here I shall introduce you to our ground rules. As many of you already know, we do not game for money tonight, not even chicken stakes. Ah, yes, I see some of you frown your bewilderment, but I tell you this is no gaming hell but a charity event we hold every year, where any money you might plunder at the table can be set aside for a better cause. Johnson holds the book over there for any pledges you might wish to make tonight to our cause, which is for the families of men killed or injured in service.' A round of applause flew up and interrupted her a moment. 'Thank you, a worthy cause I see we all agree. Well, you may say, that's all very well, but what fun is to be had about the gaming tables without stakes? Well, if you cast your eyes over to Mr Hooper our butler who will act, along with his footmen, as croupier's tonight, issuing to you winners tokens,' she held up an example and flapped the card around in her hands before lowering it. 'Now the winners, whether it is a game played by team or individual, shall all receive such a token from our croupiers for each win, collecting them up so that by the end of the night, those with the most winner's tickets may exonerate themselves from forfeits!' the crowd wooed merry at this. 'Yes, tonight some of you will be made to carry out forfeits for the winner's amusement after the gaming is concluded. So, you play this evening, not to make gains, but to save your bacon, should you not fancy the charge of having to wait upon the winners at the supper table, or entertaining us with a play act or musical demonstration. Ah, yes, I see the blushes and anxiety rise about your faces but it is all for good sport! So, as is tradition, we allow—amongst our time trusted forfeits—the top five winners to add to them, their very own forfeits. Yes, they may be anything you dare to conjure so long as they follow these two rules; it must be reasonable and it must be for the amusement of the party. Oh, and keep it polite! Happy gaming,' she declared and raised her glass, the audience following suit.

This seemed to fuel everyone into an air of fun-seeking and as we paired up and took to the tables, the room buzzed with funning and laughter; people offering up their preferences of what forfeits they should like to set and at whom, should they win. It was merrier than when we had played it in the country with less than half the number. It had arose out of our own attempts to make merry at one of the Dowagers tiresome affairs in our youth, where we would play at backgammon, chess or draughts, before we were of a permitted age to join the card tables. We got into the habit of conjuring forfeits for losers in the absence of having any stakes to raise, and so as we developed in years, so the game developed into more elaborate styles, until a few years ago, Betsy made it official and held it as an annual charity affair.

It had been the only event I had been permitted to attend in London before my coming out and had meant so much to me then: To be able to travel up to town for just this one weekend where I could be in London and amongst my friends. It was a smaller affair back then, with about fifteen of us, mainly comprised of our country set and a few suitors outside of it. It was on this account I was able to persuade my mama it was of no consequence and for a good cause that I could be permitted to go. It was also the dangled carrot that was used to bargain me into acceptance of my solitude in the country for the rest of the season.

I cast a glance about me at the company and realised I had not thought of it at all this season until tonight; it had been drowned in a sea of grand and competing affairs, paled so much into insignificance that this beacon of compromise I had clung to each year, had entirely vanished from my mind until Betsy's call yesterday. I watched Sheldon roll the die and slide his counters across the backgammon board and remembered back to one of the forfeits of our youth where Betsy beat him at the chess board and he was made to wear her bonnet and gloves for the remainder of the evening. The memory brought a chuckle to my mouth as I saw the concentration set in his as he pursed his lips and watched the dies land her, her numbers. And suddenly, I remembered *her* lips pursed and pouting as she drew me into her kisses, and as I shook this image, I came to ponder the feeling of Sheldon's kiss.

'What? Have I something on my face?' he asked me and I drew my eyes back to the board.

'Yes, determination not to lose,' I said and smiled, feeling my colour rise a shade at being caught watching him so.

'How the more disappointing for you it will be when you do,' said Betsy, sliding the dies in his direction.

I kept close to his company that evening and Betsy's too. Miss Craythorne had flocked to Martha and Beth for the draughts tables and I was relieved to need not pay attendance on her any longer. If she wanted to push her way in, she would have to do so without my assistance from now on. It seemed she was not overly concerned with attracting my notice now or claiming my company, which I thought odd since she knew so little of the others. But she was uninhibited in forming new acquaintances tonight and as the evening progressed, I lost track of the number of different partners she paired with at the tables or stood about in conversation with, spectating. And so, I came to learn of another of her talents this evening, which was one of the social butterfly and great entertainer. I listened in from time to time if she was in earshot, whilst she kept her company engaged in her stories from afar; and all without a whisper of the oryantal dans or any other strange notions she had revealed to my private company.

She was so convincing at playing the ordinary, but slightly exotic guest, I had begun to question that she seemed capable of the things she had done to me. Her perfectly composed narrative, her relaxed but confident deportment, her polite but not over flattering demeanour gave no clue to the lunacy I had witnessed these past weeks. I did not know whether to find this impressive or alarming. It was only when I excused myself to the water closet to use the chamber pot and found her waiting outside for me that I was able to reconcile the other version of her with the one I had observed all night.

'I missed you last night,' she said with not the slightest invitation to invade me at the doorway. 'It wasn't quite the same going to bed without the taste of your kisses upon my tongue.'

'Keep your voice down, will you?'

'Perhaps you could go back inside and we can talk more privately in there?'

'I do not want to talk privately with you, Miss Craythorne.'

'Oh dear, I really am no longer your Mariella. Are you no longer my Eleanor, my sweet Eleanor who has the softest mouth I have ever tasted?'

I dragged her inside the water closet and shut the door.

'Hmm, I like your dominant side.'

'Enough of this now! I cannot bear this. Unless you can behave well, I will have to send for your coachman and make your apologies.'

She held her hands up in defence. 'Calm down, I am only teasing you, you needn't be so uptight. Of course, if you are, I know a way we might put that right.'

'Hush. I do not give you leave to talk to me like this, do you understand me? I do not like it and I do not want you to say these things to me anymore. I am not *like you,* Mariella.'

'You do not have to be like me to enjoy my company, Eleanor. But whatever you say, I know you have enjoyed my company well even if you deny it. If I have pushed you too hard or too fast then I will slow the pace. If I knew you *really* meant it, I would back off altogether.'

'Of course, I mean it!'

She stepped up close to me. 'Wanting to mean it is not the same thing.'

'How dare you presume to know my mind: I told you exactly what I mean and you would do well to take heed of my words, Mariella, for it was me that put you here and it is me that can put you out again.'

'I like you better when you are vexed; you are very enchanting with the hue of anger in your cheeks. You know, it is not unusual to be frightened at this discovery, Eleanor. I felt it too at first, but you will come past it, and when you have, I will be ready to take you to the next place.'

'You will wait a very long time before I come to you of my own accord. Now, enough of this lunacy. Let us both understand each other and speak no more of this.'

'As you wish. But on one condition.'

I said nothing.

'When you go back outside, look at Mr Elmbridge, imagine doing with him, the things we did together, see if it excites you as much as the memory of doing them with me. If you dare to be even braver, kiss him as you did me and see how well you like it. If you prefer him over me, then of course I must be mistaken in what I see in you. But if you prefer my touch or the taste of my mouth, then I will be waiting to receive you, Eleanor, waiting to show the full extent of my talents at your bequest.'

I swallowed and cleared my throat. 'Very well, Miss Craythorne, if this peculiar notion pleases you, then I agree to it. There. Now, do I have your word that there will be no more of this talk?'

'You have my word, Eleanor.'

'Good, now can we at least pretend at civility for the rest of the evening?'

She nodded and I turned to leave the room before she said: 'Oh, just one more thing—' And before I could prevent her or even see it coming, she was lips pressed against me hands roaming until I found myself pinned up against the wall not knowing how I had got there.

I should have stopped her, I wanted to, at first...when I felt her hands beneath the muslin of my dress coaxing my breasts up over my stays, I brought my own hands up to prevent it, but then the stroke of her light fingertips across my nipples made me quiver and tremble so fatally, I let them fall away, found that now I pressed my kisses as firmly and hungrily against her lips as she did mine. *What was I about?* I seemed not only to remember how to perform these kisses from just our brief lesson in this art the other night, but now I seemed capable of improvising, expanding beyond my lessons, kissing at her neck and décolleté too as she sighed and breathed into my ear. There was a part of me attempting to curtail the wildness in me, in her, but every time it built the momentum to pull away, she would attack me with some new trick that set me spiralling out of control once more, and once it reached a certain level of depravity, I seemed no longer to be able to motivate myself to even try. I let her take her tongue to my breasts this time, without reluctance or displeasure, but buckled and bent against the support of the wall as she suckled at me, stirring up all kinds of frenzies in parts of me I did not know could grow so sensitive and wanton. But as I felt her teeth lightly graze the delicate skin of my nipple, my body began to grow and build with so much yearning, all I could think of was how it might be quelled. I tried to begin with, to persuade myself to stop, on account of being in the water closet and in Betsy's house and with a saloon-full of persons a corridor's breadth away, but that voice was so easily silenced in the shadow of the other which called to me to touch her and encourage her to touch me. It was this voice that was responsible for me feeling into her dress and finding the stub of a nipple between my own fingers. I was just contemplating whether I could find either the nerve or desire to suckle upon hers as she did mine, when someone tried the door handle and followed by delivering three swift raps upon the door panel. I froze at first and found I could not move a muscle, like a thief caught in the act, but Mariella called out with perfect equanimity of tone; 'Just a moment,' and stepped away from me, began fixing her dress in the glass and bidding me to do the same.

When we stepped out of the closet, I found Anna's chaperone waiting outside the door, jigging about in desperation for the pot and we suffered a scold from her, accused of prattling around with our hair and pinching our cheeks whilst others actually needed the pot. I was happy to accept this scold as she disappeared into the closet and slammed the door behind her.

I was grateful for her intervention later, although it took the entirety of the night to arrive at that head, for when we first returned to the party, my body had not caught up with my mind and continued to coil and pulse with the heat and stirrings she had whipped up in me. It was like my body was still fragile and aching for the smoothing of her hands and strokes of her tongue, even when I rolled the die or sifted through my dealt hands of cards. It would not be persuaded or regulated into compliance by my silent petitions to return to its usual ease. And even in the more bearable lulls when I managed to focus on my game, it would only take for Sheldon to brush my hand or arm in the briefest or most accidental style, for my body to set off again spooling in sensations of longing. And it was those moments I held responsible for carrying out my part in the bargain, something I had agreed to placate her, without any intention of actually doing. But I found myself studying the curl of his lips and wondering how they would look upon my breasts, how his thick pale fingers might stroke the curve of them and how it might stir me to move my hands beneath the muslin of his shirt.

Even when the winners were announced and the forfeits dealt out, I could only half listen in on them and join in at the laughter to begin with. It was this that finally began to distract me back into my proper senses and regain control of myself at last. Watching Anna and Mr Barrington play acting an operetta when neither of them were of good singing voice, Delores forced to try at the Harp Lute and the Colonel charged with performing impressions of the company in fantastic style, that the belly wrenching laughter began to gain the greater sway. Beth, Martha, and Mr

Clarke were tasked to chalk the floors in portrait style of three of the company, for which they choose to depict Anna, Betsy, and myself, all of which were unrecognisable, but no less amusing for it. Sheldon and I were dealt our penance in serving out the supper, which I felt was a light escape until we grew to the final forfeits which had been placed into the box by the winners and I heard Betsy, who had gamed her way out of any such penance, say: 'Well we have you Miss Craythorne, who is asked to select a partner of your choice to deliver us an interpretation of Romeo and Juliet.' When she cast her glance about the room and settled upon me, I pleaded with my own stare that she choose someone else: anyone else. But when she announced me, I suddenly found, returning to me in floods, all the displeasure she had so recently altered into something altogether different.

We were given costume props and prompt lines and I had Anna paint a moustache above my lips in soot ink, as Miss Craythorne had not only the pleasure of choosing to cast me in her forfeit, but also to cast me in my part, and I found myself stood in the centre of the room with all eyes set upon me, dressed in gentleman's attire, making declarations of love at Mariella's bosom whilst she feigned at playing the delicate damsel. The irony was altogether too much and I knew as I made them, how she enjoyed me making love to her in these flamboyant styles in front of such an audience. How she revelled in my heat flushed cheeks as I grew evermore conscious of the audience and stumbled over some of my lines. I had been cast in such roles before and had always taken my part with good grace and confident style, but tonight, I felt the fracture in my conviction, the faltering of my Shakespearean tone as I directed these feigned attentions to her, all the while remembering the scene we had played out privately and fearing that I would somehow give it away and the audience discover the secret.

When it was over, and the applause broke out, I thought I might pass out with the strain of holding myself so tightly together that even when Betsy took my velvet cape and Sheldon brought me a glass, I was still struggling to recompose myself. As the audience's attentions soon turned back to Betsy's new announcement as she drew another note from the forfeit box, I took advantage of the distraction and slipped carefully out of the room. I don't know where I thought I might go or what I planned to do, I only knew I had to escape the room for a time to try to recover better, before I was faced with any further conversation or compliments on my thespian skills that were as out of sorts tonight as my mind. It was times like this I wished I had some peculiar remedy or cure to rely on: Papa always reached for his brandy decanter or a cigar in such moments of anxiety; Mama always had some salts or a vinaigrette to hand, at least if she was here, I could try them, see if their medicinal powers really were as restorative as they always seemed to prove to her. I didn't even have my fan with me to cool my flaming cheeks with as I had left that in the coat room with my other things, which had served as a dressing room for theatricals.

I crossed the corridor to the staircase and slumped upon a step and held my head in my hands. I was so engrossed in my own reflections of the horror of it all that I was stunned to see Sheldon appear in front of me.

'Are you unwell?' he asked, concerned and bent down to meet me at eye level.

'No,' I said too frankly for being caught by surprise and wondered then, what other explanation I might give for my impromptu disappearance.

'Well, that is something,' he said, sitting down next to me on the step and before he had a chance to make any further enquiries, I silenced him with a kiss, before I even registered the plan to do it. It was a fairly plain kiss, compared to the one Mariella and I had been caught up in, and I did not dare to use my tongue, I only gently moved my mouth against his, caught the smell of his cologne upon his cheek as he seemed to oblige in a most retrained style. It was difficult to tell, when he drew back from it, who was the more astonished, for I felt like my body had again betrayed me in the most hideous fashion and I realised how disjointed and rogue it had become, as if it was singing to the step of a different master that whispered instructions I did not hear until it had already begun to act upon them.

'El?' he said gently, frowning at me.

'I'm sorry,' I said quickly. 'I don't know what came over me,' I said cupping my hand over my mouth as if to prevent it tricking me into any repeat.

'It's alright—I mean, there is no one here to see us but—'

'I don't know why I did it. My goodness, you must think me such a dash. Oh pray, don't think it, Sheldon, I did not mean it, I—'

'Hush,' he said gently and pressed a gentle hand over mine, 'it's alright, it's *more* than alright, but, what does it mean El?'

I shook my head despairing. 'I don't know. I can't explain. Oh I wish I might undo it! Whatever must you think of me, such a shocking thing to do—'

'Stop talking,' he said more firmly. 'You cannot think you shock me with a little kiss, now, can you? I know you are not so green to think I have not wondered at the thought myself more times than I could recollect the number.'

Oh no, please, do not begin making declarations.

'But if you wish it undone, then let us agree that it never happened, and since there are no witnesses to attest otherwise, we may put that one down to a moment of oversight.'

That one. How many more did he expect there to be? How many more could I mistrust myself to thrust upon him in this random style?

'Come, don't weep over it,' he said and wiped away a tear that rolled down my cheek and I sniffed the others back. 'You will spoil your handsome moustache,' he smiled and it drew me out of my melancholy and I joined him in the laughter.

'Thank you,' I said to him more earnestly once our laughter settled.

'What are friends for?' he said and smudged the soot from above my lips with the thumb tip of his otherwise snowy white gloves, then drew my own hand to his lips, kissed it gently and pulled me up from the stairs and said, 'Now, go and set yourself to rights and take that silly hat off, and come and receive your compliments, Romeo.'

Colt's Tooth.

June 1821. - Eleanor.

I tried my best to forget these ghastly affairs in the days that followed, doing my utmost to keep out of the way of both Mariella and Sheldon, insofar as I could. The season was starting to wind down towards its end and although there was still plenty of entertainment to be found, most of the great families were making plans to set out for the country over the next couple of weeks. A few deigned to stay in town for another six, to see the King's Coronation at the end of July, but they were in the minority, most declaring that as soon as the parliament houses were shut, they should escape the heat of the city and the rising unpleasant smells that seemed to accompany it. I was grateful we had no more than a week left in Berkeley Square after what had lately passed, and not on account of the heat, the smell or dislike of the King. It was becoming increasingly difficult to maintain my avoidance of Mariella, who was popping up more and more, not at parties, but it seemed everywhere else she could be admitted.

I had not spoken to her since Betsy's, but had stumbled briefly on her paying a call to various members of my country set on one morning or another; been out walking along Bond Street with Miss Pembroke, to catch sight of her pointing through the glass of a shop window or fingering some wares at a stall, not only with her maid, Francine, but increasingly with Martha and Beth in tow. I had even seen them riding in the Jameson's barouche one day when I took Samson out for a stretch. It had alarmed me to see how quickly she had closed in on them, and how innocent-looking she went about with them, knowing what she really was. I still flinched at the sight of them together for fear that she was trying to make up to them in the same style she had with me.

One day, when I returned in the carriage to Berkeley Square, I caught sight of them all entering Gunter's with her stepbrother and the Craythorne twins. I found this mildly reassuring and hoped that in fact I was mistaken, and she meant to keep to her word in bringing things off with Martha at least. This gave me some assurance that her tactics now were different from those she had levelled at me, and I tried to put it out of mind.

So, I trod carefully about the city, and beyond paying the odd call on Betsy or Anna, kept to other company and places I thought myself less likely to encounter her on a chance meeting. In the evenings, I had no such concern, for she remained without invitations, and so my difficulties for this part of the day were on account of Sheldon: Or more correctly, my enduring embarrassment when I was around him ever since I'd kissed him. Of course, he had behaved so prettily about it all that it was through no fault of his that I felt inclined to shrink from him, but the more good-natured he was about this contemptible faux-pas, the more it had the effect of making me feel conscious of how lacking I was in deserving his attentions. His response to my kiss had also stirred questions in other directions of thought.

I was still grappling with the possibility that he was not paying attentions to me for anything above a wish to appease his parents and do his duty. I had taken this notion of Mariella's with increasing scepticism now I understood her own motives and jealousy about our acquaintance, and yet despite this analysis, I could not entirely discount the possibility either. It was reflecting on his reaction to my kissing him that had stuck with me on this count. I don't know what exactly I had expected him to do, and I was mindful that I was at fault in behaving so, yet I expected—I wasn't sure what, but something else. Something more in return, something that gave me some clue that he had at least enjoyed my blunder.

It was true I had detected a sense of his reluctance at pulling away, it was also true that he was the perfect gentleman and exceeded my expectations in how handsomely he had forgave me it and instantly set about making me comfortable. But, I couldn't help feel that perhaps he might have took a little more pleasure in it than he had made plain to me. That he might have showed a little of the passion Mariella had demonstrated. It seemed an obscene thought, and I admonished myself for permitting it, but as we locked eyes or danced of an evening, I could not help but feel the questions rise to the surface again. I wanted to seek someone else's opinion or counsel on the matter, compare my assessment of things to their own and perhaps glean some wisdom or insight I was missing; but there was no one above him that knew, and no one that would approve of such dashing behaviour who I could disclose it to, so I could only resolve to torment myself with the idea.

It was only one evening when we were invited to a ball at Egremont House, that some trouble kicked off between him and Mr Charles—a dandy of a fellow who had petitioned his share of my dances since we had arrived in London—who had put it about that he meant to ask for my hand. I found this more than a trifle ridiculous when I heard the rumour, since I had no desire whatsoever to be leg shackled to the kind of fellow that spent more time in his dressing room looking glass than me. But Sheldon had failed to see the funny side of this when I told him as much, and had taken Mr Charles' bragging and setting his cap at me, as quite the affront, and I was forced to beg of him not to offer him out at dawn over the affair.

He had eventually acquiesced, but was in such a passion over it all night, that I realised I had been mistaken to doubt his regard. He had pulled me from the ballroom to seek my assurance that I had no interest in hearing Charles' offer to which I told him the very notion was absurd to me, and should he have the nerve to go to my father at all, then I would refuse to see him. He looked at me then and said, 'El, what happened last week at Betsy's – you've never, well, kissed a fellow before, have you?'

'God—no!' I said mortified that he would even ask the question. But I was equally disconcerted that the honest answer would have been, not another fellow; no.

This incident had seemed to reignite his determination to be selfish of my company and he had invited me to Park Lane again for dinner, invited me and Delores on no end of trips to some Gallery, Music Hall or pleasure garden. And whilst his manner remained easy and amiable on the surface, below it, I felt the steel of his intention to mark his territory and show the world what his intentions were.

Even Delores who had otherwise seemed more buoyant than usual, seemed fatigued by it all and looked to the relief of some evening soiree when she could withdraw to the sidelines in the comfort and presence of society (preferably the Squire's) to relieve her of some of the burden. She was not cut out for this work and we both understood it. She was much better suited to her role as mother's companion. But I was the last of the flock and she endured it for knowing that once I was wed, she could retire to the comfort of having no more children to play chaperone to. This was certainly the unspoken consensus, which was why the news she brought at dinner tonight came as a surprise to my mama.

The last of the removes were being cleared and the tablecloths replaced. Mama was informing us that there were plans for extending some of the season's events into the country for a few weeks. We had invitations to a ball at Ham House, a weekend at Wycombe Park, followed by another at Petworth. She was minded to accept them all and when my father assented, I saw Delores twitch uncomfortably in her seat as a footman reset her place.

As we sat over our final courses and mama continued on in an elaboration of all the various entertainments promised by these hosts, who was invited and minded to attend, and even raised the possibility of us hosting a little affair of our own at Cuddington, I could see Delores growing increasingly ill at ease. I at first assumed the prospect of keeping close watch over me for more weeks, when she was counting down her last, was all too much.

So when Mama turned to her and asked, 'Delores, I know you made mention of taking a few days leave of us at the end of the season, but it was not set at a particular date, was it?'

'It was not when I mentioned it, but I had thought the most convenient time to take it would be next week when we depart, since I should not be much missed on a travelling day and—'

'Indeed, but the thing is, it makes no sense to rattle our way down to Cuddington on Thursday if we are only to be due up at Wycombe Park a couple of days later. It would be much more convenient to spare such journeying, stay in London but a couple of days more and go directly, I think. Then on our return, there would be the space of the week you might go and be back with us again before Petworth?'

'Actually, Helena, I have an announcement to make,' Delores said, clearing her throat. 'I intended to make it privately, but since you brought up the subject and we are all here—'

'Oh?' Mama looked up surprised, but I was not, I suspected what was coming. Unlike Mama in her blissful ignorance, I had observed the flourishing of this news. I had noticed the lightening of Delores' mood, the brightness of her smile, the song in her voice and the bounce in her step more recently when in certain company. She even seemed a little younger somehow; more vibrant and less worn down than I was used to. Is that what it did; to be in love, alter you so drastically in body and spirit? It was a peculiar shift to witness in one of such years, but it became her.

'I am to be married,' she said steadily.

Mama blinked and put down her fork. 'What can you mean, Delores?' she said incredulously, as if she was funning.

Father looked up briefly from his plate and then continued eating.

This is what I had feared; this is why I had tried to awaken Mama to what was going on beneath her nose. How she had not noticed the sure but steady changes herself, I could not fathom: Perhaps because Delores spent more time at my side than hers of late. She had grown so used to having Delores to rely on these past five and twenty years that I could not imagine her adjusting well to her disappearance after such an age, a temporary one when all her London friends were about was one thing, but a permanent one, quite another.

'The squire has asked me to marry him...and I have said yes.'

Mama held her hand to her throat. 'You said yes?' she said, as if betrayed.

'Come, Helena, it is surely not such a surprise; you know we were once intended.'

'Yes, and that was a great many years ago. I thought—'

'That all hope and prospect had long expired? And so did I. But he is a free man now; it seems there can be no obstacle.'

Wrong: Mama would think a great obstacle in her attachment to Delores.

'But his wife is barely—'

'I know, and that is why I at first tried to put him off.'

'Yes, quite rightly, Delores. You must not let him sway you. You are quite proper in doing so.'

'But we also came to realise that we are of an age where we do not know how much life we have left in us, so there is no time to delay, for the sake of propriety or no.'

Mother looked like she had been slapped hard across the cheek. 'Delores, women of our years cannot just throw propriety to the wind.'

'Oh, Helena, I have waited a lifetime for such happiness, I beg you be pleased for me.'

A tear rolled down Mama's cheek, the only clue through her stiff set face that gave her away. 'I am happy for you, Delores, of course I am. But it is so sudden.'

'Yes, and I do not mean to go just yet. Sir John says we can wait until next month to fix the date.'

'Next month?' said Mama in a shriek of objection. 'But that is no time at all. The season might be over, but you know there is still much to attend—'

Delores turned and looked to me now as she spoke. 'I think we all know that we shall not be long in the wait for Eleanor offering such news of her own.'

I was now mirroring mama's expression, I realised, as my jaw dropped a fraction. 'I think that more than a little over presumptuous Delores,' I objected. 'I have no reason to expect—'

'Stuff and nonsense,' Mama interjected. 'But it is beside the point. Delores, you must see then that we will need you now more than ever, with so much to arrange?'

'And as your loyal friend, you can count on me to do my utmost. But I cannot stay in your employ once I am wed. Helena, you must see how peculiar a circumstance that would be.'

'Yes, yes I suppose so. What have Sir John's children said on the matter?'

'They do not yet know. You are the first to hear the news, so I must beg your silence to permit him to deliver it to them.'

'I see,' Mama said and I could tell from the change of her tone that she saw this as an obstacle, perhaps wished it as one, or in the least a delay. What right minded daughters and sons would not object to the marriage of their father within months of their mother's burial?

'That is why I must take leave next week; I am to accompany Sir John to give the news.'

'Well, congratulations,' my father said, having remained silent throughout. He raised his glass and toasted: 'To Delores and Sir John.'

Mama nearly spilt her glass once finding it, and after a blushing wave of gratitude, Delores excused herself from the table, leaving us to the cheeses in stunning silence.

'I can't quite believe it,' Mama said eventually.

'Well, it has perhaps come at a good time for us all, Helena, we will soon have no use for Delores anyway. At least now she can have a happy retirement, rather than have to find ways to busy herself in our service when all our children are left home.'

Left home? Pardon me? I was neither engaged, wed, or left home! How could everyone presume so comfortably that my situation would be altered in as little as a few weeks' time?

'But Henry, Delores has been with us for so many years, she has raised each of our children with us. You do not think it strange that in a month she will likely be gone?'

'I think all things run their course my dear. I thought you would be happy to see her settled.'

'Perhaps, eventually, but not now; in the middle of a season.'

'It is hardly the middle of the season, Helena, but no matter, we can soon employ another chaperone if need be.'

And this, I knew he would be happy to do. He had wanted the excuse to do as much before now. I knew he found Delores complacent in her duties and would be happy to replace her with a more 'professional' chaperone. Mama of course, would never permit it before, but now it seemed the matter was beyond her preference. I wondered if I should prefer a replacement over Delores. She was frustrating at times, and I well understood her complacency better than even my parents. But would I want a more vigilant person, a stranger watching over me? I thought of the staunch old maids my friends were saddled with. I did not fancy the prospect. At least with Delores, I knew where I stood. I cut a slither of Banbury cheese and helped myself to a cracker.

'Why don't you advertise for someone?' Father said simply with a shrug.

'Whatever for? Delores said herself she would not abandon us right away. In any case, we shall only need another few weeks at most, and it would take that long just to advertise and take interviews.'

'Then the registry perhaps?'

I wondered if papa too had sensed Delores' lack of enthusiasm and rather lethargic devotion to the role now she had her sights set towards grander things, and considered this a good opportunity to seize the moment and replace her immediately.

'And have Delores come home from a few days leave to find her position taken? What an idea, Mr Ashlyn!'

'It would hardly be taken, would it? You always manage to find something for her to do.'

Mother put down her cutlery. 'Mr Ashlyn! Have you fast forgotten it was she who saw Harriet and Caitlin through their seasons and they were the only ones I can name who made their match before their first season was even halfway through?'

'Helena, even you are not so whimsical a creature to credit their matches to Delores' efforts, I think. They secured them quite on their own account.'

'As will Eleanor. Mr Ashlyn, need I remind you things look very well for Eleanor already? I am sure we can rest assured that the hiring of a new chaperone will be neither necessary or timely at the rate things appear to be progressing.'

I almost choked on a shard of poorly chewed cracker and reached for my glass to dislodge it. Contrary to the consensus; I was in no mind at all for flouncing up the aisle in such a flash. I was too muddled to be sure of anything much at present, but I had already turned my mind to looking towards another season and in the meantime, seeing how things with Sheldon and I panned out. But even in the very best of circumstances, I would want the summer, to be certain of myself.

She looked at me with a "we both know what I speak of" expression, before returning to her plate and said after: 'But we might think of advertising for your own Lady's maid, Eleanor.'

I had quite forgotten that my participation in these matters were either necessary or welcome. 'Oh,' I said when she had waited long enough for me to express an interest in the matter.

'Watts is not getting any younger and it seems too much for her to be seeing to us both now you are out and Molly is gone.'

'I see.' It was true I supposed. I had noticed how stretched things had become with so many events to prepare for now, but I knew where I stood with Watts, and Molly too before her dismissal. Despite Watts' lack of spritely demeanour, I was reluctant to pass her over for a stranger who I could not be sure to wield any influence over. Watts could always be relied on to keep a secret for trifles.

'What do you say? A young French one would suit you far better now you are out?'

'French?' I said, thinking of Francine and springing from that thought; Mariella.

'Hmmm, Swiss perhaps to be on the safe side. What say we make an advert up tomorrow, and I will take the interviews with you once we get back to the country.'

'I think we hardly have time to take interviews?'

'True, but we will have to make the time, Eleanor, you will be in want of your own maid soon enough as it is.'

I didn't much like the implication of that statement.

'So why put Watts through the turmoil of tending us both any longer. Besides, we away to so many other places now, it is bad form to rely on our host's provisions when there is no need for you to go without.'

'Very well, but I will leave the arrangements to you.'

'Yes, I see your mind is full of other things.'

Not the things you might suspect.

'Oh, that reminds me, Mr Ashlyn, you have agreed us go to this affair at Wimpole Street, but I daresay you overlooked the fact that the Cowper's are to put on a leaving ball too next week and I have already R.S.V.P'd to it.'

Father looked up from his plate. 'Then you will have to send our apologies.'

'What affair at Wimpole Street?' I asked, swallowing my mouthful down in a gulp. I had heard no mention of this.

Mother frowned at me is if to say she expected I should. 'Some Indian themed gala, did Miss Craythorne not mention it?'

I shook my head and she turned back to my father and her features stiffened. 'Henry, you ask too much—'

I knew where this was heading and I hadn't the tolerance for the headache of it, or anymore talk of the inferiority or peculiarities of the Craythornes. I knew now that *she* was certainly peculiar, but my concern now, was that perhaps I was too. I made my excuses and went to my toilette.

A Gala.

June 1821- Eleanor.

It turned out that I was the last to know about this gala, I found out the next morning when I decided to pay a call upon Beth—if anyone was to have the details; I presumed it would be her with how much they were in company of late.

'Oh, yes we are to go aren't we, Martha,' Beth said as we sat over chilled glasses of Capillaire in the Jameson's tea parlour. 'It is unfortunate that it coincided with Lady Cowper's ballroom, but it was a very rushed affair and there was little choice in dates left. Miss Craythorne has worked non-stop to bring it off before everyone starts disappearing.'

I bet she has.

'It is to be a themed Indian affair in honour of some diplomat from the Bengal, who is to be the guest of honour and we are invited to come in themed costume should we wish it,' Martha added in excited spirits.

'How merry,' I said, taking a sip from my glass. I tried to sound agreeable to the idea as I did not want them to suspect anything to the contrary after being the one responsible for this outcome. But the dread of having to face her and in her own house, was already tangible.

'Oh, it shall be! And it's all thanks to you, you know; Miss Craythorne has told us how you inspired and directed the party at Beaulieu. What a clever idea, I suppose you never suspected the idea would be taken all the way to London society,' Martha continued.

'Not in a million years,' I replied. 'Has Betsy R.S.V.P'd?'

'Yes, she means to make an appearance, but will not cancel on the Cowper's so she will go to Wimpole Street for a while before slipping off to the Cowper's a little later.'

This was very bad news. Had it really come to this; that Betsy was willing to make allowances on her time to pay attendance on the Craythornes. I had noted that Mariella had taken a care to time her party but two hours ahead of the Cowper's, probably for the very reason to prevent receiving as many apologies, for those who were minded to split themselves between hosts. Something that I had been used to doing for weeks now, and something I wished, Mama had bargained with my father in the least.

'You are to come, aren't you?' Beth asked, leaning over the table to replenish our glasses.

'Yes,' I said evenly.

'Oh, that is good, we wasn't sure if you would,' Martha said and Beth cast her a reprimanding glance.

'Why is that?'

'Oh, you know,' Beth cut in. 'With how *busy* you are now, and of course with Lady Cowper being your mama's particular friend—'

'Did Mar—Miss Craythorne say something Martha, to give you the idea I might decline?'

'Oh no,' said Beth, but Martha had already given the answer in her expression.

'Martha?' I raised my brows in her direction.

'Oh, oh we may as well tell her the truth, Bethany. I know it was a confidence, but Eleanor has been our friend for such a time and besides, I think she will want to know.'

My heart sank, my belly contracted with anticipation. What on earth had she disclosed to them?

'Very well,' Beth said with an air of frustration at Martha. 'She did not wish us to make mention of it, but Miss Craythorne has been a little...upset, this past week,' she said carefully.

'Upset?'

She nodded, 'On account that she thinks you have quite forgotten her now and are so busy with Mr Elmbridge that you have not even had time to return her calls.'

'I see. Is that all she has said?'

They both nodded and I felt a wave of relief to hear that she had elaborated no further: For I could rely on Martha's face to show a clue to an untruth, even if Beth was more difficult to read. 'Well, I have been very busy and I have no wish to upset Miss Craythorne, but of course the season draws soon to a close and—'

'Oh, we know it,' said Martha, 'and we told her as much. We said to her, we have barely seen you ourselves beyond passing or for a brief spell over a supper room table. It can't be helped; you have so many invitations to attend and Mr Elmbridge, well, he is your particular friend now and it is of course to be expected. It was the same with Clara and look, now she is gone off on her wedding journey—'

Beth cast another disapproving glance at her and cut in, 'The thing is, Eleanor, she doesn't quite know the way of things and we have tried to explain to her that there is no snub in it, that the season can be quite dizzying with so much to attend to, and it is after all, your first. We have taken her under our wing and she is much improved, I think,'

'Well, thank you, ladies. I am grateful. You may tell Miss Craythorne I shall be attending.'

'She will be so glad,' Martha sang.

'And how are the rest of Miss Craythorne's family, are her brothers in town now?'

Martha coloured a little and nodded and Beth said, 'Yes, very well. We have seen rather *a lot* of them recently.'

'That is good,' I replied and knew from Beth's telling glance that I was correct to assume things were progressing well for Martha in that direction. This had been the only bit of news I was happy to have gleaned by the time I left. Everything else had been so very trying. I was not convinced in the least of Miss Craythorne's state of 'upset' and thought it much more like her to be using it as a ploy to win their pity and sponsorship, along with the possibility of taunting me in this passive slyboots fashion she was so adept in. But whatever the case, I must try a little harder to be amiable to her in public if I was to be forced into her ballroom.

IT CAME AROUND FAR too quickly for my liking and delivered all the pomp and ceremony we had come to expect of the Craythornes' lavish entertainments. In comparison to the usual London crushes, it was but half the number, though the number consisted of a great deal more of good ton than I had expected, and this disconcerted me greatly. If it was not for the fact that invitations were slowing down, I would fear that we might start bumping into each other in the evenings hereafter, for it stood to reason that anyone in attendance would feel an obligation to include them now. Even the Cowper's had put in a brief appearance before retreating just ahead of their own affair.

It was no doubt the novelty of it that had tempted people to come. For it was a dazzling event and in better circumstances, I knew I would have enjoyed it, but having to suffer her amongst my set all evening was more taxing than I had feared.

Even through our cordial exchanges, I found myself irritated by her presence and was grateful for the dances, to begin with, so I could withdraw to Sheldon's company and escape hers. And when he had used up the two I could safely allocate to him, I agreed to other partners without discrimination, to spare me from returning amongst her company. She did dance too tonight, however, and I realised too late that I could have afforded to sit out at least a few of them had they aligned with the sets she was engaged for. It would have been useful to have had this foresight, for not only were these Indian dances particularly exerting, but it had not fared well with Mr. Elmbridge (to whom I of course meant no injury or slight).

He had grown grim-faced by the first interval, and whilst I returned to his side during it, I could see he was not happy or to be encouraged to join in. Even Martha, who usually would prove such a reliable wallflower that he would frequently be induced to favour her with a couple of sets, was not in need of his assistance tonight, since she danced merry with all the Craythorne brothers and seemed to be on very intimate terms with them all. I hoped it would not be long before her stepbrother put an offer to her. At least then it would seem that some good might come of this disastrous association after all.

Mariella had made no secret tonight, of her satisfaction at being able to force her company on my notice and even when I was able to avoid her proximity, I caught her staring in my direction more than once or twice. It unnerved me. I did not want her, and yet I could not seem to escape her in person or thought. I wondered if I had the same effect on her; if she would sometimes think of me for no apparent reason, or catch her breath at the sight of me, or awaken from a random dream of me and almost wish not to have stirred from it? I would of course, never know nor never tell a soul. It would die with me one day along with the bitterness and shame.

The second half of the dances were harder to keep up with and not just the unfamiliar steps. I was so exhausted by the third that I really wondered if I could continue on and asked the young Mr Craythorne, if he would mind very much if I sat it out and recovered.

'Not at all, Miss Ashlyn. I should be very happy to sit it out with you if you would like,' he said charmingly, and I told him I would, for I was fond of him. He was my favourite amongst the family, indeed a very sweet natured man and was so plain speaking and infectiously jolly that it was difficult to feel Friday faced for long with him making such animated speeches and talking in styles that might convince you, you had been long time acquaintances. Although we had never spoken at great length, as I sat with him now over a cup of ratafia, I wondered increasingly how he was related to his sister at all. They seemed not only like different persons but different species altogether. He was her inverse and so disarming in his character that the further we chatted, the further I wished to keep to his merry company. It was not a fondness of any desiring affectation in the least, but of the friendliest and fondest kind of chummery. Even Sheldon took no offence to his harmless attentions and in fact paid him a great deal of his own when he re-joined us, and for a little while, I quite forgot how I had been counting my dances down to our leaving.

It took only for Mariella to join us after the closing set to throw even that quite asunder.

'Well, I am glad to see someone enjoying themselves tonight!' She had appeared from nowhere at my side.

I stepped away a stride and lowered my voice. 'It is quite the success, a credit to your family to put on such a drum.'

'That is not what I meant.'

We both know that. 'Miss Craythorne, the season is in full bloom, do you expect I would not play my part in it and hand hold you throughout?'

She narrowed her gaze and turned her head slightly to one side. 'How many parts are you playing the role of, Eleanor? By the look of it, even Mr Elmbridge is not certain.'

I checked he was still absorbed in conversation with Bertram. 'He knows I cannot dance the whole night with him.'

'He knows, but takes no comfort in the knowing, I think.'

This much was true. 'Well, it cannot be helped and I am not convinced you have Mr Elmbridge's interests at heart in any case.'

'You *know* I do not,' she spat the words with such venom even she realised too late how plain she had exposed herself.

'Mariella, I cannot believe you would show such jealousness of character, it is very unbecoming you know. And to make hints at my own friends—'

'I am not jealous! I just don't like the way he commandeers all your attention; it is like you are already promised to him. It seems to me quite an inappropriate gesture for a gentleman to treat an un-engaged lady with such a sense of ownership. I do not understand why society here seems so indifferent to what I am reminded would normally be considered quite improper.'

'I assure you, there is nothing improper about Mr Elmbridge.'

'Will you marry him, Eleanor?'

Where on earth did that come from? 'Well, if I decide to, he shall be the first to know the answer.'

'Everyone knows that he will offer for you and everyone, it would seem by their relaxed excusal of you both, expects you will say yes.'

'Was it not you that once said you did not much care for the expectations of others? Yes, I can agree with you on that head now.'

'Specifically me I suppose?'

'Look, I don't understand the sudden interest in my affairs, nothing has been spoken and nothing is changed. But if it does, you along with everyone else will surely hear of it in due course.'

'I don't want to hear of it, Eleanor. Where will that leave me? Us?'

'Us?' *Did she really think there was such a thing?* I flicked open my fan to speak from behind it. 'You cannot really believe that anything could amount to our... I mean, surely you understand that was a mistake?' I was almost whispering behind the cover of my fan now the conversation had took this turn.

Her face spoke the answer before the answer was given. 'No, clearly I have given our *friendship* more regard than you have.' She slammed down her un-sipped glass on the fire mantle and stormed off across the room and did not pause, or answer when I called out after her. I did not chase her immediately. I was still in shock at the spontaneity of this discussion and how on earth to respond to it. But as I watched her disappear through the saloon doors, something willed me on after her.

By the time I made my own exit, she was all the way across the courtyard garden and walking at a pace I had to run to catch up with. 'Mariella!' I called out as I shuffled across the straw strewn cobbles with my skirts flapping in the wind and my curls whipping up around my face. I watched her pace quicken and sped on after her. But I was grateful for the delay, I needed time to consider what on earth I would say when I reached her. I was not best practiced in apologies and nor was I sure if it was wise to make one. After all, I could not fathom what I had actually done wrong. Yes, I had been a little evasive, but I was hardly under any obligation to dance attendance on her. Besides, she had other friends to count on now, thanks to me. But because they were my friends too and we would soon all be confined to each other's company before long, I knew I must try to keep peace amongst us, whatever else, and so I paid heed to what I had learnt from Beth and Martha and considered the possibility she may have felt affronted after all, and it would be preferable to make a peace offering and part on better terms.

I finally caught up with her in the stable mews, but she ignored me completely until I reached her side. 'Mariella, don't ignore me.' I tugged at the sleeve of her mantle and forced her to pause.

'Just go back to the party, Eleanor. I am sure Mr Elmbridge must be wondering where you are by now!' she spat and tugged away.

I was tempted to do precisely that as my frustration at her rose, but I saw a glisten of a tear in the corner of her eye and quite unexpectedly I felt a hint of regret. Perhaps I had underestimated her regard for me and my injury done to her. She was a tricky one to read at the best of times, so indifferent and controlled in demeanour one moment, then recklessly unrestrained the next: it was hard to tell if she was truly fond of anything or anyone beyond the social elevation of the association. I shrunk from the thought at the realisation of how very similar we were in our polarities—perhaps that is what drew me here now to entertain her unfounded tantrum; a hint of recognition for our slight resemblance in that regard. I watched her storming along beside me, both defiance and injury in every determined step.

Had I been quite so insensitive to fail to realise the extent of her inclination? It had seemed reasonable enough that I had assumed this tomfoolery as of little consequence, certainly she had never given me any reason to contemplate it beyond that, and I was not sure I was either willing or able to think of it with any greater implication, however much I had grown to enjoy her company in those early days.

'Come, we are friends are we not, let there be no bad feeling between us. If indeed I have offended you, then I apologise,' I offered.

'Is that what we are?'

'Am I mistaken in thinking so?'

She shrugged an insulted shake of her head before disappearing through the stable house door.

I caught my breath, petitioned myself for some greater tolerance and followed her in.

She sat down on a small bench and peered ahead through the small glass windows on the doors. I examined her expression for a clue of how to approach this. Her face so blank and so plaster cast, she reminded me of an enamel cut silhouette with her long neck and pointed nose perfectly set an angle to avoid my bewildered gaze. I let out an exasperated sigh that filled the silent room more noisily than I had anticipated and then, to my horror, like a crack in freshly set plaster, I saw her expression falter, her chin quiver, her bottom lip roll up beneath the top. *She was going to cry*. It suddenly seemed uncomfortably small and confined in this place, which I had noted was the saddle room now my eyes had better adjusted to the shard of light that filtered into it, and I didn't have the foggiest idea what to say or do as I watched a tear roll down her cheek. *Why on earth did I insist on chasing after her?* I took a seat beside her on the small bench, felt for my handkerchief and offered it to her to buy a little time to think of the words.

'You must think me quite pathetic,' she said eventually.

'No. I just hadn't expected this.'

'Do you have any idea how difficult it is to find good friends when you move from one place to another every few years? How many friendships you have to put an end to?'

'No—No I do not.'

'If what is between us is going to end, then I would rather us part ways now before...'

'End?' I wasn't sure what exactly had begun. 'Mariella, I don't quite understand what has brought this on, but I am sorry if I have led you to this idea that our friendship must not continue because of my acquaintance with Mr Elmbridge. I thought some distance between you and I, would prove mutually beneficial, but perhaps I have been mistaken; I would very much like us to stay friends, if only we can settle comfortably upon that.'

'But I am not sure that will be possible if you intend to engage yourself to Mr Elmbridge.'

'Why on earth not?' I had failed to hide the outrage in my tone. I was not the grovelling kind and she had exerted my best efforts already.

She turned to face me at last but her gaze was uncomfortably sobering and I wished she would turn away again. The single tear that had bled the length of her cheek had begun to dry and her face was perfect plaster again.

'Because I am greedy, Eleanor: greedy and jealous in nature and I want you; all to myself.'

The steel in her tone and the vulgarity of her honesty should have infuriated me, repulsed me, but it did not, and this shocked me more than her very words. Instead, it sent a flare of dangerous excitement twisting through me, the one I had tried so hard to silence these past weeks. I opened my mouth to at least attempt some form of objection to her speech but I was paralysed by this peculiar enchantment she had resurrected in me.

She shuffled in closer and fixed me in an intense gaze that made me fidgety. 'Besides, I fear that I would not be able to face him with the knowledge that I have stolen the innocence of his wife to be.'

I felt a frown contort my features as I sought out the implication of this. 'But you have done no such thing, we have shared but a little kiss and—'

She put her hand lightly on my lap and I felt her hot breath at my ear. 'Not yet, but I fear I will not be able to stop myself.' She licked my ear and made me jump with the surprise. But as I pulled away to protest, she leaned in again and suckled at it, holding me firmly at the waist. My skin rose up in feverish beads of anticipation and the anger wilted as quickly as the stirrings of passion ignited inside me. I was surprised at the pleasure this strange and simple gesture provoked, but when she ran her hand across my lap, pulled the hem of my dress up to my knees and slid her palm beneath it, I froze. *Is this what she meant? What was she going to do to me?* I was paralysed by the prospect for long enough for her to travel the length of my thigh before my senses kicked in and stopped her. I cupped my hand over the top of her buried one and held it fast. 'No, Mariella, this isn't right.'

She leaned back to look at me. 'Is any of it? Is it right when I kiss your neck, or your mouth, put my hands on your breasts?'

I had no answer for her.

'No, it is not; and yet it feels—' she licked the full length of my throat and sucked my lower lip until it hurt, 'quite the contrary, does it not?'

I found the will to pull away but my body had already begun to hunger for the suggestions she had proposed to me and I could not quite catch myself.

'It's alright; we are the same, Eleanor. You and I can understand each other plainly where others might fail.' She traced her fingers lightly over my hand which was resting on the seat beside us both.

To steady my breathing was all I could manage.

'I have never known anyone like you, Eleanor: so akin to me. At first, I didn't see the similarity through all the propriety, polite smiles and prettiness that would deceive anyone into thinking you were every part the perfect lady.'

A hint of objection made a gallant attempt at forming a reply, but was quickly silenced by the growing part of me that had entirely succumb to her.

'But there is so much more beneath that façade isn't there, Eleanor?'

It wasn't a question and yet I wanted to call out 'yes' in reply to her.

She raised her hand from mine and took me firmly by the chin, turning my face slowly from side to side to examine it.

'Of course, you are utterly beautiful.' Her breath was warm against my nose as she brought me back to face her. 'No one could deny you that. But this innocence, this gentility, obedience one might assume from such a face is an utter lie, a total deception.'

I raised my eyebrows at this but still found myself immobilized.

'You are like the *Sarracenia flava*. Do you know what it is, Eleanor?'

I shook my head.

'It is a beautiful exotic flower that attracts every manner of creature to it with its handsome figure and vibrant colour; it draws them in, and once they are close enough, it traps them and devours them. The helpless poor creatures so enchanted by the charming façade, they just don't see it coming.'

I pulled away from her grip. The mood had soured and I felt my defences rising back up around me. 'I see nothing in your character that would convince me you are a helpless victim to my looks.'

'Don't take offence, Eleanor. It is an honest observation and it is that honesty between us that attracts me to you, and you to me.' Her slackened grip at my chin grew firm again and she pulled my mouth to hers and kissed me. I wanted to dislike it, to dislike her, but I did not: my body and my mind were on wholly different planes and it seemed their position could not be made commensurate for all my will.

She pulled back to look at me and closed my open mouth with a brush of her thumb. 'We can be ourselves in each other's company, let the petals unfurl and permit our true characters, true intentions be at ease. Don't you see that you are beautiful to me even when I understand that you are not mild and obedient? That in fact it is the steel beneath all of that I find far more enticing. We are women, Eleanor, but not the ordinary kind. I think you have perhaps always felt that in some way.'

I wondered how she, a stranger, could appear to know so much of my character and yet I could not deny the accuracy of her observations. I had always felt this difference she spoke of, although I assumed the struggle I had felt against the expectations of my sex something of a natural process to surmount. Mother described it as a wildness of youth, and quite unsuspecting I had simply put it down to that—a feral instinct that required refining like most of our natural impulsions. I had managed to conquer all such primitive nuances with adequate application and practice: my manners, speech, deportment, even my walk was perfected to the point I no longer had to think about it, it came so naturally to me. So long ago such struggles were won that I had quite forgotten how insurmountable they had seemed at the time, how many reminders and reprimands it took to reach their now effortless habit. Was the resistance I felt to my current struggles something different or simply a lapse in my diligence? I could not pretend the question hadn't surfaced before now. But never had I had someone else to compare it to, for everyone I had ever known seemed to manage with such ease, that to pose the very question would seem absurd. 'Even if we are alike in our deviations,' the sound of my voice surprised us both after such a lapse, 'it does not mean we should celebrate such a calamitous similarity, Mariella. Self-corruption is one thing, but a mutual corruption is simply dangerous and I cannot see how we can do anything but harm ourselves and each other in this encouragement.'

Her lips curled up into a smile and her apparent amusement began to rile me. I knew I really should have left by now and this was the perfect opportunity to make my exit. But I didn't. 'Exactly what is so amusing?'

'You still think you can master this don't you?'

I swallowed hard.

'Of course, you must try, and fail, just as I did; in your own time and in your own way—but be warned, these inclinations will not leave you, Eleanor. They will fester and grow with each passing day, with or without your consent.'

'So, what exactly do you propose?'

'Honesty,' she said simply, and this time I did not pull back when she reached out to stroke my cheek. 'There is no cure of course.'

This disconcerted me greatly, but I was not willing to show it.

'But if you are honest with yourself and adjust your expectations, you might find a way to live with it, as I have.'

'What expectations do you refer to exactly?' I realised too late that my interest had given me away and I resented the smug satisfaction with which she made her reply.

'Well, for a start,' she drew out the length of her words, 'realise that there is not a man on this earth that will ever make you feel the way that I do when I touch you.' She was playing with the ribbon that rested just below my décolleté as she spoke. 'Make your marriage match based on this expectation and you will not be half as disappointed.'

'I thought you objected to the idea of my engagement?'

'Not at all. Even I see the necessity in such an evil as plainly as the next person, only I have the sense to see it for precisely what it is and think about the kind of arrangement that will serve my purpose, as you must.'

'So why on earth have you reacted so sorely to Mr Elmbridge's interest in me? Or do different rules apply to you?'

'Because Mr Elmbridge is the wrong match for you, Eleanor.'

Her audacity had long surpassed my patience, but the confidence in which she spoke these words, not as mere opinions but with the severity of truth about them unnerved me. It was a speech I might have expected of one twice her years and yet she had all the conviction of a wise and experienced raconteur. 'What on earth would you know of our suitability?' The protest in my tone more tangible than I intended.

'All that I need to.'

'Well then you will know that he is well regarded as the greatest catch amongst the ton. So, I cannot see how you expect I might do better.'

'And yet you cannot see why, despite this, you do not appreciate the fact as well as everyone else does. Yet when he asks you to be his wife, you will accept him anyway.'

'How dare you presume to know what I feel or what I will say! I am very fond of Sheldon and have the kindest regard for him. I do not doubt that if we decide to attach ourselves to each other that our feelings would flourish a great deal better than many other marriages I could name.' I was aghast at the outburst she had provoked of me. I had never even had this discussion with myself, well not officially.

'You are wrong, you would both be quite miserable I am certain. You see, he adores you, which in ordinary circumstances, with a more ordinary woman, might indeed prove quite the harmonious arrangement you describe. But you see, you will never adore him, you will try of course and may even trick yourself into believing it, for a while... But in the end, you will crave this feeling you have pulsing through you right now. The very one that has caused you to stay and listen to so many things you did not want to hear.'

I stood up. 'You think I stayed to listen to these insults? I stayed because I made the mistake of feeling sorry for you!'

She rose too. 'No, you didn't. We both know why you are here. What you crave.' She stepped into the gap between us. 'It's alright, I will satisfy those cravings, Eleanor. If you stay just a little longer, I will show you exactly what it is I can do to you that Sheldon, or no other man will ever manage, and most likely will never so much as attempt. I will prove to you that everything I have said here is true, if you will let me.' She had worked me gradually up against the wall with small steps and I found myself wedged closely between the cold plaster and the warm pressure of her bosom.

Leave now. I warned myself.

But I did not, and nor did I stop her wandering hands that worked my skirts up to my waist, found the heat between my thighs and brought me to near collapse at the first feather light stroke of her fingertips.

'You need a husband that will not adore you, Eleanor. An indifferent man that will not be unduly concerned with whose company you are keeping when he is at his club or hunting box. I doubt Mr Elmbridge will leave your side for a moment more than he is forced to.'

I was trying, hopelessly, to follow her speech, but the words hit my ears and fell away as quickly, I could only think of the magic she was working so delicately against my writhing hips.

'A man that will not suffocate you, but permit you the freedom to come to me and let me please you like this as often as you wish it.' Her movements quickened and I sighed my pleasure into her ear which seemed to encourage her further. I had never felt nor imagined such a sensation could rise up from my own flesh and her careful manipulation of it. I should have felt disgusted at what I was permitting, wanting, enjoying, but I didn't; I cared only for the rhythm of her hand, her mouth suckling at my ear, my neck, my breast.

'See, my sweet thing, isn't that better?'

'Yes,' I groaned in reply to her whispers, collapsing against her body with the quickened strokes.

'Yes, you see, you and I are alike after all. We need a woman's touch to understand what our bodies are capable of, what will quell the hunger, don't we? Don't we?'

'Yes, yes. Don't stop,' I pleaded at her momentary pause.

'Then promise you will abandon him and be mine, Eleanor. Promise me that, and I promise to make you feel like this every day. I will show you everything there is for a woman to enjoy in her own sex, and you will not be disappointed.'

'I promise it.' I was out of control, I would have promised her anything to keep her working up this pleasure in my body so expertly.

'Good girl,' she said softly as she tugged harder on my nipple with her free hand and the violence of this tipped me into even greater subjection. The lulls and frenzies in her movements were driving me towards a despair I did not anticipate and had no idea how to brace myself for. I was dangling from the support of her body like a draped holland cover, a writhing, wriggling mess of instinctive responses that I hadn't the slightest control over, and I knew I would be ashamed of, if I could see myself from another's perspective. But I was powerless to exercise the slightest of restraint as I cried out my demands at her to move quicker against the throbbing that coursed through me from a depth I had never conceived of.

'Already, my sweet thing?' She paused, and I realised now that these pauses were deliberately punctuated to work me into even greater vulnerability.

'Please,' I begged her.

'Try to contain it just a little,' she slowed and I was on the brink of aggression at this toying with me so cruelly. Even if I had the wherewithal to "contain" this uncontrollable force that had took complete possession of my body, I would have no desire to try to suspend it. 'Do it,' I said through a gritty tone I didn't recognise as belonging to me, and was relieved when she obeyed.

As she picked the rhythm up again and failed to pause, I was incapacitated by the power of it. I could feel the strength in her tensed arm as she worked it relentlessly to please me. I could feel it coming on, although what it was and how it would manifest or end, I had no idea. What I did know; is that I wanted to go there. I wanted her to take me there. And when the shuddering began and my body was climbing and clambering all over her palm to reach the peak and prolong the pulsing, I could not believe I had almost denied myself this feeling. This knowledge. *This magic.*

I was all panting, grunts and involuntary jerks of delight that she responded to with precisely the right pace and pressure, and I couldn't imagine how many times she must have done this before to possess such skill at reading my body. Her hand slackened and slowed with the last contractions until it was just resting there, wedged between my thighs from me squeezing it so tightly in to place.

When I was sure it was over, I leaned back against the wall, released her hand and steadied myself. I was still sweating, panting and delirious, suspended in some liminal universe, but slowly, gradually, I felt the command of my own body returning to me.

What was not so welcome, was the shameful reality of what I had just done that arrived with it. I was unprepared for this, and the immediate guilt and shame that overcame me when I looked up at her made me want to vanish. A moment ago, I was sure I had fallen in love with her, now I couldn't bear the sight of her for a minute more.

'There. Now, have I convinced you?' she asked, looking pleased with herself.

I flattened down my skirts and forced my exposed breasts back into place. The humiliation of even this seemed exacerbated now. 'I have to go,' was all I said before I took off at full speed without peering back at all until I reached the saloon.

At first, the sight of everyone milling about the punch bowl and scattered about the great hall was a relief to my eyes, as was the realisation that she had not followed me back. But as I made my way through the crowds, I felt self-conscious. I reminded myself of the absurdity of my paranoia. Of course, no one could know what great misdemeanour I had just committed and nor would they. Yet I felt exposed and a heightened awareness of everyone who caught sight of me in my passing as if they knew my secret, as if they understood the disgrace that had befallen me.

'There you are!'

Sheldon seemed to apparate from thin air and I jumped, noticing him behind me.

'I turn my back for a moment and you are gone!' he complained.

'Forgive me,' I said and realised that I was not apologising for my absence but the occupation of it. 'I—I needed the powder room.'

'Are you well? You look flushed about the cheeks.'

'A little out of sorts, I think I am overtired,' I said patting them gently with a gloved hand.

'You don't feel feverish do you, you seem to be perspiring?' he said, concerned.

'No, I thank you for making such an unflattering observation,' I laughed trying to make light of it. 'I daresay it is all the dancing this evening in this heat, I am quite spent.'

'Then let me find you a chair,' he said obligingly.

Checkmate.

June 1821 - Eleanor.

I passed a terrible night: dozing through a mist of mottled awareness, twisting in my sheets, haunted by the memory, and yet, somehow; revelling in the replay of it all. I seemed to both coil in repulsion at the thought, yet simultaneously crave the pleasure of it again. The very thought of her touch sent such a persuasive yearning coursing through me, I had to squeeze my own hand hard against myself to allay it.

And as the dawn broke upon the windowpane and morning progressed in its usual style, these overwhelming feelings grew harder to avert, and I began to crave her again, despite how much the thought of her made me almost sick. And this was the greatest disparity in my feelings, as for the most part, I felt no desire towards her, no great admiration of her looks, no particular warmth of regard. Her acquaintance, I had enjoyed on a more intellectual note: Her wit and unrestrained opinion made for refreshing company, and I could not deny how well I enjoyed her many tales of exotic places in parts of the world I would likely never see, or ways of life I struggled to contemplate. But to say that I *liked* her would not be the right description at all. And yet I had been more intimate with her, than I had ever been with another, and it puzzled me. *Tormented me.*

I supposed that what she lacked in amiable qualities she made up for in other ways that were more novel in our circle. Interesting, confident women were far from ordinary here, and even though she kept a better cap on it in public, in our smaller circles, she was rather *bon mot* when she fancied it. There was a kind of charm she radiated when she was in such a frame of mind. It was this side of her I was fond of. Intrigued by.

But now, the very idea that I would have to face her again, look her plain in the eyes with the memory of the weakness she had managed to reduce me to, was intimidating. But at points in my growing arousal, the intention to avoid her and accept that I would not have her work my skirts up and soothe me again, was inconceivable. I wondered if it was usual to feel so enraptured after such an awakening. Is this what a woman could look to on her wedding night? Certainly, the prospect had improved on me, yet I could not even permit the image of Sheldon doing such a thing to me, to form in my mind. And then I remembered our conversation on the matter of me and Sheldon with dawning horror. What on earth had I agreed to? She could not be serious in forbidding me to see him and yet how could I have acquiesced to such a mad-brained request?

He would come to me today; I was quite sure he would find some small matter on which to pay a visit, as had become habit of late: A morning call, a last-minute invitation, an impromptu ride. These were things I could keep beyond her knowing, at least, if I was careful. So, I pondered why I felt such apprehension at the prospect of his coming, for it had grown customary, comfortable lately. But today it felt curious and exceedingly unnerving.

Guilt. That is what it amounted to, I realised when Bentham announced him shortly after noon, and I stared into those beguiling blue eyes, so full of optimism and esteem. I drew my gaze away almost instantly. I suddenly felt I had wronged him; deceived him somehow, despite the lack of any formal attachment between us.

'Have you recovered from last night, El? You seem better,' he asked me when Mother casually left us to finish our game of chess in the drawing room with only Watts to act as chaperone.

'Yes, I thank you. An early night is quite restorative, I find.' I kept my gaze to the chess board and moved my queen two spaces. I was struggling to concentrate on the game and puzzling over my strategy far too long before moving.

'I am glad. You were not yourself at all. I fear the season is taking its toll on your health.'

'Well, I daresay, but it is almost over. These little country affairs will certainly be a breeze after this.'

He slid his rook across the board and put me in check. 'Oh, that brings to mind the ballroom at Ham on Monday, will you go?'

'I believe mama has accepted the invitation.'

'I thought we might go together?'

'Yes, if you like,' I said quite without thinking. But then I remembered I need not be concerned; *she* would not be present at Ham House to see us arriving in the Elmbridges' carriage anyway. It had taken me a while to realise that he was only attending the season events I had confirmed on. I hadn't noticed the pattern myself since there were so many invitations to consider that no one—not even the most seasoned of ton—managed to attend them all. It was only when Betsy made the connection and rather plainly pointed out the significance of this, that I was forced to accept that he was simply enduring the season for my sake. Reflecting on this now only exacerbated the significance. 'Sheldon,' I should have stopped myself there. He looked up from the chess board and peered at me with interest. 'What is your opinion of Miss Craythorne?'

He frowned, searching for the relevance of such an unprompted topic. 'I'm not sure I have one,' he said blankly.

'Of course you do,' I said.

'I suppose she is agreeable enough, considering,' he answered.

'And her looks?'

'El, what kind of question is that?'

'A simple one between friends, I think.'

'Plain, I suppose. Why?'

'I just wondered what the chances were of her making a match. I mean, that is obviously why they are here.'

'Well, you needn't wonder on my account.' His hand was hovering just above mine as he spoke and I realised then what he thought my motive for asking such a frank question.

I picked up my king and moved it out of check, being careful to avoid any contact. I caught sight of Watts spying from above the duster she was pretending to clean with as I leaned back in my chair to put some greater distance between us. I wished I could offer him the same assurance, but far from feeling greater confidence, I was growing evermore doubtful and confused by my feelings. I looked across at his handsome face, deep in concentration, planning his next move on the board. I was the luckiest debutante in the county, in the ton, why didn't I *feel* it?

He put me back in check with a shuffle of his rook and sat up straighter. 'Well, do you think she will make a match?'

I studied the board. 'It's hard to say, if she means to, I suppose.'

'I daresay she will.'

'Is that an informed opinion? I mean, the odds are hardly stacked in her favour,' I quickly added.

'No. But she has a fair few to her advantage too,' he said simply, and quite oblivious to the intrigue he had whipped up in me.

'I can think of only one; and we all know what that is.'

'The money is not all, I assure you. What that family lacks in the way of birth connections, they make up for in status.'

This puzzled me profoundly. Had I missed some vital detail of lineage? I realised I was frowning when I saw him pause and hesitate. 'Mr Elmbridge, I do not follow, perhaps you might enlighten me, for my understanding is that you can be wealthier than the Duke of Devonshire, but it cannot buy you status, not really.'

'Not the kind you speak of perhaps, but status amongst the brotherhood works differently.'

'And plainly speaking?'

'Her father is well respected in certain circles: Important circles that go beyond the realm of the gentleman's clubs of St James or the House of Lords.'

'Beyond the realms of basic decency?'

'It's complicated, El.'

'Ah, I see, too complicated to explain to a female, you mean—'

'No.' He reclined in his seat and pressed his fingertips together. 'I shouldn't even be telling you this.'

I was curious now, but I relented. He looked uncomfortable and shifty and I was quite satisfied that he would be open with me if he could. 'Very well, spare me the details, but pray tell me: this *circle*, is it influential enough to overcome the general expectations of good society?'

He nodded and I frowned.

'Of course, everyone will put it down to her dowry and no one who understands the matter any differently will care to correct it.'

'And it will not be?'

'It helps no doubt. Why are you so concerned about it anyway?'

'I'm not concerned. Simply interested, for her sake, she is my friend now.'

'Yes, I noticed you have all relented in your snub, you even managed the impossible and brought Lady Elizabeth about.' He seemed amused at this and I scowled remembering my protest at having to make her acquaintance just months ago.

'You know, a gentleman would not remind a lady of her oversights.'

'You are right, perhaps instead he might remind her how beautiful she looks today.'

The tone changed in an instant and we sat silently a moment, eyes fixed, no words between us.

I was relieved when Bentham interrupted us and broke the eerie silence. Well, for all of about two seconds until he announced Mariella. I dropped the wooden chest piece I was holding with the surprise of this announcement and noticed it was enough to even wipe the look off Sheldon's face. *Had she heard us?*

'Miss Craythorne,' Sheldon rose and bowed as she entered and made her way to the table.

I had forgotten how to speak altogether. I wasn't sure if it was the discomfort of simply seeing her after yesterday's antics, or being caught up in the awkwardness of being found in Sheldon's company talking about her. Whichever it was, I was ill equipped for, and stumbled clumsily over my greeting. 'Miss Craythorne, what a surprise.'

'Mr Elmbridge,' she bobbed a quick curtsy in reply but her gaze was fixed on me and I knew exactly how to interpret the fire in her eyes. 'Miss Ashlyn.'

Muted rage.

'You must forgive my impertinence, but I called to see if you might like to take a turn about Hyde Park, but I did not realise you were in company.'

I smiled sheepishly. 'That is very good of you to think of me, Miss Craythorne, but I did not expect you and I am not suitably attired. You are, of course, very welcome to join us at the table. Mr Elmbridge is just about to defeat me at the chessboard.'

A tight-lipped smile formed across her mouth. 'That is most kind indeed, but as you well know, I am not fond of games. Mr Elmbridge, I hope you are well?'

'Yes, well indeed. Thank you, Miss Craythorne.' He looked at me as he said this and I watched her stifle a grimace as she re-buttoned her half-opened spencer and refused the offered chair I gestured to. 'And you, Miss Craythorne, you are well?' His tone was one of courtesy rather than interest and I knew she was far too wise to fail to see through it. But it was upon me she fixed her gaze to make reply.

'I have been *very* well indeed, Mr Elmbridge, at least I was; I think I feel a little out of sorts all of a sudden.'

'I'm sorry to hear it, is there anything I can do?' he offered.

I could imagine the kind of reply she made privately and watched her lips curl up at the temptation of speaking it aloud.

'No. I thank you,' she replied quickly, before I had the chance to make my offering. 'It's nothing serious, I'm sure.' She narrowed her eyes. 'Some fresh air will put me right again no doubt.'

'If you won't join us at the table, perhaps you will take some refreshment, instead?' I offered, but it was clear the option appealed to no one, the atmosphere was unmistakably stagnant and even I felt some relief at the prospect of her leaving, however much her presence stirred up something in my loins that made me crave her company quite against my will.

She half smiled; a pointed, contrived effort as she raised her hand to Mary to summons her to fetch her gloves. 'No, the others will expect me, I really cannot stop.' She snatched the offered gloves from Mary's hands and pushed her own inside them. 'Good day to you both.'

I EXPECTED HER TO CALL the next day once she had got over her strop, and dressed suitably in my walking dress so this time I could oblige her. But when she didn't come, I grew tired of the waiting and took Samson out instead. I suspected she was sulking and meant to make me sorry. An utter waste of her time where I was concerned: she knew not enough of my character, I supposed, to realise I was not minded to pander to such tiresome campaigns. I half expected to see her calling card amongst the others left for me when I returned home however, but this also proved a disappointment. *Fine. If that's how she wants to play.*

I didn't hear from her the day after, or the next, which I had to confess I had found mildly amusing. But I had not expected her absence at the Juliennes' charity tea on Saturday and began to find her insolence irritating. It was almost a week later when our paths finally crossed of all unlikely places, at Almack's. It was to be our final attendance at the assembly rooms before we set off for our summer departures in the coming days. It seemed only the Jamesons were minded to stay on a little longer in town. I presumed the Craythornes intended to do the same and make the most of their voucher purchase before the balls ceased in July.

'Evening ladies,' she said casually, strolling into the semi-circle we had formed around the fire mantle as we sipped on ratafia and caught up with each other's news. It appeared we were all as stunned as one another when she slipped into our notice. Unlike most things in London, this latest triumph of theirs had been kept from our hearing. Betsy cast a glare at me as if to ask, why hadn't I told her. But my mama had not made mention of it to me at all, and I doubted she would want to make mention of the fact to anyone since she had clearly been forced to relent. I watched her in the reflection of the mirror but did not turn or acknowledge her beyond a brief hello.

She was wearing a gown of crimson silk trimmed with black ribbon and fine lacework which I found both shocking and impressive on her slight, square frame, but took pains not to give it away. I meant to give nothing away to her at all tonight and keep as plaster-cast as she.

Her hair was wrapped in a co-ordinating turban with only a few wispy strands escaping on one side of her face and her lips and cheeks rosier than could be natural and yet gave no incriminating trace of rouge. She was not pretty, not handsome, but she *was* striking. Very striking, in both looks and presence, and I noted the change of tone amongst our chatter growing from one of frigid formality to one of subtle innuendo over the course of the evening. And, of course, she delivered all the usual social charm amongst the set, regaling some old Parisian tale of the origins of her dress in her usual witty narrative. I pretended to listen and threw in a few timely nods and chuckles when I noticed the others doing so, but my thoughts and eyes were searching for Sheldon. He was late tonight and I wished he was not. It was the only affair I had lately declined him escorting me to, feeling that such an arrival at Almack's a little too bold a statement. But now I wished it otherwise. If she thought her slighting me would force me to give Sheldon up, it was time I gave a demonstration of my own obstinacy.

'Good evening, ladies,' he said with a bow when he finally arrived and broke up our circle with his presence. His amiable air and gravely tone seemed enough to induce the company into a display of genteel femininity—except her of course. Although there was something telling in her eyes too as she paused and gracefully accepted the sudden decline of interest in her narrative. I wasn't sure what it was; amusement, well disguised contempt?

I permitted a brief moment of cordial small talk before bidding him to steal me away for a turn around the ballroom. Hand on top of his; I kept my eyes on hers as I strolled away from our circle in light footed strides. Even when I turned from her, I felt her gaze on me, following me, searing her discontent into the back of my head. So, I made more effort than usual to be animated and exaggerated in my manner toward him, whether we were chatting, dancing or simply staring at each other across the conversation of others. I pushed my performance as close to the boundary of decency and disgrace as my position would permit me in such wide company, and was only mildly surprised at how willing to oblige me Sheldon proved.

Not surprisingly, he was oblivious to my scheme and returned my gestures with such enthusiasm I feared he had lost the restraint of his own propriety as he took the liberty of taking extra dances and discreetly brushing his fingers across the top of my un-gloved hand when I removed them for the buffet. Even his position would not have afforded him such impertinence without expectation of an announcement to be forthcoming. But nobody seemed to notice or show concern. I pushed away the building anxiety at the thought. My intentions were otherwise engaged and I was pleased to note they had been effective. I caught Mariella glowering at me from above her fluted glass as I danced the final set with him.

She had tried and largely failed to feign disinterest in my performance for most of the evening. But I knew she was scrutinising our every move, that she was probably the only one to have noticed that brief brush of hands, to be counting our dances. I had excluded almost all other offers on my dance card except for the opening quadrille, and chose instead to sit them out in Sheldon's company. It was later, on his departure that I realised the consequences of my frivolity and the impression I had pressed on him with my complacency. There was something uncommonly fervent in the way he stared into my eyes and lingered over his farewell. I could not hold his gaze for more than a brief few seconds for fear of some declaration escaping his lips. It unsettled me. But he had not spoken, I reminded myself as I climbed up into the waiting coach.

When I saw Mariella sat inside it, I nearly jumped back out with the fright.

'Pleased to see me then?' she said flatly with slightly raised brows and I quickly regained my composure and stepped in fully to take my seat. It was our coach after all.

'What are you doing?' I asked her, checking to see if Delores was in sight. She was chatting to Lady Mowbray and not even slightly conscious of my whereabouts.

'Well, I noted you are game for a tease, I see from tonight's amateur dramatics. So, I accept the challenge,' she said expectantly and tapped the coach to instruct the driver on.

I sat bolt upright in objection as the tug of the horses shifted us. 'What are you doing? I am travelling with my parents,' I said confused.

'Well,' she leapt across the moving carriage to sit beside me. 'To answer the second part of your question, your parents are busy chatting a while. You see, my parents are ever so grateful to your mama her for securing our vouchers and have not had the chance to tell her so,' she said, pointing through the small window where I caught a glimpse of them fully engrossed in conversation with her at the roadside.

'And to answer the first.' I felt her breath against my ear and sighed with the memory of her poised just like this in the saddle room. 'I am going to teach you a lesson in how to *really* inflict torture.' And as the last syllable left her mouth, I felt her tongue set on my neck and her hand making its way up my thigh. Something inside me screamed with a long-suppressed relief whilst the rest of me berated it.

'Yes, that's right, my sweet. If you want to play such games, you had better learn some more sophisticated tactics.' She pressed hard against me a moment then released. 'Good girl, sit back for me.'

Stop her. Don't do this again. Don't give her the satisfaction.

Of course, I forgot my protest entirely as she began stroking away in that feather light motion that I had dreamt about and tried to replicate every night since this awakening, to no avail. I relaxed back fully against the back of the seat. It was better than I remembered it, even though we were rattling around a dark coach when we shouldn't have been. I was grateful for the thud of the horses' gallop against the road when those involuntary sighs began to escape me again.

'That's right: savour it, my sweet, it might be a very long time before anyone touches you like this again if you make the same mistake twice.' Even in my distraction, a shard of my consciousness was intact and understood her threat.

'Even if he knows how to please you, it's a very long wait until your wedding night. If he has even asked the question yet? Can you wait that long, my sweet?'

I mumbled a no. It was the most honest thing I had done all night.

'Do you want to feel his hands here like mine? Have you thought about his rough fingertips working you up like this?'

A splinter of contention was scratching at my pleasure. *Could she know I could not permit the thought? Could she somehow sense the resistance in me despite my affront?*

'You know he will want to touch you much more roughly than I do? Climb up right inside this tiny, delicate space with all his ferocity.' I felt a finger push up gently inside me and gasped. I was not sure if it felt exciting or uncomfortable, but when her thumb continued working on my favourite spot in some kind of strange simultaneous effort with the gentle thrusting of her finger, the sensation began to improve and my hips soon took over the pace and rhythm.

'Restraint, my sweet thing, if you don't slow down, I might venture too deep and spoil you. We don't want that, do we? You need to stay intact until you have decided what to do about your little dilemma.'

This prospect frightened me enough to obey her instructions. Was it even possible for her to cause such a thing to happen? I did not want to find out. I slowed right down but it took all my restraint. She managed to conjure indescribable sensations to stir up in me with such a slight of touch, it was indeed a kind of torture. Could anyone manage this task or was this a skill unique to her peculiar knowing? Certainly, the thought of Sheldon doing such things I could not entertain. But perhaps if he did, if he could induce me into such raptures, command my body with such ease, perhaps we might flourish after all.

'I hope he is gentle with you when he breaks you, you are such a sensitive flower.'

Breaks me? Was that really how it felt? I had irritating images of breaking in a horse distracting me from the pleasures of her touch and I wished she would shut up now.

'Of course, if I broke you—if you wanted me to—I would at least kiss you better again.'

Something told me she did not refer to kissing me on the lips. Would she really kiss me there? The thought of her mouth there almost killed me and demolished all the measured restraint I had contrived in fear and distraction in a single moment. I could feel it coming, the waves again, the control disappeared, the hunger for it violent and unstoppable. 'Kiss me there,' I demanded, screamed. But as I felt her draw away to reposition herself, I forced her hand back in place. *It is too late.* I was already there. I squeezed her tightly as my body shook with the force of it and sighed, groaned and panted against her shoulder to muffle the sound.

'That's it,' she said, slowing; kissing the side of my face, sucking my ear lobe.

When I was recovered and had fixed my skirts back into place, I tried to ignore the smug smile on her face.

Alright: you win tonight.

'Better?'

I nodded but could not look directly at her; the shame had begun to creep in as fast as it had faded at her touch.

'There is so much more we can share, Eleanor, and without the ties of marriage to stifle our pleasures. We are blessed with a freedom few women are, without the threat of destitution hanging in the balance of our marital state. But you must make a decision because this time, there will be no second chances.'

Something in her expression told me this was no bluff.

'My family away to Brighton next week. I will be home alone. London will be quieter too. You can join me there if you would like to spend the night. I will teach you more about your body by morning, than most women married forty years ever discover. But; he *must* go, Eleanor.'

She tapped the coach and it slowed and took a change of direction at her signal. I realised then, I didn't even know where we were, even though we must have been driving more than ten minutes. I lifted the blind to gaze through the window but the pitch blackness did little to help me navigate my surroundings.

'Choose wisely, Eleanor, for the wrong decision, either way, will most likely lead to insufferable regret.'

I saw a blur of lights flash through the small coach window and realised as it came into better focus that we were back in King Street and actually hadn't gone far at all. The sight of my parents stood waiting, unimpressed, sent immediate despair through me.

'It is alright, the drivers have been paid for their discretion.'

I hated the way she interrupted my thoughts with such accuracy.

'Well, providing you can find some reasonable explanation for why we have just journeyed in circles for the past ten minutes, without implicating them.' She seemed amused at this and I quickly attempted to think something up as the coach stalled and the door popped open.

'Goodnight, Eleanor, sleep well,' she said as she hopped down to the footplate and my grim-faced parents approached. I braced myself.

I told them she had asked for a demonstration of Samson's prowess and since they were so detained, I saw no harm in obliging her. Of course, they found my explanation as absurd as it sounded and berated me for such frivolity, but accepted it, no less. What else were they to have concluded: that their daughter had just been seduced by a female? I doubted they were any wiser than I was before to even think that such practices were even possible. Thankfully, Mother, who was every part as bitter over the Almack's vouchers as I suspected, was keen to blame practically anything peculiar that could be fractionally related to them as proof of the folly of my father's judgement, which suited me. So, I listened attentively to her rant for the short journey home.

'I mean, who on earth would make such a request at such an hour in the dark of night. Peculiar girl. Indeed, Henry, I don't care how much you insist otherwise, they are a different breed altogether, however many excuses you find for them!'

Ham House.

June 1821. - Eleanor.

I kept a very low profile over our last few days in London. I pretended I wasn't well and when the doctor came on Mama's insistence, he concluded my symptoms to be conducive to fatigue and prescribed bed rest. I was more fatigued in mind than body, but I was happy to accept his diagnosis for it suited my predicament. I was physically fine, and the malady I suffered with, I was certain he would not be able to diagnose or find a curative for.

The first couple of days were bliss: no early morning rising after half a night's sleep, no calls to pay or receive, no rushing about for costume changes and more importantly; no Mariella or Sheldon to contend with. The latter, I felt sorry for as he was turned away from the house with the news of my indisposition, but continued calling to leave a posy or receive an update on my health and send his well wishes. The guilt thickened as I watched him from behind a curtain. I knew that whilst my rather flirtatious behaviour with him at the assembly rooms was intended to disconcert Mariella, what it had actually done, is expose his true feelings towards me in a way I could no longer doubt or deny. He was not pursuing me for the sake of his family, or his duty and he no longer saw me simply as his old playmate; I saw it that night, in his eyes, in his touch, in his concern: he truly regarded me, perhaps was even in love with me, just as everyone else had tried to warn me. This time, I saw it for myself, knew it to be true, wondered how I did not see it before.

It was this sobering realisation that my sick bed had given me ample time to fathom out and had brought me to my senses. I would not repeat these transgressions with Mariella again. I could not pretend I had not been pleasantly surprised by this awakening, this opportunity to discover things I never knew about myself, about my own body, and yet, I knew it was not *her* I wished to share them with. Not really. I had allowed myself to get carried away in the excitement of it all, the temptation, the curiosity. But for all of the adventure, all the pleasure; the guilt and discomfort threw the whole into the shade, and it had prompted me to ask myself some difficult questions.

I still did not have all the answers and I wasn't sure if even the ones I had arrived at were correct, but the more I deliberated, the more confident I felt that this was the best course of action. I would create some distance. Mariella's would fall away naturally on our departure since she was to stay on in London a while, and Sheldon, I would not avoid, but would not allow myself to give him any further impressions that weren't borne solely out of my own true feeling and regard. It was time to be earnest, with him, with myself, whatever that meant. And with Mariella out of the picture, I had the best chance of seriously focusing on working out what that was.

I did not know whether he was the man I would, or should marry, because I had not been willing to seriously consider him in that light. My thoughts had been firing off in so many other directions I was happy to be diverted from this question. But the season was over now. Mariella would be gone. It was time. I did not know if we would end up parting as the friends we began as, or if we would find ourselves ending as husband and wife, but it was only fair that we both discovered it, once and for all.

So, the day before our departure, when he called, I ran downstairs at the sound of his horses drawing up in Berkeley Square, told Bentham to admit him to the drawing room and refused Mama's orders to return to my bed. 'I am better now, Mama, honest. I feel as fit as a fiddle now I am rested. Pray, do not let Mr Elmbridge be turned away again for nothing.'

She acquiesced and left us alone together. Completely alone. No Delores. No Watts. Not even Mary hovering about with a duster. I supposed we could at least speak plainly and that was what I knew would finally answer our questions; plain speaking and plain behaviour. That is how we would arrive at the truth. And so, when he had made his enquiries over my health and I had thanked him for coming, I knew what I must do next.

We were sitting on the sofa's opposite one another, and despite our lack of surveillance, we stood on ceremony, stiff in our seats, averting our gazes to the floor, or a portrait, or a view out onto the square when they grew too intense. Keeping our conversation appropriate to over hearing, and yet despite all these binds, there was a subtext between us so powerful in its silence, I could no longer ignore it. 'Sheldon,' I said getting up and crossing the Chinese rug to take a seat beside him, 'I think it is time we had a more serious conversation.'

His eyes widened with surprise and he turned at an angle to face me when I settled beside him.

'I know I have been a puzzle since you returned from abroad.' He did not exactly nod but I could tell from his expression that he thought it an understatement. 'But I hope you will give me leave to speak more earnestly to you, explain...'

'Of course, you may say to me whatever is in your mind,'

I smiled and took his hand in my own. 'Well, I have been reflecting these past days on...many things, and I see I have been difficult, evasive, too much... and I am sorry for it. For you have done all in your power to be patient, agreeable, a gentleman. I didn't see it before. I didn't want to see it, but I have not been fair in putting you off and avoiding the matter—'

'El, you know I am in love with you. You must know it.'

'I think I do, I have just been too frightened to acknowledge the fact.'

'I don't want to frighten you, El. I want to make you happy.'

'I realise that, and I want to be fair to you Sheldon. Honest with you. For I have not been. I will be now. I want to see if there might be a future for us. If it's possible that we might deal handsomely together not only as friends; if I could see myself as your wife. But the truth is, I need some time to understand my feelings better.'

He smiled and looked down at our hands, mine still grasping his so lightly I had quite forgotten to remove it. As I withdrew it now, he took it into his palm, brought it up to his lips and kissed it before releasing me. 'How much,' he said in earnest accents, his eyes fixed on mine, 'I wish I might do as you once did in error, and kiss you on the lips. I daresay I should not even speak of it, if I am a gentleman at all, but, well, there it is.'

I was only a little surprised at his speech. Perhaps now I had contended with far greater surprises, I was less easily unnerved. I smiled and told him sincerely, 'You are every part the gentleman Sheldon, it is I that have been at fault, and it is for me to set things right again between us.'

So, when we travelled to Ham that evening to attend our final ballroom before leaving London, I spent most of the evening in pursuit of this conciliation. Taking turns about the ballroom with him so we could chat privately, sitting out numerous dance requests on account of my recovering health—although I really did it to show him that I had no wish to dance with anyone at all tonight, apart from him. It would have proved quite the successful evening by all accounts until a sight I had not anticipated came in to view.

It had been a crush, with everyone making the most of the convenient proximity to the city and a full moon to journey under. I supposed my eyes had been all for him and much escaped my notice on this account, but how I had failed to notice the Craythornes' attendance, I did not know.

So, their transition into the ton was now complete. Oh Mama, what have you done submitting to this folly when you could have blackballed them, prevented this. They would have remained on the sidelines as they were with but a few of the local families and charitable affairs of no consequence, to admit them. Now was I to expect to cross paths with her everywhere I went? It was on precisely the assumption I would not have to, that I was able to set my mind to focussing on Sheldon and I, without her to distract me, or try to. It was also why I had been so relaxed and blasé in keeping to Sheldon's company so openly tonight. I thought us free of her observation and scheming to sway me, to hold me to ransom over ultimatum's I resented.

I almost spat out my orange wine, when I had noticed her sat quietly in the company of her brothers at the far end of the gallery. How long had she been there? She was sat in the corner so inconspicuously I was surprised to have caught sight of her at all. We shared an awkward smile of recognition and instantly I could see the contempt she tried to mask in her expression. Clearly, she had been here all night and the very fact that she had failed to mention her coming or even called upon me since, was no accident. *It was a test.* A test I had failed no doubt. And yet, I no longer wanted to succeed in.

So, when they approached me a little later, when the rest of our Cuddington set detained us in conversation, I had no intention of hiding my attachment to him from her notice or attempting to play it up for her irritation. I remained in honour of my feelings and behaved accordingly. 'Miss Craythorne, Mr Craythorne,' I said calmly, smiling. 'I hope you are having a good evening?' I studied her response carefully but she gave little away.

'Miss Ashlyn,' they chorused. 'A very good evening, thank you. Although not as merry as yours I think,' she said with emphasis in her tone and face. Nobody noticed, even Sheldon's attention had been turned in conversation with the Colonel. I understood her plainly but did not respond to it. 'Have you seen anything of Martha? I do not think she is here tonight.'

'Yes, she is dancing with Bertram.'

I turned to the dance floor and caught sight of the pair, looking exceedingly jolly.

'But I am hardly surprised you didn't notice, you have seemed rather preoccupied this evening. Felix,' she turned to her brother, Bertram's twin, who was looking between us more wisely than I felt comfortable with. 'Be a darling and get Miss Ashlyn a refill; her glass is almost empty.' I watched him scuttle off like an obedient lapdog before I could protest. There was something odd in his character, but I was yet to work out what it was. His younger brother, who was twirling Martha about in the country dance, was a most amiable creature, but he seemed evermore the exceptional sibling amongst them.

Once Felix had disappeared into the throng of guests gathered in clutches around the ballroom floor, she stepped in close to take his space and stared at me plain faced. 'I think we might go outside for some air.'

It was not a request. I followed her out with the obedience I had just mocked Felix for as I braced myself for what was either going to be an earful or an attempt at a more pleasant reminder of what was at jeopardy. I felt a shudder in *that* place at the suggestion that it might be the latter, but I was determined to ignore it. Why could I never replicate it without the thought or presence of her to prompt it? I had not so much as felt her breath upon me and already I could feel my senses awakening to the possibility when in my rational head, I wanted to entertain none of it.

When she led me out across the Great Hall, up the stairs, across the mezzanine balcony and into a dark room I could not make out the shape of, I felt an uncomfortable sense of anticipation at what might happen next.

'Surprise!' she said in a tone that allowed for no mistaking in the sarcasm it was intended with.

'Mariella, I didn't—'

'Expect to see me here?' she cut in.

'No, I mean—'

She stepped in closer and held her hand up to me. 'Do not do me the injury of insulting my intelligence and breaking your promise all in the same day, Eleanor. We both understand the situation well enough I think.'

'I am not sure that you do. I have been thinking and I am of no mind to upset you or participate in this toying any longer. Nor am I willing to cut Sheldon to satisfy you—'

'Oh?' she looked up, mildly amused by this, as if my words were made of paper and it would only take her to set a flame to them to destroy their conviction. 'I am sure that is what you want to say, what you would like to feel—'

'Stop, Mariella, this is not a game.' She was slowly edging me further and further into a corner as she spoke.

'Yet you are the one playing us off against each other, whispering sweet nothings into his ear whilst sighing your pleasure into mine.'

I was resisting the flashbacks of the memory of the last time she backed me up against a wall. 'Mariella, I do not deny it. It was wrong of me, and I mean to start afresh, with Sheldon as my potential suitor and you as my friend, and *only*, my friend.'

'You cannot have us both,'

'I have known Sheldon my whole life; I cannot simply cut him as you wish, even if I wanted to. And I don't.'

She tugged gently on one of my ringlets and twisted it about in her fingers. 'I understand that it will not be easy. Yet I am certain it will be somewhat easier than giving up the time we have come to enjoy together?'

Now I could feel her breath upon me. 'Why must you insist on making an ultimatum out of this when there is no need? I do not understand it?'

'Making tough choices, Eleanor, is part of the adult world we now inhabit. We simply cannot have it all; even if we have so far enjoyed the luxury of having everything we so desire. We have been set free from our nursemaids now, and in the real world, everything must come at a price.'

'What possible reason would I have to sacrifice him to continue our acquaintance, when I have no intention of continuing in such follies with you? Don't you see, I don't want that, not with you.'

'Hmm, you see that is the problem...' she let go of my curl and it sprung back into place, then she moved a finger to my lips, 'You say one thing with your mouth and another with other parts of your body—'

Her deliberate antagonism was becoming frustrating now and I was fast growing out of patience with her. 'Well, you will be pleased to know that they are quite in accord at last.'

'Perhaps we should put that notion to the test.'

'No, we shan't. I know my own mind and I do not mean to change it.'

'What a shame, Eleanor. Wrong choice. But you shall have to come around to that learning in time.' She was talking so close to my face I felt our lips almost brush. 'I have been patient with you. More patient than I usually am because, well, you were special to me Eleanor. But now I see that you are quite the tease, quite the disappointment, I shan't waste anymore on you.'

'Fine. As you wish it, Mariella, I will make it easier for you. If you cannot be rational and consent to being an ordinary friend then, I choose him! The loss you speak of will be all yours. You are nothing without me to help pave your way into good society and make your introductions. I was foolish to waste such efforts on you. Let us see how far you get in the absence of my assistance.'

'Oh, Eleanor, you are perfectly right; you have been quite the helpful hostess, and you will indeed be missed by our group. But, you have been *so* good in your endeavours, I am quite sure I can take it from here.'

'*Our* group.' This made laugh louder than I meant to. '*My* group, Mariella; my friends—who have been good enough to tolerate you for my sake. Not anymore. Every one of them will have abandoned you by morning. A word is all it will take to keep every door closed to you.'

'I don't doubt it. But you shan't say a thing to anyone, well, not if you want to encourage my silence.'

'You bluff, Mariella, you cannot speak of anything without implicating yourself in turn!'

'You're right. But if you are to ruin me regardless, I have absolutely no incentive not to at least bring you tumbling down with me. And you know the trouble with a family of your rank is that when you fall from such a lofty height it makes for a very rough landing. Me, I mean who am I? Who will care much for an outsider's misdeeds beyond the morning on-dit? I will simply live up to the disappointment and scandal that was anticipated. It is your name that will be remembered, far and wide. And let us not forget the other misfortune that befalls your lineage: the power you have to taint every member of your family in one single act. We will have long moved on and been forgotten when the consequences of it are left in London. Where does a family such as yours run to, to be forgotten?'

I was too stunned by her audacity to reply. I wanted to find the courage to call her bluff; dare her to divulge the vulgarities of our encounters and see if she really did have the gumption to do it, or find anyone willing to listen to such fantastic details, less still, believe them. Yet something warned me against it. Somehow, however much it defied all logic that she could go through with such a threat, there was something that told me she was mad-brained enough to try it. The very idea of all the scandal and the shadow it might leave lingering in its wake was enough to make me contain my impulse. I was likely to be a married woman before long, one way or another. I would remember this moment then, when I could cause her far greater detriment. For now, I would simply wash my hands of her.

'Good girl,' she said to me in that all too familiar tone I had been used to hearing in better circumstances. I jumped as she ran her fingers in a long trail from my waist to beneath my chin. I knew I should have stopped her, but I was speechless and immobile. 'You see the sense in us abandoning that course; for us both to go on as if none of this ever happened?'

Reluctantly, I managed a nod.

'Then we agree on something at least. I will miss you, Eleanor, but not as much as you will miss me. A shame though, you are such a pretty thing; I was quite looking forward to sampling all the delights you had to offer.' She licked my cheek and even though I was filled with a hate so violent I was nearly shaking, her touch froze me.

'Never mind, you will have Mr Elmbridge to keep you occupied now.' And with that, she let go of me, stepped back and patted down her skirts nonchalantly as if nothing at all had happened. 'Goodbye Eleanor.'

As I watched her disappear out of the room and the clink of footsteps faded down the stairs, I barely moved. Shock. I think, for I could not seem to curse or cry and I wanted to do both quite desperately.

I composed myself a while before returning to the party, and when I did, I was sorry to find Sheldon had removed to the billiards room with a party of gentleman. I looked across to where Miss Craythorne had been sat to find her now prattling away amongst the company of my friends. It was too soon to feign ignorance of her when I was so incensed. The risk of slipping up and causing a scene was too fragile right now. I hoped that this really would be the last time I would have to tolerate her presence for a while and be free of her. They might be climbing at a rapid rate, but I doubted they would get much further now until next season, they simply weren't well known enough to be invited to the kind of intimate affairs with old acquaintances we would frequent until then. So, I sought out my mama instead. 'Mama, I should like to go now, I am quite fatigued,' I complained, finding her at the gaming table playing whist with Delores and the Dowager.

'Eleanor, it is but a quarter past nine. Whatever is the matter, are you unwell again?'

'No. I just want to go home. I am bored here.'

'Keep your voice down,' she hushed me. 'You will offend our hosts. We have just started on a new game; I can hardly just announce our going. We should be finished by ten, do you think you can wait another hour?'

I nodded and sat watching the game in a sulk for a quarter of an hour before I saw Sheldon come back into the room. I got up immediately and made a beeline for him.

'Miss Ashlyn,' he said with a note of surprise in his voice which gave away his bewilderment.

'Oh, Sheldon,' I said taking his arm before he had the chance to offer it. 'I thought you might never return, how many cigars can a man smoke?'

'Eleanor are you quite well?' he asked quietly as a band of men followed through the door and dispersed into different corners of the room.

'No, I pray you get me out of here somehow.'

He glanced about the room. 'Where is Delores?'

'Playing whist with my mama.'

'Very well,' he agreed, 'let me go out first and meet me in the corridor in a few moments, alright?'

I nodded.

The relief of our escape was nerve restoring and I instantly felt the weight of my vexations begin to lift. I did not care where we went or whether I was noticed missing, I cared only to be out of there.

He steered me along the corridors which were empty save a few busied footmen who were too disinterested to pay attention to us.

'I do not know the house well, do you?' he asked me quietly as we turned and rushed along the Great Hall before someone emerged to see us.

'No, but I would rather be out of it altogether. Might you summon your carriage?'

'Eleanor, don't be absurd. What on an earth has happened?'

'Please.' I felt a quiver of desperation, a tremble of my lip that I feared would falter into a wave of sobbing.

'You know I cannot. Unless we go back for Delores and I offer to convey you home in her company?'

'No, they will not go for another half hour; they are in the middle of a game.'

'El, you are upset, what is it?'

'Please, Sheldon, don't ask me,' I pleaded.

I was relieved when he led me out of the house and beneath the shelter of a small portico beside the main door. It was night, but the moon was bright and cast its silvery light against the grand façade of the east wing.

When we stood facing each other, his face creased with the concern of his questions, a lump began to form in my throat and I swallowed it down.

'Is there something you wanted to say to me?' he asked carefully.

I shook my head. 'No, I just—' I could not find the words. I wanted to say sorry to him; sorry for a wrong he did not even know of. Sorry for a lack of judgement and restraint he did not know me guilty of. Sorry for being so tiresome and evasive, when I wanted so much to be the good companion I had always used to be, once upon a time.

'El, you are crying?'

I am crying? I dabbed beneath my eyes and inspected my gloves for the evidence. *I am.* I turned away and stood with my back to him, as I fumbled about for a handkerchief in my reticule. I could not believe this night could get any worse, but yet again I found myself yearning for an exit. A flood of tears came rushing forth before I could contain the full force of them any longer. It was the relief at last, to be away from there, from *her*, to be able to breathe again.

He spun about to face me. 'El? Good god, what's happened?' he said, reaching for me, hesitant then tentative; grasping lightly at my shoulders. I could not speak, even if I had wanted to. It seemed the longer I had held in my despair, the more gushing its pent-up release.

I was not only sobbing for what had just passed, for the venom and the shock at it all, but for what I had done, for what I had allowed and embroiled myself in. For things I could not undo, that I wished so much that I might. It all came with such brutal clarity as I remembered her glacial tone, her eyes casting daggers at me. She was a vulgar creature and I had not seen her for what she was, until now. What was worse is that I had not seen him for what he was either: a good man, a dear friend. I stepped in closer to him and held onto the lapels of his tailcoat, rested my forehead against the silk of his waistcoat and felt myself growing calmer. There was no longer as much as an inch between our bodies and I felt the warmth of his radiate through mine. It was comforting. The heat of him, the woody scent of his cologne that I had grown used to, quite without realising how familiar it was to me until now. When I felt his arms loosely envelope my shoulders, I stepped in an inch, reached my arms about his waist and sighed my relief as I felt the support of him pressed against me, encompassing me. My sobs fading into starting breaths that were beginning to regulate themselves at last. Even when they had settled to a purr against his neck cloth, I didn't move. I didn't want to.

We stood at length like this; neither of us speaking or moving, just the night breeze chilling our faces and whipping up a curl of my hair every now and then.

Good Riddance.

June 1821. - Eleanor.

Our absence from the party at Ham had not gone unnoticed. We were found out by Anna's chaperone who was evidently more circumspect in her duties than Delores, and had took it upon herself to have a footman seek us out and report our whereabouts to Mama. We were still stood in that comforting embrace, when the clatter of approaching footsteps and the orange glow of gas lamps came to our notice. We had just enough time to stand apart before Mama and Delores stepped into the portico with a party of footman. An amber orb of light dazzling us and my mama blinking in stunned disbelief. 'Eleanor!' she shrieked.

'Lady Ashlyn,' Sheldon said immediately, stepping forward with a low bow, 'I am sorry if we startled you. Miss Ashlyn was not feeling well and I escorted her to get some air, forgive my impertinence, I should have alerted you.'

'It was my fault, Mama,' I said before she could respond, 'I would not let him go and tell anyone and I was so overcome, he feared to leave me alone for even a moment.'

The entourage looked between us both.

'Footmen, our coach please, as quick as may be,' she said and when they shuffled off to carry out their instructions, she turned to Sheldon and said, 'Mr Elmbridge, I am disappointed in you and I shall not pretend otherwise. Only imagine if it was someone other than we who came upon the pair of you. You both know the consequences of such a discovery. I can only assume that your disregard of seeking a chaperone means you are minded to accept the consequences of your actions—'

'Indeed I am ma'am, you may rely upon it that you do not find my intentions lacking and anything less than in good faith, I assure you.'

'Mama, no one else has discovered us and therefore there is no need to press Mr Elmbridge. I forbid you do so. I shall not consent if you do!' I said sharply. 'Mr Elmbridge is guilty of nothing more than putting himself at my service when I was having a bad turn. I told you I wanted to leave but you would not oblige me.'

'I will speak to you later,' she warned me. 'Mr Elmbridge, I thank you and bid you good evening,' she said, and with a gentleman's bow, he bid us both goodnight.

I had expected to suffer hours of reproach once we shuffled into our carriage and made an unceremonious departure from the house. Our hosts were sent the apology that I had taken an ill turn and had to leave prematurely. My recent illness and the oversight that perhaps I had attempted to resume such engagements before I was quite well enough recovered, was spun into a compliment to my hosts in how much I desired to attend and how sorry I was for having to leave so abruptly. I hardly cared what they made of it, so long as our secret was safe and Sheldon was not forced to make me an official offer on account of it.

When the journey back to Mayfair passed in silence, I anticipated a late-night lecture and then when that passed too without ceremony, I was braced for a morning of reproach once all the grownups had had a chance to discuss and decide upon their sanctions. So, when I heard a carriage pull up outside the house, and saw Lady Elmbridge step out of it, I headed straight for the cloakroom beside Mama's small parlour: her favourite place to entertain more intimate acquaintances over their scandal broth and have secret Almack's discussions. I was not disappointed when I heard them descend into the room and shut the door, and I pressed my ear to the gap beneath it, to listen in.

'Lady Ashlyn,' the Viscountess began, 'you know I am come with the sincerest of apologies. Sheldon has briefed me, I think in full, and I want you to know that he insists I pass on his apology and assurances.'

'I thank you, Lady Elmbridge: that does indeed bring me comfort. Although Eleanor is as much at fault, and means to make no premature demands upon him, so she insists. I think she is uncomfortable with the notion of forcing his hand, and I own that so long as no harm is done it is perhaps best...'

'Indeed. Well. Perhaps it is best we permit them an opportunity to reflect on their frivolity. Sheldon has had a very serious talking to this morning and is quite aware of his obligations. He assures me there is nothing to be concerned over on any count, you have his word. I think some extra vigilance in their chaperoning might be called for just now to be certain of no repeats, however.'

'Indeed ma'am,' Delores croaked and I felt a little sorry for her having to take the brunt of the blame, knowing that she was no more at fault than my own mama.

And this apathy, this lack of setting down I knew I was deserving of, was because, despite all the ceremony of obligatory disappointment; Mama was pleased, I knew, to discover some hope of our coming together. I suppose the last thing she wanted to do, now there was finally some evidence of our progress, was to quell it with severe reproaches and limitations. It was she that had bid Delores out of the drawing room to attend her only yesterday morning leaving us quite unsupervised. It was she, I suspected kept this matter out of my father's knowing, for he hadn't shown the slightest change of mood since our return and had only expressed to me a hope that I was feeling better.

I gave no clue to having understood these facts when Mama came to me announcing we must be packed and ready to make our departure by noon.

I spent the morning directing a party of housemaids in the boxing and stacking of my best new gowns and all the other ephemera I had installed in the room on my arrival to set out upon the season in fitting style. Now I wondered what it had all been for, all the stuff I had accumulated, all the rigmarole of decorating myself with so much care, only to be leaving again, so soon. I wondered if I was to undergo the same next season, or if I would need not, by then.

But I was grateful for our going now. The season had passed in such a flash it felt we were to go when I had just stepped into the swing of it, got the measure of it all. But, to be gone from *her* in a matter of hours brought such an easiness of mind I could not wish it otherwise. And whilst we were departing for a flurry of more sedate country affairs now, I could look to them with easiness of spirit, knowing she would not be found lurking in a corner keeping watch over me. And even when I returned to Cuddington, once these visits were over, I should never cross the threshold of Beaulieu again, toss any cards from her into the grate and go on just as I did before she ever crossed my path.

It was in this mind I stood in the hall, waiting for our trunks to be loaded, bidding a silent farewell, not just to London, but to her. *Goodbye and good riddance.*

'THIS ARRIVED FOR YOU earlier, ma'am,' Bentham said when I was shrugging into my spencer with Mary's assistance. He held out a box in his crisp gloved hands.

I stole a glance about me, then took it, and thanked him before heading straight to the water closet to open it. Something told me this was not a thing I would want to open beneath Delores' gaze and I could hear her and mama on the stairs as I locked the door, sat on the closed lid of the toilet and began to unwrap it. When the paper was shed and I wriggled off the cardboard lid, I found inside it a small bunch of wildflowers tied with pink ribbon with a note written in a hand I did not recognise.

'I will wait an eternity for you if I must, now I know what it is to feel you close to me.'

It was unsigned and (thankfully) written in French to protect its contents from the servants, but I knew it was from Sheldon and it warmed me to think that I was on his mind, even when we were apart. He had been on mine fairly constantly too, which was unusual, but welcome, for it helped to occupy the space she had, more recently, come to fill. It was the perfect antidote to so much shame, disgust and brooding, to think warm and pleasant thoughts, to remember the scent of his cologne, the warmth of his embrace, the cool smoothness of his silk waistcoat against my flushed cheek. It set a kindling of anticipation through me.

He too was to break the journey to Wycombe Park with a couple of nights stay at Osterley now. And I was excited by the prospect of us being under the same roof, not only for the next two days, or the weekend at Wycombe Park, but likely in attendance at all the rest of the affairs too. I knew it must be so, for as much as Lady Jersey was a fellow patroness, a neighbour to us at Berkeley Square, I knew that privately she was Mama's least favoured acquaintance amongst the patronesses. The one she had to force herself to pay attendance on, rather than bestow it freely as she did at the Viscountess or Lady Sefton. But if we were to stay at Osterley at the Jersey's invitation, my mama likely had an ulterior motive for accepting it with such enthusiasm.

Osterley was a favourite of mine, and I had never had cause to find Lady Jersey anything but amiable and looked forward to this reprieve to spend a couple of days of leisure at their beautiful country estate. I was looking forward to taking Samson out on the park there for some serious exercise too, for it was perfect for a good gallop and I felt sorry for my neglect of him as I patted his mane waiting for the rest of our party to embark on the waiting carriages. 'Good boy,' I told him, reaching for the carrot bucket the groom had left perched on his mounting plate. I fed him a couple, patted his haunches and distributed the rest about the other horses until I was summoned to depart.

WHEN I WAS SHOWN TO my guest chamber at Osterley, and oversaw the unpacking of just a few of my things, I reached for the bandbox where I had stored Sheldon's gift box and removed it from beneath the cover of a bonnet and took the note inside it over to the fire grate, forgetting the summer heat and the cold coals that sat in it. I had planned to throw the note into the fire at the first private opportunity; I could not afford for it to fall into the wrong hands when I was still in need of more time. Less time than before, perhaps, but longer all the same. I stuffed it back into the bandbox instead and told the maids I wanted nothing unpacked from it. The flowers, I decided, I would wear in my hair this evening as a token of appreciation for the gesture, along with my favourite new gown and best pearls. I wasn't sure if we would manage to get any time alone tonight amongst the intimate party of guests, especially now we had come under scrutiny, but I knew I must find some way to signal my appreciation to him. And as I was dressed for dinner, I had the Jersey's loaned Abigail, trim the stems and place them into my neatly pinned tresses *en Camille*.

But it was not until the following morning that we were given any breathing room to speak openly. Dinner had been stiffly guarded and we found ourselves apart at the table, sitting in circumspect order of rank, leaving Sheldon to escort Lady Lillian to the table, and me in the care of Mr Grey. Now all the guests had arrived, our number made a paltry twenty or so, and this pomp and ceremony riled me as I tried to interpret Sheldon's glances across the table.

But this morning we had set out in a party of eight to exercise our horses in the vast parkland and whilst we were not left alone, we were able to keep close proximity and stall Samson and Delilah for breaks, keeping enough distance from the rest of the party to not be overheard.

'You looked beautiful last night,' he said to me as Samson took favour in a particular patch of still lush grass to chew on, which had not been scorched by the persistent summer heat. We had not had rain for most of the month and much of the land was looking parched. 'Thank you, Mr Elmbridge, I credit it to the fine flowers I received,' I said playfully and he smiled, a flash of sunlight casting over his features causing his eyes to sparkle a shade brighter than they already were. 'I shall credit it to the wearer who cause's the finest flower to look dull against the radiance of her beauty.'

This silenced me a moment and I felt not just the heat of my cheeks, but the heat that had radiated between our glances last night around the dinner table, across the shoulders of our partners. 'Well,' I said checking the fluency of my words before I spoke them; 'I recall it was your own gardener, Paxton, that told me; "It takes for the most ideal of conditions to encourage some flowers to bloom their brightest colours," so I suppose I could not help but blossom under such a gaze as yours.'

'Oh, to have leave to hold you again right now. I still smell the scent of your hair beneath my nose you know.'

'I hope we might steal such a moment again, although I think it will be difficult here. I hope your mama was not too severe on you. I am sorry you got the blame for it, I did try—'

He shrugged. 'For your sake, I could take a great deal of admonishing. Besides, Mama knows I am in earnest with you. She has always known it.'

'I wish I had her sight before now. I'm sorry, Sheldon, that we could not come to this understanding sooner. It is my f—'

'We are here now.'

'We are,' I smiled and when Lord Dash-along came bounding up beside us, we turned our conversation to the topic of the Jerseys' handsome pair of new bays.

That was as much as we were to enjoy of private conversation that day, and we passed another sedate evening in the company, a little singing and playing at the pianoforte in the evening, some chicken stake gaming and another dinner in the company of our new partners. It was dull after so much bustling about in overfilled drawing rooms, but it was the cover of them I missed now: The ease at getting lost amongst the throng, the opportunity to disappear to use the chamber pot taking thrice as long as necessary on account of the queuing and no one batting an eyelid. I hoped that Wycombe Park would prove more hospitable and concealing for us now all I could think about was him.

I MISSED HIS COMPANY the next morning, for the exercise consisted of a lady's party of walking and a gentleman's party of shooting in opposing polarities of Osterley Park. We were to travel on this evening for the Wycombe's opening weekend ball and so any horses due to pull the coaches were to be rested ahead of the journey and given only a lap or two about the paddock by the grooms. That ruled out Samson and Delilah being prevailed upon to offer us an opportunity to converse privately again.

I strolled the gravel paths and meandered about the ornamental lakes with Lady Jersey as mama and Delores lagged behind with the other ladies.

'Well, Miss Ashlyn, I hope you have had a chance to restore yourself before the ballroom tonight. I hear the season has taken its toll on you,' she said from beneath her parasol as I threw bread crusts to the swans.

'Yes, I feel very well now. I thank you,' I said carefully.

'Hmmm, the country is a welcome antidote is it not, and yet I think there is something more to account for the bloom at your cheek,' she smirked. 'Tell me; has your mama and the Viscountess's cunning plan served its purpose?'

I frowned at her.

'Oh, I daresay I shouldn't tell tales and spoil their fun, but, well what I observe betwixt you is quite an obvious love match, and so what harm can it do for you to know.'

'Know what?' I asked puzzled.

'Well, I believe after your little discovery the other night at Ham—oh don't be like that, you needn't be shy of my knowing and it is indeed a well-guarded secret, you may be sure. But you put them in quite the quandary over what to do about it.'

'Yes, well it seems they have done very little, to my surprise.'

'Ah, but there, you are wrong.'

'I am?'

She smiled. 'Well, they are of a mind that perhaps absence shall make the heart grow fonder, you see. Since you will not consent to Sheldon being pressed into an offer, then perhaps a little time kept beyond each other's reach might quicken you along.'

'I see.'

'I think they might have hit on something there. That's why I consented to let them trifle over the seating plans. It seems to have done the trick. I own the glances I have observed between the pair of you are enough to smoulder the candles down to their ends without a flame to them. It's certainly an improvement on what I noticed at the assemblies.'

I was lost for words. Could I have been so acutely read even by strangers? I wondered what else I might have given away without my notice. And to think Mama and Lady Elmbridge had been scheming to separate us and made me sit at the table with that dull fellow on purpose. I had a mind to set a scheme against them and feign absolute disinterest in Sheldon now, just to spite them. But I wouldn't. I *couldn't*. 'Lady Jersey, what would you do in my situation?' I asked, surprising myself with such boldness of speech.

'With a handsome catch like Elmbridge, I should not like to say,' she chuckled then sobered her expression. 'Child, you have youth and beauty and it will get you far indeed, there can be no question. Just look at how you have followers in every London ballroom. You can do whatever you will. If you mean to rush up the aisle in a heartbeat or spend another two seasons bringing the male sex to their knees, you may find it merry too. But in the end, what matters is what makes your heart sing. If indeed your heart is singing, as I would guess, from my own observations, then you may just get everything a debutante could hope for in your match. I see love's young dream when I look at you two. How it saddens me when I count my years to know how fast it all fades. Enjoy it little one, while you can.'

'Well, I see not how I have a hope of doing so with Mama's plan to separate us from each other's company. I own, I would not mean to be improper in Mr Elmbridge's company, but to have a little tête-à-tête with him now and then would not go amiss.'

'Hmmm. Well, here's a thing I could be brought to assisting you in: If you promise me two things sincerely.'

I was surprised at her. 'Oh?'

'You must promise me: if you behave abominably and are discovered, you shall indeed accept his offer if it is necessary he need make one, and you must never tell a soul I knew a thing about it.'

'I am not sure I would want to place such a burden on you, my lady,' I replied, but what I meant was: I was not sure I wanted to make such a promise as to committing myself to wedlock for the sake of a stolen moment when my mama would have an offer levelled at me over the slightest of trifle, and if I had such a moment offered to me in the head I was in now, I did not mean to trifle at all. I wanted to feel him close to me again. *Closer*.

'Stuff,' she said with a flick of her hand. 'You place me under no burden whatsoever, only yourself. It is for you to bear the risk, if it is worth it in your mind. Pray tell me, do you know the direction of my dressing room?'

I shook my head.

'It is the Etruscan Room, on the first floor opposite the staircase. If you are minded to have your little tête-à-tête, then get ready for the ball a half hour early and come to me there. I shall see to the rest. I shall send a note to you so your chaperone needn't fuss.'

'Oh, I don't know, though I am grateful. I fear I have caused enough trouble already.'

'Puh. What debutante worth her salt does not cause just a little? Discretion my dear, that's what it all boils down to in the end.'

Her words stayed with me long after they were spoken. Mariella had said something similar long ago and I had considered it a lack of understanding on her part. But perhaps she was right after all. Perhaps it was all a matter of discretion rather than abstinence. But I fixed my mind against accepting Lady Jersey's assistance. Not because I did not want to jump at the chance, but because I was not sure that I could trust myself to behave very prettily at all. Now I understood what my body was capable of. Now I understood what it was to feel the stifled passion between us, I could not be sure I would not cut a dash and shock him with my wickedness. My body was not easy to command at will when so provoked. It took command from some other quarter and whatever it was, it was not one of my direction.

But as I sat at my dressing room table, I changed my mind a thousand times. I wanted to be prepared for such a moment all the same. I had Watts make me up a wash for the hair, dabbed myself in Floris water and cleaned my teeth twice. I even took the liberty of adding a subtle smudge of rouge to my cheeks and lips and a dusting of candle soot to my eyelashes. I checked myself in the looking glass for any sign of it showing obvious and kissed a little of the colour off my lips against the back of my hand. *Yes, that is it;* a bloom that seemed natural, undetectable almost, but enough to set my features off a little better.

When Lady Jersey's note arrived, I was turning in the glass receiving Delores' and Watts' approving comments. Delores had not spotted the cosmetics I had smudged subtly into my skin and said only: 'Oh, how radiant you are tonight my dear. I see your health has returned to you to be sure. Pray what is that?' she said to the maid pointing to the note she carried into the room.

'My Lady sent it for Miss Ashlyn,' she said with a curtsey.

'Over here with it,' Delores said, beckoning her with a hand gesture and tearing the seal.

My heart began to race as I paused and watched her eyes scanning the contents. She folded it back up, handed it to the maidservant and nodded in my direction. 'What is it?' I asked when the maid brought it over to me.

'Lady Jersey wants your opinion on her hair style. Apparently, she means to replicate the style you wore the other night and her Abigail forgets the instructions you gave her,' Delores said.

'Oh,' I said as evenly as I could manage.

'Well, are you going to give your answer or not?'

'Of course. Are you ready to go?' I said to her.

'No. I haven't even got out of my day dress yet. Go with the maidservant,' she said. 'And make sure you escort her directly back here too, mind,' she said to the girl who gave an obliging curtsey.

I took a final glance at myself in the glass and spun on my heal and left with her. When she took me down a flight of stairs and deposited me into the Etruscan room, I was not sure what to expect, whether he would lie in wait, or what scheme had been arranged. But when I entered to find myself quite alone, I was surprised.

I took a seat and admired the decorating scheme and its rather brilliant design. It was indeed the most beautiful dressing room I had ever seen, and my own at Cuddington was not at all too shabby. I traced a finger over the shape of a pineapple finial upon the fire screen and looked about it. It was the epitome of elegance and I trifled over the figures of Grecian ladies painted in gold upon the white walls, the elegant inlaid wood furniture lacquered to such a polish the sun streaming in through the windows set it off dazzling. The door knocked and clicked open and I looked up startled. It was he, and I was surprised for I had expected at least a cue from Lady Jersey. He was even more perplexed than me by the expression on his face.

'El,' he said frowning, 'I was told my mama had summoned me.'

'Shhh,' I said getting up from my chair and crossing the room. 'I hope you are not disappointed.'

His features softened. 'No. Anything but—'

'Good,' I stepped up closer to him. He was finely dressed but missing his tailcoat. He stood handsomely set in a waistcoat of silver paisley patterned silk with his shirt sleeves showing. A gold neckcloth tied at his collar which matched his buttons. I could catch the scent of his cologne now and it sent me quite dizzy with the memory.

'Where is Delores, your mama?' he said casting fidgety glances at the decorated door he had not come through, the one I suspected led to Lady Jersey's chamber.

'Upstairs,' I said running a finger over his waistcoat lapel, 'in their toilettes.'

'Oh,' his expression eased a little more.

'Do not worry, we shan't be discovered, we are under Lady Jersey's protection.'

'We are?'

'Hush with so much fretting, you will spoil the moment. I have waited all day to cast even the slightest glance at you.'

'I've missed you dreadfully,' he confessed.

'And I. So now I have you in my midst at last, I shall take the opportunity to make amends for something I was once foolish enough to do in error.'

'What?'

I reached up on my tiptoes and kissed him softly on his mouth and drew back again. 'That one was not a mistake,' I told him, and before he could make response, I lent back in for another—although, this time, it was he who stepped in and took me by the shoulders, pressed his mouth against me with such unrelenting passion I could hardly catch my breath. I pressed my hands against his chest and matched his enthusiasm, even if not his skill, for he handled me so expertly I was quite stunned. Taking my face between his palms and varying the pressure of his lips against mine, still managing to breathe as I gasped for gaps to exhale, stroking my face with his thumbs. I felt around his waist and pulled his body closer now, so I could feel it hard against my own, the warmth I remembered, the shape of his back beneath my palms. Then when I found the courage to attempt it, I pushed passed his lips with my tongue, felt the tip of his own collide with mine, and then...then he pulled back and stared at me agog. It was then I realised my faux pas.

'El,' he said recovering, 'where did you learn to do that?' he asked dumfounded.

'I didn't,' I said quickly. 'It just...felt right.'

He drew back a little and took my hands into his own as they slid from his waist. 'Forgive me. I should not have taken advantage of you so savagely.'

'You did not. I wanted to kiss you. Don't you want to kiss me?'

'More than I am permitted to show you,' he said more soberly, concern in his eyes.

'Then kiss me again, Sheldon.'

'I cannot. I *must* not,' he said more pointedly.

'Of course you can, no one is here—'

'Which is all the more reason I should have better restraint.'

I would have continued my protest had it not been for a tap on the gilded door that started us both. 'Miss Ashlyn,' came a voice before it opened a crack and we both stepped apart. It was Lady Jersey's Abigail. 'Time's up, your chaperone is on her way. Sir, you are to wait until you are sent for before returning to your chamber.'

And with that, she pulled me into Lady Jersey's room where she was sat at her dressing table with her hair perfectly set but pulled a few strands from their pins to pose correctly, her Abigail stepping up behind her with a comb in her hand. 'Play your part now little one,' she smiled and said to me, handing me some pins and turned to the door and said: 'Miss Parkes,' to Delores when she was announced just in time to find a scene of perfect innocence set before her.

'Delores,' I said, handing a pin to the Abigail and pointing to a renegade curl. 'Am I late? Is the carriage waiting?' I said serenely.

'No,' she said suspiciously. 'Your mama sent me for you. She—'

'Come in Miss Parkes. Close the door, you shall let in a draught. Now, I must have your opinion,' she spun about on her stool. 'Well, does it suit me? Miss Ashlyn assures me it does, but I know you will furnish me with the truth, when this little one is only full of flattery.'

Delores nodded. 'It is very flattering,' she said in earnest.

'The pink or the white flowers?' she asked her next.

West Wycombe Park.

June 1821. - Eleanor.

When we journeyed in an envoy of carriages out of the gates of Osterley, I was head splitting with confusion. Part of me was full of revelry as I revisited the memory of his wild embrace, the passion I felt in his movements, the conviction. Then I tried to fathom out whether his surprise withdrawal was on account of him mistrusting my answer, or whether he really did mean to regulate our passions for the sake of propriety. I was not sure which was worse. I neither wanted him to know I had been schooled in the art of kisses, nor did I want him to mean to kill so exciting a moment. So passionate a moment, and of his own accord. I wrestled with it as I gazed through the carriage window, Mama and Delores prattling away, whilst Father tried to read the sheets of his newspaper as we rattled along.

They had seemed to accept my attendance upon Lady Jersey with satisfaction, even though I had at first suspected Delores of attempting to catch me out. Either I had been mistaken, or they had been successfully gulled.

I had decided to refashion my own hair before our departure, as well as retouch the blush of rouge at my lips and cheek, since he had somehow managed to erase it with his kisses. I found my Parisian gift box in one of my trunks and fished out the pretty hair slide he had put in it and set it just aside my fringe of curls. It was a beautiful piece of Marcasite vines, and beads of pearl, and it quite completed my retouch efforts. I had never dared wear it in the country when he gave me the gift box, for fear Mama would grow suspicious at where is had come from, but when she asked me about it tonight, I just told her I had seen it at a stall in the Western Exchange and found it pretty.

It had proved worth the extra effort of finding it, and I could not mistake the effect it had on him when our eyes met through a crack in the crowds of the busy saloon at Wycombe Park.

Despite us all setting off together, along the way, the entourage had been dispersed at various tollgates and set us all apart. And then just as we embarked on the final league, our coach had to make a stop for Father's bay had lost a horseshoe and we had to wait for the groom to tack a new one on. Something that might have been quick enough, had he not had to unload half of our trunks to find the replacement shoe.

We arrived at least an hour late for the delay, but thanks to Mama's fastidious planning, we were only a quarter hour into the ball firing off. I smiled to be reunited with the sight of him, and he appeared at my side far quicker than was polite of his company or mine. But I was equally keen to see him and have him added to my dance card ahead of anyone else, so I did not complain or make apology for our lack of interest in the rest of party.

'How you glow tonight,' he whispered as I scribbled down his name. 'You are wearing the head dress I found in Venice,' he smiled and I was pleased to see I had impressed him suitably with this gesture.

'Yes,' I said, teasingly, 'a rather dashing admirer gifted it to me. I should like to thank him later,' I grinned and watched him colour a little, a smouldering look about his gaze, and I was wondering if he was revisiting the memory I had been the whole journey here, of our stolen moment in the Etruscan room.

The problem, which became apparent only later, was that my extra efforts this evening had proved impressive to a far greater audience than I had intended, and I had spent much of the evening trying to shake off those seeking out my card. I had even resorted to enlisting Delores to my cause to spare me the indignity of so many refusals. There were of course the usual applicants to rebuff as I was well accustomed, and thankfully, Delores was well practiced in how to proceed with these pests. But there were other applicants tonight, many of which I had never set eyes on before and in some cases could barely recollect an acquaintance of, when our host brought them round. The exhaustion of it quickly outweighed the flattery, and apart from the two dances I could permit Sheldon, I spent very little time devoted to his company. I was sorry for it and I could see that he was no better pleased at this than I; I watched him sink another glass of brandy as I danced the final Reel with Mr Longhurst.

'You know,' Delores said behind her fan when Mr Longhurst brought me back. 'You will have to get used to this now, Eleanor, we might have left the season revelry behind us, but the trouble you have now, is how many acquaintances you have made throughout it and now we only increase the number of new ones.'

'I realise that, Delores.'

'So long as you do, for this is what you might expect from here on. Unless of course—' she raised her eyebrows in Sheldon's direction and I turned around to see him stood just behind us in conversation with Lord Stilingfleet, 'you have already decided where your interests lie?'

'No, Delores, I have made no firm decisions yet. I am tired and I have a pounding headache; I am quite ready to retire, I think.'

'But it is early; we have not taken supper yet?'

'You stay for supper: I have eaten enough from the buffet tonight that I have no appetite for another bite anyway. Watts can attend me,' I said in answer to the look of mistrust on her face at my suggestion of her staying. 'I'll ask Mama to attend me if that will satisfy you?'

'There is no need to disturb your mother with a simple headache. I will take you up now and take a quick supper once you are settled.'

I had no choice but to accept this bargain, so I tolerated her fussing about in our travelling medicine chest for a draught to alleviate my headache while Watts stripped me of my gown and petticoats.

'Not my hair. Leave it be,' I warned her as she attempted to de-pin the intricate design of my hairdo with her impatient fingers. Having to be summoned to sit with me was a matter she was not best pleased with and she thinly veiled the fact of her inconvenience. 'Go and fetch me some warm water that I might bathe my forehead with,' I told her, and at that very moment, Delores poked her head around the dressing room door.

'I have left you a draught on your bedside table, take it all in one go. I will be back shortly to see you are settled. Watts, you are to stay.'

That much I knew was an empty threat. She would quickly forget me. 'Very well,' I said anyway. I knew she was eager to return to the party—to the squire anyway —having been kept so busy with me tonight. The news of their engagement was still unannounced, but only a fool could have failed to notice the new license in their marked attentions.

When she bid me farewell, I held my breath to hear her whisperings to Watts on her way out; which, save a few missed syllables, amounted to Watts instruction at locking the door and keeping to my bedside until I had finished my draught and was sound asleep.

I tossed the draught into the chamber pot before they had finished talking behind the half open door and waited to hear the turn of the key, then headed straight for the changing screen where my clothes were still hanging from its frame. 'Watts, I need you to get me dressed again.'

WHEN I WAS DRESSED, I sent her to Sheldon's valet to deliver a note, instructing him to meet me outside in the patch of shrubbery to the east wing.

'Do not reproach me, I had to see you,' I said before he had the opportunity. I found him wandering the perimeter of the woodland as I slipped out of the basement Watts had escorted me to for the price of all the unwanted ephemera I had set aside in a separate bandbox on packing up at Berkeley Square.

'I am quite convinced I should, but the truth is; I am gladdened by the sight of you. I was disappointed to see you leave the party so early.'

I smiled widely. 'Well now you know the reason for it: so, I could be alone with you.'

'Eleanor.'

'Shhh,' I said, 'let us find a place to sit, shall we, before someone discovers us again. I don't think we want to be apprehended by a band of footman tonight.'

He nodded and shot a glance around us. 'I know a place out of the way,' he said and scooped me along in the direction of it.

'Is it far?'

'Not very.'

I snuck my hand in to his when he lifted his arm to guide me. 'It's alright,' I told him when he looked at me apprehensive. 'We still have our gloves on,' I smiled and was pleased when I felt him relax a little. It was encouraging to feel the slow but gradual progress we were making now. I could feel the shift in us both, mine in my marked interest of him, his in his increasing willingness to take risks. I was certain that the element of risk could be credited with some of my excitement. It felt good. Not just in the moment, but in all the hours stretched between. I knew him anxious and torn between the weight of his Mama's scolding and his own desire, but I had felt the passion contained within him now, I had felt it in the dressing room, a wildness that had been too long restrained.

We walked the water's edge of the lake with the moonlight glistening on it like polished glass. I did not mind the chill of the night air, the silence or the solitude of our company, somehow it seemed so easy between us when he was minded to permit us these private moments.

'Where are we?' I asked as we turned off the bank of the lake to follow a pathway toward a small building set only slightly back from the water's edge.

'At the music temple,' he told me and ushered me up the steps to reach the portico.

I could not make out the features of it well for it was dark and we were walking in its shadow, but I could see far enough in front of me to tread my way towards the door.

'I took the tour today to kill the time difference between our arrivals.'

This made me smile, for I remembered thinking of him as I sat in the coach, staring out the window, willing us to go faster so that I might catch even a glimpse of him before we were thrust into the party.

'I'm sure I will have the pleasure tomorrow when you are off shooting with the other men. And I shall have to remember to feign perfect ignorance of the grounds now.' The thought of the long separation we would suffer for most of the day turned stale in my mind. I reminded myself that we must make the most of the time we had together now, quite alone and quite free.

'It's locked,' he said with a rattle of the door handle. 'We shall have to make do with the bench.' He pointed to the row of stone benches positioned at intervals along the front wall.

'No matter.'

He put his jacket down and invited me to sit upon it.

'You will be cold,' I insisted, eyeing him in the pale muslin of his shirt sleeves and remembering how I had caught the shape of his arms through them earlier in the golden light streaming into the Etruscan room.

'I'm fine, sit down,' he said, and once I had settled my skirts, he joined me.

'Come closer, I shan't bite,' I was staring at the gap between us on the bench but looked up to catch his gaze: it was an incredulous glance that I translated to: *I'm not so sure about that*. And I instantly fretted over his question earlier about where I learnt to kiss. It mattered not now, for those sordid rehearsals had paled into insignificance now I had felt his, but I must not make another slip-up like that and cause him such questions again.

He moved in another inch and filled the rest of the space between us with his hand to bridge the gap. He was right not to trust me I supposed, for I knew that when I was able to muster the courage to do so, I would test us both a little more than I knew I should dare to. But for the moment, he could relax, I hadn't the nerve just yet. I was quite content to sit with him and indulge the momentary liberation of my senses that were drinking in the atmosphere of both the night and the newfound chemistry between us.

'El, I'm not sure what is happening between us, but I know that I have felt so painfully aggrieved at our separation, I have not known what to do with myself. Have you felt it to?'

'Yes, I have,' I cupped my nearside hand over the top of his as I watched the relief of my answer overcome him.

'This evening, watching you dance with—'

'I tried my best to dissuade them.'

'I know.'

'I assure you, Sheldon, I done all I could, but if I am to dance with you, I cannot easily refuse to dance elsewhere.'

'I do not blame you. But I never want to have to watch it again, El.'

'You know I could not care a whit for their attentions, don't you?'

'Perhaps, but no less they will pursue you, El, every dinner, every dance you will face the queue and I will be forced to step in line with the rest of them.'

'I'm sure it will not be as bad next time. I suppose tonight I was a new face to some of the company. It will settle now it is over with.'

'El, you did not cause a stir because you are new, you caused it because you are the most beautiful woman at Wycombe tonight, and not a man in that room could fail to notice it, whether he applied to your dance card or not.'

I did not know what to say to this, the flattery of his speech took me by surprise; not the part about the other gentleman admiring me; the part where he told me he thought me most beautiful. Of course, I knew he must think it to dangle after me so, but to hear the words...Warm flutters deep within me were stirring. 'Sheldon, nothing would have pleased me better than if I could have filled my dance card with only your name tonight, but you know I could not.'

'You could, El. If it was what you really wanted, we might settle things so that I could have you all to myself at every ball and on every moonlit night. No need for all this sneaking about. You need only permit the question—'

'Sheldon,' I said quickly, 'we have been over this; I thought you understood? It was but only days ago I read the very words on the note you sent me with the flowers,' I said taking a rosebud from the planter beside me and turning the stem between my forefinger and thumb. 'You do know how long an eternity is?' I laughed and nudged him.

He let out a long-drawn sigh. 'You're right, I did agree to be patient; but the truth is, I did not realise it would be this difficult. I still do not understand why you ask it of me, now you have made your feelings so very plain.'

'You do not understand, Sheldon, because what is open to your sex is very different to what is open to mine.'

'Well, of course, it is, but I don't see what bearing that has on it.'

'It has *everything* to do with it. Sheldon, when a man first takes his wife to his bed on their wedding night, how often do you think that the man is a nervous as his wife?'

'If that is what frightens you, we could take a long engagement, a very long one if you wish it?'

'No, that is not what I meant, please hear me out. If I can, I want to help you understand. The answer I think we would both arrive at would be that she is more likely to be anxious. But why do you think this is?'

He sat thoughtfully but did not offer an answer and I wasn't sure if it was from his discomfort at conversing on such a topic with me, or because he knew the answer and did not wish to confess it.

'It is because, for her, the experience will be not only a new one, but one she has been ill prepared for, with no training or previous experience to aid her. We both know that the same cannot often be said for a gentleman on his wedding night.'

'El...'

'I do not ask the question,' I protested and he seemed glad to be spared the ordeal of an inquisition. 'I have spent years with my tutors, not only in the education of all the usual accomplishments, but in training for this very moment, this very season. The way I walk, speak, dance, flick my fan is testament to the time spent in learning every aspect of those things to perfection, for only then can I be considered acceptable to grace the Almack's dance floor. Yet when a woman is let loose upon her debut, she knows as good as nothing about the men she must dance with, and nor does she get much time to discover it through the lengthy separations of the day and under the meticulous eye of chaperones at night. Yet from this mystery of unknowns, she is to place her whole future in the hands of one of these gentlemen, for better or worse, and entrust he will be careful with it.'

'But Eleanor, we are not the strangers you describe; we have known each other all our lives.'

'That is true, but so could claim Mr Whipple, but I do not think that qualifies him as a suitable match.' My point was taken. 'The thing is, Sheldon, all this training and coaxing, none of it really answers or prepares us for what we will feel the first time we hold each other's hand.' I lifted his hand into my lap and squeezed it. 'The first time you share the marriage bed, the first time you provoke each other's temper.'

'I could never lose my temper with you.'

'And what of my temper, can you vouch for that?'

This seemed to amuse him.

'Yes, you can laugh at it, because whether I am the mildest natured wife in the county,' he raised an eyebrow, 'or the most unruly, you are protected from the consequences by your sex and the freedom it permits you to escape me or cherish me as it suits you: To come to my bed or go to your mistresses, to pass the day in my company, or at your club. If you find that you have made the wrong choice; that is the worst case you will suffer. If I make the same mistake, Sheldon, my life could be one of solitude, misery and confinement.'

'El, I understand that, but come; we are not Prinny and Caroline. I wonder what you must think of me to need be fearful of these matters. You must think me some terrible brute if you think I would ever subject you to such an existence.'

'I do not. I think you're beautiful too, actually.' This silenced him. 'But I need time to discover the rest and learn to trust it, before I surrender the last and only, power of refusal I have.'

'Perhaps, but do not forget that even men cannot choose to recover a broken heart where they have already invested their affections. Even if, when already well aware that in pursuing such a match, he did not choose the "mildest natured wife in the county."'

We both laughed aloud at this.

'Well then, we are both learning.'

'What have you learned, El?' His tone was serious again.

'That you are jealous and impatient,' I put my finger to his lips to hush his objection. 'But also tolerant, gentle and devoted,' I took my hand away from his mouth and slid it around his waist instead and huddled into him. He put his arm around my shoulders and held me there until we finally grew too cold to stay out any longer.

'YOU ARE IN GOOD SPIRITS this morning, Delores,' I said when she joined me at the small table in my chamber for a light breakfast of tea and plum cake. I noted the bags beneath her bleary eyes. 'Late night?'

'Not at all,' she dismissed me, having not the faintest notion that I had crept back into bed only half an hour before she had retired. I wondered if she had been up to no better than me. 'Did you sleep well?'

'Perfectly,' I smiled.

'And your headache?'

And yours? I wanted to ask for she looked a little cropsick, despite her happy spirit. 'Gone—I think I must take that draught more often, for I do not remember so much as a visit to the chamber pot.'

'Oh, I am glad.' She poured us both some more tea. 'So, will you take Samson out this morning before we breakfast with the party, or shall we settle for a brisk stroll on the estate?'

For once it seemed she would have preferred me take off for a ride and spare her the need to accompany me, and I could have guessed at why. 'Samson will be tired from his journey yesterday. A walk will have to suffice,' I lied. Samson had journeyed further than West Wycombe and been well enough recovered for a morning trot. But today I did not have the time to fuss about with the inconvenience of getting in and out of my habit. I wanted to spend every spare minute in my toilette before going to the breakfast room. He had told me last night that I was the most beautiful woman here; I wanted to make sure his opinion remained unaltered this morning. Besides, this would be the most I would get to see of him for the rest of the day, and I wanted to give him something to think about during the long hours of our separation.

'What is planned for us today?' I asked on the off chance that our host might have been sympathetic to us debutantes and considered some activity that might unite the sexes, even briefly. But as Delores run off a vague recollection of tedious pastimes, I realised I had been too optimistic. I fancied a host like Lady Jersey would have paid some kind consideration to such matters, unlike this host, and I wondered if she was minded play host to any grander affairs this summer. If not, I might make the suggestion to Lady Jersey myself, I thought, when we were walking about the gardens and I caught sight of the music temple we had visited last night.

Breakfast also proved a sad disappointment. I had expected an informal buffet format where we might drift in and sit as we pleased, which would have offered the opportunity to spend at least a little time in his company. Instead, we were seated in strict order and were waited on at the table. At home in Cuddington, ordered seating was not often a problem for it was only on the rare occasions when we had out of town visitors that anyone would work to separate us much at the table. Here, it was an altogether different matter and we were kept quite apart. Unlike the ploy at Osterley where I knew the fault lay in my mama and Lady Elmbridge's plotting, this I knew was our host's preferred design and likely to follow in such a course through the whole weekend. I would have settled for the opportunity to exchange glances and smiles as some consolation, but even that proved difficult with the bobbing of so many heads obscuring the view. In the end, I gave up and starred into the oozing yolks of my eggs en cocotte wondering how on earth I might manage to pass the long hours stretched before me until tonight. I had no interest in much of these things at the best of times, but today I prepared for it to be painfully exasperating.

Once I had finished my plate, I searched the row of bobbing heads for Sheldon's and when I caught him starring past them in my direction it cheered me greatly. I looked over at Delores, who was leant over her plate, eyeing the squire between spoonfuls of oatmeal. I quickly took my fan up to shield my face from her, and mouthed for him to follow me and excused myself from the table.

'I am in need of the water closet,' I whispered to Delores as I passed her.

He found me moments later stood admiring some old family portrait in the hall and from there I gestured him to follow me on to the library which I was happy to note was still empty, save a footman laying out the papers. I took one of the books off the shelf and opened it in front of me.

'Good morning, Miss Ashlyn, I hope you slept well?' he said thumbing a copy of *Odes and Elegies* beside me.

'Very well, thank you. And you?'

'I suppose we might call it a distracted night with a lot to think upon; but a pleasant distraction no less.' He smiled and his cheek surprised me, for I had not seen enough of this side of him to expect it, but I liked it. A lot.

'What will you do today?' I asked him.

'Lord Hamilton is taking us out for a morning of shooting, followed by an al fresco nuncheon, I believe.'

'Sounds wonderful,' I told him and I meant it, for I would have much preferred his itinerary to the look of mine.

'I could find better uses for my hours if I were permitted the option.'

I looked up from my open book and smiled warmly at him and I saw reflected in his eyes, so much of what I myself was feeling.

'How will you spend the day?'

'Dreaming of better company whilst I make a hotchpotch of some water colours or needlework, I expect.'

He laughed, 'Not your forte?'

'No, and do not say I did not warn you of it. I seem to find myself better accomplished in things outside of what I am told is well suited for my occupation, except of course, riding Samson.'

'Well, if I wanted an ordinary wife, I might be disappointed.'

'Mr Elmbridge, are you accusing me of some irregularity?'

'I accuse you of being...exceptional, in every way.'

We shared another heated glance and I wanted so much to reach out and touch him. I watched his strong fingers flicking through the pages and remembered mine interlinked with them.

I looked up at the sounds of the floorboards creaking in the hallway and we strolled along the length of the bookshelves in opposite directions feigning interest in our books.

'Good day Mr Elmbridge, Miss Ashlyn,' the Duke said more wisely than I cared to acknowledge.

'Your Grace,' we both said in chorus and continued on our separate paths. When I stopped to browse another shelf, I noticed Sheldon was leant over the writing desk borrowing the use of the quill and pot upon it. If he was trying to convince the Duke of our innocence by feigning some legitimate task, it was perfectly hopeless, he already had the measure.

'Ah, there you are my dear,' said the Duke. I watched him and Lady Hester settle into opposite armchairs by the fireplace; her with a novel spread upon her lap and he with today's paper opened out in front of him. They looked content. Would Sheldon and I look that way one day?

I saw Lady Hester glance up at me and quickly I turned back to the bookshelf and pulled the closest book to me, from it. When I looked up again, I noticed Sheldon was replacing his.

He gestured to it as he slotted it back into its space and I checked that I was not watched before nodding my understanding to him. When he left, I gave it a moment before I went over and found it. I saw straight away the creased end of some paper protruding out an inch from the other pages like a forgotten bookmark. I took it straight to the table and opened it.

Today will prove too long a separation for my liking. If you find yourself in the same predicament and can safely quit the entertainment of your needlework, I will steal a moment to take Delilah for a stretch around the deer park around the hour of three. I know she will be missing Samson so much by then, that if she happened upon him in her travels, it would help her endure the wait until they can be united again.

I quickly folded it into my reticule and hid my smile.

AS PREDICTED, I PASSED the hours dabbling in water colours, needlework and wax sculpting. None of which I was skilled or much interested in, but Betsy and Anna were fond of it, and I did not fancy passing the time turning pages at the pianoforte with Beth and Martha, even if they were, for once free of the Craythorne entourage, so I settled to it anyway to pass the hours. I painted a rather poor impression of the music temple, helped Anna trim her bonnets, and gave up on the misshapen piece of wax I was working on when I realised it would not conform to my intentions. It was a good day despite this, and I realised how I had come to crave the old ways; the time before Mariella had infiltrated our group. This was too high brow an invitation to find the Craythornes on the list and I hoped many more hosts of the coming events would maintain these standards.

When I returned to my room to be dressed in my riding habit, I was surprised to find all manner of small tokens and trinkets upon the console table.

'They have been coming in all morning apparently,' Delores told me when I walked over to examine the look of them. Flowers, notes of poetic verse and a box of candied sweetmeats with various handwritten flatteries attached to them. I sifted through them all looking for something from him. "Thank you for permitting me the privilege of a dance last night." "Roses for the brightest bloom in the room!" These were definitely not in his hand or in French.

'Well?' she said, watching me. 'Who are they from?'

'I was about to ask you the very same?'

She shrugged. 'Well, I did warn you.'

I LEFT THE STABLES at two-thirty-five p.m., and even though I was ridiculously early, I still felt disappointed not to spot him somewhere across the grassland when I reached the deer park. I journeyed the whole expanse of it twice before I let my disappointment get the better of me and gave up looking altogether. It was not impossible he might have found himself unable to escape our host's itinerary or have been ambushed by the other chaperones on his way to the stables. I was not ignorant of the fact that if females had the option to offer dances or pose the question, his evening would have been as full of dancing as mine and his chamber as full of tokens. Nor of the fact that despite her being lately wed, Lady Caroline was still quite unable to take her eyes off of him and it seemed, in failing to win him in her first season, she now had her cap set at winning him as a lover. I felt a little sympathy for her; I had never cared for anyone enough to instigate the look of heartache she often wore in her glances in Sheldon's direction. I wondered now, if he had known himself to be in love with me even then, for there seemed no good reason for him to refuse her affections; she the daughter of the Duke, comely and well graced. Was that why he disappeared to the continent that spring? To avoid such ambushes and petitions? Could he really have known three years ago, that he was intent on making me his wife? With enough certainty to pass over other prospects...

'A penny for your thoughts?' came a voice from behind me, and I jumped and grasped the reigns. I turned around and saw him coming towards me on foot.

'Sheldon! Where is Delilah?'

'Too unwell to make the journey. It seems she is injured from the ride up, and cannot bear to stand upon her right front leg at any length.'

'Oh Sheldon, I am sorry to hear it. Do you know what is wrong with her?'

'Not yet, Jackson has been with her all night and the veterinarian is on his way from town this afternoon. So you will forgive me I hope, for my late arrival, but I am not as fast a walker as I am a rider.'

'I am sure she will be as fit as a fiddle after a good rest. Here, you take Samson's reigns and we will ride together. Who will see us all the way out here? This place is bigger than Longleat.'

I shuffled forward to make space for him on the saddle and was pleased when I felt him climb up behind me and his hands reach around my waist to find the reigns. My frivolity seemed to be contagious, because more and more, he was letting down his guard and succumbing to my risqué demands with increasing ease. I wondered how much longer I would need to make my mind up. It was so tempting in moments such as these to throw caution to the wind and decide to marry him.

'So were the day's entertainments as much a disappointment as you feared them?' he asked me as we took a gentle trot through the wide wooded pathways. His mouth was close enough to my ear to feel the heat of his breath tickle it and it was enough to send my senses into immediate chaos. I did not know if it was a normal response to come undone with such a simple sensation, but there was something about it that drove me to the edge of blissful despair. I leaned back into him an inch to feel it closer.

'Yes, but it did not seem so bad with this to look to.'

'Pardon me?'

'I said, it was easy to endure with this to look to,' I repeated myself a fraction louder.

'Forgive me, I cannot hear you?'

The breeze had picked up through the trees and was drowning out the sound of our voices. I turned my head to speak the words into his ear, but the timing was such that at the same moment he leaned in to say something further to me and our noses brushed lightly at the tip. The danger of this enthralled me and I wanted so much to seize the moment to kiss him. I had not tried it again last night after surprising him in the dressing room, I had lost my nerve.

'Forgive me, Miss Ashlyn,' he said straight away and drew back an inch.

I was still gazing up at him, considering how much I wished he had the nerve not to be sorry at all; to have made the most of the opportunity presented to him. I smiled, 'It's quite alright Mr Elmbridge.'

I could tell from his expression he understood the words I could not speak. I could recognise the conflict between his unbridled desire and his good breeding. I wondered what it would take to break that restraint or if it was even possible. There was a lifetime's effort of instilled propriety standing between the primal language of our bodies, and neither of us really knew how to manage it. I at least was willing to attempt it. I turned back around and reclined fully against his chest, my head beneath his chin, my body balancing between his strong arms.

The Mr Richards fan club.

June 1821 - Eleanor.

In the afternoon, we had been invited to sit on the lawns and watch the men play cricket. It was a temperate afternoon, a little cooler than the intensity we had grown used to, and I enjoyed the fading warmth of the sun as we sat upon a picnic rug beneath our parasols in our usual groupings. It reminded me of the days of last summer when we spent hours on end playing battledore championships and sipping lemonade at Cuddington. Back then it had seemed quite the distant dream to be out in the full swing of the season like many of my friends, and yet here I was, a season complete, sitting in my favourite new day dress, sipping ratafia and admiring the calves of the man who might soon become my husband. A man who had been right beneath my nose all these years.

I looked across to Lady Caroline to find I was not alone in my admiration. I never wanted the curse of wearing such a pitiful expression as I saw when she was in the company of Lord Berry. Yet the twinkle in her eye when Sheldon paid her the small courtesy of a genial greeting or smile was precisely the kind of sparkle I would always want to feel in looking upon my husband's face. I knew in my logical head, that I must manage to fall in love with Sheldon and before any formal agreement was made between us. I did not want to be the next Lady Caroline. Such an existence would be insufferable to me. And whilst I doubted the likelihood of us ever being like that pair, I knew that we must be beyond the threshold of friendship before I would hear his proposal.

Is that what was happening now, was I falling in love with him? *Is this how it begins?* Would that explain this new craving I had for his company during our separation, and the relief I felt at the sight of him? How would I know for sure if this feeling could be trusted, if it would grow or stay, with so little time to sample it?

I looked over to him to find him stealing glances between his turn in bowling the ball. I replied with a beaming smile. It seemed to make him blush, which I found odd, as I thought it my place to shy away, but he was altered in my company now. I seemed to somehow manage to reduce Sheldon—the now educated and cultured man—into Sheldon the fair haired, ten-year-old boy who wanted to give me his horse to make me smile again.

'I will certainly be taking up the music lessons tomorrow, even if I have no interest in improving my recital,' said Betsy as Mr Richards rolled his shirt sleeves up and swapped position with Sheldon as bowler.

'Betsy!' Beth exclaimed in open mouthed astonishment.

'Well, we were all thinking it, whatever you pretend. Whyever else did you spend the entire day in the music room? Even you do not favour it to *that* extent, and Martha, you play far too well to necessitate his tutelage.'

They both fell quiet at the accusation, but their lack of protest was as good as an admission.

'Hmm, I thought as much. Eleanor, you will have an honest opinion for me, what say you to the looks of the music master?'

I diverted my gaze towards him and made an effort to consider him more carefully. 'He is well enough that I can see the attraction, but I do not share it. Do you forget the Colonel so quickly?' I teased her.

'Oh my, you really are love-struck with Mr E!' Anna interjected.

'I'm not love-struck, Anna. Sheldon and I are just, re-acquainting ourselves after such a long separation.'

'Well, I don't see him re-acquainting himself with anyone else, do you?' Betsy cut in. 'Although I'm sure that madam would jump at the chance, were it offered.'

She was referring to Lady Caroline, who had seized the moment to apprehend him at the refreshment stand where he had stepped out for a glass of something. I watched her flicking her fan about and attempting her best charms as she spoke words to him that I could not hear, and he did not seem to have any interest in. He had his eye on the cricket match as he drained his glass and seemed to only half listen to whatever she had to say to him before he put his glass down, ran back onto the pitch and winked at me when he caught me looking in his direction. This pleased me. I was sure I was not entitled to such singular attentions yet, but I felt something a little protective in my connection with him now that caused me to dislike her hanging about him so grotesquely.

'Well, well, well; it seems the feeling is mutual. Mr E can't tear his eyes away from you either.'

'You speak prematurely, Anna. Speaking of which, what do any of you know of Mr Richards' character or circumstances, or have you failed to consider that small detail insofar? He could have a wife you know.'

'He is perfectly decent,' Beth said defensively.

'Oh codswallop, Beth, we know not a thing about him except that he is absolutely charming and neither of us can deny it!' Anna said as if she was about to burst, having contained it so long. 'And I do not think him old enough to be already leg shackled. There are not many like Mr E who take early to the idea, and he must not be more than a year or two above Sheldon's age.'

'Actually, his manner is impeccable; it would not surprise me if he was already taken,' Beth considered with an air of disappointment in her tone, and I imagined that was as much of a confession of her regard we might expect to get.

'Well, if he truly is so charming and of such exceptional looks, and happens to be without a wife, then he must be poor or ill connected,' Betsy complained as she flicked her fan to swat away a fly. 'Still, I am game for the finding out, what say you, Eleanor, a day at the pianoforte?'

I had no interest in the prospect, but I had been trying to make amends and reconcile our connection. 'For your sake, I will agree to it, so long as I can sing or turn pages.'

'Agreed.'

'YOU STILL KNOW HOW to play a good match,' I said to Sheldon when the end of the cricket dissipated into a leisurely integration of the players and spectators and he came to find me.

'And so do you. I remember your playing at Nork with Louisa,' he winked.

'It seems I am not to play it anymore, not publicly alas. Mother has insisted I give up all but Samson and brisk walks now I am out.'

He laughed. 'I cannot see that lasting long.'

'Nor I,' I laughed with him.

'It's a good job you have no need to impress anyone then.'

'Is that so?'

'Well, I can be excluded on account that I am already impressed. So, unless you are mindful of impressing anyone else, you are quite safe to abandon your bonnet and take up the bat.' He looked in the direction of Mr Richards as he said this and I wondered if he had caught our glances in his direction.

'Ha! Yes, well, I am not twelve anymore, so I think I will at least pretend at being the proper lady in wider circles. And you can rest your mind assured that I am one of the few, from what I can gather, who are quite disinterested in our new visitor.' I looked over at Mr Richards and I could tell that he was grateful for my reassurance.

'I fear the feeling is not mutual,' he said and I realised that Mr Richards was staring back at me beyond the small crowd of ladies that had gathered in a circle around him to congratulate him on his play. Before I looked away, he smiled.

'Well, don't mind me.'

'What am I supposed to do, cut him without cause? I was being polite, now stop being jealous, you really haven't the cause to be. Talking of which, what conversation did Lady Caroline have for you?'

'Some mumbling over an invitation to Dennings, which I politely, declined. But what I *am* inclined to do; is steal you for a few turns about the lawn whilst it is quite acceptable to do so.'

I took his offered arm and put my cup down. It annoyed me that she had the option to speak with him and offer him invitations at her leisure, whilst I had to contrive to enjoy a moment. The privileges of a married woman would be more useful to me now than after my wedding. I felt her eyes following us as we moved away for a little privacy and I made sure I was as tactile with him as decency permitted.

'Sheldon, how long an engagement do you anticipate?'

He seemed surprised at my question. 'I don't know. Would a month or so suffice? I confess I would find it difficult to look beyond that. Should I be heartened that you pose the question?'

I smiled. 'Now it is you that is fast!'

'Perhaps, but I do not think you understand the torture I endure each day on looking at you and wanting to touch you, knowing I should not dare...forgive me,' he said quickly. 'I have been too long at the punch today; the Earl is more generous and insistent than I am accustomed, with his Arrack Bowl.'

'Don't apologise, you speak of only what we both find quite the curiosity.' He stopped and looked at me with a violence of passion I was not used to, and I did not know whether it was excitement or fear I felt at the change in his demeanour. 'Continue as you are and we might just find out,' I said provocatively; I think it was the nerves to blame for it.

He took a moment to register my speech, stepped back a fraction and brushed his fringe back with a palm. 'Eleanor, you must not speak that way again in my company.' His face was serious now, his tone a tad annoyed.

'I'm sorry. I ....'

'I think I should perhaps get some sleep before dinner.'

'Must you go so soon?'

'I think I must.'

I REGRETTED MY LAPSE in speech as I sat in my chamber with Dolores, answering some correspondence from my sisters I had neglected in London, and thumbing through the increasing collection of small tokens that had gathered upon the console table. I would have much preferred to be taking a turn on the lawn with him, I thought, as I paused to look out of the window where others were still making the most of the hosts relaxation in the schedule. I could have stayed with the others when he left, but I did not want to once he was gone. Unless I was prepared to join the Mr Richards' fan club, or sit in idle gossip over fancywork with the older ladies, there was little I might be diverted with in his absence.

I was a little cross with him for his abandoning me on one of the few opportunities we were afforded to be freely in each other's company. And yet I knew the blame for it was upon my fast tongue, for I had seemed to push his tolerance a fraction too far. What I could not fathom out, however much I revisited it, was what I saw in his face today. He seemed to somehow give himself away and I thought perhaps the thought of the kiss I suggested had enchanted him, and then I sensed the restraint of his own temper in his reprimand of me. I did not know which response could be taken as the most fervent, and I needed to know, because I wanted him to kiss me again, and I wanted to encourage it, tonight.

I plied Watts with the bribe of the entire collection on the console table, in exchange for her allegiance in my plans for this evening to escape with him again. But it was a good job I was not attached to these trinkets, for I could have spared myself the trouble had I anticipated how pointless our meeting would prove.

I had noticed him more reserved at dinner due to our company and the distance set between us, but had expected the customary relaxation of manners we had recently come to enjoy when we snuck out to the music temple again. The location and the night sky were the only similarity between the two occasions as we sat upon the bench with almost a seat's width between us and little more than polite conversation with long drawn-out gaps that made me anxious.

'Sheldon,' I said, when I could not bear to continue along with the pretence any longer, 'what has changed between us so drastically that you will not even permit me to sit closer to you?'

'Nothing has changed in my regard for you, El.'

'Then what is it?'

'It was wrong of me to permit what I have, and I am sorry for allowing my own longing to encourage you as I have. It is irresponsible on my part, and it shall not happen again.'

'Sheldon, if this is because of what I said earlier—'

'I crossed the line before then, Eleanor, and we both know that I cannot blame the punch bowl for the other occasions.'

'Blame? Sheldon, there is no blame when both of us consent to it, *will* it, in fact. But if there is to be blame; then it is mine and I am not sorry for it, even if I should be.' I went to move into the empty space and he held his hand out in protest.

'El, please. Do not make this any harder.'

'It seems you will not allow me to make our suffering any easier.'

'You don't know what you are talking about, Eleanor; you speak of things you do not understand.'

I know more than you think. 'Then help me understand it, Sheldon, help me to know more of its complexities that I might sympathise with your view.'

He swallowed hard and stood up. 'If that is really what you want, El, then you will hear my question.'

'If I am what you really want, then you will answer my curiosities first.' I got up too, but walked on past him and headed down the steps.

'El—El where are you going?' He ran up behind me, but I did not wait for him, or answer his question.

'El, I know you are used to your way, but you cannot have it in this; we are not ten years old anymore.'

'It is not I that has difficulty in understanding that.'

'El you can have your way with me for the rest of our days, but not in this.'

'I see. Well, you seem to have it all worked out.'

'El, don't be like this.' He stopped me with the reach of his hand. I looked down at his gloved fingers encircled around my wrist and when he released his grip, I carried on ahead, even though the sky had broken out in a drizzle that was threatening to grow heavy. The lawns would at least be grateful of it.

He took off his tailcoat and opened it out like a tent above our heads. I could smell the musky scent of his cologne and see the shape of his well-formed arms beneath the muslin sleeves if I glanced sideways beneath my lashes.

'You cannot always win you know, none of us can.'

'Perhaps you are right Mr Elmbridge, and perhaps you are not,' I said nonchalantly. 'Either way, you know I am minded to fancy the idea, and if you hope to manage to change that, perhaps *you* are not ready to ask the question.'

He stopped and dragged me underneath a tree beside a clearing. 'You are impossible.'

'Well, we both know that already. What interests me, is all the things we have yet to learn of each other. Then we might both be a better judge of whether these things we do not like so well, might be overlooked in favour of the others we prefer.'

'You have said too much, Eleanor.'

I did not mistake the frustration in his tone, he had raised his voice a fraction more than I was used to; but I did recognise the expression on his face as the very same I had seen earlier on him when I spoke out of turn, and he'd retired. *What is the meaning of it?*

'It is too wet. Unless you want to explain to Delores why your gown is drenched, I suggest you wait it out here.'

Reluctantly, I stepped back under the partial cover of his jacket which was managing to catch the excess the branches failed to prevent. It was the closest proximity we had been in all night and it made me dizzy.

'You're right. I am cold,' I said and stepped into his vulnerable chest and pressed myself against him until I felt the warmth of his body against my cold cheek. He did not move an inch and did not say a word for the ten minutes or more that the downpour kept us trapped there.

I DID NOT SEE HIM AT breakfast, and I wondered if he had took it early to avoid me. I tried the library too on the off chance and even checked the copy of *Ode and Elegie,* but when I found myself disappointed again, I took Betsy's invitation to join her in the music room for Mr Richards' instruction and braced myself for a morning of giggling and flirtatious damsels.

I hadn't prepared myself for such a crush. The room was so crammed I imagined the other classes must be entirely empty. I found a space to stand amongst his fan club and considered giving it a few moments before slipping out.

'Good morning, ladies,' he said to silence the buzz of the room. 'For those of you I have not had the pleasure of an introduction,' I noticed his eyes on me a moment as he said it, 'I am Mr Richards; a guest tutor to Wycombe for the first time, with the honour of instructing you further in your musical accomplishments. I confess, I had planned for a smaller workshop today, so I think we might have to take a different style of tutoring this morning, so if you have any particular matters you would like to address, or particular interests, then I invite you to come forward with them.'

I half listened to his introduction as I peered out of the window and pondered Sheldon's absence.

'Perhaps a better course might be to add them to this page and we will take them in turn,' he said holding out a sheet of blank paper as they swamped him in a bid for attention.

Betsy got up and took the paper a moment before anyone else had managed to get there. I watched her scrawling away with mild amusement. It was not like Betsy to lose her moderation like this at all, so I supposed her liking for him to be greater than was usual for her. I wondered where this left the Colonel.

She had no sooner replaced the quill than had the page snatched from her grasp by another keen admirer. I wondered how any of them hoped to gain his notice or favour, exhibiting themselves as such brutes as they fought over each other to make their contribution to the page. Even the chaperones were struggling to keep them in line. I looked at his helpless face and felt a little sorry for his embarrassment.

'I hope the hour is not too early for your voice. Quick, let us warm you up,' Betsy said and I frowned my confusion.

'For what exactly?'

'To sing at the pianoforte.'

'What?'

Before I could rebuff her, I heard him call Betsy and I to the piano on account of some imagined difficulty Betsy was suffering with her playing. I watched him reading from the page and opened my mouth to berate her as he put his hands together to clap us on and I felt Betsy yank me through the crowd towards him.

'Ah, Lady Elizabeth, Miss Ashlyn,' he nodded his introduction and I wondered how he knew my name, for we had never been introduced. I smiled anyway to disguise my nerves as he took us over to the piano. I knew I owed Betsy some apology, but this was not quite what I had in mind. I had expected a handful of us about the room, not the entire female set. I stood uncomfortably at her side as I felt the weight of his stare and wished Betsy—who was fiddling with her sheet music—would hurry up. I cleared my throat as she began, and waited for my cue to begin.

'Love's blind, they say,
O Never, nay,
Can words love's grace impart;
The fancy, weak,
The tongue may speak,
But eyes alone the heart:
In one soft look, what language lies!
O, yes, believe me, love has eyes...'

I was a little croaky, but it passed with the first few notes. Then as I got into the spirit of it on the second verse, Betsy feigned some misdemeanour at the bridge that required his assistance.

'Like so?' Betsy said innocently as Mr Richards leaned over her shoulder and demonstrated the correction.

I resisted rolling my eyes to the heavens. We both knew she could play it well, and if it weren't for the fact that I was guilty of embroiling her in such favours in the past, I would have said so to avenge her for this debacle. We attempted the verse thrice before his assistance helped her *overcome* the *problem* and I was glad when the last note was struck after repeating the lines over and over.

'You sing well, Miss Ashlyn, I would like to hear more of you if I may?'

'Thank you, Mr Richards, you are very kind, but I am quite fatigued,' I sat down quickly and glowered at Betsy to warn her not to press me further.

AFTER DINNER THAT EVENING when the rugs were rolled up in the saloon, Mr Richards came over to us and petitioned for a place on my dance card. I was about to refuse him, but as

I saw Sheldon come into the room, I changed my mind and accepted. I was still furious at his day-long absence and I was certain to make him feel it.

'Miss Ashlyn, you do me a great honour,' Mr Richards said to me as I moved in to find some conversation with him.

'I think perhaps it is you that do me the honour tonight, Mr Richards,' I said, looking at all the anxious eyes upon him in the room. 'I think you will have no difficulty in dancing all night long should you wish it.'

We both laughed.

'Yes, I am sure I should be more grateful.'

'You are not?'

'I am slightly embarrassed if I am honest, Miss Ashlyn.'

'Well, I am afraid you have come to us quite the handsome, mysterious stranger into the lair of excited debutantes still fresh from the season's expectations. Still, you have survived it well considering how they have quite forgotten their manners in the fight to gain your notice.'

'And yet I seem to have escaped yours entirely, Miss Ashlyn, which I find a shame, for your company has been the most refreshing I have encountered outside of the billiards room.'

I laughed a little. 'Hmmm, well, I shall take that as compliment I think, shall we?'

'As it was intended, please,' he held his arm out and led me to the dance floor. I did not look in his direction, but I could see in my peripheral vision, Sheldon watching on in muted outrage. *Well, this is what you get when you leave a lady so neglected!*

When we had finished our set, he took me over to the table and got me a cup. I pretended not to notice all the scornful glares directed at us as we made an effort for small conversation. 'My friends are very fond of you sir, if you will forgive my saying so. They are very fond of dancing,' I said as I sipped at my wine.

'Well, Miss Ashlyn, if it will please you; I shall certainly ask them.'

'You are very good, Sir,' I smiled and watched on as their face lit up at his approach.

When our hostess came over in the interval, and asked Mr Richards to afford us the pleasure of his playing at the pianoforte, I had not expected him to accept it on the condition that I would join him in the singing. If it had been anyone else, I would have refused it, but I could not refuse the hostess, and so obediently, I followed him over to the pianoforte. We had a brief discussion on song choices as we journeyed over, and I did not fail to notice Sheldon's irritation growing restless as he stood around the perimeter with the wallflowers. *It is not nice to be kept waiting without explanation or apology, is it?*

We sang *Love among the Roses* together to begin with, but when the applause broke out, we were encouraged into performing two more pieces, all of which he sung and played better than I had ever heard them performed. He was deserving of his reputation, I realised now, and felt the honour of his invitation now I could appreciate the fact. I made sure to pay him the compliment of it when we were finished, but was relieved when he was engulfed with a procession of eager congratulators for the performance, permitting me the opportunity to slip from his company.

I chatted small pleasantries to the lesser share of our congratulators that approached me, consisting mainly of the gentleman and married persons. I seemed to have induced the cursing of the entire single female population in one foul sweep. I feigned ignorance to it. They were much mistaken to think that I had any marked regard for Mr Richards or much care for their scorn. *If you had not behaved like a kettle of savage vultures fighting over a fresh catch, then perhaps he would have applied to your dance card!*

'Well, congratulations E!' Betsy came up beside me with Anna in tow. 'Congratulations on being greedy enough to nab; not one, but two of the most desirable bachelors at Wycombe this weekend. I might have known one would not be enough for your ego.'

'Betsy!' I exclaimed. I supposed she really was fond of him. 'I have no regard for Mr Richards.'

'Well, I know that, which makes it all the more contemptible that you would have your friends endure such a display when they actually might.'

'Bets, forgive me, I wasn't thinking.'

'Oh you was; but only of yourself. Come on Anna, I am tired of our company,' she said with a contempt I could not misinterpret, and I watched them strut off across the room still cursing behind their fans. I looked over to Martha and Beth who were still watching me. I could imagine that they had opted to stay out of any conflict, and it was safe to regroup with them until Betsy and Anna had relented in their snub.

But I did not stay long; their company was no more thrilling for their easy forgiveness, and I retired early, before either Mr Richards had broke free of his followers, or Sheldon plucked up the courage to stop brooding and confront me.

I had no plans to escape my room this evening. Even though the thought of a midnight make-up meeting with Sheldon had crossed my mind; I wanted him to feel the full extent of my disappointment in his neglect of me today, so instead, I took to my bed early in preparation for tomorrow's journey back to Cuddington.

I DID NOT HEAR FROM him again until we were back home, and I was glad of it, for I knew by now he would have understood the severity of my disappointment. He left me his card the following morning, and much to my surprise, so did Mr Richards, who I did not expect to find in the country here at all, less still, paying me calls. This was a complication I no longer required; it had served its purpose, and I had no intention or desire to continue our acquaintance beyond polite conversation should our paths cross again. I had his card in my hand ready to throw into the fire when Sheldon was announced unexpectedly.

'Miss Ashlyn,' he said with a bow.

'Mr Elmbridge,' I stood up quickly and replied.

Delores wondered off to the other end of the drawing room and busied herself with some fancywork, far less inconspicuously than she might have intended, and I invited him to take a seat opposite me.

'You look well,' he said, I think, to break the ice. 'Are your family well?'

'Yes, thank you. May I enquire as to the health of yours?'

'Well, thank you.'

'Miss Ashlyn, do you think your chaperone will permit us to take a turn outside; I would very much like to talk to you more privately?' His voice was low and I could hear the discomfort in his tone as much as I felt it in the awkwardness between us.

'If you will excuse me, I will go and ask her,' I said, and he rose as I did. I had quite forgotten that I had hidden Mr Richards' calling card in my lap, when it fell to the floor as I stood up.

'Allow me,' he said as I raced down to get it a fraction too late; his hand was there upon it before mine.

'Thank you,' I said, but I could see the alteration in his expression as he rose and met my eyes.

'Actually, Miss Ashlyn,' he stared between me and Richards' card, accusing, 'you needn't take the trouble,' he said, and bid both Delores and I a swift farewell.

I contemplated going after him, but I was not the grovelling type and we both knew that. Besides, it would only encourage his belief in my guilt if I acted so out character, and I did not see the point in bending when neither of us would benefit from the effort. Instead, I decided to have Samson saddled up and escape Delores' questions which were all over her expression at this odd call.

Petworth.

June 1821. Eleanor.

B y the time I returned from my ride, Delores was gone. The squire had sent his coach for her in my absence and the pair were off to give the news of their announcement to his children. I was relieved not to have had to face the questions that had been on her lips when I had left, but I was sorry not to have wished her well. I could tell she had been anxious over it all morning. I did not know the squire's children well enough to judge how she might fare, for they were all a few years above even my siblings ages and we had never really spoke beyond cordial greetings.

It was ironic: here I was free from my chaperone, and Sheldon and I were out of charity with one another. There would likely never be such a good opportunity to scheme our way to a week of private meetings, with Mama standing in, and society so quiet. Beth and Martha had rattled back off to London together, Betsy and Anna were giving me the shrug off, and Clara was still away on her wedding journey and was not due back until next month.

If we were not due to set off for Petworth at the end of the week, it might have proved the perfect time to take a holiday, visiting my sisters. It was what I planned to do upon our return, if things with Sheldon were ill improved. I would disappear to Kent for a few weeks to see Harriet and spend a month in Edinburgh, with Caitlin. And they had the festival in August. I should rather like to go to it, for Caitlin always wrote such excited and approving letters about it, and unlike London which would be long vacant at that season, Edinburgh would be brimming with all sorts of society on account of it. Perhaps Harriet might be persuaded to come and make a party of it. It sounded like so much fun, I half wished perhaps things might not improve, just to necessitate my going to amuse myself. But it was a half-hearted thought: I was already beginning to miss his company quite excessively and it had only been a couple of days since our fall out. Perhaps if they did improve, we might go off to Edinburgh together. I was sure Caitlin would have no objection to extending an invitation to him if she understood the alteration in our friendship and his intentions.

I occupied myself with such musings as I lazed about my bed chamber, idling away the day with nothing better to do than inhabit my imagination to cure the tedium. By evening, I was so miffed over how to spend the coming days, that I had accepted to go about paying calls with Mama to announce our arrival back in Cuddington and even agreed to attend the Dowager's with her the same evening for a casual supper and a game of cribbage.

I wondered if the others were right to stay in London and stretch the season a little further until the coronation, if this was how it was to be now. The only absence I was not sorry for was Mariella's. This was my only consolation, I had thought many times as I walked the woods or rode the park, catching sight of Beaulieu from a summit or through the woodland when I veered too close to the boundary without realising. I dreaded to think of the day they would return, but hoped that if I was to journey to my sisters then I should not have any need to concern myself on this count for some months yet, and who knows, by then, I might even be married and not ever have to suffer her as a neighbour again.

At least, this was what I had thought, until we were paying a call upon Anna's Mama and she disclosed to us some news that threw me quite off guard in that respect.

'Oh, you have not heard?' said Mrs Carmichael frowning, you mean Anna did not tell you, Miss Ashlyn?'

'No ma'am,' I said puzzled. 'I have not seen Anna since Wycombe.'

'Well, you did not hear it from me mind, for the announcement has barely gone to press, but, it seems Miss Brownlow is to be wed to one of those Craythornes.'

'God forbid Mrs Carmichael, what a sorry state everything is come to nowadays,' Mama sighed and put down her teacup. 'I own, I am very sorry for poor Martha's circumstances, and were it not to *that* family, I would indeed be happy to see her rise above her circumstances.'

Even my joy at this news was blighted by the thought of the sister-in-law she would now inherit. But, unlike my mama, I was still happy to know she was not headed off as a governess or destined for an old maid's existence, and nor would she ever be forced to lie under Mr Willmott. At least something good had come from my involvement with that family. Although this private joy at Martha's turn of luck was soon overcast by another of Mrs Carmichael's revelations.

'Anna says they are to waste no time. The announcement should come any day, and upon it, they are all to return to the country so the banns may be read at St. Dunstan's and they may be wed straight away. Makes you wonder what the rush is. Anna tells me they are both very much in love and excessively happy over the affair, but I suspect those Craythornes are keen to march Miss Brownlow up the aisle as quick as can be for fear she changes her mind and they lose the connection.'

I thought it more likely that it was to act before her stepfather ended up in the Fleet, to protect the Craythornes from the Nashs' disgrace. Either way, what did it matter, they were happy and that was what was important, and so why should they wait if they really were in love. This I had found the most surprising part of the news, for even though I'd seen a mild improvement between Martha and Mr Craythorne in London, it had never seemed to me to be anything of excessive regard or feeling. And he was such an indifferent man, that it surprised me that he would be minded for love at all after all that Mariella had told me of his character: Being more concerned for his trade affairs than anything sentimental or domestic. 'Mrs Carmichael, is Anna at home?' I asked. I wanted to know when we might expect this unwelcome descent into the country, and to see if there was any sign of her or Bet's relent.

'Anna—oh you won't find her at home now the Mowbray's have that music master to stay. The pair of them have gone quite queer in the attic over the poor man. She has only been home for a change of clothes since she's been back.'

'Do you mean Mr Richards is at the Mowbray's?' I asked.

'Goodness gracious my dear, you mean you do not know? I am surprised you are not hanging about the place with them. Have you been hiding yourself away?'

'No, I—'

'She has been pre-occupied and I daresay a little neglectful of her friends of late,' Mama cut in and cast Mrs Carmichael a knowing glance that she nodded her understanding of before continuing.

'Well, you must know he's all the thing now, all those silly girls signing up for lessons and fighting over him, begging their papas to help them improve their musical accomplishments. Well, Anna did not try at least; she knew I saw right through it all. But Lady Elizabeth managed to gull her papa into taking him on for a spell before Petworth, for he is booked up now you know, for some weeks.'

'Well, what folly. I am surprised at Lady Elizabeth,' Mama said with a hint of condescension, likely on account that she was pleased to say I had not behaved in such a silly, girlish manner either, and that she and Mrs Carmichael might congratulate themselves on having bred such sensible daughters when the trend seemed otherwise inclined.

So, I left the Carmichael's in worse spirits than I had arrived there in, and now must ponder two uncomfortable realisations: That Mariella was likely to be home any day and that the chances of making things up with Bets was highly unlikely whilst Mr Richards was still about. Martha and Beth's return might have proved some consolation if it were not for the fact that I was sure I could rely on Mariella assuming the catchfart position of never being far away from them now there was to be a wedding she would *have* to be invited to. And this brought to mind another dilemma; we were likely to be invited to the wedding breakfast.

BY THURSDAY, I WAS quite willing to pay a call with mama at the Elmbridge's. I had, up until now; refused to go with her for fear of so much awkwardness should me and Sheldon be thrust together. But I had come to miss him so sorely, that today I hoped for it, so that we might have a chance to speak. So that I might tell him I was sorry. Explain to him the misunderstanding over Richards' card: For now I understood him to be at the Mowbray's, I did not want Sheldon to think I had been there dangling after him as the others were. Especially, if he was to be at Petworth too now; it made sense to clear the air ahead of it, so this issue would not grow any further out of proportion than it already had. I would stay away from Richards, I hadn't any interest in doing otherwise anyway, but I wanted him to know it so we might be at ease again. So, we might remember how to enjoy each other's company again.

But it turned out, he was not at home and had actually set off for Oxford a couple of days ago and was expected back on Friday. I hoped that meant he still planned on attending at the weekend, but I did not dare pose the question or show my surprise at him having awayed, for I did not want mama or Lady Elmbridge to suspect we were on such bad terms and subject me to questions I could not answer.

So, I wrote to him that night instead, a simple note to say:

Forgive me. I'm sorry. I miss you. I hope you will still come this weekend. I have not seen Richards and do not know why he left his card—honest.

IT WAS NOT UNTIL WE were packing up the coaches to away to Petworth that I heard from Sheldon again, with the subtle reply of his own calling card, which I assumed to be a peace offering ahead of our reunion, and confirmation of his attendance. This improved my mood a great deal, for as much as I enjoyed the company and entertainments at Petworth, it would not be the same without him. And I was sorely disappointed to learn, that not only were the Craythornes back in the country now, but had also been invited to both attend and stay this weekend. On hearing this news, I had almost considered cancelling my attendance. The thought of having to meet eyes with her again so soon, and yet after having such a nice reprieve, was too much to contemplate. But I was not to be pushed out of my own society on her account, and so I resolved to go as planned and avoid her wherever possible. Which might be easier than usual, since I was still at odds with Betsy and Anna, having not had any of my calls returned this week.

So, the prospect of having one less person displeased with me this weekend, was encouraging, and as for the time I might have to spend without him, I knew I could rely on the Earls good entertainments and numerous daughters to keep me in good company. I took my seat in the coach all the better for the happy prospects and the generous sunshine and blue skies we would make the journey in, despite Mother's sulky mood. She had perhaps not expected Delores to return last night with the announcement that her own wedding was to go ahead and the date was set for next month. I suspected she had over relied on the news going ill, failed to prepare herself accordingly and now had to contend with the fact that it would not be long before I was without my chaperone and she was without her lifelong companion.

WHEN WE ARRIVED, ONE of the first, I went straight to the drawing room to take tea with some of Sir George's children, which was always well spirited due to their sheer number. We enjoyed an hour of convivial re-acquaintance before the house begun to fill up with new arrivals, and when I saw our host doing the rounds of introductions with Mr Richards, I thought it a good time to make my departure for the dressing room and get ready for the evening's entertainments. It seemed Mrs Carmichael had been correct: his debut amongst the ton at Wycombe had set him up well; for Sir George was well known to be a generous patron of the arts should he take a fancy to someone. It was certainly one class I would be keeping off my itinerary in the coming days.

Not that it staked so high amidst the more varied offerings of sporting, art and science exhibitions open to both the men and the ladies this weekend. The invitation here, was always one well received and looked to, for you could always rely on the right balance of interesting people and offerings, dispersed with fairly relaxed and generous opportunities to mingle, and of course it was always a crush for those very reasons.

The house was half full by the time I returned downstairs, and I was pleased with Sheldon's attentive welcome of me, particularly when I noticed Mariella watching me pensively from her newly adopted corner with Bets and Anna. I returned him my most generous beam and chatted politely with him and his family at length, which pleased Mama no end as she watched on from her seat amongst the other patronesses. I knew that she had sensed something had been at odds between us by the end of the week and no doubt felt relieved we had made amends.

Despite only a week of absence he seemed much changed. He looked darker, his continental tan had revived and he had grown a stubble of hair on his face, which usually I was not partial to, but it seemed to suit his strong jaw and give him a fresh air of sophistication. I felt, from his gaze, he was equally pleased to settle his eyes upon me and even though we were surrounded by the company of others and in a continuous flow of conversation and introductions, the unspoken language between us was tangible with every glance and smile. I had expected our re-acquaintance to be slow, uncomfortable; full of explanations before we might resume such familiarity. And yet I wanted nothing more than to throw my arms about him, forget all our quarrels and tell him how much I had missed him. I could see reflected in his own eyes, the same sentiment and it reassured me this weekend was to be a happy one, despite all else.

Dinner was a leisurely affair and reliably freestyle so we could sit together and speak privately at last. The Carved Room had to be converted into a dining room in order to fit the number of tables required to accommodate all the guests and as the table filled up, it became impossible to see from one end to the other for the number of bobbing heads.

'Thank you for your note,' he turned to me and whispered once the din of the room provided adequate cover for plain speaking. 'I've missed you too.'

'Then why did you go away?'

He looked uncomfortably into his plate before answering. 'Not here, El, we'll talk, when we can. But know that all I have thought about is you.'

'I have been thinking of spending August in Edinburgh with Caitlin...I wondered if you have ever fancied the festival?'

'If you are there, I will go anywhere,' he smiled and held my gaze so intently I had to look away when I realised we had caught the notice of our neighbours. We were more careful after that and stuck to more prattling topics. He gave me a rundown of his day's itinerary tomorrow, and I was disappointed to learn he was promised to Sir George for the first half of the day between an expedition and a fishing trip on the lake. I assured him I would not be taking any music classes, but I was otherwise undecided on how I would spend my morning, and then our hostess stood and ushered the ladies along to the White and Gold Room.

I sat with Sir George's daughters over tea and pretended not to notice the congregation of my set on the other side of the room. They had arrived in dribs and drabs through the day but were now convening a catch up and exchanging news. I wondered how much my name was in the mention and when I saw Betsy making a beeline for me, I braced myself for her complaint.

'Can I sit?' she asked simply and I shuffled over to make more room for her on the sofa. 'You're quite forgiven over the Mr Richards' affair, turns out I was right all along. He is not married, but he has no money and he is rumoured to be without family: a foundling child or some such disagreeable history,' she said in the straightforward manner I was accustomed. 'My father made some enquiries,' she shrugged, 'so no hard feelings.'

This was as close to an apology as I was ever likely to receive from Betsy, I knew her so well, I could understand what was behind her words, for it was the same as what was behind mine: *I've missed you and I've tired of this now.* 'Well, he had clumsy feet anyway, if you ask me, you're all the better for knowing it,' I lied, and watched the others filter over to join us, settling into our usual spaces and forcing Mariella along one seat, which I found at least a little justice in having to bear her presence.

I was brought up to speed on the latest on-dit, which I didn't have the heart to confess I had learnt from other sources. So I played along to the bulletin with the necessary doses of surprise and disgust. The only new discovery made was that Martha had not engaged herself to Mr Craythorne of Beddington, but Bertram Craythorne, my favourite of the brother's, and this news made better sense of Mrs Carmichael's speech. No wonder they were in love and so happy, he was the most amiable creature—who could not help but fall a little in love with one so sweet tempered and always full of joy. He was like a walking dose of sunshine. A little could lift you into much higher spirits. And so, I felt happy to think that Martha really would defy the odds, not just in making a match in her difficulties, but making a love match, after all. 'Congratulations Martha, I am truly happy for you,' I told her as she coloured and clasped her hands together.

'Thank you, Eleanor. It is thanks to you, you know, that I even met Bertie. I shall never forget it. You are to be invited to the wedding and the breakfast and there is even to be an engagement party at Beaulieu for us. Oh, it is all so very exciting!'

'Indeed, it is. And you are very good, Martha, but you owe me no thanks or special invitations,' I replied.

'Oh, but I do! And I own, I would have liked to pay you the honour of attending me at the wedding, but I hope you will not mind, but I have asked Bethany and Mariella.'

So, it's Christian name intimacy all round now is it? I saw a flash in Mariella's eyes at Martha's announcement and a look of incredulity in Betsy's. 'I do not mind in the least Martha, I want you to be happy on your wedding day and it should be just as you would wish it.'

'I knew you would understand. You see, Mariella has been so exerting herself with all the arrangements—'

'Indeed,' Betsy let slip with an eye roll of exasperation. However much she had seemingly accepted Mariella's infiltration, I knew that her relent remained involuntary and superficial.

'You will come to the wedding though won't you, Eleanor?' Martha asked imploringly.

'I shall try, although I am to make a holiday of seeing my sisters soon. So do not waste a place setting on me until I can confirm the dates, will you.'

'Oh, it shan't be wasted, there is to be so many settings. There is to be no expense spared, and since it is the first wedding in the family, there is such excitement and so much fuss.'

I bet there is.

'Surely you will come, Miss Ashlyn? Martha is right, if it were not for you making the introductions between our families, it might never have come to pass. You will be quite the guest of honour, won't she Martha?' Mariella said, and I could not believe she had the audacity to dare to talk to me at all. We had not engaged ourselves in any direct conversation since Ham, and even though I understood the mischief in her question, I had not expected her to give in to the temptation so easily. To even respond to her at all, required only my best theatricals of humility and gratitude, for my disgust at this news of having to attend these affairs where she was present, was entirely authentic. I was sure I needed something stronger to endure what this evening had in store for me, but I accepted the offering of the teacup politely and braced myself to endure it.

When the gentleman emerged from the Carved Room, we were apprised of the news that we were to enjoy a little music from Mr Richards and some of his most promising pupils in the

Square Dining Room before the carpets were rolled back to cope with the overflow of dancing from the Marble Hall. I was grateful for Sheldon joining us then, for I had no wish to be drawn into Betsy's slander campaign going on behind her fan as the music struck up. I was not sure what he had done to offend her so, but she was so venomous and intent on destroying him, I assumed he must have seriously insulted her. I might not have been one of Richards' clingers on, but I could not help feel sorry for him if she was in such a head. He seemed a decent and amiable enough fellow to me, and whatever had passed between them, I was certain he could not have deserved the things I overheard her saying.

We decided to remove from the dancing tonight. It had been my idea to look at the many paintings and marble busts instead, to give us a chance to talk more intimately and avoid having to put my name down for dances when the only one I wanted to dance with, was him. We were not the only ones so minded, and the North Gallery and the Somerset Room was dotted about with other admirers to Sir George's vast collections and a few old maids scattered about the sofa's taking refuge from the ballroom hubbub. Delores shadowed us with some acquaintance I was not familiar with, since the squire was not in attendance this weekend.

It was a shame he was not, for it took us almost half the night to give her the slip at the supper rooms during the interval and we wasted no time to seize the opportunity to disappear. The house was so busy it seemed at first there was nowhere to seek refuge or escape, until we found the hall by the oak staircase vacant and stepped out of the house through the tourist entrance, closing the door soundlessly behind us. My stomach reeled with anxious excitement as we shuffled along the gravel to escape the courtyard, and up through a meandering path that led to the Doric Temple: standing out serenely white against the backdrop of trees cast into shadow as the moonlight reflected of its colonnades. When we climbed the steps beneath its cover, I wanted to reach up and kiss him, but I was too nervous, too unsure. He stepped over to a bench and sat against its armrest. I followed him over. 'What is it?' I said eventually, my voice echoing to the heights of the ceiling.

'I'm just listening,' he said thoughtfully.

'To what?'

'I believe that is the slow waltz starting up, do you hear it?'

I listened for a moment catching the rhythm of the strings. 'Yes, I believe it is.'

'It is your favourite set and yet you do not dance tonight.'

'I only want to dance with you.'

'And you shall.' He stood up, moved to the centre of the temple and bowed, 'Miss Ashlyn, will you do me the honour of this dance?'

I laughed and crossed the floor to where he stood. 'I will, Sir,' I answered, dropping a curtsey.

He stepped in close, reached around my waist, and pressed his palm into my back, drawing me in, leaving far less distance between us than was permitted in the ballroom. Our free arms met in the air above our heads, fingertips lightly clasping as we began to turn in circles, the rustle of my train sweeping the floor, the clip of our shoes against the flagstones as we rose on almost tiptoe, the stifled rhythm of the music pacing our steps. It was a blissful relief to touch him at last when my body had been aching to reach out to him all evening. I could not see his features clearly in the dim light, but I could feel him, hear the quickening of his breath as we spun a little faster, catch the scent of him as a breeze whipped up from the motion of our movements. From the first point of contact, the mood had been one of severity and intent, but as we spun further around the room, it flourished into something amorous. Our bodies crept in closer with each stride, we dropped our hands from above our heads and used them to scoop our bodies even closer, until the only part of the dance that was recognisable was the movement of our feet.

When the music fell away, we stopped where we were, forgetting our graceful decrescendo, and I lifted my chin and kissed him: a gentle motion, the snag of his stubble against my lower lip, helping to guide me to his mouth. I could not only smell the scent of him, but I tasted it now, the sweet hint of after dinner brandy still upon his lips. It lasted barely a few seconds before he pulled back, led me over to the colonnades where silvery light streamed in, then he spun me, as if we were still in the steps of the dance, until I felt him behind me; right behind me: His arms reaching to encompass me, his head filled the space between my ear and my shoulder. 'Do you know what I have been thinking of all week?' he said, a murmur upon my ear.

'No,' I said, staring out into the darkness.

'That one day...' he wrapped me up in himself a little tighter and kissed me gently on the side of my face. I felt a shiver snake the length of my neck, it shocked me. '...I will stand with you just like this, and it will be our wedding day.' He trailed his fingers the length of my arm. 'And we will dance just like that...' I felt the tip of his nose trace the length of my shoulder, my neck and then the top of my ear. '...with a private orchestra playing just for me and you.' I sighed and closed my eyes as his warm breath misted my cheek, the timbre of his voice reverberated at my ear and I broke out in quivering bumps across my décolleté. 'And I will hold you in my arms like this all night long, as you sleep.' He brushed a palm up the length of my right flank, pressed it lightly against my ribcage and I thought I might fall down with the tremor it induced in me. 'Kiss you here...' he planted the lightest of kisses into the crook of my neck and my head fell back against him, chin up to the ceiling. '...and every inch of skin that covers you, for we will be only in our skin.' At this, I let out a gasp, for my body was beginning to writhe and snake, just as I remembered when she put her hands beneath my skirts. My body was willing him, inviting him to touch me. I knew it was impossible that he could, but I craved him so desperately I would not have stopped him if he dared.

But he did not dare. When my body grew restless at this provocation, he retreated to safer ground. Stroked my cheek and held me still. And once I had calmed again, he led me down the temple steps with no more than a kiss on my forehead and left me reeling with such unquenched desire, that when I went to bed that night, I recalled the memory, felt beneath my muslin and finally achieved the tremulous outburst she had elicited from me before.

WHEN I RETIRED FROM the breakfast table and drifted into the drawing room to browse the listings for today's activities, I was soon accosted by my set. They were minded to set off for the North Gallery, where there was to be a demonstration of Maillardet's automaton writer. I went along with them after a little persuasion, for the sound of the thing intrigued me. And indeed, it was not every day you saw a doll-like machine perched at a writing table scribing poems and pictures. But when Martha and Beth tried to persuade me to going with them (and Mariella) to Mr Richards' class, I declined and sat over tea and plum cakes with Betsy and Anna in the Little Dining Room instead.

I had hoped this would prove more comfortable, without Mariella's presence to rile me, but when I realised it was to be nothing more than a Richards' slanging contest, I began to wonder what the less of evils might have proved. Before long, they returned and found us next door and Martha and Beth came back singing their praises over some musical accomplishment Mariella had demonstrated in class, impressing them rather grandly. We had heard her singing through the wall but Betsy was so vocal in her slander campaign, it was difficult to listen to either attentively.

Thankfully, I was still so much absorbed in the memory of Sheldon's attentive company last night, I felt present more in body than mind. It had restored not only my blissful disposition, but had furnished me with new hope for us. Because despite my reservations, I knew last night I had felt *it* when he breathed into my ear. My relief was not only in the realisation that such feeling existed between Sheldon and I, but that it existed at all without *her* to provoke it. It was this knowing, that made her company far easier to tolerate than before: *It is not your power after all,* I thought as I studied her and joined in the applause Martha had directed at her for this musical performance I neither paid attention to, or cared for. She could have been elected as Patroness of Almack's for all I cared now.

'Someone is quiet today,' Anna said to me once the celebratory talk faded into the usual chatter. 'I meant to ask you, where did you disappear to last night?'

I brought my teacup to my lips and took a sip. When I put it back in its saucer and looked up, I noted the interest and expectation on everyone's faces, even *hers*. In this at least, I could take some satisfaction.

'For a tour, that is all,' I said as straight faced as I could muster.

'Of Petworth?' Anna probed, mirroring the incredulity on everyone's faces.

'Where else?' I said with the same even tone.

'Surely, we have all had ten thousand tours by now, Eleanor. We have been coming here since we were in leading strings. I wonder what might have inspired you to make another inspection?' She smirked. 'And do not say it is Lord Egremont's collection.'

'Oh, very well. You may attribute it to the company I was in.' I let out a little smile which sent a contagious wave of excitement around the table. Except *hers*. Her smile was stiff like freshly glazed porcelain and, for the first time, I felt able to fully meet her stare to show her the triumph in mine.

'But Miss Ashlyn, I did not see your chaperone leave the room for at least half an hour after your departure from the supper room,' Mariella said, cracking the glaze of her tight-lipped smile and twisting her features into feigned interest.

'You are quite observant, Miss Craythorne, but the Dowager's nephew and his wife escorted us.' I knew she would not be able to account for them because she did not know who I referred to. I was also aware of their late arrival, as it was they we first stumbled upon as we made our way back to the party. I looked cautiously about the table until I recognised the relief on their faces in ready acceptance of this.

'Well, Eleanor, I think it is quite wicked of you to keep us in suspense of your intentions when we have dresses to be made and gifts to consider,' Betsy said and I recognised this as a hint that she had not been gulled.

I felt the weight of everyone's stares turn from Betsy back to me. I looked at their expectant faces and let out a chuckle. 'For goodness's sake, ladies, no words have been spoken, so you might rest assured you still have plenty of time to consider dresses, gifts and the like. Can we not think of one wedding at a time?' I moved the conversation on swiftly to enquire if anyone had had news from Clara and how her wedding journey was going.

Once we dispersed to our afternoon of activities, I had begun to question whether it was in fact easier *not* to be on congenial terms with my friends. I felt drained from our morning endeavours, and once I had the measure of their interests for the rest of the day, chose the only activity none of them had put their names down for. Sheldon was off with a party of men who were to visit Arundel to see one of Sir George's canal developments and I passed a merry afternoon with his children out on the archery field, and although I was a little rusty and out of practice, enjoyed myself immensely in such easy company. Although I had considered that a portrait of Mariella might have improved my shot in the target practice.

When we regrouped in the evening and Sheldon had still not appeared, I had to allow Charles Wyndham to take me into dinner. I was disappointed, but our hostess announced an apology on behalf of Sir George and the party of gentleman of which Sheldon was amongst. They had been late returning from their fishing trip on the lake and would dress and take their dinner in the family dining room so as not to disturb us. I was disappointed, but hoped it would not be long before we would be reunited. A day without setting eyes upon him was already too long.

When we congregated in the Marble Hall to await the start of the dancing, I was in such a gloom of spirits, I hardly noticed Mr Richards slip up beside me.

'Miss Ashlyn,' he said, 'I have not had the opportunity to even wish you good day. How are you?'

'Mr Richards, I am well. I thank you. Are you?'

'Very well. Better for seeing you, I confess. Are you minded to dance this evening?'

'Oh, to tell the truth, I am not sure. I think I may need a little more digestion time before I decide, but I know Miss Jameson was minded to dance the first half, weren't you Beth?' I said turning to her and with brightly lit eyes, she nodded.

'Ah, well, Miss Jameson, might I have the honour?' he asked her and she had her dance card out quicker than her answer given. I drifted away from them and searched the room for a sign of his coming. I saw Sir George first, emerging from the Beauty Room and I went straight out to the corridor of the Grand Staircase where I found him in conversation with a gentleman I did not know.

When he saw me approaching, he instantly made his apologies and broke free of him. 'Forgive me,' he said with a sigh, 'had I known we would be gone all the day, I would have found a way to release myself from the obligation. How I have longed to rest my eyes upon the sight of you. And as ever, you never disappoint. You shine.'

If I had thought to have an accent of reprimand in my tone, it had already faded. 'Oh, Sheldon, how I have missed you. I have been looking for you half the day,' I complained.

'I am so sorry. It has been one thing after another, and just when I thought we were at last to leave the lakes, Dalton capsizes in his boat and we have to go in and pull him out as the poor fellow cannot swim.'

'Goodness, is he alright?'

'Fine, he was not under for long at all, thanks to that Bandini fellow's quick reactions. Certainly, the kind of man one likes to have about in a scrape. Anyway, I am here now and have declined the shooting tomorrow so I can be with you. Hopefully, you shan't have me painting or wax moulding or some such fluff. Although I shan't care really. If you are with me.'

'Well, I will try to do a little better than that. I believe there is to be a lecture given by Mr Ansell on astronomy and he is to display his spectacular Orrery,' I offered, thinking it a perfect excuse to spend a morning together.

'I shall put my name down,' he smiled and turned about to see Delores approaching.

'Ah, there you are. I turn my back for a moment! Now, are the pair of you to come and dance or must I follow you about the house all night?'

'Miss Ashlyn, will you dance?' Sheldon asked.

'I would be happy to,' I said and we spent our two dances consecutively before our hostess forced us to the notice of other partners.

Mr Richards was still seeking out my company, and I, skilfully avoiding it when I took a brief break between sets. I had got the volunteering of Beth and Martha down to such an art that it had become quite impossible for him to approach me without their expectant smiles to greet him. But however well I had evaded Richards' dance invitations, he caught me out once they had finished and I sat chatting amongst the others.

'Good evening, ladies, I hope you will forgive me the intrusion but I had hoped for the occasion to petition Miss Ashlyn to accompany me at the pianoforte?'

'Good evening, Mr Richard's,' Betsy said coolly. 'It is an intrusion indeed, but we are in good spirits today, so we will forgive it on this occasion.'

I was mouth open ready to refuse him but I could see he was about to take a slaughtering from Betsy. Despite her apparently having decided against him, she didn't take well to being overlooked and his attentions to the others in our party and neglect of her were not easy to ignore. It seemed the disharmony between them was mutual and he had no wish to engage in any conversation with her. So, I agreed to one piece to spare him the assault of any further speech. He would not enjoy the forgiveness I had, and would most likely, apportion my share now I was off the hook. So, in the name of sympathy, I sang out the same rendition of *Love among the Roses* I had at Wycombe, and made a quick departure from the piano side during the applause.

Of course, I had only managed to postpone, not prevent the assassination of his character that Bets would surely have already got underway with whisperings of his background and a fair measure of biased and contrived opinion thrown in for efficacy. – It was certainly preferable to be on the better side of Betsy if you were without the position to defend yourself against one of her attacks. I felt a hint of responsibility for the fate I knew awaited him. If I had refused his dances at Wycombe like I had this weekend, it would have perhaps been easier to defend him. But I was back in our circle and did not want to come to blows in any outright attempt to support him, for I knew she would consider something more between us, or take it as an insult to injury. Besides, I had been as generous as was reasonable to expect under the circumstances and I was already going to have to explain myself to Sheldon, who I noticed, had no applause for our piece.

I knew he was brooding when he found me in the Square Dining Room, but I was also afforded a temporary pardon when the hostess brought Mr Carew over to make my introduction at the very same moment. It was but a delay.

'Miss Ashlyn, may I offer my congratulations on your duet; you sing well,' he said once Lady Arabella had made the introduction.

'Mr Carew, I have had the pleasure of admiring your splendid work this weekend, but somehow missed the opportunity to make your acquaintance,' I replied with a curtsy.

'The pleasure is certainly mine. I am giving a demonstration tomorrow, in the studio above the chapel, perhaps you will come and see my plans for an Arethusa marble?'

'Oh. I would of course have liked to, but I am already engaged tomorrow. Have you been introduced to Mr Elmbridge?' I said quickly.

When the hostess moved him on, the first thing Sheldon said to me was: 'Please El, do not sing with Richards again.'

'Well, if you can think of a better way to entertain me, I am all for it!' I said in jest, but he seemed to take me at my word. He took up my arm and pulled me through the hoards without hesitation or regard for anyone who attempted to accost us in conversation through the crush. He marched me the length of the adjoining rooms until we were in a low-ceilinged corridor where he took me up some steps and through a door that led to the chapel balcony.

It was silent inside, a meagre shaft of light filtering through the stained-glass windows opposite, the smell of oak wood and musty carpet in the air. 'Well, I assume you have not brought us here to pray?' I said, leaning against the balcony banister.

'Are you fond of him, El, tell me the truth?' His voice echoed.

'Mr Carew?'

'No. Richards,' he said as though the mention of his name left an acrid taste in his mouth.

'Not in the way you pose the question.'

'Then must you insist on cavorting around with him as though you are.'

'Cavorting? Sheldon, I have not danced with him once this weekend and have done my utmost to avoid him. But you know I cannot dance them all with you, nor can I sit them all out to please you. I did not complain at you dancing tonight.'

'I know. But it's different, these gentlemen do not simply want you for a dance partner.'

'Oh? And they have told you this?'

'They do not have to. I see it. You do not understand the male sex—the way they will think on something is quite different to the way you do.'

'So, you will have me neither speak, nor dance, nor sing with any gentleman then? It is just like Wycombe Park all over again.'

'I am still punished over Wycombe?'

I said nothing.

'El, I don't want to quarrel, I've missed you.'

'And when I missed you for a whole day at Wycombe, what consolation or explanation was I offered? Not to mention your absence in the country all week, and yesterday I barely saw you for above an hour.'

'I had to go away, El, you don't understand.'

'Try me.'

'You pushed me, El.'

'Too far?'

'Too close.'

'To what?'

'To the limit of my self-restraint and you would not heed my warning, what was I supposed to do other than put some distance between us?'

'Self-restraint? I have made no demands upon you on that head.'

'And that is the problem; you make it very easy for me to forget myself. El, when I am with you, I forget we are not engaged, and yet I want to treat you as though we are married.'

'I feel it too. I just don't want to rush into something so important. What are we to do?'

'I don't know, but I do know I want you back. I've thought of nothing else even though we have been apart so much, and I do not care if you are difficult and stubborn and strong headed...I'm, I'm too fond of you to care.'

'You have a strange way of paying a compliment to a lady, Sheldon,' I raised an eyebrow.

He did not answer but reached out for my hand which clasped the balcony. I hadn't expected this honest speech, but I forgave him his jealousy immediately, and as he stroked the back of my hand with his thumb, I felt those flutters again, stirring from deep within me.

'I like you much better when you are not my enemy,' he whispered and we both laughed a little.

'And I like you better when you show me what is really in your heart.'

'Well, that would take a great deal more than a stolen moment.'

'I'm glad to hear it.'

We stayed that way for so long, hands touching, it seemed we were making up for every moment of lost time this past week. When the sound of voices in the hall broke us apart, I was not ready to give him up. 'Let us go for a walk,' I suggested.

'Delores is probably already hunting the house for us.'

'I do not care. So long as we evade her, I can find some excuse. Please.'

He took me by the arm and led the way out. My stomach curled with the excitement and I had forgotten just how powerless it rendered me in these moments. I was not used to the vulnerability it reduced me to and all the urges that surfaced in his company. But when we stopped in some derelict place of the deer park, it got the better of me and I took off my gloves and held his face in my hands. I felt the friction of rough stubble beneath my fingertips and pressed my own cheek against it, feeling the bristle of it against my skin.

'El, what are you doing?'

'I just want to know how you feel.' I took one of his hands and de-gloved it. 'What are you so anxious of Sheldon, don't you want to know how I feel?'

'I am frightened by how much I want to know how you feel, Eleanor.'

'Don't be silly; give me your other hand.' Reluctantly, he offered me his other and I took the glove off of that one too and brought both his hands to my face.

'How do I feel?'

'Smooth as silk,' he said, stroking my cheek with his thumb.

'Kiss me,' I said then, 'properly, Sheldon, kiss me like you would if we were engaged.'

'I can't.'

'What are you so frightened of?'

'I'm not frightened El, I'm forbidden.'

'Are we not forbidden to be taking this walk alone, to be touching at all, dancing in the Doric Temple: What is forbidden can be overcome, can it not?'

His breaths had become heavy and audible. I moved in closer to him to close the gap between us and it reminded me of the sensation I had felt when she had held my body against the wall with hers: the heat, the weight, the pressure. I took one of his hands from my cheek and kissed it, then took them both and swept them down the length of my neck until they were resting on my shoulders. I leaned up on my tip toes and pressed my lips so lightly against him it was barely a kiss at all. Then I brought his palms to rest upon my décolleté. And I felt it. We both felt it. The breach. The transgression that surpassed all that came before, and caused them to pale into insignificance.

I was contemplating what I should do next when he swooped down and seized my mouth entirely and put his tongue inside it. So, I followed his example. Moved with his rhythm, began working his cravat loose, stroked the warm flesh of his neck, pressed closer into him. Felt the firmness of his chest against the softness of my own. Then I broke our kiss, took my mouth to his neck and placed my kisses there. I felt his body fidgeting against the delight and I was pleased to know I was causing it. Then his hands moved and I felt them sweep the curve of my breasts and I thought I might collapse against him with the shudder that run through me at feeling the heat of his palms through the muslin of my dress. I lifted my head up, kissed him on the mouth again then pulled his head towards my neck, my décolleté and felt the pant of him against it.

When we broke for the briefest second, I smiled at him. 'What is it?' I said to his mystified gaze.

He stepped back and caught his breath. 'El, say you'll marry me: accept our engagement and set us free.' It was his parting plea, I could sense it. The last attempt he would make at propriety before he gave in to himself; to me. I was considering what to say to him when we heard the coming of footsteps close by. We froze, but it was disappointment I felt, not fear. I had finally conquered his reluctance and the moment would be lost to us another night.

'Well, well. I knew I had stumbled upon something I should not have, but I hadn't considered it might be the two of you!' Lady Caroline was standing on the pathway of the clearing with her Chihuahua running circles around her feet. We both pulled ourselves together, fussing about with our clothes and attempting a quick recovery from the fervour we had been suspended in.

'Lady Caroline,' Sheldon said. His voice cracked over the words and his breath was still a beat faster than usual. 'It is not what you think, we, we are—'

'Courting,' I interrupted him and took him by the hand and led him away. 'Goodnight, Lady Caroline.'

'El, what are you doing?' he pulled his hand from mine.

'We do not have to explain ourselves to her.' I pulled him on towards the house.

'We need to pacify her and bid her silence unless you intend for us to make an announcement?'

'She won't utter a word, I assure you.'

'And if you are wrong?'

'She would like the prospect of our marriage no better than she liked the prospect of her own.'

'What are you talking about?'

I stopped and turned around to look at him. 'She is besotted with you, Sheldon. I see it in her face all the time, waiting to pounce, always dangling after you. You say I do not understand the male sex, well perhaps you do not understand ours.'

'Don't be absurd.'

'It's true, whether you notice it or not.' I walked on.

'So, we will not be making an announcement?'

'Not yet, Sheldon.'

'I don't understand, El. I thought—'

'But we move a little closer all the time.' We had stopped outside the tourist's entrance; I thought it best not to take any other chances so that someone else might manage to substantiate her story in the unlikely event that she spoke against us. 'Leave me here, give it a few minutes before you go back through the house and I will see you in the morning for breakfast.' I gave him a peck on the cheek and went inside.

I began my way up the staircase, mentally mapping where I was in relation to where I wanted to go, I guessed I was at the Northern end when my room was in the South. It was a big house and I was not familiar with it from this perspective. I was halfway up when I realised I had left my reticule in his pocket with the key to my room inside of it. It would have been difficult to convince Delores I had been in my bed all evening nursing a headache if I was forced to ask for her key. I ran back down to find him in the hope he had not gone yet. I needn't have worried, when I saw him through the small glass pane of the door as I approached it, he was stood in exactly the same spot looking as mystified as he did the moment I left him. It wasn't until I was close enough to reach for the handle that I saw Lady Caroline with him and something told me to hang back.

'Well, Mr Elmbridge, I didn't think you had it in you to be leading astray innocent young ladies behind their chaperones backs. I'm impressed,' she said when she was level with him.

'Keep your voice down, Caroline, I beg it.'

'You never need beg me for anything, Sheldon. But it is not I that keeps you hanging by a thread...'

How dare she use his name.

'It's not like that, Caroline. I—'

'You what? You love her?'

'Yes.'

'I see. Well, that's just precious, when is the wedding? I must have missed the announcement in *The Times*.'

'We haven't decided yet.'

'She's a tease and she is playing with you, Sheldon; you know that, don't you? It is the problem with setting your cap at the young and beautiful, they meddle with your emotions.'

'She is not meddling with me; you don't know what you're talking about.'

'Oh, but I do. I understand what it means to be driven to distraction with the desire for someone, so fervently you will bend and mould to their will in any which way to please them, but when the same is asked in return, they leave you disappointed.'

I did not like her increasing proximity to him.

He said nothing and something told me he was contemplating her speech in some corner of his mind.

Don't listen to her, she does not know me.

She stepped closer to him, so close it made me want to break my cover, but the greater part of me was curious and held me back.

'I'm sure she means you no harm, innocent little flower probably doesn't realise what she is doing to you, turning you inside out like this. She does not understand her power yet to drive a man to despair, even though she toys with it; she knows not the torture she unleashes on you when she starts you off but fails to bring the matter to a happy conclusion.'

I watched her walk her fingers up from his waistcoat to his chin and I wanted to remove her hands from him, but when he stood there without preventing it, I knew I had to keep watching.

'I understand, Sheldon. I understand what a man needs to soothe him. How long has it been since you have felt a woman's touch?' she was playing with the cravat I had moments ago untied. Right now, I could have strangled her with it.

'That long?' she said in answer to his silence. 'Poor darling. To have her subject you to such torment without the care to finish you off. You know, I can assist you, Sheldon. You just have to say the word and all that tension, all that frustration, I can make it go away right now and no one need ever know it.'

'Caroline, stop. You're embarrassing yourself,' he told her, stepping back and my relief was so immediate I gasped, but they did not seem to hear it.

'What, you are worried I will tell her or you will be found out?'

'No Caroline, I love her and the thing I want more than anything else right now is to make her my wife.'

'I can see that. I understand. But I see no reason to prevent us from giving each other a little comfort in your waiting, is there?'

'I'm sure the Duke will not see it that way.'

'You needn't worry about him. I don't.'

'I don't and nor do I worry if you open your mouth about what you saw tonight.'

'Well of course you don't, the banns will be read in church next Sunday if this gets out and I'm sure you couldn't be better pleased at the prospect from the lovesick look on your face.'

'I am leaving now, Caroline. I have heard enough. We will do each other the courtesy of pretending this conversation never happened.'

'Have it your way. But if the wait becomes too tiresome, or she breaks your heart...you know where to find me.'

In a shallow grave.

I watched him walk away and she reached down for her dog who had just left a present for the Earls gardener in the shrubbery. Her words and the anger they incited, kept me up long into the night, replaying over and again in my memory. My fury was so debilitating I could not even bring myself to see him for my key, so I sent a passing servant on the errand of retrieving my reticule instead.

Decision making.

June 1821. - Eleanor.

At three-twenty-two a.m., I was up at the small writing desk penning an anonymous letter to Lady Caroline's husband the Duke, informing him of what I'd witnessed, but leaving out the small matter of with whom. If he wasn't so distracted by all the whores he himself kept, I was sure it would not be difficult for him to work it out, but I certainly did not want to be the one to incriminate Sheldon for her indiscretions. I wondered if he would care much for the details at all, but I knew he would not be best pleased at the prospect of her carrying someone's bastard before she had done her duty in giving him an heir and at the very least, he might make that plain to her. I wrote it out several times and in several different hands before I was satisfied that my letter had the right tone of honest observation with the right balance of concern. If I wanted him to take me seriously, I knew I could not write all that I really wanted to. I signed it 'a concerned friend' and pressed the wax seal down with the bottom of the ink pot rather than sealing it with my own wafer.

I woke late the next morning and on a slightly clearer head decided to postpone my sending of the letter for now. I took it from the writing desk drawer and buried it in the pages of the novel I was reading. The well concealed edition of *Fanny Hill* that Mariella had loaned to me weeks ago that had been sewn into the cover of *Ivanhoe* to disguise it. I would send the letter in due course of our announcement, which I anticipated we might make soon if things continued well between us. That way, we needn't fear her reprisal if she worked out from whom the letter had come and sought to avenge it. I was perfectly confident now that she would not otherwise; mention a word on the matter.

When I arrived at breakfast the normality all around me confirmed I had been correct, and no scandal had been leaked at Petworth. I was pleased to notice Sheldon was quite alone at one of the smaller tables, leaning over a newspaper but not really reading it. I much preferred this relaxed breakfast format with people drifting in and out to suit themselves

'Where on earth have you been all morning, I have been here nearly two hours and taken every plate on the buffet?' he said when I took his invitation and sat down opposite him. Delores had been held up at the next table by Lady Jersey, so I took the opportunity to speak to him.

'I'm sorry, I told Delores I was unwell and she kept me to my bed late.'

'Oh, I thought you had reason to think we were on-dit and were avoiding the coming.'

'Relax, Sheldon, no one knows anything, look around us,' I cleared my throat at Delores' approach. 'Delores, Mr Elmbridge has made us invitation to join his table this morning,' I said quickly.

'How very kind of you, Mr Elmbridge,' she greeted him as he stood. 'Please,' she excused him to sit. 'I am going to the table. What shall I bring you, Eleanor?'

'I am not fit for much. Perhaps a small amount of oatmeal will not overexert me.'

When she was gone again, he leant in closer. 'What if she is biding her time?'

'Sheldon, have you reason to think she will?' I was half hoping he would put my mind at ease and confess their conversation to me.

'I do not trust her, El.'

'Nor I. But as I said, there is so little for her to gain in the doing it, and a lot more to lose in the prospect of earning herself your scorn.'

His face gave nothing away but grew concerned when she came into the breakfast room and took her seat at the closest table to ours.

'Do not give her the satisfaction of seeing your anxiety,' I said to him behind my fan and he looked away from her. She was staring beyond the Duke's shoulder. I smiled at her and turned away.

'If we are wrong?' he spoke into the pages of his newspaper.

'Then we announce our engagement a little ahead of our plans and watch the celebration of it drown out her whining.' *And sit back and watch her face and her husband's wrath when he gets my letter.*

I watched his face light up. 'I did not know we had plans. Do you mean that, El?'

'Of course, I do.' I wanted to reach out and touch his hand to reassure him, but I knew she was watching us, so I found his foot beneath the table and brushed my ankle against his.

'Then why not announce it now?—if you are sure of it.'

'I just need a little longer Sheldon, before all the formalities are forced upon us and our parents get carried away in all the arrangements. I do not want to feel the pressure of all that until we have had a little more time to reacquaint ourselves in peace. Let us have our moment privately, before surrendering it to public consumption.'

'We will have greater peace and opportunity to do so when they are busy with the distraction of a wedding to plan and willing to offer us the freedom we need to explore the rest.'

Delores put a steaming bowl of oatmeal in front of me and took her seat at the table.

'Well, what is on-dit this morning? You two seem quite the chatterboxes,' she said in blissful ignorance of the irony.

'Mr Richards,' I said to her quietly and watched the frown form across Sheldon's brow. 'It seems he is without any fortune or good family, according to Lady Elizabeth and she is minded to hark it from the treetops, to anyone who will hear it.'

'Well, I suppose it is too much to ask that he might be…talented and respectable,' she said pondering him from the corner of her eye, and I was grateful she had left out the word handsome, for Sheldon's sake.

The news had travelled well before my mention, I realised as I passed the music room on my way back from breakfast. There were the steadfast crowd you might expect to see waiting eagerly for Mr Richards' instruction of course, which included Beth and Martha along the front row. But there were ample empty seats that could not be put down solely to the competition of the other entertainments with a house as full as this one. I felt a little sorry for him as I passed him and bid him good morning. Had he found favour in Betsy, instead of wasting his efforts on me, things might have been better for him now.

I observed the same trend after dinner that evening, and could I have managed the offer of an innocent dance or invitation to the card table or even a song or two at the pianoforte without inciting the irritation of Sheldon and Bets, or the speculation of anyone else, I would have done it to spare him the confusion I saw in his face. Now it seemed that the greater proportion of his fan club had transferred over to the Mr Carew Appreciation Society. I suggested to Beth and Martha that they might make some conversation with him that might cause him to invite them either to sing or dance, but I knew they were too fearful of Betsy's rebuff to take the chance now, however much I saw the longing for it in their faces.

When I snuck away with Sheldon after our fifth game of Loo, we took extra precautions for our safety. It had not escaped my notice how lucky we had been to be seen only by Lady Caroline last night when I looked in the daylight at the spot in which she found us. The landscaping of the grounds that lacked any of the formal gardens I had been used to, had confused me into thinking we were deeper into the woodland than we actually were, when in fact we had been under the shelter of a copse, barely around the corner from the house. To ensure we did not make the same mistake twice, I had concocted a more detailed plan for tonight. I remembered from my childhood visits to Petworth; the network of underground tunnels the servants used to travel between the main house and the kitchens. Lord Egremont's children and I had often received a telling off from the cook or the housekeeper for using them in our games of hide and seek, and I was sure I still remembered the way down to them.

My memory proved unreliable, but we ended up somewhere out of the way when we came up from the damp and dimly lit tunnels.

'Well, you are full of surprises,' he said brushing down his tailcoat, which had been snagged by cobwebs on the route.

'Hmm, I cannot tell if you are disconcerted or impressed, sir,' I teased, leading us out a little way to try to work out where we were.

'Well, that makes both of us then.'

I laughed. 'Well, I haven't a clue where we are, but at least we shan't have to worry about Lady Caroline sneaking up on us again.' I noted his discomfort at my mentioning her.

'No,' was all he said, but I wondered what the unsaid thoughts were I saw lurking in his eyes. I wished he would just tell me about their conversation last night. I wanted to reassure him that the things she said about me were not true and quell the doubt I had sensed in him since. But unless he confessed it to me, I could not refute her claims without confessing I had (albeit unintentionally) spied on them. Instead, I would have to find a more indirect means of reassuring him, for I certainly felt he was in need of it tonight.

When I made certain we were quite alone and not overlooked, I took his hand in mine and kissed it. I did not know precisely where we were in relation to the house but I was certain we were far enough from anywhere to worry about being seen tonight.

'El,' he said carefully considering me. 'You know what we are doing is very dangerous, don't you?'

'I don't feel any danger. I'm sure my secrets are quite safe with you.'

'They are with me, yes. But at any moment we risk being discovered just like we were last night.'

'Is that not half of the fun?'

'Is that how you see this El, fun?'

'Of course not. I see it as an opportunity to spend some time together, but you must admit the element of risk is at least a little thrilling?'

He shrugged. 'I don't know about that. But if we really are to make an announcement soon—'

I kissed him then, lightly to begin and let him carry us off into the passionate styles he had introduced me to yesterday. I could taste cigars and brandy on his tongue, the faintest traces and wondered what I tasted like to him. Orange wine perhaps? I felt his arms scoop me in closer and the heat between our bodies. Every now and then, he would pull back a moment and utter something to me: 'You're beautiful,' or words to that effect. I wanted him to declare something more to me; a deeper truth. I don't know why I felt the need for it. I suppose I was tired of being beautiful, or at least always being defined by it. I wanted something more specific. Something more personal uttered into my ear. I love you, might have been a step too far, but something between that and you're beautiful, at least. The next time he uttered it, I broke away. 'Sheldon, what precisely is so beautiful?' I asked him.

He frowned at first but then made answer. 'What isn't beautiful about you would perhaps be the easier question to answer.'

'I do not mean my looks: I mean me.'

'El, I will not pretend that your looks do not set you apart from everyone else, and I see that you have many admirers who see that and only that...but know I see beyond that. I know you El, from that scowling wrinkle in your nose when you take offense, to that endearing sparkle in your eyes when you are happy or intrigued. I have made a lifetime study of you El and I don't intend to stop now.'

I was quite taken aback and a little distracted in wondering what wrinkle he referred to.

'You need not doubt me. I am not here under any pretences: You are as unruly as you are beautiful. As clever as you are stubborn, and as unpredictable as you are lovely.'

I wasn't sure about the calculation, but I could not argue with the sentiment. He did know me. Mostly, anyway. 'Don't you want a more ordinary wife?'

'If I did, I could have been married before now.'

'Why didn't you marry Lady Caroline—before, on her come out? I remember it being much spoken of back then.'

'Because I did not want her.'

'She was the daughter of a Duke, before she married one. I'm sure you must have been encouraged—'

'She could have been the daughter of the King! What of it if you know your own heart?'

'You speak with the air of someone who has been in love before.'

'No, I speak with the wisdom of someone who has been in love for a very long time.'

I kissed him then and felt quite out of my senses wild with desire for him in a way I had not felt before. Perhaps I too was moving to some deeper state of feeling toward him. Perhaps I really was falling in love too. If he had asked the question now, then I may well have found myself unable to refuse him. But he did not, and his words had been enough to silence us both for the journey back. We took the tunnels all the way into the house and parted through the service jib door with a kiss that held a meaning they had not before.

WHEN WE MADE OUR JOURNEY up to Kent the following morning, I realised how much I ached for him, how much I should have told him last night that I would be his wife, were he to ask the question. But we was headed on our way to see Harriet on a last-minute whim of Mama's and the prospect of the long week ahead of me without him, seemed glaringly bleak. If I had known we should be separated again so soon when we were together last night, I might have given him leave to make the announcement and prevent its delay. If it were not for the fact he had left Petworth so early, I would have had Papa turn the coach back to deliver him the news. But the opportunity had passed now, and I would have to be patient until we returned to Cuddington next week. I had considered petitioning Papa to take me back early, drop me at Cuddington on the journey, but I knew he would not agree to it. Mama might have been willing to persuade him, if she understood my cause, but she was not best pleased with me after discovering me missing from the house last night.

Even though she had kept the matter from my father, it had caused quite the exchange of strong words between her and Delores who she blamed entirely for the matter. So it seemed that everyone's mood was poor today. But even through the disappointment of our week's separation to look to, I could not help smiling to myself remembering last night. Remembering not just his kisses but that strange and compelling feeling he ignited with such earnest words. He had won me with those: not his compliments and kisses. It was that realisation that sealed my decision. I was excited to at last be decided and ready to embark on my engagement. So, as we rattled along in the coach in fractious silence, I spent the journey considering how I would give the news to him, where it should be and what I should wear. It changed moment to moment, and even by the time we were arrived at Harriet's, I had not settled on the details.

The answer.

June 1821. - Eleanor.

In this new lovesick condition, I felt the hours and days between us quite painfully. Especially when I was forced to pay attendance on Kent society. I had no wish to dance, sup, mingle or exert myself in costume changes, if he was not present. If I could not be in his company, then I wanted time alone to reminisce upon our last meeting and imagine the next. And if I was not, I wanted only to visit my sister, enjoy the rare opportunity to catch up with her and spend time with the children who always seemed to have grown so much in the time between visits. I had attempted to decline invitations to some of the smaller affairs to indulge in my romantic musings a little longer, but with mother and Delores still displeased with me, I did not push the matter and grew into a habit of meek compliance. Soon they would both be so pleased with me, they would grant me anything and quite forget their squabble and my recent misdemeanour. So, I passed the time at these affairs with my sister exclusively, not dancing at all, or even chatting beyond polite necessity.

When Martha's invitation for her engagement party came, I was pleased that upon our return there would be some occasion to draw us together again—even if it was to be at Beaulieu. If he was to be there, I could overlook that detail. I only wished that I had spoken sooner and we might be enjoying the same privileges by now.

When I woke up Friday morning to the realisation that the time had at last come, I could barely contain my excitement. I took Samson for a morning gallop on the park just to shake the excess energy from me so I could settle down enough for the journey back to Surrey. Even the thought of being under the same roof as Mariella tonight, could not dampen my spirits.

I was fit to burst when we arrived back at Cuddington, and it took all of my restraint not to go straight to him and speak in advance of tonight. But I was already on the back foot, our journey having taken longer than usual and I wanted to look my best for him, so I put my energies into the task of this instead. I was still in my travelling dress when I went straight to Mrs Oliver to make an emergency plea for her to do something with my favourite ball gown, for he had seen it before, and yet I knew it my most becoming look. I still had a couple of gowns in their boxes that were yet to be once worn, but none I liked as well as this favourite, and tonight, could not be less than perfect.

Mrs Oliver was good enough to submit to my impossible request when Delores and I made our impatient entrance into the little boutique where she was trimming lengths of ribbon for a waiting customer. But once the customer departed with her neatly wrapped package beneath her elbow and Mrs Oliver turned her attention to us, she took pity on me instantly when she realised the urgency in my plea. She turned the sign on the door to: *CLOSED* and led us through to her jumbled little sewing room at the back where I laid out my gown upon her needle-scattered table.

After some debate over what might be done to refresh it, she measured me for the addition of a cambric mock-Spencer to be sewn into the front panel of the existing fabric, which pleased me greatly because the lace up back detail was my favourite feature and I did not want to obscure it. She added a fresh ribbon, a few more darts beneath the waist and replaced the lace hem at the sleeves, which was crisper and whiter than the more tired version that preceded it. Finally, she made some coordinating embellishments to a brand-new Nakara turban I caught sight of upon a bust, and I was very satisfied when I left her boutique at the hour of four after spending the entire afternoon there.

Delores seemed as exhausted on our leaving as Mrs Oliver had in the frenzied refashioning. But I paid her handsomely for her trouble and knew Delores too would profit from her forbearance once I had the happy news to give to her later. I could think of nothing she must like more than to be free of the burden of my chaperoning at last and dance with the squire and sip tea with Mama and the ladies unhindered. She had only another couple of weeks left in our service, but would, no doubt, prefer them to be less taxing than those preceding them.

When I spent the next three hours at my toilette upon our return, I knew it was too much not to expect her to be suspicious of me. I had ordered the bath filled, had washes and lotions prepared for my hair and skin, and cleaned my teeth three times before I slipped into the muslin of my beautifully transformed gown.

'Eleanor, you cannot pretend to be up to no mischief with all this faffing about today; which even by your standards is excessive. Is there something you would like to tell me?' she finally asked as we journeyed downstairs to await the coach. I was surprised she had broken her sulk with me, that had, for the entire week, consisted of no more than rudimentary speech. I did not know precisely what Mama had said to her as they closed the dressing room door to continue the argument that had begun on my return to our bedroom that night at Petworth, but I knew it must have been most serious to silence Delores for nearly a week. 'All will become clear tonight,' I said with a smile, partly in apology to her and partly owing to my failure to fully contain my own excitement. 'But do not say a word to Mama; I want it to be a surprise.'

The truth was; I had already hinted at the surprise to Mama earlier, in order to convince her to permit my staying at Beaulieu, but I didn't want either of them to know I had told the other first and hold it against me. So when I made my petition to Mama to consent to at least Delores and I staying at Beaulieu, I slipped in the small detail that if she could manage to permit us, I might come home to her with the happy news she had long anticipated. I did not have to ask her twice, for even though she had won her way with declining to attend this event, I had been given the invitation to stay for the weekends entertainments and she no longer had the sole burden of chaperoning me now Delores was at home. This suited her now of course, for she was obdurate in her refusal to attend this time.

'I have tolerated these Craythornes and found myself complicit in your demands to accept them in my home and afford them my vote at Almack's, and now you ask me to spend the weekend under their roof? Well, you ask too much, sir! I will not do it for anything!' she had bellowed at Father at the dinner table on Tuesday when we received the invitation. It was not like Mama to be so severe in her rebuttals—dramatic; yes, but menacing; no. But her outburst on Tuesday had left him in no doubt that this was one of the rare occasions he would have to concede to her, and he did.

On any other occasion, I might have applauded her small victory and admired her obstinacy, but not this one. I was no better pleased to be a guest of the Craythorne's than she was, but I wanted to spend every possible moment with Sheldon this weekend and I could not have cared if it were in the Cuddington tavern so long as he was there. 'Mama, please do not cancel Fathers acceptance. The Elmbridge's will be staying the whole, why can't we do the same? Even a polite token of one night perhaps?'

'Well, to have you do your Father's bidding! I am ashamed of you Eleanor!'

'I do not do his bidding, Mama, I do my own. I must have the opportunity to speak on a very important matter with Mr Elmbridge this weekend. A matter that might give us all some happy news we have long awaited.'

She checked my expression for authenticity. 'Eleanor, has he asked the question?'

'Not exactly...not yet. But I think he shall this weekend, if only I can give him the opportunity to do so.'

She clapped her hands together and her features softened. 'Well, I cannot see the harm in *your* staying. I mean, you are well acquainted with the daughter, it would not be in bad taste to permit you and Delores spend the weekend. But Eleanor,' her voice grew grave again, 'no more slipping from Delores' notice. That is my condition.'

I was surprised that she was prepared to send me under Delores' supervision after last weekend's calamity, but I supposed the comfort of the idea that I would be an engaged woman on my return appeared worth the risk. After months of plotting, it seemed at last our Mama's plans were to finally come to fruition.

UNFORTUNATELY, DELORES had other priorities tonight and decided to prove her worth this evening with uncharacteristic rigour in her duties of my protection. I had not considered how intent she was in restoring Mama's faith in her, but she would not hear of any reason, protest or excuse tonight. She told me she had the authority to bring me instantly home at the first sign of concern and given it would take less than ten minutes to courier messages betwixt them here, I acquiesced. She was my shadow at every turn and my attempts to lose her even for a brief visit to the water closet or buffet table were unsuccessful. I was shocked at how determined she was to prove herself the good chaperone that we all knew she was not, but apparently, was capable of being. When the squire's arrival failed to divert her from her watch of me, I began to realise the severity of the problem and started thinking of alternative means to escape her. *Of all the moments to pick to do your duty!*

Sheldon was as surprised by the change in her as I was. I could see the bewilderment in his face as he collected me for dances but I could not enlighten him on the cause of it for we were not given a moment in private. Beyond the fragmented conversation during our dances, we were interrupted or overheard at every moment. It was devastating after such a lengthy separation to have to speak on small insignificant matters when I was bursting with the temptation to tell him the thing he had longed to hear. I had even considered the idea of trying to whisper it to him during our final set, but by the time I realised it would be the only opportunity we would be afforded, our dance was spent. It was a torturous anti-climax to a day so full of anticipation. I wasn't sure if I wanted to cry, scream or scowl at her for it by the end of the evening when the last precious moments of being in his company were about to expire alongside the hope of a single stolen word or kiss.

I had tried to signal my regard for him all night with my eyes and with my fan and I had not mistaken the language of his stare which told me my looks had pleased him: The subtle but tender pressure of his hands when we danced the waltz, the love-drowsy glaze about his eyes when I caught his stare. But it was a poor consolation for what I had planned, as I trod the way up to our chamber having bid him a reluctant goodnight.

I stifled sobs as a housemaid unpinned my turban and undone all the clever work we had contrived only hours ago. And when I was down to my shift, I lay in bed restless awaiting the signal that Delores was asleep on the day bed in the hope I might manage to creep out to him before he retired. He had joined the gentleman in the billiards room on my departure, and I could not be sure at what hour he would retire. But the sound of her flapping about with papers at the writing desk extinguished any hope of that by the hour of two, and I knew I must submit to my exhaustion, accept the painful defeat and look to the relief of the morning when I could behold him again.

I did not wake until late the next morning and found all the men gone off in a shooting party before I joined the others for breakfast. It was another blow to my delicate mood and I felt little inclination to participate in anything else today despite the entreaties of my friends.

Tonight, I knew, would prove as impossible as the last. Perhaps worse now the house was somewhat emptier and there would be less opportunity to get lost or linger amongst the crush. The prospect of another day diminishing into failure was soul destroying. I wanted to be alone with him for just a little while so that I could explain to him the proviso on which I was ready to hear the question: I wanted a two-month engagement, no matter what coaxing or tricks my mama (or his) might attempt in marching us up the aisle before the month was out.

This would permit us to travel up to Edinburgh for the festival and enjoy a little time unhindered, rather than be trussed up in wedding gown fittings or engagement parties. And—this being my most persuasive reason—so we would have time before the wedding, to reacquaint ourselves better; this new version of 'us' that was quite altered. To see how we went along in the coming months. To detect if we irritated each other or wearied of each other's company. To be certain that the jealousy I had noted in him would be pacified by my acceptance of his proposal. If he was to be over jealous of me and curb my freedom after we were engaged, then I knew that would come to bristle over time. And finally, in the hope that before the two months expired, I was able to say whole heartedly and in absolute certainty that I *knew* myself to be in love with him. It needed to be above suspicion or folly. I must *feel* certain of it.

In the absence of this knowing, it was impossible I should accept anyone. I would rather cry off an engagement than be stuck in an ill-suited marriage contract. Of course, it was my hope that that would not be necessary at all, and now I knew it possible I *could* fall in love with him, that I even might be, it was becoming every day, more an act of precautionary prudence than sincere concern. No less, I would have my way or make no vows. So even though desperation of circumstance had permitted me to consider it, I knew it would not suffice to ask Delores for a private moment with him, for the few minutes I would be permitted—likely with her ear pressed against the door—would not be sufficient for such a discussion. Neither could I have such negotiations in her presence, or she would bid me hold my tongue with such conditions. Nor could I risk, however small a risk I thought it was, telling her he desired an interview with me and then him declining to meet my terms. Right now, the only thing helping me escape everyone's contempt was that they believed it was he and not I, responsible for holding up progress. A lie that was contradicted by every look and gesture he afforded me and would not hold out much longer.

But to come back bearing news of the surprise that we had engaged ourselves, would be just the thing to keep everyone happy and abandon such suspicions. So, I must find a way today, to speak alone with him. I needed a change of tactic. I could go to him before dinner in his toilette. No one would suspect such an outrageous scheme, not even Delores if I timed it by the moment she was busied in her own. To be prepared for me trying to shake her off of an evening was one thing, but to vanish from the bed chamber at such an hour she would never conceive of...

AFTER BREAKFAST, I took the trouble to pay some small bribes to the housemaids in order to find out which room he was staying in and then another to stage the necessary distraction of his valet at the appropriate hour. This at least was easy work since she left me quite at ease with the servants and it was all arranged amicably. We would not have long, but we would be alone.

It was all set by midday: everything in place for my great escape to him. All that was necessary now was for Delores to be as reliable to our routine as was usual and for me to hope that everyone else was too busy in their own toilette to be wandering the corridors on my short journey to the east wing. It seemed the wings had been divided as much by sex as possible, beyond the married persons. I had noted the instant we arrived that our room was beside Mariella's. Thankfully, I had seen next to nothing of her beyond passing acknowledgments, despite this unfortunate proximity. On the other side was Martha and her mama, no sign of Mr Nash and it seemed that she too had seen the prudence in ministering to her daughter's future at last and embracing the Craythorne's with the meekest amiability.

When the clock chimed the hour of five and Delores did not look up from her fancy work, I began to feel anxious as the maid shuffled about our portmanteau's waiting to dress us. It was customary for Delores to go first since she was not usually much above fifteen minutes and that period could barely account for my hair design. But she seemed unconcerned at the chiming of the clock today. Had she sensed something in me to cause her suspicion? I had tried to be so very careful and discreet. But Delores was not as easy to gull as my mama. *She* was not blinded by maternal bias.

In an effort not to let my apprehension show, I busied myself with feigned interest over choosing gowns, pairing shoe roses and fingering ornaments: Holding them up to myself in the looking glass, turning at angles before discarding them for another choice. When she finally disappeared to the side dressing room with the maid, I left quickly. I knew I had no more than twenty minutes at best, before she would notice me gone, but it was all I needed to state my position and steal a celebratory moment with him. And even though I would be for it on my return, with the news I would bring back with me, I would be forgiven in an instant and Mama need never know. I was shaking with the excitement as I trod carefully along the corridors, cautiously about the corners, my ear pricked at every turn. Tonight, we would be free to make our announcement to the whole of Cuddington and could no longer be kept apart so cruelly. There seemed a perfect justice to it being here, in Beaulieu too.

When I arrived outside his door, my stomach sank with an unanticipated gurgle of nerves. I was not the nervous type, but the rules did not seem to apply to this scenario and as I lifted my hand in front of me to knock; I saw it trembling. I inhaled deeply to steady myself. *I can do it. I want this.* Then I heard coming from it, some distinctive sounds that were certainly not from his lips, although I could not recognise the lady's cries of adulation, so breathy and ragged I could not make them out. I stepped back quickly into the recess of an alcove to give me time to think. *Incompetent maid!* I was furious. How difficult could it be to remember the correct room of a guest when your entire day revolved around the task of maintaining their comfort? To give me the direction of some married person's! The thought of them being interrupted to find me at their door! I felt near to nauseous at the prospective embarrassment. What would I say in answer to their puzzled faces? Sorry, wrong room! I was looking for Mr Elmbridge!

I looked along the hall and considered which door might actually be his. It was probably one of the ones either side of it, but I could not take the chance and nor could I see any sign of any servants about to assist me. My heart was still recovering from the surprise of my close scrape. Time was slipping fast away. Delores may have already discovered me gone. I could not return empty handed. *Damn maids!* I would have my veils back for this.

I was bracing myself for the disappointment of a fruitless journey back when I heard the click of the handle next door. Felix Craythorne emerged from it and I did not know whether to be relieved or horrified as he stood checking his pockets in contemplation as I pressed my back flat to the wall. *There are worst people I might be found out by, at least he is a dull-witted type of fool,* I thought as I stood wedged behind the ornamental figurine of Guinevere and the cold plaster of the wall behind me. I held my breath as he passed and prayed to be spared the embarrassment of his discovery. When he walked straight past me quite without noticing, I knew I should make a quick escape as his footsteps tapered off. I must have been ten minutes into my time limit by now and he could have been anyone. But...but now I could rule out his room and the conjugal chamber, it seemed that the third door *must* belong to Sheldon. I had invested too much not to go to him now. I looked at the closed oak door a few feet along and imagined him behind it and the surprise on his face at my arrival, then the relief and celebration of it when I gave him the news. *It's now or never.* I checked the safety of the hall before stepping out from behind Guinevere, headed at full speed in its direction when I heard another click of the door handle and was forced to run for cover again. This time, there was no alcove to jump into and as Lady Caroline stepped out of the first room, we were both equally aghast at the sight of each other.

'Miss Ashlyn?' she said as she walked quickly in my direction fixing her hair.

'I, I am lost,' I said more guiltily than I intended.

'Oh dear. No, you are not, he is in there,' she said with a conceited smile that in a single moment fractured all the hope I was filled with. I closed my open mouth and went straight to the door she had come from as she disappeared around the corner. I didn't even knock or check, somehow, I *knew* that this was indeed his room; the servants had not been mistaken and those noises I now recognised as belonging to her. I turned the handle and barged straight in, stumbling through the door, clinging to the doorknob for support. When he turned around to see me, I knew, for all the wrong reasons, that it was not I he expected to see there.

'El?' he frowned and quickly fastened the waist of his trousers he was busied with. It was all he was wearing. 'What are you doing here?'

I looked between the sight of him, his naked torso covered in a light sheen of sweat, his hair tousled; the sheets of the bed a twisted clump upon the floor.

'I wanted to see you. I had something to tell you but...it doesn't matter now,' was all I could manage before the tears began to bulge in my eyes. I turned back around.

'El, El don't go. I want to hear it,' he said chasing me to the door.

I stopped and looked him square in the face. 'I no longer wish to tell it.'

'Oh god, El, please don't say that. It means nothing.' He closed the door shut behind us and lent palms pressed against it, his elbows above my shoulders, his breath against my nose.

'Perhaps to you: it actually meant a great deal to me—and to her too I expect.'

I reached behind me for the handle and he held the door firm. 'Please El, it's just sex. I do not care for her. You know my heart and my future is yours, has always been yours.'

'Well, I hope it was *good* sex, Sheldon, because it has come at a heavy price to us both. Now, let me go!' I fought to free the door handle but when he removed his hands, he put them on me, and held me there against the door.

'El, what on earth are you talking about? This changes nothing, stop talking nonsense and tell me you will be my—'

'Remove your hands from me, I do not like where they have been!' I said with a venom that persuaded him to relent. 'I am not stupid, Sheldon. I am not naive enough to think you would not have been preoccupied these past years as much in petticoat pursuits as you were in your travels, but this? Now? *Her?* You ask too much, and I will bid you let me out before I scream!'

It was an empty threat of course. Now I could think of nothing worse than my being found here in his room with the evidence of passion all around us and being made to engage myself to him.

He assumed something of a beggar's pose. 'Please El, just let me explain... A man has needs, we are beasts, I confess it, but it does not change the matter that we are in love and should be married.'

I forced my words through the constriction of my throat, a lump so obstructing I could not swallow. 'A woman has them to you know, but no one likes to speak of that do they? Well, now you needn't trouble yourself with such conversations or the burden of such a duty.'

His colour rose. 'It was because of your fast and uncouth passions I have ended up in this state of desperation! Do you have any notion of what you do to a man when you subject him to such torturous torment? Letting me kiss you and touch you when I must refrain. Staring into my eyes with invitations and promises you do not even understand. It is *you* I wanted in my bed tonight and every night for the past three years, but I have had to bear it as well as I could. And now, now after such a wait you withhold yourself from me, toy with me, when you have it in your power to say the word that can free us both...'

'Very well: you were promised an answer. No is my answer. Now, let me go.'

'Damn it, Eleanor. I will not hear it. I came all the way back from the continent to take your hand; three years I have waited. You will not break with me over such a folly!' His face changed and it scared me so much that it took me a moment to react to him when he scooped me up and carried me to the bed. I began fighting him as soon as my senses came back to me but I was too frightened to kick up a dust and be discovered now.

'Get off me, Sheldon,' I snarled through gritted teeth as he dropped me onto the bed and climbed above me.

'I love you, El. I will not lose you,' he said as he clambered over my kicking, wriggling body attempting to settle it with the weight of his.

'You lost me when you took her to your bed!' I spat loudly before I remembered the volume of it.

'I'll never take another woman to my bed a day of my life now I can have you El. You are more than all the women in the world,' he said, placing kisses over my neck.

'You think I want your kisses now?'

'I know you want this, El. I have seen it in your eyes. I have felt it in your touch. I want it too. Let us not wait another moment.' Now he set his kisses upon my décolleté. I slapped his head and fought them back off, 'I do not want it anymore. Not now. Not with you!' I growled. But he did not relent and I grew more violent in my resistance.

'You toy with us both, El: I know you want this too. Why else have you come to me in my chamber?'

'I wanted to discuss our engagement, not offer myself to you!'

'I love you, El. Say you love me.'

Suddenly the danger of the whole situation became very real; this would be my future if I let this progress. This is the impression I had allowed him to form. He had me as a dasher and I could not dispute it. Curiosity had been my curse. But I would not allow a singe from the flame to permit the fire engulf me. It was not too late to remove from this situation—yet. 'I cannot say it. I HATE YOU!' With a strength I did not know I had, I hit him hard around the face and I saw the surprise in his eyes when he looked back up at me. 'I will ask you one more time, Sheldon, get off me. You disgust me!'

The sobriety of the moment seemed at last to dawn on him. This was no play act of timidity or propriety. I meant it and in that moment he understood. He got up straight away and made a feeble attempt to replace my dishevelled clothes before he turned from me and sat back-facing me, on the edge of the bed with his head in his hands. 'I cannot win with you, El. What do you want?'

Quickly, I pulled myself up and patted out my skirts. 'To be free of you,' I said and when I stepped away, I felt his hand grab hold of mine and I shook it off with such violence I thought my wrist might dislocate.

'El, I'm sorry,' he said, looking up at me, and in his face, I saw the shame now, the realisation.

'So am I, Sheldon, you were the one man I thought stood apart from all the others, but you truly are all beasts,' I spat, and when he put his hands back over his face, I left without looking back at him.

When I found myself padding carefully along the hall, Guinevere glaring at me, my relief faded as I remembered I still had the journey back to my room to navigate through my bleary, weeping eyes and the prospect of Delores questions. I had barely turned the corner of the first corridor when Mariella emerged from some direction behind me and I jumped at her words.

'Are you well, Eleanor?' she said to me more kindly than I had been spoken to by her in an age.

'I'm fine,' I said with my gaze still to the floor and carried on determined up the corridor.

'I thought I heard you screaming,' she said and I wondered where she could have been to hear me so well when her room was over in the west wing where I was staying. I stopped and looked at her carefully and did not see the guarded indifferent expression I was used to observing lately, but the giving away of some kind of concern in her eyes.

'Don't be ridiculous, your ears must be deceiving you,' I said and carried on before the tears fell.

'I must have been mistaken,' she said gently but persisted beside me until we passed the staircase and I reached my corridor.

'Indeed.' I wanted to tell her to get lost but it seemed impossible to in her own house, so I held my temper and then as Delores stepped out of our room just ahead, I felt the final crack in my nerves that I knew would make me come undone and I could not bear it.

'Eleanor, where on earth have you been?' she said with her hands on her hips, and a look that told me that as soon as we were alone, she would have severe words for me.

'Forgive me, Miss Parkes,' Mariella cut in, and I realised her time to avenge me had arrived at a most untimely moment. 'I needed some help choosing my gown and I could not think of anyone better to help me with it. So, I'm afraid I am to blame for stealing her away. I was just bringing her back to you. Thanks again Eleanor. I will see you at dinner.'

'Well then, we had better get you changed into your gown if we're to be on time for dinner.' Delores said satisfied and I could not work out if I was more overcome with relief or bewilderment. As I bid Mariella a feigned farewell, I tried to examine her for a clue to what had just happened but she was wearing her porcelain gaze and I could not guess her thoughts. But the contemplation quickly left me when I stepped into the dressing room for my toilette. I was full of only one matter now I was at last safe to permit it, and I sent the maid for some lotions so I could finally let out my tears.

A squiffy mistake.

30th June 1821. - Eleanor.

I didn't make much effort in my toilette tonight; I picked out one of my plainer gowns and had my hair pinned back behind a Bandeau. After dinner, I went straight over to Bets and co. and decided I would hide away amongst them for the entire evening. Saying little. Paying attention to little. The images of Sheldon and Lady Caroline spiralling in loops about my head.

I gave Delores strict instructions that I would not dance tonight on account of a feigned injury to my ankle on coming down the stairs, but I knew she didn't believe it. She understood the change in my mood even if not the cause as she looked between Sheldon and I, at the dinner table. I purposely stalled to cause us to be late for the seating so I would not be forced to sit with or greet him, or be questioned as to why I had not. But I felt his eyes on me the entire time and I refused to meet them even once. The very thought of him disgusted me and I knew that it would take a long time to shake this feeling, and right now I wanted nothing more than to forget everything.

If it had not been for the dreadful prospect of returning home to Mama empty handed, I would have insisted on our early departure. But I was not ready to bear anyone's questions or disappointment, when I had yet to reconcile my own. My only comfort was that the only persons to know of this matter were all invested in keeping it secret. Lady Caroline, I knew, as I was forced to bid her an acknowledgement of feigned equanimity at the table, was relishing in my torment and would have loved nothing more than to have their little ménage on-dit. But she had little choice than to tow the line for her husband's sake, and so I was to suffer only her privately understood gloating smiles; which I did my utmost to return when I must, and avoid wherever possible.

So, I sat sipping claret cup with my back turned against the dance floor so I would not have to see either of them. I made quite the perfect wallflower alongside Bets and Mariella as the others moved interchangeably between their seats and the dance floor in accordance with their invitations. But when the Colonel arrived, even Bets abandoned me. I supposed she was keen to reignite things in that direction now she had turned her face against Richards. I wished tonight she would not dance and would entertain me with some witty conversation or gossip to divert me. But most of my time was spent over disparate exchanges with Beth, and in uncomfortable silence with Mariella. We had not spoken since her odd rescuing act earlier, and although I knew I probably ought to thank her for it, I could not bring myself to find the words.

When Mr Craythorne finally came to take Beth up for the German Waltz, leaving Mariella and I quite alone and staring at each other, I begun to consider what I might say to her. I cleared my throat to speak the words when I saw her nod beyond my shoulder. I turned around to find Sheldon stood behind me.

'Miss Ashlyn, please, will you dance with me?' he asked with all the chivalry of an innocent gentleman.

I could not believe his audacity. 'I'm sorry, Mr Elmbridge, I have had a very long day and I am quite fatigued,' I said with as much composure as I could summons, for I was quite aware of the eyes that were upon me as I spoke the words, which did not exclude Delores', even though she was but a row away in subtle observation.

'Please, just this one?'

'No. I don't think so, Mr Elmbridge; why don't you ask Lady Caroline, she seems to be without invitation,' I suggested and turned back around in my chair before he could detain me any further.

'Well said,' Mariella remarked when he had gone. 'Don't let her get to you,' she added, and this I could not ignore.

'What do you mean?'

'I saw them, Eleanor, last night. I'm sorry.'

'Last night?' *So today was not the first...*

'I saw her go to him in his chamber and I did not know if I should come to you, for things have not been kind between us and I did not know if you would think I was meddling.'

I drained my glass.

'Something stronger?' she said, when I put it down. I nodded.

She returned with two generously filled glasses of Arrack punch for us moments later and even though I hated the stuff, I sunk it quickly.

'He is a fool, Eleanor...' she said drawing her chair closer to me and leaning in, '...but do not take it personally; this is what men do.'

'Yes, it seems you had them sussed long before I, so I suppose you can say you told me so now.'

'I could, but I would rather tell you that I have missed you.'

The words chilled me. I had cut my feelings towards her (ill and otherwise) completely these past weeks to make the bearing of her company easier. I knew I should say something kinder to her admission, but it would take me a lot longer to thaw out and understand my regard for her now.

'It is good of you to say so, but I thought our friendship quite extinguished.'

'Well...let us just say it is not only men who can behave like fools.'

I laughed a little at that. 'Thank you for earlier.'

'It was no trouble. Now, what's say we take some drinks to the games table and forget about all this nonsense?'

'It is the best offer I've had all night!' I said and followed her over to them. We sat down and joined a new game with the dowager and Delores. I remembered when she could not even play the game, nor be admitted to the dowager's company, and it seemed such a long time ago suddenly. So much seemed changed. As the cards were dealt and I drunk another cup of Arrack punch, I realised I was thawing, albeit slowly.

We played for chicken stakes: I lost two games and won the last. 'Don't deal for me. I think I will end on a winning streak after my luck today,' I said to the offer of a fourth match.

'That goes for me too,' Mariella said.

'Well, that leaves just us dear, I'll deal,' the dowager said to Delores and I knew she could not refuse her, even if my desire to escape her surveilance no longer had merit.

When I rose, I suddenly felt the effect of all the cups I had taken, but feigned a pained expression on account of my ankle when Delores raised her eyes to me; my head was in quite the spin and I had to use the table to steady myself.

'Well, I do not think either of us are in a suitable state for returning to the party, do you?' Mariella said, taking me by the arm to support me and leading me away. 'Shall we take a little air on the balcony to freshen our senses?'

'Delores will not permit it,' I told her as I trod carefully with her assistance. 'She is under strict orders to keep me in her sights and the dowager will not keep her long detained if she grows suspicious of me.'

'We can soon see to that,' she said and stopped to whisper something to her brother as we passed him.

'He will keep her busy,' she said and took me out through the half open doors.

There were only a couple of other people out there, busy in intimate tete-a-tete's, and perfectly uninterested when we sat perched upon the top stair of the balcony steps. I thought I might fall down if I didn't sit down first. The airing did not seem to improve my dizziness but I was too relaxed to care much now. I accepted another glass of something fairly strong Mariella had the footman deliver to us, and the frustrations of a miserable day, slowly began to fade into the balminess of the air.

'What will you do now?' Mariella asked as we stared into the black of night and sipped from our glasses.

I shrugged. 'Go to Edinburgh, enjoy the summer to its fullest and see what comes of it.'

'And Mr Elmbridge?'

'I do not know. Right now, I am not best placed to consider it because I am not yet beyond the shock. Certainly, I do not expect to be making the announcement that was planned this evening; for some time, if at all.'

'Oh my, I hadn't realised how fast you had progressed.'

'To tell the truth, it seemed to happen very quickly. I have been a fool.'

'Of course, you haven't; he is the fool in this.'

'Perhaps, but I have been fast and imprudent in our courtship, Mariella. I thought I was safe in my doing so because everything seemed so certain between us. I suppose I must learn the lesson of misplaced trust from it, whatever else.'

'How fast exactly?'

'Not enough to do any enduring damage at least, just that of my pride, I suppose. The only witness to anything is that wretched woman, and she shan't breathe a word of it after everything that's passed.'

'Well, thank goodness you have not bound yourself to him before you are decided on your course.'

'Yes, although I doubt it will alter enough to make a difference in the end. All men are beasts. I realise the truth in that now. But I am to marry one of them eventually, and despite all this, I still fancy him one of the lesser kind. Besides, I fear my regard has grown beyond what I had expected, and I am not sure I can dismiss it entirely. That said, I am sure he should endure a great deal of suffering at the possibility and a great deal of wooing in bringing me around again!' I laughed, and it was definitely the cup to blame for it, for there was little of heartfelt humour in me right now.

'You know it does not have to be inevitable. What I said to you before; your position; it affords you a certain luxury in enjoying some of the comforts of a husband whilst freeing you from the oppression of one.'

'Oh Mariella, I do not think I would be best served by an indifferent match: If this is how cruelly I can be injured by a man whose affections I have won, just imagine what could be bestowed by one that holds not the slightest care for me. Besides, I do not think my family would ever forgive me if I pass up the opportunity to make our family's connection to the Elmbridges, not now.'

'And what about what you want?'

'It is not so different from their wishes. I suppose I wanted to secure the perfect husband and live a happy existence aside him. I realise now that he does not exist.'

'It depends what you consider a perfect husband. In my mind, he is the type of man who is so much busy in his own affairs, that he has no mind for how I entertain the hours of his absence.'

'Mariella, you speak of wild and impossible things.'

'Not impossible, Eleanor, and not too late to reconsider.'

'No, please do not set out upon this scheme of yours again. I confess our dalliance was not unpleasant, but I do not feel as you do about it, and I certainly do not think any person should be repaid so poorly by his wife as to endure such goings on under his own roof.'

'I once thought the very same thing you did, Eleanor. It took me a long time to permit myself the idea that it was more than a dalliance, and even longer to accept that it could not be kept silent forever.'

'I am not like you, Mariella, my path is in front of me. I have simply tripped along it somewhere but I will find my feet again once I am recovered from the mishap.'

'Well, in that case, perhaps I can help you in that direction: There is no better aid to recovery than a good distraction from the misery.'

'Oh, what do you have in mind?'

'A mutual satisfaction; for the folly of it. Quite without any obligation beyond our own immediate amusement.'

I laughed at her bravado. 'I cannot.'

'Why: Haven't you missed me as much as I have you?' I felt her hand around the back of my neck pulling my ear towards her mouth. It sent shivers through the core of me and I struggled to catch my breath to answer. 'Yes. But I am attached now, in theory at least,' I told her, but it did not prevent her from pulling me in closer to feel the warmth of her breath at my ear.

'But that didn't stop him, did it. You would be, simply, evening the score?'

This much was true.

'Why should you deny yourself the relief he has enjoyed? In any case, he will be none the wiser for it... and you know I will not disappoint you.'

I looked about us to make sure we were not watched. We were not, but I noticed beyond the patio doors the sight of Lady Caroline sniffing about Sheldon in the hope of some attention. He was sat drinking port wine by himself and in no mood for conversation by the look of it. But the sight of them, even in an innocent circumstance set me off again. Images of them both together, the sounds of her pleasure rising out from the room, the workings of my own mind in filling in the details; it all began to swim about in the fog of my inebriated head. I turned away to the sound of her voice.

'Ignore her, she is nothing on you and he can see that as well as anyone. You're special Eleanor in ways that are rarely beheld. Make him suffer; give him something to miss before you allow him the pleasure of you again.'

'You are right: I will make his sufferance a long one.'

'Good girl.' I felt her lips faintly brush my ear. 'Can I show you how I've missed you, Eleanor? Will you let me take you to my bed now and make you feel my apology here?' she ran her slender fingers across my neck. 'Here?' over the full curve of my breast, '...and here.' I gasped as she cupped between my thighs; a firm pressure, a gentle squeeze before releasing it and trailing her fingers away along the length of my thigh. I could feel the pulsating pick up its own rhythm and the heat blazing from me was not just the effect of the cup. So many nights I had been pressed against him, feeling the ache in that place she touched.

She stood up and I followed suit and took the hand she offered to steady me. 'Come, we can forget everything for a while.'

But as I turned to follow her on into the saloon, I found myself accosted by Mr Richards at the door.

'Miss Ashlyn, I was just coming to find you, will you be so good as to dance the next set with me?' he said in that polite, unassuming way I admired in him.

'Yes Mr Richards, I think I would like that very well,' I replied and was pleased to make him smile whilst simultaneously managing to make Sheldon look up from his seat in horror.

'Miss Ashlyn?' Mariella tugged at my elbow, noticing the delay.

'I am to dance the next set with Mr Richards,' I told her. I shall come to you after.

'You are slurring your speech, Miss Ashlyn. I don't think you are best disposed for dancing now, do you?'

'Forgive me, Miss Ashlyn. I did not realise you unwell. Please sit down; I will get you some water.'

'Unwell? Nonsense Mr Richards, I am perfectly game for a dance.'

'I think, Sir, that would be very good of you,' Mariella intercepted and I watched him speed off to summon a footman.

'Why did you do that?'

'You are not steady on your feet and your speech is showing up your cups.'

'Fustian! I am going to dance. I feel very inclined to it. I have not felt so well all day!'

'I don't think such a public diversion is what you want in this state, Eleanor.'

'Nay, a private one would be much more fun if Mr Richards will entertain me in one.' I laughed and she scorned me with her expression.

'You must go to bed!'

'With Mr Richards?' I suggested and laughed as her eyes widened.

'I have missed some joke?' Mr Richards put a glass of water in my hand.

'She is not herself, sir. Drink it,' she directed in a tone I was better used to accepting from Delores or Mama.

'Tell me what I can do to help?' Mr Richards said to Miss Craythorne as I swallowed the water and complained of the plainness of it.

'I think you must help me to get her out of here as quietly as can be managed.'

'No, Mr Richards, we are to dance!'

He looked between us perplexed.

'What has she had to drink?'

'I do not know, but far too much I think.'

'Mr Richards, it is very bad form to ask a lady to dance and then snub her!' I reminded him, pulling myself up from the chair she had pushed me into and taking his arm up to steady myself.

'I have no wish to offend you Miss Ashlyn, truly, but—'

'Good, then do not!' I mustered all my strength to pull him on towards the dance floor and away from Mariella's crowing, and when he protested again, I said to him, 'You are a very handsome man, Mr Richards, have I told you so before?'

'No, Miss Ashlyn, and I wish you would not do so here.'

'Whyever not? Don't you find me handsome?'

'I think, Miss Ashlyn, with all due respect, you would not wish to have such a conversation with me in your better mind.'

'Oh Mr Richards, what if I would like nothing more than to spend the evening in your company enjoying much more than your conversation?'

'Eleanor!' Mariella scowled at me and I noticed her appear at my other arm with a squeeze. I let her drag me back from the dance floor and through the saloon, but I refused to release my grip on Mr Richards. I could barely navigate the steps well but I kept up with them. In the blur of bodies, we worked our way through, I saw Delores, dancing with Felix Craythorne, which I at first thought was some strange trick of my bleary vision. Then as we got to the other end of the room to make our way out, I saw Sheldon suddenly at my side.

'Miss Ashlyn,' Sheldon said in the same desperate tone I remembered from earlier. 'Mr Richards, unhand her sir!' I heard him complain and I held firmly onto Mr Richards' arm.

'He is helping me!' Mariella interjected. 'Can't you see she is not well? Now, she has nothing to say to you Mr Elmbridge,' she said, which was probably just as well for I was in no mood to say anything cordial to him.

'Please. Miss Craythorne, this matter is between us. What is wrong with her?'

'Us? Would that "us" include Lady Caroline too?' I let out an involuntary slur.

'El, you are cropsick,' he said and I laughed at the look on his face.

'And you are the cause behind it,' Mariella whispered with reprimand in her tone. 'Now, if you don't mind, I need to get her to bed before it is noticed. Excuse me Mr Elmbridge,' she said, marching me away, and I laughed again for I knew we were not going upstairs to sleep and the justice of it was tangible.

'Not with Mr Richards' assistance! Let me help.'

'Sir, forgive me but what can you mean?' Mr Richards protested, and as I noticed Sheldon reach out towards me, I pushed his arm away. 'You sir, will not lay your hands upon me!' I told him. 'Mr Richards, however, may...'

'Do you want to cause a scene, Mr Elmbridge?' Mariella said through gritted teeth.

'Of course not!'

'Then move out of the way and let me get her out of here. Mr Richards can convey us as far as the stairs; now, make yourself useful and find a footman and direct him to relieve Mr Richards.'

'Then, for god's sake, look after her,' he said and backed off.

'I assure you my care of her will be far less careless than yours has been, Mr Elmbridge. Goodnight,' Mariella bid him with anything but civility in her tone.

'Well, that was famous!' I laughed as we struggled towards the staircase.

'It was nothing; now, let us get you out of the way before you are seen. Mr Richards, you have been very good but you may leave us here. The footman will come any moment.'

'Yes, of course,' he said, freeing his arm from my grasp and as he did so, I stumbled on the first step and nearly took Mariella with me.

'I'm sorry, Mr Richards—' I felt her pull me back up, '—but perhaps you will need to help me in the meantime: The servants' stairs,' she said, looking about us and nodding to him the direction. 'We may carry her from there out of view.'

She pulled us through a jib door and once we were inside, asked if he was able to carry me up the staircase. I laughed aloud at this idea. 'What a funny thing to ask him,' I said. 'I am quite capable of—oops.' I lost my balance and felt him catch me before heaving me up in his arms. 'Well, Mr Richards, this is a very cosy arrangement,' I teased, gathering my arms clumsily around his neck.

'You must lead the way, Miss Craythorne: I cannot see a thing,' he told her and I saw the shape of her ahead of us in the darkness.

'You, maid: Turn away at once. You did not see a thing! Now, give me your lantern and find a footman to come at once.' I heard her say to someone I could not see and then noticed through my bleary eyes the shadow of a glow of light flickering ahead.

'Mr Richards, you smell very good,' I said as I rested my dizzying head against his neck to try to alleviate the spinning.

'Thank you, Miss Ashlyn; please stay steady.'

'Steady: Now, there is something to converse on, the steadiness of one's character.'

'Ignore her, Mr Richards, she is full of nonsense tonight.'

'Actually Mariella, I feel less full of nonsense now than I have in weeks! I can see everything so much clearer now. I mean, Mr Richards, I own I understood why you were admired, but never so much as in this very moment. I wonder how well you could kiss me? I patted his face to find him in the darkness and placed my lips against a stubbly patch of skin.

He stopped on the stairway. 'Please, Miss Ashlyn.'

'Eleanor!' I felt her grab me by the chin and turn my head. 'Stop it at once! This is most irregular. Mr Richards is trying to help you, now, stop impeding him.'

'Oh, I would very much like not to impede him at all. Mr Richards, I give you leave to do whatever you will with me. What shall you choose?'

'I shall choose to take you to your chamber.'

'Now, that I like the sound of!'

'And leave you to your bed so you can rest and forget this whole affair.'

I prodded his chin gently with my finger. 'How disappointing; I was rather hoping you might have some better design.'

'She really does not take her drink well. Miss Craythorne, you must take better care not to let her get into such a state again.'

'Oh, yes, of course, I am a mere woman, so I must be in my cups to speak so to a man. I mean it's all very well for a man to make such advances but—'

'I mean no offence—'

'Well then hear me, Mr Richards! I insist that you take me to my chamber at once and awaken my senses to the delights of your sex.'

'She is better ignored, sir. She will tire of these hysterics if you pay her no mind.'

'But I am not tired at all. In fact, I have quite enough energy to undress Mr Richards and see what tricks he has to teach me. I am a very keen learner, sir. Tell me, will you make a student of me tonight?'

'For goodness sake, hold your tongue, Eleanor! Sir, I am very sorry for you, but you must know this is the cups talking.'

'It is quite alright, Miss Craythorne. I know enough of her character to discern she is not herself. I really am only concerned to save her the memory. Pray where is your footman?'

'You know...'

'I have no idea! But we are nearly there now.'

'...It is very rude to speak of someone as if they were absent when you are in their presence.'

'My apologies, Miss Ashlyn.'

'I will forgive you, Mr Richards, for I think we might kiss and makeup rather passionately.'

'Take her in.'

Brightness flooded my eyes and I sensed we had come to some other place.

'You can put her on the chaise.'

I saw her now as she went back to close the door of my chamber. I remembered the look of the stylish Parisian décor as I tried to settle the focus of my gaze on something that didn't seem to be moving. Then I felt him lower me, and as he released me, I stole his hand. 'You cannot go, Mr Richards, I do not permit it!'

'Miss Ashlyn, please let go of me. I must take my leave.'

I grasped at his cravat and was surprised when Mariella snatched it from me and slapped me swiftly across the face.

'Miss Craythorne!' He gathered me up and examined my face; I felt the sting in my cheek and held my hand to it. 'There is no need for that I say!'

'I am not trying to upset her; I am trying to bring her to her senses!'

'Miss Ashlyn, are you alright?' he asked gently. 'I do not think that's the way Miss Craythorne!'

'No. I fear I am not very well at all,' I replied as I felt my head rush from side to side as if the contents were at sea on a storm. I felt his palm at my forehead. 'Have you some smelling salts or some such remedy?' he asked.

'Stop fussing. She will be fine; she simply needs to sleep it off. Now I must bid you go: if someone discovers us, we will all be in a great deal more trouble than this.'

'No, Mr Richards please don't leave me with her. I beseech you.'

He held my hand. 'Miss Craythorne is right, you need to sleep, you will feel better in the morning and I cannot stay here.'

'Please, she will not take care of me at all; you would not believe the things Miss Craythorne—'

'Mr Richards, perhaps you might try to settle her a moment whilst I find a servant.'

'Can you not ring the bell?'

'It is broken.'

'Fine, I will wait with her.' The door slammed shut and I felt relieved to be alone with him. 'Miss Ashlyn, are you going to be alright with my going; would you like me to find your chaperone on my way out?'

'No! No, sir, you cannot go to her. Just stay with me, will you? Please. I feel so very odd.' I rested my head against his shoulder and felt him cradle me against him. 'You will be yourself again soon, now rest.'

I must have dozed off awhile, for when I awoke to him peeling me away from him, Mariella was back in the chamber with her Indian maid servant tinkering about in her spice box.

Best laid plans.

30th June 1821. - Mariella.

It had been a tiresome effort to bring it all about so carefully, but I knew as I watched her enter the dining room with red rimmed eyes and a pallor that matched the plainness of her dress, that this phase of the scheme had succeeded.

I watched her all night from afar, waiting for my opportunity to get her alone, but it was not until Colonel Delaware arrived and swept Betsy out of the way that I found my path clear. She was as cold and frigid to my reception as she had been to Elmbridge all night, but of course, I had the advantage of her being in my debt. Not that you would have guessed it, since she had not bothered to utter a single word of thanks through our slight exchanges. I was beginning to despair of all my efforts when Francine came to tell me Giles was arrived. I had begun to grow anxious at his coming he was so late.

I met him on the vestibule and reached out to embrace him. 'I am glad you are here at last,' I said, releasing him.

'Well, I hope I am not too late. I have had a terrible time of it getting here. The coach cracked a wheel and I thought I would have to go on horseback the ten miles.'

I could see he was in one of his black moods. 'Oh, how horrid; but you are here now, and I have made good progress,' I said sweetly seeing his interest piqued and leading him straight into the small parlour, out of sight.

I set about explaining to him how it had all gone off with setting up the meeting between Sheldon and Lady Caroline; how Eleanor had discovered them and reacted with all the expected outrage and heartache. How the next part of my plan was proving more tiresome, but I was, as ever, confident in my powers of persuasion.

'What a clever little thing you are,' he said, kissing me lightly on the cheek as I poured him a brandy and took his gloves from him.

'So, how shall you bring about the rest of the scheme if she is so distraught?' He took a long drawn-out sip and sat back in the Chesterfield.

'Oh Giles, how poorly your sex understands ours. You know there is no better cure for heartache than a diversion, and who better to show her some compassion and offer such comforts...'

'You think she will go for it after how much she has taken against you?'

'You of all people should know better than to underestimate me. I can be very persuasive when I'm minded to be.'

He smiled and decanted the next glass himself.

'I have already paid her the service of an alibi to her chaperone which she will be too grateful of, to snub me. I will find an opening to show her some small sympathies and then when she is ripe for the diversion, I will offer it to her, which is where you are needed.'

'So what will you have me do?'

'You will come to the guest chamber, next to my own when Geeta brings the message to you. I shall have all prepared, you need only be found in the wrong place at the wrong time.'

'And you are confident that will be enough?'

'Oh, believe me, when Delores finds her in such circumstances, she will do the rest of the work for us.'

He took a cigar from his case and I pushed the candlestick towards him so he could light it. 'I must get back. Make sure to stay about the saloon. You must be at the ready when the moment comes.'

'You may count upon it.'

I smiled. 'Enjoy the entertainment for now; await my instruction, and if all goes well, by morning, things will be much altered.'

A curl of cigar smoke spiralled above us. 'What about Elmbridge?' he asked when he had finished exhaling it.

'Leave him to me,' I said and raised my glass to his.

WHEN I RETURNED TO the party, I saw her sat dismal-faced where I had left her as Betsy and the Colonel prattled merrily and remained quite oblivious to her pitiable sulking. It took no time at all to encourage them to join the others in the dancing and at last the way opened and I ushered her off to the gaming tables with the offer of good stakes.

As I sat at the card table, feigning enjoyment in this odious game, my eyes searched out Giles, who was watching from above his glass as he spoke with Felix.

'You must be in need of a top up too, Miss Ashlyn?' I said, snatching up her glass along with mine and summoning the footman.

She nodded vaguely as she frowned over her fanned cards and when the footman came with his tray to unburden me of the cups, I deliberately dropped hers and watched it smash to the floor.

'Forgive me, Ameet, let me help you,' I said to him in accents of apology as he knelt to recover the broken pieces.

'Leave it to me madam,' he said and then I bent down to whisper to him as I gathered fragments of the glass stem: 'Take this draught and put it in my cup with the punch please, Ameet—I have a terrible headache but I must entertain. Be discreet now.' He nodded and awayed at once with the vial tucked into his gloved palm.

'How clumsy of you, Miss Craythorne,' Eleanor teased when I sat back up at the table. 'I think the anxiety of the game encourages your cups,' she said, gloating as she laid her deck upon the table and swept away her winnings.

'The night is young,' I replied with a gleam of mischief in my eye I was sure she caught, but seemed suddenly wasted as I followed her gaze over to Sheldon who had been accosted by Lady Caroline again. I could almost see the naked images of the pair dancing in her eyes. If she had but known the trouble I had taken to set it up, she might be a little more sympathetic of him. She might too have noticed I had given the game away to her and her triumph at the cards a shallow one to the stakes that were really being raised. It perked her up no less, and it seemed worth the endurance of it to bring her back to more congenial spirits.

'Don't deal for me. I think I will end on a winning streak after my luck today,' she said as the croupier cleared the table ready to deal a new hand.

'That goes for me too,' I added, taking our replenished drinks from Ameet and switching hers with the draught.

'Come now, ladies,' said the dowager complaining, 'Delores, you shan't disappoint me I know: I must have the chance to make a comeback. Double or quit?'

'Here,' I said, pushing my remaining tokens over to Delores. 'Perhaps your touch will prove luckier than mine. You have all reminded me what a novice I am.' And when I noticed Eleanor had nearly finished her cup, I said quickly, 'What say we take a turn?' I had approximately twenty minutes or so to get her out of here before the draught took its effect.

'Actually, I think I am ready to dance now,' she said and I felt my stomach sink.

'Come Miss Ashlyn, you have snubbed your would-be partners and they are all making merry. Perhaps we can encourage some invitations for the second half. Shall we at least get our circulation flowing? These chairs do nothing for my posture.'

She nodded her agreement and I came up beside her to take her arm as it suddenly became apparent that she had already begun to suffer the effect as she used the table to steady herself. I swept her away with a promise to Delores to stay about the saloon and felt the unsteadiness of her weight sway me just a fraction as she faltered at my elbow. I stood firmer and checked about me for any notice, but all eyes were fixed upon the freshly dealt cards and I padded away with enough grace of step for the pair of us. This woozying was premature and yet she still seemed to have her head.

'Look, there is Mr Alversley,' she said, stopping. 'I think he is without a partner and should like to dance.'

'Oh yes,' I said, pulling her away. I had not time for too much honey tonguing if I was to remove her before it was noticed. 'I think you must take some air first for you seem a little giddy. We don't want Mr Alversley to think you in your cups.'

'You are right; I think I shall sober a little first.'

I stole her through the open balcony doors and was pleased to find it quieter and too dark to notice her clumsy footing out here. All the same, I settled her upon the steps and set to work in seducing her as gently as I could against such time constraints. I knew she had none of the regard for me she once did; I had long seen him pilfer it away, inch by inch: Her eyes ever brightening in his direction and ever dulling in mine. And however much vexation he had earned himself today, I could see the longing in them still; despite how fiercely she pretended to set her face against him. She was hurt, to be sure: angry no end—yet beyond that fiery sparkle beneath her lashes, there lurked something of great feeling and it unnerved me slightly. If I could not prevent their coming together when she had no notice of him, it did not bode well now he had her heart within his grasp. Still, where he had heart, I knew I would excel in other quarters. He might have had her kisses but I could tell from her excitement as I sighed breathy teases into her ear, that he had been remiss in taking advantage of her naïve enthusiasm.

I traced my fingers along her thigh and confirmed my suspicions. Whatever her words were telling me, her body betrayed something altogether different. I wondered how long she had swelled and moistened at his kisses to be left always disappointed. How many weeks had it been since I had last unburdened her of such frustrations? *Long enough.* 'Come, we can forget everything for a while,' I said, pulling her up from the steps once I had stirred her up adequately to be certain of her compliance. It had been harder won than I expected, but as I felt her leaning at my elbow and trying to keep pace with me, I felt the relief of my victory tangible. The promise of a no-strings-dalliance proved more effective than trying at making love to her and romancing her into bed when she cared not a fig for anyone but he, and when I pitched it as such, I realised my faux pas and changed course. A parting amusement had a finality about it that seemed to appeal to her better. The irony was painful; how little she knew herself better off in my hands than his; not that she would ever discover the comparison now, I thought, catching sight of him as I held open the balcony door to go back in.

He looked so miserable it was in this instant I realised the weakness in my plan and thought quickly how to improve it. I must get *him* to cry off, not her. She was too cotton-headed with sentiment to be trusted to break with him once her anger settled, even if her chaperone laid the charge at her. He would do everything in his power to bring her back about. But his reaction would be better insurance than Delores' if I could encourage him to discover her there with Giles. His honour would make it impossible not to cry off, no matter what his feelings were. Although it could end in quite the mess, I considered: offers of duels and so forth, which was a complication I could do without and I'm sure Giles would not appreciate. Delores summoned first, and then perhaps once Giles was out the way, Elmbridge could be gulled to go to them and make up his own mind at the scene before him. I was certain he could work out the rest.

The excitement of these refinements to my plan quickened my steps, as did the increasing weight of her staggering at my side. The saloon was still thick with dancers and so I sought to navigate her about the perimeter of the room where we could take cover in the crush. It had all gone so well until this point, and then I noticed her lag behind and turned to find Mr Richards petitioning her. *You great pest!* I mumbled inwardly and pulled her on.

But she was of another mind and paused shaking me off. 'I am to dance the next set with Mr Richards. I will come to you after,' she protested, a slur at my ear.

She was undeterred by my objections, so I turned my efforts to him instead, pleading her inebriation, and just when I had enlisted him to my service in helping me to get her out of public view, she grew wild and began saying such shocking things to Richards, it was hard to tell who was the more astonished. It did at least lend to my cause and Richards made himself agreeable in taking up her other arm and placating her on towards the hall. We had barely made it out when I heard Sheldon at our backs and I was certain all that had been recovered, must now be lost. He was flying into a rage at Richards, Eleanor into one at Elmbridge and I levelled my attack at him, realising that we would soon have the saloon pouring out into the hall to discover the disturbance. 'Do you want to cause a scene, Mr Elmbridge?' I scowled.

'Of course not.'

'Then move out of the way and let me get her out of here. Mr Richards can convey us as far as the stairs; now, make yourself useful and find a footman to relieve Mr Richards, will you?' I took a breath to compose myself as he relented and set off on his errand, but when Richards and I reached the stairs and guided her up them, she came tumbling at the first step and it took both our strength to catch her. I redirected him towards the service staircase, realising that the only way she would get to the chamber is to be carried to it, and since I could not manage it, I succumb to having Richards do it for me.

It was a less of evils to choose from now, if I was to recover the scheme at all. The last thing I needed was anyone else about as she passed into a stupor. But there would be no hope at all if

I did not quickly get her to the chamber. Yet, if Richards witnessed her complete incapacitation, then it would render the whole set up impossible if he could vouch for her. However, if I hung about waiting another moment for a footman, I would be risking her ending up in a comatose heap on the stairwell and everyone set about in a panic.

I instructed him to follow me up with her, hoping all was not lost. It was only when he had hoisted her up and she got up lively again I felt a little reassurance this still might work. His close proximity seemed to reinvigorate her and as I navigated us up the staircase, I heard flirtations spring to her lips I never thought her capable of. If it were not for how much was at stake in these vital moments, I might have laughed out loud at her vulgar speeches and Mr Richards' desperate attempts to keep his composure as she fussed and groped at him. But my humour soon faded when we finally got to her room and Eleanor refused to let him go. I was almost ready to cede to defeat as I tried to prise her away from clutching at him. When I slapped her around the face to shock her into letting him go, it seemed even this was set against me.

'Miss Craythorne! There is no need for that I say!' he bellowed and I realised whilst it seemed to do the trick in bringing Eleanor out of her hysterics, it seemed to have quite the opposite effect on Mr Richards who took great offense to my approach and stood between us protectively.

In the end, I left them to it and set off along the corridor in a panic to find someone to fetch Giles. I did not know what to do now to recover this, but he was the only one I could rely on to assist me.

Cropsick.

1st July 1821. - Eleanor.

When I woke up with a start, it was dark. The candles had burned down and the curtains were drawn. I rolled onto my side and felt how cruelly my head ached and throbbed. I sat up and searched the darkness for any sign of the nightmare that was coming back to my consciousness in a hazy mist. A Jackal bearing its teeth. Woodland. Slipping in the mud and trying to climb a tree as it pursued me. It came in these flashes, out of sequence, almost beyond my grasp, but I could feel the harrowing effect it had imprinted upon my senses as I recovered my breath. I looked about the room and remembered where I was; Beaulieu, and then it came back to me, the liquor, the sickness, the...I was distracted by the sudden notice of how full my bladder was and how keenly it threatened, so I mustered up the energy to get out of the bed to find the chamber pot, even though my body protested at the effort.

I could not find a lamp or candle in the unfamiliar room as I stumbled around trying to co-ordinate my sleepy body and navigate in the darkness. So, I went over to the window where a thin stream of light broke through a gap and was surprised as I pulled back the heavy drape to be flooded with bright sunlight. My eyes struggled to adjust to it and I squinted my way over to the washstand to find the chamber pot, fearing I would soon be too late.

As I relieved myself of the burden, I jumped at the notice of Mariella fast asleep on the day bed to the far side of the room. Why was I in her chamber and not with Delores? What exactly had happened last night?

Despite my surprise that we had shared the room, I felt a little relief that she was on the daybed, besides, the sight of her presence comforted me. I preferred it to the thought of being alone with all the emotions of a haunting dream still swimming around my head. Far too many cups last night I thought might have some bearing on how ragged I felt. I remembered then, in fragments, the drinking, the swooning, the laughing, Mr Richards. 'Dash,' I said clutching at the recollection of clinging to him in the saloon and then trying to shake off the horror of the memory. And then some other piecemeal flashes came through the fog; she had embraced me outside and I had agreed to let her take me upstairs to fulfil her indecent promises. It was only then it occurred to me that I was completely naked. I looked about the room to see my clothes strewn across the floor and I instantly felt the sting of regret. What had we done last night? Had I let her do those things to me I promised I would not permit again? I remembered those sensations she had stirred in me out on the balcony that had weakened my resolve, but I could not piece it all together in my head.

Then as I replaced the heavy chamber pot, I noticed the blood-streaked colour of it and realised my menses had come on. Of all the inconvenient timing, my courses would come on when I was in someone else's bed, quite unprepared for the calamity.

It must have been very early, for when I peered into the water jug to clean myself up, it was empty; the maids had not yet come. I grabbed my chemise from the floor and wriggled it over my head then went over to her on the daybed. Whyever did I not return to my own chamber, and what must Delores think of my absence?

'Mariella,' I called, leaning over to her bed. 'Mariella!' I said again, reaching out and shaking her.

She groaned and blinked at the daylight. 'What is it?'

'I need a belt and rags.'

She sat up and rubbed her eyes. 'What are you talking about?'

'My menses have caught me by surprise and I did not bring any with me, do you have a belt I could use?'

'In the top drawer,' she muttered into her pillow and I went off to find the thing and arrange myself.

When I was in better order, I roused her again. 'Why are you sleeping on the daybed and why am I in your room?' I wanted to ask her why I had awoken buck naked, but I was not ready to face the answer of that so early, with my head still in a stupor.

'You were ill, I could not leave you so much in your cups. You were as sick as dog last night!'

I could still taste the stale punch on my tongue.

'What time is it?' she asked.

I searched the mantle for the clock. 'Almost six o'clock.'

'Whatever are you up at this hour for? Close the curtains and go back to bed.'

I was happy to oblige, for I felt like I had hardly slept a blink despite the many hours lost to me, so I went back over to close the curtains and settle back to sleep a while. Hopefully, I would make more sense of everything when I was better rested.

I was just dozing off again when the door rapped and made us both jump.

'It is too early,' Mariella complained, come back in an hour.

'Miss Ashlyn,' I heard Delores' voice; it was not the maids. I sat bolt upright and by now even Mariella was sitting up to force herself into consciousness.

'Delores, why so early?' I asked when she came in, feeling in sudden terror that she would be in want of an explanation I did not have to offer her. She came straight over to me and noticing Miss Craythorne on the daybed, said low. 'Forgive me, it is a most irregular errand, but Mr Elmbridge insists he must see you at once. I have tried to beg him come back later but he will not hear of it.'

'Sheldon?' I tried to cast my memory back to last night.

'Tell him I will be down in an hour.'

'Well, I own I would prefer it too, you are hardly looking your brightest at this hour my dear, but he is just outside the door and very determined. I have warned him that he had better come with *very* serious business in mind to inconvenience us all so much in this most irregular way, and he assures me that he has, so, where is your peignoir my dear?'

I held in a very long sigh. I could not believe he had given me so little time to cool off before attempting to push his question. One I had already answered bluntly enough. I was still in a rage and not ready to relent. The audacity of it, and such an insolent request was enough to mind me to refuse him flatly again. But I remembered all the promises made to mama and Delores only yesterday, and could not see how I could decline to even hear him. 'Very well, help me then,' I said in answer to her expectant expression, sending her for my gown and slippers in my unpacked Portmanteau next door.

When she returned, she sat me at the dressing table and brushed my hair out, dabbed me with Floris water and then said, 'My, I think you had better clean your teeth perhaps,' handing me the tooth powder.

My mouth was very foul tasting and it was a relief to taste something fresher than the stale residue of liqueur and vomit on my tongue. I caught a glimpse of Mariella as I used barley water from the carafe to rinse out my mouth. She was sat upright on her bed now, looking desperate to ask me something but daring not to in Delores company. I spat into the bowl, ran my tongue across my teeth to test their polish and Delores pinched my cheeks to give them some colour and I could see the necessity for it, even if it did catch me by surprise.

'Well, Miss Craythorne, we must have somewhere else to go, have you not a sitting room or some such in these apartments that we might use?' she said evenly and I was grateful she had not asked why I was here at all, even if her audacity in directing Mariella within her own house was a little shocking to us both.

'Of course, take the door through there,' she said obligingly, pulling back the sheets and pointing its direction.

'A small parlour room?' Delores said. 'Yes, I think that will do much better. What a mess you have made in here, ladies. Miss Craythorne, perhaps you could ring for the maid.'

I SAT IN MARIELLA'S small parlour stiffly in my chair when Delores announced Sheldon and made a very swift exit. I might have been a little more self-conscious of my own appearance had the sight of his not shocked me so much. *It seems I was not the only one too much in my cups last night,* I thought to myself as he settled into his seat opposite me, dark half-moons beneath his bloodshot eyes.

'Mr Elmbridge, you look very tired, are you sure you wish to have such a conversation now?' I asked in a last-ditch attempt to put him off.

'Eleanor, I have not slept a wink all night, you must know why I am here.'

'Yes, well I had thought you would have given me the courtesy of a little more time to allow the memory of my discovery to fade a little better.'

He frowned. 'Your discovery? Eleanor, I beg you to tell me in earnest, what is between you and Mr Richards?'

His question puzzled me so much it took me a moment to even answer him. 'Nothing whatsoever—why should you ask me such a thing?'

He leaned forward in his seat. 'Do not toy with me, Eleanor, can you not see how anxious I am to have the whole?'

Instinctively, I leaned further back in my own. 'I own I can see it, but what I cannot understand is how you dare to ask me such a thing after it was you—'

'Last night, Eleanor; I saw you.' His eyes were wide, something accusatory in them.

'I own I was in my cups and the memory of the evening is a little hazy, but I can tell you for a fact that nothing inappropriate passed between me and Mr Richards if that is what you mean to suggest.'

'He took you up to your room.'

A vague memory of me clutching at him caused a little heat to rise in my cheeks as I remembered that my speech had perhaps been undesirable, but that was all. 'Yes, he did but I assure you, that was all there was to the matter.'

'And when you were alone together?'

'Alone?'

'Do not tell me you was not, Miss Craythorne told me herself that she had to leave you a while in his care whilst she got help, I think you were quite ill.'

'Yes, I was, so how you can imagine Mr Richards made any advances upon me in such a state I cannot imagine!'

'I saw you, Eleanor,' he shook his head, 'you were in your bed quite naked, your clothes about the place, the bed...'

My heart sank as two realisations became clear to me; he was in here with me last night and had seen me naked and indeed, I had been up to no good with Miss Craythorne as I feared! It was then I suddenly realised what Mariella's constipated expression was trying to tell me. 'I hope, sir, for both our sakes you do not mean you would dare look at me so inappropriately without—'

'I simply saw from the view of your bare shoulders!' he held up a hand in protest. 'I would not—'

'Well. Whatever did you come to a lady's chamber for? I own I do not remember your coming.'

'You were quite asleep by then. What concerns me is the period you spent between then and Miss Craythorne leaving you quite alone in Mr Richards' charge.'

'Well, I cannot remember every moment, for I spent a great deal of time in being quite silly and then quite sick, but I can tell you this: nothing untoward passed between Richards and I. I cannot believe you would dare come and ask me such things after everything...' my voice cracked and trailed off as I felt a lump form in my throat.

He pressed his face against his palms and sighed through them. 'Oh El,' he said exasperated, 'I want so very much to believe you but the evidence was all about the place.'

'Evidence? I think you are gone quite mad.'

'Well, it is no surprise, I am about to make you my wife, the next Lady Elmbridge. If there is the slightest chance—'

'Oh, is that so? I own the more I hear from you the more unlikely I find that!'

'Please don't say that. I know I have wronged you and I am so very sorry for it I cannot begin to tell you. But please El, you must see that if—'

'If I have behaved as abominably as you have?'

'Yes...there are more serious consequences that cannot be so easily overlooked.'

I laughed sardonically at this. I don't know if it was the stifled anger or the audacity. 'Of course, I am a female after all.'

'You could have a child!'

This time I laughed raucously. 'Well, let me explain something to you: it actually would require me to lie with him and as I told you before, that DID NOT HAPPEN! And if it is evidence you require, then how does this serve you, I am currently indisposed so what you say is quite impossible!'

He looked as uncomfortable at this admission as I was in saying it, but my fury got the better of me. 'Oh, would you like to see for yourself? I mean you have already seen me without my clothes so what harm can it do now?' I said, gesturing to my skirts.

'Please. Let us not quarrel.'

'It was you that came here to pick one under the guise of something altogether different from what Delores tells me.'

'I did not. I came to clarify so that I could dare hope to still make such a request of you.'

'Well, you really know how to set the mood for such an event.'

We both sat silently a while before he eventually come to me and drew up my hands in his. 'El, I know I have been a fool and I am sorry for it. But you must see that I have loved you for so very long and waited an age for this day to finally come. If you can forgive me, if you can permit me to spend the rest of our years proving to you my earnest wish to make you happy: Please consider me despite these past days and be my wife.'

I had planned refusal, failing that delay, but there was something in his speech, in his eyes, that cut through all the heartache that had bound so tightly over my emotions, that I realised I could not. I felt a tear roll down my cheek and went to catch it, but he lifted my chin, wiped it away with a stroke of his thumb and kissed me lightly on the forehead.

'I am sorry to have injured you. *Truly.* Let me set things right between us.'

'Oh Sheldon, however did it go so badly? I own I wish I had let you ask me it all those weeks ago, if I could have foreseen how sadly things would turn.'

'Does that mean your answer would have been yes?' he peered at me hopefully.

'Yes, it would have been and I think perhaps it still can be, if—' I said pointedly at the noted brightening of his expression: 'If we might at least take a reasonable engagement to permit us to put all this folly behind us and remember each other a little more fondly again before the date is set.'

I could see the tears form in his eyes as he broke into a smile so wide, I quite forgot all the anger I had been quelling. Unlike mine, his did not fall, only glistened in them making them seem brighter. 'Do you say yes?'

I nodded and I was grateful of Delores' foresight in bidding me clean my teeth for he kissed me on my mouth with such unbridled passion I was taken quite aback.

'The date is not to be set for a while though, in fact, not for two months' time,' I said when he finally relented. I needed to be certain and to forget this monstrous faux pas.

He agreed and swept me up for another.

DELORES, WHO I HOPED had not had her ear to the door given all the things that were said, bounced with excitement when I went back into the chamber and nodded to her questions that yes, he had asked and yes, I had accepted.

'Oh, my dear,' she scooped me up and I realised I was much too fragile this morning for all this ceremony. 'We must get ready at once and give your parents the happy news!'

I agreed that we would on the proviso she afforded me a little time to take a small breakfast—the effect of the alcohol had left my stomach growling. I still felt quite nauseous but a plain breakfast I thought, might settle it. I also felt such an emotional and literal wreck that I needed a little while, just to sit with my thoughts and attempt to put them in some order. It was when she disappeared to ring the bell, that I first considered, in the light of day, the arrangement of the chamber. It was apparent that we had enjoyed quite an evening up here that I still could not remember at all and it puzzled me. Although Mariella had seemed to abandon the chamber swiftly, I knew I must wait for her return and speak to her privately. 'Delores, won't you have the rest of my things brought in here? It is so much more comfortable than our little chamber and Mariella shall not mind a bit.'

'Very well, these bells are still not working, I shall find a maid and send her to you. You would think they would at least fix the bell before setting guests up in the room!' she complained and set off with a bounce about her step her complaining could not disguise. She was relieved. She was soon to be free of me.

I sat down at Mariella's dressing table and contemplated the mess. I was disappointed with myself for getting into such a state that I could not retrieve the details and more so for permitting these things to occur between us again. However out of sorts I was last night, in my right mind, I had no desire to encourage any further transgressions with Mariella and I sorely hoped she did not take this dalliance as such an indication.

When Mariella came back in, I was already dressed and sitting over a small breakfast of buttered toast and tea.

'What was all of that about?' she said carefully, checking that Delores was not about the place.

'*That* was Sheldon and I becoming engaged,' I told her steadily.

'Then I congratulate you and wish you every happiness.'

'Thank you, Mariella,' I smiled, grateful that she seemed not to have taken offence which reassured me that what had passed between us last night had not revitalized the idea that this dalliance would be reinstated.

'I think this must mean that you and I will no longer...' she said as if reading my mind.

'No. I mean, you understand that we can be friends, Mariella, but nothing like what passed last night can ever happen again now I am to be married.'

'Last night?' she frowned.

'Yes.'

'But nothing at all did pass between us last night. I own, I had hoped that it might be possible but you were so much out of sorts that I realised it would not be and then when I came back and you were asleep to bed, I had no mind to disturb you.'

I felt a frown contort my features. 'You mean we did not at all?' I put my teacup back in its saucer even though I hadn't sipped from it.

'No. Whyever did you think so?'

I looked about the room and begged my memory for a clue. 'Then why did I awake this morning to find myself quite naked and my clothes all about the floor?'

'I thought you must have undressed yourself. I mean, I thought it an odd thing for you to manage, since you could barely walk and Mr Richards had to carry you all the way.'

'Mr Richards.'

'Oh yes,' Mariella cut in. 'You will not want to see him again after your encounter last night!'

'Whatever can you mean, did something unhappy pass between us?'

'Well, from what I saw of it, you will be quite horrified at the things you said to him, but he assured me of his discretion.'

'What you saw of it? We were with you, I remember you scolding me.' I held a palm to my cheek.

'Yes, more than a few times, you were quite out of control! Thank god Mr Richards had a soothing effect on you because you had settled down quite well by the time I returned.'

Sheldon's accusation came instantly back to me. 'Returned? Mariella, how long were Mr Richards and I alone?'

'Only a short while: fifteen to twenty minutes or so, I imagine. I had to go and get a draft to purge you of the alcohol, you were so very ill and there were no servants about and what with the broken bell,' she shrugged.

The memory of retching over a bowl returned to me and I felt my stomach lurch at the reminder and pushed away my toast. 'But why did you not send Mr Richards for help? You surely must have had a thought for my reputation?'

'I tried to but you would not let go of him. When he tried to settle you on the chaise, you clung to him and refused to let him leave you. I own in the end I had to slap you smartly across the cheek to try and bring you round.'

As she recounted it, I suddenly remembered the sting of it, but it was not that which disturbed me so ill.

'I am sorry to have done it, but it did seem to affect you a little and I did try to be quick, but on my way, Sheldon accosted me and then Delores took a lot of gulling and when I come back, you were asleep, Mr Richards was gone and I could not wake you.'

'Wake me?'

'Yes, you were out like a light. I tried to stir you but you wouldn't come too and then Geeta had to help me give you the sickness draft and you were so violently sick I thought you would never stop! You do not remember it?'

'Yes, yes some of it I think, but I cannot think clearly, my mind is in such a haze and I had such a terrible nightmare.' I pressed a napkin to my lips, deciding breakfast was concluded. 'Mariella,' I said carefully, 'so when you left me, I was dressed and on the chaise with Mr Richards and when you come back, I was asleep, in bed, unclothed?'

'Yes.'

'And you are certain you or one of the servants did not undress me?'

She nodded her head.

'And Mr Richards had returned to the party?'

'Well, that was the mystery, although I did not pay too much mind to it at the time as there was so much else to tend to. After you were sick the first time, I had to move you both into my chamber to have the entire guest room cleaned down in fear of Delores returning to such a scene, for there was vomit everywhere. I left you both upon the chaise in here, and yet when I returned, you were settled into my bed. I own I thought it very odd, but assumed you had grown tired and wanted to sleep. Besides, I was quite exhausted by it all, I just settled for the daybed.'

'What was the mystery?'

'Mr Richards was gone when I returned, and I thought he had seen you get to sleep at last and did not want to wait around once he knew you safe and sound. It was only when I found this,' she went over to the dresser and pulled a blood-stained handkerchief from it. 'I thought it very odd and I thought perhaps someone had been hurt.'

I took the offered handkerchief and saw the initials C.R stitched into the corner of it, down the centre run a streak of dried blood. 'Mr Richards?'

'Yes, very odd, but all seemed well so I did not concern myself with it. I mean, the bed was all in such a mess, I did find that a little strange. But considered you may have had a fitful descent into sleep.'

I stood up from the small table and ran over to the bed.

'What is wrong?'

I pulled back the sheets and saw a small, speckled blood stain in the centre of it. 'Where did you discover this handkerchief?'

'On the side table, why?'

'I do not know precisely I just—I need my journal, I need to see the dates of my last menstruation.' I had given the matter no thought at all, but I paused then, realising I had said too much. I could not tell her that there seemed to be a big chunk of the evening I could not account for, that I thought I had only had my courses a sennight or two ago, that I could not explain why I was undressed and why I feared it could be my blood on Mr Richards handkerchief. Instead, I just replied to her puzzled gaze: 'Mariella, I feel unwell, I need to go home.'

'Are you alright?'

'No, no I don't think I am.'

'If this is about you and Mr Richards, I shall not breathe a word of the matter, you have my promise.'

'What about Mr Richards and I?'

'Well, you must own the things you said and did, were hardly—'

'What things?'

'Well, you must remember trying at kissing him, telling him you would like him to take you to bed and show you the tricks of his sex, that you would have him do what he would with you...'

As she spoke the words, the memories came back so hauntingly clear that I had thought myself gone quite mad. Whatever had I done? 'Mariella, can you give me Mr Richards' direction, I think I must...give him my apologies.'

'Well, the clerk must have it somewhere for he sent out all the invitations. I will go and ask him. But, do you think that is a good idea, to go to him now?'

I did not think it a good idea at all, and even if I had, I was in no fit state to journey to the London address she later supplied me with, in search of answers, less still, chance being seen in the light of such precariousness.

WHEN WE GOT HOME, I prayed my parents would still be in their chambers so I could take a moment to compose myself before I faced them. I was about to give them the news they had longed for, and yet it was tainted with doubt as I replayed Sheldon's accusations over Mr Richards, which at the time seemed so outrageous, but had since grown in ambiguity with each little memory or reminder of what went on last night. But once Grantley relieved us of our pelisse's and bonnets, before I could make excuse, I found myself pushed through the breakfast room door to present my news to Mama and Papa who were sat at the table, chatting over tea and plum cakes, and I realised that through their eyes, the world remained unchanged.

'Good morning Mother, Father,' I greeted them as nonchalantly as I could manage and forced my mouth into a smile.

'My dear, you are home early,' Mother frowned and Father followed suit. 'I didn't hear the coach?' she was looking through the morning room windows which gave a reasonable view out to the front of the house.

'We walked the way,' Delores said, coming in behind me.

'Whatever would you walk for?'

'It was a shorter walk than the waiting for the groom to have the coach ready at this hour and we were in a rush.'

My father put down his cup and my mother's eyes brightened with anticipation.

I took a seat opposite and Mary set me a place.

'I thought we mightn't expect you 'till after church my dear, is everything well?'

I cleared my throat. 'Yes of course,' I lied.

'Very well indeed!' Delores added and I could see her bursting with the need to relieve herself of the account. 'Eleanor brings news.'

'Oh, I say?' Mama sat up straight.

I cleared my throat as their eyes settled on me. 'Sheldon came to me today.'

'And, what did he say?'

'They are engaged!' Delores clapped her hands together and I was glad she relieved me of the need.

'Oh, Mr Ashlyn! What happy news! I told you, did I not?' Mama exclaimed, sitting up taller: Peacock like now.

'Very happy news indeed Eleanor, I congratulate you,' my father said and even though I could see the satisfaction behind his gaze, I knew I could rely on him at least not to fuss and flap around as Mama and Delores had begun to in exaggerated congratulations.

'Well, only this morning, Papa agreed to us holding our own ball in three weeks' time. Now, I think it must be an engagement party! What an occasion, but so much to do.' Her eyes were wide, begging to be asked the details, but her own excitement too impatient to allow an adequate pause.

'Oh, I don't think we need to go to all that trouble, Mama?' I replied with as great an effort as I could conjure. I reached for the coffee pot and busied myself with buttering some bread although I had no appetite now. I had expected her to be puffed up with excitement but I had such a pounding head I had no patience with it.

'It is no trouble at all. If my daughter is about to come the next Viscountess Elmbridge, I say there is every need, and no end to the trouble we are willing to take to celebrate such an occasion in a manner befitting it. We are to hire the dancing Maestro, isn't that right, Henry?' she probed for confirmation, catching her breath.

'Yes dear, if you like,' he said.

'What say you to this Mr Richards? I had thought of asking him to play for us, he is rather exceptional, but what with all this bad business about his family, well I just don't know.'

'Mr Richards?' I looked up from my plate.

'Hmm.' I watched her scrawl a question mark next to his name.

I finished up my cup of coffee and went upstairs before I could be drawn into any further arrangements for the party that I did not want, for the engagement I had made thinking myself innocent of all charges and now...now I was not so sure.

Then I remembered my journal. I dropped my reticule upon the bed and rushed over to the escritoire and pulled it from its hiding place beneath the table top. I was sure I had last had my menses around the middle of the month. I remembered it particularly because it came on our departure from London and I was most inconvenienced by the fact. I thumbed through the pages to find the correct entry: June sixteenth, two weeks ago. Then I lifted up my skirts to examine the belt and check I had not imagined it. Beyond the mildest dry stain, there was nothing else to note. If I was not on my menses which stood to reason, then there was only one other reason why I should bleed from such a place and the prospect made me so ill, I had to go to my bed and lie down before I fell down.

I ran the events of the night through my head again and no matter how much I willed the memory to return to me, the gaps to be filled, the doubts quelled, I could only find more and more questions forming. Was it possible; could it be that Mr Richards took me up on my lewd suggestions? I could not believe it of him for a second and yet, I knew he had a tendré for me. Would he really have been so savage as to seize such an opportunity? Or was it my own being so fast, being so inebriated and so angry with Sheldon that I induced him to comply with it? I could not answer to any of it, but there was one person who could, and somehow, I would have to find a means of asking him.

I sent an express out to his rooms in London but, later that day, the return came back to say he was out of town. At first, I hoped he may have took a room in the Greyhound or the Harrow for the purpose of the party last night, but my inquiries there also returned empty. Either Mr Richards had boarded the night in some other place and not yet returned home, or, he had returned home and gone away again all in the same day. I could not help but wonder if his purpose was to escape my questions or the scandal of my remembering. Although I did not remember at all, and this was the rub.

In the gaps of despairing over Richards and tolerating Mama and Delores' excited flapping, I slept away the hours. I felt ill: of mind and body. I did not know if it was the drink or the distress. Only that I felt an insatiable need for rest and escape.

I FELT ONLY SLIGHTLY improved the next day, and when I was summoned from my bed on account of Lord Elmbridge and Sheldon being arrived to deal in the business of the marriage contract, I wanted to vanish into another realm altogether. I was not ready to see Sheldon again so soon. It was hard enough to contain the disparity between my anger and acceptance, and now the very real prospect that his suspicions about Richards might not be so unfounded after all. It was all too much.

'They are out shooting in the park with Papa presently,' Mama said, standing over me in the bed and petitioning me out of it. 'But I have instructed the kitchen to have a nuncheon set out for their return. What is wrong? You look tired. Watts, some lotions and salts I think. Come, come, we want to be ready; they will be back soon.'

I took as long as I could reasonably manage in getting ready with a flustered Watts trying to work double time on me. I needed to buy time to think, to train myself in how to act without giving away my doubts, to prepare answers for questions he may yet throw at me. But once I had exhausted my excuses of 'it's too tight,' 'it's the wrong colour,' 'too heavy,' 'too formal,' and just about every other thing I could think of, I looked at the pile of dresses mounted on the bed and decided I didn't much fancy going through it all again any more than Watts.

Something had died inside me now and it included the affection I once held Sheldon in. What had killed it exactly; his betrayal or the potential of my own? Perhaps just the prospect of marching down the aisle with such burdens and deceit to take into our marriage. Whatever it was hung over me gravely and his impending presence only exacerbated the feeling. If I was to keep up such pretences without faltering, I would need to keep my distance from him until the wedding day and yet all the freedom and opportunity were now poured upon me to do precisely the opposite. I picked up my bonnet and dismissed a disgruntled Watts before making my way down.

But my timing couldn't have been worse, or better in Mother's view, judging by the look of relief on her face as I took my seat at the table on the front lawns. The men were emerging through the trees in the distance, guns hanging at their sides, the dogs racing a little ahead of them.

'There, you look much better, my dear,' she smiled at the sight of me. 'Take up your fan, dear,' she shoved it into my hand. 'And try to look...pleasing,' she said, patting her own curls into place and re-adjusting her parasol.

I did as I was told and held in a sigh. I knew what was coming and could see no way to avoid it. I watched the servants at work around the large summer table; folding napkins and checking the shine of the glasses. When I turned back, the men had walked half the journey and were only minutes away. I looked at Sheldon, his head was shining with sweat and his cravat was loose around his neck, his braces pulling his shirt in tight about the centre of his chest so that it was hard to deny he cut a good figure. I should know it by now, I had seen him half naked after all. But my reluctance had never been based on his looks; in truth, I had been blind to them so long that I wondered how I had not seen before how handsome he was. A part of me wished we could go back to such innocence. Return to the time before all this bad business had ensued.

'Bess!' I put down my fan and bent over to pet the dog as she ran to my feet.

'Really Eleanor!' Mama said exasperated.

'There's a good girl, Bess,' I ignored Mama and carried on stroking the scruff of her neck. She wagged her tail and panted before shaking out a torrent of yellow hairs all over me. Pretending not to hear mother gasp, I fed Bess the remains of the plum cakes from the table with one hand and patted the hairs out with the other.

'Gentlemen,' my mother transformed her disapproving face into a smile.

'Ladies, good morning,' Sheldon and his father greeted us. Papa was busy offloading their guns to the gamekeeper and calling the dogs to heel. I gave Bess a final pat as she departed and looked up to see Sheldon stood over me, his fair hair pushed messily aside, his face bright, beaming at me. He certainly seemed better rested than at our last meeting.

'Good day Lord Elmbridge, Mr Elmbridge,' I said to them both with my best conjured smile.

'It is indeed,' he said more pointedly and did not break his gaze even when I found it uncomfortably lingering.

'I thought you might be hungry after your exertions; I arranged a spot of nuncheon,' mother said flipping a blasé hand towards the summer table which I knew she had gone all out in arranging.

'You are very generous, Lady Ashlyn,' said Lord Elmbridge. 'Let us get cleaned up and we will join you forthwith.'

I watched them walk away and relaxed again.

'What on earth is wrong with you today girl?' Mama said behind her fan when they were out of earshot.

I hid my hands in my lap. 'Nothing, I feel I might be coming down with something,' I said quickly.

'I don't know, you have always had such a strong constitution, but lately you have been so unlike yourself. Perhaps you are not eating well enough, I thought you seemed to have lost a little weight. I will have Cook put you on a fortifying diet until the wedding: that should solve it.'

I agreed for the peace of it.

When the men returned, we removed to the large table and sat opposite one another. I could feel his gaze upon me as I ate. The prattling and inconsequential talk rattling off of everyone's tongues but mine. My mother was particularly vocal and I supposed Lady Elmbridge's absence and Delores being out to town to be fitted for her own wedding gown this morning made it all the more resounding.

I had hardly spoken a word nor paid much attention, but I put in the occasional nod or: "Hmmm, oh yes." And had, for the most part, ensured I kept my mouth so full with food or drink that I did not leave myself open to much beyond that. It was only when Mama brought up the subject of our wedding journey that I renewed my interest in it.

'Any thoughts on where you might spend it?' she said to Sheldon.

'Wherever would please Miss Ashlyn will be agreeable to me.'

I put down my glass and smiled. 'Well, I think you must be tired of travelling Mr Elmbridge after your tour. Perhaps we might think of somewhere not too much out of the way,' I said to attempt to cull the topic. I knew that we would soon be faced with the solitude of each other's company and since it was the first opportunity we had had to speak privately at length, I would broach the subject then, use it to fill the space as a substitute for the topics I wanted to avoid. I had thought the scenario through several times, yet when he invited me to take a turn with him once we had finished our meal: I knew I was no better prepared for it. We walked down to the lake which I was glad of since I could feel my mother's eyes on me until we reached the woodland and were out of sight.

'It is a beautiful day, is it not?' he stopped.

'Yes, it is,' I hadn't noticed.

'El.' He turned to me but I kept my gaze low and did not meet his eyes. 'I know I am far from forgiven in your mind despite all the arrangements, but I promise you, I will earn it.'

'You are. I told you it is quite forgotten.'

He looked at me incredulously and leaned in to kiss me. His lips were light upon mine and I did not wish to encourage it beyond that, so I did little more than oblige him.

He pulled back to look at me. 'Oh El, is it really so bad you can no longer bear my kisses?'

'Of course not.'

He walked away from me and then turned around and walked back again. 'Damn it, El, I am not a foolish man and neither a stranger to you, so please speak plainly.'

'Very well, I may need a little time, to forget the memory,' I said quickly, preferring him to think that was the cause of my reluctance than the alternative. 'I'm sorry. I am trying. It's just hard to remove the image from my head.'

'I understand,' he said more kindly now. 'I will be patient if that is what you need. But know this,' he held my chin up so I had no choice but to meet his gaze, 'I love you, El, you and you alone, and you have made me the happiest man in England accepting me. I promise you, whatever it takes, ours will be a happy marriage and this will soon be forgotten. If you love me, then it can be overcome. Do you still love me, Eleanor?' he paused to allow me the opportunity to answer but I could not.

When the silence lingered too long, I forced the words from my mouth. 'Of course, I do.'

He smiled and kissed me on the nose. 'Then let us look ahead to happier times. Starting with where you would like to journey for our honeymoon. I recall you had a wish to go to Edinburgh for the festival?'

I had so many wishes now, but none I could dare to speak of. 'Yes,' I nodded.

'LADIES, WHAT A SURPRISE,' I greeted Betsy, Anna, and Beth when I joined them in the drawing room after being brought news of their call.

'Miss Ashlyn—or should I say—soon to be Lady Elmbridge?' Betsy smirked, and I managed a chuckle to throw her off the scent of my true feeling. If anyone would likely see through me and detect it, it would be her.

'Well, let us not put the carriage before the horse. We are barely engaged and yet I see the news has reached you.'

'True, but you cannot expect it to stay quiet when your mama is so very vocal. Anyway, you see we come ahead of the pack. We were eager to offer our congratulations first.'

That's why you are here. You wanted to jump the queue to claim your position of attendance before the others. 'You will take tea?' I offered serenely.

They nodded and I had Mary pour it for us before dismissing her.

'So, has the date been set?' Anna said, and I could see her hunger for the details of it all, but I had no desire to recount them.

'Yes. The negotiations are done, the announcement to follow.'

'Well, congratulations. We all knew it was coming but you certainly like to keep us all suspended in the wait, you devil!' Betsy's tone was light, playful, but her meaning was clear.

'Well, I supposed it was time to give everyone a change of subject on-dit.'

'You certainly have, and not a moment too soon. I had begun to worry you might have strung it out a little *too* long,' she admitted.

'Well, you know me Bets, I hate to be predictable, but no harm done.'

'No,' Beth said quickly.

Always the pacifier, I thought, but her reassurance was comforting. If there was any hint of a whisper about Richards and I in circulation, I could certainly rely on them to know it, and since they did not, I felt assured that Mariella had kept my confidence. I lifted my teacup to my lips but couldn't stomach it.

'But you have certainly ruffled a few of the old dame's feathers,' Betsy continued. 'Although little you need care for it now.'

'Yes, I see that. I had the pleasure of bumping into Mrs Colborne paying Mama a call this morning and she made no secret of the fact.'

'Hmmm, well no matter, you are above it now whether she likes it or no.'

If only I was. I still had the small matter of convincing Sheldon of my virginity to attend to, so in the scheme of things, it offered little consolation.

'So, what are the plans?' Anna leaned forward in her chair.

'We are to visit St. James' next week to book the hour, but our mama's have it in mind for the twenty-seventh of July presently, to coincide with the start of the coronation events. She thought it best to pick a time when society was already headed back to London and besides, there are so many wedding dates now, she had to have a care to navigate around them so as to not step on any other toes.' Their eyes lit up with excitement. *A wedding to look forward to and me out of the way within a single season.*

'You waste no time then: Probably for the best under the circumstances,' Anna smirked.

I nodded. It had not been my decision, but in the light of all that had since passed I realised it for the best. *I had no time to spare.* The long engagement I had made Sheldon promise, was overthrown with my assent in favour of the quickest possibility, now I knew how urgent the situation.

'So have you decided on any of the *other* arrangements yet?' Betsy said carefully.

Specifically the bridesmaids? I wanted to sigh.

No, not yet, but they are underway. You shall be the first to know when the matters are finalised.'

Betsy smiled widely at this and Anna looked a little put out.

Yes, you have got what you came for, now you can leave.

Improvising.

30th June 1821. - Mariella.

'Is it time?' Giles said when I pulled him into my chamber.

'No. It is all gone disastrously wrong! I need your help, nothing is running to plan. Mr Richards is next door with her now and she will not let him leave.'

'Be calm —panic will get you nowhere.'

'But it is all gone to ruin Giles, all my hard work.'

I could see from his slightly clenched jaw and the way he bit down on the corner of his lower lip that this was not an option in his mind, anymore than in mine. 'Mr Richards you say?' he frowned and I hushed him for fear we might be heard through the wall.

'Do not trouble me for explanations now. We have no time to spare or all will be lost and there won't be another shot after this. Suffice to say, she was falling all over the place and he carried her up for me and now she is all over him. You must think of how to get rid of him, Giles and quickly, before she is noticed missing.'

He stood quietly contemplative and his docility was almost enough to send me into despairing sobs. Then he said, 'What if, we do not get him to go?'

'What?'

'Well, you said yourself she was all over him, and he is far from indifferent to her. Maybe if you leave them alone long enough, they will bring off quite the perfect scene without our interference?'

I considered the implications a moment. 'What, and have Delores force Richards into making her an offer?'

'I very much doubt that; I mean from what we know of him, he has neither money nor birth to recommend him. I'm sure with him as the alternative choice—'

'Yes, I see: That's it!' I said clapping my palms together at this stroke of genius. 'I shall seek out Sheldon now and it will be enough to cause him to retract his offer instantly. He is already jealous of Richards and suspicious of him, so I'm sure he will not require too much coaxing . But what if Richards does not take the opportunity? He gives her the brush off. I own I know it's only for decency's sake, but still, if he does not give in to temptation then however improper he should be found there, it is not enough proof...'

'He does not have to, does he? So long as Elmbridge is adequately suspicious. All you need to do is make sure the right kind of scene awaits them. Get him to help you undress her for bed or some such thing, then make excuse to leave them: That is the precise point to have them discovered.'

I was not certain it could be made to work, but I saw the merit in trying at turning this misfortune to our advantage. Besides, with Giles out of the picture, should there be any matters of honour or duels arising, they would now be offered in Richards' direction. 'Very well, now, go to my maidservant and tell her to bring me a purging draught. I must keep her from falling into oblivion too soon. If she carries on with the kind of speeches she is making to him, Sheldon will not fail to get the measure of things in an instant. But she is close to passing out.'

WHEN GEETA CAME TO find me, I was ear-pressed against the wall with a carafe listening in on them for a sign of mischief. I had heard nothing for a while and hoped that such silence signalled the right moment, calculating Giles would be well on his way to the basement bell board by now. I was to ring from my room as a signal that he must bring Delores and Sheldon up instantly with a concern for Eleanor's inelegant state. I needed only to take a peek to see how things were progressing and give Geeta the nod to return to my room and set the bell off, for I had only cut the cord to the one in her chamber.

However, when I opened the door the slightest crack to get a view, I did not expect to come upon the image of a sleeping Eleanor cradled in Mr Richards' arms much like a child would be cradled by a nursemaid. Foolish man! I was about to close it again when the floorboards creaked and he looked up in my direction.

'Miss Craythorne, at last!' he said and I had no choice but to come into the room and feign attendance upon them. 'Is she better?' I asked gently.

'Yes, I think so,' Mr Richards answered looking up momentarily as he stroked her hair. 'She has been asleep for a while now, though she is fidgety and fretful at times.'

'Mr Richards, you are very good for taking care of her: I am so grateful to you.' I turned to close the door shut behind me, offering Geeta a glance that signalled she must not pull the bell, leaving her outside in the hall, in wait for such a moment I may give the signal. It was certainly not this one: Such a scene would not do to be discovered; it seemed more akin to something from a sickbed gathering than a site of improper passions. Whilst his presence could be considered inappropriate at best, there could be nothing indecent construed from it. Not when he could explain it all away so satisfactorily.

'Mr Richards, will you help me put her to bed?' I have sent my maid to bring a purging draft but I do not think it would do any good to wake her now she is at last peaceful.'

He stared at me strangely. 'I do not think that is something I should assist in; where are your servants? There seems to always be enough of them about until you want one.'

'Coming soon: the party delays them and the bell pulls are broken in some of the rooms, so it is as ill-timed as you can imagine. But if you could at least help me to convey her to the bed, I will manage the rest myself.' This he could surely not refuse.

'Very well,' he agreed and lifted her a fraction from his shoulder to shuffle up in his seat. 'But then I really must be off.'

'Yes, we have detained you long enough I fear.' I helped him ease her off of him as much as necessary so he could slide out from beneath her lolling weight, then I went over to the bed to pull back the covers so we could lower her into it smoothly. If she was to be found beneath the covers, it would certainly add to the ambiguity of the scene. I went back to the chaise and bent down with him to heave her into his outstretched arms, but she was a dead weight now and flopped all over the place as I attempted to roll her onto her side to better manoeuvre her. It was then the plan came undone: Eleanor broke out in a coughing fit, proceeded by an aggressive bout of vomiting that we were not well poised to avoid. We were both alarmed as the streams of vomit projected violently from her, whilst she lolled about, semi-conscious of the fact. 'Get a bowl,' shouted Mr Richards as he forced her to sit up enough through her involuntary sputtering about.

I took the bowl from the washstand to catch the remainder of the onslaught, too late to spare the carpet or any of our clothes.

'It's alright, you will feel better for it,' Mr Richards comforted her, sweeping her hair from her face and soothing her with lulling tones which seemed to settle her again. 'I think you must get her a doctor,' he said more gravely.

'For being too much in her cups, sir; how well do you think that will go with her family?'

'She is ill. Look at her colour.'

'She is foxed. This will improve her, like you said.' The last thing I needed was for him to go running about downstairs calling out an emergency. Besides, once Geeta had given her the charcoal draught, she would soon settle down. On that thought, I went back to the hall and whispered to her to go and fetch it, pretending at using the bell pull in another room where it was working. She went off immediately and soon came back with it prepared. We were both grateful when this came to pass. Eventually, the vomiting subsided and she was roused enough to take a glass of charcoal water, before slipping back into sleep.

It was only then, reassured that there was no more serious emergency requiring me to alert anyone else, that I considered what could be done now to recover the plan. I looked about the room, all the carpet and our clothes covered in vomit. Eleanor in an agitated slumber and Mr Richards looking gravely concerned, that I saw there was no hope in pursuing this line. I would have to get rid of him altogether and manage this myself.

I had Geeta open up the doors that connected to my chamber and had Mr Richards help me carry her through to it. No one would be convinced of anything beyond the truth having occurred in a room carrying the stench of vomit and all of us covered in it.

The servants, who had finally appeared at the sound of the commotion, set about the task of cleaning up the mess in the guest room and tending to Eleanor in concert, and I decided that Mr Richards' services were of no further use. He was only a hindrance now to my newly forming idea. I must get rid of him and quietly. I offered him the use of my dressing room to clean up in and had Geeta relieve him of his jacket, which had taken the worst of the offence. 'She will see to it, you freshen up in there.' Whilst the servants saw to bringing him up a washbowl and cloths, I went through his jacket and took from his pocket a handkerchief with his initials embroidered into the hem and slid it into my bodice. *All is not lost.*

He did not notice it missing when he returned from the dressing room looking fresher, and thanked her when Geeta returned a cleaner jacket to him than he had left it, a few damp patches still drying, the only clue. 'Well, you will need to send it to be laundered when you go home, but the worst of it is done. Although Mr Richards, if you are returning to the party, perhaps I can offer you some of my brother's cologne to disguise the smell?'

'Thank you: No. That won't be necessary. I think I will go straight home.'

This relieved me from the effort of orchestrating this part of the plan—he would need to seem to be missing for a good deal of time if his whereabouts was to be called into question to corroborate my tale. 'Mr Richards, did you drive here?'

'No, I came by hack.'

'Then you will let me have you conveyed home in our coach. Ameet, come here, will you?' I summoned him a manservant to make the arrangements for him.

'No need to trouble yourself on my account.'

'Not at all, Mr Richards; it is the least I can do after all your assistance tonight in this unfortunate business. Go with Ameet, he will take you back down the servants' staircase so you can avoid the bombardment of Elmbridge's questions; he accosts my servants relentlessly to know the whereabouts of you both. My father's valet holds him back from coming up and finding out for himself.'

'Does he indeed. Well, perhaps I should go and explain the case to him and settle his concerns.'

'Do you think it wise, sir? Mr Elmbridge does not seem like the kind of fellow one would want to be on the worse side of. I mean, I know you have been nothing beyond the perfect gentleman, but he—'

'All the more reason to have the business out with rather than let his suspicions grow wild.'

'Well, I hope you are good with your pistols, sir, I hear he is quite the shot and not shy of offering a man out upon his honour.' This bluff I hoped did not run contrary to his character, I hardly knew enough of him to guess, although it seemed to me just the kind of fluff men like Elmbridge would see fitting to such circumstances.'

He was thoughtful and his gaze wondered over to Eleanor where she sat slumped in the dressing chair with half a dozen maids supporting her limbs whilst the other half dozen sponged and pawed at her with cloths and towels. She was down to her shift now and he turned about at the notice of the detail.

'Her colour looks a little better does it not?' he said and I nodded. 'Perhaps you might set Mr Elmbridge right on matters. It has been a long enough night.'

I smiled approvingly. 'You may rely upon it. Now, sir, let me not detain you further. I think the maids are quite ready to undress her now. Go along with Ameet, then instruct the groom to convey you to your address. The rest you may leave in my hands.'

'That is very good of you: I thank you, Miss Craythorne.' He turned at the door, 'You will send word to me tomorrow, and tell me how she does?'

'If you desire me to, sir. Leave your direction with the groom and I will send a note.'

'Much obliged.'

'But I think Mr Richards, Eleanor will be quite horrified by these events in the morning when her senses return—perhaps you might spare her the embarrassment of happening upon you again, for long enough to forget it a little.'

'Yes, yes of course.'

'I trust our secret is quite safe?'

'It is. I would never do anything to harm, Miss Ashlyn; you have my word.'

When at last he was gone, I directed Geeta to clear my chamber of all the other servants. I wanted no more witnesses about than necessary. When she returned, we struggled between us to convey her to the bed. 'Come now little princess, time for slumber,' I said lifting her up from the pillow enough for Geeta to undress her. Save the odd mumbled complaint at being disturbed, she seemed much better settled and lolled around oblivious as we stripped her down.

'Geeta, how quickly can you have her dress made good?'

'By morning madam.'

'No, that won't do. You must bring it back tonight; just deal with the vomit patches and fragrance it. And when you go down, have Barton bring up a bottle of wine and two glasses, being sure to pass Mr Elmbridge's notice on his way. Oh, and bring some pigs blood too if you can find it.'

Unintended consequences.

July 1821. - Eleanor.

As the days passed with more exhausted options and no progress, it begun to dawn on me quite seriously now, that Mr Richards had fled and there was only one reason I could think of to have caused it. He had lay with me that night, whether by my design or his. No more bleeding had come to substantiate any hope that my menses were to blame, nor any explanatory memory to discredit the encounter. And whilst coming to terms with this, I was still acclimatising to my engagement to Sheldon and the horror of him discovering on our wedding night, the truth of the matter. I could not bear the thought and yet it was only when Mariella reminded me of a possibility even worse than this that I realised just what a terrible fix I was in.

'I mean, so long as you are not with child, it is possible you could trick him into thinking you are Virgo intacta,' she had suggested when I relented in giving her the whole. She was the only person I could afford to, for anyone else would scold or disown me for the very possibility.

'With child?' I was astounded. 'Surely not, not just the once and on the first attempt I—'

'Well, once is all that is required. I suppose you will have to sit out the wait to be sure.'

'Good grief, Mariella!' I got up and crossed the room. I suddenly seemed unable to sit still in the chair. 'Whatever will I do?'

'I suppose you must abandon Mr Elmbridge and marry Mr Richards if it is as bad as that.'

'I do not want to marry him,' I said defensively.

'Well, I do not see what else is to be done; if you tell Mr Elmbridge, he will cry off, and Mr Richards will have no choice but to marry you to reduce your family scandal to one of an embarrassing match over one of a ruined daughter!'

I peered out of the window, taking in her words and all the harsh reality they gave birth to. 'I cannot marry, Mr Richards. My mother would never forgive it; she would disown me.'

'Then the only other choice you have is to marry Sheldon quickly, before the pregnancy gives you away. Then the child can be a well-timed wedding night miracle!'

'Mariella, you astonish me. I could not deceive an innocent man into thinking him a father to a child that is not his own. How cruel a trick!'

'Well, unless you think he will marry you with the knowledge of the pregnancy, then I cannot see what can be done?'

'Impossible, he is the heir of Elmbridge.'

'Yes, I see the difficulty. If you are carrying a boy, it will become his heir. How can he do his duty if the child is not his own blood?'

'Surely, if I was with child, there would be some sign of it by now?'

'Not after a week. Perhaps after a few you might become sick?'

I thought back to Harriet and how sick and poorly she was in her confinement. Mama and I had gone to Kent to sit up with her through the worst of it. If I was anything like my sister, I would not be able to hide the fact for long. 'I must find a physician who will see me privately and conduct an exam.'

'Oh, I see, I thought you meant to remove the pregnancy.'

I looked up. 'You think it could be done?'

'Well, I would not trust a doctor to the task, too many ghastly stories in that business even if you could find one willing. But in India, the midwives have a special medicine they can give you to take each day until the job is done. I have not heard of any ill effect to this remedy. But we are not in India.'

'What about your Indian maidservant?'

'Geeta? Well, I own she is a wonder with most things but this, I am not sure it is in her knowing.'

'But you could ask her?'

WHEN SHE CAME THREE days later with a pungent smelling liquid dispersed into several vials, I at last found some hope that this may not end so ill after all. That was until the sickness began and my menses failed to arrive punctually another week later and then I realised: unless this draft was effective, it was all ruined.

'How long will it take for this medicine to do its work, Mariella? I am so very sick I fear I will not be able to hide the matter for much longer.'

'So, it is as we feared. Oh, my Eleanor, I am so sorry for you!'

'I don't need your sympathy! I need your help...please.'

'But what is to be done? The draft should have done its work by now; I'm sure of it. Unless, unless we were too late beginning it? Or the ingredients perhaps, I know she could not obtain them all here and improvised a little.'

'Then a doctor, Miss Craythorne. You must help me to find one of those doctors or midwives who can end this by other means.'

'Eleanor, even if we could find one without attracting any suspicion, these matters are so perilous, you could die if it all goes ill—'

'I think I shall die anyway if I cannot! What life of poverty and disgrace will I have to bear as wife to Mr Richards or living out a lie with Sheldon knowing it is not his child? The wedding is less than a couple of weeks away. Oh, what a terrible mess! What can be done but try to find a willing doctor?'

'There is one thing...but nay you would never hear it,' she said shaking her head.

'What Mariella? I will hear anything if it can help.'

'Well, if you cannot marry Sheldon and you will not marry Mr Richards, perhaps you could find a husband neither so high the heir issue will be nothing to answer, nor so low it brings such disgrace and ruin to your family.'

'And where exactly do you think I will find such a man, woo him in time and still come out of this well?'

'There is someone, I can think of.'

'Who?'

'My stepbrother.'

I laughed out loud at this.

'I know he would not be an ideal choice in your mind, but I do know him a good sort of man and he has no title to trouble himself with the issue of the child's father, but he does have all the comforts you could expect, and even though your family may not be thrilled with the connection, I am sure they would much prefer it over the alternative...'

'You have gone quite mad, gull your own brother!'

'No, not gull him. Simply put the matter to him openly.'

'And why ever would your brother wish to do me such a service, knowing the circumstances! A ruined bride and a bastard child!'

'Yes, it is a great deal to ask of anyone...but I know my brother, and I know he thought well of you. He is not for the folly of marriage in the usual sense; he is married to his work. But he is a practical man and wishes to do his duty and make a good connection.'

'You are actually serious.'

'Well, unless you have a brighter idea, or are resolved to Mr Richards.'

'You truly believe that if I was wild enough to permit you to entrust this knowledge to your brother he would actually consider it; for the sake of a connection?'

'I own, I may have to use my influence a little to bring him about, but once he has considered the matter practically, I cannot see what he would trouble himself with. He is not the romantic or sentimental type, so a good match so simply arranged would spare him the efforts of my family trying to match-make on his behalf, which he cannot bear. Besides, he is still disappointed over

Martha. Bertie swept her quite away from his notice and he hasn't made any effort to look to anyone else since. I think he would be happy to settle things quickly before he disappears abroad again, knowing his wife could oversee the estate in his absence. Like I said, he has no title to pass on so it would not be such a travesty should you bear a boy. Although I own, he will want sons of his own, but what better assurance of having some knowing before his wedding night, that his wife can do her duty?'

I did not know who was the more insane, her for formulating such ideas or me for taking heart in the possibility that I could be saved from either extremity of my alternatives. 'Miss Craythorne, what sort of man is your brother, I own I do not know much about him at all?'

'A straightforward kind I suppose, he has little time for anything beyond his business or sports, so I can't pretend he will be much about you. But he would install you very prettily indeed and do his duty. He has plenty of money and he is not ungenerous with it.'

I had not disliked him precisely, but I could not pretend to have found his company at all diverting. But bear him, over all the calamities...if he was much away, how well this might suit me, left much to my own devices. Mama would dislike it but she would be practical if she knew what was at stake and Father, so long as everything was settled well, would forgive me it, in the end. 'And you, you could bear my marriage to your own brother after all the folly that has passed between us?'

'Yes, if it would spare you calamity, then yes, I can. You are my dearest friend; so it a sacrifice I will be happy to make. Besides, we will be family.'

This disturbed me more than the prospect of wedding her brother. Would she think that having done me such a service, I would be forever in her debt and my gratitude know no bounds? Would she use her position as my 'relative' to dangle after me? I should rather marry Mr Richards. 'Miss Craythorne, I am very grateful for your pains on my behalf, but I cannot consent to this scheme, however kindly thought. It is not fair to Mr Craythorne. I must find another way to...'

'I see. Well, don't be hasty Eleanor, think about it. You have time yet.'

Did I? I was sure that it would not be long before Watts went to Mama with her concerns of finding me at the sick bowl, there was only so far my petty bribes could endure in a matter this grave. The vials, although I had taken them steadfastly, were running low and the prospect of any hope in that direction fading fast.

I HAD REVERSED MY DECISION several times by the evening, interspersed with the idea of making a wild attempt at seduction with Sheldon before our wedding, and even reconsidering Mr Richards' circumstances. His prospects were poor, but my dowry was good, and I liked him at least.

We were at the Elmbridge's tonight for a celebratory party in honour of our engagement. Mama had lost out to the Viscountess as host in this, but was to have the Wedding breakfast, which went some way to placating her despite the elaborate plans she had long been arranging. Toasts were raised, smiles and well wishes at every turn and I did my best to play the blushing bride-to-be as inside I crumbled with doubt and despair. Even as I filled my dance card that night, I considered all my partners for the position. Would any of them prove a better alternative to Richards or deceiving Sheldon?

Mr Vane was so indifferent a character and known to be such a rake that I could perhaps bear delivering such a deceit to him without great conscience. But nay, however much I could ignore his rakish pursuits, his drinking and gambling would not be so easy to disregard. Mr Fortescue was of the gentry, genteel enough to not be thought vulgar even if below me, but too much a man of virtue to commit such an act against him. Then there was Mr Seymour, who I supposed would be similarly disposed as her brother; practically minded but instead of being consumed in trade, was equally compelled in Westminster: This would certainly prove the better bargain to my papa, but I disliked his opinions so much that I did not think we would go along easily.

I looked about the hall; every other eligible bachelor was either too young and skittish to seriously look to marriage yet, or of title and in need of an heir. There was of course old Mr Willmott, I entertained the thought for a brief moment and scolded myself for even permitting the thought. Could it really be true that my need of him was now greater than Martha's? She soon to be married and for love, to all our surprise. Wilmott would not live a long life, but I knew I could not endure the prospect of sharing a bed with a man of his years, however short lived. And it was this mental torment, going back and forth and round again that I think was to blame for inducing me to do what I did then.

Sheldon and I had escaped the party after the dances and took a private walk along the park. Delores was pre-occupied, so lazy she had become since our announcement and regaining mama's affection, she might as well have given me up already. So it was easy to escape her, and now it was known we were a match, no one seemed particularly interested in surveilling us anymore. This newfound freedom had even caused Sheldon to become more daring and steel more than kisses from me when we were safely out of sight. I had not wanted or meant to go for this very reason. The taste of his kisses now was such a very stark reminder of our mutual deceit, they were anything but sweet. Every look and touch seemed tainted by this invisible curse; the one he was ignorant of and I consumed with. But I could not let it show. I had to mediate the disparity between my interior world and exterior façade with more skill than had ever been called upon me to demonstrate. I could not afford to let him suspect anything was anomalous. Even though I feared my sudden forgiveness of the Lady Caroline affair might have caused him suspicion, it had not. With Mr Richards having made what seemed to be a total abandonment of society—that at least, kept him quite out of mind for Sheldon, even if it haunted my daily thoughts. No less, in these private moments where the intimacy I had only weeks ago longed for, was now set at frequent intervals, I struggled hard to play pretend, and yet tonight, I knew I must conduct my best performance yet.

We were sat on the grass by the lake in a woody spot, a balmy night with the warmth of the sun still in the air, despite being a little way past sunset. I was pleased to find no resistance from him when I started kissing his neck and loosening the buttons of his waistcoat. Quite the contrary in fact as I felt his hands roaming the curves of my body without restraint.

'Oh El, you are so beautiful,' he said to me between his laboured breathing that I felt against the back of my neck.

I kissed him more hungrily and felt him yield, the wildness in his touch growing, the exploration of my own expanding. He was on the edge now. I wished to feel the same. Knew I might have if it were not for the hindrance of all that had come to contaminate what was once sacred. I must play along anyway. Find a way through. A way to tempt him to abandon all restraint and take me now, before my wedding night. The thought frightened me as I felt the urgency in his kisses, the feral roaming of his hands. Despite what had passed between Mariella and I, it had ill prepared me for what must pass between a man and woman. I had done it before. I reminded myself and yet I could not remember the slightest detail of how it went with Richards, although I carried the consequence inside of me. Beneath where his hands brushed my body, the evidence lay, hidden for now, but not for long. It was this that propelled me on to bring his hand up and rest it at my bosom. His clammy palm against the skin of my décolleté. His breath ragged.

'You can touch me,' I whispered into his ear. 'I know you want to. I want it too.' It was enough. He stroked and grappled and planted kisses upon my chest. It should have felt nice, I was certain it should. But I could only think of him pawing over Lady Caroline in such a fashion and I had to quell the thought for fear of it bringing me to the nauseous condition I spent much of my days in now. It was not just the thought of where his hands had been, or the rage that inwardly smouldered beneath my acquiescent smiles. It was something far more daunting: The realisation that I was bound to him now and I no longer knew if that was what I wanted. When I thought of Lady Caroline, it reminded me that I did not want to be her a year or two down the line, making desperate petitions to find the satisfaction and comfort my husband could not give me. Of course, I hoped that in time it would prove otherwise. But as I felt him feasting on me, my body unmoved and unresponsive, I could not help but worry I was making a huge mistake.

Nonetheless, as I felt his passion building, I compelled myself to be guided by it and I managed to work down the top of my dress enough to free my breasts from it. I felt the air against them instantly as the boning of my stays pushed them upright from beneath. When I pressed my exposed bosom lightly against his chest, it had the desired effect and surprised him into checking that he had in fact felt my breasts against him. 'Oh Sheldon,' I broke our kiss and sighed the words to encourage him.

His hands were timid now, I knew for my sake, as he cupped me softly with both his hands. It felt odd to have them there and yet I knew I must grow used to it, perhaps even try to enjoy it.

'Have you thought about it, Sheldon, how I look beneath these stitches?' I reached back up for his mouth and tasted the increased appetite on his lips. I put my hand inside his waistcoat and felt for his chest and run my hands over it through his shirt. *Follow my lead, touch me.*

'Is this truly what you want, El?'

'Yes,' I said and replaced his hands that had slipped away. He looked down at them, at me and his expression changed to expose the beast inside him.

He threw his jacket down on the floor and he did not need to ask; I pulled him down upon it, upon me.

'I'm going to hell for this if you cry off and don't marry me, El,' he muttered as he seized me with his hands more firmly than moments ago.

Well, that makes two of us at least. 'I won't cry off,' I said to reassure him. Within moments, his mouth was at my breast, his hands beneath every stitch of muslin as he stroked the length of my thigh, my flanks, my navel, but painfully avoiding the place he must if we were to progress. I tried to encourage him, rolling my hips and letting my body do the pleading. Whilst it was pleading for progression, inside I pleaded for endurance. Neither were answered and so I considered how to move things along. This time, I let my hands do the roaming. I had an idea of what I was looking for but I did not know what to do with it when I felt the stiff bulge beneath the cloth of his breeches. I stroked it pensively, the violence of its strength and size frightened me as I explored it better and I understood the horror *Fanny Hill* described in my novel. What on earth would I do with it now? I paused a moment in the hope he would take over the instruction but instead he pulled my hand away entirely.

'El, stop, stop it,' he said, catching his breath. 'This is too much, too far; let me be gentle with you,' he pleaded and pulled his hands out from the layers of muslin they were entangled in and moved mine away. I supposed I must relent in case it gave way to suspicion that I was not quite as inexperienced as he assumed me. I retreated into kisses, contemplating how I was going to provoke him to completion. I was impressed by his self-control for I could sense his desperation fighting against the tide of his restraint, even though his touch was feather light gentility now. I sighed at these caresses. They felt nice, welcome, and helped me to forget a moment, the objective of this task. 'Touch me everywhere,' I whispered against his mouth. He paused and pulled back to consider me. I wondered how much he could see of me in the moonlight, I could just about make out the shine of his eyes.

'I'm already yours,' I said to encourage him. 'I will soon be your wife.'

He lowered himself back down and shuffled so he was now fully on top of me. I wriggled and parted my knees to make space for him to sink between them. I felt the weight of him there, pressed upon that magic spot and it sent me momentarily dizzy. He was moving against me, I felt the fabric of his clothes pressed into the heat of me and wondered when he would undo his breeches. The thought of this was forbidding, but it seemed the best way: Out here in the night where no sheets were to be inspected to give a clue to my lack of virginity. No way for him to see clearly in the darkness and I could only hope that he could glean no other clue when he entered. Mariella had told me she thought it unlikely, that it took a few occasions to properly yield even once you were fully breeched. I dared not ask how she knew, but I needed her to be right in this. *Everything hung in the balance.*

'Teach me Sheldon, teach me what it is to make love with our bodies,' I said when he had started moving rapidly against me, the friction of the clothes beginning to chafe a little against my delicate skin.

'Soon,' he said still moving. 'On our wedding night.'

'I cannot wait that long,' I said as convincingly as I could muster. 'My body is yearning for you. I can't make it stop.'

He paused suddenly and I thought at first something was wrong but he did not move away. He just laid rigid against me panting as if to steady himself.

'Sheldon?'

'I'm sorry.' He shifted his weight a fraction.

'Open your breeches.'

'Is that really what you want?'

'I want you to soothe all this aching here.' I brought his palm down and pressed it into the heat of me. Instantly I jumped and cried out at the sensation. This was one of the few reactions born of authenticity. But it was not the shock of innocent ignorance he thought it, it was the reminder, the memory.

'My god, you are ready for me,' he said as he stroked me.

'I am.'

He drew up to his knees and started to unbutton himself. I swallowed my fear with the relief of knowing in a few moments, my mission would be complete and my problems behind me. *You can do it. You must bear it.* The promise of normality lay just the other side of this. I might even look forward to our wedding day now. God knows I was tired of being dragged to the houses of every person we knew to announce my engagement whilst trying to prevent myself casting up my accounts between dances. For it all to be over, the worry, the fear of discovery, the turmoil of making impossible decisions. In this one act it would silence them all. This is what I reminded myself when I felt myself shrink in fear at the sight of him unleashing himself and moving back onto all fours above me. His misguided poking at my legs as he struggled to blindly find his way. 'What shall I do? Do you need me to help?' I asked when he seemed to be struggling to find the place.

He shook his head.

'I love you,' I said to him next and since it wasn't meant in earnest but in encouragement, I would have refrained if I had understood the effect it would have.

'Dear god,' he said as if pleading forgiveness and quickly climbed off of me, still panting. 'El, I'm so sorry, you must forgive me,' he said, covering me back up quickly. He was perched on his knees tucking himself away.

'Forgive you? What are you doing? I want you; I want this.'

'If you mean it, El, let me take you back to the house, to my bed.'

I sighed my disappointment and sat up. 'It's too dangerous, we might be discovered. Take me here, take me now.'

'It isn't right.'

'Is it not enough that I am here with you now offering myself to you? How long have you waited Sheldon, to feel me? To know my deepest places?'

He sat contemplatively. I could still see the beast lurking about in the back of his jaded gaze considering the prize for his deviance.

'No, El, this must stop,' his tone was angry and I was too frightened to make a further attempt, so I let him get up to his feet and help me to mine.

'Don't you want me?' was the sudden question upon my lips before I could prevent it. I was immediately embarrassed by it but I knew he had heard it because his face changed.

'El,' he reached for me and I shooed him away. 'Don't be like this. I want you more than anything but not like this, not like—'

'The cheap whores you are used to desecrating,' I finished his sentence for him and began to walk back towards the house. His arm sprung out in front of me to make me stop.

'Stop it, El, we both know you deserve better than this. This is surely not how you envisaged it.'

'Are you sure? Have I not acted well enough the part of the whore to convince you this is perfectly adequate?' I spat at him more violently than I meant to and regretted the outburst instantly. *What was I thinking?*

'El, you don't speak like that; stop it, it does not suit you.'

'I thought you lie with Lady Caroline because you could not have me, and now you can you refuse to...'

'Come here.' He gathered me up in his arms and the greater part of me that needed his embrace gave way to the part that wanted to push him off of me.

'El, please understand; I love you too much to reduce you to this.' He stroked my face. 'On our wedding night, I will take you to my bed and lie with you beneath the softness of the sheets in only our skin before I make love to every part of this beautiful body. But I will not do it before and you must forgive me for losing sight of the matter.'

'The blame is mine.'

'There is no blame. When you are in love, it takes a will of its own and we have both been at its mercy. But now we must compose ourselves and wait for the moment we can enjoy the pleasures of each other in comfort, not amongst the rough ground of the woodland before we are even wed.'

'Alright,' I surrendered.

It was then, in the sobering morning light of how close I had come to being so desperate as to trick Sheldon into a liaison that I might place the pregnancy blame on him, my own shame rose so poignantly to the surface, that the decision was made. I would tell Mariella to petition her brother, and if he agreed, however unlikely it seemed, I would cry off from Sheldon and marry Mr Harper-Craythorne of Beddington. This settled in my mind as the less of all the evils presenting themselves to me. None of them were ideal; none were without their price and none were what I would have hoped for. But I must face the consequences of my actions now. Not gull someone else into such acceptance without their consent. That wasn't who I was. Desperate I had become, yes. Tempted I had become to finding a way out. But, whether by act of circumstance or some other supernatural obstacle, I still had open to me, the choice in how to deal in this. I would do it in as much integrity and honesty as was available to me and would not live out a lie or in perpetual discordance with my own conscience.

If for some mad brained reason Mr Craythorne was amenable to the scheme, if the full transparency of the circumstances was made plain to him, then this, I could live with. This would permit me to sleep at night. What would not, was lying next to Sheldon each night, knowing the pregnancy he would dote upon was not his to celebrate, knowing the child he would take pride in would not be of his blood. He loved me. I knew this. However ramshackle a way he had of showing it; I knew it to be true. To deceive him so cruelly was too much. I realised that now.

The matter that plagued me next was how to break with him. If I told him the truth, I would break his heart and if I could not give him a reason, I would break his heart. The first would have the additional effect of turning him so far against me in understanding my betrayal it would be impossible to bear; the latter would torment him sorely when I wed Mr Craythorne.

'Well, his heart may well break, but at least that he will recover after a time, and marry still and have his own heir,' Mariella said when I gave her my answer and presented her with my next dilemma.

I had not considered it in this light. I was so braced for the effect of him seeing me wed to another that I had not considered how ill I would find the prospect of having to see him wed to someone else too, someone who was not me, someone who would take my rightful place.

'Don't distress yourself so cruelly, Eleanor. By the time he has overcome his heartache and is looking again to his duty, you will be long married, your child protected. And think of the freedom you will own by then.'

'I cannot think of anything to look forward to, you must see how dreadful it all is.'

'Yes, I do. But take comfort. I will go to my brother directly and see if we might settle this.'

'Thank you, Mariella, truly, you are the only one I could turn to in this and you have served me as the greatest friend. No matter what the outcome of your interview, I am grateful for your trying.' It was true. We had a very curious history and our relationship had been anything but smooth. But despite this, at my lowest hour, in my moment of need, it was only her I could turn to and she had not failed me yet.

Where there's a will...

30th June 1821 - Mariella.

Within half an hour everything was in place. I had waited for the servants to finish cleaning the guest chamber before setting the final touches. I had no choice but to leave her in my room now, but there must not be any sign of us having been in her room at all if I was to convince Delores of our alibi, which I was still mulling over. I tucked the corner of a sheet beneath her arms so it was obvious she was naked beneath them from just a glance. Setting out two glasses of wine on the side table, I drained them both to about half and took a moments respite to rehearse my story. I looked about the place: on the floor I had left her shimmy in a heap as if it had dropped from her body and been stepped out of, her spot cleaned dress a few paces farther. I had rustled up the bedding so it was in disarray and even took the trouble to lay upon the bed beside her to leave an imprint in the pillow. 'Eleanor?' I called to test her consciousness. When no reply came and I felt satisfied the scene around the room looked adequately suspicious, I went downstairs to seek out Sheldon.

I saw him lurking at the bottom of the stairs in the main hall as I rounded the last flight and composed myself, accordingly, pretending not to notice him until he came upon me.

'Miss Craythorne, where is Eleanor? Is she well?'

'She is asleep, quite exhausted.'

'But she is alright?'

'Yes; no thanks to you.'

'She told you then.'

'She did not have to. You think I cannot recognise a broken heart when I am left to pick up the pieces of it.'

'Is she recovered?'

'Well, that depends what you mean. If you mean, is she recovering from all the cups she sunk to swallow the pain of your deception tonight: then yes, but as for her heartache, that is a matter I doubt will be so easily remedied.'

'I did not mean to injure her. Damn it, I love her.'

'Well, you have a funny way of conveying the sentiment. But by and by, that is a matter betwixt the pair of you. But if you want my advice; you will leave her well alone and give her time to forget this travesty before making any demands upon her. Now, if you will excuse me, I must find Mr Richards, have you seen him?'

'Mr Richards, whatever for?'

'He left his handkerchief in her chamber and I thought I must return it to him before he goes?'

'What was he doing in her chamber?' he demanded and stepped fully into my path so I could not avoid the question. Little did he know I had no wish to avoid it.

'Helping me convey her upstairs before someone noticed her state!'

'That is most irregular Miss Craythorne, have you people no sense of how things are done? That is a servant's task. What possible reason could you have to permit Mr Richards' conveying her to a bedchamber. I sent the footman like you asked?'

'Mr Elmbridge, I do not like your tone. I had very little choice in the matter since the servant I sent you to call did not come and she was falling up the stairs!'

He looked at me mistrusting, 'Miss Craythorne, I warn you, if you are lying or covering some—'

'Mr Elmbridge, how dare you! We both know the art of lying is better left to your sex!'

'Where is Mr Richards?'

'As I said, I do not know. I presume he must have re-joined the party, but after how vulgarly you spoke to him, I would not be surprised if he decided to leave.'

He narrowed his eyes with suspicion dancing in them. 'And what do you want with him now?'

'To return his handkerchief, he left it in the room.' I held it out as proof and he snatched it from my grasp to examine it.

'Is that blood upon it? Is someone hurt?'

'I do not know, Sir; that is why I am trying to find him. Certainly, Eleanor is well. She was fast asleep when I came back.' It took a moment for the penny to drop before his eyes widened and I felt his fingertips pressing into my arm. 'Do you mean to tell me you left them alone together?'

'You will bruise me, Sir!' I scolded and he let go of me.

'You left them alone?' he repeated his question with half the volume and double the urgency.

'Only whilst I found the servants and went to my maid to have a draught made up.'

'You foolish girl!'

'I could hardly leave her alone in such a state. Besides, she would not let him go. What would you have had me do? You saw the state she was in.'

'I own I cannot believe this. I knew it was mad brained of my parents to accept your sort into our society! How long were you gone?'

I ignored the insult. 'I don't know exactly... Twenty minutes or so. What does it signify: she was quite well when I came back, fast asleep in fact which is a great improvement on how I left her for she was quite hysterical, saying all sorts of odd things to Mr Richards. I own, I do not know what magic he worked upon her but he seems to have quite the winning touch with her and she sleeps soundly now.'

'You will take me to her right now, where is she?' he demanded, resuming his grip upon my arm and urging me back up the stairs.

'Mr Elmbridge! Unhand me at once. I shall not take you! You yourself have just set me down for the very same.'

'This is different, we are to be married.'

Oh, I doubt that now.

'Whatever is the matter?' Lady Caroline came upon us quite without our notice until she slid between us with a perplexed frown upon her face. 'Sheldon?' She gave him a searching glance: 'Let go of her.'

Reluctantly, he did and I rubbed the pressure marks from my flesh.

'This is a private matter Caroline, you need not concern yourself,' he told her in the same acerbic tone he'd used on me.

'You are causing a scene, what has gotten into you?' she said, quite mortified.

I cleared my throat. 'Mr Elmbridge wishes me to convey him to Miss Ashlyn's bedchamber, your Grace. I have told him I cannot.'

'Indeed?'

'Don't look at me like that: I simply wish to ascertain that she is well.'

'Then perhaps you will let me go and spare you the inconvenience?' she offered, although we all knew the object of her real concern.

'Fine, then you will take my valet with you and he will report back to me.'

'Very peculiar of you Sheldon, but very well.'

I led them all up to my room with Mr Elmbridge's valet in tow and opening the door just a crack to find Eleanor still fast asleep, I ushered them in with a finger pressed to my lips to shush them, holding Sheldon back at the door before closing him out. Lady Caroline went straight to the bedside, cast a perfunctory glance over her and headed straight for the door. I had hoped she would pay notice to the clues around the room, but she did not seem to notice or care, and simply went back out and told Sheldon everything was well. It was only when his valet pulled him aside and whispered something to him I could not hear, that he leapt up and charged into the room himself. I took no pains to prevent him at all and was relieved to see the clues did not escape his notice as he lifted the glasses and eyed up the dishevelled bed.

'Whatever are you looking for?' Lady Caroline said, piling in behind us.

He ignored her and lifted Eleanor's shimmy from the heap on the floor and said to his valet: 'Go search the house for Mr Richards at once!'

'Sheldon, what is the meaning of all this?' Lady Caroline crowed about after him in protest. He ignored her still as if oblivious of her shadowing his every move and went over to the bed and lifted the sheets just a fraction to make out her nakedness. His face was a perfect picture of horror and with it came the relief of knowing all my efforts had not gone asunder. *It was done.*

'Who undressed her?' he demanded.

'I own I do not know Mr Elmbridge: I assumed she undressed herself for she was already in bed when I—'

He was so completely stunned that had Lady Caroline not pulled him away and insisted he did not do such un-gentlemanly things as to look at a lady beneath her sheets, I was sure he would have lost his senses entirely and struck me.

'I think, Sheldon, we must go!' She pulled him from the room before he could say another word.

When they were gone, I sank instantly into the nearest chair and congratulated myself that the first part of my plan had succeeded against all the odds. And how odious it had been. How glad I would be when this business was all settled and I could enjoy my just desserts. Heaven knows I had earned it. I took a few moments to reconsider how it had gone and felt certain the cat had been well set among the pigeons. The only thing that could jeopardise it now was Richards' account. Which reminded me that Elmbridge's valet, at any moment would return to his master to tell him Mr Richards could not be found. I got up and decided it was time to seek out Giles and give him a progress report. I charged him with the task of throwing Elmbridge's valet off the scent and finding a means to occupy Mr Richards abroad some place for long enough to escape any questioning. Or worse perhaps, if Sheldon caught up with him and proved as good with his pistols as I had convinced Richards. A few weeks should be adequate to keep both he and Eleanor in the dark for long enough to induce one of them to cry off, after which, it mattered not.

I WAS BUSY IN MY OWN toilette when Lady Caroline knocked at the door an hour later, inquiring after what the cause of all this drama was. 'Mr Elmbridge is so very out of sorts but he will not tell me anything? I own I cannot keep him contained much longer.'

'Lady Caroline, I do not know myself, and it is not my place to say: but he seems very suspicious of Miss Ashlyn and Mr Richards. I have tried to tell him there is nothing to be concerned of, but he will not hear it, you saw for yourself.'

'And you say there is nothing going on, truly.'

'Not to my knowledge, and I have Miss Ashlyn's confidence, so I cannot see how it would be possible.'

When I had bid, a rather perplexed Lady Caroline goodnight, I pulled out the daybed and settled into it. The final phase of my plan meant that I must be there, ready to plant seeds of doubt, the moment she awoke.

The Proposal.

July 1821. - Eleanor.

It took no time at all for Mr Craythorne to pay his call and this left me very little room to reflect too deeply on the details of it. It was perhaps for the best because when I saw him come into the drawing room and take a seat on the sofa opposite me, I could not help but wonder what the less of the evils would be. A ruined woman or a wife to a man I did not know and I did not care for a jot beyond the ordinary.

'Thank you for your visit, Mr Craythorne, it is very good of you to come.'

'It is my pleasure, Miss Ashlyn. I hope you are well?'

'Yes, thank you.'

'I am pleased to hear it. Now, would you permit me to speak openly with you Miss Ashlyn?'

'Yes,' was my answer, however much I stiffened in my seat.

'Then I shall come straight to the point: I am a simple man, I own. I do not possess any great talent for romance or conversation but,' he sat forward and interlinked his fingers, 'I mean to take a wife and set her up as prettily as she would wish. I would like it to be you I can call my wife.'

I cleared my throat. 'I think Mr Craythorne that I must be grateful that you do, for you know the circumstance I find myself in.'

'I do and it is of no consequence to my offer Miss Ashlyn. I had come home to find a wife, although I am told I have made very little effort in the attempt. But it seems we both find ourselves in circumstances that would be well remedied by such a union and beyond that, it would be a great honour to have you as my wife, and to have settled things before I go abroad at the end of July, would be my greatest wish.'

I thought it unlikely it could be managed so soon but was heartened by the idea of his imminent departure. 'Where must you go?'

'To Venice, I have some very important business to attend and I fear I will be gone some months with all the trouble the Ottoman war is causing to trade lines. I hope my absence will not affect your answer, it is not the greatest start to a marriage I expect, but—'

'No,' I said quickly. 'It will not. I would be very happy to accept your offer, Mr Craythorne. I think it will suit us both very well.'

His smile was wide and reached his eyes. 'I am truly honoured.'

'I ask one thing though, if I may.'

'Name it.'

'I would like us not to announce our engagement too soon, if you please. I should like to visit my sisters and let the scandal of all else cool down before we proceed.' I kept even in my tone. 'For you realise Mr Craythorne; that when I cry off from Mr Elmbridge, it will indeed result in a scandal after we have been so much in each others company.' He nodded and I pressed on, 'It would seem a shame, to taint our announcement with the bad business. So, I wonder if we might go about it quietly, to begin at least.'

'I understand.'

'Of course, my father will be in a rush to settle things when he learns of my crying off. And of course, if you are to away so soon, we must not delay it much, but he will not be persuaded by my reasoning; but if you were to bring about the idea—'

'Say no more Miss Ashlyn, you can leave it with me. I shall pay him a visit as soon as I might.'

'I will need a couple of days, Sir, to break off with Mr Elmbridge.'

'Well, of course, Friday then, not a moment before.'

'Thank you.'

'Now, if you will forgive my haste, I must bid you farewell. I am to away to town presently but I'm sure we must meet again soon, there is much to arrange.'

He kissed my hand and left me then, and far from feeling apprehension or regret I felt remarkably at ease with his blunt and easy composure. Mariella was right in one thing it appeared: a frank and loveless match could have its advantage, and whilst I was far from happy at my need to be rescued, I was grateful to her all the same, that I had been.

Of course, this realisation had brought me swiftly to the next; I would now have to officially cry off from Mr Elmbridge and suffer the fall from grace that would ensue from such an act. It was a sobering consideration but knowing that it could now at least be put quickly to rights made the prospect somewhat easier to bear.

'I CANNOT FORGET, SHELDON,' I said to him on our morning ride the next day. 'I cannot move beyond what was between you and Lady Caroline, however much I have tried, it is of no use. I beg you release me from our engagement for I know our marriage shall never be a happy one now.'

'El, how can you ask it? After all that has gone between us: after all that is still promised? I told you she was nothing to me and I meant it. What can I do to make you believe it?'

I thought his pleading words might break me. *I have no choice.* 'I cannot put it out of my mind. I thought I could, but now I realise that we would be so very unhappy to begin in such a way.'

'Please, El, think of what you are saying?'

'I have done little else. I'm sorry.'

'Dash it, El! You truly want me to cry off over a muslin fling? Is that what this is really about?'

I nodded swallowing back my tears. 'If you have a care for me at all, Sheldon, I wish you would make this easier—'

'You will be ruined you know, after all that has gone before!'

I nodded again. 'I know.'

'You have lost your sense, Eleanor. I do not know what you are about but I know this is not you! Pray tell me what has happened? Is it Richards?' I think my face betrayed me before my own admission. I nodded as streams of tears that could no longer be held back came flooding out in gut wrenching sobs.

He held his hand across his mouth and said nothing for so long I wanted to snatch up Samson's reigns and disappear entirely. *What have I done?* What had I brought to bear upon us all over a school girl tantrum. I was not ready to be a mother. I could barely govern myself.

'Well, now you have settled the score I suppose. I shall convey you home. If you would be so good as to permit me the day to break the news to my mama first, I shall tell her we have called it off.'

'Of course. Thank you,' I said feebly.

I sat out a while in the woodland to collect myself and recover from my sobbing before going back to the house. I kept as much out of everyone's way as I could and when the day turned into the next and there was still no sign of any news, I grew ever more restless. I sent a note to Mariella to insist her brother delay his interview with my father until further notice. I could not have one piece of shocking news delivered ahead of the first. She followed up with a visit while Mama was out paying calls and I had Watts send her away with an apology. I had considered sending an express to Sheldon to enquire and pondered whether to attempt to broach the subject myself over dinner that evening. But all of it seemed impossible. It was when Mary came to tell me I was summoned to the drawing room for the sake of a visitor, my heart sank at the realisation that the time had come to face the music. I suspected I might find Lady Elmbridge there, come to bring Mama the news, but felt instantly mortified when I found Sheldon there himself. I checked my mama for a sign and puzzled as she excused herself with a smile about her face.

'I did not think you would call here again,' I said, feeling uncomfortably aware of myself and not knowing whether to sit or stay standing.

He was stood back facing me, staring out of the window from across the room and didn't turn at my coming in. 'Nor I.'

I took a few slow steps in his direction. 'Then why have you come?'

He turned around suddenly now and I noticed how unlike himself he looked. How long since he had shaved or set his hair in style, the clumsiness in which his cravat was tied, the heavy look about his eyes. If it was possible to wear your inner turmoil externally, his seemed to be a good case for an example and it cut me hollow to see it, to know I was the cause of it. 'Because,' he said without lifting his gaze beyond a glance to locate me, 'despite it all, a part of me hopes and prays for some miraculous explanation you might give me to help me overlook the facts. Because I want a reason to forgive you, to excuse you, a reason to still become your husband and find that all is not lost as it seems to be now.' His eyes shined with bulging tears and it astonished me so painfully I did not know where to look or what to say.

'Oh Sheldon! I despise myself for all of it, truly. But I could not let you go on believing in a lie. I am not who you thought I was. I let us both down and because of it I have ruined everything, so how could I ask you to forgive or love, what I myself cannot abide?'

He looked at me squarely now for the first time. 'I have always loved you, you know I have.'

'I did not know the nature of it to begin with, I own. But believe me when I tell you that when I did know it, for certain, I meant to be earnest. And I am so very sorry for causing you pain. I wish I had just told you the whole that day when you suspected me, but the truth is, I was so foxed and delirious I did not remember the slightest detail myself until your saying it to me.' I dared to reach out to him but lowered my hand mid reach. 'You deserve a better wife.'

'Do you love him, El?'

'No! How could I? I barely know him and somehow that only serves to make it seem so much the worse, for I have thrown it all over for something so insignificant.' Even he could not doubt those words to be spoken anything but honest. Each one of them passed through my lips like shards of glass.

'Then why?'

'I was drunk and I was angry.' I was crying now and he stepped in close to me. I felt his hands wipe the tears from beneath my eyes.

'If I had not upset you so ill, none of it would have happened.'

I couldn't say the words although I could feel the dependency of my answer in his stare. Even if I could release myself from the blame of it, I could not escape the fact that I was carrying Mr Richards' child. Could I endure such a scandal as he had the power to wield if I trusted the matter to him? Even if I could, I knew my family could not.

'Tell me, did I drive you to it?'

'What difference does it make?'

'The difference of me finding a way I can forgive you of it.'

'Even if you could, it is too much to ask, it is no use.'

'What do you mean?'

'There are consequences for a woman Sheldon as you yourself said: We do not have the ability to forget such a mistake as easily as your sex.'

'Of course, I know it! Do you think I have not considered the fact it will not be an innocent maiden I take down the aisle? I detest it, deplore it with every possible fragment of my being, but it is done now. Just as I cannot retract my misdemeanours with Caroline...'

'It is true. But we both know that the consequences reach quite beyond my innocence.'

'You cannot mean?' He pulled away from me.

'I do not know,' I lied, for the disgust in his face was so ugly it scared me. 'But it is a possibility I cannot ignore and neither can you.'

'Miss Ashlyn,' Watts came into the room and dropped a curtsy.

We both looked at each other and wondered if we had been overheard.

'What is it?' The aggravation in my answer was badly disguised.

'Miss Parkes is wondering what keeps you, what shall I tell her ma'am?'

'Whatever you must, just keep her away a while.'

'Sheldon,' I said when I was certain she was gone.

'How long until you know the effect of the circumstances?'

'I'm not sure.'

'Don't you keep dates of such things?'

I was surprised at his candid speech but made no objection. 'I have never before seen the need.' As every lie was spoken from my mouth, a little more of me died at the saying of them. I could not tell him that even though I was still only a little way past the due date, I was already subject to regular bouts of nausea and sickness. It would be too much to let him have the whole in one great hit. I already saw how he struggled with the half-truth.

'Then we must wait a while and see what becomes of it.'

'What good will it do?'

'Because if it as not as bad as all that, then we might still be married.'

I was speechless. He was quite lost and out of reason reckless I knew, but this? 'Sheldon, I am ruined, child or no.'

'You are not ruined if it is not known what has passed, and if there is no greater consequence to it by the time the month is out. Can't you see: I cannot give you up.'

Cat's Paw.

July 1821. - Mariella.

'Send out the servants,' I said when I arrived at Beddington Park and was received in his study. The excitement was born more of seeing my part in the bargain fulfilled at last. 'I require a private audience for the news I come bearing!'

'Well, that is serious talk, I presume you bring news of our little princess?' he said, putting down his papers and dismissing the footmen with a nod.

'I bring you the news you have been hoping for.'

'You clever little thing, is it true?'

'I am come on an errand, to petition you to rescue our poor little friend from ruin and make her an offer.'

'I own I did not think it possible,' he smiled, impressed.

'Ah how much you underestimate me, Giles.'

'So, she was convinced to believe she had carried on so ill with Mr Richards after all?'

'Yes, and now she is of a mind that she is carrying his bastard child and you will take it on.'

He nearly spat out his mouthful of freshly decanted whiskey.

'She is with child?'

'Calm down, of course she is not, how could she be?'

'Then whyever would she say so, you said yourself she had been fast with Elmbridge.'

'Not *that* fast Giles. So, rest assured, there is no child. I simply helped her along with the idea that there *could* be and when she took the idea up, it took little effort to assist her.'

'How?'

'Oh, a draft of box myrtle, red raspberry leaf and some other recipe Geeta prepared for the purposes of making her nauseous and delaying her menses. It seems to be working a treat in any case, she is thoroughly convinced of her ruin and her sad fate.'

'Well, I did indeed underestimate you. But how did you get her to take the stuff?'

'Oh, that was easy; once her mind was set on the idea of her condition, she asked me to seek out a medicine to rid her of it. I simply obliged, with a somewhat different remedy.'

'You wicked little minx,' he said more impressed than appalled.

'Well, my part is done.'

'Then I think we must set up a little meeting to be sure of her and if all goes well, I may visit her papa before the week is out.'

'Well, I shall leave all that to you. I have certainly exerted myself to exhaustion. I am in need of a holiday after all this scheming. I hope you do not forget that, Giles.'

'My dear, as if I could. It is all thanks to you and I am ever in your debt.'

'Just do not forget your part in the bargain, Giles, a marriage of convenience, nothing more.'

He held his palms up: 'Precisely as you say.'

'Any word on Richards?'

'He is safely tucked away in Cork, arrived but a day ago. All is well.'

'And he suspects nothing?'

'You are not the only one with such powers of conviction you know.'

'How much did you pay him then?'

'I? I paid him nothing at all. Mr Fitzgibbons however, rather generously had his man of business arrange a draft for 200 guineas for his procurement for the next three weeks. The poor are always made agreeable by such sums.'

'Three weeks Giles, you had better get to work, that is barely time enough for the banns to be read. You know how these slow country folk like to hold fast to their traditions.'

'It was the most he would agree to, he is promised to some other London family thereafter and would not be swayed. It shall do if she is as agreeable as you say. In any case, a Special License should hasten things along.'

'What about Elmbridge? I hear he is as mad as fire and still tries to coax her into a change of heart. You cannot think he will take kindly to your offering for her the moment his back is turned.'

'What do I care for the Elmbridges? They have served their purpose as far as I'm concerned. The rest is by the by.'

'Papa will no doubt see it differently. Oh well.'

The Parson's Mousetrap.

July - 1821. Eleanor.

It had been days since Sheldon's visit and there had been nothing to signal anyone being any the wiser. He really did mean to still have me if he could, and yet I already knew it was too late to hope for such an outcome, the draft having failed miserably, despite my faithful taking of it. I had reconsidered trying to find one of those midwives that could manually assist in disturbing the pregnancy since the draught did not seem to be working, but I didn't know where I'd even begin in the asking, and Mariella—my only confidante—was entirely against the scheme on account of the risk to my health. She had been around every morning to ask after me, and I was grateful for her concern and service in relaying messages over to Beddington to delay her brother, but I needed her help in *this*.

I was grateful too for her assistance in securing Mr Craythornes's offer, but I knew now, Sheldon really did love me. To be willing to still have me after this was testament to it, and if I cried off, I would hurt him beyond anything. And yet it was my regard for his strength of feeling that made it impossible to withhold the truth any longer. It was torturing us both. It was time I faced the ugliness of this task and put us both out of our misery.

I arranged a meeting with him on the Epsom Downs that afternoon, although I had had to walk half the journey, as bumping about on Samson's back had exacerbated the vomiting, and after a second interruption to my ride where I paused to throw up at the roadside, I stayed down and led him by the reigns the rest of the way.

When I finally reached our muster spot, I could see Delilah's glossy chestnut coat glinting in the sun's rays in the distance. He was probably looking for me. I was sure I must be above half an hour late in the least. I tried waving and calling him but he was too far away to notice, and so, reluctantly, I led Samson over to a tree stump to climb up and remount him, hoping my stomach would tolerate a quick jaunt over.

I was wrong. By the time I reached his notice, I was already feeling the tell-tale signs of another vomiting fit, my cheeks tingling, my mouth filling with excess saliva, my head light and delirious.

I managed to slide down from Samson's back just in time.

'El?' came his voice over the gallop of Delilah's hooves.

He found me crouching over a patch of bramble, retching the contents of my stomach, which I was sure must have been already cast up in the last hour. But the relief was immediate and as the last waves settled, I felt steadier, clearer.

'You are ill?' he said. He was crouching next to me now with his hand upon my back.

I wiped my mouth with my handkerchief and stood up shaking my head. 'No, Sheldon, I am not ill. I am pregnant. I'm sorry,' I said.

'Lord, tell me it is not true.'

I clamped down on my lower lip to stop it trembling as I saw all hope drain from him. 'I wish I could.'

He shook his head, refused to meet my eyes when I reached out to comfort him, then kicked a rock across the grass and sank onto a fallen tree trunk and began to cry.

I was astounded. 'Sheldon, I hate to see you like this.'

He looked up briefly. 'You've broken my heart, El. I don't know how to put it back together.'

I joined in the crying now too and threw my arms around him. Held him whilst he shook and trembled and whimpered in them. It was soul destroying. How had everything good turned to ash in a heartbeat?

'Does Richards know?' he said between sobs.

'No. I have not seen him and do not mean to again.'

'I'm going to kill him.'

'Sheldon, please, don't speak like that. What good would that do?'

'It would make me feel a damn site better.'

'No, it wouldn't. It would get you hung. What use are two dead men? Where is the justice in that?'

'There is no justice, don't you see? If there was then we could be together.'

'Sheldon, promise me you will not.'

'I cannot.'

'Well then, you might as well kill me to for I am as much to blame.'

'No, you're not; he should have acted like a gentleman and not taken advantage.'

'Perhaps then, I should have acted more like a lady.' This silenced him for a while and then he said more calmly:

'You know, it might only be a little girl.'

'It might,' I agreed.

'If it is a girl, it would not matter. We could overcome it.'

'Yes, we could. But what if it is not?'

'Let us have a long engagement and find out.'

'Sheldon, we cannot wait eight months unmarried when I will be showing my condition in but a few.'

'You could go away. We could go away together and pretend we are married. I shall get you a ring and could rent us a house somewhere—France perhaps.'

'My parents would never consent prior to our wedding, and even if they could be persuaded to, what then? We grow fonder in love, live out the next eight months as man and wife and then I bear a son and you cry off?'

'You could give it up, no one need ever know.'

'I would know!' I said aghast. I might not be thrilled about my circumstances and nor did I know what it was to bear a child, but something told me that in the moment of so doing, with a child in my arms, I would see only *my* child—not Richards bastard or Sheldon's threat to the lineage, but my own son. If that is how it would be, then I knew that giving him up would be entirely out of the question.

'We could find him a good home. I would pay for his keep, settle on him well but—'

'You ask too much, Sheldon.'

'We will have many sons after for you to love and cherish.'

'Think of what you are saying, Sheldon. I cannot abandon my own child. However inconvenient it is.'

'Then you clearly do not share my feelings, for I would do anything for you, anything to save our marriage.' His tone was rising in aggression again.

'Fine, then you make the sacrifice: You marry me now as planned and take the fifty-fifty chance that I may have a girl or boy.'

He sat thoughtfully for a moment then said, 'You know I cannot afford to take that risk.'

'And neither can I!' I cried.

We were both silent for the next few moments, the stiffness of our bodies and coldness of our distance now, stark against the balmy air and woodland birdsong.

Then he got up eventually, brushed out his coat hem and said, 'Then it seems there is nothing more to say.'

'No.'

'Then I bid you good afternoon, Miss Ashlyn.'

AN EXPRESS CAME LATER that evening from Nork Park. Mama nearly swooned at the reading of it and it was only when Delores pulled the letter from her grasp and read it, that I realised what it was.

'Is it true Eleanor?' she said as she held out Mama's vinaigrette to her in one hand and scanned the letter in the other.

'What does it say?' I asked, putting down my fancy work.

'Lady Elmbridge says: "Sheldon came home today bearing me the most ill news after his ride with Eleanor this afternoon. It appears they convened a meeting where it was mutually decided they should call off the wedding. He will not tell me why. Perhaps you will have better luck finding it out and see what is to be done." Well?' she demanded.

I nodded and broke into tears. It was amazing there were any left with how many rivers I had already cried on my way home.

'How could you, Eleanor!' cried my mama.

'Please tell me this is not over, Lady Caroline,' said Delores, and Mama frowned her bewilderment.

She knew? How could it be. I was certain no one else could. 'Yes, it was one of the reasons,' I confessed.

'What *about* Lady Caroline?' Mama interrupted.

Delores sighed and sat back down in her seat. 'I did not want to mention it before. But there was talk, only amongst a couple of the chaperones mind. I managed to persuade them to hold their tongues. They had noticed Lady Caroline dangling about after him weeks ago, all the way back at West Wycombe Park.'

'Well, what does that signify?' my mama cut in.

'It turned out that at Beaulieu, things took an altogether different turn.'

'How did you know?' I asked her.

'I didn't; until I went to town last week to visit Mrs Oliver's and I ran in to one of them with her charge: Mrs Tumble. Anyway, she said there had been talk below stairs that had reached her notice, it appears Lady Caroline had been visiting his bedchamber.'

'I cannot believe a word of it. Servants' gossip and nothing more. Sheldon would not—'

'It is true, Mama.'

She looked at me stunned. 'You mean he has told you so?'

'Yes, I have it as a fact.'

'And you knew this all along?'

'I did. And I forgave him it.'

'As you must my dear. You cannot hold an unmarried man to account for such dalliances. You are not yet man and wife. He must give it up now you are soon to be wed.' She put down her vinaigrette on her workbox.

'Well, at least she is a married woman, better that scenario: she can do you no harm,' said Delores.

'The harm is already done, on both sides. We have both said some unpleasant things to each other and despite our efforts in the trying, the fact is, it cannot be overcome.'

'Well, of course it can,' Mama sat up in her chair.

'I had hoped the same. But we are both decided, and I have agreed to release Mr Elmbridge of his obligation.'

'Stupid girl!' Mama cried out.

'Perhaps. But he is in accord and there is nothing to be done now.'

I did not stay around for the onslaught when she ran off in search of my father to report it to him and have him "talk some sense into me." I ran straight out of the house, through the woodland and collapsed into Mariella's arms in floods of tears when she found me in the reception room waiting for her. 'It is done,' I told her. 'The wedding is off.'

'There there,' she said, cradling me upon the floor where I had sunk to my knees in despair. 'It shall be alright. You have done the right thing. You could not have lived with yourself if you had tricked Mr Elmbridge into raising Richards' child.'

'Oh, but had you seen him, Mariella. I have broken his heart and I fear my own is breaking too.'

'Be at ease: You shall recover and so shall he. Give it time to settle.'

'I don't know, Mariella. He wants us to have a long engagement, to see if the child is a boy. He says he will make arrangements for it if it is so, and perhaps I should have consented, for everyone is so upset. My mama is furious and all hell is broke loose in the house; and it is all my fault.'

'No, it is not your fault. Mr Elmbridge brought this on himself and now you are to bear all this suffering. It is selfish of him to ask you to give up your child. He cannot love you if he asks it. Even my brother does not ask it and neither of you are the least bit in love.'

It was true. If Mr Craythorne could accept the child, surely, he should be as willing. But it was not the same, Sheldon had so much more at stake in the bargain.

No less, by the time I left, feeling a little more at ease, I agreed that if Mr Craythorne would leave it a couple of days to let the dust settle, he may proceed to my papa with his intentions.

Although even this was not to run smoothly. The next day, I was disturbed from my moping by the announcement of Betsy's arrival. It was all I needed; to have to face her puffy eyed and sleep deprived. She must have heard the news. She confirmed the same instantly.

'Eleanor, is it true the wedding shall not go ahead?' she asked before I had even taken my seat beside her.

'Yes, it is true.'

'My goodness, you look a fright.'

'I feel it,' I said, sinking down into the chair.

'But why? Anyone can see the pair of you are destined.'

'It is complicated. We are not as well suited as we once thought.'

'Surely better suited than you and Mr Craythorne!' she said, failing to hide her disgust.

'What?'

'It's all over town: that Craythorne has offered for you?'

Impossible. I knew Mariella would not break my confidence and it would not be in her brother's interests to mention it before he had even approached my father.

'Please tell me there is no truth in it—or at least that you mean to decline.'

'I have not decided,' I lied.

'You cannot be serious?' she said with such a look of incredulity, an expression I was becoming well accustomed to in this house already.

'Who told you?'

'About three different people this morning alone. If it was not bad enough trying to defend your character over the rumours of you crying off from Sheldon, but even I cannot help you in this quarter.'

'I did not ask for your help, Betsy. You need not defend me.'

'And nor shall I attempt to now I know you are out of reason senseless!'

'So, you are to abandon me.'

'You leave me little choice.' She stood up from her seat.

'Martha is happy, you have not abandoned her. She is to marry a Craythorne and you are to go to the wedding!'

'Do not compare your circumstances to Martha's! She had little choice, she was in desperate straits. It is not Martha who had any better prospects, it is not Martha who has been parading around on Elmbridge's arm for weeks taking the liberties of an engaged woman, it is not Martha's name that is on-dit in every quarter over crying off, and in the next breath, before the heat has even cooled on that topic, you are back again now with this Craythorne talk.'

'No. It is not. But I have my reasons, Betsy. I assure you I do not take it lightly.'

'That's may be, but you think society cares for that? You are ruined, Eleanor. Just the Sheldon situation alone, and now you want to add insult to injury. Well, you are on your own.'

'As I always have been!' I cried and left the room, ringing the bell on my way out.

MARIELLA WAS NOT SURPRISED to hear the news of her brother's offer being all about the town. She herself had been busy all morning trying to find out the culprit, which had turned out to be a housemaid that had overheard a conversation and decided to tell all the others; and so, it had travelled from basement to basement at lightning speed. She had just been down with the housekeeper, ordering her dismissal when I arrived. She assured me that her brother had every intention of honouring his offer, and so I need not despair, and I beseeched her to have him pay attendance on my father as soon as possible, before my parents got wind of the gossip. But it could not be done. We took the carriage together directly over to Beddington to bid him to return with us and speak to my father at once. But when we arrived, it turned out he was already away to Portsmouth on some business matter and would not return until Monday at the earliest.

There was nothing more for it. I would have to tell them myself before it come to their notice through some other means.

WHEN I RETURNED HOME and was met with the expected scold from Mama, I was prepared for her. I snatched off my bonnet and waved away Mary's fussing hands. 'I have been to Beddington Park.'

'On your own? Were you seen?'

'No, Mama, I was not alone and I was not seen. I went to see Mr Craythorne.'

'Whatever for?'

'He has made me an offer.'

She turned immediately to Mary and nodded to dismiss her before pulling me by the arm into the parlour. 'What kind of mad brained scheme is this?'

I released my arm from her grip and sat down on the nearest sofa. 'The only one open to me now, Mama.'

'No; no it is not! I told you, Mr Elmbridge will forgive you your temper and may even reinstate his offer if you will only humble yourself and see sense.'

'I have seen sense, Mama. I am ruined. Everyone is talking about me and if I don't put things right quickly; then we shall all suffer. Mr Craythorne and I are very certain that this arrangement will be—'

'Mr Craythorne and I! Do you hear yourself?' She paced up and down in front of me. 'Nay, I cannot permit this madness.' She was shaking her head despairing. 'We shall go to Nork Park and you will tell Sheldon you are sorry. You did not mean it. That is how this shall be fixed.'

'It's not madness, Mama.' I could hardly convince her it was love or affection nor tell her it was a rescue attempt: 'A practical choice.'

'Practical. Since when Eleanor, were you ever of a practical mind? And since when was marrying so beneath your touch a matter of pragmatism when you have the future Viscount's heart?'

What could I say? 'Mama, whatever was once between Sheldon and I, has since been tarnished beyond all reconciliation.'

'Lady Caroline. It is all over and done with. It was but a trifle. His mama told me so herself. She is frightful of his health he is so distraught and you are no better. We shall go directly to Nork Park and the pair of you may talk it out and set things to rights.'

'We have tried. It cannot be.'

'But come, Eleanor, can you really think it a good excuse to write off such a winning future?'

'Yes. I cannot begin a life with someone I cannot trust. Someone who has already shown himself capable of such habits. Someone whose affections are so easily—'

'Eleanor, Sheldon assures his mama that whatever was between him and Lady Caroline is quite over. He has given his word and lest I remind you, you had given your word to be his wife after the knowing of this. If you ever want your word or your name to count for anything again, then I suggest you take a leaf from his book and commit to it.'

I felt a tear roll down my cheek. I wanted so much to tell her the truth. To tell her that the actions I took were to do right by Sheldon, not to punish him as it may have seemed to everyone else: To spare him the burden and shame of an illegitimate child.

'Forgiveness, my dear, is something all wives must become practised in. If you think it otherwise, you shall be in for a sad surprise whomever you wed.'

'I can forgive him, Mama. I do forgive him. I simply can't go on with him in the way I once would have.'

'What nonsense. Of course, you can. You decide now in that hard headedness that you will not, but if you do not, and you do not realise it soon before Mr Elmbridge offers elsewhere, then you will come to regret it, Eleanor. Who do you think will want to make offers to you after this?'

'Mr Craythorne *has*, Mama. I don't know why, but he is not put off by the scandal of my crying off and I shall accept his offer,' I said as evenly as I could manage.

'I tell you why. Because they are mushrooms! Unspeakable social climbers who neither know or care for what is proper. That is why he is indifferent. Oh, I do not doubt he would be happy to take you off your father's hands and get his connection to good society, for that is the only ticket his money cannot yet buy him.'

Of course it was true. I knew full well that this arrangement went beyond charity. That his willingness to overlook my sins was in exchange for my willingness to overlook his class and what he stood to gain from the rising of his status through our union. But he could have offered to Beth or someone else and achieved as much without the burden. He meant to help me, and in return I would help him. 'Oh, to the devil with it, Mama. I am tired of your prejudice. They have been kinder to me than the family you wish to push me on.'

Her face went grey with this affront. 'Sheldon is not himself; I own I do not commend his behaviour, but Eleanor, you cannot imagine your fate a better one to marry into that family over the Elmbridge's?'

'Well, it does not answer since the Elmbridges have quite abandoned me. So, you tell me what else I am to do?'

'Give him time to forgive you, Eleanor: men do not like to be told when they are wrong, less still by a woman. He will come to you and make amends for it all when he has calmed down and see's sense. At this very moment, Lady Elmbridge assures me she is petitioning him to settle things, and I know she will bring him round. But what good will any of it do if you accept another offer before he has the chance to see beyond his anger.'

I held back a sarcastic laugh. 'Oh Mother, can you and Lady Elmbridge not see how much you have exhausted this notion in our matchmaking. He does not want me and I do not want him anymore. You must tell my father to expect Mr Craythorne on Monday morning.' I got up.

'Eleanor—'

'Please, Mama, just tell my father if you will. I cannot bear to look at him any more than he can bear the sight of me. I will soon be off your hands and everyone will be glad.'

I went then to my chamber and poured my heart into the pages of my diary for the remainder of the day.

I WAS SURPRISED TO be summoned for church on Sunday. I had not been out again since the day of Betsy's revelation, and I had therefore been spared the inconvenience of facing the scorn of society insofar. I did all I could to get out of it, but it was apparently non-negotiable. In but a day's time, Mr Craythorne would arrive to speak to my father and then I would be willing to face them again, once the news of our confirmed engagement would extinguish the other whisperings of my name. Yes, it would be ridiculed and puzzled over; a nobody in place of the future Viscount, but my married status would make me respectable again all the same, and I would not be ruined.

But even this line of persuasion would not suffice and Mama brought Watts into the dressing room to have me made presentable for church.

'Your father says we must go and show the town that we do not hide from them, that there is nothing to hide from,' she told me.

'But there is every reason to hide from them, Mama, you know what they are all saying, don't you?'

'Yes, and you brought it on yourself so what can we do but bear it.'

So that was their game, some tough love strategy to make me face the music and see if that did not change my mind.

And so it was, we went off to church as we always did, and when the coach pulled up and I saw the streams of parishioners pouring through the gates, I felt unusually nervous. The only small consolation I could comfort myself with was that at least some of the more important realms of society were out of town and I would not have to face their looks. But I was unhappy to see that the Elmbridge's had remained. The Elmbridges would often be found at their seat in Oxfordshire at this time of year, but I could only presume that this bad business had held them back.

My parents put on a good show of things and, as usual, stopped and chatted several times along the pathway, which usually didn't bother me, but today, I just wanted to get in and out as quickly as we may. As they stood talking to the Chamberlains for what seemed like an age, I studied the shrubbery that lined the winding pathway for the diversion. I was hiding beneath my bonnet and I didn't want to catch the eye of anyone, who in great number was congregating all around us, so I did my best to look preoccupied. I followed the yellows and lilacs of the beds with my eyes until they met the grey of the rocky walls that enclosed the church grounds. If it were not for all the mossy, tilting gravestones that interrupted the horizon, I was sure it would make quite a beautiful picture on a day like today; the sky clear and the sunlight upon the grass giving it the pomona green lustre of vitality. But even the fair weather couldn't improve my mood. I was kicking up the gravel beneath my feet with impatience when I looked up to the sound of the Elmbridge's introduction. My heart sank when I noticed Sheldon looking uncomfortably at me from behind his parents, who were chatting amiably enough to mine. *So, it was a combined tactic then.* I wanted to disappear instantly. I saw him in the image of his disgusted thwarted face, even though his expression was placid now.

'Miss Ashlyn,' he greeted me with a tilt of his hat.

I saw mama look up from her conversation with the Viscountess, but I did not linger on it.

'Mr Elmbridge,' I replied, keeping my face as much turned away from him as I could politely manage.

He came over to me and ushered me out of earshot with a few steps back. 'I think we must talk if either of us are ever to have a moment's peace,' he said keeping his voice low.

I took a few more steps back to be sure we were not overheard. 'You are being constantly pecked at too, I see.'

He nodded.

'If only they knew how impossible our position, perhaps they might back off and let us nurse our wounds and move beyond this. But you know I cannot tell them.'

His expression was pained. Had the sobriety of our separation been as hard on him as on me, or had his mama simply boxed his ears harder than even my own?

'I should not have said those things to you, I know, and I am sorry for my conduct. I own it to be every part as hideous to me as I know it was to you. But we cannot talk now.'

I was grateful he could admit that much, but it wasn't enough to alter anything betwixt us. Our predicament remained unaltered by tokens of regret or apology, heartfelt or not.

'I am sorry about the Lady Caroline confession—Delores already knew—'

'I don't care about that; it is nothing to me. Everything that was of value, is now lost.'

It seemed laughable now, to consider that a fortnight ago I believed my world to have collapsed over what now seemed such trivialities as his conduct with Lady Caroline. I would have given anything to have only to face such simple dilemmas as coming to terms with that matter. *That* I could have recovered eventually. My injured pride could have healed given a little time. I was innocent then, naive enough to take his folly personally, when I now realised that he was doing nothing more than being true to his sex. I had seen enough of society to understand that it was merely the way of things, and as Delores had told me, better his dalliance with a married woman than some more worthy opponent. But it mattered not now; my own misdemeanours could not be so easily erased or forgiven, however much we wished it.

We both jumped as the church bells began to chime out above us.

'Eleanor, come along,' I heard my father's voice. I looked up having quite forgotten them all and broke my conversation off with Sheldon. I could see that however much my mother was willing to overlook the matter for the sake of setting us up, my father was not so forgiving. In his eyes, Sheldon had lost a great deal of credit in his conduct and whilst I was sorry for him taking so much of the flack, I only hoped that it would make Papa more receptive to Mr Craythorne tomorrow.

We walked over to their beckoning; I couldn't even manage to feign a smile or some other veil for their benefit, it seemed impossible now. But we fell into step of the slow-moving line piling into the church.

When we reached the door and our parents were busied in small talk with the rector, he turned to me and whispered. 'Will you wait for me after the service?'

I wanted to refuse, I wanted to make an excuse; I wanted nothing more than to get back home quickly to avoid any further conversations with anyone this day. But I knew the sooner we cleared the air, the sooner I could put this matter aside and try to focus on what must be done. I nodded my agreement and exchanged a brief greeting with the rector as I funnelled in through the door.

I looked for a seat away from him as my parents took up the remainder or the nearest aisle, when I felt someone tug at my arm from behind, it made me jump over zealously – my nerves were oversensitive today. 'Mariella!' I gasped.

'How are you bearing up?' she asked.

I took my seat on the bench beside Miss Martine and Mariella sat down next to me and leaned in close. 'Just about. I'll be glad to get home.'

'I didn't expect you to be here.'

'No. I have been trying to lay low,' I leaned in and lowered my voice, 'but it seems my parents and the Elmbridges will stop at nothing to put us in each other's way.'

'I suspected as much.'

'The sooner tomorrow comes and everything is settled, the better.'

'Indeed. I saw you speaking with Mr Elmbridge.'

I quickly picked up the hymn book in front of me to steady my shaking hands. 'Not here,' I said, before I noticed how my tone had piqued Miss Martine's interest and disapproval.

'He still means to persuade you.' It was a statement, not a question. She was watching him as he found a seat two rows across from us.

'It's impossible now.'

'SHHH!' Came a voice from the row behind and a stout faced woman peered at us unimpressed.

Mariella turned about and stared at her with violent contempt until she looked away.

I was grateful for an end to this conversation here with the sideways glances I could feel being cast in my direction. I hadn't even noticed the service had begun. I quickly stood and bowed my head for the prayer. The words drifted over me, my mind raced over everything inside it. I was not sure if I felt better or worse off for Mariella's proximity. Certainly, to have even one friend now was reassuring, but it would surely only fuel the whispers about her brother's offer. Of course, by tomorrow, the news would be officially out, but I did not want to face it here and in Sheldon's company. Certainly it was on this head he wanted an audience with me after and I dreaded how it would go. 'Amen,' I chorused. When I opened my eyes, I caught Mr Elmbridge looking at me from across the aisles and I felt the pressure mounting in my temples from all around me. I turned the pages in my hymn book, glancing over at Miss Martine's to check the page number I had missed. The organ blew into tune and the room burst out in song all around me, echoing about the lofty ceilings.

'What will you say to him if he reinstates your offer?' Mariella whispered from behind her hymn book.

I brought mine close to my lips. 'I will have to tell him the truth I suppose.'

'Are you sure that is wise?'

'It will be confirmed tomorrow, anyway. I only hope it will keep 'till then.'

'You are making the right decision you know. It is a hard one of course and I know my brother must seem dull to you, but others have married under circumstances far worse than this, and he will be an easy husband to go along with.' This last sentence coincided with the end of the song a moment too late and it was immediately clear that as the music fell away, her voice had filled the room with this last statement plainly enough for everyone close to hear.

I cut her a very deep glare before looking around at the gawping expressions. I felt my cheeks ablaze as the whole room turned eyes upon us. I didn't dare look across to my parents to capture their reaction. I put my head down and ignored the quiet mumblings that had erupted around the hall in response to Mariella's faux pas.

We didn't speak again until the service was over, and when it was, I rushed out as quickly as I could to avoid the curious looks and gossip following fast behind me.

'My goodness, Mariella!' I said, unable to hide my fury when we stepped out into the church yard. 'Have a care for goodness' sake. There are enough whispers about me without you adding fuel to the fire.' My mother had already warned me with a flash of her eyes that there would be words to have on the way back.

'I'm sorry, Eleanor; I will set it right.'

I stepped back. 'Set it right! And how will you do that?' I said through gritted teeth as passers-by fell silent at the sight of us.

'I will explain it was a misunderstanding—that we were speaking of somebody else, Martha perhaps: that would set it right.'

I pulled her aside, over to a quieter part of the yard. 'Just like that, you believe a scandal can be so easily recovered, with everything that has passed this week, you think any of them stupid enough to be taken in?'

Before we could discuss the matter any further, I closed my open mouth and forced it into the most even expression I could contrive as I noticed Sheldon close approaching.

'I will leave you to it.' Mariella made her exit on cue and I hadn't a moment to even consider what I would say to him before he was in front of me. I could see the questions on his lips before he spoke them.

'So, the rumours are true then?' His fury was tangible. 'You will accept Craythorne's offer?'

'What else can I do? I can hardly marry Richards.'

He fell silent.

'What of it now anyway? It is all ruined.' I felt a tear escape my eye and swept it away with a gloved finger.

'Well, perhaps you should of thought about that.'

'Don't you dare: You did as much with Lady Caroline. Worst in fact, because it was not just the matter of one occasion was it Sheldon? And she a married woman. But that does not answer does it because it is acceptable for you to act so abhorrently, but dare I do anything remotely like it and I deserve everything I get. Well, I don't have the luxury of Lady Caroline's protection should she end up in the same condition at your hands.'

'I own what I did was bad of me. But Eleanor, you were playing with fire taking such risks.'

'Yes. Because of my sex, that is your only argument against it and you know it is such a poor one. I do not care anymore, it shall all be settled tomorrow and I will marry Mr Craythorne to save my name, and you will waltz around unblemished for your sins. And yes, he knows on what terms his offer is made, and makes no objection.'

'Good god, Eleanor! I am heir to my father's title. Can you really think it possible that I could wed you as easy as he when you are carrying some other fellow's bastard that I would have to carry off as my own, make my heir.'

This at least I knew was not a possibility. 'Oh, keep your precious dignity Sheldon, I would not ask it, and I do not want it. Tomorrow, we can draw a line in this and both be free to move on.'

'I can't move on.'

I didn't know what to say to this. I cast a brief glance across the churchyard. All around me, I could hear the whispers and feel the hot gazes of nosy gawpers upon us. This was nothing new in itself, but now, now the question on everyone's lips referred not to a simple matter of when I would marry, but to whom.

'Please don't marry him, El.'

After that exhibition, it was clear that to marry was the only decent way out of this debacle. Marry or ruin. I saw my mother crossing the lawn to reach us. 'I have to go,' I said.

'Come to Nork Park at three-o-clock, please. We need to talk. My parents are not at home.'

'I cannot, Sheldon, there is nothing more to be said.'

'Just this one thing: is all I ask.'

'I will try.'

'I will bid you good day, Miss Ashlyn,' he said as Mama came level with us and I bobbed a curtsy and watched him depart.

The words, or more correctly: the rage that blew up on the way home once we were safely out of sight in our carriage, rained over me like a shower of fire sparks. Stinging once in a while, but mostly burning out before they even touched me. I sank into some part of my consciousness that seemed removed from it all: A place of retreat in my mind where the questions and scolds were like a distant blur against my hearing. Just like sounds above water when you are immersed beneath it.

Alternative arrangements.

July 1821 - Eleanor.

When I arrived at Nork, I was anxious and questioning whether to turn Samson back around again, but tomorrow I was to be engaged, so if there was any chance at all of Sheldon having a change of heart, this was the last opportunity to hear it before the point of no return. I trotted on towards the stable yard and handed the reigns over to the groom. Sheldon was already waiting to meet me and convey me up through the rear entrance to the house.

'I'm so glad you came,' he said in far more genial spirits than those we last spoke on. I tried to warn myself not to read too much into this as a sign of hope, and yet as we trod our way up to his study, I could not help but feel a little optimistic at how much more like himself he seemed: Like *my* Sheldon again, not the jaded version I had recently become more familiar with. 'Where are your family?'

'They left for Buscot after church. They need a holiday; this has left my mama quite forlorn.'

'I'm sorry to hear that.'

'Have a seat,' he said, closing the study door, and I was confused at the formality. I had assumed we were headed to his study to find a private place to talk, but now I knew the house was empty, I could not understand it.

'I have a proposal for you,' he said, taking a document from the desk and handing it to me.

'What is it?' I said.

'A contract.'

I scanned the document.

'Would you like something to drink?'

I shook my head. 'A contract to be your whore!' I threw it onto the desk. 'Well, that exceeds everything.'

'No. You could never be that to me,' he said, rushing over to my side. 'I love you, El. It is the only way open to us now. You will have a house in Oxford and two hundred a year, it is the most I can do until I inherit. Then I could make it a thousand. Damn, I don't care if you ask thrice as much.'

'You are serious?'

'Of course, I am serious, El, don't you see? It is a way I can protect you. A way we can be together, and you will not need to marry Craythorne or anyone else.'

'By becoming your courtesan? Can you actually hear yourself?'

'Do you know the pains I have taken to have this drawn up in such a rush and on a Sunday?'

'Well, I am very sorry for your inconvenience, Mr Elmbridge, had I known the purpose of your cause, I should have told you not to waste either of our time. I have never been so insulted in my life!'

'El, come, you know I don't mean to insult or offend. I just—I just want to find a way to be with you.'

'Oh Sheldon, it cannot be, don't you see that now? It is over. Our chance for happiness has long departed, and if you think either of us would be happy with such an arrangement in the long run, then you are quite mistaken.'

He picked the contract back up and tried to press it into my hands. 'Please, just say you will think about it.'

'I would be lying. I cannot even consider it. I have brought enough despair to my family as it is and that is without them knowing the whole. I mean to do no more. I shall be engaged tomorrow and it shall free us all of this abhorrent misery.'

'No. El, please, you cannot mean it. It is me you love, not him.'

'I know that, and that is why it shall be the hardest thing I have ever had to do, and yet it must be done.'

'So, you really will accept him?'

'My child needs protection. He offers it. It is a simple bargain; my happiness for the protection of my child, for the protection of my family. It is no different from what you must do to protect yours, Sheldon.'

He sunk into the chair I had risen from, hands in his head, despairing. 'I cannot lose you.'

'You cannot keep me, not as your wife, your courtesan, your paramour. I am not Lady Caroline. I mean to be faithful to Mr Craythorne and do my duty in return for his.'

He sat up. 'Then give me tonight.'

'What do you mean?'

'You will be beyond my touch by morning, but let us have just one night together. What can it matter now? The damage is already done. Let me love you tonight and if by morning you still want to go ahead, then I shall not stand in your way.'

'Sheldon, that is not fair to either of us.'

'Don't you want it? Don't you want to know what it is to be truly loved. Not like those cheap tricks Mr Richards gulled you into. Or the duty you must perform on your wedding night. Know at least, what it is to be held close in loving arms.'

It was true, there was nothing to be lost in it now and yet I knew it a bad idea, even as he stood up and drew me into his arms. But the relief of his kiss was such an antidote to all the pain, the misery and the conflict, that I let him lead me up to his chamber in a flurry of broken kisses. Gave my back to him to undress me, and when I found myself lying naked alongside him beneath the sheets, I wondered how I had allowed this. But it was too late, he was kissing his way down my body, savouring it as if to capture the memory. 'Sheldon, we must not,' I said once I had found the courage to speak.

He answered with his hand pressed into the heat of me and I found myself unable to say anything for a moment. 'I'm scared, Sheldon,' I said eventually.

'Of me?' he said looking pained.

'No. Not of you. Of it. I don't remember anything about...'

'You needn't. Let us take it slowly. There is time enough to work towards it. I shall lead the way,' he said and the next thing I felt was him move my hand towards him until I felt the bulge of him in my grasp, his hand guiding mine over the shape of him. It felt strange. I wanted to withdraw, but then he gasped so loud and almost collapsed against me, and I knew he was feeling the pleasure I had known before, and felt I owed him this much at least. Then as he released my hand from his grasp, I continued the motion he had trained it in and felt his hand travel to the place that caused me to gasp as audibly, and I almost forgot my rhythm, my task. His touch was so overdue I lasted no time at all and within moments, I was climbing those familiar waves of uncontainable delight, my breaths heaving, my body shaking, my consciousness slipping into some other realm. His mouth at my breast, his hand in perfect coordination with my demands as if he could read me like the notes off of a music manuscript. It lasted to so long I thought I might never stop trembling. But when I felt the shift of his weight, opened my eyes and saw him above me, I sobered quickly. I don't know why I was so frightened but I felt it starkly and begged him stop when I felt him attempting the task. 'I'm sorry,' I said to his perplexed expression. 'Is there some other way I might—'

'Let me look at you,' he said and lifted up on to his knees, replacing my hand upon him and I picked up where I had left off as he began to mirror the movement and sounds I had just created; thrusting, groaning, his eyes falling heavy but determined to drink in the sight of me: A sheen of sweat glowing upon his chest, the muscles of his torso contracting as he moved. He was so handsome, I had never really appreciated just how much, and it saddened me to know it now. But I did not dwell, I felt his demands for me to hasten and so I did, until he forbade it, wrapped his hand about mine and prevented me from moving whilst he caught his breath. I wasn't sure if he was finished. If it passed more subtly for men, and then I realised he was not, as he permitted me move slowly again and then said: 'Give me your mouth instead.'

'My mouth?' I said as he pulled me up. Then I realised what he intended as he drew my face down towards the swell of him. It seemed an impossible task as he pushed gently passed my lips, but I tried to figure out what he wanted, which was made clearer as he grew more restless and began to thrust himself into my mouth, so fast, I felt I might choke. I tried to draw back but he only sank himself further into me, and when I lifted my head to get up, I felt his hands on the back of my head, pressing so firmly into my scalp I could barely move for the force of his thrusting against my face and the strength with which he held my head fast. I started to panic then and move more forcibly away, but he adjusted his fingers, knotted them in my hair so tightly that I daren't move again for fear my scalp would tear away. So, I endured the slam of him, repeatedly, the gag reflex that was causing me to retch, the more wayward jabs at the back of my throat that became increasingly painful until my throat filled with hot liquid and he began to slow at last, groaning with such volume I knew this must be the end.

He held me there a few moments more as I tried to swallow down the liquid that kept filling my mouth until it seemed he was growing limper and I suddenly could release my jaw a little more comfortably. Then he let go of my head and sunk back on top of the pillows, panting. 'Come here,' he said looking up briefly and beckoned me into his open arms.

Tentatively, I lowered myself into the space and he gathered me up saying: 'Thank you. That was amazing. You are amazing.'

I could not share the sentiment as I wiped my mouth and massaged my scalp carefully. But I was glad I had brought him relief and settled back into the warmth of him, felt his gentle kisses at my forehead now and then. I rested my hand upon his chest and felt it clammy beneath my palm, the heartbeat rushing beneath it at accelerated speed.

We must have fell into a doze after that because when I opened my eyes again the courtyard clock was chiming the hour of five. I sat up and disturbed him from his sleep. 'I have to go,' I said. 'I have already been gone two hours.'

'Oh, don't go yet. We haven't even—'

'I am never out this long on a ride, they will grow worried if I am not back soon.'

'Let me convey them a note. Say you have stopped in at Bets or something.'

'Bets,' I laughed. 'She would not vouch for me now.'

'Come here,' he pulled me into a kiss that soon grew into passion and I prised myself away when he began to travel to my breasts again.

'Sheldon. I can't stay.'

'But I am ready for you again, see.' And I felt him swollen against my hand again. 'Let me make love to your body this time. We have had our little warm up, but I need to be inside you.'

'No, I don't want to, Sheldon,' I said trying to sit up again. 'My parents—'

'Shhh, you just need a little more persuasion,' he said and he sunk below the covers and I felt the wetness of his mouth against me. The shock of it began to stir me, but I knew I must not let it take course this time. Not only would I be in more trouble than I could cope with right now if I spent a moment longer, but I did not want to be in debt to his favours anymore, now I knew what it was to return them. So, against all the will of my body, which was of quite another mind when his tongue begun stirring me in ways that even exceeded the last pleasure, I pulled him away and sat up.

'You do not enjoy it?' he said puzzled.

'I do. But I cannot be any later.'

'Then quickly, let me just feel my way inside you. It shan't take long, I promise it.'

'No, Sheldon. I have to go.' But as I spoke the words, he fought past my closed thighs and slipped his finger inside me, just like I had remembered Mariella doing before. Except that time, I had enjoyed it, this time, I was so much out of the mood now, I just wanted to be gone.

'Look how wet you are, you deceive us both. You are ready for me now,' he said, withdrawing his fingers and licking the shine from them. 'It shan't hurt so much this time, not with you so well prepared. If that is what is worrying you.'

I did not remember even the pain of Richards' actions, so this did little to convince me. I shuffled across the mattress to get up. 'It is not that,' I insisted. 'I told you, my parents—'

'Five minutes more shan't make the difference and I will convey you home to make up for it. I will ride Samson for you alongside the coach—'

'No,' I said more severely and stepped onto the floor.

'You don't want me, is that it?'

I began gathering my clothes up from the floor. 'It is not that.'

'You didn't mind letting Richards take a poke though. If only you had been so standoffish with him—'

'Don't start ruining it, Sheldon!' I said despairing. 'Let us part as friends.'

'As friends?' he shot up from the bed and came behind me and I felt frightened in that instant. 'If I meant anything to you, you would not have let that filthy music master fill you with his seed,' he growled through gritted teeth and I ran towards the door, clutching my clothes at my breast. He slammed up behind me before I could open it and pressed me up against the panels of wood so they pressed cold against my naked flesh, the heat of him at my back.

'Stop it, Sheldon! This is not like you.'

'I am not like me anymore! Don't you see; I am dead inside!'

His breath was hot against my ear. 'No. You are hurt now. But it shall pass and you will return to yourself. Give it time.' I was actually repeating Mariella's words, for even I had no faith in what

I spoke. We were both altered now beyond return to those innocent days, clutching beneath a tree to try out a kiss.

'Is that how it is for you? Is that what you will be thinking on your wedding night when you let Craythorne have what you deny me now. God, I have a mind to just take you,' he said with such violence of tone, but also in the way he reached around my body and clasped his hand between my legs so he caused me to stand on tiptoe. 'Why should he have what is mine,' he pressed me so tight to the door that I was cheek against it and unable to move. I felt the bulge of him fight between my thighs, looking for the right place, as he clutched his hand to inch me closer.

'Stop it, Sheldon! Stop, you are hurting me,' I screamed.

'Don't you know, this is what happens to whores?' he said, and I knew there was no talking him down. It was as though I did not know this man at all. It was not *my* Sheldon. My beautiful and tender friend, pressed behind me, thrusting himself now between the clench of my thighs in frustration, because I had clamped them so tightly shut, he could not enter me. I felt the anger, the force, the pain with every movement as he slid between my thighs more furiously. I held onto the door, cradling my palms in front of my face to stop my cheekbone bumping against it. He must have taken this shift in my movements as another attempt to escape him, for he clutched my hair spitefully again and started up saying vulgar things into my ear. His lips were wet against my temple.

'You will let other men go where you forbid me,' he snarled and I felt hot tears roll down my face, that were not only falling from my eyes. 'You act like a whore, then men will treat you like a whore.'

I stopped listening after that, I could not bear it, the sounds of his insults mixed with the sound of his tears and grunts of his pleasure. It was all too much to bear and when I felt him quicken and release, I was relieved that it was done.

When he stepped away and sat on the bed, his face flushed and tear streamed, I said nothing to him. He was a sorry sight to behold and I wanted only to get home and forget this affair. I picked up my shift and wiped away the dampness he had left trailing my legs and got dressed as quickly as I could manage alone.

When I slipped into my boots and released the door, he looked up and said, 'I'm sorry, El. I'm ashamed of myself.'

I said nothing and left the room and only let my tears come thick as I rode Samson at a gallop.

The contract is binding.

July 1821. - Eleanor.

I gave my parents the story that I had taken a little tumble off of Samson and it had taken me a while to walk the journey back. It accounted for my bloodshot teary eyes and the slipshod state I returned in too, and they accepted it. They advised me that I was not to go out riding alone anymore beyond the park. The easing of this restriction had been on account of my protected status as an engaged woman, a status I reminded them would be reinstated tomorrow and the reason why they needn't go to the trouble of finding me a replacement for Delores now she was to go.

'Eleanor,' my father said to this. 'You seem awfully certain that I shall consent to Mr Craythorne's proposal.'

'If you don't, Papa, then do not be surprised to find me eloped one day,' was all I said and walked from the room, ignoring my mama's indignation and locking myself in my chamber and crawling into bed.

IN THE MORNING, I HOPED for the best. Dressed prettily, I waited patiently until Mr Craythorne's carriage set him down on the drive at midday. As I watched him emerge from it, standing tall in his neat blue tailcoat and hessian boots, I tried to shake the thought that I would soon be in the kind of proximity to him as I had been to Sheldon last night if this scheme was to come off. I pushed away the thought. After everything that had passed, I was only firmer in my resolution to commit to this, should it go favourably, and overhearing the arguments bellowing up from below the floorboards last night between my parents, I assumed it would. If Mama found it necessary to kick up a dust, it meant my father was not opposed to the idea. Most likely, he would be relieved to hand over the responsibility to Mr Craythorne at this stage.

This suspicion was confirmed when Mr Craythorne joined me in the drawing room and made his proposal.

To my relief, no time was wasted in the settlement negotiations which were not overly arduous. I was advised when I joined my parents in the study to hear the terms of it, I was to have a pin of three hundred pounds a year, which I could have no complaint to. The jointure allowed for a small estate in Sussex that Mr Craythorne had been left through his mother's inheritance, as well as one thousand a year she had also bestowed upon him. It was presumably a good bargain by how much improved my mama's mood appeared, even if my own relief was owed to altogether different reasons.

The wedding had been set for two weeks' time. We were to be married at Beddington Park by Special License. My parents had easily given over the grander plans of St James' and a wedding breakfast at Berkeley Square, in favour of a quieter affair in the country with only close family invited. It was thought St. James' would be too pretentious after so much trouble and a quieter affair would be more suited to the circumstances now. This, I knew would be Mama's stipulation. Her friendship with the Viscountess was so fragile now; she would prefer a low-profile affair and excuse to restrict invitations to relatives only. It suited me. I had no desire to be forced to play act amongst a society that secretly scorned me, but would play the pretty to my face now.

He would instruct a wing of Beddington Park to be opened up for us for the purpose of the wedding, but since so much work was required to bring it about, we would stay in the new London house he had rented until he awayed, and I could take apartments at Beaulieu whilst he was in Venice so the works to our own apartments at Beddington could be brought up to a more habitable condition for our return. This I felt unsure of, but made no protest. I could always remove back to Cuddington on his departure and hope that Beddington was liveable by the time he came back. A lonely London in summer would have to do if that failed.

As much as I was grateful of Mariella and had grown familiar and fond of her family, I had no wish to live with them or to be subject to her passionate outbursts should they resurface. For all she had done for me these past weeks, for being the only person I could trust with such secrets or rely on for help; I was ever grateful. But I could not help growing anxious in thinking of her own considered gain in this arrangement: Of the words she had spoken about convenient marriages permitting us a cover for such fancies betwixt us. And whilst she vehemently denied it, I felt sure she saw my marriage as a gateway to more frivolity between us rather than a cause for greater propriety. More intimate access to me as a relative. More excuse to play companion and divert me with her brother's regular awaying. Of all things in the marital bargain, this possibility disturbed me the most. As it stood, I could avoid her advances by declining invitations or taking advantage of keeping to more formal spaces where we might be overheard or discovered. But the same barriers could not be so well maintained amongst the household if I was a part of it. I took heart in knowing that we did not repeat such intimacy *that* night—however regrettable that I had spent it with Richards instead—but that I had given her the impression I was open to it, still distressed me. Did this notion encourage her to hope? How could I tell her that my feelings had altered so drastically since Sheldon, when she had been so good to me.

Before it had been easy to press the point and endure her sulking, but as family, I dreaded to think of the discomfort it could cause and the suspicion it might arouse if I was forced to make plain my feelings in no uncertain terms. I must hope that I could maintain the boundaries comfortably, for as a friend I liked her well, as a lover I felt entirely cold. Lord knows I had partook in my share of reckless folly these past months and oh, how I had paid for it; but I meant to learn from it and go on wiser from here.

I was about to become a woman; to be independent and free to pursue life on better terms, have a purse to match it. I could happily forego frivolity in pursuit of discovery of a world I had been kept back from. I tried to see beyond the dread of my wedding night and into a future of days commanded by my own wishes, especially when Giles was absentee. Days filled with visits to museums, libraries and exhibitions. Trips to family and friends afar and to fashionable resorts. Journeys to Paris and beyond, eventually. For this, I was joyful, excited and ready to embrace this new turn. My wifely duties, I hoped, would prove a minor price for such freedoms, and I could already see our time would be spent so much apart that we could go on quite famously together under such circumstances.

So, with such thoughts in my mind and all the financial arrangements settled to everyone's satisfaction an announcement was on its way to *The Times* presently.

There was only one grumble I had in all the arrangements, which was the temporary employ of a chaperone until the wedding, to replace Delores. She had set the date of her own wedding in view of it coinciding with mine and Sheldon's. The delay of course, to me now being married two weeks later to Craythorne, could not have been foreseen, nor could Delores be expected to delay her own wedding arrangements, to see me through to mine. So, with my wedding but a fortnight away, my parents had set as a condition for their assent, that I would submit to a lady chaperone my father would commission, who would "ensure" I was "well attended" in the meantime, so that *this* engagement period would leave me quite beyond reproach.

This, I was certain, was my father's doing. But I did not argue it, for I could hardly blame them for wanting to protect us all after all the calamities I had managed to bring about in only one season. It stood to reason they should wish to guarantee I might see it through to my wedding breakfast without further incident. It was just as I wished it too, for I could not have hoped for things to have come about so well, after how poorly they had looked on the prospect of our engagement only days ago.

This was a speech I tried to deliver to Mariella the very next day when she paid a call to give her official congratulations. She was so full of enthusiasm for our becoming relations that

Mother, who was doing her best to bear up to this new connection as well as she could, was more than happy to let us out to the park with a servant, to be relieved of the talk.

'Oh Eleanor, I am so excited. We shall have so much fun,' she said once we had walked out to woods.

'I wanted to talk to you about that, Mariella,' I said carefully, considering how best to phrase things. That I did not care to receive her unnatural attentions ever again, I could not say after she had been so helpful to me of late, but that to deceive her own brother so ill in repayment for his saving me from ruin, I did tell her: 'You see, so much has passed now that I cannot risk anything else going ill. If your brother was to discover us, it might all be undone.'

'As if he could: He is never about! But I accept your terms, Eleanor. I would not wish things to be compromised any more than you. And after all, we have become good enough friends to be satisfied enough, have we not?'

I smiled with such relief. 'Yes.' I could not quite believe her equanimity. I wondered if she too felt the moral obligation to her brother now it was to be official.

'So, I suppose we must begin to think of the other arrangements. There are parties to arrange, and your wedding ensemble to think of, and your wedding journey...'

'I believe it is all in hand.' I did not tell her my family wished to hush the affair as much as permissible, or that I would wear the dress that had already been commissioned for my wedding to Sheldon.

'Oh?'

'Well, except the wedding journey of course, with your brother being abroad. He tells my parents we shall make a belated one in the Autumn when he is returned.'

'I see. Well, I'm sure you must brace yourself for a few amendments: My parents will be quite ecstatic when he breaks the news to them and will no doubt want a large engagement party in the least.'

'You mean he has not already told them?'

'No. He means to do it by way of a surprise. He will wait for the announcement to be published in *The Times,* and I have been tasked with the duty of placing it on the breakfast table for them to discover, the morning it is in print.'

'I see.' At least someone would be celebrating this mesalliance with genuine feeling. If it could bring nothing above relief of recovery in my own house, at least it would bring happiness to theirs, I supposed.

'So, what say we take the coach into London, go to the Strand and visit Ackermann's this afternoon to browse the prints. You surely shan't tell me that even the decor for the rest of Beddington has been chosen overnight? I can show you your new London home too, it is on Half Moon Street.'

'I'm afraid I cannot. I am strictly prohibited from leaving the park now until my new chaperone is arrived, so there is no hope of them permitting me that far away. Besides, I can hardly risk going too far abroad with these bouts of sickness to conceal.'

'Chaperone?'

'Yes, my father is determined this match will not fail or come under any scandalous scrutiny, and so I must do the pretty.'

'How insufferable.'

'It shan't be *so* bad. It is only for a couple of weeks. To tell the truth, between the nausea and all the whispers about town, I don't have any desire to leave the house much beyond what I am compelled to. I am already dreading facing it out again at church on Sunday. I cannot wait until we are settled in Beddington and beyond the reach of our local gossips here.'

'Well, like you say; it shan't be for long. They think you ruined for crying off, but they too, will soon see the announcement and the Sheldon affair will quickly be forgotten and all will be restored.'

'I hope so. Father says as much, but you know these things are never *really* forgotten. I mean, the details may fade from memory, and yes, my engagement will help to expedite the process: but the stain of scandal never really washes away.

'Well. Since none of your friends will be of your new wealth or status yet awhile, you may amuse yourself with their obligatory deference to make them atone for their snubs.'

I laughed at this. It might be true in theory, but in practice, I would always be the unfortunate friend who made a condescending match, and married woman or no, I should never gain the respect I would, had I been Sheldon's bride.

I SAT IN THE PARLOUR with Mama eating some vulgar dish that was part of the fortifying diet her and Cook had devised for me, when she slid the open copy of the Times across the table: "...*the engagement of Giles Harper-Craythorne, of Beddington Park to the Honourable Miss Eleanor Ashlyn, daughter of Baron Westcott.."* I nodded and pushed it back towards her and observed how she winced over the reading of it. It was there in black and white, yet it seemed so surreal. All of it. I was supposed to marry Sheldon, not this man that I knew nothing of and my family and friends found so low. I folded up the newspaper, thinking then of the merriment around the table at Beaulieu today. I wished I could feel so. And whilst I could not conjure anything beyond a sense of relief, I knew it was for the best, and not just on account of my concealed pregnancy. Sheldon had showed me a side of himself that had forever altered him in my mind, and though it broke my heart to think it, the truth was, even if I *could* marry him now, I would not choose to.

THREE DAYS AFTER THE announcement in the paper, and we had almost no well-wishers come to pay calls, except for the Craythornes themselves, and Martha, who technically would be one too by next month anyway. There'd been no sign of Betsy and co. competing to get round the quickest to claim the place to play attendant under the guise of congratulation. And few responses to the letter's we sent out retracting the invitations for what would have been Sheldon and I's, this week. But, I had at least noticed a lessening in the studied glances on the rare occasions I went out to Mrs Oliver's or to the registry with Mama to see if there were any chaperone's that had instant availability. I had been happy to see there was not. So, Mama was to try the ones in London instead, where she hoped for a better response and I hoped that by the time she found someone, it would be pointless.

It had been decided, despite the Craythornes' enthusiasm for the occasion, we would not hold any engagement party at all, since the wedding was so close and Mr Craythorne so very hard to pin down with his business affairs taking him all over the place. His trip to Venice had been delayed by the wedding now but he seemed no less occupied for it. In truth, I knew that there were limits to what Mama could endure, and had my marriage been to Mr Elmbridge, there would have been no end to the pre and post wedding celebrations with all the bells and whistles. But who could she hope to invite to a ceremony of such degradation. For that was what it was; in everyone but the Craythornes' minds, and yet we were all to proceed under the guise of subdued celebration. I did not mind the subtlety. I wanted to get through this affair as swiftly and smoothly as anyone and put all the rest behind me, increasingly so as I came to ever closer scrapes in hiding my sickness.

Far from the fairy-tale notions I had nurtured over the years about my perfect wedding, perfect husband and all that accompanied it; it had been reduced to little more than a means to an end. The only clue to my former notions, the beautiful gown I stood in at Mrs Oliver's for fittings, that had been designed for my wedding in St. James'. The cost of it and effort on Mrs Oliver's part had been too vast to justify its cancellation at the last minute, and so it was to stay, however exorbitant it seemed for such a humble occasion.

Whilst no parties were to be thrown beyond the obligatory wedding breakfast, we were compelled to make our best effort when Mr Craythorne was in town and make a few worthy appearances together, to make a good show of things. And so, dutifully, we attended a couple of country assemblies, Delores' Wedding Breakfast, danced a few sets and accepted sparse congratulations from those willing to bestow them. We were careful to avoid anything where the Elmbridges might be in attendance, but it was unlikely, since I had heard on-dit that Sheldon had removed away to Oxford with the rest of the family. It saddened me to hear it, for I knew the announcement must have prompted it; yet I knew it for the best.

As the days went on and the news wore thin, I was pleased to find myself quite forgiven, on the surface at least. I was perfectly aware of the ingenuity of my reception in most quarters, but still it made it easier to bear if I must. To be tolerated was perhaps as much as could be asked under the circumstances. Martha and Beth at least could still be relied upon for company and Mariella of course sprung to my allegiance as devotedly as Betsy, Anna, and Clara created as much distance as they could. I cared little. How trivial such politics seemed now I was facing much more significant matters. However, when I learned that these three were to decline attending Martha's wedding if I was to be present, I volunteered to stay away, rather than force her into a predicament. 'But we are to be sisters now,' Martha said. 'Family. It is only right you should be there.'

'So, we shall celebrate privately and you shall not have to take a side.'

A delayed response.

July 1821. - Eleanor.

After weeks of receiving no response to my many letters to Mr Richards, I was surprised when Grantley brought the mail, to find a letter from him. I swallowed my mouthful of chocolate in a gulp, snatched it from the salver and vanished into the water closet to open it.

Dear Miss Ashlyn,

I hope you will forgive my delayed correspondence, I have just this night returned from Cork where I was employed by the Fitzgibbon family for the past three weeks. It was a last-minute affair, so you will forgive my not bidding you farewell in the proper style, but I did not know I would go until the very day.

I have on my return to London read your letters and I am sorry to have not understood your anxiety to hear from me sooner, or I should have endeavoured to send word to you before now.

I hope I can put your mind at ease, by telling you that the events of the evening in question were nothing to signify and are quite forgotten in my mind. I am not sure how much you can recall from the evening as you will forgive me for saying that you were quite unwell, but nothing as improper as you fear, occurred between us at all.

I own that our conversation was perhaps somewhat out of the ordinary owing to you not being quite yourself, but beyond that, I can reassure you that there is nothing to concern yourself over, and it is quite forgotten and forgiven in my mind.

I do hope this letter finds you well and now I am returned to London, you will find me at your disposal should you wish for any further discussion in this regard.

Yours, Mr Richards.

I threw it straight into the fire and watched it burn to ashes. I was quite beside myself to take in the words. If I was to trust his assurances; all of my fears, all of my weeks of worry—which for the most part had expired—could now be put to rest. But it was also possible that he was lying, whether to spare me the embarrassment of my forward behaviour, or to cover the tracks of his own deception. His alibi of employ by the Fitzgibbon's could be little more than a cover for his running off for fear of being discovered. I considered this a moment, attempting to put myself in his head. *What would I do if guilty of such a transgression?* It seemed to me that his decision to run away and evade such inquiries would indeed point to his guilt, but why then, would he come back so soon if he was guilty of taking advantage of me, with or without my consent, as the case may have been? It seemed impossible to me, knowing what I did of him, that it could have been without my consent.

It was true that I did not know him very well, yet I felt sure I had the measure of his character as one of decency. Yet the failure of my own memory left me uncertain. I weighed it up, thinking, as objectively as I could, of what I could remember; that which was undisputed in my mind. It amounted to the many attempts I made, some verbal and others more tactile, to seduce him and his continuous rebuffing and diverting such advances. I could not recollect a single instance of anything to the contrary, even if it did seem apparent to me that he was fond of me, perhaps above the ordinary.

As I revisited the fragments of that night, over and over, exhausting them until I was certain, I could not conclude that anything *he* did that evening was untoward. Then I added to that the possibility that he was engaged by the Fitzgibbon's as he said, and was now returned to London and at my disposal to answer questions, having taken pains to reply directly upon his return. These would all seem to point more towards his innocence. But it was in all the unknown and unaccounted spaces that suspicion could flourish and so I realised then, that I must find out unequivocally, if the Fitzgibbon's of Cork were a material fact, and if they were, whether he really was with them these past weeks. I thought instantly of Aunt Orlagh and knew I must find a private means to see her as soon as possible.

My aunt and uncle were not easy to pin down at the best of times, living between London and Ireland and always seeming to well utilize their time here in engagements of some kind or other. I at least knew them to be planning on staying in London for the King's Coronation, and so I knew that if I acted soon, I might catch them.

We were due back in London anyway on account of the very same, as well as to take interviews for the chaperone position. Mama had short listed five and they all sounded a dead bore and I was reluctant to go with her. But since Delores was now gone, there was no one to attend me and so I was not given a choice. But if I was to be forced to go anyway, I might as well use my time wisely. I was of no mind to go to Richards' address and confront him, despite his invitation. But my aunt, would surely be able to point me in the right direction to finding out if Richards' story could be trusted.

Three days later, I found my aunt at home in Saville Row, Mama having permitted me out for a walk with the housemaid.

'Well, how nice of you to pay me a call,' she said, a little surprised to find me in her drawing room. I was only grateful to find her alone.

'Well, I was out walking and thought I must call in since I was so close by. I hope you do not mind?'

'Mind? Don't be daft. It's a pleasure to see you, to be sure. Now, will you have tea? Or perhaps something cooler?'

Once we had sipped on lemonade a while and chatted over small pleasantries, I waited for a casual break to slip in the question: 'I was wondering aunt, do you happen to know of a family in your hometown, the Fitzgibbon's?'

She mulled it over before answering me. 'To be sure, the name is familiar, although I cannot say I can place it precisely. Why, my love?'

'Oh, nothing of great consequence. Only a friend of mine is looking to procure a music tutor and had given to her the name of one, referencing the Fitzgibbon's as one of his recent patrons. Since she is not familiar with the society of Cork, she was not able to verify it.'

'Oh, I see. Well, let me ask your uncle when he returns and I shall see what I can discover for you.'

I smiled. 'Thank you, Aunt, that is very good of you.'

'No trouble at all my dear, now, tell me; how have you been bearing up? I know there has been a lot of unpleasant talk...'

I took a long sip from my glass. 'I have made some foolish decisions, Aunt, I don't deny it. But I think it shall all work out well now.'

'Aye. Well, you won't be the first young lass, or the last, to get carried off into the season's merriment my dear, but I'm sure you have learned what you ought to be careful of it now.'

I nodded. More than what I could disclose, yes. More than I ought, I was unconvinced. It seemed to me that I had ought to have learned a lot more and a great deal sooner than I had, upon reflection.

'Well, don't look so down hearted dear, I do not reproach you. I know full well that you're a good girl but such receptions as you've received can...disorientate you, in the beginning, when you are new to such attentions. But, you are to be married now.'

'I am.'

'So, tell me about your husband to be, I hear he is a man of rising means but a very successful one.'

'Yes, I believe so. He has inherited Beddington Park and renovates in presently, but he is still a man of business and Mama does not like it well at all.'

'Aye well, your mama is, shall we say, not in favour of upsetting the order of things much. I suppose she must have taken it hard.'

I nodded.

'She will come about, my love. Everyone will in the end. Once you're married and settled, it will all be right and dandy.'

I smiled, grateful. She was an easy ear and even though I was fearful of her taking more than I had given in my enquiry, I was sure that even if she did suspect me of some other motive in wanting to find out about the Fitzgibbon's of Cork, then I could at least trust her to bring such questions directly to me, rather than flaunt about such suspicions. I wished I could have entrusted more to her. Her warmness made it easy to feel tempted to, but I knew I must remember that her allegiance would lie first to my father as her brother and only second to me, if I was to divulge anything warranting any serious concern or suspicion. So, I held my tongue and took leave of her, having spent a good half hour talking more of ordinary things and rendering my enquiry a minor passing thought, rather than the object of my coming.

Her response came a day later: my uncle was aware of such a family in Douglas, a middling, merchant sort who could have been the family referenced. She gave the direction as Vernon Mount, in order I might query with my *friend* whether that was the address given on her reference. In keeping with this story, I proceeded directly to address such a letter to the Fitzgibbons, as follows:

Dear Mr Fitzgibbon's,

Forgive my lack of prior introduction, but I write to you with regard to following up a reference given to me and hope you will not mind my writing to you to ascertain its validity.

It refers to a Mr Christopher Richards of London, Music Master, who I am considering taking into my employ. He lists you as having been one of his prior engagements of recent, and as such, I hope to make enquiry as to your satisfaction of his character and merit and whether you wish to make recommendation of him?

I would be incredibly grateful if you could furnish me with your reply.

Much obliged,

Miss E. Ashlyn.

I realised that from the moment I sent it, that I hoped for not only a response, but a certain kind of response, although I could not entirely fathom why. I knew I should be angry, incensed at Richards, determined to go to his rooms (were it not so dangerous to do so) and seek out the interview he offered me, seeing with my own eyes what I made of his demeanour and his answers, yet somehow, I did not feel so inclined. At least, inclined for the sake of curiosity and knowing, but not for the sake of some angry interrogation as I was sure I should feel.

I realised eventually, what lay between this discrepancy of feeling, uncomfortable as it was. It amounted to my knowing, that whatever *had* occurred between us that night, that the likely guilty party was myself. That whether he had encouraged or acquiesced to such an encounter, that it was my own vulgar behaviour that had accounted for his taking such liberties. I did not feel that it was a just end that I should be lumbering about his child as the justice of it, whilst he enjoyed the luxury of going on with his life unscathed, but I did know that had I not said and done such forward things, he could never have dared to hold such a willing impression of me. That it was this impression, that I myself had given him, which lured him to me and permitted whatever passed to be possible.

So, whenever I was caught with a bout of the horrendous sickness, my ears burning for gossip, or falling into melancholy at the prospect of my second-rate marriage, I caught myself at the point of cursing Richards, and reminded myself that I had led him to my bed in a flurry of wanton kisses and demands. That it had been my responsibility to safeguard my virtue, and it was my disregard of this duty that had rendered me in such a condition. He may not be blameless, but if I had learned anything these past weeks, it was that men were more driven by their carnal appetites than I had ever previously thought or known. An image of Sheldon and Lady Caroline formed a mist of interruption in my vision as I gazed into my nephew's story book, from which I was reading from.

'Are you alright, Aunty Lelanor?' came his innocent glance, searching my face, head cocked at an angle as he fidgeted in my lap.

'Yes Bertie, quite well.' I smiled and turned the page, conscious of my attention drifting.

Coming to Kent to stay with Harriet a while, was one of Mama's better designs. I knew it was intended as much to get me out of the way of whispers as well as resolving the issue of my being un-chaperoned now Delores was gone. Our interview's had failed to find anyone in want of less than a fortnights work, but its efficacy reached far beyond that. As nice as it was to escape society a while, it was being amongst my sister and her family at such a time that I found so restorative. My sisters' love had always been my greatest affection and their loss to me one of my greatest afflictions. I still remembered the day Lord Osborne had scooped Harriet away from us in Berkeley Square after the Wedding Breakfast and how cruelly I cursed him and beseeched her not to go. 'We have already sorely felt the loss of Caitlyn,' I remembered saying to her, 'and now I shall renew that loss with your going and double it.' We both cried a while, for she was sad to leave us all behind too, being grateful at least, that unlike Caitlyn who was removed to Edinburgh and unlikely to make the journey often to see us, she was at least, only going to the county of Kent. Kent seemed to me then as good as Edinburgh for little difference would it make to me that she was there rather than Scotland when I looked for her in her chamber or to go out riding or walking with on the Park. But at least I could see the benefit now that I could not then. Two hours in the coach was certainly not the ends of the earth and well worth the rattling about to see her. I would make more of a habit of it once the wedding was done. Go to Edinburgh too to catch up with Caitlyn. All such things I would be at liberty decide upon without reference to Mama, Delores, or even my husband whilst he was away.

I had just finished reading to Bertie when Harriet came into the room, balancing little Grace upon her hip, 'Come now, Bertie, Nanny is to take you to wash for dinner.'

'Oh Mama, I am not hungry. Let me stay with Aunty Lelanor, will you, Mama? Please?'

'Later Bertie, you may come sit with us a while after your dinner,' she said gazing warmly at his animated petitions and ushering him towards Nanny who was stood waiting to take them off to the nursery.

'Go on now, Bertie, go and eat up so we may carry on our story after dinner,' I said, pressing a kiss to his warm chubby cheek and setting him down off my lap.

'Do you promise?' he said.

I held out my pinky and waited for him to link it with his own. 'It's a bargain,' I said and watched him pad over and take up nanny's hand.

'You have a way with him,' Harriet said, sinking into the chair beside me.

She looked tired but in a contented way. I hoped motherhood was something I would find contentment in, however ill timed. 'I have missed you all,' I said, setting the book on the nearside table, checking the teacup that had long grown cold.

'It's good to have you here again. It has been too long since we have had a proper chance to speak.'

'Harriet, if Mama has set you up to finding out—'

'Yes,' she interrupted me, 'of course, she has. But I hope you know me better than to think I ask in that pursuit.'

I nodded.

'I just want to know you are alright.'

'I am,' I said steadily. 'Well, I am going to be,' I corrected myself for my sister knew me well enough not to be easily fooled by the façades that sufficed for others. 'I suppose I am looking towards when all this business might be a horrid memory and I can concern myself with happier occupations.'

'It will,' she said reassuring. 'Everything passes eventually.'

I looked forward to counting this chapter of my life amongst the list.

'So, I am told Mr Craythorne has written up a generous contract and seeks a Special License for the wedding.'

'Yes, a very large pin, I own I had not expected it.'

'Generous. He certainly seems unequal to Mama's complaints about his character and means to do things in quite the proper style.'

'Father is satisfied with the settlement. Mama accuses Craythorne of over-compensating, says three hundred pounds a year for a pin is nearing the vulgar.'

We laughed a little.

'Well, that is Mama for you,' she said. 'But never mind all that, Ellie, are you happy? Is this what you want?'

I shifted uncomfortably in my seat. It seemed happiness came in relative degrees. 'I want what you have, in the end. But I realise, it may take time to come about. But you are happy aren't you, Harri?'

'Yes, yes I am. But being a wife or becoming a mother is not without its challenges and miseries either, Ellie. But if you love Mr Craythorne, or are persuaded you wish it so, then they shall balance themselves out well enough.'

I could not tell her that neither concern could signify at this point, that the point of no return had long since been trespassed upon and to be spared at least a total disaster I must be satisfied to be on cordial terms with Mr Craythorne. To come to love him seemed both unlikely and undesirable to me, but to go along comfortably with him, I was content with—would have to be in any case. 'I cannot say I know much of love, but I hope to be happy with the arrangement.'

'You are still disappointed by Sheldon?'

More than I could ever tell you. I nodded.

'He has shocked us all, I think. I cannot pretend to be surprised at Lady Caroline for she was always dangling after him, but I own, I expected better of Sheldon, for I know he has loved you such an age.'

'Well, it is all history now.'

'Is it?'

'Of course.'

'I mean really, Ellie; do you speak from your heart or from your hurt?'

'Both perhaps, but we were ill suited. I suppose what I feel the most is the loss of a dear friend, a brother of sorts, and I am sorry for it. But in truth, if everyone had not been so intent on pushing us together, I do not think we would be in this situation now. Did you know?'

'Know that he would propose to you?'

'Yes, but before my coming out. Did you suspect our parents' intentions before all this?'

She shook her head. 'No. I only knew that I had seen in him an attachment to you many years ago and wondered if was cream pot love or something more serious.'

'It seemed I was the last to know then, for what it's worth now.'

'Sadly, I think Sheldon will live a long time in regret. You at least might be spared such a misery if your feelings are as you say...'

They were. I knew that now. My own regret was in ever permitting our friendship to be tainted and perverted by such a course when it might have been otherwise. But there was no going back. We had crossed the point of no return on our last meeting. What had once been a beautiful possibility was turned to ash; twisted into something ugly and tainted with so much misery I could not even bear to think about it anymore. But no less, I could not help feeling that the notion of walking the aisle, or the prospect of my wedding night would feel somewhat less daunting at his side over that of Mr Craythorne, now I understood clearly what kind of intimacy I was to be placed in with a complete stranger. I only hoped that lack of familiarity would be compensated by a less tenacious experience. I pushed away the thought. It seemed the nearer the day drew, the more unnerving the prospect became and my previous optimism harder to conjure.

When I went to bed that night and searched for my things that Hawkins had unpacked for me, I began to panic, realising I had, in my rush, forgotten to pack the vials of my draft. I was seized by instant horror as I pulled out drawers and searched the tabletops. Whilst it was clear that they had not proven their efficacy as yet, even after more than two weeks of taking them religiously, I still lived on the daily hope that at any moment they could prove worthwhile. The hope grew more and more dilapidated with every passing day and every bout of violent sickness that I battled to hide, but at least whilst I kept to the dosage, it existed. I was now fifteen days past my menses and was minded that if no result was produced by this elixir by my wedding night, I would give up on it. Now, I thought, turning out the insides of my travelling trunk once again, I would not even have remote hope to console me.

WHEN HAWKINS CAME IN to attend my toilette, surveying the room with a puzzle about her face, I decided I must abandon the matter. I told her I was looking for my favourite lotion as she considered the mess about the otherwise neatly kept room. As she brushed out my hair at the dressing table, I reasoned I must let it go and accept my fate. This child seemed destined to come and so I must stop resisting. I could hardly send back home for the vials anyway, and even if I did, by the time they would take to arrive, I would be on my way home, for I was only to stay a few days to be back in time for the final wedding preparations.

Despite my distress at this oversight, I had managed to keep to high spirits here. My sister's company was enough to help me forget my troubles a while and as my stay began to turn towards its end, I found myself wishing so fervently not to have to return at all. We had rekindled our sisterly companionship with every passing day and I enjoyed the simple things again, our walks, our rides, the games we would play with the children and cosy evening chatter that fell more easily now we had grown used to it again. Another thing that improved my mood immensely was that I noticed I was no longer prone to the regular episodes of sickness. They had persisted for only a day into my arrival before vanishing entirely. At first, I had put it down to some temporary reprieve, considered whether a change of air or in routine had helped since I had found myself much more active in taking long walks or running about playing games. But as the days rolled on, I felt no sign of the nausea at all, as if I was entirely returned to my former health.

Had I not been so preoccupied in my company, I might have considered it more carefully, but I had little time for reflection here and so I did not consider it at any great length until I woke one night in a violent fit of monthly colic and a liberal stain of blood all over my sheets. I was ill prepared, being the middle of the night and having brought no rags with me. After attempting to staunch the flow with a rolled-up shift and sleep aside the wet patch of the bed, I had eventually succumb to ringing the bell for a hot brick when the colic had become too much to bear. I had tried to work out whether the measure of blood or discomfort was above the ordinary—it seemed impossible to know, since the beginning of these spells were always so marked with pain and heavy blood. Could the draught have finally succeeded? I inspected the flow of it at regular intervals, fearing that it might be marked by the expulsion of something disconcerting, or, as I had heard stories of before, causing me to bleed to death in my bed.

It was this bout of panic and obsessing over such possibilities that led to me crying out in a fit of tears when Hawkins answered the bell and agreed to fetch me the hot brick and fresh sheets and rags I requested. I should have thought better than to make such a show of things to my sister's maid, so when Harri came in, blinking off her slumber and concern in her face, I realised instantly that Hawkins had gone to her to raise her concerns.

'Oh Harri,' I said in answer to her questions, 'I am so much sorry, it wasn't meant to happen here.'

'What wasn't meant to happen? Ellie, you are frightening me.'

'This,' I said pointing to the bucket full of bloodied linens Hawkins had discarded as she had cleaned me up and changed the bed.

'Don't be silly,' she said relieved, how could you help it. It will soon wash out. Whyever should you upset yourself so over a few spoiled sheets?'

'It's not the sheets,' I told her, bursting into another rush of tears.

'What then?'

'I cannot tell you, Harri, you will be so cross with me—'

'Cross with you? No. Why would I be?'

I bit down on my trembling bottom lip.

'Ellie, what is it? Tell me at once,' she said more severely and then going over to the bucket and examining the sheets, 'Ellie!' she said with less patience. 'What are you not telling me?'

'I'm sorry.'

'Ellie, tell me this is your menses and not something else?'

'I didn't mean to—'

'Good heavens, what have you done?'

'It was just a draught—'

'A draft of what?'

'Something to help rid me of—'

'No. Hawkins, Hawkins!' she called out now, her face flushed and streaming too. 'Send for the doctor immediately,' she cried, then ushered me back into the bed, checking as she did that I was not bleeding through the wad of rags I had set in place to catch the bleeding.

'Oh Ellie, you should have come to me.'

'How could I? I have disgraced myself,' I sobbed.

'Never mind that! Your health means more to me than *that*!'

This sent me into a flood of tears and whimpering I could not contain and she crept aside me on the bed and held me as I felt my body tremor with the weight of releasing them.

'Does Mr Craythorne know?'

I nodded.

'So that's why it was all so rushed. Oh Ellie, if you are to be married soon, why did you make such an attempt?'

'I was scared, I did not know then that it would turn out well.'

'Is that why he has offered for you?'

I nodded again. I could see what she surmised and preferred her presumption to the horror of the true account. If I corrected her and told her it was not Craythorne's doing, I knew she would assume it Sheldon's and how could I tell her it was not his either? Any leniency in her judgment of me may not extend to that level of transgression. And so, I permitted her to assume a lapse in my conduct towards my husband-to-be as a comparatively better alternative to the truth.

By the time the doctor arrived, we were both calmer. The hot brick had brought me some alleviation and the blood, had seemed to be flowing in the normal measure.

'Eleanor, Dr Lambert will need to examine you more thoroughly than you may be used to. I will stay with you,' she said and helped Dr Lambert lift the sheets to around my knees before taking up my hand and clutching it. 'Just try to relax.'

I did try, but could not manage it. The natural inclination to shut up my knees was not easy to overcome as I felt his uncomfortable prodding.

'Miss Ashlyn, how long since your last menstruation do you say?' he paused to ask me, mid-prod.

I scanned my memory back to my diary entry. 'Six weeks now, Sir. '

'Hmm. And you say you believe you were with child?'

'Yes.'

'Could you be at all mistaken?'

'Perhaps. But I have been sick for some weeks now, maybe three of them. I am not entirely sure, it certainly feels like it might have been forever.'

'Is something wrong, Doctor?' Harri cut in.

'Well, I cannot see any signs that would suggest a loss, or a pregnancy at all. If I am not mistaken, I would say the hymen is quite intact, although I cannot say with certainty as it is difficult to tell during menstruation.'

'You mean I am not with child?'

'No. It appears you are not, nor likely to have been.'

I was perfectly mystified. 'But the sickness and my missing the monthly curse...'

'Possible they are unrelated.' He withdrew from me and pulled the sheet down.

'Miss Ashlyn, have you been through any distress of late or any other illness?'

'Yes, she has been distressed,' Harri answered in my place and I added that I had not otherwise been ill.

'I see,' he said as if that accounted for it.

His assessment of the situation seemed to be that my worries and distress had caused a hysteria of sorts that had disrupted the normal routine of my menses and could have even accounted for the sickness and nausea. He was of an opinion of some certainty that the question of being or having been with child was impossible but, he would come and check on me in a few days' time when my bleeding had lessened and he could make a better examination of me.

I might have been more relieved if I was not so perplexed and increasingly horrified that I had now needlessly, as it seemed, made such confessions to my sister who seemed just as discombobulated by it all as she launched question after question at me. In the end, she resigned to leaving me to sleep from the drops Dr Lambert had left with me to help calm my nerves.

IN THE MORNING, HARRI told me she had sent an express to my parents to say I was ill—nothing to worry over—but the doctor thought it best I refrain from travelling just yet.

'Thank you, Harri, truly.'

'You know I hate lying, Ellie. I am sorry you have put me in the position.'

'So am I,' I said sincerely. 'I should not have come here with all my troubles. Forgive me.'

'Yes, you should. You are my sister. But you should have been frank with me Ellie, from the off.'

'I was scared. Everyone has shunned me and thinks ill of me. My set have abandoned me, save Martha and Beth. Papa barely looks at me. Mama is so sullen faced I can hardly bare to look at her.'

'Come here,' she said, the reprimand in her face softening, and gathered me up.

WHEN I RETURNED HOME a few days later, having been given the all-clear from Dr Hawkins and furnished with a story of hurting my back in a game of hoop racing, I was sad to be without my sister's company. Cuddington was quiet with Delores gone, Papa out shooting, my mama making calls, and me—not wanting to join her, or sit about with the new toad of a chaperone she had finally found and brought home from London—keeping much to my quarters. One thing that had pleased me on my return however, was my response from Mr Fitzgibbons, which had arrived during my absence.

Dear Miss Ashlyn,

I write in response to your recent enquiry over Mr Richards' employ with us.

I can confirm that Mr Richards did indeed attend us for three weeks in Douglass, where he was employed in tutoring parties of ladies in the accomplishment as well as making occasional concerts and recitals.

I can recommend him on account of his talents and service rendered to us during that time, and having been given his recommendation from an acquaintance in London myself, I can with confidence assure you of his merit and proper conduct.

I do hope this information is helpful to you.

Sincerely,

E. Fitzgibbons

It was as I had hoped and expected. Dr Lambert's assessment had persuaded me that I had not been with child after all. That I was still Virgo intacta and that my presumed condition had been borne out of my own worry and distress. It seemed implausible at first to accept this, so convincing had my symptoms been, although he assured me that such "episodes" were not unheard of in his experience, even Queen Mary I had been rumoured to suffer such an episode. So, it seemed that I had had it all quite wrong.

Between this, and now Mr Fitzgibbons response, it seemed I could at last acquit Mr Richards of any mischief. Although relieved by this and not least the reassurance of my innocence too, I now realised something that suddenly seemed worse: I was engaged to Mr Craythorne over nothing but a paranoid whim. To know I was not pregnant was relief enough but to know that the possibility of it was never in question hit me hard now as I sat but days away from my wedding. Here I was, unsullied and without child and inching closer towards the aisle every day, when it was no longer necessary. There was nothing to be done. To cry off now, after all I had subjected my family to, after all the bad business with Sheldon; I would have to go through with it whether I liked it or no. But I could not think of it without wanting to go to him directly and beg him retract his offer, even though I knew it pointless.

I had even considered bringing Mariella back into my confidence and asking her if she thought he would be so inclined to release me. But it seemed a risk too great to chance now. To be twice engaged and twice disgraced would likely mean a match even worse than he, or perhaps none at all. Even Sheldon, who might be minded to reinstate his offer, was not the version of the Sheldon I once wanted to marry. Not now. I was not sure if I could bear any more regrets, and I knew full well my family could not. So, I held my tongue around Mariella as she renewed her visits to me now I was back. I told her: yes, I was still suffering bouts of the sickness, when she asked. No, still no sign of the monthly curse, and just about anything else I must, to permit her believe all was unaltered. For it had occurred to me that perhaps if Mr Craythorne learned of the truth, he might think me guilty of some plot to lure him into making his offer and withdraw it anyway. Sometimes the possibility seemed to me a tempting one, others a fragile curse that I might be made to regret. One thing I did know for certain; is after coming so dangerously close to my own ruin, I must learn to be more careful.

I had, however, considered the idea of crying off more seriously as the prospect grew closer, but the more the reality was brought to bear on me, the more I tried to persuade myself of the advantages of the match. I would be free from continuous chaperoning from this Mrs Mason who I disliked excessively, and the hen pecking from Mama if I wanted to take Samson for a ride, or walk a league on my own. With the pin I was to have at my disposal, there was much I could do to entertain myself. I could visit my sisters and friends at will, spend weeks at a time, making a journey on from one place to the next. I would have so much unguarded time with Craythorne tending his business; the only question was what I wished to do with so much liberty.

So I consoled myself with this when I was forced to suffer the small family dinners put on in our honour as the wedding loomed ever nearer. I did not let out a clue to him that anything was amiss when he swept me up for dances or invited me to take turns with him. Inwardly of course, I was as indifferent towards him as could be, yet I must be happy to exchange a little peculiarity for my part in the bargain. And by the time these days had passed and the ceremony arrived, a fresh start awaited me and all the bad business that had cast so much shadow on me and my family, must soon dispel.

Sunset.

July 1821 - Annalise.

Summer in Cuddington might have started badly, but had flourished into something beautiful and melodic in the past month. The weather had blossomed into perpetual sunshine and the gardens alive with such colour and density that it was a pleasure to look out onto them and take in the air carrying the scent of floral perfumes with it.

There had been spring cleaning and canning to tend to in the day, but the lighter evenings and earlier finishes had given way to regular opportunities to enjoy an evening stroll in the woodlands or sit a little while in the kitchen garden under the guise of collecting and tying the herbs. The key was to keep a low profile. The consensus seemed to be that so long as the staff weren't seen to be roaming the estate with free license and were either out under the appearance of some duty, or discreetly lost amongst the woodland, then the upper servants would seem not to notice the increasing vacancy of the servant's hall after dinner. Even during the daytime, small liberties were permitted once the main chores were tended to and they had been unusually allowed a group half day off after church last Sunday and had all ended up sneaking off to the far extent of the lake where they picnicked on bread, cheese, and grapes, where some of the men even took to swimming in the sun glistened waters. It had looked so inviting and refreshing that Annalise wished she could swim, seeing them splash about all afternoon in such merriment. But the water terrified her and she refused Will's offers to teach her it when he held his arm out, droplets trickling down to his fingertips and his bare skinned chest beaded with water streams. 'You can trust me, you know, I won't let you come to any 'arm,' he said imploringly.

'It's not you, Will. I don't trust myself not to fly into a panic and drown us both in an instant,' she said, holding a hand across her brow to see him against the glare of the sun. It would have perhaps been better had she not looked so carefully, for the sight of him so handsomely set before her had not left her mind much since. He was in knee length breeches and nothing else, a warmth of tan across his skin that made him seem golden in the sunlight, his eyes even bluer than usual. Even when they had sat about the herb garden that evening with the others, drinking cider from the farm which one of the farm hands had procured for them, she could not unsee him in that image now.

'Are you alright?' he asked her as he refilled their cups from the keg perched on Paget's barrow cart.

'Yes, quite. Why do you ask?' she replied taking the refilled cup from him.

'I dunno. You just seem a little quiet.'

'Sorry. I'm just, enjoying the peace, wondering how we might manage giving all this up when the Ashlyns return.'

'Well, we'll 'ave next spring, eh? And who knows, by then you might even trust me enough to come in the lake with me,' he winked and sipped from his mug before staring into its contents and swirling it about in his hand.

Annalise was considering the unlikelihood of this when Fanny and Maggie came bounding into the garden in excited shrills.

'Paget, wheel the barrow out behind us; we're going into the woods to have our dinner over a fire!' she shrieked and Maggie opened up a sack that she had rolled up in her apron, carrying a stack of sausages and mutton chops.

'We'll roast 'em ourselves on the fire,' Maggie said, pleased with herself and wrapped them back up. 'Jack's bringing some ice up from the icehouse and Susan's bringing some sugar plums, come on, they've already started the fire up.'

'But what about Grantley, he'll sniff out a fire in no time and probably think we've got poachers or vagrants on the land,' Thomas sat up, lured by the excitement in their faces.

'Nope,' Fanny said self-assuredly. 'He's given himself a day's leave to visit a relative—Jibber's just dropped him at the posting stop. He'll not be back 'till tomorrow evening and you know Crawford won't venture out 'ere after sunset.'

Thomas stood up which prompted the shuffling of the others to their feet, abandoning the herb bundles they'd been lazily tying and picking up their cups to bring with them.

'Well, you coming then?' Will said, holding his hand out to Annalise, and in that moment, the image came back to her with startling piquancy and though she had meant to decline and offer her excuses, she found herself nodding instead and taking his hand and heaving herself up to follow the rest of the group who were already bounding out of the walled garden ahead of them. 'That's the spirit,' he said, and she could not ignore the feeling as he pressed a palm gently to her back and escorted her out.

They followed the others across the lawns in the direction of the wooded periphery as the sun set into a pink and amber haze over the treetops. Will's hand was still in place and his proximity as they walked seemed to grow ever closer. Had there been anyone behind them, she might have pulled away and tried to create a little distance, but they were the last to lag along as the others disappeared into the clearing a fraction ahead.

'You know, you look so pretty today,' he said to her as they navigated the log and twig strewn woodland floor, leaving the fading evening light behind them. 'There's just one thing missing,' he said and paused, reaching down to pick a flower and tucking it behind her ear. 'There,' he said and held her cheek loosely in a cupped palm as he examined her.

Annalise smiled and he gazed so warmly into her eyes she wasn't quite sure where to look.

'Hey lovebirds,' the hallboy jeered throwing a stone the other side of them, 'come on.'

She was grateful for the interruption as Will chased him off through the trees in jest before waiting for her to catch him up. But as she watched him through the evening, his eyes twinkling in the glow of firelight whilst his other features shrunk into shadow, the smell of rosemary splintered mutton rising with the smoke plumes as they sat about holding their sticks over the flames, she pondered over what might have happened if they had not been interrupted. She was veering dangerously close to falling into Molly's example and she knew she must try harder to avert it. But it seemed the more she tried to fight against the flow of his attentions, the more she found herself being drawn into secret musings of admiration as he laughed or smiled in her direction. She sat back against the stump she had settled on as the dripping mutton fat caused the fire to crackle and she withdrew her stick and checked the colour of the meat to examine its progress. When she looked up to set it back over the flames, Will was watching her and she wandered if he had been thinking the same.

They ate and drank amid a happy flow of chatter as the fire fell to glowing embers. They finished by singing ditties against the sound of hooting owls and the stirring of other creatures before trotting off to bed in contented spirits.

That's why there was an air of foreboding in the morning as these last stolen moments of bliss were counted down and the house was prepared for the family's return tomorrow. There were all sorts of ideas and plans flying around on how to spend their final evening of liberty as they tried to hurry through the day's chores. But even in the anticipation of it all, there was an undertone of urgency and dread as the reality crept upon them. The fear of the daughter's expected wedding announcement had created a sense of anxiety over the preparations that were anticipated to shortly descend upon them in the height of the summer heat without any of the respite they had grown accustomed to, to help them bear it. Cook had already been making up provisional shopping lists and menus to get ahead of herself and the guest chambers had been given an airing and clean linens.

However, when the Ashlyns' carriages rolled into the courtyard the next day and no announcement was forthcoming, there began a hope that perhaps she was not to follow in the usual trend and be married so soon after all. There had been no mention of dinners or parties at all and in fact they were to be off again on Friday to set out for Petworth, leaving them another balmy stretch of leisure to themselves. This had taken the sting out of their return and the routines and strictures of servicing the family's needs seemed bearable for this knowing, and even though the liberties of early finishing and estate wanderings were temporarily suspended, the staff remained in buoyant spirits, anticipating the return of their summer evening pastimes.

THE DREADED NEWS OF the announcement came a couple of weeks later just when everyone had been comfortably lured into a false sense of security. The daughter was to be married to the Elmbridge's heir and Lady Ashlyn was planning an extravagant engagement party that had shattered everyone's hopes at swerving the chore this year. To add insult to injury, whilst the Wedding was to be in London and the rest of the house spared, the kitchen staff were to be carted up with them to assist with the Wedding Breakfast.

Annalise did not mind this idea much. She had never been to London but had always wanted to see it, even if it would be mostly through the carriage window as they journeyed as Poppy had enlightened her. 'There won't be a moment outta that kitchen I'm tellin' yer. They're a stuffy bunch that London lot, even Cook refuses to go and put up with the French chef they hire. That's why we shan't get out of it. It'll be all hands on deck.'

'But it is only a few days Poppy. How bad can it be?'

'You'll soon find out with ten of us sweating and poking about in that tiny basement kitchen with its steam fed cookers and the stench of London heat. And you wait 'till we have to roast in that stuffy attic at night with all the other maids, on truckle beds there ain't no room for.'

'Still, we might get to see the Cathedral and some of the grand buildings.'

Poppy laughed and chucked the giblets into a bucket before she filleted a chicken breast with the ease of a knife through warm butter. 'You're such a romantic.'

It was true, she supposed, but she meant to make the most of it. If it really was as bad as all that, at least she could enjoy her imaginings a while longer until the bubble burst. Besides, she had been privately relieved at going and escaping Will for a bit. Things had grown so intense lately she was frightened that another free spell of the family being away, might just be enough to tip them both over the edge. She was certain that he had meant to try at kissing her the other day whilst she joined him on the morning dog walk. It had been a bad idea to go, and yet he was so persistent and she wanted to go, wanted to spend these precious spells of time under his warm gaze and smiles. Just not beneath his embraces—that was the line she feared there would be no going back from and yet the one she knew they were coming ever closer to breaching in these private little meetings that had seemed to flourish into increasing routine in the family's absence.

At least if she was to be away for some of it, by the time they returned, such opportunities would be extinguished by the family settling to Cuddington for the rest of the year. Besides, she had agreed to share the role of tweenie with Maggie when the family returned for good and would have no time at all to spare then. There had been no real loss to the household tasking on Molly's leaving with the family away. But once they were back in situ, her absence would be felt and meant more work for everyone else. So it was agreed that the housemaids would see to the daughters bell calls and toilette's, Maggie would tend the morning fires and water boiling, and Annalise would turn the house down for bed, snuffing any fires and lights out whilst a new housemaid was advertised for.

Annalise had wondered whether or not to approach the subject of being considered herself for the position, and advertising for a replacement kitchen maid; but she had only been there five months and wondered if it would seem a little pretentious to fancy herself for the position so soon. She had thought it might serve better to prove herself to Mrs Crawford before making such a suggestion, and so she accepted the tweenie tasks on top of her kitchen work with good grace. There had not been much to do anyway with the fires out for summer and only the candles to snuff upstairs when the family were at home. Maggie had gotten the worse end of the bargain and yet she didn't seem to mind it at all and was as chirpy as ever when she joined her at the kitchen table after breakfast.

'You'll never guess what,' she said as they set about scrubbing the carrots.

'What?' Annalise said, setting out the basins.

'Don't say anyfin will yer?'

'Maggie, you know I shan't.'

'Well,' she said cutting the leafy tops off four large carrots in one chop. 'Fanny overheard the Ashlyns talking and, it turns out the wedding's off. We shan't be going to London at all.'

'Do not believe everything Fanny tells you, Maggie. Does anyone else know this?'

She shook her head.

'Well, I suggest you keep it to yourself and if it turns out to be true, then everyone shall know it anyway soon enough.'

It transpired Fanny had been correct. There was to be no wedding now and the atmosphere above stairs was reported to be exceedingly tense according to the housemaids who kept the servants' hall alive with gossip and musings over it that evening. Fanny offered reports of the Ashlyn girl sobbing, even though she was said to have cried off, and her parents arguing and Lady Ashlyn sulking with her husband and her daughter. It all sounded quite tragic to Annalise as she sat with Will and Poppy in the kitchen to escape the noise of it all. If there was anything Annalise would regret in trying for the housemaid's post, it would be leaving behind her friends in the kitchen and having to be about the perpetual whisperings of the family's affairs, which she neither approved of, nor took any interest in. Will seemed pleased that she was at least going to be staying here and not going to London now, even if the hopes of another reprieve had been dashed with the Ashlyns cancelling their wedding trip to London.

They were not the only ones cancelling plans. Cook flustered about the kitchen the following day in such a foul and peevish mood as she rummaged through the larders and sent notes back and forth to the farm to see what could be mustered to feed the family in the coming days now they were to be dining in. At the same time, she was cancelling orders and menu's for the party, which had thankfully, not been delivered or procured yet, but they would soon be lumbered with if she didn't act fast. Everyone had felt the stress of her mood and were only too happy to be sent off on errands conveying messages to escape her. Annalise even got to enjoy a rare trip into the town to procure some emergency supplies the farm were unable to supply. The groom conveyed her in the trap, despite her willingness to walk the journey.

It had made the return to their duties a startling misery and the light-hearted mood of their summer respite faded so fast she had wondered if it had ever happened at all it seemed so distant now.

They had just recovered from all this disruption when Cook came in and announced that there was now to be a wedding after all, but beyond the other Ashlyn children coming home to stay a couple of nights for the ceremony, there was nothing more to cater for. No breakfast, or engagement party.

'This,' Maggie said, 'was cos the daughter had let them down with her choice of 'usband.'

'Oh?' Annalise said surprised. They were sat in the kitchen garden shelling peas for this evening's dinner.

'Fanny said she's marrying some fellow beneath her now, not the Lord from before, and it's caused a right scandal and that's whys Lady Ashlyn's not putting on any of them fancy do's she usually does and letting it all go on at the 'usbands 'ouse instead. Fanny says she's ashamed and don't want no folk making a fuss about it.'

'Is that so. Well, Maggie, Fanny has an awful lot to say and I'm not sure it's her place to tell it.'

'Yeah, I spose. She said you and Will might be married one day at this rate. Is it true, Anna?'

This she had not expected. 'No Maggie, it is not true and I would beg you not to repeat it for it might get me into the kind of trouble Molly was in if reaches the upper servants.'

'Oh no! I shan't say a thing. I would 'ate it if you left. You won't, will yer?'

'No. At least not for a very long time I suspect.'

Weddings Bells.

August 1821.- Eleanor.

This was what the season effort was all about after all: weddings. It was not coined the marriage mart for nothing. The season providing the means and the wedding the ultimate ends. Clara had returned to the country as Mrs Allerton, Delores was now to be addressed as Lady Hambleton, and Martha was to be married in the morning. I was to follow close behind her. As we stood in church for the final time the banns were to be read, I felt the distress of my circumstances increasingly severely. I was to be spared the banns on my own account at least since the Special License was now obtained, the problem was: I no longer wanted to be wed at all.

I was happy for Delores and Martha, their union had the elements of a love match with the added advantage of being raised up and spared a lesser fate. Mine was lacking in both aspects, although I could not afford the plunge into even more social disgrace. Crying off once had left me tolerated but privately eschewed, twice would leave me quite beyond recovery. This is the mantra I played to myself as I sat at the pew and the clergyman's words poured over me:

'I publish the Banns of marriage between Bertram Henry Craythorne of Cuddington and Martha Jane Brownlow of Ewell. If any of you know cause or just impediment why these two persons should not be joined together in Holy matrimony, ye are to declare it. This is the third time of asking.'

The customary silence and wide-eyed glare of the vicar ensued before everyone was free to exhale and move on to the final hymn. If it was up to me, I would not attend church at all. But my parents were resolute that I must continue to show a brave and smiling face each Sunday, against all the whisperers and slanderers. I did not care for their opinions anymore. But I knew I owed some duty to my family in reparation of disappointing them all so sadly. It was only I who truly knew to just what an extent I had come close to causing such unthinkable scandal that would have done far greater damage than that already suffered. This was the rescue package, and I knew I should be more grateful for it.

In the afternoon, Mrs Oliver came for the final dress fitting; and Mama, my new chaperone, Mrs Mason, and Watts crowded into my small dressing room to see it. When she had finished pinning a few more hems and tucking a few rogue pleats, I stood there—mannequin like—with everyone telling me how handsome I looked, what an excellent job Mrs Oliver had done. I agreed with them; it had after all been commissioned for a Viscount's bride. But beneath the fine lace and silk, the half smiles and blushes, I was struggling to hold myself together. Wondering how I would get through, if spinsterhood might be preferable to vowing my life to a man I knew next to nothing about?

I had refused to see Mr Craythorne anymore beforehand. The revelation of my Virgo intacta state had begun to grate so sorely against me the closer it got. I declined to go with him to Beddington to choose a room in the house as he had requested. Or to suffer any more of his parent's soiree's where I was paraded about like a new acquisition, an impressive trophy for their visitors to admire. I was too frightened that now I was no longer in need of rescuing, if I was too much about him, I would find a reason to dislike him and throw the whole thing off. And secretly, I hoped that my indifference might tempt him into withdrawing his offer. But it had not. However much I shunned and avoided him, did not return his cards... he remained complaisant. It seemed Mariella was right; he was an indifferent man and had either no care, or no understanding of how I cut him. She had warned me as much, and I told myself that if there really was no way out of this arrangement now, I must cling to the fact that a man so disinterested would be a worthy prize.

This was how I convinced myself to sit at church, how I got through the dress fittings, invitation writing, and finally the vowels that I uttered, pledging myself to Giles Harper-Craythorne, a detail that was new to me and I frowned over, as he stood in Naval livery, his hand clasped over mine. It was surreal to me, the words I uttered, the compliments and congratulations I received, all so far removed from me. Like an evasive dream, it did not feel real. Even when I had stood in the mirror that morning, I hardly recognised my own reflection in it.

My dress was beautiful; ivory silk and beaded cuffs. Daisies in my hair and my mother's finest pearls hanging from my ears and neck.

'You make the most beautiful bride, my dear,' Mama said, arranging my veil about my shoulders and stepping back to smile. Behind the pride in her eyes, I could see her other thoughts: *What a sad waste: you were meant to be Mr Elmbridge's bride.* I wondered if her grief had been greater than mine in it all. For even though I felt deep regret, and foolishness, I did not feel the type of lovers' heartache I was sure I ought to.

'Beautiful,' Delores and my sister chanted their confirmation when Mama stepped aside.

I didn't say a word. I could not afford to open my mouth for fear that the only words that would come forth from it would be: 'Stop the wedding, I cannot marry him,' or some such plea to that effect. It all felt so wrong now. So needless... and yet I was already bound. Something from the deepest guttural depths of me said it was not too late—yet. But it was. If I turned back now, we would all suffer: Everyone in this room and many beyond it, tainted by my insubordination. I looked at their smiling happy faces. *I must do my duty...I must.*

'Well, I had better get dressed myself now, will you manage, Watts?' Mama said.

'Yes ma'am,' she grunted and continued prodding at various folds in my dress.

When Mama went, taking Delores with her, Caitlyn came to me and lifted the veil.

'You look like a princess,' she said, clasping her hands together. 'You always used to say you were one.'

There was much I used to say that no longer felt like my truth. I could not bring myself to share in the joke. The best I could manage was a thin-lipped smile.

Caitlyn looked me over and dismissed Watts with a nod. 'Harriet has just arrived, she'll be up to see you in a moment, she's just settling the children with Silvia,' she continued. Then she put her hand on my forearm. 'It won't be as terrible as you imagine it to be, you know. Not once you have got used to it.'

I wished I could believe it. Somehow, I could not. I could not explain exactly why. My reluctance seemed borne more out of some deeper sense of instinct, rather than reasoned logic. When I presented the case in logical form, it seemed there was no particular case for anxiety. Yes, there were better matches, but I had settled on a comfortable one. And yet, the feeling that plagued me, seeming to almost shrink my very heart, could not be persuaded by any such argument.

'I was nervous on my wedding day too: I thought I might not make it to the alter in one piece,' she laughed a little. 'But the fear itself turned out to be worse than the actual day,' she smiled, moving a strand of hair from my face. 'You'll do fine.'

'Oh Caitlyn, I do not know if I can go through with it. I wonder if I am making a very great mistake. I mean, I know so little of Mr Craythorne after all, indeed it was all so very rushed.'

'Eleanor, it is your nerves speaking, and quite natural, but pay no head.'

She hugged me then and I prayed she was right. I felt like I was about to walk into a mistake from which there was no return. But the feeling didn't shift, not when I entered the Great Hall, not once I uttered the vowels, or signed the register.

It was a fairly small affair, the Wedding breakfast only slightly better attended than the service, and I was grateful for that, if nothing else, as I struggled to maintain my composure amongst the company.

We sat about the dining table with my family and his, Delores and the squire and a few of Giles' friends; about thirty of us in number. Champagne and a feast of a wedding breakfast set before us, raised glasses and speeches of congratulation all about me. I was grateful for the Champagne at least. This was all I could partake in with any sincerity. The acquiescent smiles and rudimentary nods or replies were entirely contrived. I was not happy and no amount of congratulation or well-wishing would alter that. I was perhaps relieved, that at last I had made right on my transgressions, but even that mild consolation was tainted by the more sobering realisation that I was to go to bed tonight, with a total stranger. That I was his property and subject to his wants and needs. If he was as tenacious as Sheldon had been, I did not know how I should manage that well at all. At least I had feelings for Sheldon then. When I looked at my new husband, I felt vacant. And yet I knew I must do my duty to him tonight, the fear was all consuming.

WHEN THE HOUSE AT LAST grew quiet and the visitors finally departed, it was already past five-o-clock and I was quite fagged on account of the early morning and excessive champagne sipping. I had initially thought it would help me through the day, and it did to begin with. But now only a thumping headache and unquenchable thirst remained.

I was already in my new chamber, the maid having at last stripped me of all decoration and dressing me in the plainest of day dresses I could find. Anything, anything at all to make me less desirable to him was welcome. So, I had asked her not to fuss about my toilette, made no protests to her unpinning the elaborate design the friseur had spent hours fashioning, and did not accept her offers of cold compresses to my eyes to alleviate their blood-shot looking whites.

When he came to my room shortly after her going, I felt instantly alarmed. Surely, he did not expect me to perform such duties already. It was not even six-o-clock yet. I had permitted myself the luxury of thinking I had a few more hours to mentally prepare myself. This, was above all other things, the most dreaded in this arrangement.

I was at the writing desk, making thank-you notes for the wedding gifts when he came into the room. I sat instantly upright and stiffened in my seat.

'I see you have settled in well?' he said, hovering at my shoulder.

'Yes, I thank you. Your staff have been most attentive.'

'My staff? *Our* staff my dear. I am happy they are looking after their new mistress well.'

I felt his hand upon my shoulder and did my best not to flinch.

'You are busy?' he said examining the papers upon the desk.

'Well, we had so many gifts I thought I ought to see to the thank you notes before I quite forget what came from whom.'

'Yes, yes you are quite right, we must not seem ungrateful.'

'No,' I agreed, sensing some more sinister edge to what he said, but being too preoccupied by his proximity to pay mind to it.

'Have you many left to do?'

I felt myself baulk at the question. I knew what was next to come and yet I had hoped somehow it would not. 'Quite a few,' I sighed.

'You are tired I think,' he said, brushing a palm against my cheek and this caressing felt so unnatural, such an invasion. 'Perhaps you can finish this in the morning?'

'I am, and I have such a terrible headache.'

He crouched down beside me. 'Perhaps then you must think of taking a nap before supper.'

I hoped he did not mean to suggest joining me in it. But when he took up my hand and kissed the ring he had only this morning put upon it, I froze and an answer would not come forth. My aversion was strong, more powerful than anything I had ever felt before. Even when Sheldon had pressed me into his chamber door, I did not feel this much foreboding. I didn't know why, or what exactly caused such repulsion to rise at his advances. He was not a disagreeable man, and whilst he was far removed from my personal tastes, he could not be called either unhandsome or uncharismatic. But there remained something that compelled me to shrink away from his advances. An indecipherable repulsion.

'Perhaps you would like me to have a supper tray brought up to you instead?'

I did not know how to answer. The prospect of sitting about the table with him again was unhappy, but at least Mariella would be there. 'That is good of you, but I think I will be well enough, if I just take a little rest now,' I decided on.

'Whatever pleases you, my dear. I shall let you get some rest and will see you later.' He pecked me on the nose and left the room, leaving me quite stunned with a vague 'yes' upon my lips.

Once the relief of him going washed over me, I began to feel regretful. He had behaved towards me with the generosity and attentiveness of an exemplary husband and yet I had rewarded him so poorly for it. It was not his fault, after all, that I felt so indifferent to him. His intention had been to save me from a terrible scrape, how was he to know that by the time we were announced I would no longer be in it. I still had to face *that* confession yet. But it seemed ill timed, it could wait until tomorrow. It would surely bring him joy to know that I was neither ruined or carrying some other man's child after all and that would go someway to pleasing him. I realised then if I was to be the good wife that I meant to be, to be worthy of his generosity, I would have to convince myself to try harder, to see him more favourably and attempt to overcome my aversion with some self-inflicted persuasion.

Wedding night dread.

August 1821.- Eleanor.

I was grateful to Mariella for agreeing to stay with me on our wedding night. Accommodation at Beddington was scarce, owing to the renovation works, and what remained of it, quite unfit for habitation. It could not have answered to have invited guests to stay, yet she did not mind a bit. It seemed the natural solution to my lack of companion now I had dispensed with the formidable Mrs Mason, and my even more pressing lack of near acquaintance with her brother. With her about to soften the uneasiness of our being such strangers, it felt somewhat less daunting, and supper was not nearly as taxing as I had expected. But as the moment of dread approached and I dismissed the maid who had been tending my bedtime toilette, I suddenly felt too overcome to be separated from her.

'I am sure I cannot manage it, Mariella, the thought of it. No, it is too much. Pray do not leave me alone with him. I know he is your brother, and I mean no offence, but I am quite unfamiliar with what is required of me. You know I do not remember a hint of what passed between Richards and I,' I added quickly.

'Nonsense, you will remember exactly what to do when the moment comes. You could just close your eyes and imagine it is me touching you.'

This suggestion did not improve the prospect at all. I felt my eyes swell with the threat of tears and a gasp of despair escape me.

She put her palm against my cheek and said more seriously; 'Indeed it will be over so quickly, you will barely know it is done. If it was such a ghastly task, then how could it have passed so forgettably with Richards, however in your cups you were?'

I caught my breath and nodded. I could not tell her that it did not pass betwixt us—she was an ally I could not afford to lose. 'It is true, and yet it gives me no comfort. But no matter how I ponder it, I remember nothing beyond his carrying me up the stairs.' What I did remember in startling clarity now, is what had passed with Sheldon at Nork and I could only hope he would not expect such favours. 'Oh, it will not do! I am not sure I can go through with it.'

She placed her hands upon my shoulders. 'Do your duty this night, and I am certain he will leave you be thereafter. Men do not treat their wives so poorly as to expect a regular occurrence; they have mistresses for that. From their wives, they want only issue.'

I considered her point, it was true that from the little I knew of such intimacy there were few married persons I could name that seemed to be tied to the marriage bed, and many seemed to be absent of any affection at all. There were the exceptions of course, they also came to mind, but were scarcer in example. Even Caitlin, married only four years had expressed to Harriet that since the birth of her two children, the Marquis had not come to her chamber in a great many months. I suppose two boys was enough to satisfy him as to the security of his estate.

If I could just bring myself to get the thing out of the way, hopefully I would be like my sisters and fall instantly with child, and it would surely not be so bad after that. If I could manage to bear a son quickly, there truly would be no need for him to pester me beyond it. In better circumstances, I would not have wished to bear children so hastily; indeed, I loved to ride on Samson too much to be bogged down with the burden of pregnancy. If what I had seen of my sister's confinements was anything to go by, it seemed a miserable bore and restricted so much of what was to be enjoyed in diversion. And I was independent now, I could spend my time in so many things that had been forbidden or regulated; I was not ready for an interruption before it had really fired off. But to do my duty swiftly would relieve me of further burdens, and so I must wish it.

Tentatively, I shrugged out of my robe, let Mariella brush out the lengths of my hair and anxiously climbed into the bed. When she departed, I knew he would come soon. I felt an unsettled stirring in my belly. I could find no desire in my body or senses to embrace the task with equanimity, less still desire, but I wanted to declare it over and as I watched the clock on the mantle turn over half an hour, I grew despairingly anxious.

I listened for footsteps, checked the door was left unlocked and used the chamber pot several times before I resolved he was not to come. Perhaps Mariella had reported my anxiety and he had taken pity on me this night? I did not know whether to find the possibility a blessing or an insult. I was relieved at the prospect of being let alone, and yet dreaded the idea of having to repeat the routine tomorrow instead.

As another quarter hour passed, I resolved to snub out the candle flame and try to sleep in this strange, unfamiliar bed. But no sooner had I settled into a comfortable spot and felt the promise of sleep on the horizon, I heard a cry and raised voices. I sat up bolt upright in the bed and listened hard; did I imagine it? Was I dreaming? No, it came again: muffled sobs. If I was not mistaken, the sound of Mariella's sobs.

I got down from the bed almost slipping on the steps and searched blindly in the dark for my robe and slippers. Gently, I opened the door and searched for any sign of a servant who might make inquiries and spare me the need. There was no one about. The sobs had petered off into a dull snivel and I knew something quite terrible must have come to pass to bring Mariella to tears. I feared some dreadful accident or the like. I was distressed at what state I might find her in. I padded carefully along the hall, trying to remember in the dark the way to her chamber, but when I got there, there was no sound and when I opened the door, she was not inside it. Then I followed the trails of whimpers until I came to what I was sure was Giles' chamber. Then I heard more clearly the voices behind the door. 'Please do not weep so,' I heard Giles say.

How terrible, I thought. *Had some urgent news come of some family calamity? One of their relatives ill, or worse: dead?* Yes, it explained it all. Mariella must have received the word of it and took it to Giles to deliver it to him. Perhaps whilst I was lost to an oblivion of nerves and trepidation, an express was delivered. How dreadful, and on such a happy day for the family. I was about to go in and offer my condolences, but then it struck me that it would be an uncomfortable thing to enter Giles room uninvited, husband or no. Perhaps even to encroach on their grief in a private matter of this gravity would be too much this soon. Yes indeed, I would go back to bed and wait to be told of it. I could then offer Mariella my comfort and Giles my condolences in the proper manner befitting such circumstances. I turned to find my way back to my room as I heard such a strange sentence it caused me to pause and consider it.

'You knew this moment would come, Mary. I can hardly take a wife without the complication can I? It is my duty,' he said.

'I knew it, but I did not know how sorely it would affect me. Please. I beg you Giles, do not go to her,' came Mariella's desperate reply.

My heart sunk. This was not about some family calamity at all: She had told him. She had let her emotions gain advantage of her sense and she had warned him away from me. Not to spare my distress, but her own. She was jealous of him and it had pushed her to confess the unsavoury secrets of our past intimacy. I felt suddenly sick. How could she confess such a thing to anyone? It could not answer that she would do so savage a thing on such a night as this. I too felt disgusted at what must pass, but it was she who persuaded me to it in the end, and now this...

'I have no choice. What will she think if I cry off? By gad, on her wedding night!'

'She would be relieved, I know that much.'

I almost let out an audible sigh. How could she say such things that I had told her in confidence? How indeed could he seem to take the news with such equanimity? It was the strangest exchange I'd ever heard. She was warning him off of his own wife, in his own house and he was attempting to placate her.

'Well, that's by the by,' he dismissed. 'She will expect me because it is the proper thing, and if I give into you and decline to go, she will suspect something and then what will you say?'

'I will think of something, anything...just let me stay with you tonight.'

My ears must have deceived me was my first thought at this odd reply. Stay with him? But why...

'Let me go to her, deal in the business as quick as I might, and you can wait here for me.'

'Huh, and you come back to the bed with the stench of her about you? I thank you no.'

'You are quite impossible, Mary; I don't know what I can to do to please you. You are obstinate tonight and I am not in the mood for it! Now, let go of me and I will have the business dealt in.'

'I won't,' she refused, and then the sobs were renewed.

I shook my head in disbelief; there must be some strange explanation I had yet to work out. I was exceedingly tired and spent a long time at the Champagne after all.

'Let me deal with you instead, Giles. No one knows as I do, how to please you.'

'Not now, let go.'

'I'll let you do your favourite thing,' she said in what seemed some winning appeal that silenced him a moment before answering: 'When I am returned.'

'Damn you! You will take it now or not at all!'

I could have swooned and perhaps I might have if I did not hear footsteps padding up the hall bedside me. It was Digby, Giles' valet, and I knew as he approached me that my hopes of leaving undiscovered had now expired.

'Are you quite well, madam?' he said, his weasel-like face glowing in the amber light of the lamp he carried with him.

'No,' I said with all the equanimity I could contrive. 'I—I must see my husband.'

'I will let him know, ma'am, and send him to you directly.' But before I could reply, we both heard Mariella let out a deep throated cry which startled us.

'Ma'am, please: go back to your chamber and I will see what is the matter.'

'No, I shall stay,' I told him, and without warning, he stepped in my way and tried to spirit me off along the hall.

'How dare you!' I exclaimed. 'Remove your hands from me, Sir!' I pulled away from him. 'Do you not understand your place?' I said a little louder than I meant, but with so much noise rising out of the room, I did not think it could be noticed.

'Please, go to bed. I will manage this,' he insisted, but I did not heed him. Instead, instinct took over and before I thought the scheme through, I pushed past him and burst into the room.

I could not tell who was most suspended in surprise: me at the sight of a half-naked Mariella on her knees with her hands clutching at Giles' breeches as he sat in the wing back chair; they as they noticed me; or Digby as he attempted to pull me from the room. It was a scene nothing could have prepared me for, and even though I wanted to speak, make some communication of my bewilderment, my shock, my disgust, I found myself utterly speechless.

'Eleanor!' they both exclaimed, and whilst Giles' tone was one of alarm, Mariella's held a peculiar hint of relief about it. He pushed her away from him and relaced his half-undone breeches. 'It's not what it appears.'

'I do not want to hear of it,' I said then, and relented in my struggle with Digby and let him escort me through the door before shaking free of him and bursting into a sprint towards my own chamber. I heard him call out after me and then his footsteps quicken against the floorboards. He gained on me as I fumbled to find the door handle in the dark, but just in time, as if my prayer was answered, the door lurched open and I turned the key to lock it behind me. I leaned against the wall and caught my breath, hearing him call out for me to let him in and trying the door handle.

'Go away,' I told him, and then it was Giles' voice I heard next.

'Eleanor?'

'Leave me alone, I do not want to see you,' I told him through my tears.

'Eleanor, I just want to talk to you... Explain.'

'No, you can say nothing to answer for what I have just witnessed. Now GO AWAY!' I screamed this so loud I surprised myself. But it silenced him, the door stopped rattling in its frame and I heard footsteps taper away.

I supposed however much he wished to offer me some impossible explanation for this scene, he wanted less to disturb the house further and have to explain the cause. Although, if his valet's actions were anything to go by, the servants had quite forgotten the proper order of things under this roof.

I stepped away from the wall, climbed up on the bed and let my tears out. *How could she?* I did not know precisely what to make of it all, I owned, but there was nothing that could possibly be explained that could in any way redeem the fact that I had just seen Mariella attempting relations with her own brother. And if the peculiarity of that was not terrible enough, she was preventing him from my bed, not because she was jealous for my sake as I had supposed, but for his.

I had never credited her with deep sentiment or kindness, but with me, she had of late, proved changed; softer, gentler to me and I had took it for some deeper care she had come to find in our renewed friendship. She had been there for me when I could turn nowhere else. Assisted me with so much calamity. Could it have all been a lie? Nay, surely it could not. I would have detected it before. But it was despair I heard in her voice, desperation I saw in her eyes and she was not sorry to be discovered as he was. I saw it: I could not deny the look of defiance in them. It spun my thoughts into such a pounding headache, I willed the prospect of sleep to relieve me of it.

———— ❦ ————

IN THE MORNING, I WAS perfectly startled when I opened my eyes and found him sitting in the chair beside my bed. I almost screamed at the shock. The curtains had been drawn open and the washstand set up, a tea tray awaited me on the small table. I realised the maids must have let him in. I sat up to see if any of them were about, but they were not.

'Do not be distressed,' he said gently. 'You must forgive me the intrusion, but I had to come. We need to speak about last night. I owe you an explanation.'

The image reformed in my mind. 'Oh yes, to be sure you do.'

'I know it looked very ill to you.'

'Ill? She is your sister! What can you be about?'

'No. She is not my sister.'

I thought I might faint. I had entered a madhouse to be sure. 'What can you mean?'

'She is my cousin; my aunt's daughter.'

This surprised me, but still, I did not like it. 'If she is your cousin, then why have you led society to think you siblings?'

'It is a long story, and I shan't bore you with the whole.'

'Oh, I think you shall, for I do not know how to believe a word that comes from either of your lips anymore!'

'Very well, as you wish.' He leaned back in his chair. 'My mother has been long dead. My father, that is; my natural father, was a married man, who was not married to my mother. I was the result of an affair between my married mama and the Chevalier di Barosini. It was a scandalous situation at the time, and there was nothing for it than for each of them to disown me and preserve their positions. For a while. I was kept here at Beddington under the guise of a tenant's son. Later, when it was feared my looks too suspiciously reminiscent of my mother's, I was put into the care of my aunt, a young spinster then, who had nothing to lose in taking me in as her charge. I knew nothing of the fact of course, until I was of age, when my aunt declared it to me and bestowed on me a sum offered by my parents in way of compensation to me. I used it to buy a naval commission.'

I gasped, my fury had transformed to something more like pity. 'Did you not know them at all?'

'My father would not acknowledge me in the least when I eventually found him out. My mama did eventually, but too many years had passed to make anything of it. Except Beddington I suppose, it was the property she had through her marriage jointure, and she had willed it to me just three years before her death. But I had no need of it 'till now.'

So this was the mystery of his birth. He was not the squire's son or heir as the rumours suggested; it was all smoke and mirrors.

'I was brought up by my aunt and later Mr Craythorne too when my aunt married him. We moved abroad thereafter, and no one knew any better there, so it was said I should be known as their son, to keep things simple, and so it was. Mary and the boys had not been born yet and before they were out of the school room, I had set off to make my fortune. I did not know any of them again, until I visited them in Paris just a year ago.'

'Very well Mr Craythorne—Giles,' I corrected myself. 'I see your circumstance, and indeed I have a deal of sympathy for it, but you cannot imagine that this in some way compensates for what I witnessed last night—'

'No, no I suppose it cannot. But at least you know it is not quite as bad as you thought it.'

'Perhaps, but if you are in love with Mariella and she is, as you say, your cousin—why did you not just marry her? Why put me in the way of it?'

'I own I did not mean for it to turn out this way. I do not love her, not that way.' He sat forward a little now, leaning in. 'Mary is a dependent type. Having not seen her since she was a babe, I knew nothing of her character when I was reunited with the family in Paris. She became fond of me, and I thought it in quite the proper way that families might be so inclined. I was mistaken. I should not have let things escalate into such a fashion, but she was wilful, persistent.'

I knew enough of her character to accept this easily enough.

'I had never meant to marry her or anything of the sort. I told her as much, many times. Our connection is not one of mutual regard, as you saw for yourself.'

I suppose I could vouch for that too.

'She has some very peculiar ways...'

I flinched at this.

'And sometimes I think she is not of sound mind at all. But no less, she is family and I have a care for that sake. I had hoped that London would settle her. I hope to see her well married off. It would do her a great deal of good and prompt her to release her attachment to me. But as you see, I have not managed to see her well positioned yet. It has been an arduous task to tempt her into society and she makes no effort to try for it at all,' he sighed the words. 'I doubled her dowry myself, in the hope of finding her a good husband to settle to.'

'I see.' That's why she had her face set against the marriage mart. She already had her sights set upon what she wanted. But then why, why had she encouraged me to marry him?

'Now,' he continued, 'I had not expected to find you in the compromising circumstances that I did, it was quite above anything I expected to find out, and I own, I was not in any great rush to take a wife until I had seen Mariella wedded. But she refused to make a try for it. And when she told me about your predicament, I felt obliged to do the right thing. Mary seemed so fond of you and so sad at your despair, I felt sure that if she was to accept my marrying at all, then it would be to you, her dearest friend. And you had been so good to her, paid her notice and sponsored her along when other doors remained closed to her.'

Yes, and this is how she thought to repay me the favour!

'I thought my proposal would be quite the thing to offer us both a happy solution. And I own, there was an advantage in my mind, that if I was set apart and married, I could at last bring Mary round to cutting them ties with me. I hoped she would see there was nothing to be done and that she must settle on a match herself.'

'But she will not.'

'She will, eventually. Only it may take her time to accept the circumstance. I hadn't realised you would agree to her being at home with us on our wedding night. When I learned of your invitation, I feared it an ill-idea, but how could I refuse my new wife the want of her companion?'

'I did not know it could matter then.'

'Indeed, how were you to know? And how could I begin to tell such a story to my new wife? It was quite beyond me. I hoped there would be no further need to. But there it is.'

'I wish you would have told me sooner.'

'Yes, I see it was wrong of me. But it alters nothing. Later, I will send her home to Beaulieu and she will behave herself under her parents' roof. I will go presently to London to open up the house I have rented there whilst the improvements are made good here. I no longer think it sensible to stay at Beaulieu. That way, we can remove quickly, which I think will make things much easier on everyone.'

I nodded.

'I had planned to do so on my return from Venice, but I see that now Mary is quite out of her senses; the best thing is to expedite such arrangements and for us to be removed from her society altogether until she accepts the circumstances. It is plain she will not whilst we remain under the same roof.'

'Very well,' I said with some relief. I had no intention of spending another moment in her company anyhow. Giles might be somewhat less blameworthy, and he may even think her a sorry case to be pitied, but I knew different. She had lied to me. Strung me along and pretended at being my friend whilst all the while lusting after her own cousin, then encouraging me to marry him. It all made sense now. It was too much to even think it. Did she believe that her encouragement of our marriage would lead her into some comfortable ménage betwixt the three of us? Surely, she could not be so mad? Or perhaps it was her wish that I would fulfil the role of the indifferent loveless wife, not as she had suggested, for the sake of our continuing dalliance, but because I would be too unconcerned over her continuance in her cousin's bed! I did not know anymore, but I had seen enough of her antics to realise she was not of ordinary sense and could not be trusted. To away from her was the best thing for it, and the sooner the better.

'With any luck,' he added, 'left alone in the country, boredom might turn her to finding a husband.'

That I thought most unlikely. She had never shown the slightest interest and whilst I had allowed myself to be flattered into thinking it was on my account, it was obviously not out of any aversion to the male sex. Perhaps that was why it was a safer bet to distract herself with a female; there could be no impediment to her affection for Giles. Such a passionate dislike for her began to grow in me now that it unsettled me. 'And what shall I do, once you have packed her off and departed for London?'

'I need not go right away, you may go with me if you wish it, assess the decor and furniture together?'

'No,' I said flatly. 'No, I think we cannot afford the delay under such circumstances. You must go directly to London and I think, perhaps I must remain here until you send for me?' I might have been able to forgive his portion in this debacle, but it would take time for me to digest it all and permit him near me now.

'Surely you cannot stay here alone, with no company and not even a proper house to enjoy with all the works ongoing?'

'It is certainly not ideal. But what else can be done? I can hardly appeal to any relatives to stay for I will be instantly questioned so soon after our wedding day. They will know something is wrong. I shall not be able to hide it from them so well. And I can hardly come with you and stay in some hotel, with me still so much scorned by society. I have been on-dit for so long that I can only hope that now I am married and much out of sight, they will find some other thing to talk about and forgive me in time. But putting up at a hotel, even briefly, no, it will only bring further disapproval and bring me back into their thoughts. Once you have furnished the house there, and we are respectably settled, it will not matter.'

'Well, I cannot like the idea of leaving you here alone. But I do not wish you to suffer any further distress after all that has passed. So, if it will please you to remain here, I shall leave this afternoon and try to make quick work of bringing it about so you may join me as quick as may be.'

'Thank you.' I felt some genuine gratitude for him granting me this. As much as I did not feel comfortable in staying here alone, to afford me some space for reflection was a kindness that touched me. I could feel no distress on his account, for he meant nothing to me, but Mariella, all her deceit, all the confidences I had entrusted to her, I felt distraught.

'What if, Giles, she lets out the secret of our coming together, the Richards' incident—'

'That, my dear, is why I must go gently with her and cannot throw her aside harshly and vex her. You have suffered enough scandal and it is my greatest wish that there will be no more sufferance on your part. But Mary can be quite a live wire, so we must have a care not to provoke her resentment. Let me deal with her gently and I may yet protect you.'

I nodded. 'Thank you, Giles.' I was truly grateful for his consideration. Perhaps that was why, against all my physical instincts to permit it, when he got up from his chair, sat down on the bed beside me and began stroking my face, I could not refuse him.

'I am so sorry, my love, that things have taken off on such a footing.'

I smiled outwardly, but inside I wanted to crawl away as he advanced. I felt my body slipping further from his grasp and had to will it to stand fast. But he was my husband now, and despite this bizarre revelation, he had been honest in his explanation, patient with my ill temper, considerate to my wishes, understanding of my feelings, where many may not have been. So when I felt his kiss upon my lips, I willed myself to try. I accepted them with as much equanimity as I could muster, the taste of his tongue invading my mouth, the wondering of his hand about my shoulder, my clavicle, my décolleté. It startled me to have him touch my breasts; I flinched and gripped the blanket, squeezing it in my fist. But I permitted it, endured it as best I could.

I realised quickly, as he shifted position and I found myself beneath his weight—grateful for the blankets still between us—that even his delicate kisses at my neck, his tender stroking of my nipples; that I could not find myself earnestly open to his advances. My body would not be stirred by his attentions to it, like they had when she had practiced such things upon it, when Sheldon had brought me to even greater elation. Now, it wanted only to recoil, shrink away, dissolve at every stroke, every lick, every murmur of his satisfaction.

I do not want you. I did not know how to make myself comply, not beyond the physical strength of holding myself there instead of fleeing; frozen, breathless until my lungs bounced up to gasp the air for fear of expiring. I think he took such gasps for pleasure, they encouraged him on. How could he know they were little more than the natural urge for my body, my physical body alas, to instinctively fight to breathe, to live; when my soul felt so much inclined to want to die now, right here, in this bed.

He stood up then and I dared to open my eyes, wondering if my prayers had been answered, if he suspected this too much for me, after all the recent excitement. But no, my guardian angel had seemed to abandon me, for he got up only to remove his own clothes.

I stared into the ceiling. I think I may have been begging it to somehow intervene, to fall down upon us perhaps? I did not know. But as I traced the hairline cracks in the plaster, it remained unmoved. Then I could not keep my glance fixed upon it when I heard him unbuttoning his breeches, the weight of them fall to the floor, his feet stepping out of them. I should not have looked, but I did. I think I wanted to know my enemy. To understand what would attack me so cruelly. But when I looked upon him and saw the culprit, so swollen and violent looking, I wished I had not. Even once I squeezed my eyes shut against the sight, I could not unsee it. I found the strength to lift myself onto my elbows. *I can not do this.* I must get up. I must go. But he met me at the halfway point and gathered me up in his arms, pulled me gently from the bed as he kissed me: Lifted me out of my chemise until I was standing there before him; cold, despite the warmth of the summer morning, shivering, unable to move now. His examination of me unnerved me further, his brown eyes roaming me, up and down, widening at the sight, darkening with intent.

Why didn't I run now? He stood back enough in his evaluation to permit me room to flee. My feet would not obey me; they remained firm against the fibres of the rug. With every attempt at beseeching them to move, they seemed to sink only further into the floor, until I could feel the flattening of the pile, the edge of the floorboards running beneath the rug, pressing into my soles.

'You are truly something,' he said to me then, and I read the change in his demeanour, a power in his stare that told me he was intending to make the most of his new rights. How I was not sure, but I knew he meant to enjoy it. He pushed me gently back upon the bed so I landed sitting on it and realised only then, my feet were able to move. I could not feel the floorboard cutting into them anymore, only the indentation it had left behind. Then he was above me again, his heaviness, the prickling of his beard scratching at my chest, my navel, my...

I did not know whether I should be grateful for his diversion to such places for I had expected next, the force of him trying to enter me with that violent swell that looked impossible to fit within my body.

'Relax my love, I see you are not ready yet, but let me help you along,' he said between kisses at my thigh, and then he lifted my legs quite asunder, parted the tangle of hair and when I felt his tongue, hot and wet where he had parted it: I let out an involuntary gasp. This was not *only* a gasp of horror, although I wanted it to be. I felt betrayed by my body's response. How could it wish to jerk itself closer to his feasting mouth when I wanted so much to crush him between my thighs, before kicking him away and fleeing. *Curse you.* I did not know if I directed this to him, or to my own flesh; to those parts of it that sought to draw him in as I fought somehow to bear him. I felt a hot tear escape and stream into my ear, my instinct was to find my hand and wipe them away, but when I lifted my head to do so, I realised he could not see me. I could only see the tufts of his thick dark hair between my thighs. My thighs: they were moving and thrashing around in peculiar jerks and circles. I could not believe I had not felt them, but then all I seemed to feel was his mouth, his tongue, his rhythm. I stared at them a moment in disbelief, as if they did not belong to my body at all. I tried to steady them but they continued their erratic thrusting and jostling. I was ashamed of them. Why had my body abandoned me like this? I knew this too—even my very bones—belonged to him now.

But I still thought that in physicality, I still possessed it, I still had command of my own limbs. It seemed I was wrong about this too. They were jolting and moving so fervently now, I felt totally disjointed from them. His pace quickened, and so my body quickened. I felt a push, it must have been a finger pounding inside of me. It jarred at first, he moved it slower for a few beats before quickening, then he returned his greedy mouth to me, sucking me in so hungrily I thought he might swallow me up entirely soon. Oh, I wished he would stop. *PLEASE. Let me be now: Abandon this wicked assault, I do not want you. I do not ...*

Then I heard a scream, or was it a sigh, an imploring gasp? This too belonged to me, although I had not summoned it, given it permission to leave my lips. It grew louder, more musical, more breathy, more desperate. I stopped fighting against it; suddenly I could not anymore; something built so powerfully within me it suspended my body entirely and now I—no, I could not bear the thought to flourish—*I wanted it.* I suddenly needed his mouth precisely where it was, no: closer, his finger deeper, faster. I too had abandoned my conscience. Had I signed away my soul too, on that register? *Eat me then. Eat me whole. Bludgeon me with your violent parts if you must. I will let you. I will welcome you. I will even try to enjoy it, just—just don't stop what you are doing to me. Not now, not yet...*

It was only after those violent waves crashed into ripples, then fell away altogether, that I wanted to swallow up every thought and feeling I had allowed to lapse into such depravity. When he crawled out from between my legs and they fell flat like jelly upon the mattress, I recoiled at what I had permitted. I could smell the scent of myself on him as he towered over me now, his kiss slimy and repugnant on my lips as he lowered himself and pressed himself against the place that had just moments ago, felt so vast and now had shrunken once more into nothing but resistance. *God no.*

'Relax my love, you are quite ready for me now,' he said, a whisper upon my tear-filled ear.

He was wrong. I would never be ready for him. No matter what tricks he played to win the cooperation of my body, there was something deeper within me, even beyond my physical presence, that I knew would not allow him in; that had battened itself against him. I dug my fingers so deeply into the mattress I felt my nails bending, snapping at the edges as he pushed against me, trying to find his way. He could not, that part of me—whatever it was—had regained its composure, clenched against his efforts, would not permit him in, no matter how much he persisted in trying to persuade it.

'Relax, my love, it will make it easier for us both,' he said, his tangy warm breath misting my face.

I turned away, stared into the headboard, my body turned to stone. Then after a few more failed attempts, he repositioned himself, lifting up on to his knees, pulling me closer against him so I slid an inch further down the bed until I felt a stinging pain, a pressure building. 'Please stop, it hurts so cruelly,' I begged him. The tears were coming fast now, my ears overflowing with them.

He retracted a little, his attempts more gentle again, but he did not stop the trying.

'If you would relax, it will not hurt for long, just this once,' he told me, impatience in his tone.

I was certain it would hurt forever.

He continued on, the stinging was now burning hot and mounting pressure I recoiled from. As he attempted to push, I felt my body clench and push back. As his attempts grew more determined, so too did my own avoidance. 'Let us try again tomorrow,' I pleaded. 'It is too much painful now.'

'It must be so this time, but we must endure it,' he said with less consideration in his tone, and this time when I jarred back at his attempt, he held me fast about my knees and pulled against my resistance, his fingertips carving imprints in my thighs.

I let out a cry, I could not tell how far he had breached me, but I knew it was not yet done for he was still pushing: I felt I might break apart if he persisted. I should have confessed to him that this was my first time. Perhaps he would have been more gentle, thinking this my second. He hushed me and concentrated on his task, steady and persevering and this time when I used all my body strength and begging to deter him, he did not respond to it at all, as if he did not hear me and poised himself to make his most contrived effort yet. I screamed out, so loud that I had thought, when the door burst open, that a maidservant must have heard me and come to my aid. But when I saw, charging across the room in a fit of fury, Mariella, her hair let out around her shoulders in a wild mess, dressed only in her shimmy, I thought I could never be so glad to see her again.

Instantly, he let go of my knees.

'How could you!' she screamed at him, running towards us. 'You promised me you would not,' she cried, pulling him from the bed and beating her hands against his chest.

'Mary, get out of here!' he said with a force of such anger it would have frightened me to be the recipient of it.

I took the opportunity to dart from the bed, gathering a sheet around my nakedness.

'Mary, Mary!' he was shouting as she pounded her fists about and he attempted to contain her. 'You thought you could keep me from knowing: had that Digby lock me up and keep guard over me!'

Lock her up? She had gone quite insane. I could barely keep up with her words; they were erratic, muffled at times by being pressed against Giles chest as he tried to hold on to her. She kicking, flaying her arms, moving so wildly I did not know if I should go to fetch some assistance. Then Digby came bursting into the room, but there was something not right looking about him. He was dishevelled, unsteady; his hair was flat on one side and was that blood, yes blood trailing down his neck, his hair congealed in its thickness. I screamed at the notice and Giles and Mariella looked around now to see him too.

'You!' Giles roared. 'How could you allow this?' he said accusing.

'Forgive me, Sir, I...'

'I hit him swift around the head with the fire irons,' Mariella said with a lunacy about her tone that matched the wildness of her looks now.

Digby held his head, feeling the blood now and examining it between his fingers.

'Yes, and if you think of stepping near me again, I will kill you next time!' she growled at him.

Giles had managed to hold her fast now, in a strange kind of lock that had his arms about her shoulders in a vice and one of his pale, hairy legs wrapped about both her ankles, so all she could do was fidget and complain. If the spectacle of this had not been so bizarre, Giles naked and me so much relieved to be free from that torture, I might have been more frightened; I should have been. But for a moment, I felt such great relief to be interrupted that I did not mind that it was on account of such a scene. I did however feel concerned for Digby, and gathering my sheet tighter about me, I grabbed a towel from the washstand and offered it to him. It was then her eyes settled on me.

'You!' The growl in her voice was so unnatural I dropped the towel. It was feral as if originating from the throat of some wild animal, not her small mouth.

I picked it up and gave it to Digby, stepping away from her direction.

'You bitch. You seduced him.'

'I did nothing of the sort,' I said in protest, but wondered why I did.

'So, you got what you wanted did you?' This; she directed at Giles and quite rightly, for I certainly had not wanted such an ordeal, not even the bit I had been momentarily tricked in to thinking I did. The shame of this memory caught in my throat.

'Mary, I warn you, stop this now,' Giles said, his impatience rising, his body fixed strong and firm against her renewed attempts to escape him. I was grateful he had her contained now; for I knew it was me she wished to get to, I who she would attack next if given the chance.

'You think yourself so much above our touch don't you?' she scowled at me.

I said nothing.

'And yet here you are, letting him defile your body even though you do not want it. Still, you will have him, take what is mine.'

'He is my husband, Mariella, not yours.' I should not have said this, I realised a moment too late, for it drove her beyond forbearance, and she broke free of Giles a moment, running towards me with him grasping after her.

I did not know whether to run or launch my own attack upon her, so much fury I felt at her deceit and contriving. I had not asked for this. It was her that pushed and pulled me to the idea. If I had not been so desperate, I would never have been brought to it in a million years. I could not say it of course. If it was reassurance she wanted, I could have put her quite out of her misery and told her that I did not want him, not a bit, not in the slightest, that he was all hers, so long as she kept him from assaulting me so vilely. But I could hardly tell her as much in front of him. Right now, I wished never to set eyes on either of them again.

She got close to me before he caught her, snatched her up just inches from me as she launched herself in my direction. I wondered what she might have attempted to do to me if he had not wrestled her back with so much force.

'And now you protect her!' she growled, tears streaming down her cheeks. 'What about me?'

'Mary, please.'

'Do you love her, Giles? Do you?' It seemed more accusation than question.

'Mary, enough of this now. For shame!'

'Or is it just your hunger to break her that compels you so?'

So she had seen enough of his attempts at trying and yet she thought me already broken by Richards, I was perplexed but could correct neither of them. I was embarrassed to be seen in such a circumstance. Could she not tell from my face, how much I did not want him to succeed in it?

'You stink of her!' she said slapping his cheek and this momentary lapse offered her a chance to spit in my face.

I wiped it with the corner of the sheet I had been clinging to.

'So you let him taste you then. Even though you refused me.'

I was shocked at this strange shift and then embarrassed, remembering that neither Giles or Digby knew of what had passed between us. 'Mariella, you are quite mad,' I said. 'I think you must go!'

'You, you think *you* can tell me to go!'

'I, tell you to go,' Giles thundered in. 'You will be packed off this instant and will not be welcome here again,' he warned her, and I supposed this increased fury in him was confirmation, that she had not yet confessed to him our past intimacy.

'I will go nowhere,' she spat. 'Not without telling her the whole'

He put his hand about her mouth now. 'Eleanor. Go into the hallway and call down to the servants, tell them to bring a number great enough to restrain Miss Craythorne and get someone to wait on Digby before he swoons.'

I looked over to Digby, he looked grey.

I did as bid, and imparted to some unknown face in the stairway, the information.

It took only moments for them to descend into the room, busying themselves about it. I don't know what had occurred in my absence, but Giles had been pulling on his breeches when I returned. Mariella sat now in the chair, unrestrained but still simmering. He warned her with a flash of his eyes not to think of leaving it when she saw me come back in.

I did not know what to do. I felt I should remove to some other place but this was my room.

He led her out of it once he was dressed, and I did not know or care what he had said to manage to contain her. But later, when I watched from the window, the carriage pull up, loading her and her things into it, I felt both relief and fear simultaneously.

She was gone at last. But he was not.

I was washed and dressed now. I had spent an age cleaning those parts of me I felt he had tainted. Soothing my injuries. I was not certain he had managed to do the deed. What I had learnt from this assault, knowing now how agonising the sensation of such an attempt, was that Richards was undoubtedly as innocent as he protested. It was impossible I could not remember such a thing. I had felt none of the soreness and pain I suffered now. Surely, no matter how inebriated, such a jarring assault would have roused me from any number of cups. I ached and throbbed so painfully I had taken to sitting upon an arrangement of cushions. I did not know how I would bear it again and I could not think of it, or I knew some rash attempt to flee into the unknown would win the better of me.

So when he summoned me for dinner that night, I kept an even temper and prayed he would not subject me to a repeat.

'Eleanor, I do not know where to begin in making my apology for such a calamity.'

Forget that, make your apology for trying to force your body into mine. Make promise you shall never try again and all the rest can be quite forgotten. 'It was a most irregular scene,' I said, looking up from my plate for just a moment.

'I know. And you have borne it all so well. I thank you for such grace.'

Then leave me be now, I beg you.

'She is gone now and shall not return.'

'How did you manage it?'

He sipped from his glass before answering. 'I told her that I would go to her parents and give them the full account if she persisted.'

'I see.' I was not convinced even that would have won her compliance. 'And will you, if you have to?'

'I hope I will not. But, if I do, then I shall do it for your sake.'

My sake? I prayed he was not working up to some declaration of regard that he thought might lure me into another try at the marriage bed this night. He was supposed to away too, had he forgotten? 'Well, let's hope the threat of it proves sufficient. I hope we will be removed to the London house quite swiftly, Giles. I must insist that we get away from her knowing where we are. Cuddington is not so far away from here.'

'And, first thing tomorrow I shall leave to make the arrangements. I would have set upon it today as planned but Digby was in need of a day's rest before journeying.'

'Is he alright?'

'He will be quite well, once recovered.'

'That is good. I still can't believe she would do such an abominable thing.'

'Well, you do not know her like I do,' he said and I agreed it, wondering to what extent he understood us to know each other now. Had she elaborated on her earlier speech in some spiteful fit about what had passed betwixt us before? If she had, he did not seem angered with me for it. I suspected he would have known her to be the instigator in any case.

The rest of the meal proceeded in relative quiet, with occasional prattling. I watched as he chewed on his beef, trying to shake the memory of his mouth so hungrily attacking me. Trying to shake with it, the shame of my allowing it to draw such responses from me, however brief. I told him I was tired when we left the table. So much fatigued and feeling quite unwell from the day's events, I must go straight to bed, straight to sleep.

I was not sure if he took my hint or if it would be enough to ensure my peace tonight. But I felt increasingly more hopeful as I lay fidgeting in the bed, the clock ticking on. One rather enduring kiss he had subjected me to on parting from dinner had caused me some concern, but I took it now for a parting conclusion, rather than a threat of his coming to me later for more.

WHEN I AWOKE TO THE suns glare, I instantly searched the room for a sign of him. He was not there and I had made it through the night, unscathed. So long as he did not mean to make a breakfasting habit of it as he had yesterday, I might feel relieved.

I got up promptly and dressed before the maids came in, to avoid being discovered in a vulnerable circumstance. I had left the drapes open all night to ensure the dawn light would wake me ahead of the household. If I was up and setting about on things, I was sure any such repeats of yesterday might quickly be avoided. So, remembering from my tour on that sporting day, I found my way over to the west wing and took an interest in the works as the men began to set upon them for the day.

It was a strange feeling that plagued me as I took the housekeepers escort around Beddington. Tragic almost; remembering doing the same just a few months ago, back when it was irrelevant to me: this place, this house, him. Back when the world was mine and possibilities infinite. I remembered, as we inspected the same rooms I had with Martha and Delores. I had envisaged Martha here—not me. And yet, here I was discussing the progress and plans, learning the shape of my new home, being introduced to my new staff.

It felt like one of those times in childhood when I would fall asleep in one place and wake up somewhere else, having no awareness of how I had miraculously moved from one place to the next. If only I could travel backwards over that bridge of time as quickly as I had travelled towards this fate.

What would I have done differently? I pondered as Mrs Pemble lifted some holland covers to query my preference for the rearrangement of some sofas. Would I have accepted Sheldon's offer back in those early days of his return? Would I feel any better being married to him, now? No. Not after how he had demonstrated his *feelings* for me. Knowing what I know now, I would not have engaged myself to anyone at all. I would have settled on another season next year.

I had been two days married now. I should have been filled with happy thoughts and hopes of new beginnings, not feeling like the world had collapsed around me, just as this house seemed to be doing.

'This is to be your private parlour,' Mrs Pemble said, leading me into the next room. 'It has one of the finest views over the parterre,' she added, with some of the enthusiasm I was quite obviously lacking.

This room was still intact, a pale blue and yellow damask upon the wall, a round table to fit four facing another large window overlooking the formal gardens. 'It is a very pleasant view,' I managed, and whilst this seemed to appease her, I was sure I must seem terribly ungrateful and disapproving. How could I tell her that it was not the house I disapproved of, however dusty, worn and faded.

Mrs Pemble was talking me through the staffing arrangements when he found me in her parlour and announced himself off to London within the hour.

He thought we might take a luncheon together before he left and it seemed a reasonable request to do so with him promised far away from me soon.

But my prattling over details of the house and asking after the London one, did not throw him off for long. When the plates were cleared and we removed into the drawing room, I expected him to go now, not to sit so close to me on the sofa as I tried to concentrate on my sewing basket.

His kisses were gradually increasing, his caresses of me no longer subtle.

'Please, Giles,' I said, feeling his hand wonder to the place that still ached with tenderness. 'I am in so much pain, I cannot.'

'But we did not manage it,' he protested a little.

'Didn't we?' I said more aghast at this than I meant to let on. So the worst *was* still to come.

'No, my sweet. You were too much anxious I think.'

'I'm sorry. I did not think it would be so uncomfortable, I...' I wanted to explain to him then—that it was my first attempt, that I was not having Richards' child after all—before I thought better of it.

'It cannot be helped. Perhaps, if we permit you a little time to recover...'

'Yes,' I agreed quickly.

'When I return, we may try under more relaxed circumstances.'

'Indeed, I think once I have had a chance to restore my nerves, it will make all the difference. It has been a very taxing couple of days.'

'It has. But you must know how tortured I am to have come so close.'

'Forgive me.'

'Perhaps, if you could just offer me a little relief, I could go on to London quite comfortable in the wait for you, my love.'

No, please no.

'But I have already told you, I am so much injured—'

'And I do not mean to make matters worse for you, if you could just perhaps, take me in hand instead.'

'I do not know how,' I lied, alarmed at this suggestion.

'I will teach you,' he said, placing my hand upon the bulge beneath his breeches.

I do not wish to learn.

'That's it my dear,' he said lifting my hand in strokes over the shape of it. If this was all, I could stomach it in exchange for yesterday's request. He relaxed back on the sofa and when he let go of my hand, I continued the motion as he groaned in relief. If it had remained so, I could have bore it better. But when he opened his breeches and put my hand inside them, instructing it beneath his own, I wanted suddenly to strangle it. It was the same art Sheldon had guided me in, but I had not minded it so much with him. But now, I did not like how it felt, or the smell of it. I prayed he would not make the other request Sheldon had of me; that would be impossible. But I closed my eyes and continued. Even when he snatched my breasts out of my dress, the neckline drooping beneath them so he could look at them as I serviced him, I remained attentive to the task, remembering it would soon be done, he would soon be gone away. But it took all I could manage to continue when he demanded such squeezing and fast thrusting and poured all over my hands and my skirts his wetness. I thought I might throw up.

I assumed it done then, taking his offered handkerchief. *Go now, please.* But he did not. Instead, he laid out upon my lap, recovering himself. I was pleased my performance had been sufficient, for it was over now. I had done my duty and he could at last be gone.

An old friend in a friendless town.

August 1821.- Eleanor.

My first night alone in the house was lonely, eerie and filled with sobbing into my pillow until sleep finally alleviated me. The next couple of days passed under a mist of sombre numbness where I did little beyond ride on Samson and pour my heart into my diary. But by the time Giles' express arrived, saying the house was now staffed and furnished and ready for me to join him, I was better composed. I had only half a week to contend with before his ship left for Venice. I was certain I could keep him from my bed until then.

I had devised a story that I had been tended by the doctor in his absence over a bleed, just as I had, albeit in error, at my sisters. I had still not found the moment to confess to him the truth of my condition and when my menses arrived, it seemed the perfect cover to keep him away. I knew the servants could corroborate the story if I left enough clues, and so I stopped hiding my rags and had the doctor called. Albeit only for my nerves, but no one else was to know the true cause.

When I arrived in Half Moon Street, I furnished him with the tale that I had been advised to take bed rest and do *nothing* to disturb the child until the bleeding ceased.

He took it with relative equanimity and made sure to keep me well tended by the servants so I could rest, but was soon demanding *other* favours, and so I bore them as best I could. As my menses dwindled and there was still a couple of nights to account for before he awayed, I did my best to dampen the soiled rags, and refused the maids changing my sheets in order the staining could be kept convincing. It had sufficed, just about. But he was growing ever more tactile and tender with me and I felt such guilt at deceiving him. I knew I must use the time of his absence to come to terms with my duties before he returned. He deserved better from me, he had been nothing but decent and yet I repaid him so poorly for his efforts. Even if I had permitted far greater liberties than before, I could not seem to submit to *that*, or to returning his "I love yous.".

We had been married but a sennight and although we were less like strangers now, we were hardly yet friends. It was a curious circumstance, to be both intimately connected and naturally distant. But it was not until his parting night that this delicate balancing act felt truly breached, when he insisted upon no favours tonight, but something that seemed only fractionally less difficult to abide; to sleep in my bed with me. I hardly slept a wink, stiff and back turned to him as his naked flesh flanked my body, his arms gathered around me and planted kisses upon my shoulders. I cried quietly once he was finally asleep and stared into the gloom of the room, willing morning to arrive.

When it did, and his valet sent up a message to say he was to be late if they were not departed within the hour, I felt so much relief I struggled to quell it. Even the parting kisses he smothered me with seemed more tolerable for knowing them the last for over a month.

IT WAS A GREAT RELIEF to at last be free of him, and I felt instantly lighter as I watched his coach rattle up the road and beyond my sight. I could breathe again. I was alone. There was not even a chaperone to keep tabs on me. And suddenly I was reminded of the *why*—why I had endured it all, the light at the end of the tunnel, the calm after the storm: I was at last, my own master.

And whilst I was excited to be in London as my own mistress and without Giles to encumber me, it soon seemed lonely. The less of the evils indeed, but far from ideal. Society was scarce now, the London streets radiated with the swell of pounding August heat, the Coronation had passed and had sent most of society back off to the country or one of the spa resorts. I paid a few calls anyway and left a few cards to see if anyone was still about. I had hoped Miss Pembroke might still be about. I had not seen her since the Season's end, for her family's seat was somewhere in the North of England and we had agreed to write since the distance would not permit visiting. In the midst of everything that had happened since, I had quite forgotten to respond to her letters and could not recall the date on which she meant to return. I walked around to Cavendish Square anyway to leave a card, and cringed as I looked over towards Wimpole Street on my journey. I knew the Craythornes were in the country, for I had told Giles not to send for me until he was certain Mariella remained out of town. But even the thought of her lagging back and lurking behind one of the windows as I passed it, made me shiver.

I spent a few hours perusing along Bond Street, but it was quiet and soon grew boring with only the maid for company, so I returned home minded to take a light dinner and write to Caitlyn, who had said I would be welcome to come and stay with her in the summer for the festival. I hoped her offer would stand at this short notice, but I would have to hurry on account of the length of the journey, if I was to be back in time for Giles' return. I had not broached the topic with him, since I had hoped London would prove a little livelier than this, but now I was here, I knew I would struggle to fill the days. Why shouldn't I change my plans and travel to Edinburgh and amuse myself at the festival. That was the whole point of being at liberty, after all.

To my surprise, however, when I got home, I had received Betsy's calling card in my absence. I was surprised that she knew my direction, or wanted to make contact with me at all after how things last stood between us. But no less, I returned it and found her ready to make amends. It turned out the Mowbrays had been delayed in leaving by her father's health, but would soon head off to Cheltenham so he could take the waters for his gout just as soon as his physician declared him fit enough for the journey, she had explained to me over tea.

'Well, do not waste our morning conversing on my family's health, you must tell me; how goes your marriage?'

'Yes, well enough, I think. I mean, it has been so full of distractions, we have had little time to well acquaint ourselves with Giles so busy...' I was going to say with his business responsibilities, but then I remembered my company. To feign some ignorance over the matter in favour of her old friend was one thing, but to speak so openly on it would be quite beyond her tolerance. 'Busy setting up Beddington for us, there is a great deal to be done. He means to hurry it along so I might be established there soon.' This I knew to be a more favourable course and it was not wholly untrue.

'So you won't go abroad with him? I thought you would jump at the chance...'

'Not this time. He travels by merchant ships and says it is no way for a lady to travel. But he assures me we will make a wedding journey on his return, in the proper style.'

'I see. Well, it leaves you quite conveniently free in London, and I own, he has established you prettily enough here; but what will you find for diversion at such a season?'

'That I do not know, it seems so very quiet here now. I have not seen a soul since I arrived and certainly did not expect your card...'

'Well, there is that Wedding party at Cavendish House in a couple of weeks. I know much of society shall rattle back up for a week to do the pretty. You may look to that at least, if you are still here.'

'That's true.'

'How long will it be before you can settle in Beddington? I mean, surely it cannot be so bad you cannot stay there at all?'

'The house has been shut up for some time; it was rented out for a great many years before Giles inherited it.' Again, I sensed dangerous territory so I turned its direction. 'There are some parts of the building that are not structurally sound, but the wing in use is simply tired and in need of refurbishment. I am advised that to have our quarters renovated will not take much longer, and we might return there as soon as that much is done whilst the rest of the work continues. We may take a trip to Brighton during its course in any case and make a holiday of it before the weather turns.'

'Indeed. Then will you not retreat to Beaulieu for the meantime? At least there, you will have some society and your family close by of course.'

'No. I am quite sick of the place. It is not ideal to begin a married life under someone else's roof.'

'I see. Are they that intolerable to live amongst? Nay, forgive me. I meant no offense.'

'Not especially,' I said as evenly as I could contrive. 'But it is not my home and I feel so very foreign there.'

'Yes, to be sure you must. Well, London it must be for now then. I'm sure it will all come about soon enough. In the meantime, there are a few still in residence, although they thin out by the day and none of them, except Lady de Whittaker, plan to remain beyond the week.'

Lady de Whittaker-Hollingford; an eccentric as she was known, had no regard for society's ways or etiquette, she was a singularly unusual female, especially for her years, which must be quite beyond her late fifties now. But her position was so great that she was tolerated all the same: the former Duchess of Middlesex, top drawer ton, whatever else. It was said she came away a widow with most her property returned to her, and a handsome jointure, by her husband's untimely death, which amounted to no trivial sum, since it was well known she was an heiress even before her marriage to the Duke. She had not remarried after his death, despite being a young widow and having a great many dangle after one of such esteemed wealth and connection. A tale of her as the most hunted bride of decades ago, still held infamy.

But she could not be caught. Instead, she suited herself in whatever way she chose, whether society liked it or nay. On the few brief occasions, I had spoken to her, I found her very agreeable, but Mama had no taste for her and never took up her invitations or made calls there unless it could not be avoided. My sisters and I had always been advised to do the same. That is why when Betsy first advised me Lady de Whittaker was to get a party up out of the remains of London society before the week was out and even the dregs vanished, my instinct was to decline. If my mama heard of my attendance, it would seem to add insult to injury after all else.

'I own, I would not go either for want of something better, and even that would not usually induce me, only the Colonel is to go, before he departs for Malta and so I find I must accept the invitation with equanimity. They are close relations you know.'

'The Colonel...I sense progress in that quarter?' I smiled.

'Not entirely, I confess—well, we have been too long friends, so I will speak openly to you—he has made me an offer, on the quiet mind, but he is called to the garrison at Malta and so we have agreed to make no announcement until he returns and we can be married. He had hoped I might marry him before and go with him, but I don't think the climate would suit me.'

'I see. I am happy for you, Bets. I hope he will not be long away?'

'Who can tell? I would rather him sell his commission and not go, but he insists he must not sell out this soon. He is a second son after all and has only three thousand pounds a year to rely on, and heavens knows we could not get along comfortably on that. But his brother's health is so poor everyone regards he must inherit the whole someday soon, and I would rather he would just sit out the wait than keeping going off with the army. But there it is. I must concede.'

'Well, they say the course of true love never does run smoothly. We both know Giles was not my first choice.'

'But are you in love?'

'Not in love precisely. But it proves a practical arrangement. He asks nothing much of me and yet he does everything that is proper to establish me.'

'Well then, for a person such as you to say so, then it cannot be so bad.'

'Such as me?'

'A romantic. Well, do not take it so poorly. I meant no offense of course. I just meant with all that business with Sheldon, you seemed quite swept up in him and no one could make sense of you taking up with Craythorne.'

'No, I suppose.' I knew she referred to how forward I had been, despite her not knowing the half of it. I suppose I must have seemed quite love struck then. 'Sheldon was not constant in his affections to me, Betsy. So, to have a husband without such complication of affection has some advantages.'

'Yes, I heard the rumours about him and Lady Caroline. Stupid fellow. He regrets it sorely now, I know.'

I felt sorry at this. He had taken all the blame and never disclosed my part in it. 'I hope he will find someone who makes him happy in the end.'

'He has no mind to, it seems. He joins the Bucks volunteers regiment and leaves for Malta with the Colonel, I believe.'

This astonished me. Sheldon was not the military type. 'Really?'

She nodded. 'The Viscountess is heartbroken at his going; thinks he has lost all sense and reason, but the truth is, it is thought it will do him some good, he is so much altered for the worst of late. His papa, expressed to mine—privately of course—that he feared he would grow more reckless if he did not agree to assist in his commission. He drinks and gambles and was even caught bare knuckle boxing in Oxford.'

I felt so saddened to hear this, I could barely compose myself.

'He was a fool; everyone knows it; but he did love you, Eleanor, and he suffers his penance to be sure.'

I nodded for I could scarcely speak.

'Still, they say all is fair in love and war and at least we are not at war for once. I daresay it will do him good.'

I could see her hunger for my response, perhaps in hope of a hint of my own regret. As much as I knew she thought him foolish, I know she thought me equally as foolish for crying off over such a trifle. Betsy was far too pragmatic to see the sense in ruining a good match on account of feelings. And yet I could not tell her that was only a factor, not the cause. I certainly had no wish to dreg up what was passed, so I turned the direction swiftly, saying. 'So, you must give me Lady de Whittaker's direction so I can pay her a call: like you, what else have I for my diversion now I find myself alone in town.'

'Yes, indeed she will invite you if she knows you are here. But I doubt she does: I would have hardly known it myself, had I not spotted you out walking as I set out for Hyde Park this morning.' She consulted the clock. 'It is too late for calls now, but tomorrow, I think, we can go together if you would like?'

So that is what we did. And as I sat in the lavish drawing room at Grosvenor Square, taking tea with Lady de Whittaker, I could not help but feel Mama had been needlessly harsh in her disregard of her. That was to say that whilst the rumours of her candid countenance seemed quite well justified, and there was no denying her an eccentric, I could not help admire her for the very things she was accused of falling out of favour for. She was so content and comfortable with her ways it seemed impossible not to esteem of such a disposition. Whatever she might be thought, she certainly cared not a fig for it, and I considered how much better society might be if we all took her leaf from her book.

Having secured my invitation, Betsy and I departed, for she had some errands to run on her father's behalf and I wished to go for a peruse along Bond Street to collect a few of the things I had spotted yesterday, now I had occasion for them. I had more money in my pin than I should ever know how to spend and I could no longer quell the small excitement at finding some new thing to buy with it. So I had Birch set me down at the corner of Bond Street and told him to wait for me. I was a married woman now and quite capable of perusing the Western Exchange and Burlington Arcade without his escort, even if I would need to send for him to carry my things to the coach when I was done.

It was just as I was admiring a pretty shot silk parasol in the window of Rundles that had caught my eye in passing, when I heard my name, that was my old name alas, called just ahead of me. I looked up and frowned until the person drew nearer and I recognised Mr Richards beneath his top hat.

'Miss Ashlyn, what a pleasure to see you after such an age,' he said when he had gained on me.

It was strange to see him again, knowing all that had (and had not) passed since our last encounter. To think I had thought myself to be bearing his child. I remembered the shock, the anger, the apology and felt almost shy to look at him now. 'Mr Richards, how do you do? But I am not Miss Ashlyn anymore, I must correct you.'

'Forgive me, I did hear the news and yet seeing you so unexpectedly threw me quite by surprise. May I offer you my congratulations.'

'Thank you. Yes, you find me stuck here in town whilst my husband aways. What a friendless place it is after the season's end, I had never known it.'

'It is indeed.'

I noted something more than he meant to give away in his down turned countenance and hoped he did not feel resentful of my prior accusations, for I had never bothered to make reply to his letter. 'Have you been much busy since?' I did not want to bring up the issue, 'Since I last saw you?'

'No, not much at all, I confess. I have a little work to occupy me with my pupils, but most of them are away now and I have not had another engagement since my return.'

'I am so sorry to hear it Mr Richards, it seems very unjust, for you play so magnificently. What will you do?'

'I will go on as I do for now. Perhaps remove to some other place for the rest of the summer if I can find a position, try to re-establish myself there.'

My heart sank for him. Could he know that his decline was all down to Betsy's meddling? I thought not and yet he must have caught the gist of things even if not the source of them. I hoped he did not think I had any hand in it. I felt some sympathy with his cause for he truly was a talented master and should not have been so poorly treated by those that would hold themselves out as his betters. I still did not fully understand why and I knew better than to ask it now. A thought formed in my mind then as I remembered Lady de Whittaker's gathering. Had she not said herself she was struggling to come up with the entertainments at this season? 'Mr Richards, will you be in London on Friday?'

'Yes, I shall.'

'Then take my card, I am at Half Moon Street. I make no promises, but I might know of just the thing if it is not too late. Will you call on me tomorrow and I can tell you then if it is of use?'

He took my card and offered me his thanks, saying he would very much like to pay me a call, whatever the outcome of my enquiries, for he had a great deal of time for me. I wished him good day and continued onto Bond Street. I reasoned that if anyone was to disregard this nonsense of his birth, then it would be Lady de Whittaker. She might of course already have engaged someone by then, so I must move fast, for I was certain if she only heard him play, she would secure him for Friday's party, and if anyone could re-launch him a success; she could.

—◦◦◦—

I GATHERED A VERY PRETTY number of parcels and boxes through the course of the afternoon and although Birch seemed less than impressed at having to wait so many hours for me, and then to load so many things into the carriage, I felt quite pleased at the diversion.

I took a small dinner before having the maid attend my toilette: I was to go out tonight after all. When Lady de Whittaker had invited us to her card party this evening, Betsy had been quick to decline on both our accounts with the greatest regret that we were promised elsewhere and of course would otherwise had loved to join her party. These, Betsy warned me, were a dreadful bore with all types of society permitted entry and she had considered herself to have done me a service in declining on my behalf.

I would have to find some reason for being able to alter the arrangement, but I would go, and safe in knowing that Betsy wouldn't dream of attending such a paltry affair in such company; for I must find an opportunity to give Mr Richards direction to her, not only without delay, but without Betsy's knowledge if we were to remain amicable. She would not forgive me it, if she knew my intentions to correct what she had took pains to bring about, and she would never understand my meddling. But the truth was, I liked him, and after all the bad business I had almost believed him capable of despite his innocence, I felt guilty. It seemed unjust to see him so long faced, having done nothing to deserve it.

So I got to Grosvenor Square a little ahead of the invited hour, which I'd daren't do in other company, but my brief, yet enlightening meeting with Lady W. this morning assured me she would not be at all inconvenienced by my forwardness.

'Mrs Craythorne, how splendid; you came after all.'

'Yes, I—' I had rehearsed the story in my head but as she cut me off, I noted she did not care for it and I was relieved of the need to make excuses.

'What a turn of luck, you see Mr Sawyer sent his apologies this afternoon and the party has shrunk now to such a meagre number, I was of a mind to cancel it altogether. Still, no matter, we can play a few rubbers still and raise a little gathering. Have you any friends to send for Mrs Craythorne, bring our party to a better number? I will send a horse to the Major presently and see what he is about tonight.'

How outrageously irregular, I thought, to arrange a party, then come close to cancelling it at the last, and then beg me to help in her last minute efforts to bring it off. I did not know whether to laugh of feel embarrassed. But then another thought came to me: 'Yes, yes, I do in fact, although I am not altogether sure of his direction, some rooms on Old Chapel Street I think, a Mr Richards, do you know him?'

'I cannot be sure, the name rings a bell but I cannot place him. Still not to worry, I will beg Ellis to go there after he has called on the Major, if he can find out his direction that is.'

It was the most irregular thing, but she carried it of so comfortably there was no choice but to accept it with good humour.

We sat about the drawing room chatting whilst the tables were set up for a few games and guests starting arriving casually in dribs and drabs: about twelve of us in number by the time her manservant returned with the Major and the news that he could not find out Richards' direction.

'Ah, not to worry, Ellis. I thank you,' she said and turned to me, 'well, perhaps next time you might invite your friend along. Still our number is well enough now to get up a few games at least.'

'Yes. It is a shame I cannot remember his direction, I had hoped to introduce you to him. You see Mr Richards is a most talented Musician Lady W. I am sure that is why you must have heard his name.'

'Is he indeed—I daresay it was he at that Wycombe affair in June?'

'Yes, yes it was he, do you remember him?'

'Yes, I do now I come to think of it. The one that all the debutantes were dangling over, even some of the old maids as I recollect it,' she laughed. 'But then there was all that talk and I own I never heard of him again.'

'Yes, well it was a silly thing really.'

'My dear, the ways of the ton are all rather silly don't you find? I myself do not care for it I must say, except the races; I have a great deal of time for that tradition. But the rest! Tuh, what a song and dance it all is.'

I smiled at this, holding back my laughter. 'Lady W., I was wondering, since you mentioned you were still arranging the entertainments for Friday evening, if you would perhaps think of Mr Richards, if you did not mind all the talk.'

'Mind that, not a bit. But could I hope to engage him so shortly? If he is a good as you insist, and I cannot recollect him so very well I own, for at my age you see—'

'Yes, to be sure, he is busy seeking an engagement to move on to the country for the summer, I saw him only this morning and he said so, so I know he will not be engaged for the evening.'

'I see. Well then, it is settled. If you give him my direction, he must come to me tomorrow and play something for me. If I am happy with the interview, he will give a concert on Friday before supper. I have already engaged the orchestra for the dances afterward so that would not do, but a concert before we sit down to the table would be quite the thing.'

Mission accomplished.

WHEN MR RICHARDS CALLED the next morning, I was very happy to give him the news and Lady W.'s direction, and he was happier still, to follow up on it. I was just bidding him farewell when Tibbins came in and announced: 'Miss Mariella Craythorne.'

I almost dropped my fan. It could not be. And then there she was, smiling sweetly in the doorway and then noticing my company and looking suspiciously between us. They exchanged a polite but awkward greeting, and Mr Richards excused himself promptly, and then I was left quite alone with her.

'What do you mean coming here, how dare you show your face,' I said when I heard the front door shut.

"There is no need to be so out of temper with me, Eleanor. I came to see you to offer my apology.'

This was rich. 'Oh, for what exactly: the lying, the deception, the interference in my marriage, which exactly are you here to apologise for, because you cannot imagine, even in that twisted head of yours, that we have anything more to say to each other!'

'I realise you must be out of reason cross with me, and I cannot blame you.'

'No, you cannot. And so, you must accept the consequence of your deeds and realise I cannot bear to look at you a moment longer; you disgust me.'

'I do realise that. But since we are family now, I am certain we must find a way to move quite beyond these issues, so we might get along amicably.'

'Family, yes I see how intimate a family you are now, and god forbid Giles should ever find out that his cousin was so busy with her hands beneath my skirts before our wedding, I do not know how it could go. He is as mad as fire with you, you know.'

She hid a wince at this before composing herself. 'I shall never tell him *that*, you may be sure of it.'

'I do not know what I can be sure of after all else. But I do know that your cousin is a dutiful man, and when he returns from abroad, we shall make a crack of things, and it would be a much better thing if you were not around.'

'I see, he is gone then. When does my cousin return, precisely?'

'If you do not know, then I can only suppose he had no wish to tell you, and so do not expect an answer from my lips. Now if you please; I have calls to pay this morning—'

'Yes, I see you are having no difficulty keeping company in Giles' absence. What did Richards want—to check in on his little one?'

I shook my head despairing. 'You really have no limits, do you? There is always venom on the tip of your tongue. Well, I do not care to hear any more of it, and I would bid you take refreshment and be gone by the time I return.'

'I see how it is. Well then, you leave me no choice. If you will not play nicely, Eleanor, I will have to tell him the whole after all.'

'You would not dare!'

'No, no not in ordinary circumstances I would not. Just think how uncomfortable it would be for us all and after such a beginning. But if you will not see me, and Giles is in a rage with me, what else have I to lose in the deal?'

'And why do you think that is, Mariella? This is just the kind of style that earns you enemies instead of friends, if you could only know the difference you might find yourself much less disappointed!'

'I daresay, thank you for the lesson, Miss Society. I wonder how long that title could bear through another scandal and one *this* messy—I mean, you recovered surprisingly well through the Sheldon affair, so quiet the truth was kept, but then I suppose they could not know just how much you had promised him and just how intimate you had become, nor the true reason you cried off, even though the official line—'

I stood up to leave. 'You are a hideous creature. Truly. I could not believe such a person could exist until I met you!'

'Hmm, but am I the only one guilty of such a charge? Shall we put the facts out to the public test and perhaps we could measure against each other; who out of the pair of us might come off the worst in it?'

'*If* and it is a very big if indeed, your word would carry a hint of consequence over mine, with you the poor relation, you forget that you will harm not just me, but your cousin, your parents and yourself; for if you were not already a poor case for a debutante as it was, this would indeed finish you entirely. You overlook that I am married now, so what can be altered in my fate?'

'Very true. Which is why I would prefer it not to come to that. I mean, I don't care a dash for the marriage prospects, as you know, my interests lie elsewhere. But to harm my family would not be my greatest wish, but nor would it be enough to prevent me, and on that you can rely.'

I wanted to tell her to go to the devil with her threats and yet something in her eyes assured me they were not empty. 'Your cousin said you were quite mad.' This displeased her and threw her a little out of countenance, but it passed fleetingly enough.

'Well then, you had better not put it to the test. Now if you please, I should like your footman to take my things down from the carriage; I think I might stay the week and wait for news of my dear cousin's return, if you will not tell me when.'

This was too much. 'Very well, if I tell you, will you at least go away until then? You cannot think we will have anything kind to say to each other in the waiting.'

She smiled widely like a Cheshire cat and though I had never felt compelled to attack anyone in my life, right now, I wanted to wipe it clean off her face.

'Yes, I think that sounds agreeable, after all, it was Giles I wanted to see. So tell me when you expect him and I will have my horses rested an hour and then I will return home.'

'By the end of September, all running to plan.'

'Very well. You can expect me then. Now, who must I call to get some tea around here?'

I rang the bell for her then left at once. I didn't even have time to get Samson saddled up, so impatient I was to be gone from the place. I would go and see Betsy; she would know how to divert me. But no that would not do for she would see something was quite wrong in my countenance and force it from my lips. Who could I confide such a vulgar affair to? *Lady W.*

I walked in the direction of Grosvenor Square, wiping the tear streams from my cheeks and trying to think what I might say. I could not give her the whole of course, but perhaps I could just offer her a hypothetical quandary of what could be done when someone was blackmailing you. I was going through various schemes in my head and was not at all aware of my surroundings when I bumped right into a gentleman who must have been walking in my direction.

'Good grief. I am so sorry, Sir!' I said regaining my composure and nursing an ache in my jaw.

He looked up after gathering his top hat from the floor. 'It is quite alright—Mrs Craythorne?'

'Mr Richards. My goodness, I am sorry.'

'We must stop meeting like this,' he jested and brushed some dander off his hat with his gloved hand. 'You are hurt?'

'No, just surprised. I will be fine.'

'But it cannot be, you have tears in your face?'

'Not over that bump.'

'Then something else?'

'Yes; something altogether different. Now, do not let me keep you, you are headed to Lady W.'s I trust?'

'Yes. But it can wait.'

'No, it cannot wait. It is just the thing to bring things about for you, so you mustn't keep her waiting. I will be perfectly well and I am heading there anyway.'

He persisted enough to induce me into a quick and brief outline of my troubles with Mariella, not in the whole of course, for I could not disclose certain details to anyone, but the general gist of our mutual dislike of each other and her interference and unwelcome visit. This he took with impressive composure for his sex, before resting his gloved hand gently on my forearm and telling me with a light squeeze: 'When your husband returns home, you must insist he forces her to depart. If this does not come off comfortably, then you must insist he take you away someplace she will not know. She will grow tired of the chase eventually.'

'Yes, I am sure you are right, and I will certainly petition him to that end when he returns. Thank you for your kindness, Mr Richards, you have caused me to feel much improved.'

'Glad to be of service.'

With that, we set off to Lady W's together where Mr Richards undertook a brief interview and performed a winning rendition of Mr Moore's *Last Rose of Summer,* as well as some of his own compositions, which left Lady W. suitably impressed and me a little breathless with the way he looked at me when he was singing.

He took his leave with Lady W.'s confirming him for a concert on Friday evening before the supper and I was so happy for him. If he brought it off well, it could resurrect him as quite the thing amongst the ton again, in spite of Betsy's efforts. *Betsy*—this detail I had forgotten to tie up. 'Lady W., I am so pleased it went well.'

'Yes, I must thank you for your recommendation, Mrs Craythorne. I had quite forgotten just how commendable he is. I owe you a great debt in arranging this so promptly before the party.'

'You do not indeed. In fact, I should be grateful if you would not mention it at all.'

'I see, like that between you is it?'

'No. No nothing of the sort I assure you.'

'No need to assure me, Mrs Craythorne, it is none of my concern, and I own, if I was of your years, well I could hardly blame you...'

'Forgive me my lady, but you are truly mistaken. But your confidence in my making his recommendation—'

'Can be assured of, Mrs Craythorne. Now how about a rubber of whist since you are here?'

One rubber turned into many, and I was surprised to have spent so long out when I walked back with the escort of Lady W.'s footman at nine-thirty p.m. She had insisted upon it, following our discussion over my lack of Abigail or companion, which she owned was at times a dreadful inconvenience, but quite the necessary evil in town, even by her standards. So I accepted her offer of assistance in procuring one or the other in the least.

I departed company with the footman on the doorstep of Half Moon Street and was alarmed to notice the twitching of the curtain as I felt for my key. She had promised herself gone by my return and I could not have delayed it any longer to permit her adequate time to do so. I considered making a swift turn and venturing over to Betsy's, but it was an impolite hour to descend upon them uninvited, and whatever else, I did not want Mariella to think me intimidated by her, or that she could drive me out of my own house. So I headed in and was surprised when Tibbins took my Spencer, at the disconcerted glances between him and Mrs Birch, the housekeeper.

'Is everything well, Tibbins?'

'Yes, ma'am.'

'Is my cousin gone now?'

'No, ma'am.'

My heart sank. And then I noticed a top hat and cane on the hall stand. 'Mr Tibbins, is there a man in this house?'

'Only the master, Miss.'

I felt some relief at that but I was perfectly mystified, he should be well on his way to the continent now. 'Where is the master, Tibbins?'

'In his chamber, I believe ma'am. I will tell him you are home. Shall I send for some tea for you in the small parlour.'

'No, thank you. I will tell him myself.'

'Ma'am, I think you should allow me to—'

'No,' I said, pushing past him and towards the stairs.

When I arrived at Giles' chamber and found Digby hovering about outside it, I made instant sense of Digby's discomposure and reluctance to let me in. I refused his petitions to wait outside and when denied access to the main door, went into my own chamber and came through the adjoining dressing room doors to find him and Mariella in the bed together, mid romp. They looked up surprised and Mariella smiled unashamed, her naked body bobbing up and down as she sat astride Giles who, did not seem to share her delight at my timely appearance.

He threw her off almost instantly and gathered a sheet around his waist, 'Eleanor, Eleanor...'

I locked the dressing room door behind me on the way out and steadied myself. I had no doubt she had persuaded him, but how could he be so vile?

'Eleanor, let me out,' I heard him call.

'I have nothing to say to you, you both disgust me.'

'Just leave her Giles, what does it matter, she needs to understand how it will go,' Mariella said.

'Get off me,' I heard him say to her and I moved quickly through my chamber, back down the stairs and straight out of the house without a thought for any of my things or where I was to go. All I knew is I was not going to stay there for another spell of their lunacy. I could not care a whit why he was home or even who he was in bed with, so long as she was not under my roof.

I scuttled along the streets quickly, keeping my gaze low. It was late and even though it was still bright with evening sunlight, it was setting now and I had no wish to get into a scrape being seen about on my own. Instinctively, I headed over to Grosvenor Square and looked for a light in Betsy's windows, but they were dim. I thought of going to Berkeley Square and having Bentham open up a part of the house for me; but he would suspect me and alert my parents, and it was the first place Giles would think to look for me. So it was with sheer desperation and night fast setting upon the quiet London streets, that I made the short journey across to Lady W.'s, where I burst in to her in a fit of tears and gave her, almost, the whole.

I don't know why I felt I could trust her with such details, perhaps a lack of care for the consequences in the fit of it all, or as later proved to be true, the assurance that Lady W. would take all of this quite comfortably in her stride and have a room set up for me there with an invitation to stay under her protection until I had calmed down.

So, as I sunk into the freshly made bed with a low light burning, I felt reassured that I could be let well alone here, for he would neither guess at my whereabouts, nor would he have the ability to get past Lady W., even if he should discover it. But no less, I cried myself to sleep with the quandary of how this could all be settled between us. If he would not make her go, I would be forced to insist on a separation.

Mr Richards.

August 1821. - Eleanor.

I slept well at Grosvenor Square, despite spending a while puzzling over Giles' impromptu return and apparent *forgiveness* of Mariella. I was not sure what had been discussed between them to affect this change of heart on his part, but I knew now, neither of them could be trusted. If she was not to be banished from our home and our company hereafter, I was done with the pair of them.

Despite being quite on edge; he did not discover me the next day as I feared and I kept to the house to ensure it remained that way. I was happy to have the diversion of the party to look to tonight to take my mind off all the madness and I checked and double checked that there were no other Craythornes on the guest list.

Lady W. was sprightly company, despite being busy in her arrangements and was good enough to include me in her tasks wherever she could. As I helped her decide upon the arrangement of furniture, check the menus for the dinner and organise the wines, I realised just how fortunate she was to go about her business so independently. It was no wonder she never chose to re-marry; she had every comfort at her disposal and no one to please beyond herself. What a rare and unusual position she found herself in. One I considered many women should like to enjoy. I was growing ever more convinced that this was the ideal circumstance and feeling ever deeper regret at embroiling myself into such a contract. But it was the stone after it was thrown and dwelling upon it seemed futile.

WHEN GUESTS BEGAN ARRIVING at seven, it felt heartening to be in company again after so much solitude. Better still, most of the company was unknown to me and I enjoyed a relative sense of anonymity as Lady W. introduced "Mrs Craythorne" to several new acquaintances to whom the name meant nothing, where the name Ashlyn would be instantly recognised. A few of the ton, which I had previously only known by face or fleeting recollection surely would know me though, but many seemed to be of the gentry, and it was refreshing to have new connections that neither knew, nor likely would care for the gossip of my recent circumstances. If it was not for Betsy and a few other well-known attendees, I might have forgotten the last few months entirely and thought myself fresh into society with a clean slate. No inane smiles angled at me, slanted sneaking gazes as I passed, or the hum of whisperings following me about the room. I felt lighter once more; not returned or recovered perhaps, but partially reclaimed.

Just as I knew he would, Mr Richards proved equal to the opportunity and kept the party aptly entertained with his musical talents through the course of the evening, and I was pleased to see that he seemed redeemed from Betsy's character assassination. She however, seemed piqued by his presence, whispering to me as we took our seats for the concert: 'I see he has crawled out from his rock again. Well, trust our host to be unfussy in her choice of entertainment.'

I made no reply and was grateful for the Colonel taking his seat between us at that precise moment and being spared the need to answer. There was a time when we could rely on being in sympathy with each other's sentiments, but it seemed we had grown more accustomed to being at odds this year. I liked the man and did not want to see him suffer, whatever his backstory. However unfortunate, he could not help his birth and he had never pretended to be above himself at all. It was everyone else that raised him on that pedestal before hatefully kicking him off it. And he had never been anything less than kind to me, so how could I consent to his slander campaign when it was within my power to counter it.

It was heartening to see that he was well appreciated by the rest of our company, though. Compliments and applause at every interval, a general buzz about him afterward, with everyone wanting to detain him in conversation. Even the Colonel shook him by the hand, much to Betsy's chagrin. I presumed she had no wish to express her opinions on Richards to the Colonels ear for fear of him sensing the jealous roots which they sprang from. I kept to mixed company so she could not fill my ears with them now, and when we were called to the dining room, we were set a few spaces apart, providing a welcome distance.

I sat between the Major and Mrs Beckett, the former I met at the little card party previous, the latter a new introduction, and both I found pleasant enough neighbours to sup with. In any case, with Lady W. presiding over the table, the conversation was always lively and stimulating so that it hardly mattered where you were sat, so long as in earshot of her speeches. And so, there was a great deal of chatter, debate and laughter about the table throughout. Nothing like the stiff formal dinners you might expect to sit out in such a grand dining room as this. And I realised in this moment, I felt happy. For the first time in an age, I felt comfortable. I was pleased to observe the same in Mr Richards' countenance. A lifting of the anxious hue I had noted in his face more recently.

Our eyes met, quite by accident, over supper. His smile warm at the sight of me, and I knew he was grateful for my meddling in restoring him. But it was not just gratitude I read in his stare, I realised as I removed my glass from my lips and offered him a smile in return, there was something altogether quite beyond gratitude. I returned to my plate before it was noticed, but when I turned to answer the Major, I caught him watching me still. 'No, Sir, I am not familiar with the Land Tax Act,' I answered, but my eyes were drawn to further along the table to those eyes that drunk me in so entirely, and thereafter could be no mistaking the purpose behind the many furtive glances that followed.

Could it be, the handsome Mr Richards still had a tendré for me? Had my notice of him been so poor throughout the season that I had not realised that whilst the misses of the ton dangled after his every step, I was the only one whose company he sought? I reflected on our brief conversations, a trifle of dances and duets at the pianoforte—that were for my part—offered in either pity or politeness: But what of his reasons? And then there was of course the Beaulieu affair that had been so embarrassing and ghastly on my part, that I had quite forgotten that it was him pursuing me for dances and putting himself at my service that night that was the greater thread of the story. Yes, it became clear now. I had been so distracted by Sheldon, so distracted by *her*—the thought of her made me shrink with repulsion now—that I had not noticed it. Even in his kindness to me, I had been too preoccupied to read the warmth in his gaze for what it was. Was that why Betsy had been so cruel? Had she noticed right away and resented us both for it? I crushed the thought and went back to my conversation with the Major although another one entirely was forming in my mind as I spoke to him, increasingly distracted by the view beyond his shoulder. As Richards cast connotative glances at me, I felt something kindling: the prospect of revenge turned over in the pit of my stomach as I sunk another glass and reflected on the idea I had at first shook into silence. *He wanted me.* I squeezed the lemon wedge over my fish, finishing with a few shakes from the salt and pepper pot, but it was not food I craved as I forked little parcels into my mouth. I was protected by my marriage now, and having not yet consummated it, how sweet would it be to serve Giles his desserts and let some other man go before him? *I oughtn't.* The injury to me had been done on her account, her faux friendship and deception. I had not the slightest regard for the man I had married and not an inkling of jealous feeling could be coaxed from me for his sake. It was her who riled me with her deceit, her I still remembered drawing him into her embrace and petitioning him to take her, her who I thought a dependable friend and confidante, her whose image bobbing up and down disturbed me. I felt a burn in my chest and realised as I swallowed, I had blindly taken up the Major's cup in error and sunk the lot before realising it: Brandy, straight and a half full glass, I recalled as I composed myself from the shock of it. 'Forgive me, Sir!' I said ashamed. 'I had thought it my cup.'

He smiled amused, impressed perhaps. 'Dash it, help yourself my dear. I own I did not think ladies had a taste for the stuff, but as you please.'

I felt the liquor-laced heat escape my breath and flourish in my cheeks. I returned to my wine in the hope of cooling it. The Major summoned a footman for a refill of his own. 'And for you, Mrs Craythorne?' he gestured, and I refused his offerings on my behalf and found my gaze drawn back to Mr Richards who was having a similar difficulty holding a conversation with his neighbours; his eyes constantly drawing away from them. His distracted attentions and contemplative smiles in my direction had strengthened my resolve to dare at my most seductive efforts. They were out of practice perhaps, but not entirely forgotten. I narrowed my eyes a fraction and peered up through my lashes with just a hint of a smile on my lips as he stared at me. Each time, my gaze a little bolder, lingering a little longer as my confidence in this affinity grew. I watched him grow more and more distracted, then restless, almost entirely ignorant of his company, the conversation falling away from him, word by word, syllable by syllable.

I twisted the stem of my glass between my fingers. *It's working, you still have it and this is one power which cannot be taken from you.* I smiled as the prospect unfolded in my head.

When I removed to the withdrawing room with the other ladies, a number of strategies had formed in my mind as to how I might proceed in my cause. But when the gentlemen regrouped with us, I had not resolved on exactly how I would execute it. I considered we might play a game at the table or I could attach myself to someone in his circle and speak to him like that. I could approach his conversation directly, but it was too explicit and would not answer. Besides, Betsy's gaze was upon us and I wasn't completely sure of him yet—I hadn't the stomach for rejection. So, instead, I decided to look for an excuse to walk in his direction and pass the opportunity of approach, over to him. A fleeting look about the room spotted the Carpenters just announced. I made my excuses to the ladies and headed straight for them.

I was careful to keep my eyes fixed on them as I passed him even though I could feel his gaze on me and felt powerfully drawn to it.

'Mr Carpenter, Mrs Carpenter, good to see you again. You are both looking very well,' I said when I reached them. I was careful to position myself in clear view of him and as I leant forward to kiss both their cheeks, I locked eyes with him. A fire ignited inside me from a place I had lately thought dead. But as the flame of anticipation struck up, I recognised it instantly as passion; the reckless, dangerous kind. I was going to do something wild tonight, I could feel it.

I stepped back a little and chatted small pleasantries to the Carpenters all the while keeping him fixed in my view. He hadn't looked away once yet and it seemed we had reached the point of challenge, waiting for the other to advance the next move. I excused myself from my company and went over to the fire mantle and feigned interest in the portraits, to make myself available to him. He didn't keep me waiting long. He left his company and strode towards me, purposefully, confidently. He was not typical of the sort of man I might normally be attracted to, but he was agreeable and handsome and for some reason that I had not yet fathomed, I wanted him, now.

'Does your evening go well, Mrs Craythorne?' he said with a smile that translated to something far beyond a simple greeting.

My lips turned up into a sultry smile, quite of their own accord. 'Good evening, Mr Richards.' I held out my hand and when he took it in his and kissed it through the satin of my glove, I knew I wanted to feel his kiss elsewhere.

'I have wished for a chance to speak with you all evening,' he said as he lifted back up and let go of my hand. 'But I could not find the opportunity.'

'Yes, likewise,' I told him as coolly as I could manage given how hot my blood was rushing beneath my skin.

He arched a puzzled eyebrow as if trying to read my direction. 'I must give you my thanks for your patronage; I have already been sought for six new engagements tonight.'

'I am very glad to hear it, Mr Richards, but I cannot take the credit for that; it is all of your own doing.'

'Well, if it was not for your arranging the opportunity.'

'You may credit me with that much, but it is not I who has impressed them with my talents. Anyhow, it was the least I could do. You were poorly used, Mr Richards, and I own it was most unjust. I am only glad Lady W. has the good sense to pay no mind to such nonsense.'

'What nonsense?'

It had not occurred to me that he did not know. 'Well,' I said thinking how to be tactful on the subject, 'whatever occurred betwixt you and Lady Elizabeth, has prompted her into a slander campaign against you—you did not know?'

'Nothing did pass between us. It seems that has been my crime then, only I had not known my sentence.'

'I'm sorry. I thought you knew.'

'I knew that Lady Elizabeth was offended by my rejection of her advances, she made that plain enough. But no, I did not know she was campaigning against me. Well, it explains much.'

'It does not matter, you are talented and admired; not everyone will listen to her prattling you know.'

He smiled warmly at me. 'I see that.'

I gave my now empty glass to a passing footman. 'You played so very beautifully tonight, I confess, I find myself quite enchanted.'

'You are too generous. But I am pleased to have managed to enchant you, Mrs Craythorne. I had thought that quite the impossible task and rather beyond my talents.' I saw the shade of a wicked thought darken his gaze and his smile faded into something more sobering. 'Will you dance tonight, Mrs Craythorne? I would be very honoured to claim a space on your card.'

'Well, I had been minded not to, but yes, certainly I will for your sake,' I agreed.

When the strings of the orchestra started up a little later, he came to claim me and we danced a merry cotillion together. The steps of the dance, wherein I would usually find the merriment, were not on this occasion, responsible for it. It was the dance between our glances, smiles and unspoken thoughts that provided the thrill. It never failed to amaze me how much could be conveyed without the utterance of a single word.

By the end of our set, I had extinguished every doubt in reading his intentions toward me, and any uncertainty as to whether this was what I wanted. I was of course nervous; the incident with Giles had left me uncomfortable with the whole idea. I suspected too that I was acting out of internalised rage at my circumstances. And yet, beyond it all, I knew when I felt his hand brush mine, or caught the scent of his cologne, that there was something undeniably compelling between us. Something I hankered to explore.

'Thank you for honouring me, Mrs Craythorne. You must let me find you a drink,' he offered when we had finished, leading me over to a chair where I refused to sit down.

This was my moment. If I did not act now, I may not manage to contrive another. 'You are kind, Mr Richards, but I am quite flustered, I wonder if you might be as good as to escort me to take some air?' It was a feeble ploy, but all I could think of with haste.

He offered me his arm. 'Please.'

As he led me through the saloon and out into the hall, I felt the prickle of nervous anticipation overcome me. I had not noticed that the doors were locked here after eleven, and we must risk discovery in asking for them to be opened or give up the idea of taking the night air. 'Uh.' I patted my cheeks, they were hot, but the dancing was not to blame.

He stalled to look at me. 'You are not well? I shall find someone to open them.'

I laughed considering the dread he must feel at such a prospect of my inebriation after last time. But I was not ill or foxed. I felt clearer minded in this moment than I had in an age. I knew exactly what I wanted in this moment, I needed only the privacy to make it plain to him. 'Indeed, I am well. An open window and a quiet place to sit down for a moment will suffice.'

He looked about and turned the handle of the nearest door coming off the hall and took me into it. It was in complete darkness, no candles or fire burning, but as my eyes adjusted to it, I could tell from the moon gleam upon the lacquer wood desk that we must be in the study.

He dispatched me to the nearest seat then set about to open the windows.

'Do not go,' I said impatiently, rising up at his side and quite dispelling the myth of my frailty. I felt a little light-headed, I owned, but it was not from the Majors brandy.

He looked at me quizzically and I could not read what was behind his eyes. *Had I gone too far too soon?*

'Then I will not go. Shall I sit with you?' he gestured to the sofa, but I did not return to it. I had no desire for conversation and thought I had read a like-mindedness in his impatience. 'I think we might do better than that,' I said so boldly I amazed myself. Then I noticed a slowing of his breath, a smouldering glare I felt more clearly than I could see, and a seriousness in his expression that was on the cusp of faltering. Then came his kiss, tender but full of a passion; quite unmistakable. I wondered how long he had considered bestowing it upon me. How many times I had not noticed that detail before. I returned it with equal affection, and felt the pressure of his body against mine as we leaned in closer to each other. 'Mr Richards,' I said, pausing. 'I think we are about to do something quite outrageous, in fact, I wish it.'

I had stirred up something wild; almost primal in him. I sensed it now, what I had at first mistaken for reluctance.

'I would like nothing more; but we might be discovered here?'

'I realise it, but I do not care a whit, do you?'

'Not for my sake, only for yours.' He took me by the arm and led me out of the study in some other direction. Perhaps I should have been more cautious, more nervous, more reserved; but the overarching emotion was wild determination. I was going to let this man take me somewhere and fuck me, and nothing would prevent it.

I AWOKE THE NEXT MORNING feeling quietly smug. I knew Lady W. had quite the measure of things but would not address the subject, so we were quite content to go along discussing the highlights and success of the evening without reference to my impromptu disappearance coinciding with Mr Richards'. She had a mind that since I had nothing to do today, and she was used to pleasing herself, that I should like to come to a circulating library with her later on. Whilst I had much else to occupy my thoughts, and was still concerned over bumping into Giles, I could offer no good reason as to why I should not accompany her, and I had already expressed to her my love of reading, so we were to finish our breakfast and depart directly. But we had neither expected the announcement that my husband and Mariella had called and were waiting in the receiving room downstairs. How could they guess at my being here? It was quite impossible that they should. Someone from the party must have given me away.

'Well, my dear,' Lady W. said, putting down her cutlery. 'I can either have Crampton send them on their way. Or, we can go down there together and see what they are about? I mean, they have chased you out of your own home, but you do not have to show them any conquest in it.'

'I don't want to see them, it's true, yet I don't want them to think me in hiding. No, I must face them out.'

'Excellent. Then let us send for some tea to be taken down and we will join them directly.'

When I sat opposite Giles and Mariella on the small sofa, I expected to feel more anxious, but under Lady W.'s protection, I felt quite untouchable. In fact, I could hardly keep the smile off my lips as we exchanged formalities. Lady W.'s deft handling of the conversation kept their intended direction of the conversation quite beyond their lips. I said little beyond occasional brusque answers, as flashes of the evening's events were replaying in my mind; the smell, taste, and feel of Mr Richards still tangible to my senses.

'Eleanor tells me you were supposed to away for a period, Mr Craythorne, and you must know London is no place to be abandoned at this season. So I am very pleased to have her companionship in the interim and I will of course take very good care of her,' Lady W. told him with that tone of mild insistence that warned everyone it was neither a request or petition, but a simple fact of the circumstance, whilst retaining far too gracious a manner to be accused of any dictatorial air.

I watched him stiffen in his seat then remembered how Mr Richards had pressed me flat against the parlour wall and lifted my skirts to my waist. We could still hear the din of the party next door: the muffled chatter, the stifled timbre of the orchestra, the shuffle of dancing feet against the marble floor. But in my ear, I heard his breath, rasping as I felt the swell of him enter me. I did not expect to feel anything of pleasure as he breached me, but his other tricks of arousal helped me bear it readily. It was a worthy discomfort I thought, when I stared at them across my teacup, knowing I had given this gift that was due to my husband to someone more to my liking. It was the thought of them last night that encouraged a steely determination in me to embrace it: To push through my nervous anxiety and the discomfort. To leave Mr Richards with such a fond and vibrant memory of fucking me that it would be the only thing on his mind whenever he was in our company. For I meant him to be in it much more often. If Lady W. could throw a gathering and further his prospects, so could I. I was at liberty to host my own parties now and procure my own entertainments, and I intended to.

This thought pleased me a great deal, the advantage of him knowing how well he could thrill me, how much I wanted him above my husband. I thought back to all the words I had whispered into his ear last night; some arising from my genuine surprise but mostly from my desire to leave precisely the impression I knew would humiliate Giles the most. 'Oh my, I have never been handled like this... Oh why doesn't my husband make me feel this way? ...Oh Mr Richards, you are a marvel...' followed by the most vocal attempt at orgasm I had ever expressed, despite not achieving one, and his trying to quiet me.

I knew part of me wanted someone to hear me and discover us, to find me leant up against the wall with this man inside me. To see their face at the realisation of my pleasure, my betrayal. But no one had come. Even when the deed was done, there was time still for him to kiss me affectionately and fill my ears with his tender regard. It was only when we departed the small parlour and made our way back to the saloon, that Betsy had offered us a conspicuous glare as she lingered in the saloon doorway with the Colonel. Part of me had damned the irony that should we be suspected, it would be by her of all people, but another part, the vindictive part of me, almost wished it.

'You should know I depart for Beaulieu today,' Mariella said eventually and Giles looked up from the plate of offered biscuits to check our reactions to this news.

I hid my creeping smile behind my teacup and took a long drawn-out sip before replacing it and giving my answer. 'What welcome news,' I said and stole a fancy from the plate and bit into it.

Mariella shot Giles an uneasy glance. Of course, neither of them could suppose for a moment I would bring Lady W. into my confidence to the extent of sharing the details of such a disgraceful affair. And yet for the most part, I had.

'I have reconsidered my trip to Venice, Eleanor. I thought perhaps I might delay it until September once we have spent some time in each other's company. I must instead go to Dublin next week, but thought we could go together and make something of a late wedding journey of it?' Giles said then, and I realised from the outrage in Mariella's widened eyes that this news was new to her. The thought of displeasing her so much in accepting this invitation brought me close to considering it, but I could not forget his part so easily, and nor did I trust that she would not set about some scheme to join herself to it. I was just trying to find a reasonable objection, when Lady W. intervened.

'A business trip, Mr Craythorne?' she asked.

'Yes.'

'Well, you surely cannot find that a suitable wedding journey for your new wife? Whatever will she do for society? You cannot mean it, I'm sure.'

'I thought you might employ a companion, Eleanor?'

'Lady W., are you free to make such a journey at short notice?'

'Well, I own I am. I was quite resigned to remaining in town, but, Dublin you say? I could perhaps be persuaded to take the sea air and you know the society in Dublin is not all that bad at this season.'

I bit my lip to hide the laughter forming at his nettled expression. 'Perhaps you are right,' he said then, before this line of conversation grew quite out of proportion. 'I had not thought it through. Perhaps on my return from Dublin we can make a wedding journey of your choosing instead,' he counter offered.

'Bath?' I suggested, feeling certain that no one in my circle was likely to be found there.

'Very good choice,' Lady W. offered, approving.

'Bath it is then. We shall journey the day after my return which is anticipated to be by next Saturday. I trust I can leave the arrangements to you my dear?'

'Yes, I will set upon it presently,' I said, smiling at him but directing my stare at Mariella who I knew, was exercising every effort of constraint to keep tight lipped against the fury I saw behind her poker-faced glare. Her hazel eyes, darkened like glowing coals, the only clue.

They took their leave shortly after, and I could tell that they did so, having achieved none of what they had set out to, and endured a great deal more than they were used to in Lady W.'s company. As if that hadn't been enough to taunt them, they were left pondering the disconcerting possibility of whether or not I had confided any personal details to her.

I thanked her profusely as we watched them leave from the drawing room window. 'I owe you such a great debt...'

'Nonsense, you gave me Mr Richards' direction and so I think we can consider things settled. Now young lady, what is to be done about this pest of a cousin? I cannot like her in the least. I have known her sort before and I must tell you, she is not to be trifled with. She means to dangle on you know, despite your marriage.'

'I know, and she is indeed a slyboots. But I cannot see what is to be done when he permits her so much leave to interfere.'

'Well, one advantage you do have, Eleanor, is that his eyes are all for you; that much he gave away, but that chit does not at all like it for she sees it too. She will become desperate if he hopes to abandon her and there is no knowing what such a person could do if she has nothing left to lose in the bargain.'

'But if that is true, then why does he permit it?'

'The male sex, they cannot bear our more sinister ways, it is far too complicated for them to fathom. Half of what we can see in her intentions, has likely not even reached his notice, the other half he would sooner give in to her whims and quiet her than deal with the complication. Now, we must think of a way to distract her, it is only then you can be alone for long enough to make a go of it, and I think then he will do all you ask of him to dispel her.'

'Do you really think so?'

'Without a doubt. So, you must go to Bath together and we must find a way to make sure she cannot join you there. But Eleanor: Mr Richards will have to be dropped.'

I felt a flush rise up from my neck to my cheeks.

'A man like your husband is far too proud to have another man interfere in his marriage bed, so if you want to make a crack of it, he must never find out, and you cannot see Mr Richards again if you mean to make a try. The last thing you want to give him is a reason to turn to her and the pair team up against you.'

I nodded my agreement, even though I felt some disappointment at having to cut him so instantly, having just begun to form some fondness for him.

'Not even discreetly, Eleanor. If your husband gets a sniff of it, this could go very ill for you indeed and that chit will have him precisely where she wants him, mark my words.'

So it was with this superior wisdom Lady W. imparted (and I was readily willing to trust), that I ignored Mr Richards' card when I received it as we were about to leave for the circulating library. It saddened me to do it. I was very fond of him and even if I must curtail such risky interactions betwixt us, I should still like to remain his friend and sponsor. But I at least needed to make a try at rescuing my marriage before discarding it to my mounting heap of failures.

I was forced to decline many more too in the coming days, and took great care to stay out of his way. I felt quite sorry for it as I watched him from my chamber window, having been turned away by Crampton again. But there was nothing for it, however fond I was of him. I must turn my efforts to more serious matters and win my husband out of her wicked clutches and set the both of us free of her poison now. Of course, I still did not care for Giles or nurture any hopes of an intimate marriage, but one without her inclusion was the least I expected. Otherwise, it was enough for me to have my independence. In this short time, I had grown very attached to it, and had no wish to have it superseded by an over-jealous or lovelorn husband. But to win him well enough to rid her from betwixt us and go on amicably, would suit me very well. I felt certain it would him too, especially having suffered the demands of an emotionally deranged Mariella for such a time: the simplicity of my measured affection would surely be found quite refreshing.

So with Lady W.'s assistance, I began to put in place the arrangements for Bath. She had been good enough to permit us to stay in her own house there, which was comfortably situated in the Royal Crescent and was quite wasted to her at this season, for she much preferred the quiet lull of London over the swarming crush of Bath at the height of summer. I was fast learning that Lady W.'s preferences often ran contrary to the ton's seasons, not because she was not fond of society, but had a preference for society outside of the ton for the most part. She had her favourites and exceptions she compromised for, but on the whole, she prefered to suit herself, and she planned her engagements in such a fashion as to take or leave them as she fancied.

It had become somewhat clear to me on our visit to the circulating library as to why this might be; for she was a woman of many surprises and had not simply gone to return a book or find a new one, but to meet in secret with a similarly bookish group of ladies to discuss, not the nuances of Byron's latest work, or even some scandalous original publication of King Lear, but to discuss such topics as social reform and politics and other such topics I knew nothing of at all. I was suitably shocked by some of the things I could make out in the very lively conversation that ensued between the ladies, which was far beyond any talk of the latest patterns, fashions or on-dit's as I had been used to overhearing in Mama's small parlour as the patronesses sat over their scandal broth.

It was suggested that there must be a very subtle petition to every husband, brother or father who had a seat, to support the efforts to abolish the salt tax. It was also decided upon, who would take over the role in teaching the parishioners their letters now Miss Jenkins was away in the country.

My head was in quite a spin when we left and Lady W. directed me along the Burlington Arcade and perused a few of its offerings in the shop windows as we passed them.

'You know Eleanor, I knew as soon as I saw you, you were not like all those other chits. I daresay you are quite shocked by our little gathering, but I know you will not be in the least offended, because I see something quite above the ordinary in your character, even if you have yet to grow into it.'

She did? This I was not convinced of, but I smiled along anyway.

'When you are ready, my dear, I think you will do very well amongst us. So, you must not forget me when your husband whisks you off to Bath on Sunday. When you have tired of him and of whatever society is to be found in a place such as Beddington, you must look for me and we will have a more serious interview then.'

As if I could forget her, less still tire of her. There was no one else like her. She might have been beyond my own mama's years, but it was hard to consider them alike, so singular was Lady W.'s character and strength of mind.

'Now, I recommend that we pop over to Half Moon Street tomorrow to see if that pair have kept to their word and she has vacated the house. You know, you are very welcome in my house, but you must not become a stranger in your own home. And you must talk to the groom about having that handsome horse of yours moved over to Grosvenor Square so we might go out to Hyde Park in the mornings, do you agree?'

'Yes.'

'It's settled then. Oh my, what a charming bouquet that is.' She paused and pointed out to me as we went passed the florists.

WE WENT TO HOUSE THE following day and found it quite empty, and Tibbins quite put out of countenance by having to take such an interview as he suffered at the hands of Lady W.: someone who was neither his master or mistress and yet seemed to harness all the authority of both combined.

On leaving, she said to me, 'I fear Eleanor, that Tibbins is not to be trusted.'

'Oh?' I said surprised as we alighted her carriage and waited for Samson to be saddled up with her bays.

'I do not want to make you uncomfortable my dear, and I own, I could be mistaken, but I read something quite disagreeable in his character. It would not surprise me at all if he had been given orders by Mr Craythorne to report on you in his absence.'

I had not given such matters any thought, but remembered now how he had tried so persistently to divert me from going to Giles' chamber that night when I found them in it. 'I think you are right, but what can I do about it?'

'Nothing much, it is a little early on for you to be changing about the whole staff; just be careful in your dealings with them and be aware of who is about you when you are in company or private conversation. But it brings to mind something else we have neglected, and that is the outstanding matter of your lack of Abigail.'

'I confess I quite like the lack of having a shadow, I have only just begun to enjoy the feeling after leaving my chaperones behind me. I am not sure I am ready to give it up so soon. And society is so thin now, and I am under the protection of your company, so what harm can be done to wait a little longer?'

'Hmm, well I hate to admit it, for I sympathise a great deal with your attitude my dear, indeed it reminds me of my very own all those years ago when I became a wife. But having gone about such things in all the wrong way, I can tell you dear; there are some things that cannot be easily overlooked. Besides, London is no place to be walking about alone, and I say it out of concern for your safety more than for the sake of your reputation. You cannot think I did not notice your coming to me on every occasion unattended and on foot?'

'It seemed such a short journey to make.'

'And were you with your maid, so it would be. The trick is, not to find a replacement for your old chaperone who suffocates your movements, or reports on you to your husband or whispers your secrets to the other staff. Nay—that is every part as ugly as you imagine. But select a person for the task who is most agreeable to you and most importantly, who will be loyal to you, and you alone.'

'But how will I find such a person, let alone keep her loyalty when it will be my husband that accounts for her wages? And surely, should I earn her scorn, she might be turned by any bribe.' I thought of Watts and her willingness to accept bribes in exchange for keeping secrets from my mama.

'Well, first you must find someone whose character or circumstance would make them most likely to oblige you and share your sentiments. That part I may be able to assist you in. But then you must make a friend of them and situate them so prettily in position and in your confidence, that they would have no more desire to leave you, than you them: That is the part you will have to manage alone; but if you bring it off well, it will serve you a lifetime. You know, not all servants are open to bribing and tattling. My own Abigail is a dear friend and companion to me and when she is retired, I shall be very sorry, for she has been with me since I was one and thirty, you know.'

SO, IT WAS SETTLED, the acquisition of such a person was to become the sole occupation of my remaining days in London before Giles returned and I awayed to Bath. It was no quick task. We undertook countless interviews of potential candidates Lady W. had sought on my behalf, inquiring amongst her rather peculiar connections we had met with at the circulating library that day. The result had been endless hours of reading characters and taking interviews, and just when I had begun to think it impossible to find a suitable person for the task, in came Isabelle Rosen, a girl of similar years to my own, whose demeanour did not strike me as overly excitable, nor dreadfully dull as I had found the remaining number.

It turned out she had been in some social disgrace of her own in having her last mistress's husband take a fancy to her and pay her unwanted attentions, and as a result, was finding it very difficult to find a position and was looking ever more destined for the school room if she could not find a means to escape it. This appealed to me quite favourably: that we might rescue each other from uncomfortable circumstances. It would surely set things up on the right note. She had an even manner and I admired her straightforwardness. She was not of genteel birth, and I liked this even more, for I knew no one would likely know or hold sway with her.

'Miss Rosen, can you assure Mrs Craythorne, that you will not only guard her confidence and interest with your life, but that you will also undertake to act in her behalf as a spy for her interests?' Lady W. posed this question, I suspected, to test her resolve.

She took a moment to consider her words, but she did not falter: she looked squarely at us both and said: 'Ladies, I will not pretend to have any particular skills in this direction, but I will tell you this; I need this position and will do practically anything my lady asks of me to keep it, that is about all the assurance I can give to that end, but as for the former, I know what it is to be betrayed, and I can assure you, I have no wish to be such a vulgar character as to betray my own mistress.'

We shared a glance of satisfaction at this speech and I offered her the position there and then. Lady W. assisted me with the contract—which was just as well, for I wouldn't have known where to begin in the arrangement of such papers, since Mama had meant to teach me such useful things but they had gone quite asunder amongst everything else.

So, I was very happy to return to Half Moon Street the next day with my new companion at my side: her things still packed and ready to make the journey to Bath the following day. We were not yet comfortable friends, but I liked her well enough and saw the potential for it. She had an easy manner which I found to be uncomplicated but also perfectly well graced. And yet I sensed a hint of fire in her character, so I knew she would not prove a dead bore, nor lack the gumption to stand up to Tibbins if needed.

I entered the hall with Miss Rosen feeling quite relaxed and confident as I instructed Tibbins that her things would need to be taken up and a room prepared for her, for she was now in my employ. He did not like the circumstances thrust upon him in such a way, I could tell, but I was mistress here and he would have to grow used to the fact. But it was not his voice that made an answer.

'I think Miss Rosen must take some refreshment whilst we have a chat.'

'Mama?' I said in surprise, turning to see her approaching me. 'But I did not know you were in town.'

'No, and nor did I intend to be, and yet what choice did I have when that horrid Craythorne girl, of all people, decides to pay me a call yesterday, advising me you were installed with that bluestocking in Grosvenor Square and quite estranged from your husband.'

Mariella, you will drive me to strangle you if you continue with your tricks! 'Lady W. has been very kind to me, Mama, and does not deserve your contempt, but perhaps your thanks for she has done everything right by me and quite without any obligation to.'

'Right by you; keeping you from your own house?'

'Keeping me? I sought her aid, and dare you have the stomach to know the precise details as to why, for you would not have patience with them.'

'Then if you were reckless enough to make such a show of yourself, she should have had the good sense to send you home to your husband! But what could be expected of such a person as she who cares nothing for the rules of society.'

'Well, I cannot imagine what she has ever done to you to make you speak so poorly of her, and if you must know, she did tell me to come home to him and that is precisely why I am come.'

'I see. So, you are quite happy to take her counsel then?'

'I am very grateful of it for no one else will help me, will they?'

'What precisely requires so much help, Eleanor? You are married now are you not; and whilst I have no sympathy with your choice...'

Tibbins balked at this and I realised he did not like this statement, and though I had little care for him, I ushered mama into the nearest room anyway, as she continued her protest.

'... It was your own choosing and so I cannot know what you must expect anyone to do now you have made such a connection.'

'Mama, I found my husband with someone else in his bed and she will not go quietly.'

She went momentarily pale before a rage of colour flashed back into her face.

'Well, what on earth did you allow such a thing to happen for?'

'Allow? Whatever made you think I would? It was a great surprise to me and I have had a time of it getting rid of her.'

'How can this be? So soon. Have you done your duty Eleanor?'

I swallowed but could not answer.

'Good god. What can you expect then? He is a man, but a newly-wed man above all others, should not be forced to seek his rights elsewhere.'

'Forced?' Could I really have forced him to do such a thing? I remembered the same in Sheldon's speech, how he claimed I had forced him into Lady Caroline's embrace. I was growing ever cynical of this alleged power to compel men into the beds of other women.

'Well, what can you expect if you go running off to stay at another house like that?'

'I don't know, Mama, perhaps nothing more. But it does not signify, we are to away together to Bath in the morning and I mean to set everything right.'

'Indeed, you must. Now, we will set off for Cuddington presently and show all the tittle-tattles that the rumours are quite unfounded and you and your husband go on perfectly well.

Mariella, what mischief have you set about the parish? 'I cannot go now, Mama. Giles is expected here in the morning and we leave forthwith.'

'Your husband is returned to Beaulieu last night to face such news as whisperings about unspeakable goings on in that woman's house.'

Mr Richards? This I could hardly believe; how could anyone in Cuddington know: *Betsy.* I could not believe her capable of it, and yet who else was present who would report such news back to Cuddington? 'Why is Giles at Beaulieu?'

'Well, he could hardly come here himself with all the on-dit. I said I would come for you instead and discover the truth of the matter.'

'Well, there is nothing to discover, Richards and I share a musical passion, nothing else,' I lied.

'Well, let us hope your husband accepts the case.'

And so, with some reluctance, I agreed to return to Beaulieu with my mama and Miss Rosen that very hour. I had no notion of how I would bear being under the same roof as that witch, and yet what choice did I have but petition my husband to believe me and make an effort to compensate the lie. In any case, it was only one night and we would away in the morning. If he would not go, I certainly would. I had Miss Rosen now, so I could travel with or without him; depending upon how he took the news. And it was the reassurance of having her with me at my side that persuaded me to agree to go to Beaulieu at all. The inconvenient thing about the rush of it all was that with Mama's presence in the coach, I could not adequately brief Miss Rosen of the circumstances or the kind of house we were about to enter. I would have to find a quiet moment on our arrival, to explain the circumstances and warn her of the great enemy I had in Mariella, for she would not like Miss Rosen's presence at all and would surely do something to try to gull her.

AS IT SO HAPPENED, Mariella was all sweetness and grace when we arrived under my mother's chaperone. She was a woman of so many faces; I had quite forgotten this one. Giles took the news of my employment of Miss Rosen with indifferent equanimity as I found him in his uncle's study, swirling the half-drunk contents of his brandy around the bottom of his glass. He put it down but did not look up.

'Sit down, Eleanor,' he said blindly and for a moment I felt like a naughty child about to receive my father's reprimand.

I took off my shawl and settled down to the armchair. 'I have everything settled for the morning's journey,' I told him brightly, glancing furtively across the table.

'So, you think we are still to go?'

'Why ever shouldn't we? It was you who thought it a good idea to escape that persevering cousin of yours and permit us some time to get better acquainted. Although I see even that has been neglected. I should rather stay in Beddington with all the hammering and dust, than spend the night in this house with her, as you well know.'

'That cousin of mine brings me news, Eleanor; news of your flirtation with a Mr Richards. The same man she insists is the father of the child you are carrying.'

I had so long grown used to the mistake of that fallacy, that for a moment I forgot they still believed it to be true, and almost disclosed as much. I caught myself swiftly. 'Well of course she does, how very well that would suit her cause.'

He lifted his gaze to me for the first time and made a study of me. 'So, you deny it?'

'Deny what? You already knew me to be carrying a child, you cannot pretend you thought it Mr Elmbridge's or else I would not have broken with him. I was simply talking to him, hardly a crime.'

'A handsome fellow she tells me, is he not?'

'He is, but if you dare to insult me with the idea that I would engage in an open flirtation with a man so much below my touch when I am not out of reason cropsick; you are quite out of your senses. Yes, that's how I ended up in my condition: I was drunk and so much out of my wits I could not even remember it.' Now this he seemed to consider. For what could he know of my character having spent so little time in my company. He would at best have the measure of me by the example of my mama's poorly stifled snobbery, or of Mariella's deranged and jealous reports that could not be relied upon. I remembered what Lady W. had told me about the male sex and them having little understanding of a woman's tricks and so I thought to try it out on him. Perhaps I might have felt some remorse at this elaborate deception if it were not for the fact of what I had learnt of his relations with Mariella, despite all he had explained and promised to the contrary.

'So, you say you are wrongly accused.'

'Yes, I do. And I say she had a damned nerve to make such things up to put me out of favour with my husband, so she might lie with him in my place. God Giles, can you not see what she is about? You told me yourself she was quite mad and I have seen she is quite capable of any scheme that keeps your connection. Well, it won't answer: she can go to the devil, for I am at my wits end now with all her tricks. If you will not sever your ties with her and give our marriage a chance, then I will not fight it, I will let you alone to it and be done with the pair of you.'

'Let's not be hasty, Eleanor,' his tone levelled out to something more reasonable. 'I had no option but to ask you and now I have, I can see what she's about. We will set off for Bath in the morning and make a holiday of it, as is your wish.'

'Thank you. That is all I have hoped for from the off, and yet you have been away to some quarter or another.'

'You shall have your wish; I promise it. Now, you must be tired from your journey. I will see you at dinner later and you can tell me of the arrangements.'

'What, with her there?'

'No, I will see to it that it is just the two of us—how does that suit you?'

'Not as well as it would to leave this house and go to Beddington instead. What is one night amongst dust sheets and rubble?'

'Trifling. But since half the roof has fallen in this week, we have little choice but to put up here until morning.'

'The roof? My goodness. Very well,' I agreed, and even though I did not want to respond to the kiss he then directed at my cheek, I permitted it for the sake of the great relief I felt at having come out well from the interview.

When I came upstairs and found Mariella in my chamber with Miss Rosen as she set out some of my clothes for me to choose for dinner, I was not so well disposed.

'Get out of here. You disgust me,' I told her instantly and held the door open in wait for her going.

'Such manners in front of your new companion, Eleanor? Or is she already accustomed with the depravity of your habits, like I am. You know, Miss Rosen, you had better hope she doesn't want you to provide the services I used to for her.'

I flashed her a warning glare but noted the alarm in Miss Rosen's eyes at this.

'I am quite happy to provide Mrs Craythorne with any service she wishes to charge me with.'

Mariella let out a roar of overzealous laughter and I thought I might be driven to strangle her in her own house at this rate. 'Please don't pay any mind to this lunacy, Isabelle. I have it from her own cousin she is quite mad and I am inclined to believe him.'

'That might be so; but it was you that begged to have my hands between your legs. Oh and I remember how you forced my face their too, begging me to taste your—'

That much was a terrible lie. I grabbed her roughly by the arm and marched her towards the door more violently than I thought myself capable. 'I have asked you to leave so many times; I cannot believe you have misheard me.'

She pulled herself free of my grip when we reached the door and caught me out with a move I had not anticipated; she pressed me flat against the door and made a savage attempt at kissing me and taking my breasts painfully violent in her hands and squeezing them so hard I pushed her so angrily from my person she fell down on the floor with quite a thud.

'See what a brute your mistress is, Miss Rosen. You had better come to me later and learn all the things she will expect you to do for her private pleasure else she might end up treating you as poorly if you cannot manage it.'

'I think you should go now,' was all Isabelle said in reply, but I read something of grave disturbance in her eyes.

'I am so sorry I had to bring you to this house Isabelle, it is a house of lunatics I confess, but I did not realise it until I was already wed.'

'We are not to return here, are we?'

'No, no, the house in Beddington is being renovated at this very moment. I will insist that we must return from Bath to that house or to Half Moon Street, but nay I shall not spend another night in this one when we return. And please do not be concerned, those things she said...'

'Impossible things. I pay no heed to it; but I must tell you, I find her company quite intolerable and I hope she will not come here again tonight.'

'You can be sure of it. If you would like, we could set up the day bed in here tonight and look out for each other?'

She looked a little unsure at this, could she suspect me of commissioning such vile services from her as Mariella had tried to convince her? 'I promise you, I have no such peculiar requests of you, Isabelle.'

'Of course not, I will move my things from the attic at once.'

WHEN I JOINED GILES in the dining room that evening, I had not expected him to be able to keep her away, but maybe our little episode earlier had served to show her I was not going to take her efforts of sabotage lying down. I took the offered chair and received his compliments on my looks and began on the white soup.

'So, my dear, what time are we to go tomorrow?'

I put down my spoon. 'I thought nine-o-clock would be convenient. But pray Giles, I do not understand how you come to be at home when your ship was set to leave for Venice?'

'An issue with the ship's cargo my dear. It shall sail instead on Wednesday all being well. But I am minded, after the start we have gotten off to, that it would be better to delay my going and permit us a time to get to know each other better. It was short sighted of me not to think of it sooner. But there you are. It has all come about now.'

'I see,' I tried to stop the disappointment showing in my face and returned to my soup before saying: 'I must tell you though, Giles, if we are to have even the remote hope of improving on this start, Mariella must stay out of the way.'

'Well, the thing is my dear, we are family and that makes it all the more difficult—'

'I mean it, Giles. She is insufferable and family or nay, if I do not have your assurance that she will not be a feature of our marriage and indeed our life at all beyond doing the pretty when we must, there shall be no future for you and I.'

He coloured a little but seemed to quell it. 'Let's not be hasty my dear, she is of no consequence to us and I do not mean to let her upset you any further.'

'Upset me? She has already distressed Miss Rosen and I was minded to leave that very instant and go to Cuddington for the night and meet you in the morning.'

'Calm down my love. There is no need for that. I shall deal with her. Rest assured.'

Yes, I have seen how you *deal* with her, I almost said. 'Well, I shall have Miss Rosen in with me tonight to be certain of no more of her mischief.'

'As you wish it.'

Jealousy.

August 1821 - Eleanor.

I left the table feeling reassured. I had not expected him to be so accommodating or to show such consideration, after his interrogation, but he seemed to have taken it all in his stride. I was looking forward to confirming to Isabelle that the journey to Bath was to go ahead as planned and we need only get through this one night here. I knew she was sadly disconcerted by Mariella's behaviour. But it was the last either of us would have to tolerate, I thought with some relief as I made my way back to my quarters. I mounted the last flight of stairs, walked past Guinevere's bust and glanced in passing, at the door that had once been Sheldon's guest chamber. I considered as I continued on to my own, what a turning point that day was for us both, although neither of us realised how poignant a moment then. Perhaps if we had, we might have chosen differently.

When I arrived at my chamber and saw Isabelle's truckle bed set up in the corner, I smiled. It was a great comfort not to be alone here. I called out to her as I closed the door behind me and when no response came, I presumed her still supping in the servants' parlour. But as I went about the apartment, I could see none of her things. The worn floral tapestry bag that had been perched on the tabletop, the bandbox and small trunk she had had the footman carry down from the attic. Perhaps she had tidied them away before going for her supper. I looked about the room for them, opening cupboards and drawers, bending to look beneath the truckle bed and in corners and cubby holes where they might be stacked, standing upon the bed steps to survey the tops of taller furniture. *Nothing.* It was when I repeated the same in the adjoining dressing room I began to grow concerned. There was not a trace of Isabelle's things about the place at all, and I had seen them brought in with my own eyes just an hour ago. A dreadful thought struck me then: had she abandoned me? Had Mariella's demonstration disconcerted her so much that upon reflection she found she could not trust me or bear to spend even a night in such company as Mariella's. I could not blame her for that, but had she told me so, I would have sent her to Cuddington for the night if I had known it that insufferable to her.

It might not be too late to catch her, for she would have to seek out someone's help to convey her on. It was not like London here; the streets could not be easily walked or navigated, with their desolate winding tracks and non-existent gas lighting. In the very least, she would need to seek out a hack or look for the direction of the nearest posting point. I left the room and hurried back downstairs to find the housekeeper. I hoped with all my heart that as I navigated the quiet corridors and stairways that the housekeeper would tell me she was still at the table or some such place below stairs. But when I had a hallboy send for her, she stared back at me blank faced and reported not to have seen her at supper at all. I thanked her with a dreadful sense of foreboding and diverted back up towards the dining room where I had moments ago left Giles to his cigars and brandy. But as I took the eastern corridor towards it, I watched Mariella slip into the room through the door ahead of me, unaware that I was approaching at a distance behind her. So I stalled and waited for the click of the latch before stepping up to it as soundlessly as I could and pressing my ear against the keyhole.

'I got rid of Miss Rosen, a twenty-pound draft on your bank did the trick,' she declared triumphant and I heard the scrape of her pulling up a chair.

My heart sank, could she really have abandoned me so cheaply? For her to leave on account of her discomfort was one thing, but to desert me by bribe. I would have paid her twice the sum to not abandon me here this night. But it was not just the money, I knew. I had seen the damage done by Mariella's accusations; I had only hoped she proved to be of as much substance as I had first credited her with.

'Good. This source of yours, how certain of this affair with Mr Richards is she?' Giles replied.

'Why do you care? You have what you wanted from the bargain.'

'She is my wife, Mariella. In society's eyes she has made a fool out of me within a week of our wedding. I won't have it.'

This was an altogether different turn of what he had shown to my face.

'Well, Betsy assures me they were both missing from the party near to an hour or thereabouts. But what should you care, no one else can corroborate her story except the Colonel and she does not want him involved, so she shan't put it about.'

Giles mumbled something I could not hear.

Betsy, oh Betsy, how could you?

'That is not all, is it? I see it in your eyes, you are not satisfied with containing the gossip of it, you cannot bear the thought that she has lay beneath the handsome Mr Richards, can you?'

'I warn you to stop your goading, Mary.'

'And yet you never minded my having to prepare her for you. I see it all now: you want her, don't you? You long for this holiday in Bath to ravish her and win her heart, that is why you never mentioned your plans to me.'

'No, I do not. Stop being so sentimental, it doesn't suit you. I simply mean to ascertain the truth. She insists upon her innocence and I wish to understand if she is telling the truth or not.'

'You liar,' she began weeping and I struggled to contain my own surprise at this hearing. *He knew.* He knew about our shameful encounters; he had put her up to them.

'You absolute bastard,' I heard her say. 'I did everything I could to bring her to the aisle for you; got you everything you wanted and now you want more?' I sensed a change in temper and spied through the small keyhole and watched as she launched herself at him and began throwing her fists in the air until they landed on his chest.

'Enough,' he said with a calm but warning note to his tone.

'Enough? It is never enough for you, is it?' she continued to lash her rage out upon him.

'Calm yourself, you are irrational,' he said more firmly, catching her fists in his hands. But she did not submit, she grew more violent, more emotional, and more erratic.

'It's not enough to have won your connection, to have your seat in parliament, your country mansion and London town house. No, you want the full package, don't you? A trophy for a wife and an heir to your kingdom and perhaps even a little love between you. Hmm, yes, I see it all now. And tell me, Giles, where do I fit in to such a pretty picture? What is my recompense for so much labour in your behalf?'

'You have your position as my mistress and all the benefits that entails, of course. Until you make a match of your own.'

Mistress. Is that how this was to go? Had it been anyone but her I might be grateful to her for taking on the duties I was more than happy to dispense with. But I would not have her about me for anything.

'A match? How dare you use me so poorly. You promised me you would protect me from having to marry if I did this for you; you said we would be together!' she screamed and with this, he seemed to lose the end of his resolve and slapped her swiftly across the face with the back of his hand until she fell to the ground and collapsed into a torrent of tears.

'I am sick and tired of your demands. What has happened to the days where women knew their place?' he thundered. 'Now, get out of my sight before I throw you out.'

I heard a shuffling and saw she was back to her feet. But far from head towards the door as I feared, she took up the decanter on the table and threw the contents over him. 'How dare you speak to me like that,' she snarled and held the decanter poised as if to strike him with it. 'You said you loved me. You said we would go abroad together and leave your wife sitting pretty keeping house. You promised we would go on as we did in Paris, but freely abroad, somewhere we were not known. It was all a lie wasn't it; that's why you wouldn't have Martha when I encouraged you in that quarter: You wanted *her.* You knew even then how it would go.'

'I told you what you wanted to hear. You did not actually think I meant it, did you?' There was the hint of a laugh about his tone which she caught, sending her into a rage of a different class, launching the crystal decanter at him, he dodging it by a fraction and it bouncing against the back of the chair before shattering against the floor in glittering shards. I could not make out at first what happened once he got up from his seat but the noises startled me and then they came back into my view, him dragging her by the hair across the floor, towards the door from which I spied through. I leapt back from it in an instant. For a moment, wondered what I should do: the scene was so appalling to watch, I had to hold back from intervening. Whatever she was, whatever she had done, I did not like to see this brutal treatment of a female. Then all fell quiet and I dared to look back in. She was arms wrapped about his knees sobbing her apologies to him. Seeking his forgiveness at which he let go of her hair, broke free and walked away from her. If it had continued beyond this, I perhaps would have gone running in to break it apart, but it seemed it was over now. Giles straightening out his clothes and collecting his glass of brandy from the table where he had left it and Mariella nursing her pained cheek and a broken spirit.

I stepped back and tried to understand what all of this meant. Could he really have commissioned her to do this to ensnare me? Had they marked my card so long ago that everything that followed was only a means to the end they had in sight for me. Could it be? Could anyone be so vulgar and corrupt of their sense to embroil an innocent person into such a mad scheme? I thought she had sought me out as a friend, not as someone who could sit pretty as his wife whilst they gallivanted about abroad under the cover of our marriage. It beggared all belief to me. I would go to my parents and tell them the whole, see if there was some means by which this arrangement might be annulled; it was after all, little more than a great deception.

No, I could not.

After all that had passed, how could I have such intimate and unnatural things made public? Even if I could bear it, and I was not certain I could, how could I bestow anymore scandal upon my family? It would not answer, it was too late and whilst the corruption was theirs, the naivety was my own. I looked at the gold band around my finger: it was done; there was nothing for it but to go on as if I had not heard a word of the thing. Hope that he would keep his commitment to her and they might disappear away together on their travels. In any case, it would prove a happy outcome for me if things took such a turn. I would assist in it, encourage them together, befriend Mariella again and keep her in the way of us, make him honour his promises to her. For however sadly I had suffered in my part, the fact was I had sealed my own fate in this and so I must remedy it myself also.

I would go to bed and rise early to take the post into Bath alone. Lady W.'s butler would not permit him to enter the house, if I could only send word to her in time. Since it seemed he had his own mistress to take care of the bedroom affairs, they could console themselves together in whatever vulgar ways they might prefer and let me alone. *Oh, Isabelle, I wish you had not abandoned me at such an inopportune moment.* I must find another person to attend me to travel to Bath alone now, but how could I find someone in time? As these many things bewildered me all at once, I did not have my senses quite about me as I began backing away from the door and tripped over the feet of an old, armoured statue and felt it come crashing down upon me as I fell to the ground. What a stupid and unfashionable ornament to have, I cursed the thing as I clambered out from beneath it and found Mariella and Giles standing there, looking down at me. *Good God.*

'Are you harmed, my dear?' Giles said.

'Not a bit. What a clumsy fool I am, I should have brought a light with me,' I said as Giles coolly offered me his hand and I took it to pull myself up. 'I was just come to see if anyone knew where Miss Rosen had got to and I tripped over this great beast of a thing!'

'On your way to us?' said Mariella suspiciously.

'Yes,' I told her flatly and busied myself in neatening up my ruffled clothes. 'Now, have you seen Miss Rosen?'

'Yes, I have; but you already know it don't you, Eleanor, for you tripped in quite the wrong direction for one approaching this room, but in perfect style of someone leaving that direction,' she said accusatory and as Giles studied the scene, I grew nervous.

'What nonsense,' I insisted, but I had nothing more to offer. 'I better call someone to set this to rights and find Miss Rosen myself if you will not tell me where she is—'

'I will take care of that.' Giles put out his arm to prevent my going and it was only then I accepted I had lost this one.

'Very well. Then I must go to bed, we have a very long journey in the morning and—'

'Then I will come to you shortly, my dear. It has been long enough, I think. Now, won't you go and get comfortable and let me deal in this matter.'

I smiled. 'Of course, I shall get ready for bed presently.'

I went instantly to my room, locked all the doors and began packing up my things. I could not remain here and I did not care how late I would have to sit up to await the moment, but I would go to Cuddington as soon as it came about, whatever the hour. I wondered what time Mr and Mrs Craythorne might return from their dinner party tonight. I checked the clock on the mantle as I packed my bedclothes away. It was only ten-o-clock, I doubted they could be expected for another few hours yet. Once they returned, I could go to them to ask for a coach to Cuddington. I would not tell them why, for even though they had always been amiable enough to me, I doubted they would believe the truth of what was between Mariella and Giles and even if they did, the last thing they would want is to send me off home to tell the whole of it. I would give them some story about having forgotten something there. No that would not do, they would offer a servant's going. I would tell them I had received a note from my mama, saying my father was ill and I must go to them. Yes, I would scribe the note myself and show it to them—I knew my mama's hand well enough. Then pay the hallboy to say it was delivered to him.

After a half hour had passed and I had everything packed and ready, the forged note sealed and powdered, I took a few good coins from my reticule. I had the keys in my hand to unlock the door to set about delivering it when it knocked and I paused.

'Eleanor, Eleanor?' came Giles' voice but I did not answer or unlock it. Instead, I padded soundlessly backwards and sat quietly upon the trunk I had just packed. I would have my father's man come and collect my things tomorrow if need be. If they were at least assembled it would be a simple undertaking.

'Eleanor.' His voice came again and again and then a sound I was not prepared for, the turn of a key, the latch releasing and the door crack open.

I got up instantly. 'Giles!'

'I thought you were asleep, my love. You weren't ignoring me, were you?'

I swallowed a deep gulp and backed away from him as he came towards me, something in his eyes warned he was not in the mood for play acting and it made me very uneasy having just witnessed his temper.

'Forgive me, I was just in the dressing room: I must get undressed and I will be right with you,' I said, slipping the keys back into my pocket and hastening my steps towards the dressing room. I checked before I closed the door behind me, that he was not following me in. He was not. He took his jacket off and hung it about the back of a chair and as quietly as I could manage, I released the latch, drew the right key from my pocket and turned the lock. I repeated the same to open the adjoining door on the other side of the dressing room which clicked louder than the other had and I hurried to make my exit, not expecting to find Mariella waiting beyond it. She launched herself into the room and towards me.

'Aren't you glad I took the initiative to procure the other keys now, Giles?' she said and I turned around in horror, still quite speechless, and almost walked into his waiting arms. I jumped back, but then I felt her behind me. I was sandwiched between the two and had nowhere to go. 'What is this?' I protested. But they closed in on me until I almost stepped upon his boots and felt her breath against my neck.

'I told you she had heard the whole, didn't I?' Mariella said to Giles. 'Fully clothed. No doubt you found her things packed up? What would you do without me, Giles?'

'You can leave us now, Mariella,' was all he said in answer to this, but I did not like his tone.

She screwed her face up in a scold, 'You think this will be some romantic moment now, after all she has learned. Well, fine, good luck with that, you will regret not having my help for she will fight you for it now.'

With this, she turned to leave and, as she opened the door, without thinking it through, I panicked, saw my exit and pushed past her to make a run for it. I must have hit my head against the frame because for a dizzying moment, all was lost to me. But when he pulled me to my feet to examine my forehead where I could feel the throb of a bump, we were back in the dressing room with Mariella prattling on; telling Giles she had told him so, and if he wanted to bring this off, he would need her help. He must have agreed to this, for when I got steady on my feet again and begged him let me sit down a moment for my head was in such a spin, he did not dismiss her. It was she who pushed a stool behind my knees and instructed me to sit. And when I did, she began unbuttoning the back of my dress.

'Do not touch me,' I warned her, snatching the nape of my dress from her bony fingers.'

'Well, there are no maids about, all sent to bed, so who else will help you?'

My heart sank, there would be no one coming to interrupt us for a time yet. 'I think I must see a doctor, I feel quite unwell, my head—'

'Nonsense, don't believe a word of it, Giles, if you want your way with her, it is now, or give up the idea and let her go running off to Bath in the morning!'

This seemed to decide the matter and as she set about unbuttoning me again and I rose to escape her, he caught me in his arms and held me still that she might continue. 'Husband, you will not let her touch me! Let us go to bed then and send her away, I beg of you.' Tears were in my voice and I could not prevent them, I sensed something quite beyond anything coming as I recalled various points of their conversation earlier.

They were in this together.

Yes, she was mad but so was he to set her to undertake such tasks. He was not an innocent victim of her obsession but the director of her mad behaviours and endeavours. She did it out of some twisted tendré for him, but he had shown brutal coldness in using her so poorly in the scheme and clearly did not return her sentiment. Did I really want to be left alone with such a man, even if she was such a vile creature? I felt a rush of cold air hit my skin as my dress fell to the ground, the ruby damask fabric the colour of the blood on my fingertips, and suddenly I felt very aware of my body. He was drinking in the sight of me and stood back to get a better view. I felt instantly sick. She was tugging at the laces of my bodice and when she pulled them loose, I held it instinctively against my bosom like a shield.

'Don't be shy now, we have both already seen those beauties,' she purred at my ear and I shouldered her off of me and stepped away.

'I do not need your assistance, I can manage myself!' I said but she ignored me and tore the basque from my hands; and there I was, stood before him with nothing but the thin gauze of my shimmy. When she tried at lifting this from me, it was too much to feel her hands tugging at this last thread of dignity. I fought against her, to what end I did not know, but I fought her hard for it and it was only when I showed a sign of getting the better of the bargain that I felt him pull me apart from her and drag me away into the bedchamber. 'Unhand me,' I cried, but no matter how much I kicked, screamed and tried to wriggle from his grasp, I could not break free, I could not petition him, I could not get out of the room, even if I did exert myself to good effect.

When he flung me onto the bed and told me, 'Enough!' she climbed up behind my head and pinned my arms to the bed with all her body weight so I could not wriggle free.

'You are hurting me!' I spat at her and tried as Giles lifted my shimmy to expose my body to his eyes, to bite her wrist. The feeling of his clammy hand clasping at my breast, shocked me so much I quite forgot this course entirely and begged him to stop.

'I have been patient with you, Eleanor, so very patient and yet you will deny me my rightful claim.'

'I have never denied you! It was you that did not come to me when I waited on our wedding night and we all know why that was! Just not like this, I beg of you, not like this... Send her away and I will come to you willingly.'

'How very romantic. Now, what do you think, Giles; quite a wiry tangle you must fight through, but she is very sensitive to a frigging if you find her parched.'

I stared at Giles in disbelief, he knew this? *He planned it,* I remembered. I felt his hand slither between my legs. 'Is this how you mean to treat your wife?' I exclaimed as I felt his fingers pressing inside of me just like the doctor had done that day in Kent. 'What are you doing?' I demanded, squirming from him.

He ignored me and I lost it then, and put up my best fight yet, kicking him away so violently that even when he managed to wrestle my ankles into submission, I broke free of her grip and grabbed her by the hair as she tried to reclaim me. Then I felt his hand enter me more violently and in the momentary gasp of pain that distracted me, she pulled out from my reach, slapped me hard across the face and pinned my shoulders beneath her bent knees with such pressure I thought my neck might snap.

'You twisted creatures; you will kill me!' I screamed and she relented just a touch so I could at least catch my breath. 'Take me then, be the vile beast I have discovered you to be, but if you think I could ever love you or want your hands upon me now, then you are sadly mistaken. Oh, and Betsy informed you quite rightly, I was gone about an hour with Richards.' This made him stiffen and pause and I laughed. 'I can still feel the ache of him inside my deepest parts! Yes, I lied to you too. He fucked me so well at that party it left me with a far better impression of the act than your pathetic tries.'

At these words, he withdrew, stood up and began furiously unfastening his breeches in a rage that began to frighten me. Mariella, who had quite relented, and hovered above me in enjoyment of this speech had a smile upon her lips as she watched his colour flare hot crimson.

I was getting to him. It seemed to be the only thing to take effect. So worn out with thrashing about, I continued with only my speeches: 'Oh, I hope you might measure up to Richards if you mean to put that feeble looking thing inside of me. You might even still catch the scent of him there, a trickle of spending should still be about to ease your entry, no need to exert your hand sir. Take a sniff of your hand, tell me if you smell him on it. Perhaps this time he really has left me with child, his seed must be nicely rooted by now. You see, I was not with child before, after all. I had forgot to mention that. Nor had he breeched me at all...until Friday night that is. You are not the only one who can keep secrets.'

'Oh, but you mistake things,' Mariella cut in. 'We already knew that; it was you that was so easily gulled into believing otherwise.'

I tried to hide the genuine shock at this revelation and press on. 'Well, we'll call it a self-fulfilling prophecy then; for he definitely did break me and spend his seed this time. You will feel it to be true for yourself Giles, he has eased your path for you. I see you have already realised the difference.'

'Good. We shall make quicker work of it then. Well Giles, what are you waiting for, get this over with for goodness' sake.'

He discarded his pantaloons but hesitated.

I contrived a laugh. 'He does not want me now. What a shame. Is the thought of Mr Richards going before you, putting you off?' I teased him.

'Turn her over,' he said to Mariella then and I felt instantly afraid.

'Giles, you mustn't, she is funning, to be sure.'

'You think I am going to risk fucking her when she could end up bearing me his bastard.'

These words should have comforted me and I thought perhaps my tactics had paid off, but the change in his tone made me fearful. There was an unmistakable threat about it and I did not know what he meant to do. Thrash me perhaps?

'Giles, I agreed to help you because you said you only wanted to plant an heir and be done with her. If that is not to be this night, then let her alone and try it next month—'

'Turn her over, god damn you!' he shouted and she obliged him, pulling at me and wrestling me until I found myself face down on the bed and held there by the weight of her body. I had spent so much energy fighting them that my bursts of resistance became less effective. When I felt him lift my hips to poise me for his entry, I realised he was pressed against me in altogether the wrong place, and mustered up all my remaining strength to shuffle forward, but I could not do it with the weight of her upon my back and him holding my hips so fixedly. Then as I tried through muffled petitions into the sheets, to tell him this was not the right place to enter me, I was silenced with pain as I felt him tear into me; into my back passage. I thought I might die with the agony of it as I collapsed completely onto the mattress and felt him pound at me so violently I could only sob and wince through these jarring assaults. I was sure I must have suffered such terrible injury I would not be able to move, even when he was finished.

When he was done, I could not even turn around to say anything to him. I stayed with my face pressed into the mattress even when she climbed off my back. My degradation was complete, my injury so profound I could not have believed it possible and I could do nothing but weep as I heard him redress himself. 'If you ever think of fucking another man again, you will know what to expect,' he said after a time. 'Now, clean her up and lock her in!' Then I heard his footsteps on the floor and the door close behind him.

'Well, get up then, it is done,' Mariella said impatiently.

'I cannot move!' I told her through gritted teeth and unrelenting sobs.

'Suit yourself then,' she said nonchalantly and then I heard a splash of a jug and felt her dare to take a cloth to me and start washing me. I had no fight left in me now. What did it matter to have her wiping at me after all I had just endured. Every humiliation possible had already been dealt to me, what could this signify? I felt her pull my shimmy back down to my ankles and then she said: 'Sit up.' but I did not.

'You brought it on yourself you know, you shouldn't have teased him like that.'

Now I did turn about to look at her. 'Mariella, if you love him, why do you let him fuck me.'

'You must do your duty. He will let you alone after, he has promised it.'

I stared at her. 'You know that will never be enough for him,' I spat.

'Don't flatter yourself. You are a conquest not a pleasure. He wants issue not your body.'

'Oh, that was why he spent an age taking his mouth to me that morning you interrupted us at Beddington.'

She looked up at this. 'What?'

'Yes, you forget. You arrived late for seeing it for yourself if I recall. I see you remember it now, you know I am not lying. Ask him about it if you wish. And then how he made me undertake the disgusting task of handling him the very next day.'

'Novelty, that is all.'

'I would have thought it might have worn off by now...' I could see her growing increasingly unsettled, but I was more inclined to win her support than simply anger her now. It was clear to me who the greater enemy was. 'How can you love a man like him?'

'It is none of your business who or how I love.'

'But you see it always will be whilst I am in the picture. You will dangle after him, he will dangle after me: Is that how you wish it to be?'

'Stop your chattering and drink this, it will ease the pain,' she held a glass out to me.

This was beyond anything. 'Pain? And what do you care for my suffering after all the wickedness you have caused me to bear?'

'It was just a suggestion, do not think I care a hoot whether you drink it or not; you deserved everything you got. Sleeping with Mr Richards—even I had not thought it as bad as all that, even when Betsy told me she suspected something quite serious between you but, well now I can tell her she was quite a good judge of things.'

I sat up and hugged the small of my tummy in as it felt like everything inside of me might fall out. 'Nobody deserves to be treated this foully,' I said as I gently pulled myself from the bed to ease the pressure: I felt aching at every angle of me. 'And you would not dare, to make such a fool of your cousin as to set the word about.' I managed to stand up straight and hobble over to the washstand.

'You are quite mistaken you know, I don't care a fig for any of that, it is only him that means to make himself respectable, you must see that I could want nothing more than to destroy your precious character.'

'Then let me go.'

She fell silent and put the glass down on the washstand in front of me which was full of some amber coloured liquid. 'You will not be able to sit if you don't take it, so choose your sufferance if you will. I shall leave you to it.'

'Leave the door unlocked and I will be gone by morning. If you do not care, then let me go willingly, leave you to him. There need be no battle; he is all yours!'

She seemed to mull it over.

'Oh, I see: you are scared of him, of his outrage,' I goaded.

'No, I can handle him just fine, and in any case, it will be worth the scold to be rid of you, I own. But you are full of tricks, Eleanor, and I would not trust you not to wake the whole house up in a fit if I let you free.'

'You think I would want to stay under this roof for even a moment?'

'It is late, what will you do?'

'Use the shortcut through the grounds, please Mariella, I give you my word I will not disturb anyone if you can give me a passage out, all I want is to go home. You will never have to see me again. I will go away where he cannot find me.'

'Drink it and I will do it,' she gestured to the glass.

'What is it?'

'Something to calm your nerves, and settle your pain. A little insurance that you will not fly into a rage and set off a panic.'

The irony was astonishing after all I had seen tonight. I took the glass and peered into it and without further delay, sunk the lot.

'Good. Now, get dressed and leave it ten minutes. I will leave the door unlocked and the servants' entrance unbolted, take the backstairs. But if he catches you Eleanor, you are on your own and I will deny the whole.'

I did not get properly dressed, I only threw my clothes on in haphazard fashion and found my slippers, nor did I wait ten minutes after her going, the liquid had got to my head so fast I felt almost instantly delirious and knew my time was limited before the spinning in my head and the pain aching through my body won over my senses and rendered me incapacitated. So, a few moments after, I made my exit. Following her directions, I slipped through the service jib, shuffled down the stairs with a great deal of trouble and found my way out through the service exit we had often used. It was only when I burst out into the cool night air did I feel some relief and hope that I could escape him. I saw a light burning from one of the windows above and clung closely to the wall as I passed it before using the last of my fight to run into the woodland where the pitch darkness engulfed me. My body fell weak and after stumbling my way as best I could remember, I felt entirely out of my senses, my eyes straining against the darkness, my body struggling to hold up its own weight as I clung onto a nearby tree trunk and then I was spent.

An Inclement night, part 2.

August 1821. - Eleanor.

When I woke up to rain falling on my face and a wicked wind stirring up in the trees, I had thought it all some terrible nightmare, until I tried to move and felt the ache from my insides. I was at the bottom of an oak tree, cradling its lumpy roots, my clothes soaked through to my skin, my slippers lost to me and a pounding in my head so dreadful I felt reluctant to lift it at all. But then I remembered that I must still be on Beaulieu land, and I had no idea how much time I had lost or if he had discovered me gone. So, I forced my feeble body up from the ground, lifted my heavy, rain drenched skirts and began to run. When would I ever cease running from one thing or another?

To be continued...

Next in this series...

Diary of an obstinate, headstrong female. Vol. 2: Appetence.

A failed marriage.
A longing for escape.
An unexpected romance.

With her girlish days of blind innocence behind her, Eleanor finds herself more than just physically bruised, as she attempts to battle through her darkest days in the aftermath of an unprecedented Season.

Fallen from grace, traumatised, friendless and alone, there seems little left to live for and even less to find meaningful occupation in as she vows never to return to her husband after his vile treatment of her.

Far from being where she expected to be by now; prettily situated and much at her own leisure in a marriage of comfortable convenience, Eleanor's future has never been more uncertain.

Taking refuge at Cuddington might keep her safe from her husbands attempts to reclaim her, but shunned from society, dropped by her friends, and sinking her family into ever deeper depths of disappointment with her failures, it is a bitter-sweet refuge that soon has her longing for escape.

Just when all seems lost and bleak, something unexpected begins to emerge from a most unlikely quarter and reminds Eleanor that life is still worth living, love is not dead, and not all new acquaintances are worthy of mistrust.

Will this emerging new relationship help to restore all that was set asunder and show her what it really means to find friendship, trust, and love?

Available now.[1]

---

1. https://www.amazon.co.uk/gp/product/B09TQ264WR

www.ingramcontent.com/pod-product-compliance
Lightning Source LLC
Chambersburg PA
CBHW081138020726
47504CB00009B/1910